# Hind's Kidnap

DZANC
BOOKS

Also by Joseph McElroy

*A Smuggler's Bible*
*Ancient History: A Paraphase*
*Lookout Cartridge*
*Plus*
*Ship Rock: A Place*
*Women and Men*
*The Letter Left to Me*
*Exponential* (essays—in Italian translation)
*Actress in the House*
*Preparations for Search* (novella)
*Night Soul and Other Stories*
*Cannonball*
*Taken from Him* (novella)

# Hind's Kidnap

*A Pastoral on Familiar Airs*

**by**

**Joseph McElroy**

DZANC
BOOKS

Dzanc Books
5220 Dexter Ann Arbor Rd.
Ann Arbor, MI 48103
www.dzancbooks.org

Published 2021 by Dzanc Books

ISBN-13: 978-1-950539-31-4

Cover by Daniel Benneworth-Gray

for it is not so much to know the self

as to know it as it is known

    by galaxy and cedar cone,

as if birth had never found it

and death could never end it

*A. R. Ammons*

# Faith,

## or

# The First Condition

*i*

Hind surprised a tall old woman in his vestibule one morning shortly before the mailman came. He had hurried down the three flights of marble stairs, the heel of his palm on the cool black rail, his long legs wishing to play the stairs three at a time; for he was going round the block to his wife Sylvia's to make up his differences with her—and he was late, though he had not told her he was coming. But then the old woman, long-limbed, white-haired, black-eyed, much taller than Sylvia, was in his vestibule forcing a folded slip of paper into the grille of his postbox. She was one of the few women Hind had seen who came up even to his shoulder. She appeared not to be startled by his height.

He drew the note from the grille's crenate bars and read, "If you're still trying to break the kidnap, visit the pier by the hospital." The old woman had gone back onto the street.

Hind ran after her into the mild air, but she walked fast, and he had so much to say to her there in the middle of the city that, noting a certain commotion across the street, he stood still. Over the sidewalk and beyond to the middle of the street spread blue-and-yellow-speckled the new-leaved shadow of the ailanthus that grew next door and leaned partway across the front of the undertaker's brownstone on the top floor of which was Hind's (formerly Hind's, Sylvia's, and little May's) apartment. An avenue bus southbound passed the intersection at one end of his block—brakes exhaling—and he knew it would stop out of sight in front of Neighborhood Drug. The tall woman, who now disappeared around that corner, must be catching the bus. Hind's right arm reached out.

But right across the street from where he stood, two shaggy-haired young men were forcing a brown-and-white heifer up the four steps and toward the warmly polished, opening, dark wooden door of the advertising art director's studio. Bricks glittered white, sky moved hugely in crisp windows. For a second the animal seemed carved, so stiff had its structure of hide and bone become. Forehoofs scraped upon the first step, and the heifer's forehoofs had to jerk one two up to the second, up up to the third, though its rear hoofs stayed braced.

Also the new plane tree was present, meager and nondescript for all its advance billing. The little freelance janitor Knott (everready to tell why he suspected Phil the druggist of giving him not pork insulin but the European synthetic) stood in baggy green work pants with his key-packed tortoise-shell horseshoe chained from his belt, squinting down at the two big Parks Department men the city had sent with the tree, who sat on the curb resting their cigarette hands on high-tilted knees. By now they would have learned which of the brownstone and the rust-red, green-gray, pink, and blue brick houses Knott looked after, for Knott would always give you an account of himself. So far the men had not relaid the thirty cobbles in the tree's plot.

Hind heard for the first time since five A.M. the bubbly Ow Wow Ow Wow Wow of the Police Emergency Service siren come up the avenue at his left, and he imagined vehicles fading to the side to give way, his own long arms stretching over the heights and depths of the city to whatever injured or dead or suicidal person or persons the truck was going to. Wifely Sylvia said, "Keep your perspective, not everybody needs you." But everything said "perspective" nowadays; and this very morning he had thought he'd break the conversational ice by reviewing a peculiar thing or two she had broached concerning a new perspective expounded by this English artist Plante she had spent the night with.

But the tall old woman's note, rescued from the grille's crenate bars, said, "If you're still trying to break the kidnap, visit the pier."

But now, around the soft form of a boy, a beating music approached. The unzipped fly of his olive Wranglers seemed a vent through which horns, nasal reeds, and percussive gut worked out their inescapable process from a transistor's cage the boy held in his pocket. This music dropped busily under a Hydragena ad, not all of which Hind caught: "...do smog and smoke wilt your makeup?...Hydragena works, I said works I said...Get into perspective...slip out of your city skin—" over which came up electric strings housing, clothing, inhabiting the last two syllables of the trade name as if, after being interrupted to take on passengers, the train now continued and engine and rails digested "*jee*nah jeenah *jee*nah jeenah." And Hind thought that the muse of the communications media is a catholic muse, her airs exoskeletal tokens explaining, though only explaining, vast reaches of soft inner mass.

The heifer bawled twice in a ragged octave; then, as if to look far away, it bent its tough neck to the right, toward where Hind had seen what would be the old woman's bus cross. The heifer bawled at a higher pitch, angrier, more resigned, longing for the field of the home company from which it had been rented. (If you want to break the kidnap.)

The boy, the tree men, and Knott observed the herding. In the illegally parked cars on that side, drivers appeared from behind high-spread newspapers to look; at eleven they would no longer be fair game for the police wrecker.

In a second-floor window of the ad art director's a golden haired model cupped an oblong mirror as she drew a slow line along her eyelid. In the next window of the studio a girl nestling a phone between shoulder and jaw felt for something in her bag and smiled and talked.

The two Old Chestnuts, one with white-tipped aluminum cane, the other with his black plastic messenger portfolio, held onto a railing and stared down the block at the mailman's untended bag suspended in its rubber-tired pushcart. The dainty child Rain, whose grandfather couldn't make the stoop, waited by her areaway railing for the mail; she was in second grade, she ought to be in school today. "Hi, Jack," she called, "I start recorder lessons at the Music Clinic tomorrow." She waved to Mrs. Fordham, who was waiting for the other-side mailman and looking at Hind. (If you want to break the kidnap.) The Fordhams lived in a third-floor walkup. The fact that Winky left home three or four nights a week and at five A.M. could be seen walking back in his carefree bare feet, his socks hanging out of his jacket, was incomplete without the other fact, that, noticing he had come to his building, he would look up, and she, who had had them confiscated by her friend the newsdealer, dropped her husband's weather-curled loafers down to him, and he put them on and went upstairs to sleep away the night's memory. Heather Fordham had a stern, pleased face the times Hind was up early enough to see her stand at the window before dropping Winky's shoes. She liked being up early. To Ivy Bowles, her tea-buddy at Neighborhood Drug, and also to the druggist's wife Phyllis, who ran the fountain, she retorted, "You got to live with what there is"; she had married late, at fifty. Hind thought he knew Heather as well as he knew the facts of the kidnap, or as well as he recognized the timbre of Rain's uncle's car's twin-trumpet Italian air-horn, which that grinning universal pal visiting Rain's grandfather once a week elbowed perhaps by accident getting out.

Hind must act on the old woman's note, for as old Dewey Wood liked to say—though no paper had yet consented to print—"You can save only in the ways offered you, and these you can't regulate." Consequently, the pier. Had the old woman seen Hind there? Her form was clean and functional as a branch, a fine lone figure.

In his vestibule he should have been able to reach and detain her. But it was at street level, so there had been no outside stairs for her to go down before reaching the sidewalk. Sylvia's damn common sense would ask why he didn't speak to the old woman. Distractions Syl particularly taxed him for giving in to were often those which, if pursued, might lead like old children's tales to the very responsibilities she herself believed in. "Say that again?" she said, though indeed she too might speak confusingly and sneak a trick through when she wanted. To her common garden variety of sense you replied that you couldn't shut your eyes to the world, any more than erase your own name, and if the reason Hind relinquished his private kidnap inquiry five or six years ago was cloudy or odd, the old woman's note wasn't at all cloudy. *If* you still believe in the kidnap. (And Syl thought marriage was for better not for worse.)

And if you didn't resume the search, who would? Sometimes, even without being able to prove it happened near you, you felt at your very elbow an interruption like the bird that between iron uprights occupied three inches of sooty white fire escape across the street, the sparrow you sometimes saw in the far side of your eye from the study window: Hind turned his head to see, and often the sparrow then tipped off the railing and turned into a dead thing diving at the sidewalk; yet at the end of the fine stem of its descent the thing turned into a brown bird and was superbly swung away toward its other special perch; and when it got there to its own sycamore twig and shook the buttonballs, it was again a peering sparrow.

Six years ago he had cared about and tried to live through the kidnap the old woman's note must refer to. He gathered into his memory the equivalent of many ring binders full of data, hoping to break through onto the clear ground of what happened. Long after the police of the region gave up on the kidnaped child, Hind persevered. He advertised in papers, even looked abroad. The child's violet birthmark, his Magic Bean Bag, dusty window sills—and Hind's reward was only a ring from an inspector who wanted to know why in God's green earth Hind was in the case, it was as good as closed.

"But in a city someone can simply disappear"—and Hind had omitted one step of logic, as his guardian would have been quick to point out.

"Wait a sec," said Inspector Praid, "the kid's parents are dead, you're cognizant of that; and his other known relatives are irrelevant; and to all intensive purposes, the *kid* is dead, there seems to be a slight goof on the ransom. So this has to be for the files, the report can't *be* complete. Forget it, Mr. Hind."

Hind was going to say, "But what proves that a ransom was ever even asked? Which means, you see, that—" however, he said, instead, good-bye. To which Inspector Praid replied, "And by the way, the city's just where you *can't* disappear."

Hind, as he told his overbearing friend the architect Madison Beecher, was used to acting, not being acted upon. Which was about to be their friend Oliver Plane's little trap at the university, for his now renowned noninvolvement was drawing administrators and grammarians from all over that cubic Campus City (as the plant was called) smack onto Plane's trail when as a rule they'd not have known him from one of his older students. The old woman's message meant that after virtually forgetting the kidnap for months that became years, Hind would start again, again be a moving watchman. He must simply wait for this new word on the kidnap he had long ago let go.

The old woman was very tall. Was this something? Hind himself was a sixteenth either way of six-seven—but what was six-seven nowadays, with televised basketball? The old woman—messenger, agent, or even ultimate party—came just to his shoulder, thin and strong as a branch.

You believe, trust, even would cleave to, a tall man sooner than a short. Which usually put Hind, according to the guardian (as if *he* was responsible for Hind's height), one up. On the other hand, it is better to be understood than to be believed, unquote the guardian.

The old woman looked unfamiliar; but Hind believed he would know the voice if it spoke.

Long, strong, dry limbs—Hind identified her perhaps too readily with the kidnap message she brought. But those old strong entrails her words had alone the meaning that counted; and the means by which the note had come to his box mattered less: Yes, the identity of the bleak woman tall as his shoulder bone and possessed of a rocking, straining competitor's stride quite like Hind's ungainly own when hurrying mattered less than the words she had turned up to give him.

So he would take a towel and a book, maybe a watercress-and-tongue roll, and lie out on the pier in the growing April sun and wait for a sign.

Originally, years ago, he had felt he was right, guessed the police were bored, imagined the child had been, simply, taken; inferred that if ransom was still at issue it was an essential ransom less symbolic than money and final as the child itself, even more lost now its displaced parents were dead, though they had indeed been unfit parents.

Hind could not tell Sylvia the kidnap had begun all over again. This would then seem to have been why he left her last summer. But he didn't want to spend a lot of his time somewhere unbeknownst to her. He would say he was taping people at the pier. Immigrant backgrounds, idioms, erosions, chat.

He'd phone, not visit her as he'd been going to this morning at the moment he surprised the long-limbed old woman in the vestibule. But he and Sylvia and his little girl May had to get together again. If they all did not, then he was bound to grow into something else. But if he didn't finish the kidnap, who would? And if he didn't, he would likewise grow into something else. If the kidnap case didn't matter, neither did he. He imagined, on either side of him, low earnest shoulders of children, and his hands on the shoulders, looking after the shoulders—city shepherd.

The girl who handed him his tongue roll to go said, "Can I ask you a question?"

Hind said, "Six-seven."

And now, what was this pier? He had been observed. But before the delivery of the note, how many times had he dropped by this pier? Three or four. Who had watched him? Hind had seen everything. It was the same now, except that now, across the river in another borough, a crane ground and flowed through its slow job with a chain and wrecking ball. From here, its spinning arbor was invisible even when its cable or a pocket of grease caught the sun. Hind watched the crane swing away from a lofty gray façade now bereft of the edifice it had been part of. Hind watched the gooseneck pivot, then reverse, as the ball began to follow, pivot back toward the wall and wait while the pendulum wheeled into its new cycle of inertia, the chain stiff as a vector; and at last, with superintendent skill, the inclined crane, its transverse and longitudinal parts so fine against the sky they looked drawn by a draftsman's hand, waited at the wall as the steel ball made its arc and struck from the stone a puff of dust.

In the other direction—between Hind's pier and the hospital—a crew were planting foundations and pipes in a spacious hole at the center of whose area stood a forty-foot-high steam rig housing a drop hammer. And between all this and the pier ran the Drive, a nearly complete belt that followed the shores of three intersecting rivers which made this borough, Hind's borough, an island. Beyond the island, the harbor; beyond the harbor, the sea. Your fellow residents mostly ignored the city's association with the sea; few looked toward the sea except when they spent vacations at beaches beyond the old city limits. The city became other than its named self, became the very coast of which it had been part.

In any case, the picture, thus—Hind stared at the cement below the beam he sat on: hospital, construction, Drive, pier, river (one of the three), and across the river in another borough the crane and wrecking ball. You knew where you were. Sometimes a fore-and-aft-prop helicopter crossing the river took your eye from one object to the next. Hind tried to make out the manufacturer's name on a nearby cleat.

If you were six-seven everybody knew where you were.

The pier was in fact two piers divided by a slip. On the larger one, a cement plaza, were parked eleven baby carriages. From an unidentified transistor Hind heard over the slip a famous southpaw say, "Pitching? It's the name of the game." What was this city's name? On chipped, faded, initialed green benches over there sat middle-aged and elderly men with bared breasts who pushed their faces toward the sun. The smaller pier—Hind's—was narrow, also floored with cement, and not cluttered with young mothers and small fry; it was connected to the larger pier only by a walk at the landward end.

His own berth was one of the rutted beams framing the pier's two lengthways borders and its river end. Alternately on his stomach and his back, he lay on a faded olive towel Sylvia had left. And he listened for whatever it was he was meant to hear.

He foresaw but did not really wish to forestall the inevitable.

He began to think of himself as a regular.

He would be forced once more into being someone's confidant, perhaps merely because he made someone nervous: "You're a pretty tall boy there. Say your name was Hind?" The name "Jack" would lead to the inevitable, illogical "You're quite a beanstalk."

He looked at his legs. They were, of course, the longest, or tallest, legs on the pier. Even twenty years ago his limbs had in a way blinded him; from an over-all length of twenty-seven inches at birth, he had by the age of fifteen reached seventy-three. During the laps and laps he logged in the choppy waters of the pool at school—and as, off the one-meter board, he tucked violently into a double somersault then snapped full out to a slight backward lean which inertia swung so he slipped feet first into the water upright (hands pressed along thighs, legs never then quite perfectly unbent)—he knew he could never stop his growth, knew he'd add more inches whether he smoked or did nonbreathing headstands or tried to give his arms and torso and thighs and calves the compressed fullness of a weight-lifter's neat body, like Siggofreddo Morales's, the public high school diving champion in those days. As the winter solstice approached, indeed all through midwinter, Hind tried to blight his energies; but he grew and grew, right down to his animal toes and their vegetable nails. At fifteen, seventy-three inches; now, years later, an apparently full stand of seventy-nine or seventy-nine-and-a-half, depending on day-to-day weather.

The pier regulars didn't look at him much unless he stood up. At first none of them—not even Ivy Bowles, who talked to anyone and read the paper out loud—could take Hind enough for granted to say, "You're a tall man, son," or "You grew, didn't you!" or "Let me give you some Unicap Vitamin Capsules, Slim," or "How's the pressure up there?"

The third day of the pier watch the old man in brown trunks with a hard-looking growth of belly and blue words tattooed on his shoulders said when Hind got up to stretch, "You must be basketball." And Hind said that he was just tall, but that indeed he had often been asked to join teams.

"See what *I* got," the man said. "Fresh from the hospital, look at this." He pointed to the mauve stripe zippered down his middle from breast to abdomen. It covered up a place where something had been taken out or where what was still there had been rerouted. But hadn't the old man implied, "We're both freaks today"? Yet he would rather be Hind's height and whole, and see down his front not the zipper-line of stitch welts but merely these long lateral wrinkles Hind's slouch renewed each day. His name was Charley and he had come thirty years ago from southern Poland.

From how the people sometimes stared, any of them could be the lead implied in the old woman's note. Or would it not be a person? A private hydrofoil with a drydock-like frame of two-by-fours across its bow-stem took businessmen up the river and out to the marine basin three times a day. Would the contact be an event? Along the edge of the Drive a fellow tried to start his motorcycle by running beside it, and as soon as he swung onto the seat, the motorcycle slowed down as if it could run only in competition with the man. Or was the contact the nature of this place? At lunchtime both piers filled up with white-coated hospital employees who sat and watched the river traffic.

Hind observed the regulars. He came to know their habits.

The body pumping push-ups near him was Buck Field. He had short legs. Cheating a bit, he dropped down too fast, fell so sharply Hind worried he might jam his chin into the cement. At first Buck seemed to use as a metronome for his calisthenics the pile driver's bong whoosh bong whoosh bong whoosh in the hospital yard; but then he let the mechanical beat edge ahead of his own; and the slowing tempo against the faster pulled Hind's attention toward him. Hind couldn't keep his mind quite clear when this happened; he counted the push-ups thirty-six, thirty-seven, -eight, -nine....The pile driver cut, leaving silence like echoes, and Hind, almost hearing the next blow, felt its eventual sound hang broad above him in the spring air. Buck Field came for his workout at ten forty-five, and by the time he had done his last set of leg raises—a pale vein starting out on the left side of his flat abdomen—an hour had gone by.

Charley, the man with the shiny new scar, got after Hind first. It was the fifth day. Charley's questions seemed to arise from the paper he was reading. He crashed it down from in front of him asking Hind for an authoritative answer concerning the news item. Yet the item would point also to Hind.

"You know everything, you're young, tell me: baseball bat boys at spring training Florida, when do they go to school? They get taken away from their family; they kid around the Grapefruit League till middle of April, then they come up north with the team, the season opens, but when do they go back to their families? I mean, when do they go back to school? Steal them away from school, school is what they ought to be. I pay taxes for public school, I used to pay *taxes*."

Kids. Abductions. Can kids be deduced from income tax?

Or, throwing down his paper and clamping swollen knuckles over the edge of the beam he sat on, he asked Hind something even closer to home.

"Why don't a kid have a right to grow up right?"

But did he want Hind's answer? He supplied his own: "Because they get ahold of him in this new school built out of blue and yellow bricks, and they teach my grandnephew not spelling and long division but dances. One night he got his knees up and kicking his foot around in a circle, you know what, we did that where I come from in the mountains in eighteen-ninety-six when I was small and didn't have this scar. In my schoolhouse with the bush blowing against the shutter and such woodwork on the outside like you don't see no more, with the boards slanting up to meet in the center like a whole lot of upside-down V's—we had no window glass...Because a kid here don't learn what he *got* to know, he don't stand on his own feet, they give him a load of manure he should get along with other people and folk dancing, and he never learn to do nothing for himself, no more than the coloreds. Initiative. Same with the government now. Big government like my radio says it has you from womb to tomb. I say they kill these kids, their spirit, there's no training. *I'm* not kidding. Because my grandnephew just as well stay home, I teach him spelling, long division, but the school board takes him away *where*? To hold hands and do a folk dance that was old as the hills in eighteen-ninety-six. Let *me* get my hands on him *I* teach him. I never see my grandnephew, they never ask me over."

And the speed with which he now brought up his paper in front of him seemed to make the relevance of what he said even odder. But Hind couldn't know. Charley—his name was Charley, Mrs. Bowles called him that—did not seem confidential.

Hind looked at the others around him, browning, sweating, still. Radio music measured time. The marine offshore forecast came every half-hour.

The morning he had found the old woman at his mailbox he should have ignored her and proceeded around the block to see Sylvia. (Sylvia worked at home designing dust jackets. Along the top of a low white bookcase leaned oblongs of color finished in gray card-board frames.) Yet he had been so ready to forget the clear, cold black stair-rail descending under his hand; forget the differences between the now almost defunct business his landlord-undertaker ran in the bottom two floors of the brownstone and the life Hind lived in the top, rented floor; forget the precisely known distance between the undertaker's and the six-floor walkup Sylvia now lived in.

Charley's volunteered remarks on kids and abductions might not mean a thing. The kidnap was so long ago.

From the start of that first inquiry long ago he had thought the kidnapers might evade the law for years, yet assumed that no two of the facts growing in his mind were far apart. Much depended on how you put them. Language is the trap: unquote Hind's guardian, whose name had been different from Hind's but who had been like a father to him. As a child you lived far into the future: as you grew, your name "Hind" would change and when you were a grownup your name would have turned into your guardian's. Out of warm reverie Hind blinked forth upon the sky; for a second he didn't know which was cloud and which was the momentarily pale blue, as if overhead were an unfamiliar map on which land and sea were distinct, though which was which wasn't plain. He woke in the middle of one childhood summer night thinking about his height and hearing a woman say to the guardian, "It's very well to preserve your feeling for her, but adopting her child was going a bit far. Unless you've a wife to help." The guardian's life seemed whole, with a beginning so long before Hind it seemed huge and ancient, and a future as destined, collective, and collected as his fourteen or fifteen thousand books or as his neighbor's mother's privately printed Christmas gift to all her friends, a glossy-plated essay on sumac-dyed weaving wool in old Portsmouth, New Hampshire: a wholeness automatically Hind's since he was the guardian's: but as impenetrable as Jackie was himself indelibly adopted.

Seven years ago, as if by memory, he had been able really to see the days through which the kidnap approached; he oversaw the plan though he couldn't spell it out; heard the jays in that deep country scene throw proud squeezed voices through the pines and oaks toward the house in whose kitchen window a tan Abyssinian tom, lean and crisp, looked up through the pane at a nest in a fork of a rhododendron that at two or three points grew against the pane; heard the jays' squawk fly through the sheltering green above the jagged windows of sunlight in the cool-shaded grass and patches of ground with sweet needles.

The tenth of that subtle month the doomed parents made their final move to this house in the country. The thirteenth, in the hardware store in front of two banks of trowels with dark wooden handles, he and she put on a quick, alert argument after the proprietor had tried not to take sides on what hose to buy, vinyl or rubber. "You can see how countrified *we* are," the woman said, "you can see how much *we* know about living in the country." And her husband said to her, "I came out of the city because my child had to breathe, and if you don't help us live in the country, you can go back." But she merely said, "He commutes." A long, new month.

Hind thought almost anyone could without too much stretching make sense of the narrative examples set down in clumps in his mind. Not that he could not merely enjoy the facts in themselves; they were rich, simply alone and singly: the initial trip to the country–the purchase of the stone house–the final move–the hardware scene–the incident of the wall–the appearance at a nearby newspaper-store-soda-fountain of an unidentified, dimly described female friend of the husband (possibly a cousin by some early, now dissolved marriage): she asked how to get to the house, and was told by the big man in the green-and-black-check jacket (whose skinny boy and girl ate chocolate doughnuts hiding behind his legs) that there were two routes to the house through the hills, and that four miles from the house they came together and became one road. Someday Hind would think luxuriously about these facts divorced from the kidnap by then solved.

Meanwhile the folk on the pier hoped for an accident on the Drive. The mildest peep of tires not holding brought eyes up and heads around. When Hind heard the start of a really good skid's wheeling treble, he felt like sticking his arm straight out sharp: he often stuck out his arm at curbs in case a pedestrian beside him put a foot into the street with a car coming.

"Funny there aren't more accidents on the Drive," said Ivy Bowles. She read from her paper: "'Air Pollution

Study Group Reports Increased Hazard.' 'Acid Man Attacks Child.' Except again they say it wasn't acid, they don't know exactly what it was, something new. But it works." Mrs. Bowles laughed.

When she read articles she read so slowly Hind wondered if she made it up. "...a little girl—why would you throw acid on a little girl's face? Here comes the colored wino." Mrs. Bowles was looking down the pier.

Hind was on his back. He closed his eyes again. He watched his pink, sun-blurred hand save a child's face from acid that had been intended to clean the face of personal traces. And three drops sank into the back of Hind's hand and turned it into a claw-wing expertly composed and fuselaged by a film team's property man, a claw with raised green veins. Yet when Hind took away the child and turned him around to see the face, it had nothing precise and personal, nothing familiar, on it. But this might be the effect of the pier, to which Hind was now returning as fast as he had dropped off into what Sylvia would call fantasy: can't dance at two weddings with one behind: he couldn't hold onto the child and its hands and face and its promise, and at the same time return to the pier and old Ivy Bowles' talk. Far away the child's face was being pressed this way and that, retreating into space and suffering atmospheric drags, flesh losing hold but never holding a new shape. Hind blinked.

Ivy Bowles said, "He tried to bum a Popsicle from the Puerto Rican. Now he's coming to bother us." She spoke for the whole group of sunbathers. She kept an eye on the colored wino. "They like sweets," she said. "'Course vanilla's a type of dope."

When he reached the end area where the regulars were, the colored wino, who called himself Berry Brown and whom Hind sometimes saw early in the morning at Mitropoulos's Always Open Coffee Cup, did not address them. Instead, he went to the very end of the beam where Charley sat and Ivy Bowles now lay on her side. Berry Brown was being independent and prim today. He knelt on the cement, leaned over the beam pressing his stomach on it, and stretched so that his legs straightened and he balanced on the toes of his basketball sneakers. He went further, and his rubber toes teetered up just off the cement. Ivy Bowles said, "Watch him go in, he's down there grazing on the lichens." Berry and his girlfriend, who waited for him now on a bench on the other, larger pier, shared a suitcase–blue, molded airplane luggage made of amazingly lightweight polypropylene. This was what Berry Brown was getting, from a crossbeam four feet above the water.

He unlocked the two locks, snapped the latches, and lifted the lid. On a pile of things he found a neatly folded pair of dirty white athletic socks. These he put carefully on a beam by Ivy Bowles. Then he locked the case and lowered it over the edge of the pier to its crossbeam. He didn't look at anyone but tramped slowly back down the pier. On the other one his girl tipped up to her mouth a bottle in a brown paper bag. You assumed it was a bottle. (If you're still trying to break the kidnap.)

Yesterday Berry Brown asked people one by one all the way along Hind's pier for two filter cigarettes. Charley had stared into his paper and said, "I don't speak to him. Let him stand on his own two feet. 'F I had my way, I'd take care of him." But Brown, who empty-handed would have been forced to save face by purposefully going down after his gear, was saved by Ivy Bowles, who handed him one cigarette even as he turned to speak to Charley. Then Berry flared his nicked Zippo at her but she wasn't smoking. That was yesterday; today he had come and gone as if the regulars weren't here. He was stopping again at the white ice cream wagon; the Puerto Rican shook his head; he needed a shave. Berry Brown was still talking, but the Puerto Rican was looking at Hind, or in Hind's direction. He jingled the little side bells as if to emphasize a point to Berry Brown.

Charley said, "Over on the bench he got every morning newspaper there is. You bet he don't pay money for them. Every paper you ever heard of."

Hot air from an apartment incinerator chimney made the higher gray edifice behind it float on the shimmer. Noon traffic on the Drive was heating up, slowing. To get to the pier from the other side of the Drive you took a foot overpass; or if you came from a few blocks uptown headed for the brief walk that ran along the river, you took your chance beating the traffic, there was no light. The walk ran from the Drive end of Hind's pier to the right for seventy-five yards and then smack into the construction firm's on-site office, a green Mariette house trailer parked broadside to the walk and parallel to the Drive. What were they working on? Now, with clement weather, five drunks took the benches along the walk or sat on the ground up against the trees and from that level in a helplessly subtle tone of lupine deference accosted passers-by.

Buck Field tried to keep exercising when Berry Brown came over to the regulars' pier to dance. But it turned Buck's rhythm into something else. Berry put his hand which concealed his transistorette to his large, delicately arced ear so the ear seemed through some physiological turn to be a fluting pipe, and he did a step Hind couldn't quite understand, there seemed to be no repetitions. Berry danced at first as if with a partner, his girl stayed on the other pier. He bowed, extending to the rear (like a holed-out golfer bending for his ball) a leg whose foot's toe tapped left, right, before swinging through to do the same in front; but the other leg then would not respond in kind but did, not this Greek beginning again, but, to the same beat of his own and to the continuing hustle of the heavy prefab music, now the cocky thrust forward of a Twist stance, his knee rolling over and in, over and in, before he twisted round into the air like a skater better than Hind had ever been.

"Oh, don't pretend to be high-spirited," said Buck Field, who then turned and smiled so at Hind that Hind thought once more that Buck might be the contact implied in the very tall old woman's note.

Berry stopped. "You afraid of personal contact. You afraid of my rhythm. You think all black men got rhythm. You with you Air India kit. Well I have *not* got rhythm."

Buck lay back and did a leg raise. "I got an assistant waiting to go to lunch, and I got two more sets to do here."

When Hind was on this pier, Berry Brown, except for his few visits across, was always from his pier watching the regulars, even when he was tipping up the paper bag. If Hind got to his feet to have a casual look around but ostensibly to stretch, and especially if he got up abruptly, he felt Berry Brown's eye go with him. Hind's sense that the eye stayed with him was like his sense during high school soccer games his guardian came to watch years ago. His guardian called soccer Association Football and if with a goal kick Hind found one of his halfbacks or better still a drifting winger, the guardian would analyze it later and call it a "useful" kick—he had given three whole years of his life to living in England.

When Hind glanced at the sideline to catch his guardian's approval, the face would look away shyly. One day Hind stood at fullback thinking as usual about how Coach Blum, the Spanish teacher, thought of him only as Hind's Height. "We've got Hind's height at fullback. His height is good for defensive headers when the ball goes loose up in the air by the goal mouth, and good for stopping the offensive looper toward the corner because you can't ever depend on an opposing forward being caught offside; good, too, for–" Blum used long, informative sentences in his half-time talks–"good, too, for psychological effect not only as a sort of moving goal post in your way but just as a tall man." The guardian stood on the sidelines; the game was degenerating, stockings down, shirt-tails flying, neither team holding possession. No matter what his guardian said, Hind would not have made first team if he'd had to rely on his left foot or on snappiness of reflex (though indeed he ran terrifically fast once he got going). He could catch from a standing position some of the high balls kids of normal height would have to catch with a bicycle kick; and though he couldn't run circles round the circles enemy forwards tried to run round him, he would plant himself in the way, and the inside or outside left would usually fail to beat Hind, for Hind would make a long leg reach out farther than even experienced forwards envisioned. What he loved about fullback–as opposed to how his partner de Forrest felt at left full, for he was mainly a frustrated left half and a would-be play-maker–was that you protected. The men were yours. When the heat was off and the halfs and forwards charged at each other far upfield, Hind was protecting the whole interest of his team. His guardian was looking at him, and the second time young Hind caught him watching, the guardian shook his head in sage approval. But the herd now broke for Hind's goal and Hind's center half tried a skidding hook tackle about as effective as Hind and Maddy Beecher when they pretended water in the school pool was a basepath and went running off the edge into it as if sliding into second base. Hind's right half was being outrun by the man with the ball, Hind bounced on his toes and tried to know exactly when to challenge this opposing outside left whose jinking run now began to slow. But out of the ground almost, or out of nowhere,

Hind's left half was there, and now, in for an instant the very same rhythm as the dribbling enemy winger, he met the white ball with its green-brown stains but spun it up with enough height and English to go back over his own shaggy black head. The little left-winger was round the halfback trying to get possession again, with only the ball and Hind between him and the goal. He had never really lost his momentum when Hind's halfback had blocked him, and now, as the ball bounced high, he went up wildly tilting for a bicycle, and slashed his shin through the air as if he would break the ball before it ever found the nets: but Hind was there very simply with his shoe, his other foot barely off the ground; and as the enemy forward missed and Hind's shin deflected the ball, Hind's instep caught the whipping shin of his man, who fell as suddenly as a diver disappears into the second part of a front-dive-with-a-delayed-one-and-a-half, fell onto his side, and started to make a screaming noise and rolled onto his chest. And Hind had broken the leg so cleanly the bone beneath the calf muscle prodded the skin. Out of the corner of his eye Hind had seen de Forrest recover the ball and begin, with eager, balancing elbows, to angle upfield—but two staccato trebles from the ref stopped de Forrest. What had been painful was not the agony of the boy, who had mysteriously turned into a sick person, but rather the way Hind had now been defended by that watchful eye from the sidelines, the fascinated partisan guardian, who now approached.

Ivy Bowles put down her paper and her magnetized lorgnette magnifier and, lying down full length, turned on her side, her back to the river, her right leg (tan, knobbly) resting neatly on the left. "That's the insane wing of the hospital right back of where the men are working."

The pile driver had started again; Buck Field was doing jack-knife leg raises.

"What's your first name, Mr. Hind?" asked Ivy Bowles.

"Jack," said Hind.

The pile driver cut again and Buck Field said, "You got a good body, you obviously keep in shape."

"*You're* educated," said Ivy Bowles to Hind—she hadn't asked him what he did—"what should be the punishment for mutilation and disfigurements? That little girl with the acid face doesn't look the same any more; it's like her real face has been taken away. They should execute a man does that to a child. What do you think?"

"They should cure him and *then* punish him," said Hind. "He's crazy, but punishment doesn't mean anything until you really have something to lose but he's lost his mind: cure him, then punish him."

"What sentence would you give him, I'd cut him down to size," said Ivy Bowles. She saw that Hind was staring at her old legs, skinny, puffy thighs.

"I'd make him replace the other face, I'd make him find it."

Ivy Bowles squinted at Hind as if trying to see through what he said, or almost to hint to him that she had something to tell.

"You're an only child, I bet; or anyway you don't have children."

"One," said Hind, nodding, grinning.

"Then you must be an only child to talk like that—imagine not deterring a man who throws acid in a little girl's face! Execution's a deterrent. Any more than a family man spends all day sunbathing off by himself."

"I *was* an only child. That is, before my parents died and left me to my guardian, and he's dead now."

"You don't say," said Ivy Bowles, "and you're a grown-up man. Well, you were joking about that sentence."

Her head was on her arm. The way she lay sideways she looked as if she could be blown away by the wind. So early in the spring hers must be a lamp tan. Dewey Wood at the health club uptown wore ski goggles in front of a bank of lamps; his skin was slipping, but Mrs. Bowles was unwholesomely trim. Hind didn't want an argument with her; he hadn't been joking about the punishment. She didn't seem to be the kidnap contact implied in the old woman's note, but on the other hand why should this contact be sympathetic, and might it not turn out to be the original tall old girl herself?

Or was it the mildest background thing one didn't bother to look at? The soiled white jacket of the Puerto Rican ice cream man. Or the pattern of pile driver hammer strokes in the work area by the hospital. When the Circle Line boat came by with its load of sightseers circuiting the island, he had heard a loudspeaker but didn't listen to what it said. On the river now a man seemed to be staring at Hind, or the pier—a man leaning against the stern pilothouse of a great barge—the *Cape Rose*. Upriver, under the charcoal-gray tracery of the old mid-city bridge, another kind of boat came fast in Hind's direction. On the other pier a helmeted lead-line tester in bell-bottoms was calling data to a man in a dark suit who cradled a clipboard. At the Drive end of the pier, a pregnant girl in shorts and halter was breaking precedent pushing a small stroller toward the regulars. Ivy Bowles eyed her.

"There you are, breeding as fast as she can, coming onto the small pier. I see what we're going to be by July."

At noon a tug from the south tied up for lunch. It drifted against the beams of Hind's pier, and the sunbathers opened their eyes and got up on their elbows when they felt the massive budge. If seat belts were being used, Hind would have supervised their fastening. Hind believed that the tug's movement caused a huge compression within the substance of the pier. Two fat women slowly and observantly were devouring submarines inch by inch.

One day, just as Buck Field finished his squats and just before the tug came for lunch, a young man with rimless glasses, high black pompadour, white-on-white open at the throat showing a white T-shirt, black chino trousers, sheer white socks, and tasseled black loafers, sat down near Hind. Wired to the oblong object in his breast pocket was a biscuit-shaped mike he cupped in his palm. Smiling sweetly, he did something to the object—a tape recorder—in his breast pocket and opened a paperback entitled *Guerillas of the Spirit, or You Can't See the Good for the Trees.* Hind couldn't hear what was being said into the mike, but the young man—he was perhaps three years younger than Hind and had eyes as dark brown as Hind's—was reading from the book. But after only a page, and just as Buck Field was removing his khakis from his Air India bag, a big man in his mid-forties came onto the pier with a bottle and a reflector that opened out like a triptych book and proceeded to take off his gray sharkskin lounge suit (with double vent fattening his behind) and every stitch except for a gray rayon bikini like the one Hind's old friend Oliver Plane wore at the health club uptown. The young man with the tape recorder looked up from *Guerillas of the Spirit* and smiled sweetly at the newcomer and then emphatically frowned at the bottle of Scotch. After which he went back to his job.

The big man was monkeying with his bottle. His great torso was shining.

But the bottle was a radio and the dials worked laterally at the base of the neck. Music came from the bottle. Buck Field said something. The man fingered the radio's repertoire; for two seconds Hind heard Handel's bagpipe air.

The young man stopped reading and said to the man with the radio, "I'm trying to record."

"So I'm giving you background music." The man didn't look up. Then he did, and stared.

"What I am saying cannot be heard over your so-called background music. I'm sorry."

"My music is free," said the man, hunching forward comfortably and tilting his head sideways to eye the young man. (And the swerving logic played in Hind's memory like one of two familiar events so alike he would confuse them.)

"It's breaking into my work," said the young man with the tape recorder. "I record books for the Baptist Blind, I give up my lunch break to this tape recorder"—he smiled and shook his head—"when I get out of my office at five-thirty, I have to go to school; otherwise I won't be able to make it here in the city, I'm from the sticks"—he grinned—"so some of my recording sessions have to be fit in during lunch break, that's the way the ball bounces."

The man in the bikini had brought the bottle up close to his ear and had turned away from the young man, who now changed his tone and said, "Control that radio, hear?"

"Don't sit up so straight," said the radio man, "what's the matter with you, really listen to this here." Then he snapped his eyes toward the young man and said, "Hear the vibes, I guess we're coming to the overture, buddy." He grinned too hard at the young man.

Two Orientals whom Hind realized he had already seen here turned off the promenade into the regulars' pier and approached at a steady efficient pace. The big one was dressed in a black suit, the little one in black trousers and a hospital employee's white jacket. Their faces were full-chopped, very similar; but the picture they made was in their proportions, which appeared to be identical: next to his small companion the man in black (hardly as tall as Hind) seemed massive. But when you forced your eyes to see scale, not size, then these two Orientals on the pier were twins. There was something like this sometimes at the health club uptown. And now, too, in Sylvia's remarks on the new antiperspective as expounded by the Englishman she entertained at her flat. In her words the theory seemed so familiar Hind heard his heart snap recollections too dark to see, and in his nose and the inboard bank of each eye socket that old rinse simplified all congestion in a leavening embrace like childhood or death. But he could get no further, it just was not up to him, he was at the mercy of his memory. The Orientals sat on the Drive side of Hind, the tape recorder on the other side between Hind and the river end of the pier. The dispute was louder, but against some of the words these two Oriental men now exchanged, the dispute became a background. The importance of what they said seemed to magnify the soft wash of a dozen forgotten wakes among the mossy pilings under the pier. The light breeze had swung round from the draped intricacies of the near bridge upriver, and now came from the whirring Drive.

And now Hind believed what he heard: he was hearing what he wanted to hear, or what the powerful old woman who had left him the note wanted him to hear—ranks and ranks of long-lost people associated with the kidnap fled into his mind; and he cursed these Orientals for not speaking up: "...Utopia Boulevard"—nearly visible, nearly–"...Partridge and Company...Jordan Marsh"—the Boston store to whose blanket department the wrapper label had been traced, which led in turn to (and the small Oriental said it)–"the bungalow outside Lynnfield"–deserted on a small lake in or near the model suburban townlet, red or yellow with lots of white trim; neat little residential loops, sometimes another level and a ramp up to the garage, the Huckleberry School, the bank, the golf course, Nibur Paint and Hardware, The Village Footman, Lynnfield Cleanser (a ticket? a memory?), the Village something Restaurant, The Pioneer Shoppe (where Hind received notice instead of information, and was later tracked from there by the Mass. police)–"because," the small Chinese said, "the...Peoples Drug Store..."–the one in–which one in?–Baltimore, where two alleged adults had been seen openly with the child, each holding a hand; which hand?

The Baptist unplugged his mike, wrapped its cord, and said in a higher-pitched voice, "People in the city don't know how to act. Someday I'll go back home."

"Go, go," said the beefy man listening to his Scotch bottle.

The big Oriental said something ending in "-she Laurel"–which had to be the last name and second syllable of the first, of Hershey Laurel, the first time Hind had heard the name said in how long–*Her*shey Laurel, it had to be–the boy kidnaped, the closed case.

At this instant, seeing the small Oriental point to his lips to shush his friend, Hind turned away from them and checked if the long-lost child's name had been picked up by the regulars and the combatants; but they had as promptly turned their attention to the skidding car or cars, and as the shriek of hot rubber sank in the air, the man in the bikini grinned fixedly at the Baptist recorder and said, "Too bad no accident, eh? Too bad no accident: So you sacrifice your lunch hour to tape-record propaganda for blind people to be entertained, but you want an accident like I do."

"Anybody give me two filters and a light?" said Berry Brown, who Hind saw was standing with one sneaker up on the beam by the frayed edge of Hind's towel. "I'm out of fluid."

"Gave it up, man," said Hind. But Berry Brown had addressed himself to the group at the very end of the pier.

The wind had shifted. In the corner of his eye, Hind saw the Orientals.

The young man with the tape recorder rather too slowly and not menacingly enough took two steps toward the man in the bikini, who mincingly with the same bad grin took four toward him. The Scotch bottle sang behind him.

When Hind carefully turned back to the Orientals, fearing they had walked away, they were both looking in his direction, whether at him or at the dispute behind him he wasn't sure. They were not talking.

There were scuffs on the cement, the Orientals tensed, Hind looked back at the end of the pier to see the man in the bikini with the big chest prevent the young tape recorder man from getting past him to lay hands on the bottle radio.

"*Don't* call me a Christian," the young man cried, "I'm a Baptist!"

"They're crazy," said Ivy Bowles, and drew her legs in and grasped her shins so she seemed perched on her beam.

The young man was now pushed staggering backwards; the older man was heavier and stronger, though fat. Charley the old Pole gripped his beam. A man across from Hind picked up his things and walked away in his undershorts. The young man with the tape recorder moaned trying to free his arms from the other man's grasp and push back.

"You was going to mess with my property," said the man in the bikini.

"I'll throw it overboard where it belongs," said the young man, and shifting his weight to the other hip he caused the bigger man to fall past him to the beam just to the right of where Ivy Bowles had been huddled. But she, to keep him from reaching her, rose up on astonishingly live legs and looked like an animal backing off or a tree come to human hovering life for the second she took to lose her balance and lean very straight-spined back onto the air, then start to jack her head toward her feet before disappearing from the sight of Hind, who now stood up. But Berry Brown was quick, and Hind's chagrin not to be her savior was stopped by his exhilaration at seeing Berry Brown lope long-leggedly forward as if he hoped to swing across the river to where the crane and wrecking ball were knocking down the gray façade, then find, as if he were a broad jumper, that he had not enough room for a final full stride, take the interrupted step and therefore be forced by his rhythm to bring his other leg forth in a grand step which prevented him from diving—which would not have been advisable in any case, for lifesavers must try not to submerge and must therefore go in feet first, feet preferably scissored, arms out—and bring off a stagger vault which made clumsiness sudden virtue, and perhaps it was the style in which he entered the water that made him howl triumphantly, though he howled too late, for he was hitting the water, he was partly drowned out by his splash and by a new, stronger noise from Ivy Bowles.

Hind was at the edge watching Berry Brown do the cross-chest carry, and Ivy Bowles now was looking neutrally across the river.

The Orientals weren't around any more. Hind hadn't kept an eye on them. He took a step or two toward the Drive, stopped, and looked at the foot overpass, and imagined his moving eye had caught just the memory of the two men's presence leaving the foot overpass on the other side of the Drive. He had lost them. Was this loss implied in the old woman's note? Was this lesson that he should have taken his prize and ignored the fracas at the pier's river end?

Many people on the other, larger pier were looking. The young mother on Hind's pier was coming with a huge green-flowered towel, it must be six feet.

How could he use the words he'd heard? He thought he knew the old sequence, but thought he must now use the known names freshly. How could he use the words he'd heard, without the Oriental men who had spoken them? How do you use what you have?

When he was very young he was so tall for his age he hesitated to fight other boys. Yet in processions, as if administering a touch of punishment *de haut en bas*, he kicked their calves from behind. The boys never deigned to plot against him—Maddy Beecher, who was beginning to be friends with him then, had said that the fact that Hind had a guardian protected him—Hind's foster father; the boys never plotted against him even when they formed a cadre of Minute Men in the spring of 'forty-five. ("Fight in the mountains at a moment's notice, vanish unbeknownst.") The Minute Men—Fourth and Fifth Formers—made special allowance for him (despite his racially objectionable height) because he was a foster child and to be pitied. But he was, as nearly as he ever could be, angry, on behalf of his guardian, who was as real a father and thus possessed as real a son as any Minute Man family might boast.

At a swimming meet Hind had been slightly thrown off by the idea that the lights would fuse just when he left his third and final approach step and rose from the harsh cocoa matting to jump for his take-off spring—then lights out. His guardian came to the meets. Later they discussed, say, Siggofreddo Morales's form, not Hind's poor third, or his cowardly choice of a summer-vacation back flip for one of his optionals.

The young mother with the voluminous towel said, looking down into the water at Ivy, "The poor dear!" Hind heard Ivy say out of sight below eye level, "The slime is unbelievable, you wouldn't know it's a salt river."

Their purpose, whatever it was, had carried the two Oriental men off fast. Hind couldn't leave the pier yet. He went to the edge next to the young mother, and looked down at Berry Brown and Ivy.

Sometimes the kidnap seemed to have started in his head before actually happening in fact. His guardian had given Sylvia and him a beach party before they left for Europe almost seven years ago. They weren't married, and, of all people, Sylvia went shy when the guardian wanted to book their hotel rooms everywhere. He would have footed the trip even if he had known, as Sylvia knew, why Hind was really going. The guardian had probably never known of Hind's devoted interest in the kidnap, possibly hadn't known of the kidnap itself.

Why should another beach party much earlier seem also to fall within the kidnap? It was just after college, and the guardian corralled some of Hind's friends, and all but one stayed at least one night in the house. Maddy Beecher and fiancée came, and dangerous Cassia Meaning; and the guardian not quite quizzically enough criticized Maddy for planning to marry so young. Bee Bee Barker came with her canvas athletic bag. Ashley Sill got tight on the beach and complained that Hind's guardian had blackmailed him into driving all the way from Maine. Oliver Plane's girl drove him out from the city, and he said he had come only to have a look at the guardian's tenant.

He meant a portly Japanese youth who lived on the beach in the former bath shack which the guardian had equipped with two electric burners. The Jap wasn't exactly a tenant; he didn't pay. There were a wife and three small children, though at the time of the beach party these four were away. And there was his talent. The guardian was always referring to it. "You see," he argued with Bee Bee (who looked away while he spoke), "there is such a thing as inborn character, however true all our patient views are of the ambiguous collaboration between genes and circumstance."

After the guardian got the fire started, the Jap came out of his shack and waddled grinning toward the group, and the guardian in his finely pressed jeans walked quite a distance with his hand outstretched–he'd thought the Jap was coming faster than he really was–and then they shook hands at last. The guardian, still holding the man's hand, swung gracefully round using his left hand and arm to sweep open an avenue of excitement leading from the Jap to Hind and his friends–though the gesture didn't quite work, for naturally the guardian's right hand kept hold of the other man's right, so the guardian's right arm with the fringes of the suède frontier jacket hanging down partly blocked the other man's front– and said, "I'd like to introduce you to the distinguished Japanese poet"–and the name. The Jap put his left hand over his eyes and giggled. Later, as Hind knew he would, the man recited the same old translation.

The guardian cooked, no one could help. Hind tried to take the guardian's hand off the handle of the bean pot: "Let one of the girls cook." But the guardian merely switched his hip round and bumped Hind down onto his knee in the sand. And Bee Bee Barker said, "You wouldn't catch me cooking dinner"–she was the same even today, though she had someone to do it for her.

The guardian insisted everyone sing a song. Later, in the middle of the Japanese poet's recitation and the dark, the guardian went swimming.

With surging hips and swaying thick shoulders he waded out. And when he came to the narrow crest of the high bar he dived into the dark.

The fire didn't carry far enough. Bee Bee Barker's big silver flashlight found him floating toes up, but by then the recitation was over and the guardian had been in the water for a while. He pulled his toes toward him without his knees breaking the surface, so he looked, from head to toes, about three feet six. Indeed, in any case, he was already a good five inches shorter than Hind by then.

Why hadn't Sylvia appeared for such a long time? For so many years? Hind was twenty-seven when he met her.

A good girl. Bugged by something, she'd nag once; then, if it didn't take, she'd drop it. "I should think you'd want to know about your parents, especially since they were friends of your guardian. *I'd* want to know. You've kept their name." But the guardian told what there was to be told and left the subject open and Hind closed it. One father, if he was good, was enough for any man. Furthermore, family tree surgery ends in dull, smug self-interest, and there's so much helpful work you can do for other people, let *them* know you for what you are. "But–" said Sylvia, and stopped herself–"Oh, I'll shut up."

Once under a street lamp in Cracow, she had known his thoughts and caught his wrist and warned him–before she married, before she got pregnant, before a sequence of unmanageable distortions happened to him–"Give up that child, abandon the kidnap. Or else you'll give me up and your own children." By then he knew that both kidnap parents–Sears and Shirley Laurel–were dead, and he wanted to know why. The hourly trumpets began to blow from the cathedral tower in the square a block away, and Sylvia turned and walked ahead of Hind, and said, "This damned Laurel thing isn't your business," and five fellows who had just stepped from the university students' club's ground-floor window opened a path for her and laughed.

Why shouldn't Sylvia, then or now, understand that he had made something dreadfully simple out of the case? The case and the manner in which, unsolved, it had finally been closed with a confident disclaimer from headquarters—this was what all their lives today were about. Sylvia didn't give him credit. A pile of, a compost bed of, a formulaic sound of complications—made into something richly simpler. He wanted to find a child. The child had in fact been kidnaped. The case had been closed, though never broken, and the evidence the police publicized was inconclusive. Sylvia had seemed to love Hind most when she seemed suddenly to change her mind and instead of continuing to call him off the chase told him he should go on, but told him in a demeaning way: "Someday you will get to the end, the real end of it: you'll find out why you started the hunt in the first place." But what in effect was her love when it grabbed away the very nature of the search and put in front of him a new one? He was through saying, "If I don't do this, who will?"

Sylvia said, "You see that everything is like everything else." (She couldn't say anything plainly; *she* didn't see everything was like everything else; she meant that, in her opinion, *he* saw thus.) Well, how really could you not think everything was like everything else? Not that you made much out of the Coast Guardsman in chambray and dungarees who wheeled onto the pier a small generator and for forty minutes prepared to spend the five it finally took him to drill a mooring hole through the cement. *And*—not that you made much out of the young man recording for the blind—the voice moored the tape to the book, which had been written by someone far away, perhaps dead and plowed under by now; the voice then moored the book to the blind person for whom the book might not necessarily have been intended. But "Hold it!" Sylvia was always saying to his mind. But she knew she was buried so deep inside him he couldn't hear her. The Medical Group doctor—Sylvia insisted on the Group rather than a private physician—had told them they were cardiographically almost identical. (Even though so different in size.) Hind came back to her crimping touch. Maddy Beecher said his wife Flo was his "conscience," which was going a bit far. But Sylvia's knowledge of Hind was always in his mind ready to work.

Over a hot bath she suspended her wool dress on a wooden hanger on the shower rod; she de-creased the dress, the moisture worked on it. He knew the exact articulation in the upturn of her earlobe at its fore edge, like the more regular lobes on the leaves of his guardian's imported snowberry bush. (Pale Ashley Sill's lobe lacked any hang at all; it grew vegetable into his jaw skin.) Hind knew her just as painfully as she was invisible to him. The dark insides of the body you lived in all your life—the heated, stemming parts; the esoteric heart valves or the pancreas—esoteric because they existed only in the hospital where you had them looked at.

Parts you couldn't send out like the bubble a voice disengaged from itself. *Was* the voice a bubble?

The phone call from America had been switched from Cracow to Ostend to London. It reached him in London, the voice of his guardian's remote cousin whom he had not met but who had once or twice been pretty short with him over the phone—Hind, the gratuitously adopted ward, the heir plucked out of nowhere. But this time there had seemed no animus in her voice. She spoke loudly, flatly, slowly, she prepared Hind for the essential news of death, but whether in the style of a ruthless narrator or in spite of herself out of deference to his feelings he had never after been able to decide. He couldn't find anything to say, and when she said, "Are you still there?" he nodded. He had never met this cousin. The guardian made no effort in that direction.

The guardian's death had made Hind change plans instantly. But Sylvia may not have understood at the time. At least he canceled the search, canceled it the moment he heard the voice on the phone saying the guardian was dead. Why did Sylvia speak as she did while they waited for a plane at the London airport? There wouldn't be a plane for them for at least three hours, and they sat hunched on a backless leather bench feeling the twilight outside despite the lighting in the waiting area. Instead of saying something respectfully appropriate, which Hind would never have insisted on as she well knew, but which he nonetheless would have expected, Sylvia told a story about a billboard. Why should she call attention to herself? Was it to make him feel better? His guardian was dead. Or was it to get his eye onto her, now that the kidnaped child had been replaced by the guardian? Hind enjoyed the story, it made him forget to change some money, forget even the purpose of the flight. He was seeing her tale vividly; it intervened between himself and the distant guardian. With Hind on the left, Sylvia seemed sensitive to the standing, black metal ashtray near her right knee, and to the man's hand that came slowly over there to tap off an extension of cigarette ash. (It was one of those long Russian cigarettes that were two-thirds recessed filter.) Sylvia would look at the hand, and hesitate. Did it take her out of her story? Did she wish not to be heard by the hand?

She was ten, walking a hot, tar road in New Hampshire, the surface billowy and broken; the town patched the potholes and hoped they would go away. At the head of the rise the road turned through a disorderly stand of red and white pines. Then it started a steep downgrade, but Sylvia stopped and was looking away into the vale and beyond it to a house on a hill and beyond to a clump of gray hills. But her view was stopped, for she couldn't keep from staring at Lyons's billboard, which she knew so well. Her father, when he saw it, always grunted as if repelled, but she hadn't cared that it wasn't beautiful, or in a way had thought it almost was—which Hind could understand, having had similar comfort from an intricate mechanized billboard you saw just as you went bumping up cobbles onto one of the city bridges, with regular-featured couples moving hinged thighs up and down and shoulders forward and back, offering each other glasses. Now the hand with the cigarette ash came near Sylvia's knee.

Lyons was a local market gardener whose family had been on his land since sixteen-thirty and whose own roadside trade grew so big it finished his bulk business with nearby supermarkets. Before Sylvia could even remember, Lyons's brother-in-law from California had had designed for a billboard a giant string bean, humanized, motorized, and gripping a comparatively miniature stalk from which presumably it had been picked or had picked itself. The bean had sun-ray eyes and wing arms, and a waist, and it was sitting in a red tractor and had a crescent of faded yellow grin. But Sylvia knew all this and liked it; she and her schoolmates couldn't see why the art teacher told them not to give their fish eyelashes and kissy lips, or their bears long pants. The bean's stalk drooped aging dark green leaves like reptile skin, but that didn't bother Sylvia, ten years old.

Hind and Sylvia sat in a waiting room, or part of the great complicated hall where there were waiting-room benches and information counters and moving stewardesses in red-white-and-mauve uniforms, and small children bustling on errands knowing exactly where their elders would be when they returned. The guardian was dead.

"No, a Farmer Pan didn't stand up behind a bush and reach for me." Nothing like that. "No, I suddenly saw both a real bean. Yes, the real bean. Not that I ever said to myself before that day that the bean was human. Just that I never said openly to myself that it was not. But now not only a real bean, but a—do you see, Jack? And someplace in my ears the approaching motor I heard was the tractor getting ready to move out of the billboard; but the main thing was, the bean was not human. And as I was letting myself dream there in the middle of the road, the tractor motor got loud, until, a moment soon enough, I knew the sound came from behind, and there was a car suddenly round the corner behind me driving through the pines and it would have hit me or I would have forced it to drive off into who knows what, if I hadn't dived off the road and onto a stiff bush that killed my arms. And I was grateful the car didn't stop but went on down that steep hill. Because I wanted to keep thinking about the bean billboard. This story isn't about animated vegetables, you understand that." She had left something out of her story: *both a real bean*...and a what?

The Orientals were sitting on his beam near the place where he always sat. Today they wore dark green business suits. The identity of their proportions limb for limb seemed increased by other kinships: each man had a fat crease halfway between collar and barbered temple, and when they rose as Hind passed he noted that the thickly dressed hair had a large-toothed-comb pattern. One man must be all of two-twenty, the other much less—the jawline lost in that fat crease. Hind sat down on the low beam and let his giant legs out straight. A great skinny wood doll at rest, that was him. If the men looked back they might see he wasn't taking off his trousers. As they reached the Drive end of Hind's pier they were far enough so their identical scale made the smaller seem merely farther away than the larger. They turned left, passed the Drive end of the larger pier, ignored two gray drunks gently begging from a bench, and turned right up the steps that led to the foot overpass. Halfway over, they turned almost toward Hind and leaned on their hands on the railing looking down at the cars. Hind got up, took his Baggie-bagged sandwich out of his towel, kicked off his sandals, unzipped his fly, and eyed the overpass in time to catch the two Orientals disappearing down off it on the far side. But in less time than Buck Field said it had once taken him to do sixty yards on the extended straightaway of his splintery board track at school, Hind was ready to go.

Their trail went through Hind's own street, as if they would drop him off at home. One of the tree men was back inspecting the new tree, and Knott said, "Tell them the druggist's wife put a wire halter around the neck of that sycamore across the street and it's killing it." The undertaker's main door was open, but as usual nothing was going on. Carmen La Branche had put out the garbage can with two long slats propped either side, to save a parking spot as if for a hearse but in fact for the boss himself. Hind's private entrance door was shut. He could see part of his Anglepoise lamp in his top-floor study-window. On the sidewalk above her basement steps Mrs. Knott sat in the collapsible aluminum chair she had won at the supermarket. Her Persian tortoise shell sat on the step next to the top visible only from its shoulders up. Mrs. Knott didn't seem to know her cat was there. Both looked straight on into the street and hardly acknowledged Hind as he passed following the two men of similar scale.

These two talked in profile; they had paused at the traffic light. They smiled at each other, the two half-smiles in profile together making a whole. The light went green, and they didn't notice.

Carmen La Branche or La Grange, the handyman for the undertaker's brownstone whose top floor was Hind's, appeared up to Hind's left and headed across toward the light where the two men had stood. Jerking his arms up at the elbow, almost as energetic as one of those piston-hipped walkers who made the annual twelve-mile borough race, Carmen came across Hind's sight and thus seemed to set off the two men Hind was following, for they saw that the light had gone green and they started across. They didn't hurry, it turned red halfway over, and Hind heard two vehicles adjust to the fact of these strolling men by shifting down to an argumentative second. Carmen passed across out of sight to the right, in the opposite direction from the vehicles, which now appeared as the light turned green for them and red against Hind. The two men and, a moment ago, Carmen could have been killed, and the two men between them had a clue-lead. The two men were going slowly; now they stopped to shake hands; the small one looked back toward Hind and pointed. The companion looked and smiled, though whether at a remark or at Hind or something in the area around him, you couldn't tell. They went up the street; they weren't saying good-bye yet, anyway not separating.

There in front of him Hind saw the past, guarded by one of its moods. Yes, when his past was ten. Football helmets with white brows tapering to wingy points at each temple contrasting with the maroon leather of the rest. He smelled the new helmet in his sleep, imagined the inside webbing on his scalp when he sat in the old bathroom at school. When he gained the starting spot he wanted, he was amazed. Saturday morning the school field seemed so big partly because you went there by the loosely assembled brown-and-gray bus, though the field was still in the city, not in the suburbs even. Old Buddy Bourne, the lower school coach whose arm was as big around as his neck, and who alternated between first and last names rather haphazardly, took Hind aside with Lief Lund, whose parents when he was seven took Lief to Hardangerfjord in Norway late in the spring for the whole summer; Buddy said, "Hind—same goes for you, Lund—if you receive, head off toward Liefie like you're going for the far sideline, but then, with Liefie crossing behind you, you hand it off to him, Jackie, get it? Same for you, Lund, if you receive. They'll never look for a reverse on the kickoff." But then, though Hind did indeed receive a slow-motion end-over-end, he forgot the plan, for Lief went out of Hind's mind completely when Hind, on taking the kick and digging off upfield, saw directly before him his friend Byron trip flat on his face.

Which, to Hind, as he thought back, had had no meaning. It had merely forced. Even now, years onward, he heard Lief pounding toward him saying, "Hey, Hind, shit!" Still, all Hind had done was stop in the middle— "Hey, at least gimme a lateral!"—but no kidding, at the very start of what might have been a victorious kickoff return devised by old Buddy Bourne...whose voice Hind also could hear now, "Oh *no*, Hindie! Don't forget!" Hind, at the instant when the meaningless trip of his friend Byron had jolted into his vision, shifted the pigskin to his left arm and stopped short to reach down and slip his right hand under the fallen Byron's left armpit, saying, "You O.K., By?" and Byron looked up, screwing round his head.

Whereupon Hind had been hit left and right; yet the tacklers' own forward motion had swung their hips and legs as they tried to hold Hind, so he had enough freedom to try to slip away forward. But then, wanting to run, though still forgetting Lief (who, he learned later, had stopped behind him and was standing with his hands on his hips), Hind lifted a knee only to fall over Byron, who was trying to get up.

Coach Bourne yanked Hind. Bourne's upper lip sweated in the cool, late autumn air. He sat on the bench with his gray sweatshirt hood up. He didn't know how to begin to tell Hind what he thought of any boy stupid enough to forget that great play, and bastard enough to jeopardize the team's endeavor, even life and limb, to stop for a fallen teammate. Hind was sorry for Buddy Bourne. This stocky, broad-backed, well-conditioned coach kept returning to the matter during the game, most of which Hind sat out. "Hind, Hind, Hind." There were two–"Jack, Jack..."–two kinds of guys out on any given field–"How could you do that to me! Your head was in the cotton-picking clouds!"–two kinds–one that adhered to the pregame plan, the other so hopelessly green.... Hind hadn't the courage to listen all the way through to old Buddy, who was possessed of small grammar and the most casual pronunciation and whom the guardian once or twice heard with scarcely hidden embarrassment (though you might ask, To whom did Buddy belong, Hind or the guardian?). With Buddy in mind, but with tacit politeness, the guardian said, "Language is what you build on, Jack, so best get it right."

The two bums (drunks, alcoholics) at the Drive end of the larger pier, who had desultorily begged as the Orientals passed, had seemed simply gray. Faces? Suits? Position? in the composition?

Now Hind shot up his right arm at the curb lest the girl beside him step off into the street and be killed by one of two automobiles coming. But where were the big man and the little man? To his right, a block away, on this side of the street—and Hind now ran for them—they could just be seen descending the subway steps. The office girl held a brown paper bag with a dark mark of wet on its side; one of her pink plastic Friday curlers peeked (poked, stuck) out in front of the edge of her pink headscarf.

When he pulled up at the head of the steps panting, the two Orientals were already down, and out of sight. He felt for change, got a piece of folded paper—what?—and drew out three nickels.

# ii

A weekend's worth of brass-brown tokens punched in a pattern suggesting ornamental buttons lay overlapping in the wooden dish under the change booth window. The student evidently knew the pudgy, middle-aged, poorly shaved crew-cut man in the booth. The bulb behind the grilled window brought out a single silver hair that grew straight off the man's wrinkling forehead. As Hind held out a dollar at waist level, the older man said sharply, "But Sir Isaac Newton he said that an effective acts only according to the powers of that which receives its action, not according to its own powers." Then he looked at Hind blankly.

The rumble of a train coming was now clearly a local from downtown. At the corner of a white-tiled wall, one of the two Orientals—Hind couldn't tell at first it was the small one—stood talking. His big friend appeared to be hidden around the corner, and they appeared to be discussing the wall or something on it.

Now, with its strained couplings trying to crash loose, and a kind of screaming hum as if due to the tunnel squeezing, the train broke into the station.

"Two, please," said Hind loudly, and the student began sliding each token up out of the dish and off into his hand.

The man in the booth went on, "When I finish the Great Ideas at the Library, I'm going to take Education."

"Two, please," said Hind above the grinding of the train. "I'm in a huge rush."

"There's always another train, buddy," the man said. The student dropped the last token off into his hand and moved not for the turnstiles but the stairs; he wasn't taking the train, just buying tokens.

The train doors slid open and Hind heard gathering steps advance on the turnstiles. He took the tokens and his change—the man had already returned to his paperback. Hind took three great skips to a turnstile token slot, but slipping in the coin (feeling on his fingertip the exact roughness of the coin's perforation) and hearing the deep, designed cluck as it landed in place, Hind had to step away from the turnstile because Phil the druggist, chewing Clorets, was there in a breeze gaily batting through as if the old wooden arm were the winning runner's tape at a track meet. But what had wood to do with tape?

"Big Jack," he called over his shoulder, walking for the stairs.

"My token!" Hind called to him, and turned back to the turnstile and was met by a woman who deferred to him scowling.

The train doors went, as Hind cut between a couple who had gotten off. But when he thought he had lost the two Orientals, there they were in front of him smiling, the small one in front of the big one, both hauling on the canvas guard to hold the door for him.

He was in, and the car jolted, and he grabbed a white pole. The Orientals were going into the next car. The connecting door in this car banged to after them.

Hind had to see them. He didn't want to be as noticeable as boys with lank hair who stood at the door that led between cars and stared into the next car covering curiosity with grimness. From a casual angle—Hind was slouched against the panel door of what would be the engineer's cubicle if this car were being used as the head of the train—he could see enough. From the knees down you couldn't miss the Orientals' wide, dark green trousers, black socks with yellow clocks, and black, pointed wingtips. The big Oriental's feet were comfortably crossed at the ankles. Now the small one slung his left leg over his right knee and kept it gently jerking. A backhander slapped twice into Hind's view accenting a point.

At the express stop they got off and went downstairs, apparently to get a train east under the river since they passed up a waiting westbound.

They were examining what, because of its location, should have been a map of all the city's subways. But whatever it was it looked strange. Hind wasn't close enough to see why. But he did see which part of the city they were arguing about. Was the crux the spot they kept jabbing? The big one looked around him suddenly with a mournful eye; he probably wanted to ask someone. Hind would be happy to direct them. He knew all the streets and corners, heights and depths. Meanwhile the little one wrote something on the disputed spot. When the big one read it, he laughed and swayed.

They went to a chocolate machine, and from the hip each leaned slightly left and went up under jacket tails to pull a bright steel comb from the right hip pocket. One in front of the other, tall behind small, they combed their thick, glistening hair in the chocolate machine mirror. Hind put his hands in his pockets, increased his slouch, and went to the map.

On it he hardly knew his own city. If you took a thing like this layout seriously, you would get around about as fast as the young man with rubber knees on Hind's block, who used aluminum crutches and marketed with a red-white-and-green knapsack on his back strapped there by Heather Fordham and filled for him by the vegetable boy at the A. & P. But the map, even in its present state, could probably be read.

From twenty-five yards, and because of a raw yellow light bulb so close to Hind's eyes it obscured the map's titles and legends, Hind hadn't understood. But now the blue-banked gray sea holding blue isles became relatively clear. Much of this laminated map had been knifed to strips and peeled down to cardboard, so it looked like a collage. On pieces of actual map and on cardboard were cut and penned girls' and boys' names and initials. For some seconds Hind's concerned eye raggedly toured a two-dimensional terrain of rough promises and unflinching factual reports. Near what would have been the area where Hind and Sylvia lived, a girl's round hand read, "I live here"—in two other boroughs, the same in different hands, one narrowly fine and regular, the second large and open and buttocky, both female.

There were old-style phone numbers, often with explanations: "UR 2-2222 goes the limit." A seven-digit phone number had three shaky concentric circles round it as if it were a topographical isobar. Below one nine-stop stretch of untouched Independent Subway ran a heavily amended equation: "Lorraine plus Louie equals love love love"—under it: "equals beauty and the beast," crossed out, followed by "equals the square root of heaven." One male hand—like a roving duck hawk preying with powerful speed on city pigeons—had visited twenty spots: "Nuts"–"No"–"You wrong"–"Never happen"–"No no"–"Six of the Storks scored off Honey La Grange Xmas Eve"–"Viva" with what must have followed torn away–"Never"–"Never Happen." The same hand had added above a caret between the "was" and the "no" of "Corinne was no virgin" the familiar nostalgia of "never." Half a mile to the west, "Want to get your ass broke, meet the Storks Friday 10 P.M. corner of Jewel and–" the other coordinate destroyed. "Corinne and Dawn they are nympho ask the Storks."

Hind studied the darkened, confused triangular area where the small Oriental had worked his ballpoint in the upper right corner. Initials and dates clustered at all angles; the eye, making its own smooth stroke, might if it tried divine a whole clock face inlaid with intimations of rectangular forms—rocks clustered, angling every which way. "Henny blows the greatest reed." "Henny's combo blows the greatest sound." Hind couldn't tell which of many marks the Oriental had left in this area. His eye wandered. "Block party Monday. Dancing on Northfield Avenue." A painfully slow map, if you studied it.

On the other hand, using it you could really make time around the city. "A.B." is within easy finger distance of "December, 1964," which itself can be reached easily from the centermost "never" or from "U R in Kicksburg," though a few concentrics rose up like venereal eminences in the way.

The noise, the growing noises, around him made Hind feel he could concentrate more easily. Trains coming, people coming, the city coming, had to be understood.

But if the city was still here in this originally laminated map he tried to follow, then certainly a gray gulf had overtaken her; or she had had slipped across her, as through geologic fault, a gray plain; or—and when he saw this he was afraid—all two hundred square miles of her urban complex had had laid on it one great dirty piece of war-torn paper.

The train sounds came together into a kind of unison in order to stop.

They had stopped, except for the electric humming. Hind watched a small boy getting off break against two adults boarding the train; half-falling, the boy made it onto the platform, and Hind's right arm automatically shot up. The door was closing, but the sound was augmented, and Hind looked toward the platform on his left, the map and boy before his eyes. And there, too, the doors were closing. But did he know which of the missed trains the Orientals would be on? Almost surely, because of the train they had changed from, they'd have been taking the right-hand platform, the train outward bound from the city center. He ran to the nearest window of this train but he didn't see the men. He walked along the train looking, but it had started, and a crowd of schoolchildren–three o'clock–stood in his way laughing at each other, so he couldn't run. He had lost the Orientals. The other train was moving out. He thought surely they weren't on it; they were on this. The dingy black-green of the train's sides seemed clean because of the train's speed as the last of it passed and was suddenly beyond Hind and about to disappear round the turn just past the red light at the outgoing end of the station where the tunnel resumed. When the tail car of a subway train was suddenly past you, like that, almost unexpectedly, there came a hole in your balance and you felt like falling into the space that was no longer occupied by the train, and, like a new recruit to the army of arm amputees, you had to consciously think about standing.

But to his surprise–and as he heard the noise and glanced round–he was aware that the light he'd been looking at had now turned green, a new train was following on top of the one he had missed. So it was possible he could catch the Orientals. The headlights were visible at the bend just beyond the incoming end of the station. The new train now came on. But as it entered the station, though it slowed slightly, it didn't stop, and as its cars passed him Hind saw they were empty of passengers. In one car a workman read a newspaper.

Yet now the sound of this second train receding was sustained by the sound of a third. And this one was coming, not from the other direction and onto the platform

Hind didn't want, but surprisingly on the same track as that of the train he'd missed and of that second, empty train that was being moved to the other end of the line for repair or because of schedule adjustments. And this train was stopping. If the one after the one he'd missed turned onto the express track and passed the one he'd missed, then this third train he was now boarding might catch the one he'd missed, come close enough so he could see up the line and check who got off at the next station, and if the Orientals got off, he could get off himself when his train arrived. But curves might stand in the way. Hind walked rapidly through his train, heading for the front. The train was moving, too.

He was at the front window and at once feeling the momentum from years ago. The train couldn't stop—any more than a car on a superhighway, if the car couldn't claim an emergency—but you were perfectly in charge of the tunnel, you didn't care if the train turned out the tunnel or went straight downward rather than horizontal with a slight upward run. Years ago—and he did it now—he could concentrate in such a way that he could cause the car's interior lights above and behind him right and left to drop away far behind, and he could pull around him like earth the tunnel's night; or the tunnel was like a stationary train windowless and with a white bulb every fifty yards. If you knew how to do it, you could stand in what Hind thought of as the gulleys of the tunnel in such a way as not to get hit by the train; or if there was a catwalk, you could swing up. If you were in the path, you must try to jump high just at the moment, and link yourself onto the little front chain; but the thing was not at the last instant to be distracted by something on the tunnel walls: a light bulb or a grating or a sign. Years ago, here would be Hind running the train from this window, or in charge of it; he wouldn't exactly be running it, he would be in charge of the mysterious, seldom-seen

motorman who ran it in his sealed-off cubicle in the
right front corner of the lead car, the cubicle whose plain
panel-door Hind had sometimes leaned against when he
was keeping watch out the window. And sometimes he
was right out in the tunnel in the resounding darkness,
but it was different from the plunging dark of the school
locker room in November as you came in from the cold
sunny spaces. Traveling to the Saturday children's
concerts in mid-town, Hind and two friends elbowed and
wedged (sometimes as a tactical trick released pressure
by suddenly standing aside hoping their former force,
transferred in reverse to the friendly obstacle, would
cause the latter to lose balance and fall away, leaving a
space) at the front window—till at last they sank together
in a tight compromise, the boy on either side pressing
the center and tilting his head so that as he contentedly
saw down into the tunnel his outside eye would be higher
than his inside. But two or three stops later the three
would fight again, and one of his friends might complain
that Hind was too tall, he ought to stand back and see
over. Which made Hind want to get behind and kick their
calves. But now there was no one with him, not even his
little girl May, who loved the subway.

The tunnel disappeared, the train rolled up into the
open air, which muffled the train's noises; in a siding or
yard freight cars crowded together blindly; the train rose
toward the first of the elevated stations. Down through
lattices, ladders, grilles, of track and girder, Hind followed
a yellow taxi and then two girls of indeterminate height
crossing the street in its wake.

When the train reached the mid-point of the first big
curve of track, Hind saw not far ahead two trains side
by side moving in the same direction as his own train,
though more slowly. Then the one in the middle track, the
express track, the nearly empty train with the workman

reading the newspaper, accelerated and passed what had been the first of the three, the one in Hind's track, the local track, the train that had come first and that Hind had missed. Now that they were all out of the tunnel in the open air with three boroughs visible and back across the river the skyline of the mid-town area Hind was coming from, he thought he would catch the Orientals.

A man laid aside his tabloid when the train stopped; as he walked out onto the platform another man rose nonchalantly and, eyeing Hind as the doors rolled shut, stepped across the car and snatched the newspaper.

Even if the inspector on the phone thought the case should indeed be reopened and thought these Orientals had in fact been discussing Hershey Laurel—the boy kidnaped seven years ago just in time for his fourth birthday—might not Inspector Praid be apt to give up? If, for that matter—or in that case—Praid was even around now. You could retire quite young if you joined the force young enough. Bee Bee Barker called the police "the tool of the immense American ruling class." Praid might say maybe the Orientals didn't take that particular—as if it could be a *general*—train, maybe they remembered an errand and so, when Hind was watching the map, had sloped off up the station stairs to the exit. And the public had been so terribly touched when just after the kidnap the father made a taped plea for help and the police played it on the radio at rush hour with the traffic report. People wrote letters of sympathy. With the help of Sylvia's editorial hand and her Tombow Signpen-P Color Set, Hind could have drawn Hershey Laurel to tally almost exactly with the photo released to the papers.

Hershey had been almost four, with, for a child, quite a deep, humorous chin. He had hazel eyes. He had lucky moles on his back like Sylvia. He was always hooking up and turning on the garden hose, and on rainy days his mother couldn't keep him out of the kitchen sink. He had been three feet six, his hair his father's peculiar grayish-brown. One Sunday shortly before the kidnap, he had got rather close to some boys playing softball in a field, and when the batter cut wildly at a change-up—the ball not even floating up to the plate till the anguished swing was complete—the bat had slipped from his perspiring, thoughtless hands, sailed a few feet, and struck fascinated, un-moving Hershey Laurel at the crest of his left eyebrow. At the time of the kidnap the stitches were rawly visible. The kidnaper or kidnapers had come during the day, a sunny day that ended in rain. The Laurel house was a mile in from a devious road, which at the point at which it met the Laurel driveway was four miles from a fork, each of whose two roads led to the village of Long Corners. Hershey's mother said she had pinned up her laundry, written (which made three times in ten weeks) a letter canceling her membership in a book club, and gone down to the pond seventy-five yards from the house to study her Greek lesson. She would not have heard whatever conversation Hershey certainly engaged in with his abductor or abductors, one of whom may have stood watch; Hershey's mother would have been just visible from the house. If there was no conversation, there was in any case no cry. None of Hershey's toys were taken—or, only a beanbag of which he was fond. If he didn't carry the beanbag with him when he was on the move, he left it on one of the sills in his room.

But now, years later, everyone had forgotten the boy.

At this moment, with the train Hind trailed in sight if not reach, and going at the same speed as his so if you looked solely at *it* you thought it wasn't moving, Hind feared that Sylvia, who wouldn't carry even her Medical Group card, would be unidentifiable if she had any accident—a slight, quick glance from a precocious fender (a bit of a knock, a touch of concussion, a measure of fatal shock); and now his landlord the undertaker—whom he rarely saw—seemed to be losing his identity through lack of funerals, though he was now involved in the control of a gymnasium-restaurant.

But where was Hershey's public now? It had written to newspapers in response to the father's police broadcast. The public was, of course, everywhere. And where would the boy Hershey be? Searches were simply dropped. In effect you just kiss Hershey good-bye. What if Sylvia was alone when she got hit? What might become of Hind's little May, and Hind not there? of May's precociously complete sentences.

If the Orientals went much farther, the three of them would be getting to the elevated stop near Maddy Beecher's offices, the Santos plant. Even now, four stops down, Hind could see Maddy's small, private tower, though not the considerable grounds.

The Orientals' train had come into the next station. Hind looked up the track again just in time to catch that train as it stopped and, presumably, doors opened. Hind's train now moved, crept, barely tended—can a train loiter?—hung, was going, so slow you thought it would have somehow to stop in order to go faster. But now it did stop, with a falling jerk back, all fastenings gently shrugging back, groaning. A man recovered his footing and continued to look at an Asthma Panic ad.

At least five passengers were off the Orientals' train, and perhaps a child with three adults, though Hind couldn't perfectly follow them since they in turn were partly blocked by two others—women, who now separated—for only one of them could slip ahead of the three others to the stair. No, there were five, and there was no child, it must have been a shadowy overlapping motion between the legs of the adults: "hard-to-see distances," a mirror designer's ad copy might read. At the health club uptown on a crowded Wednesday night you saw configurations of men in (under, and of) glass—mirrors angled within mirrors. Looking up the track, as far as he could see, though now pretty sure that that station there wasn't it, Hind hungered for what was going on there. Neat, how a separation of travelers, a passage of passengers, an assemblage of forms, emptied a platform, disappearing downstairs as down, yes, one of the dickering wood chutes in the cubic maze Hind and cool-fingered Cassia Meaning devised on rainy childhood afternoons for marbles to roll around through. She and he fought over those marbles of his—the cloudy green-lemon jasper, the bright cat's-eye, the clear ruby with its smudges of cracks inside, the great variety of kinds he usually kept unsorted in a deerskin sack the guardian had brought him from a tiny factory on the far side of Mount Mary. And Cassia would run away with a handful and open a window and say, "Possession's nine-tenths of the law."

The Orientals' train started; Hind's train started. They seemed controlled by the same transformer.

He should have stayed at the pier, perhaps the Orientals had nothing to show him now. There was this constant danger of letting things lure you off course just by being themselves.

Or might he be like the little woman Bella Church whose house and garden he now could almost see as he looked to the northeast of the famous mail-order house at the steel-and-concrete doughnut structure, a new branch of the world's biggest department store—"shop" was what Cassia Meaning called all the big stores when she came back briefly from England last Easter. Greatest or not, the emporium's branch doughnut had to accommodate an exquisite architectural bite, having commanded and in vain again commanded the little woman to give up her undistinguished backyard at a big price. The house would have had to go too, but the yard was what was desired. But her dog, her small and fat and quite humanly irritable white-and-black mutt, spent several hours per day outside their green-tarpaper-roofed home fussing along from bone to bone digging and undigging, almost oblivious of construction crews and elevated trains. Bella Church had fought for her dog's rights. He used the whole garden, she said, almost every foot of it; and Hind loved her when she wouldn't sell, and shouldered his gear and came out to tape her. "Yes," the guardian would have said, "character, inborn character." She would not sell even if they found something under her place. But the store did build its spiral-ramp-and-carpark-skirted doughnut—plans were too far along—and when the men came to the garden where Boy planted all his bones, they neatly cut from the-as-yet-not-fully-existent building a monumental bite. Boy was deaf, so though he lay panting by the fence on the other side of which the earth-moving equipment ground and groaned and a steam rig struck again and again, he heard almost nothing, and surely nothing that interested him, heard little of the pile-driving, the voices drinking coffee, the generators and cranes, the wreckage and waste banging down the company's wooden well-shaft.

People got on the Orientals' train at the next three stops.

At the fourth the Orientals got off. Hind's train seemed just as impatient as Hind, and his own fellow passengers were standing ready at the door even while the Orientals' former train was getting out of the station.

The Orientals were looking at newspapers downstairs, almost as if they were waiting for Hind to catch them up.

Suddenly here they were idle. An accident? Were *they* one? But as Hind resisted the wish to let out his legs, and instead, feeling like a potato racer about to fall, or a hobbled horse, or a leg-hobbled swimmer strengthening his arms twisting (frugging, shaking, swimming!) down a championship pool, he stepped the stairs one by one so he felt fussy from knees to waist. Well, the smaller of the Orientals looked in Hind's direction, turned back toward the magazine rack, and shrugged; then nudged his sidekick and led the way ambling round the corner. If Hind could only say to them, "Whatever may have lured you into the Laurel case, whatever you may be getting out of it, I don't blame or care. All that's in it for me is to save the child, even at the expense of not knowing wholly why what happened. If you are being used, I care not. Can't we get together? Are you not laying a trail for me? Does the old woman act as agent for the kidnapers or against? Am I to die?" If he went on like that, the next thing would be, "I am terribly sorry for you."

The old pounding spring of pity enough to float his head off his neck if he didn't hear what he wanted to hear, and if he didn't tell all, made him forget he wasn't at all going to spill the beans. For he knew himself. He was quite shifty no matter how dearly he liked each man and woman moving in his head.

Hind went a bit fast. The big Oriental had something in his shoe, and when he stopped and leaned against the Santos-Dumont fence that had just begun at the third corner from the station and would go on for half a mile this side, he had stopped to put his right ankle across his knee and with a wince jam his right shoe off and look up into its toe; and Hind couldn't simply also stop. So he strolled past the scuffing and heavy breathing. He was ahead, moving slow, and now heard the Orientals come on behind him.

Over the stone-piered grand entrance to Santos-Dumont's grounds, a neon mustachio arced ready to go on at sundown. Hind did not pause inquisitively at the gate; the tailored gray guards would ask him who he was. But

Hind walked still more slowly, and looked, listening to what came on behind. Santos-Dumont's low, clean-cut blocks might have housed Oliver Plane's classrooms, his students, for the style was the same. One wall of one building was growing green fur. S-D's fence-to-fence lawns were as clean-cropped as the greens at the country club Ashley Sill and wife had bought far away and now ran. The fence of high, fine white-metal sticks made a xylophone sound in his moving eye, like that sculpture Sylvia had shown him in London, whose inner and outer aisles of tubes shifted and mingled as you walked around watching; and Hind's right-hand fingers tingled in memory of the tightly held stickball stick clicking black areaway bars, each bar impeding the stick as it dragged off onto the next bar—like the valve-like impeder stationary atop the fortune wheel the Sunday Hind's guardian had said that for education's sake they would go out and try the Bowlacoaster at Greenland Parkette.

But Hind should have turned; for the sound of the Orientals walking had turned, had gone away. And as Hind gracefully turned to the fence, grasping a rod in each hand as if to look through into S-D, but rather searched rapidly to his right to see which building the Orientals were going to—only to find that, just as at certain angles with the sculpture Sylvia had taken him to, so here—but no, it wasn't so complex, the bars naturally became intervalless...He turned up the fold of paper in his pocket. The list: he had forgotten these worries: "Ash, maybe a book of poetic impressions of golf course, greens for grazing/ Oliver, instead of destroying ungraded papers, study one student/Cassia, try to get married, i.e., bring self to accept English men you actually do like, Renn Redfern or Avery Storm will propose if given chance/Get Maddy into shape, get to join Fieldston Health Club (five free massages for getting new member)."

Maddy Beecher tended to look out a window rather than at Hind. From Maddy's white-walled office on a modern hill just ten land miles from the center, though easily within the limits of the city's harshest urban growth, you could see in three directions. Maddy's desk faced the west window, which was even wider than the south or north. In his swivel chair past and present found shape: steel and white enamel plasticompo and the button that ran the swivel won only a tense counterpoise from the truth that this chair was in idea the same swivel Thomas Jefferson invented. Viewed from an approaching helicopter, Maddy Beecher's office, a white concrete block, perhaps like a huge clamping nut just thick enough to hide its bolt, topped the rambling but cleanly conceived cubic volumes of The Center for Total Research, of which Maddy Beecher was Curator, Director, and "God knows, chaperon, chief robot, even circulation librarian if you want me."

"Your"—only rarely "our"—"operation" (as his superiors called it) had grown from being an adjunct of their far-rooted firm to a status now nearly mysterious in its fame. Santos-Dumont Sisters, Incorporated— "Plastic Values for Basic Goals"—had intended Maddy Beecher's little setup, in its ostensible detachment from commerce, to advertise their concern for the Past, for the disinterested imagination, for the American Story ("The Plot," Maddy called it). But the Center got out of hand, and the overseers, pretending shrewdness, gratefully let Maddy alone. He was fond of saying, in a tone whose loyalty he couldn't disentangle from its levity, "Our plant is overgrowing." He said it to board members and other superiors who phoned with vague, respectful questions, and he may not have meant to distinguish, in the word "plant," between SDS and CTR.

· · ·

Westward he could see the mid-city profile through what was now often, as he reminded Hind, approximately a number four haze.

"Maddy," said Hind a moment after entering the office, "I've reason to believe—"

"Is it still our same old city?" Maddy said. "Where is the face of the earth?"

They looked at the armed point of the granite and Indiana limestone hypodermic thermometric thing that was the tallest there far away, and at the solar-Gothic snout near it, and at the blue, shimmering utility of the elegant cube in fact nearer the river Hind had come under than you could easily see from the distance that now separated Hind from mid-city. At Maddy's elbow, by his Holographone—which took dictation and returned it to him printed in his own hand—there was magnetized to the desk top the single tiny button that of all the (as Maddy put it to Hind) doodads here most quaintly suggested what tricks contemporary techne knows. For, at a touch, followed by the relevant number whispered, Control would send up, projected (and of course blown up) on his then suddenly uncabineted screen against the east wall behind him, any microfilm on file. There were no stairs to his lone, topside office—only the cramped antique lift he had had copied from the Florence *pensione* he had once booked Sylvia and Hind into against the guardian's advice.

"Maddy," said Hind, "I've reason to believe that two men—"

"Look," said Maddy quickly, pointing to the white Formica table in front of the north window. On it was what seemed a model city. "No one knows whether I'm just on the jury, or contracting privately, or selling my approval to a young architect (it's a long story), or devoting myself to improving the city. Look at this."

"What I came to say," Hind began again, "was that I've reason to believe—"

"Haven't we all, if you *insist*," said Maddy, and he waved his hand between them as if to get closer to Hind. At either end of the model was a hyperparaboloid space frame: "Infinitesimally undulating surfaces kids will play on, or a sheltering wing for rainy days." They looked fanciful for the function served, they looked like ramps leading nowhere, or an experimental (a pilot)airplane, or like white South American bats, their membranes taut and smooth.

You wouldn't imagine animals walking across this. Or only clockwork (docked, inoculated) Schnauzers on extensible leashes. Now, take London: within sight of St. Paul's there are badgers living.

On Maddy's table a stray snapshot showed a fat, transparent chair. "We make the Perspex for the legs. The chair inflates."

Hind started again, hoping an indirect approach might get him discreetly back to the Orientals.

"The young designer you spoke of when I saw you last time—"

"What a memory!" said Maddy. "Which designer?"

"The English one who thinks in cylinders, reverse towers, stacks, silos—build down rather than up, and glassed over or covered by an electric field at the surface. Spinal elevators," Hind finished, pleased with his image.

"Procedural problems too hard, ripening people up for the idea, but then he had a nervous collapse for a week or ten days and came out of it convinced he'd been wrong to, well, bury these buildings, and he threw human dignity at me all one afternoon. I *liked* his reverse towers, you see, and he ended telling me he hated me for liking them, he ended the conversation incoherently, the kid infuriates me after all I did. He spoke of human dignity and burying conspirators in old Venice head down heels up, and he said, 'I am not like you, I do not like you.' Grabbed his plexiplast helmet and off he went. But he called me up a week later. I'm sure I figure in his plans."

"The one," continued Hind, who hoped to force Maddy onto the Orientals, "who wants the electronically variable glass–do away with shades, switch your windows transparent, turn on the sun–"

"Does anyone on earth besides me Jack collect people's lives like you do? God what you recall!"

Yet Maddy would not recall Hind's interest in the kidnap, Hind could bank on that.

As if idly, Maddy jabbed at a panel in front of him and a gust seemed to blow up in front of Hind a number made out of blue-fiery dots.

Another button could inexorably panel up a steel sink over which hung a collapsible strainer with a pale heart of lettuce in it. (Now, had the old woman put Hind onto the Orientals in order to get him to Maddy but Maddy wasn't giving anything away?) On the steel draining counter that was part of the sink unit lay a substantial loaf of gray pâté flecked with fat.

"I get up here into the tower, you see," said Maddy Beecher, "and with an iceberg lettuce and a pork terrine and a can of mandarin oranges and my hammock"–Hind did not see the hammock–"I'm able to fight it out alone." Maddy smiled, as if at himself. "Fight it out alone, all I need is a Bowie knife and leggings and a duck horn." He smiled and held it.

But Hind knew Maddy had told the truth. The directors had expressed doubt about Maddy's proposal to virtually isolate his single-room tower. There was his one-stop, private elevator which only he and his secretary, he thought, had the key to. But even the elevator didn't dismiss from the directors' minds the idea that Maddy's deliberate isolation, this state of being physically almost cut off from certain crash programs developing all through the "operation," might become some macabre assertion of power at an unspecified time in the developing future. The truth was, Maddy was pretending to be alone, to be simplifying, perhaps in honor of the simplicity of his paycheck.

It had begun to rain, as if the haze had condensed.

"Well, I look straight out over the city and, as if I were speaking to my girl, I say to myself, 'It's all yours, Mad,' and so much of this, you see, is touched by area redevelopment pilot consultation projects Santos and I got involved in—and I'm at the top, or *a* top of a kind, even though it's often, on a jury, only one vote. 'It's all yours, Mad,' I say, as if I were my girl, 'yours to make into high-rise-green-space.' But then I almost don't care. I'm not a callow architectural student any more."

"*Then*?" said Hind. "When?"

"No: 'then' in the logical sense, 'then again.' You sound just like your guardian and I thought you'd rebelled against all that language snobbery. Well, as you see we shan't administer—create—what could be; instead, we'll build on the same principle which"—and Hind was guided by Maddy over to the south window—Hind disliked Maddy's supervisory elbow-handling and contact-arranging—"on which *that* thing"—the long suspension bridge across the harbor-entrance channel—"was done. Been done before. Be done again, unless I make a miracle of organization in the career of our young English friend, but he's getting cynical. I found him a rent-control two-and-half with one wall bare brick, and a fireplace and one room air-conditioned, but he keeps it like some strange nest, mattresses all over the floor. You can't imagine how he puts in his time, he's been stopped now by two city agencies and one national foundation. But America is open-ended, he keeps on saying, you build the American house unfinished with the concept that you'll be adding to it, whereas the ends are closed in Europe, houses are made finished (well that last is nonsense, I don't care which academic says it who doesn't know what life is like in the field). So talk to my young protégé if you can find him and you'll hear some of what we could be doing to ordinary people, remaking them." Maddy said "we" as if he were still a practicing architect instead of a sixty-four-thousand-a-year coordinator—the first member of their college class to be really big. But neither Hind nor Maddy missed the point, and they both knew.

But Maddy wasn't quite thirty-five, and he spoke of retiring to pure architecture.

"And will you listen to this bridge John Plante the English boy *could* be building that no one here is brave enough to build." Maddy waited, as if listening. "Say, why did you drop up?"

"I lost two Orientals I was trailing," said Hind, "and I may have lost them in Santos, or I may not."

"This has been hell all day," said Maddy, "they won't leave me alone, the birds downstairs. We had this strange phone call—"

"I say Orientals' rather than Japanese or Chinese or—"

"You wanted to tape them."

"Not these. I wanted to find out if—if they came in here—"

"Everybody enters here one day: do you know how far I've gone from those magical edifices Professor Braintree invented in class?—oh Christ, *you* didn't go to *architecture* school with me, what's the matter with me!—this is how far I've gone: Santos-Dumont's a holding operation mainly,

I suspect; they buy all sorts of outfits all over the world, the latest is a string of Oriental language schools, and I'm halfway, unwittingly, in charge of researching this extension holding policy, which and what and where do we buy, *I* an *architect*—that's it: polity has become policy— and the policy I am supposed to be halfway in charge of the researching of has for its motto 'Simplification of Frontiers'—you see, all barriers between Santos-D. and the outer world are to fall. But I'm not dead yet. The bridge I referred to..." Maddy knew he had not quite captured Hind. Maddy stared at the slanted dash dot made by flashes of rain the breeze couldn't swing away. Hind was sorry for Maddy. Maddy would not force Hind to tell about the kidnap. Maddy was thinking about the bridge and his English protégé. "Instead of that bridge over the channel, he'd have thrown clear across that water a great white slow fold of reinforced concrete. Cars would wake up into a tunnel-like trough, while on the high narrow edges of each upward fold pedestrians could contemplate suicide with such a view the bridge would become famous as a walk, a communal street; it would in fact be a street, the way the Brooklyn Bridge was meant— think of using folded concrete like that, without a single pier, without the old dreary suspension drape."

"I have to go back," said Hind.

"Of course you do, of course you do," said Maddy, "but who I ask you around here—at our shop, or in this city— knows about architectural cowardice?" Maddy was at the sink stuffing his lettuce and richly streaky pâté into polyethylene monogrammed "MB."

"My secretary gave me a whole set of these."

The sidewalk beyond the west fence of Santos displayed three people who seemed at this distance to be walking Indian file; they were equidistant from each other; they didn't seem to know each other; the man in front had a newspaper on his head; all three squeezed their shoulders in close to their necks; the third man was quite a lot shorter than the first two. They seemed to know where they were going, but Hind wondered anxiously if they knew which was the closest subway.

"And if I had to find John Plante fast, he could be roller-skating in the middle of mid-town traffic. Needs organizing. Suppose I got you in touch with him, he's going to be important. He runs around with a boy and girl he says want to level the whole city."

"I'm going now," said Hind.

"So am I," said Maddy, stepped back, pressed the button, and put his palm up against the moving panel as if to help it along. "Pretend to save that for tomorrow lunch but throw it out as soon as I get in in the morning." Hind did not tell Maddy it was Friday. Now there was just a wall where the sink had been. "*You*," said Maddy, "will come to dinner tonight. Our nine-year-old genius will tell you a bedtime story, *his* bedtime. I want you to hear him yourself, though I could retell one of his stories to you to give you the flavor—and maybe I will on the subway."

"I can't come to your house tonight," said Hind, which sounded like something they might have said to each other at the age of nine or ten.

"Look, Jackie, I know you're not with Sylvia, don't think you can hide that state of affairs—"

"I myself told you Sylvia and I weren't together," said Hind, who could have kicked Maddy Beecher.

"So what if you did. Flo is making geranium cream with blackberries—the geranium leaves you just wouldn't believe."

"Your little boy can tell me his bedtime story another time."

"He's been on a serial lately. I'll tell you the earlier parts on the subway; then you can hear him in person. He gets drowsy telling his tales to us drunks, and often he drops off without actually finishing. But you haven't been over in months."

"We met last just under a year ago."

"I've phoned, though, I think."

"We've phoned each other three times, alternately."

"For a time the child simply wouldn't go to bed, he argued us out of it, he was irrefutable, we were upset, I thought I'd look foolish if I clobbered him. Then he said if we would actually pay attention to everything he said and answer questions later, he would go to bed if *he* could tell *us* a bedtime story. He has his price. What is a child's price, and can you pay it? *Will* you pay it? Well Jackie, I wish I knew what to say or do about you and Sylvia and the kid. I saw Syl during the winter, you know."

"I want to catch one of his stories some night, but I'm busy."

"You wouldn't believe how they literally carry you away, they're fabulous. No story's good if it can't carry you away, eh? On the other hand, sometimes he gets off science fantasy onto social reform with a twist: can you imagine a nine-year-old sitting in your lap telling a story about the death house at Sing Sing: says he's not sure capital punishment's a bad thing. Calls Grimm kid stuff."

"I like stories I've heard before."

For instance, the story of Shirley Laurel's neighbor in that cramped green landscape. Hershey's mother Shirley—hating the country, hating the city.

The old woman's note could not mean nothing. But Hind had been commanded. Or by implication so: a command here seemed to him less credible than a pitiable plea for help. There hadn't been exactly despair

or danger in the note. The invitation—no, command—
hung wholly on the condition, "If you're still trying to
break the kidnap." And at the moment he read the note,
he *hadn't* still been.

If Hind now, after one of those long delays in your life
that are afterward inexplicable, went on and tracked the
child, now older but still a child, what would happen? The
value of the search needed no outside support. It certified
itself. But what would happen to the old woman, black-
eyed, tall, with a tight white bun? She was a different
physical type from Sylvia.

Then at last Hind would find the child in a crowded
arena, a circus or a play or a crucial sports event, each
side stalking the other, the crowd out of its skull. And
no one except maybe Sylvia could effectively receive his
revelation that this child had been kidnaped, and the
child himself would have been so "treated" that very
likely the child might not recall his abduction. Or if it
all turned out well, maybe the long-limbed crone would
become a sweet-lipped princess.

"If I could do all my business from the country—and
sometimes this job gets so disembodied, so unearthly you
might say—why I'd stay there and come in about once
every six weeks. I could hop right in onto this roof and
never have to go below. The landscape *here*—" he waved
to the window—"is pretty rough on an architect's eyes.
Not that there's any future in domestic architecture; give
me brown boards and shingles and shutters, and the attic
where it should be, and the lake and the island and one
thousand pines. But it would be complicated living in the
country. I guess I'd give up Santos, or did I say that? But
how could I? Then I wouldn't have a salary. Every man
has his price. Can't have a wife and *two* mistresses. I don't
know if I've got this job by the tail or *it's* wagging *me*: I
make policy."

A private corridor led from the lower level where the elevator let them off, to another elevator that ran in what Hind believed to be a slanted shaft so you got on in the middle of the silent-halled building's mass, felt yourself during your ride rounded and made gently tentative by the swinging strings that adapted a Lully pastorale, and ended at transparent doors on the ground floor. Where, instead of an electric eye, an inaudible sound ran between two short, delicate posts that looked like silver-headed ebony canes.

Doors opened; the drizzle was now mist-fine and drenching. Not how sun drenches (unquote the guardian, who felt himself to be language's last sentinel and said Hind wasn't *like* a son to him but a lawful (or rudimentary, or documentary) son).

Hind ticked off famous people who had been very tall. Sir Basil Henriques, six-seven, founded a settlement house in the East End; then he and Lady Henriques went to live there. A revered social worker.

The man who bought the blanket ostensibly for the kidnaped Laurel child was likewise tall.

A new, dark green subway waited at the platform. The high hum of the generator continued, and Maddy and Hind sat quietly. The trembling current of sound died, and there was the pause which Hind had thought was like Sylvia. The train jerked and started.

A spring of clammy air passed through Hind's ankles. Maddy looked at him in the glass opposite. Maddy would never let you do anything for him. At college he believed in communal study and would gather fellow students together the night before an exam to swap definitions. What's a chimera? An individual, organ, or part consisting of tissues of diverse genetic constitution and occurring especially in plants and most frequently at a graft union.

Now he gave a children's architecture class biweekly in a Negro school. (*Children's* architecture?) To make the kids more conscious. Of. But Maddy had dropped architecture; he conceded that.

Above the window in which Hind and Maddy had been staring at each other an ad said, "Her phone will never ring again. She has a Deltaphone now, and Deltaphone *warbles!*" The young woman in the negligee had a turn of quizzical satisfaction around her unrouged mouth. "'*Warbles*'?" the guardian would ask, and right away make up one of his impossible equations used to train Jackie for part of the national college exam he would have to take one day. "Telephone is to warble as a member of the subfamily *Silviinae*, say the black cap, is to...what?" But the guardian never rode a subway in his life. Building had been to Maddy Beecher at one time as green was to an ivy leaf. And once, years ago, old-fashioned descriptive linguistics had been to Oliver Plane as carbon to a plant.

Hind's high school biology teacher Dr. Skoldberg, with sober, fat jaw, would have made the course pure botany if it had been up to him. "O.K.," he said, "O.K."–which Hind's guardian called bad, bad English. And then very fast, blurring his words in a hiss, Dr. Skoldberg would say, "What's this, what's this, what's this?"–the words a polite reference to students whispering, though if you were a visiting parent you might think Skoldy referred to the spectroscope he used for the experiment he loved. He had boiled his ivy leaves, which Hind sometimes snitched for him from the wall next to the handball courts; Skoldy then soaked the green out of them in alcohol, watered his green alcohol, added benzol, finally decanted his chlorophyll extract, which by now was floating on top of the alcohol, which itself had gone yellow.

Lights out. "O.K.," nasally, quietly, quite confidently.

Dr. Skoldberg flashed his chlorophyll on a screen. "What colors should we see at each end of the spectrum? Maybe you know, but I'll tell you: violet and blue. Do you see them here? Do you? Well, maybe you know, but I'll tell you." He was simply shepherding Hind and the rest through the experiment he loved. But Oliver Plane, shaggy brown hair down threatening his eyes, liked to cut into Skoldy's favorite. Plane interrupted. "The ends of the spectrum, the violet and blue, are blacked out, because..." and he held up to let Dr. S. think *he* could resume; but as soon as Skoldy said, "These high frequency waves—" O.P. said, even faster than Dr. S. had said, "What's this, what's this, what's this," "waves are in fact *used* and absorbed by chlorophyll; red and"—which Oliver now pronounced blasé French—"*orange* are practically obliterated, erased, frigging annihilated; whereas green is loud and clear because—" and he'd stop before tuning into a cruelly choral duet with persistent, self-absorbed, hopeful, good Dr. Skoldberg:

| | |
|---|---|
| S: | (repeating the formula) "We call plants green—" |
| OP: | "We call plants green because they use..." |
| S: | "Because they use, because paradoxically they use green—" |
| OP:<br>S: | "Least!" |
| OP: | "'cause green's what they reject—" |
| S: | "Reject just as soon as it hits—" |
| OP: | "The upper ce——" |
| S:<br>OP: | "——ells" |

The glimmering highlight of Skoldy's trip to England was finding some fragile yellow Hairy Bird's Foot on a Hampshire golf course. He stumbled onto it while listening to and smelling the sea. Oliver Plane could have hurt him deeply if Dr. S. had not been content to receive an intruder's help in hatching that experiment.

Hershey Laurel's father Sears faced rather too coolly a similar assistance. Hind would never have allowed Shirley to be so deviously at large. She simply ignored Sears' promise to rebuild the pond wall. There came a day when neighbor Ken Love's wife Beulah was on the line and Sears Laurel wondered how many other subscribers were on it too. "Your wife not there? Then I'll have to speak to you, Mr. Laurel. Now my husband Ken has built two walls already this month, with milking and his firewood business, and he's got too much to do." But Sears could not admit the truth, and simultaneously as he heard little Hershey outside trying to count five while his beanbag was in the air, Sears asked himself why Shirley had not answered the phone. "He can't start a third wall for you, Mr. Laurel."

Hind's and Maddy's train came into the sun. The relatively clean window seemed newly opaque; but in it those cars neatly running up and down the overpass grade were neither far nor near. When it was crowded, the Fieldston Hotel Health Club gym mirrors within mirrors did that to members. Sylvia's demonstrations had puzzled his eyesight perhaps.

What with the new concentric vents in the subway car, you hadn't the noise of the old-time summer fans whose blades would always bear a furry mold of grease-stuck soot. A small, fatty old man in voluminous brown pin-stripe trousers and tan poplin windbreaker with bottom buttons undone stared at Hind's size-fifteen feet. And as Hind retaliated by boring fascinated into the man's stomach and thought he might again try to tell Maddy it was imperative to check on the Orientals, Maddy began.

"Not—"

"Louder."

"Not that my young Englishman is taken in by the talk of the one who got him onto roller skates." Maddy jerked around. "But *you* knew Christy Amondson—who's still almost your size, not quite your height, and still I hear can be seen skating the Heights and maybe God knows most of the city in the course of a good month's regular skating."

The train stopped in a station and Hind's voice burst into the car. "He had a kind of mandarin calm rolling along with his hands clasped behind his back. We used to think he was tall because he skated with kids who were much younger—and comparatively they got younger and younger—and his style made him seem tall."

"The English guy," said Maddy, preoccupied. The old man's gaze at Hind's feet had become a shifting attempt at defense; he knew that his stomach was being stared at.

Maddy was describing again what he had shown Hind before they left. "You don't affront a jury, and Plante did. I couldn't help him, though he says I could have, I couldn't." Before leaving the S-D office Maddy had taken a folder from a cylindrical drawer of his desk, found what he wanted, leaned over his desk, looking carefully at its surface, and pressed a camouflaged and countersunk button. He forgot and began in his normal voice, then lowered it to a murmur—he couldn't get used to the whisper the electronic gadget was geared to. "Eleven zero zero six zero zero five zero zero three one."

As he pivoted to face the east wall, he registered with a smile and a unity of head-dip and leg-swing and foot-stop, the simple rightness of it all as the cabinet doors hissed open: on palest olive paper.

The color was visible only to someone who knew the original document or was as well briefed as Hind. On palest olive paper was laid out a floor plan for a floor of a now rejected apartment block. Down the upper right was the Lighting Legend, explaining a scheme of radiant wall illumination John Plante said he had dreamed. He had had to go in jeans before the full jury at one of the later meetings and berate the members for fearing growth; he said he'd researched them all and had found that every one of them except Maddy Beecher commuted from at most a small town, none lived in the city or roller-skated. "Jack, he was afraid the jurors would think simply that he was a good architect who saw some useful point in designing low-income apartment blocks. And he had to add, as if it had been a germ of his work, some truculent theory about designed evolutionary accident"—Maddy was saying the same all over again now next to Hind in this subway, which Maddy made a point of taking, rather than use the S-D limousines—"and about the pressure on the human tenant to alter the shapes of his rooms as the life of the materials of which the apartment house would be made changed from year to year. You don't affront a jury, you don't, you just don't."

The woman in the ad looked toward Hind but not truly at anything, as with Deltaphone nestled against her yet very visibly articulated ear—a lobe to hold in the lips—her charmed eyes conjured the person she talked to.

"So now," Maddy was saying, "John Plante if not roller-skating is lending himself out with wrecking bar to various friends who live in railroad flats in good neighborhoods and want walls knocked down."

"Could I have seen him at the pier when I was sunbathing?"

Maddy did not ask which pier. "He's everywhere except at a drawing board. He's even met Sylvia."

The elevators at Maddy's stop had gone self-service since Hind had last been to the Heights. In the crowd Hind saw three elderly men he knew.

Two blocks down a short man with feet pointed out came striding across against the light swinging his arms strenuously. The rush hour traffic report from police helicopter number four from a radio welled and faded; then as the man passed, Hind saw in the hand at the end of one swinging arm a long white transistor.

Maddy took Hind's elbow and walked him into the middle of the street. Maddy pointed to a five-foot square of black iron grating and the circular sewer cover almost tangent at the far end. "Think back to Sunday years ago. Christy didn't want to play hockey, and we stopped and I decided we would have an expedition. Just then Christy's father came walking along grinning the way he always did, and before Christy saw him Christy said, 'To qualify for the expedition you got to clear the grating and the sewer in one jump,' and Mr. Amondson kept grinning and said, 'If Christy tries that stunt I'll confiscate his wheels indefinitely,' which surprised me—and I imagine you too, Hind"—Maddy had an annoying habit of saying your name to you all the time—"for here was this man who was always grinning at us but never saying anything. I knew we'd all of us *except* Christy have trouble trying to get over that space, maybe crack an ankle—this space, look at it, untouched—but you and I knew Christy could and would, and probably had trained for it, but we were sick of playing hockey, the regulation puck Flo's father gave us was skipping, then landing on end and rolling down into someone's areaway, or down the sewer by the parish house, and we couldn't find a wire coat hanger in the gutter—"

Hind raised his elbow out of Maddy's grip.

Maddy said, "And the wood block we'd been using split. And we liked Christy, but then his father said this, and kept grinning; it was ghastly."

"No one I saw," said Hind, "ever skated the street the way Christy did it. Like ice, or invisible electric tracks. I wanted to help Christy, and I wonder if you didn't, too."

"I still see him on a Sunday if we're not in the country. He's around."

"There he was," Hind was recalling somewhat nervously, "every second or so rocking slowly from shoulder down to knee, then back to the other shoulder, knee, back and forth, beautiful. I *thought* maybe he'd never stop. And I bet it isn't only Sundays now. We called him '*that* weird.'"

"You got that, too," said Maddy.

"At school," said Hind.

"Naturally."

The Beecher child Eddy had decided to turn in early, he said he felt under the weather; he was not to be disturbed; he had gone to bed without any supper. He knew more current events than Berry Brown, whom Charley condemned as a "colored wino" when Charley once again failed Berry's daily quiz for not knowing where the marchers had gone from Selma. Maddy and Hind sat drinking whisky for a fairly dull three-quarters of an hour, Maddy knew nothing about any Orientals; then Flo came in from the kitchen and asked some irrelevant questions about Sylvia and Hind's little girl. (May was just as smart as Eddy.) As Flo was returning to the kitchen, a very small woman named Marina was introduced. Hind's old friend Bee Bee Barker had told Marina to meet her at the Beechers' for dinner, and Flo carried off the surprise well, she had never met Marina nor had she been notified by Bee Bee.

Maddy was talking. "I haven't seen Jack for months and suddenly he turns up today looking for a couple of Chinamen."

Marina brought her drink toward her mouth. "You married?"

"Of course he's married," said Maddy. "That's why he's looking for two Chinamen."

"*Were* they Chinese?" asked Hind.

"Marriage," said Maddy, "seems very often a kind of criminal act. I haven't figured out just what crime."

Flo called, "Do you feel we've collaborated?"

"Marriage," said Marina, "is self-mutilation."

"*I* liked it," said Hind, "but I've been kind of selfish."

"You an only child?" asked Marina loudly, looking away toward the kitchen. "You marry late?" Her short upper lip gave the teeth a bared look, the corner-creases of the mouth took on a judging downturn, her left arm dropped out straight, over the chair arm.

"I'll explain," said Hind patiently.

"Oh," said Marina, bringing her cigarette up abruptly as if in self-defense, "don't do *that*!" Then she tried to shrink away biting her lower lip, hoping to hide the apparent force of her words, and she brushed in the cigarette ash newly broken onto the lap of her gray-green cord skirt. Did the Orientals lead to Maddy Beecher only so he could lead Hind to Marina?

Hind was doing an embarrassing thing, reaching far over toward her chair at first as if to make a point, then bringing fingers together as he always had to remember to do swimming; and when Marina leaned the other way against the far arm of her chair, Hind flipped his thumb over as if merely using his hands to talk. He wanted to get hold of her.

Maddy spread his adminicular arms—his third dark Scotch in hand—"Maybe *I'll* explain."

"Dinner's done," yelled Flo from the kitchen.

"Our stove," said Maddy, "clucks and snaps, and olive-green lights go off, you name it. A gift from Santos-Dumont Sisters."

Hind tried to stare Marina down and succeeded.

"An only child, yes," said Maddy with a difficult smile showing not the just subtlety he hoped but faint discomfort due to some physical cause. "But not only without brothers and sisters. Without parents as well."

"My talent," said Hind rising, "was to care rather than be cared for, to herd rather than be heard: now shut up, Maddy."

"I don't think Hind knew his parents," said Maddy to Bee Bee Barker's friend Marina. "He was too little. I suppose he knows them now only in the...foreshortened distortions of...some—"

"So what?" said Marina. "What did anyone have more than him?"

"—of," continued Maddy, "a baby. For that is all he was when he was adopted."

"Adopted," said Marina.

Hind nodded, but she was looking at Maddy, who was looking through his glass toward the dining room.

There you were, two or three years old, tired but in bed a bit too early you felt, since the spring evening was warm and you were in the country, and you thought about two things while you worked a foot free of the covers yet did not kick them off the rest of you: first the two black butterflies you saw chasing each other higher and higher just as either your father or your guardian called you to supper, and it doesn't matter except to the impoverished recollections of some foraging historian who will never do your life's sequence; and the other thing you thought about while recollecting the dark busy play of those wings here now in bed was, is, the arrangements of steps now being taken by the adult walking near your two- or three-year-old door, then nearer, then away far to a place characterized by pause, then closer still and more slowly, and you plotted the strokes of movement as if no one set of steps occurred before another—that night either the female present is seated through all this walking, or there isn't a female present and the adult walking is, so long as no other male be there, *alone*. And at last, as you are tired tired tired, the steps arrive at your door and stop.

"The beans are limp," cried Flo.

"And Jack," said Maddy, "had a now late uncle who everyone thought would be guardian, but no, it turned out Hind's father, perhaps with a fine, antique ideal in mind, had designated a nonrelative as guardian, and it stood up in court. A bachelor, too."

"That's misleading," said Hind. "My guardian must have been very close to my parents."

"Dinner," said Flo from the dining room. "You are always going around telling other people's stories in front of them. It's Jack's story, not yours."

"It's Jack's story," said Maddy quietly and happily, then drank down his drink and got up.

"Bee Bee won't touch beans," said Marina, "so I don't cook them any more."

Anyhow Maddy had not finished his story. Hind did something all the way through, almost no matter what it cost. The guardian had set that example, he never let a job go uncompleted or be completed by someone else; and whenever Hind forced himself to follow that example—or, better, when after unconsciously persisting in a job, like taping "Naked Voice," for example, he later studied his acts and found he had been fruitfully copying his guardian, he submitted to a blind happiness as obscure in its fullness as were Sylvia's semiannual anxieties, April and December. Sylvia wouldn't ask for her sip of his beer till there was only one sip left, or a pull on his final cigarette of the night till the lit end was nearly burning his long nose. On the other hand, Maddy started projects he then left to someone else. Which was not a good example. For instance, a children's architecture-orientation class, optional in an almost all-black school uptown.

When Hind left, later than he thought he'd wanted to, Maddy held him up by the elevator. "There were those Orientals I think you said. They supposed to work at my shop?" Hind heard the elevator seem to flap above. The story was too long for this few seconds; he couldn't start with Maddy, who didn't perhaps care anyway.

"The trees he plans for this development will never do, and reverse skyscrapers and also normal apartment blocks—the trees would be hybrids that could grow very fast, you could *see* them going up when they went up, they'd stop at about a hundred feet and wouldn't need tending and would have plenty of low limbs for the kids." Maddy yawned, putting a hand up on Hind's shoulder. "You're silent, for you. I think I"—he yawned—"forgot something I wanted to say."

"I'm sure," said Hind.

As the elevator door slid smoothly open, the impatient jab of the buzzer came—and before he turned to shake Maddy's hand, Hind looked inside and saw the button lit for a higher floor.

Was Maddy's skeleton sinking within his body moment by moment? But he kept talking, like the old man, Dewey Wood's pal, who nearly died in the sauna bath. "This friend of John Plante's," said Mad, "the boy not the girl—they're all roller-skaters and she's got her lovely long legs like a crane—no kidding she spends a lot of actual skating time standing on one leg with the other sort of wound around—and anyway I mean *legs*, not just long—the boy in question"—Maddy yawned—"has it in for me. Maybe worse. Plante says the guy will do something to me one day. I've sold out, you see. It's just that the kid misunderstood something casual Plante said about my giving up art in order to sell plastic values. Flo and I had the three of them"—the angry buzzer came again twice, frowning and twitching—Hind got a foot in the elevator—"the three of them here in the house last month, hmmm, the day Christy Amondson's dad got pickpocketed. And Plante's friend went off inspecting Flo's kitchen and the incinerator chute outside right here"—Maddy pointed to the olive panel that went quietly with the mauve-on-mauve flocked wallpaper.

"Thinks I've sold out." The buzzer again once. "*Plante* thinks. Says we *might* have planned the God's Country Complex so we could *add* to the apartment buildings when we needed more space, and says the space-frame wings waste acres of space, and he talks about well you could at least have designed them for ice for undulating skating or sled trials. And says, like a squirt, 'Well, Beecher, think of those poor cliffdwelling bastards locked into the great pieces of replaceable turd you supervised the cheap design and erection of.' It's not as if I don't know what he's talking about; he treats me like I'm an architectural student who had the same term project he did. I told him it's easier to tear down when you need a bigger building. Flo and I designed the summer place so as to add to it; we built toward the rest of the big ledge, you never came up to see it—not that a summer camp is hard to plan that way…I'm not drunk, Hind, just very tired."

"I know, Mad," said Hind. Go back to S-D in the morning, not now in the dark; get under the neon mustachio; an S-D helichopper would be standing by on the evergreen lawn near the furred wall.

"Well, I know you know, but you don't understand what I struggle every day. Through. At my tenured eminence and salary, *I* have to be barraged, infiltrated... programed into these procedural phone calls that no one knows how to deal with."

Yet here was the whole trouble: not *enough* ordinary human routine for Maddy now. "Night, Maddy." The guardian saying on some psychic, higher floor, "Collaboration between circumstance and genes, yes: but character is the basic, if one only knew what–"

"Night, Hind, Jack, last name first, whatever your name is. If–" Maddy stopped the live door with his hand–"if those dewy-wise young idealists making their condescending survey of other people's incinerators– well, *my* incinerator is what I mean–knew what life is really like, they wouldn't accuse me of deserting architecture. The girl, the one with long legs, chimed in with a word or two about every building should express the maker's love, so you're living in his love, I ask you, but the little commercial fronts near the bridge?, what about them?, but Plante shut me up and told her to shut up. If he knew my everyday problems, what it means to be thrown into, as our dear bitchy rainyday girlfriend with the game leg Cassia used to say–"

"'Total disarray,'" said Hind.

"Yes, thrown into total disarray by a mad phone call that may have had an English accent, who insists that some genius my staff never heard of called–"

Buzzes had steadied to a patiently angry one every two seconds; Maddy's hand went, Maddy's face still talking was for a second a puzzled or earnest portrait in the circle of glass–"Lowell, Lawlor, Laura, came to work for us."

Lowell, Lawlor, Laura, Laurel: Maddy relevant after all: Hind jabbed Maddy's floor as Maddy relayed the Laurel wordgram, but the elevator rose in response to the person or persons above, and to check the three L's you required not Maddy but the relevant personnel at S-D. But of course there was so much *to* Maddy that the kidnap plot wouldn't let you for the time being pursue. Skip him for now.

As the elevator rose, Hind heard "Night" murmured below him like part of the dank air of the shaft.

But when he came into his own street, the pier cycle leading to Santos seemed lost. Maddy would have been easy to put to sleep tonight if his little boy Edison had felt like telling a bedtime story. Maddy's talk had been so full of irrelevancies Hind thought this stage of the kidnap revival would need indeed to be sealed off from Maddy's little troubles. All evening he would come back to his own administrative policy puzzles, his deep boredom, his wish to make demands on the S-D Sisters though unsure which demands; he must resent Hind turning up like this freelance in midafternoon.

It was unthinkable that Hind could not finish this stage.

Imagining he followed the Orientals into Santos, was *he* in fact the followed by virtue of some exactly planted emptiness into which he kept falling? and had the big and little Oriental, now asleep somewhere in the heights and depths of the city, safe once more from the daily danger of car accidents, though breathing airs which even the editorial fabrics of their muscles and lungs could not disarm, had the big and little Oriental led Hind, a known giant, along the lattices of track and the plots of pavement directly to old friend Mad Beecher?

When Hind came into his own street no one was in front of him. Only the four street lights, two on either sidewalk, staggered; only one lighted window on the ground floor of the ad photographer's studio; only the beetle rows of tight-parked cars, along which, after school, children ran, shooting across at each other. A part of the merged noises of the city came from the bright glow in the avenues that crossed the east and west ends of his street. He had one eye on the small spaces between the glinting cars on his left, and one on the stone stoops and areaways on his right. Up here somewhere— here in this house on the top floor—Good Queen Rain, so crowned by Mr. Fordham, slept on her little stomach perhaps dreaming about tall Hind, her hero.

Now a familiar figure came out under the undertaker's awning and turned her face half toward Hind. If it was not the old woman's face—and Hind caught the flashing white hair, and thought he saw long limbs—it was someone so like her that this was in itself significant. She turned toward the other end of the street, to the glow of the avenue at the east end of the street, and she walked awkwardly fast. Like the old woman who had left the note. With arms at her sides like Hind.

Even at this distance Hind could see that Carmen La Branche had left only the small vestibule light on, and Hind was sure there was no funeral and therefore no one sleeping the night on the ground floor and so no reason to believe the main, the business, door had been left unlocked. So the old woman could have come out of Hind's entrance, which might mean she'd left a new note.

Hind trotted. He looked for a cop, lest a cop note his hurry. When he reached the undertaker's he saw that he could catch the old woman; she was just at the avenue corner.

The note was more important. If there was a note.

Tall, yes, and slender, the old woman did not look back and now turned the corner. Or did she look back as she turned? Or merely look up the avenue for a downtown cab? The avenue was, of course, now one-way. Now a cab came, Hind saw it skip across the intersection of the avenue and his street, then slow sharply to slip past the restaurant on the corner, likely stopping for the old woman.

*If* there was a note.

Sylvia loved old cabs with cracked, cool leather. At three A.M. of a Sunday, in sidewalk slush waiting for a cab, he in his straw sombrero with the shredded edges, Sylvia in her fedora green and feathered, swayed holding on to each other; as the vacant cab neared, the man added his "Off-Duty" lights and drew out into the center; but when, discus-style, Hind slung into the cold street the Sunday *Times*, which on the still air sailed not at all like a discus out into some of its parts, Sylvia without looking was into the street rushing to pick up–no, not the whole paper–merely "the Magazine crossword, stupid," she had answered his anxious call.

Fixed between two of the crenate bars of the postbox grille, the new note was in the old place.

The box was so small and the top-hinged door so tight you often had a job to pull down and out the longer pieces of mail; Sylvia bruised her knuckles extracting a magazine.

"Hooked with a wood," Hind read aloud, "into the forest, it will lead you well beyond the pier–if you're still interested."

She began to sound like the guardian when for his summer treasure hunt he devised almost hopeless clues to go with his ingenious snaps of roots and bogs and thickety vistas and his familiar hand going into the narrow cleft of an unfamiliar tree trunk. Ashley Sill won second prize the once he had been persuaded to visit Hind: a National League baseball with autographs of all the Giants curving along seams and crossing to meet each other.

Why did Hind not run after the old woman?

The motive of the person who was involving him in this hunt all over again would be important in the scheme. But at this stage Hind would only follow the track, he would save this other question for later, as if it were some stamina he'd need.

From his own entrance-hallway Hind went through the side door into the front ground-floor funeral parlor. Carmen had left the tiny night light on the lectern by the desk; the white letters designating the name of the last funeral had not been picked out of the black rows in the small sign that stood up from the higher end of the lectern. The undertaker hadn't had a funeral in weeks. And the last came in in the afternoon and only for one night and disappeared in the early morning cross-town traffic. Sometimes some of his mail would be misdelivered to the undertaker, and Carmen would sometimes leave it on the desk. A folder on the desk said that "Jaundice knows no season" and that the fluid here advertised was the recommended arterial fluid for a jaundiced case and would overcome yellow discoloration without turning the body green. But Hind's landlord had not done his own embalming for years, the trade embalmer did it at the center. There was no mail here for Hind, no one was sleeping on the two scuffed and cracked red leather couches; Carmen was home with his family, and probably so was the undertaker, who sometimes went on the town and used the funeral parlor for a *pied-à-terre*. He said to Hind, but not glumly (for the man was rich—"like you, Señor Hind," he said), "People just not dying, stiffs in short supply. But I made mine years ago."

When Hind would pay his rent, an old man would be leaning back on a leather couch, sometimes two or three. They would interrupt their half-sleep, catch their respiration in mid wheeze, and squint and blink at Hind in the low light as he crossed the long room to place the business envelope on the undertaker's green blotter. It wasn't even the television they came for, but the carpeting and the nineteen-thirties furniture, also the landlord himself, old Irish, old neighborhood, who when he came in two or three times a week would berate them and give them a drink from the bathroom cabinet and tell them if they didn't stay off the couches they would grow into them or if they didn't stop lounging around, what with business, he might just up and plant them.

On the cover of the jaundice-fluid folder was a black-and-white lino or woodcut print of a snow-sleigh drawn by a dark, swift horse about to turn his heaving shoulders sharply round a curve that led to a snow-covered bridge; white-heavy pines filled the left foreground, and over the black river a bright farmhouse with too many windows lay a bit nearer than a couple of mysterious, bunched barns. No other additive or arterial fluid needed with this "total" fluid, though you might use Clot Disperser, should drainage problems come up. Or down.

The night warm but going cool; the top floor, with or without Sylvia, stuffy. Soot caressed his bare soles; Hind could think of nothing to compare to the heat of the night.

He went to his ordinary old black telephone to call the Smith Answering Service. But he might, then, have to phone some more tonight; tonight he did not resent the fact that communications from his various contacts should be so smoothly translatable into the intimately business tone in which the colored girl on duty at this hour Friday night turned "Mister" into the allegro form "Mist'" when she responded to him. He called her Smitty.

Yet then he did phone, only to find that Sylvia's father had phoned long distance station-to-station, and Sylvia had called asking if Hind had gone to visit Ashley Sill, and Smitty was proudly saying she told Sylvia she was unable to give out data of that nature, when Hind summarily hung up.

He had his bathing trunks on, and he lay down in them. Despite the cramping form of shoes still sensible upon his now bare feet, his feet could breathe. In the summer they felt his height.

Again at the window he was in time to see the ad studio's light go. And from the front door into which had passed stubbornly the heifer three, now four, weeks ago, came suddenly the familiar figure of the girl all in black-striped, white vinyl—soft helmet, dark dark glasses, thigh boots, stiff coat A-flared. She went to her motorcycle in the shadows of the ad studio steps.

No, Sylvia wasn't going to douse the bedside lamp. She had made it with an earthenware jug, a corked fixture, a burlap shade. Sylvia wasn't here. He wrote a letter at her flat months ago and when she read it she said, "Why not *ask* me whether I send love to whoever you're writing?" He didn't see she was kidding. She played with him.

He wanted some of those painkiller pills the guardian happened to have in his raincoat in a plastic tube when Hind's shoe broke the little left-winger's right leg. Trying to go to sleep, Hind heard for what seemed a long time an apparent collaboration between the clock ticking on the bureau to the left of his bed and, to his right, the framed picture ticking against the plaster wall. Then, for a time, he would hear the picture only, or, to be exact, its wood frame. This ticking couldn't be due to air current; the air of the late-spring night was slow. The answer must then be some tremor from inside the city, perhaps in the city's construction a sway or cycle the picture's inertia didn't receive. Was there a cadence of the city audible only to the true citizens? Quote unquote, Mr. Wood, old Dewey Wood, whose right calf's prickle of blue varicose he thought he was shrinking in the sauna room at the health club uptown. When he quoted his newspaper contributions ("passing simplicities of a very private citizen"), Oliver Plane, behind his hot, sweat-wet, sweat-stiff atrocity sheet, tilted his head up barely enough to eye Dewey over the top edge: "There is below the brouhaha," said glistening old Wood, his balls hanging over the cedar bench, "a true music of the city audible only to her frequent citizens; you in your vest of clay are vouchsafed in the..." Adapted to this room at the undertaker's, and this time, it could read, "...in the picture's tick a hint of the old harmonies other real citizens hear naturally." Did the cycle tick from the very design of the picture itself? The guardian had had his eye on "Jack, my young beanstalk" always: on the soccer fields, in the swimming pools, even at Sunday school (though he never visited) and over the business of the Jesus-puzzle portrait which Mrs. Daisy Deal called a delightful Christian game just right for her class, but which the guardian regarded as obnoxious and misleading and not to be tacked up in Jack's room. "Yes, *character*!" said the guardian. "But the tragic point is, you can turn away from your real nature."

Hind, curling, stretching, pillow-flipping, crossing ankles, swimming on sand it seemed, turning over, lying again down carefully on his loose genitals, pulling hairs, splitting—not *that*, not *that* one, no, please, splitting imagining splitting—the forearms of his delicate (precocious?) little girl May tucked asleep round the corner (who endured fairy tales politely but preferred thrice-told true tales of Hind's and Sylvia's childhoods), Hind now saw he wasn't hearing the clock: it had stopped. Its luminous dim circle was in Hind's memory part of Sylvia's hand. She would set the clock before bed, because he sometimes set it wrong when he bothered. She would wind and set that clock. While he looked now at the silent clock, Hind listened to the tick of the picture against the wall turn stage by stage into his billowing mind. The sheep wouldn't count, but he heard their horns, and he knew he had almost begun to sleep. Sylvia's hand was upon him. He hadn't after all split his little girl's forearms, he had imagined them and kissed them—Sylvia was commending him for being such a good father to May and her little arms, but as for splitting he had split hairs, he had been to the paintbrush factory on the S-D side of the river that Maddy was putting some of his own cash in, and Hind saw how the firm split ends of hairs in the flagging machine so you get in the end of each bristle two or three tiny fishhooks you call flags that help the brush hold more paint and at this concern to which Hind went to get a tape for "Naked Voice" a new new (and secret) p-r-o-c-e-s-s puts into the flags already made, infinitesimal flaglets, an extra which nobody else knows how. "Hooked with a wood into the forest, it will lead you well beyond the pier." Hind knew he had begun to sleep. He could sleep into the middle of next week.

And it was indeed more than two weeks till he could break away from "Naked Voice" and think about the second note and then decide to go off north to Ashley Sill's golf-course-country-club, which, through a great glass window guarded outside by his wife's imported bay tree, Ash, poor Ash, looked bleakly at in his letters to Hind. Yet Ash had only the books to keep, for he and his wife hired help to run the pro shop and keep the greens not too fast and the fairways weekend wide.

Hind went on a weekday to miss the traffic, and the sky turned clear blue as soon as he crossed the city limits and approached the state border.

The distance to the Sills' was three hundred miles. Hind drove it in seven hours, stopping only for gas, though at the point on one major artery where he pulled in, his need for fuel was not immediate, and therefore he didn't exactly obey the signs along this artery that said, STOP ONLY IN EMERGENCY.

## *...*
## *iii*

And if he nearly stopped at the point in the state next his where there was that state's (thus billboarded) FIRST ALL-ELECTRIC HIGH SCHOOL—for he had planned one day to tape grouped voices there—he still found himself drawn on up the Thruway. The clue clearly meant the Sills' place, and he had neglected Ash for months—but he would have had to discuss his separation from Sylvia—then also, as dreamy, acid Ash would have forgotten by now, the golf-course-country-club-pasture complex, above which on a knoll loomed the Sills' huge ginger-bread, was so arrestingly near—nineteen miles near—the crossroad newspaper-store-soda-fountain eight miles from the kidnap house, that Hind could go again easily in one sweep; then, too, the graded landscape of the now totally connected and thus endless Thruway was something to finish, or to find the rim of if not the end of—not something to abandon. Hind smiled, the Thruway was so calm. Calm as Sylvia's deodorant smelled, which was called Calm and billed "Dry as a desert breeze." She had left an almost full can, and there was some left even now, for Hind didn't use the stuff.

Hind remembered a shortcut he had not realized he had forgotten, and, at a rise whence he saw glimmering in the sun a shopping complex and some neon gumdrops saying SEARS AUTOMOTIVE CENTER, he left the main way eleven and a half miles from the Sills'. And soon he was driving along the east border of a cultivated pasture full of black-and-white cows. The unfenced border was open to the black, country road. Hind stopped the car, turned to the left window, and took some long inhalations. He felt he smelled the wild oil of the red cedars, the violet of their berries; *let* Sylvia the country girl say the oil couldn't be smelt and anyway had nothing to do with the berries but rose up in the wood and through the needles—and she wouldn't say "rose up" either.

Further on, he stopped again. The yellow-and-brown of the house Ashley lived in with his gardener wife could barely be seen above maples on a ridge close by what marked the southern reach of Sill territory. Beyond that pasture and toward the house, their golf course began. He thought he found the sun-flash from their gold Protestant rooster he knew stood on the top tower of the old house.

A bird on the gravel shoulder twitched round profile to watch Hind. On the other side of the road, animals: two brown-and-white heifers stretching stretching for grass till they had to move a hoof; a giant Belgian workhorse tossing flies out of his shining blond mane; a self-absorbed Shetland grazing with his hose aired practically to the ground. Hind put his nose back out his own window and thought he caught the click of a golf shot. The air was so sweet you forgot the car. A strangely silent jay flew straight off its branch and up the road; Hind didn't see birds here in the country quite as precisely as he could the sparrow that came to his fourth-floor ledge to tap at the pane, a wedgelet of horn emerging from a live piece of gray. Cars seemed to bother birds less than people—be precise, says a guardian voice—as if to the bird the car was natural.

Hind's legs bothered him as he drove on again; he kept wanting this mild plain land, but he had to get on; but he had to stop to look and smell, get some for Sylvia and May. May would sit off on the brink of that sand trap talking to herself. But he must get to the Sills'. He shifted his right knee, slipped his foot off the gas, and was jerked against the wheel. Sometimes during long drives he was sure he started to grow again. The body used the zigzag posture to hide its insatiable growth. When Hind was a sub on the jayvee basketball team at school, the coach's son aged five or six would come to him during the game where he sat on the bench with his knees sticking forth, and the little boy climbed him, so to speak, got onto one of the knees, got onto the other, sat on him blocking his view. Hind was an object.

Here was the seventeenth fairway, with a wood on the far side beyond a narrow high rough. It was impossible for Sylvia to be more absent from his life, he had thought—and especially because her flat was so close to their old one in the undertaker's where Hind lived. But if she now found him renewing the kidnap, playing games with two-dimensional Asians, treasuring words that went, "Hooked with a wood into the forest, it will lead you well beyond the pier"—if she knew, her mind would send him even further away. Again he was stopping; the main highway ended this road a quarter of a mile ahead; but here was the seventeenth green, and two elders in possession of it.

From Hind's angle the green looked circular, as svelte as Maddy's indoor practice "carpet." One man stood at its edge, leaning on his putter. The other, as slim and white-haired (-thatched, -capped) and unearthly, rested on one knee with putter extended on the green ground toward the hole. Flag and stick lay pointed west. The player raised his club handle and caned himself up to standing, and Hind gave a soupçon more gas to keep from stalling. The player was over his ball now, pigeon-toed, knock-kneed, round-shouldered, keeping the odd eye again again again on the hole as if to catch it moving. (In the old days, when Ash was new here, he had in fact changed cup locations without warning under cover of night, but few members could in any case expect to hit the green from very far out, and the course's only tournaments were club or member-guest.) Behind, the partner was standing letting his club gently swing from his fingers. The man putting gave his clubhead two preparatory jerks and Hind shifted to first, and, as the elderly, elegant, white-haired man showed in a certain final rigidity of buttocks, shoulder-hunch, and knee-knock that he belonged to his ball and had forgotten about the score he'd finish the round with and cared only for his finish here on seventeen—though maybe only for the stake per hole—Hind let out the clutch, depressed the accelerator pedal, and on the elderly man's ultimate twitch back then through to give the stroke, honked the horn twice moving slowly off, and saw in the very corner of his eye that he had drawn blood.

Across the intersection ahead, cars passed right and left up the main way. Behind him, a blue car's open trunk-lid was a blue vista out its rear window.

Did he inherit from his guardian the nearly possessive wish to finish things for others? His great, the guardian's great, relaxed hands smelled, and in Hind's dreams tasted, of citrus, the blood oranges the guardian took for strength, the big greenish Italian lemons. Yet he wasn't handy. What would he be able to do at the undertaker's, the plain, clean old brownstone concealing its ills if you didn't go inside and upstairs and try to jam the sash chains back into the splintery bed-grooves where they were supposed to run? If the guardian, officially dead by the time Hind and Sylvia moved into the undertaker's, were to hear the moan at the faucet's root in the bathroom, he'd not have tried to check the washer or, first, turned off the basement valve; he'd have twisted the faucet handle left and right, then tried with mean-eyed concentration to jiggle it. (It need not be clear just what he might have done with his life had he not taken on himself the burden of a foster son; the guardian's many friends must of course have been right that he had given up remarkable chances in order to adopt and raise Jack. Jack thought it out during the second half of a dull scrimmage in which he and de Forrest had hardly one defensive chance, and there the guardian stood at the sideline—education, mind, force, looks, money, just watching—a rainy day, the ball lobbed high down the center and Hind and de Forrest converged, but then an idea seemed to form at the intersection of two distances and Hind let de Forrest handle the return, the center half watching de Forrest knowing de Forrest would like to bypass halfs and forwards and dribble clear through to score—the idea was simply that Jack must for one thing show the guardian that like father like son did apply here, he had a real son demonstrably his—but an enemy halfback faked the ball away from de Forrest and gave his own inside left too long a lead on a pass; and Hind had to come in and did, and so could not finish the epochal plan that had just occurred to him.)

To get to the Sills', Hind had to drive out into the main highway again, go off at an angle from the Sills', then find the paved narrow road that led back in to the fork, one branch of which continued to the clubhouse-pro-shop-putting-green-complex, while the other turned up the hill to Ashley's house. Hind passed a low school of blue bricks that had a spun, un-bricklike shine; bright-jacketed books stood ajar in windows. Two miles down the highway Hind slowed to watch for the turn. A lanky child in jeans, her top bound in a bikini bra, passed him on a silver-bright, stick-shift Spyder accompanied by the high-voltage guitars that came from the radio clamped to the crosspiece of her high-rise handlebars. She pedaled in time.

Ashley was standing exactly as he had been the last time Hind had appeared here (though not the last time they'd seen each other): at the window picking his ear with a key, his eyes up, his long Norse jaw pulled in toward his collarbone. Hind had a long Norse jaw just like it, though since Hind was far bigger than Ash and they were in proportions almost the same scale, Hind's jaw was absolutely longer.

Without greeting Hind, Ash shyly went right into a continuation of an argument they had been having six months before when the ad studio's rented microbus had started beeping to get past Ash's double-parked desert wagon: "But city people don't know how to *do* things—how do you clean carbon off an oil furnace ring? or if a sink backs up, the city person is just plain impractical—"

"*You* wanted a resident herd of *deer*," said Hind now as they sat down in the living room. "You got the idea from the Hampton Court Park golf course when you were in London with Cassia."

"You remember too damn much, what good does it do?" said Ashley, staring at Hind's long shoes. Ash was even thinner than when Hind had last seen him. His wife was in the Big Garden.

"You said you would make me resident deerherd."

"All right, all right, I may have said that." Impatient for some change in himself brought about by himself; eager, bored. "One of my final efforts to be agreeable."

The groundskeepers had predicted deer droppings if Ash's plan should be acted on, and the pro foresaw a new slowness and stealthiness in the way some members would play the course (clubhead socks over gun muzzles.) Hind had said yes ah yes yes; but what he had then irrelevantly told Ash's wife Peggy she had proceeded to use against Ash: that as with a lone dog, so possibly with a player who had hooked into the woods or even hit and (strolled straight to) his green: deer might close a diminishing circle then hoof him to death. Therefore, no resident herd of deer. Ash didn't much care. It was the city he kept on about before and now. Hind tried to return him to immediate matters.

"The children?" asked Hind. Who would be clue-bearer?

Ash shook his head. "Working, always working. Never have time for me. How long can you stay? Unless you stay three nights at least—"

"Not possible—"

"Unless you stay three nights you may not even set eyes on them. They haven't even time for me. Hop teaches woodwork. Daisy—"

"Hop's eleven now," eagerly, tentatively.

"Yes," said Ash, "I believe he is. But you see, the main thing, he's a teacher. Woodwork to deaf children. How come so many deaf children just around here? Sundays when I want to sit around and talk or take in a movie in town, he's busy. Well, what the hell, I've got a lot to ask you about the city."

"What? *since* my phone call?"

"I can't ever think of things in a spur-of-the-moment phone call."

"What *does* Hop do Sundays?"

"Teaches, and goes on botany walks and photographs the pasture—you name it, he uses his time frighteningly well. The Sunday teaching is an added burden for me because I have to drive him in with his carton of culture games and illustrated history lessons in the form of advertising cartoons, and the eight-year-olds at the Unitarian Fellowship think he's wonderful, so I have to sit in the car till it's time to go home; Hop and Daisy have to be in town at nine, but the Sunday papers from the city haven't arrived; so there I am, waiting, with nothing to do and too much to consider." Ash's voice was testy again, "Now *you're* going to answer some things."

But of course what Ashley Sill needed to talk about was himself, not the city he felt guilty having left.

Sometimes, Hind thought, eardrums pounding, I understand everyone.

"What's Beecher up to? He still with Flo?"

"Up to everyone's business. Makes a lot of money, judges architecture competitions, protects young talent by means of elegant Bloody Mary brunch parties, manipulates even the colored kids he teaches architecture to at a grade school—does it with slides, takes the kids from corner to cornice to window to angle, slowly all over a building, clicking the remote on his rotary projector so he can sit down among the kids, all the time building suspense, missed his vocation."

"At six figures a year?"

Erect in an old slat-back, Hind looked out over the white bells of the hydrangeas. The long messy living room was full of light; the room was a corner of the house and had windows on two sides.

"Peg gardening?"

"Peg is among the flowers," said Ash. "I don't know the names any better than when we moved here. Isn't it deathly quiet? Yet you can't even hear the mower down the hill. I've learned a bird or two, I watch them from upstairs. I'm sure they don't sing for kicks. They're sort of insane, birds; in fact I don't believe they really like the country."

"It's beautiful here," said Hind. "You'd be crazy to make a change."

"I couldn't. No. I could."

"If *I* could tear myself away—"

"*You!* You long-legged Samaritan."

"Peg's got more money than I have." Hind was going to say that Sylvia would never stand the country, whether she worked or not. But he didn't know how much Ash had heard about the unofficial separation. "I have thirty phone calls a day at least. I could do with a year on your course, give me a greenskeeper's job."

"But the simple life is not simple, even with money," said Ash, and started a new Lark with the old one. "Because here in the fresh air with only those birds and the quiet sound of Peg's lopping shears turning up on one side of the house then suddenly disappearing, then moving steadily in the same spot, then suddenly turning up *behind* me, then suddenly right in front of my bay window where I was standing when you drove in—mind you, she's good with them, sticks them out in front of her and they seem to operate themselves—but what other noises are there? The man from below about the locker-room fruit-juice machine. Maybe a heavy wind down on the course in the middle of the night. Or you get in the middle of a hot noonday a truck accelerating in second but so far away that it seems like it's going off under a hill. And all the time thinking. Not like back home in the city, for in the city there are gaps *in*side you the city fills up but here the gap *out*side gets *in*to, and you think about your every move, life becomes shall I go to the upstairs library and check last year's world almanac. But what happened to Ollie Plane, and what about you, what are you after, more voices? Is Ollie Plane sitting talking to students in that mid-town saloon?"

"I've got to see him," said Hind. "He teaches at the university so he has time off, but he never phones me. But I hear about him from Maddy Beecher, who sees him for lunch at the club and once took him along to a gallery on a Saturday afternoon but Plane disappeared while Maddy was talking to someone he always sees on Saturday afternoon in one gallery or another, and when he phoned Oliver later he didn't answer. You don't want to hear about the damned. There's not one of us wouldn't give it all up to have the privilege of—hooking into one of your woods and tracking the ball all day."

"What wood? A club? or woods in the sense of trees?"

"Well, then, *you* tell *me*—where might one hook into trees?"

"Stop trying to make talk. I know you didn't come here just for a change. Either you're being compassionate to your old lost retired pal or you're using me to do something. Whatever happened to the old fellow we walked with that weekend I came to the city?"

"You mean Dewey?"

"Dewey Wood. The old boy who said that about the gas fumes."

"He could use a country cottage like this."

"So what if I have got fourteen rooms, I don't use them. That wasn't how he struck me. He sniffed the bus exhaust outside the antique shop we didn't go into—the warm, sweet bus exhaust, he inhaled it—and said, 'Well, that's city life,' and gave this sickening sweet smile."

"At the health club," said Hind, "he lies on the benches in the sauna and stays in too long." Had the management fixed the crack in the narrow panel along one side of the sauna room? Heat would get out.

"Peg catches me not breathing, even out here in the clear. She says, 'For God's sake breathe!' But she's too busy to stick around to see if I do. Everyone's too busy. I could crawl into a tree and no one would miss me."

"Do you let Peg treat you like a kid?"

"Sure. Just like I'm letting you treat me like just an old friend you pay a visit to. Here comes Peg. We're going to have a drink before lunch."

Who had involved Peg and Ash in the new search for the old child? The reference to golf and forest could not be mistaken; Sylvia would never send him on a wild-goose chase up into the country for the fun of it, and she was off him now anyway, and it looked as if this time she would divorce him; yet the message delivered by the old woman came from someone who knew Hind's life.

Peg had lines of dark earth under her fingernails. She had on golflike, but spikeless, brogues and green wool socks. Long ago Ash announced he had not married for money; and Hind knew this to be true. Ash married Peg because Peg had a purpose; it was to live in the country. Her parents had used to come here summers; so had Ash's parents, but she and Ash had never met until a college glee club concert in the city one Christmas: they had both been singing, he for his and Hind's college, she for hers. There had been two rehearsals, one performance, one reception, Ash's reckless racing on the park's public ice, Peg's silence at two cocktail parties, her straight spine as she sat on a sofa.

Peg left her cranberry vodka on the stone ledge under the bay window, and went to the kitchen to finish lunch. She still at thirty-six wore her yellow hair in a long plait. Fingernail dirt or not, she seemed unable to dishevel herself. Over her shoulder she said to Hind and Ash, "Finish up."

*That* was it, or at least *one* thing. Whoever sent the messages through this old woman could seem to force the new hunt from time into place, both lead and drive Hind zigzag over an apparently foreknown course: but Hind would do the finishing, he it would be who would put the period (the full stop, unquote the guardian).

Peg was spooning Hind another helping of string-beans-and-almonds, just as Sylvia made them. "They're good." "They're only frozen."

Ash told a story: "Maddy said when you won the small cup for most improved sportsman in the junior class at school donated by that rich florist whose son died of an unsterile needle in an army hospital, and when Beecher and Oliver came up and congratulated you, you let out on top of your smile a small whimper—"

"Why?" said Hind.

"And he asked, 'What?' For he thought the whimper was a word, and you said, 'Nothing,' and again according to Maddy the whimper broke out."

"I guess I'm tougher now." Did people do a lot of talking about Hind, about Hind's answering service, his estrangement from Sylvia?

Hind had of course felt that whimper in his throat and behind his eyes, like that sinal rinsing after a difficult dream. The phenomenon the day the boys had congratulated him wasn't easy to explain. He didn't want, or couldn't take, their congratulations.

Peg stayed off the Sylvia issue so carefully she made Hind nervous. His foot touched hers under the table. She said, getting up, "You say you're taking a break from the 'Naked Voice' program, but I have to watch what comes out in your presence, you're dangerous." She seemed to smile, she was shy. "You might be wired for sound." There! She'd tried to joke.

"But," said Ash, "she knows you never take a break, you're always on something, that's even what Sylvia said when she phoned." Ash might be referring to a recent call or one long ago, you couldn't always tell if his sense of time was confused or he was merely casual.

Hind would not if he could help it talk about the city to Ash. For Ash's persistence would then turn to resentment that Hind had *not* left, nor Maddy nor Oliver nor even in a way Cassia Meaning, though she had changed countries. And furthermore if Hind let Ash lead him up avenues and across parks and high in richly wood-appointed brass-operated elevators up into nineteenth-century apartment houses where old Polish gentlemen, deprived of manorial forests but not of summers in Dubrovnik, gave patronic soirées for displaced violists, for mordantly unsuccessful cartoonists, for teams of girls and a young architect desperately turned sculptor, and for poets—why, right there, on the word "poets," as if words were people, Ash would suddenly be tired and ask, "What do they write?"—which would be Ash's way of punishing Hind for Ash's own poetry or lack of it. And the pity Hind had for Ash would be in danger of growing into the old rattling sack of hard, tactical words Hind often forgot about, the readi-bag of put-downs, retorts like obituary briefs stored for when friends went too far, words that swelled at a certain place in his body that he had thought was filled by terrible sympathy for others. And if Ash got talking of the long poem he had stopped starting to continue, he would get at Hind and say, "Maybe I'm not the poet you took me for, but where's your wife?"—and Hind, thinking that all these friends who were each like him in some respect (jaw, ear lobes, off-center widow's peak, a faintly pigeon-toed inswing of the left ankle, hoarseness when tired), and tied to him as fully as the placental city, the private mongrel Boy, the photosynthetic skyscape, the invented but really old tales Mad's adult child maintained from night to night afraid his dad would feel a duty he'd be too dull to shoulder, Hind thinking all these ties most tight at the times when out bloomed the bag of crystallized vitriol and he found himself damning these—"Where's your wife and kid? A man's initial responsibility—" but Ash probably would not finish, and instead would plunge off to the living room to turn a record high enough to erase friend and wife. Once upon a time he might capitalize every noun in an epigram. Or drink for a week: "The only way, way to get down, down deep into, into yourself, your self and the past that's hiding like, like an octopus behind,

behind you whichever way you look because unless you drink you can't turn fast to look everywhere." (Why does an alcoholic friend make you feel guilty?) O.K., O.K., Hind went "deep" with Ash a few times but Ash talked of himself, and Hind in any case could not see any point in diving, as it were backward, into deep glue or into a flat, live barricade you could grow on like a dog-fanged bat turning into furry-tailed foliage.

But lunch was pleasant, and Ash and Hind, at Hind's suggestion, toured the golf course later.

He must find out what he was intended to find out, without openly consulting Ash. This privacy was kin to finishing, Hind must be the one to do the finishing.

At the fifth, sixth, and eleventh, a hook off the tee could land you in woods. That is, if you were right-handed. But the eleventh had woods on both sides of the dog-leg halfway to the green, even if the trees on the right side were sparse.

The first time they were lying in bed together, Sylvia discussed the disadvantages and advantages of Hind's height. Then, putting her fingers on his chest, she said, "At least you're not left-handed."

"There's nothing in there," said Ashley Sill, watching Hind stroll toward the trees.

Sparse but deep—just as on the other side the stand was dense and shallow.

Ash joined Hind as a twosome now played through. The ball hooked, but the stroke had been wrongly aligned toward the right-side trees where Ash and Hind stood, so the shot bent into the center of the fairway, carrying just far enough into the dog-leg for a clear second shot to the green.

Hind looked among the trees; though dense, the stand was so shallow as almost to be a façade; from outside you thought it deep. Hind heard the click of the second man's shot. Moving among the trees Hind stared up respectfully, touched bark. "Let's go," called Ash. Something seemed to begin to fall whisperingly from high up, then stopped.

A woodpecker knocked, and a jay squawked.

"They don't even know I run this place," said Ash, watching the two men march by. "Come on, you've seen the wood; let's look for the twelfth tee. This whole layout is one of my life's rewards. My wife bought me, a nongolfer, a golf course."

"It's a good investment," said Hind, leaving off his inspection of the trees.

There was a token in a hollow, or some keepsake tacked onto a tree in an envelope; or there was a message. Or was the whole clue two (over two) weeks ago merely a means to get Hind to Ash Sill? Now, he had just called this golf course a kind of consolation prize and *he* had been, still could be, something of a poet; and the *poet's* old prize was a *laurel* crown! Had Ash told something? Hind took it up: "Not only an investment: you like overseeing these golfers. It's *your* pastures they lose their balls in, it's your woods they lose themselves in, your course they think about all week; where would they be without you?"

"Here," said Ash. "And so would you. You didn't come because of *me*."

Hind could give Ash a progress report, if Ash knew her, on Ivy Bowles, who wasn't coming along as well as expected but was at home now being looked after by her brother-in-law. Hind's thirty-five phone calls a day weren't small selfish fantasies, they were palpable voices of people Hind served. Was it not, as with the guardian, a matter of withdrawing when formerly needy friends did not need you so much any more? Of course. Way back in grade school at the time of that football game, he was already as tall as Buddy Bourne and plainly exceeding him hour by hour; and after the kickoff incident, Bud said, "You let us down," and Jack Hind had the feeling that this squat muscular Buddy sank away, always looking upward angrily, sank.

"Look, Ash, I wish you wrote me. Here I am visiting you because you're afraid of what would happen if you took a bachelor weekend in the city."

Ash's tone changed. "You mean you did come just to see me?"

"Perhaps that is sentimental. You said yourself I had something on. I'm making a sort of search, and this area happens to be of interest."

"You recall we aren't so far from the kidnap place you let yourself get involved in. Sylvia almost wouldn't marry you."

"You're happier not remembering those days and the city."

"Don't you organize my happiness, Hind. You don't know beans about me. What are you hunting this time?"

Ash wanted to hold Sylvia over his head; Ash had heard. But could Ash know about the renewal of the kidnap, the kidnap's renewal, the renewal of Hind's kidnap? There was in that wood something that would complete this latest clue, and Hind wasn't going to let Ash put his pretense of proprietorship upon that grove of trees and what they held.

Once, Hind let himself in for Ash's control, and he could never risk it again; his determination was a part of his sympathy for Ash. He knew Ash. They had taken Ash's car to the city for a weekend away from college; the guardian had not been told. And returning up one of the freezing, deserted parkways Ash had gone to sleep driving. The heater rattled, and Hind was drowsing, and as he fell asleep he seemed to himself to fall into a mind, presumably his own, that moved even faster than the old Plymouth convertible with its rusty clamps so difficult to get on when you wanted the top up. Hind was waking as the accident happened, waking as slowly as the accident was fast. They were half over the little curb and onto grass. As the car seemed so slowly to stop, the windshield on Hind's side received a slow, broad caress from a crystal bush of confectionary branches and, continuing to wake, he thought that those ice threads running over frosted glass were a delta he and Ash drove toward. But the scintillant points along the dogwood branches (hence, according to the guardian, necessarily round-leafed dogwood) were due to a highway overhead lamp, and if the car had been moving faster, it might have hit the lamp's post; but before that the glass might have split into Hind's face. Hind drove the rest of the way, knees upspread either side of the steering shaft, buttock bones more and more tired in the seat that, no matter how hard Hind tried to move it back, would not release from the close position Ash had it in.

Peg had filled the house with flowers when they came in from the eighteenth. What kind of flowers? No, what mattered was the group of scrubby jack pine in that unthinned part of the left-hander's wood at the dog-leg of the eleventh hole, and what most mattered was a thing up on one trunk of a twin-trunked-branching white birch within the pine group.

Hop and Daisy would stay in town to attend a meeting of Future Parents, Inc. Before dinner Ash said he didn't mind being used by Hop and Daisy, he simply wished they could acknowledge his presence in the house and tell him what they had done the preceding week. "At least they're my own."

Car horns and shouts could be heard from the direction of the club. In the late-afternoon light the roof of the main building could barely be made out from the south window of the living room, where Ash and Peg and Hind stood. It seemed there was a scuffling fight.

"Let them work it out themselves," said Ash. A bartender and a young man to play records behind a big screen painted with figures of musicians—these two were enough. "The club's cooperative; if they dig up the driveway gravel with their arguments they then have to face what happened to the driveway, and then they're sorry, they have a nice sense of the integrity of this place. You know, they use their cars to argue, they back up forty miles an hour twenty yards to retort to something a fellow member has just done with his car. I'd like to disappear into this background, just disappear, become the scene. What does your undertaker do about parking if he has a funeral on, and—?"

"His man Carmen La Branche puts the garbage can out front with a five-foot strip of three-ply leaning either side. The advertising girls park their scooters and motorbikes everywhere, and Carmen is always moving them, and the girls stand at the windows watching, or down on the sidewalk looking out at him from behind their goggles, and Ash, in cold weather they have black-and-white vinyl masks to go with the rest of the outfit; and of course they'd never say anything to Carmen."

Peg walked away toward the kitchen, saying, "He's trying to take what doesn't belong to him, and the girls just take it back."

"See what I have to live with," said Ash, continuing to watch the clubhouse roof below. "Why don't you come and take me out of all this, Hind?"

"If I ran this club," said Hind, "I would see that it was run, I'd be down the hill there making sure."

"You would participate, I know, head and shoulders above the rest. And what would you have, *who* would you have at the end?

"If you only knew."

"I do know," said Ash, still gazing down the hill. "What you've recently done and what you're up to right now."

Hind would not be lured into an account of his work in the city. It would upset Ash too much. But Ash would never leave here.

By the fire that distant evening on the youthful beach while the guardian floated offshore, Hind looked at Ashley sitting hunched on the sand: the long ears with lobes growing immediately into his upper jaw; then his low, long, though not jutting jaw almost between his knees with a mouth above it so comparatively small it seemed pursed; then long fingers with ridges along the nails, he saw two of the nails well enough to make out the ridges he had seen—there was a medical reason for them; his old, Ash's old, cashmere sweater (Hind had bought the same one exactly) as always tucked in at the waist—for what? for clarity? or because Ash dressed his torso fully before getting into his trousers? And Hind then, with tough Bee Bee Barker singing what she called political shanties, had had the wish to pick up slight, difficult Ash and stand him on Hind's shoulders, which must be alone close to six feet above the ground. Lights stood a mile offshore, seeming not to move, and Hind knew they were the Coast Guard picket boat and the Chief who was sneaking in to check on his boys stationed at the lighthouse. Where was the guardian? Ash was perhaps not listening to Bee Bee's song; he looked as if he might be thinking over the job Hind had asked the guardian to get for him—here, the end of college. He pitied Ash's inevitably smaller head, and he thought of tossing Ash out to the guardian thirty yards off the beach. Even if it *would* be rude to Bee Bee and her unaccompanied song. But Sylvia was then behind and put one leg then the other, bare and soft and smooth and from the fire warm, over his shoulders and sat on him using his head as a saddle horn is not intended to be used.

"We ought to swap places," said Ash, still watching the roof of the country clubhouse and listening to the arguing horns and the slice of gravel. "You could live here with Peg in your fantasies; you could follow your clients around the course like a shepherd, imagine you were committed to a decent job."

"I am trying to find a kidnaped child," said Hind with a justly modulated gentleness. "Isn't that enough to do with one's life?" Ash turned away from him and went to the phonograph and put on a record the substance of which Hind did not even notice.

At dinner Ash did not seem to pursue Hind. He did discuss the brief swing through botany Hind had taken during his junior year of college. "If you could get the right fidelity amplification and find the correct place on the stem or blossom or root, you could record not only the sound of growth—you could pick up plant thoughts, plant dreams, plant experience."

If the old woman's group, or she herself, had planted the clue in the crook of a tree there in the left-hander's wood, would the Sills then have seen someone? Were they possibly acquainted with her? had she come perspiring to their door to ask for a drink, opening a book to show newly pressed wildflowers, or saying the bird she had watched had drawn her onto the course and did they mind? And why did the two clues in this, the kidnap's, second wind take for place Hind's old pals?

And so it turned out that in the evening Hind did talk about the kidnap, and Ash was easier to be with.

They parted at the Sills' bedroom door. Ashley had finally forced Hind to admit the kidnap to conversation.

"But what did you think was the motive?"

"I still do. It was that he, she, or they wanted *a* or *the* child."

"Wanted? Not money?"

"I proved long ago it wasn't money, just as I settled my own mind that the child did not die. But you say 'wanted'? Yes, I guess that's it. And the parents weren't happy, but that may not matter."

"And you expect to solve it in the city? Yes, I suppose you do."

Hind looked down at Ash and changed the subject: "But you said you had a thousand questions, that's what you said when I arrived. You didn't think them up just since I phoned this morning."

"But I knew you would phone," said Ash, too quickly, his hand on the knob.

"You knew I'd be coming?"

"Knew you'd be coming."

"Who could have told you?"

"I knew you'd be wanting to use us, I didn't know for sure how."

"*Use* you! What the hell do you mean by *that*? Surely you don't know the old—"

Ash had his hand on the knob, turned his head to look at the knob. He seemed constrained to wait until Hind had said something.

"Then did a person tell you I'd be coming here?"

"Yes, of course."

"An old woman," said Hind, without a question in his tone.

"Yours."

"I know her?"

"Sylvia, Hind, Sylvia."

Hind preferred to nod, and bob his head from side to side as if happily bewildered by the mysterious surprises of life.

He went next door. Ash still had not turned the knob, and as Hind stepped into the guest room he was to sleep in, Ash stopped him with "Will you accept my gift of information?" People were talking about Hind, but what good was it to him? Think of the admiration of the guardian after his death! Botanist, adviser, Independent, sportsman, idealist. He had been taken up after his death by a group of people on the Heights, who often talked about him, often sent to Hind for information about the guardian that Hind simply did not have, or asked for letters Hind would not give, or offered morsels of information which something in Hind made him pretend not to want.

Hind guessed that the kidnaper or kidnapers had adopted a simple motive. Had this child been taken just as that tiny baby (but not tiny enough!) in Denmark? A first! for never before in Denmark had a baby been kidnaped for more than two days. Hind had had cause to infer that a woman had done *his* kidnap, just as in the Denmark case. How far, though, could you pursue the parallel? The Dane had suffered a miscarriage, but told her husband she had borne her baby. Was that it? (Where was *he*, away? It was the sort of story the papers wouldn't get wrong.) A neighbor saw how big the new baby was. The police took it from there. Three months too big for eleven days.

Hind dreamt he had a miscarriage and down the john went ripe heads of familiars and peers, till he had, tweaking his neck, the citrus fingers of the guardian. And Hind woke, at first forgetting his car was parked on gravel near a golf course and lying almost beside him were Ash and Peg. Did they talk about him in there?

Round and round his neck was the old ring of cool sweat.

Round and round his head the old part-heard conversation. He was around five, for this memory was early and
few of his secure memories dated earlier than that—only
perhaps some isolated scintillation of adult eyelashes in
a summer backyard under a male (yes) cherry tree where
sparrows tattled, or a woman's hands on his slick shoulders in a steel washtub in what may have been the same
backyard and the same summer. But apart from these abductions of past into present, little else shone up from
depths below the five mark. The old part-heard conversation had an echo, as if it had been held often; at its root
in time it had a meaning inversely proportionate to his
five-year-old ignorance of its point; or, in the few words
of it that lasted on his heart's tongue, had he fundamen-
tally guessed what they, the guardian (yes) and a woman,
in retrospect likely the divine and beautiful Thea, talked about?—Thea, he fancied her as his future mother and
later, at nine or ten, as the object, giver, and possessor of
his present lust; she had not minded his seeing her un-
dressed. But *was* it Thea talking to the guardian? He was
in bed, five, he had woken with a ring of sweat round his
neck—which meant that however long he had slept he had
had a dream; and he guessed it had had to do with earlier words of this very conversation, which after all was
not much of one…."Well, say I'm blocked, then—I don't
mind what words you use, maybe you're right, you may
not be pure gold but you're no dope. So: say I'm blocked."
"I haven't noticed it at bedtimes, Foster." "Getting married is not simply going to bed." "Sometimes it's much
less." "Jack's mother knew that kind of talk was nonsense, and so do I—and so do you." "I'm sick of you invoking her." "What can my words about her mean to you?"
"That *child* in there that you adopted." "I can't really tell
you why I'd rather not marry. Call me blocked, with your
jargon." "Ho hum, Foster. If you change your mind, say
the word….Well, I bet it's something simple, like a heart-
to-heart discussion you and she once had….Ah, dear dear

dear. I won't propose to you any more, Fossy....Make you a nightcap?...a nightcap, Fossy?...Fossy?...whisky and fizzy?"

He could not go back to sleep, the lucid moon passed through Ash and Peg's curtains. Hind dressed, and fastened at his belt his needle-point pencil-beam, and went out to the moon-drenched, moon-rinsed, lunaroid golf course.

Maybe near the crotch of a certain tree, a small animal ate the clue that had been left for Hind, some fox-cheeked, lemur-tailed night owl busily at home.

The old woman had sent him off on the quest; then why did she seem to be ahead of him rather than back at a starting point? True, she was at the mailbox grille; but more, she was out ahead trailed by him just as much as he trailed the growing boy Hershey Laurel he had abandoned for six going on seven years. The mind's fierce fuss, forever discontinuous.

At night the course was wildly smoother, wildly fixed. His mind must take possession of it. Did the game's renewal renew also the original risks? Will the child be killed; will child be killed if ransom not paid on time, if not paid at all, or even if ransom *is* paid? Will kid be permanently harmed, maimed, brainwashed, strange?

The mere hunt for Hershey Laurel had at first long ago one fringe benefit: namely, Hind's running guess how the *guardian* would judge data Hind was acquiring: for Hind had kept the quest secret from him, which gave Hind the chance to *envision* what giving it up to his guardian might mean: so Hind didn't have after him the guardian's power of good sense and narrow, upward reasoning; therefore Hind could titillate himself thinking what the guardian would infer from this juncture or that parallel. What would he have made of Sears Laurel's unwillingness to go look for his wife when she vanished three days after the kidnaping? or to have her questioned when she came back at the end of a week? The police didn't listen when she broke down and attacked Inspector Praid's reporter friend for referring to the case as "Hershey Laurel's" (later as "little Hershey's") "kidnap": She broke down, "As if it was his, as if it was his, as if it was his. It belonged to him like *his funeral!*"

The golf course lay for the most part like an "L," its angle the farthest point from the club buildings; but that contour was so tempted out of shape by the several "S" lines of tee-green-tee that from a helicopter you might see, instead, an amoebic or a glovelike hand.

Hind's shortcut, prepositioned during the afternoon tour, took him through two roughs and across two fairways; thus, he came to the eleventh tee not from the tenth green but from the direction of the clubhouse now seemingly so remote. His foot kicked something light—weightless, white; a paper cup. When he turned to look back at the lower and higher silhouettes—the club buildings, the Sill house—he saw a light shape become a tree's, or go behind a tree's; or was the paper cup still in his eye? Unquote guardian: "'Tree's' incorrect: inanimate object cannot grammatically possess."

He ought to be afraid; he saw the white again as it again fell into or behind a tree. The dark of this kind was something Hind didn't worry about. But this something cold-blooded in him was not ungenerous. He was scared, or used to be, of the light being doused as he reached up, grew up, branched up, into a dive at the school pool. But the dark of the moon, and these part-human trees, and the hollow-solid intimacy offered by the recently abandoned paper cup did not scare him: they were part of the inheritance which through his responsible curiosity he had come into; this was the way to the boy Hershey. Maddy Beecher wanted John Plante to be different; but his want came from fear that Plante was real, while he himself went only so far as to teach colored (Negro, black) kids architecture once a week.

The trees and their earth were part of the moon sky. Hind could dribble a soccer ball slalom through these trunks, they would not stop him with branch or root.

Hind listened for the white shape following him. It had not reached the edge of the left-hander's wood. He stood in among pines feeling his right direction. He found what he wanted, the V-shape of branching trunks, the sickly white birch. It had been an ornament to a small wood that was now full of skinny pines. The ground was not crisp; his high, weatherproofed shoes purchased in the Trading Post down in the subway station made only a soft emphasis upon the ground as they moved toward the birch. Hind was going to climb. Through a perfectly aisled gap in this wood he could see through across the narrowed fairway to the right-hander's wood, where a great elm like a narrow vase of flowers opened into the sky.

He did not have to go to the top of the birch, only to a point up one of the two branching trunks at which a rope had been tied and a piece of cardboard or paper stuck in between rope and tree.

Coach Blum said, one day when Hind was having trouble coming close in to the board at the finish of his dives, "Slow the whole thing up. Think you're not really leaving the board, you're only extending your arms and then your back and ribs and abdomen upward, and some time in the future the board may let go of your feet, the balls of your"—*There*, indeed, was worry number two in the school pool particularly at meets: the first was the light going off at the top of a dive; this second was his feet growing into the board and he going up and spreading grandly like a tree. It improved his diving (as Blum said it would, adding, "Tell your guardian what I said and see if he agrees"): on a twist or half gainer you let your feet wait and follow as if slowly. But Hind kept worrying about the tree. Yet it was, as the guardian would say, a mere mere fantasy.

This time when he looked the white shape came out from, rather than going into, a tree, and stood quite human at the edge of the wood and at the edge of a great moonlit area.

*Let* him be followed; he was followed by something smaller than he. He could climb to the spot on the tree as easily as, in this sea bottom, one huge solitary grouper fish rose to nose a giant, tough old plant.

He started up: on top of a sloping limb rather than slung under.

Another fringe benefit in the mere hunt for Hershey Laurel of itself was knowing, as when Hind had married Sylvia, that he entered a new and necessary range, terrain, field, plot, tract which only he entered and where nothing could follow. So now, up along the branching trunk, Hind was not a rustic poacher in danger of being taken or having his own act finished by someone else. The sound he picked up from the edge of the wood was not going to shoot him through the heart. He was free.

"You somehow," said Sylvia just the night before their marriage, "do lack a heart, even though it seems impossible. You applied to be a Brother to an underprivileged kid, and you already do so much else. But you're kind of heartless. I wish I knew what I meant, because I love you, and I love you not merely because you're tall."

Hind heard the sound nearer, he was pulling and shinnying, and now he had a harder time keeping on this upper side.

He breathed hard and thought nothing. But then the sound came so close it seemed to be rising in the air beside him.

He grabbed higher and got the rope, and felt it and its short frayed end, then back to the stiff, barklike piece apparently tied. Rescue the clue, and one clue deserves another.

He knew perfectly well who the shape was, though not exactly what she would say. So when the flashlight came at him he said, "Ah, there you are, Peg"–though all he saw of her or hers was light–"would you train it where my hand is."

She was angry, at last. She kept Ash on short leash. But what of it?

But the tied thing wasn't tied, it was a piece of peeling bark; when he jiggled the ring of rope toward him, the bark was seen to be growing out of the live tree.

"Ash started to fix a swing for Daisy but that branch, that trunk, was obviously too vertical, and there wasn't another one of the right kind near enough to tie the other side of the seat. I told him but he didn't listen. And then he cut the rope rather than untie all his knots, I don't know why. No doubt *you* know the deep reasons why. And here now in the middle of the night you've got your legs wrapped around that birch breaking off bark and staring at it like a hungry animal." Hind had soft hair along his cheekbones under his eyes, and had thick eyebrows: what must he look like? This woman shot woodchuck for stew, Hind had seen a frozen bag of it.

"There's nothing on this bark, I thought it was paper or cardboard." Was the clue in another tree? Or perhaps– Peg was talking–perhaps the clue "Hooked with a wood" meant all along the oversized fishhook that used to be stuck in the scaly bark of the hornbeam by the Laurel pond, deer browsed the twigs. Shirley ran a line across from the hornbeam to the trellis where she grew red and white and blue morning glories. Hind was now standing in front of Peg, and when she kept her long light on him he unclipped his pen-light and needle-pointed her.

Eyes at night, in a hooded white sweatshirt like the one he worked out in at the Fieldston Hotel Health Club, and white jeans; and she was coldly talking to him. A woman develops good wooden thorns to keep from simply being grazed on, but Peg mistakenly thought that being on home ground she would win.

"Ash would have told you if you'd asked about the tree. You're the type of listener who gives people a chance to talk but never the right kind of chance if they're as gentle as Ash."

"I wanted to stay off the city," said Hind.

"Off Sylvia, rather. And Ash can talk about the city without going nasty and turning up the stereo."

"Maybe he'll come see me, then," said Hind, "or would you object?"

"He came back from the city last week, he was there for three days."

"Why on earth didn't you phone me?"

"You mean–"

"Why didn't *he* phone me?"

"He did once. He phoned Oliver Plane several times, at different places, health club, university office, a private theater Oliver's girlfriend works at, and something called the Chapel of Laughter; and left word for him and *was* left word; but Ash never caught him till the evening he left the city to come home. They saw part of the show at the theater–you no doubt know all there is to know about the show–Ash liked it–and they had a short time to talk afterward, and then Ash got in the car and drove right out of town and got here at five-thirty A.M."

"My answering service didn't record him."

"In the morning he said to me, 'I still want to know where I went wrong: and when I asked Oliver Plane, he laughed and so did the girlfriend, but I didn't mind them,

I liked them,' that's what Ash told me. He's in a corner; I don't think you can understand that."

"Why, naturally I understand," said Hind, "I've tried to say the right thing ever since I got here. Why doesn't he rush into the face of his boredom and take up golf?"

"I'm cold," said Peg. "I shouldn't have come down here. Ash played now and then. He sliced one into a car windshield off the seventeenth tee; and later on he threw his wedge down the old well in the little wood on the hill behind our house, where it's getting rusty."

Hind was moving with Peg, he wanted to touch her strong neck and find out exactly what her waist was like. She had meant to rebuke him, but Hind had gotten her off her aim, he was ready for her even if it did mean thinking double. They stopped again, or Peg stopped, as if hoping Hind would not go on with her.

The words had been, "Hooked with a wood into the forest, it will lead you well beyond the pier."

"*Well*," an unexpectedly personal idiom.

But the clue meant something else. Hind said, "I'm off in the morning."

"It's morning now," said Peg.

Hooked with a wood. The wood, Ash himself. "Hooked" could point to the hornbeam.

Drawn to Ash in order that you might be drawn on to the kidnap area so close.

And above all: the unused well which Shirley Laurel told Hershey to keep clear of: the well on whose split, wooden lid, the day before the kidnap, she had found Hershey's beanbag and thus had known he'd been playing there: he came round from behind a tree and she saw him and cried out that she was going to throw the beanbag down the well, and he came pelting toward her, his eye on the beanbag as if it were a bagful of treasure: running at her with strange independence, and though running hard talking not yelling as if he possessed independent controls over his motion and his voice: please don't throw the beanbag away: she was going to whack him but was touched by the importance he set upon the bag.

The morning of the old woman's first clue, Hind should have torn it up and flung it in Carmen La Branche's carefully disinfected garbage can outside the undertaker's—Hind's garbage can really—and gone as planned round the corner to Sylvia's to heal the breach once and for all.

Better even to follow the heifer through the ad studio's door then than.

But he'd finish what he'd started, the way the guardian said.

Peg was away ahead, headed toward the clubhouse complex, on up to fast-slumbering Ash busy entering his dreams against the charging count of each day's devious life. But she stopped, and turned to say some more to Hind. He stopped again, and she raised her voice.

"And why shouldn't he keep doing what he says, looking for the point where he went wrong?" She moved on.

Hind called, "I didn't say there was anything wrong with doing that."

"He asks me and asks me." Peg stopped and turned and started walking again; stopped and turned around; said, not loud, "The sooner the better, you overgrown..." She was walking.

Ash had asked Hind many times before. "Where did I go wrong exactly?"

What did you tell a friend? "*Do* something."

Tonight Ash had begun again. "Sometimes I think the single turn that was the wrong one was to take your guardian up on his offer."

"He could have started you," Hind had said. "It could have meant meeting people; it might have been interesting; he offered it to me too, and I had some other things I was interested in."

"To be his paid associate," said Ash, "in the Independent Advisory Service for Eastern Colleges."

"It might have worked," said Hind.

The guardian had become obsessed with the idea that college boys—but of a certain class—weren't given psychic (as opposed to actual) time to see which were their true talents; so he was going around the New England colleges as Independent Adviser; and Ash was to be liaison, attaché, secretary, branch-adviser, back-up man. The deans looked on.

Ash found Peg and the golf course and the bay window. She never knew what to say about his poems, she liked them. Ash found his simple way to green country.

So it was off to kidnap territory first thing in the morning. The Laurel land had changed hands, three times in the six going on seven years' break between searches. Peg did not look into him, she merely disliked him. Nor did she look into the kind of words he used, or any words: she would scorn his clues and Hershey. Perhaps after all Ash *was* a captive.

Could the old woman have known what would pass between him and Peg? How much did Sylvia know of the old woman? Or did Sylvia *know* her?

Peg hoped he would go right away, he was trouble and she smelled it.

So he would. Ash would not have been happy in city air, noise, rift. Ash saw a different city and thought he had fouled his own passage at some now hidden turn, and that but for that he would be moving from café to studio to stadium to library to high-speed elevator to concerts and intersections and newsstands where he flipped the familiar and nameless newsdealer the price and stood in the used air rereading headlines in a cold breeze, feeling brush past him some feminine scent bearing the image of a soft wintry cheek.

Light not yet gold was coming slowly through the trees near the seventeenth hole. What had been that putter's score Hind had surprised? Did the score belong to the man? But which of those elderly men was which? For they were almost twins, slacked and serene.

Peg had gone behind the clubhouse complex but now appeared going up the path to her house. Finding people was such a damned job, but had to be done: who else was about to do it? And so, through the clue that brought him to the Sill estate, he had learned through Peg through Ash a fruitful meaning of the clue: wood, Ash, forest, well, hook, well: Shirley Laurel and Sears Laurel were dead: but the land they had owned was not: and Hind had faith that Hershey wasn't either. Tomorrow—already today— this renewed clue would go on becoming itself—at the crime's scene. But it was not the only scene of the crime, this kidnap spot, this plot of ground where two people and a child had moved a precise number of years ago. Dewey Wood would understand, for he often said in the sauna and at the bus stop, breathing what he said were the sweet fumes of exhaust, that he should have married again if only to have a child. Only to have a child. Should have hooked some gal in order to have that kid.

Turning out of the Sill road into the branch highway, feeling in his chest the need of coffee and in his heart the damp cleanness of the dew on the car hood, Hind recalled in detail a birth Sylvia witnessed. Her friend was on acid and her heart was far away; the crux was, she felt no tearing, searing blow-by-blow in her womb at the body- splitting intrasection as the baby labored unloving out and out, and Bee Bee Barker took color Polaroid shots one after the other, sixteen in all. But what Hind had wanted to know was, how thick (widthways, densewise) was this background of pleasure the child tried unknowing to twist forth from, and was this child's new air still that of the background even when this child was at last hideously free?

Peg would be glad not to have to make breakfast for Hind. The tune on the car radio had been played recently in the Fieldston Hotel Health Club and in the mirrored elevators in the blue-brick high-rise where Lief Lund lived. Hind heard old Dewey's light reed baritone la-la as he did squats with eighty-five pounds across his shoulders. Old Charley from the pier could stand some light reconditioning on the blue-scarred belly he loved—no dashing about, just routine hip rolls prone, and some standing side lifts with the dumbbells, fifteen-or twenty-pound, and maybe a swim, with the girls from the girls' gym up on the solarium floor. But why round up everybody you knew and get them to join the Fieldston? To keep yourself in free five-buck massages? Never simple selfishness. Eighteen years after The Betrayal of Buddy Bourne, Lief Lund had turned up at an eggnog blast—now it must be six years since Hind had laid eyes on him—and when Hind got Lief to remember the kickoff return, Lief simply said, "I wouldn't have handed off to you if *I'd* received, I'd have run like you." But that hadn't been the same brand of selfishness as Hind's now. If Lief Lund, with those prosperous, thirty-five-year-old eyes moving carefully in his lamp-and-ski-and-sea-tanned, sluggish face, could look from mid-town out to Hind's speeding purpose on this country highway, Lief would not recall Hind's stopping in mid-runback to pick up Byron but rather would say, at a level of fifteen to sixteen thousand dollars a year, "Jack Hind always did go off the beaten track," followed exactly (of Hind) by the same thing Lief said of the book on anthropology his wife gave him each Yuletide, "Interesting"—a sternly tolerant, attentively walnut-paneled "interesting." (His college major.)

To which Bee Bee Barker, in another track, branch, line, lane, road, dead-end of Hind's brain, was saying, "But for Christ's sake, *is* it interesting when you reach right in and grab hold of a piece of it? '*Hind*'! Where do you get a name like 'Hind'?" Yet her harsh warmth was like Lief's grin-lines about the mouth: He had put them there, they hadn't happened happily.

Hind jabbed the station selector, a combo's long, peering note ended by discovering a sudden blow of staccato horns, followed by (as if the instruments and their world had gone down the gullet of) a sweet bass saying, "Five-eleven in the A.M., friends; you heard me out there, five-eleven—oops, twelve."

Hind punched off. He needed gas, but LUBRI-CITY hadn't opened.

In this phase of the reopened case he cared only to look at the hornbeam and the oaken well-cover. The neighbor's golden hens with whom Hershey had tried to play one day, and the big, ruddy neighbor himself—Ken Love—with his chain saw off and on all day, and his factory-outlet green-and-black-wool lumber jacket stuck in front with bits of bark, and his visits to Shirley the days Sears Laurel commuted fifty-six miles to the coast—these Hind could not now afford to think about, though since he approached by this route he would bypass the intersection via the old dirt road Love seemed to rule. It wouldn't be (as the guardian would put it) in the great biological narrative a "sport" for Ken Love or one of his many children to be suddenly there standing when Hind drove by the overgrown entrance to the Loves' private way.

Indeed, Hind stopped at this entrance. The sky was the solitary blue of dawn, and Hind heard a cow bawl. He drove on.

He was going to the end of the dirt road, past the deserted little bungalows—some of this land Love's to sell to the city people more and more coming up here looking for bargains—past the last rusty mailbox to the final road.

At this intersection Hind stopped again, delaying the approach. A gray-blue rock-dove walked slowly across the end of Love's road directly in front of Hind's car. Still sick, badly sick, Ivy Bowles was confined to feeding pigeons off her bedroom window ledge; a central post office near her had electrified on all four sides certain protected ledges, and the pigeons were dying like nothing. Ivy spoke guardedly of a friend on the inside, a sorter, who might help. Hind told her the fine, high, sooty old edifice in the financial district would soon come down, and with it the high, guardian finials whose overflowing curves and grand grooves almost a century of pigeons had claimed unchallenged; but Ivy cared about pigeons not finials, she said, birds not buildings—and by the way, what *was* a finial?

From the driver's seat Hind couldn't see the pigeon any more, but when he turned left into the terribly familiar road that he hadn't touched for over six years, the pigeon was walking the left shoulder. A small dark bird in a tree watched Hind pass. Maddy's little boy had had from Hind—delivered by mistake to Sylvia's— The Child's Compact Micro-Tome of Tek-Knowledge, complete with projector/viewer for the tiny rings of film; so little genius Eddy Beecher—eight that Christmas, now nine—could place that bird in a few seconds.

There were people living where the Laurels had lived. The name on the mailbox did not interest Hind. Unless they had built, unless someone was already up tramping about or fishing in the pond for groggy horn pout, unless there was a willing dog out all night or now let out by a member of the family or capable of letting himself out by a swinging trap door, Hind at this hour ought to be able to go down past the garage, along the piny rise near house and pond, to the hornbeam—and the old oaken well—without calling attention to himself.

Troughs along the shoulders of this private drive were as before, and Hind watched ahead for the rise in the road where it alarmingly became a rounded, five-inch eminence of rock that because of its breadth looked more like a foot. Hind's buttocks ached, and he thought he would like a dip in the pond and then Cassia Meaning on the six-by-seven tree bridge he and the guardian built years ago. And if wind came while he and she were up, the semi-impeding wedge-blocks would release and, with the going of the boughs of the two great trees that grew so unhealthily near, the platform would ride gently also.

In the same five-car port built long before the Laurels, were a serviceable sedan and a high old Jeep pick-up. The snowplow you rigged onto the Jeep's front piston-lift lay, rested, was, on blocks by the rear wall. The shingles would have to be done, and at least one tire on the sedan was bald, and the dewy lilacs beside the carport needed pruning.

Hind passed down the grass past the garage and felt he was coming home. Like Winky Fordham, eyes on the ground, soothed and simplified by his long night in the bar. Like Oliver Plane, taking a lightheaded, unwashed walk in the dawn air and feeling refined, *not* by the love he had gotten from some girl who he didn't care whether woke up in his absence or not—refined rather by having done three hours in his bed to earn his golden independence.

Hind so wanted a telling mark on tree or well or between, that he nearly failed to leave the usual and nearest route right past the house.

Who lived in the gray, natural-shingle summer house now? What insignificant name had been on the mailbox? The Laurels had just finished having Ken Love put in fiberglass insulation, when Hershey was kidnaped.

Hind passed through pines along the mid-line of the familiar hill's slope, and the clothesline was up, from hornbeam to trellis, and on the other side higher no doubt than the lady of the house could reach was the now rusted, still oversized fishhook. To the tree's right, fifty yards off, the pond; and beyond it the now finished wall; on the left, on higher ground fifty feet off, the plain well. But if you could forget perspective, the well was simply smaller around than the hornbeam (which Ken Love said was called ironwood). Hind once paced off the fifty feet; now they seemed trivial. The grass needed a cut, the dew darkened the toes of Hind's boots. The great hook was on the well side of the tree, the other side from the trellis. The tree was hooked from the well.

As he went to the well he heard what he took to be a door come open, the ill-fitting storeroom door; but he would not divert his path even with a confident over-the-shoulder glance of inspection like the raccoon's that didn't trust the guardian and ran slowly away from the food he put out for it. ("Yes," he would say, "character! But the tragic point is, you can turn away from your real nature. This is the real idea of my College Advisory Service.")

As Hind bent over the well-cover noting the same degree of split, and the circular, mole-brown knot that exactly marked where the late Shirley L. said Hershey had left his beanbag, and as Hind squeezed into his imagination's hand his own cloth beanbag in which each trapped childhood pellet lay so clear he had faith he could find each tangible hidden one again—he heard in the solvent air a woman's voice call for the second time, "What're you looking for?"

She was leaning way out holding the doorposts, feet rooted inside the threshold. She was dressed in blue jeans.

Hind said, "Sorry it's so early. I knew this place six years ago, I've been over it twice before and I was driving by, so I took a look and hoped no one would wake up."

"My husband's way ahead of you, out fishing since four; I don't go back to sleep. Come in, have some coffee."

She was slight, and her agile behind was too small, and she had fragile wrists and ankles; she was already very tan. Closer, her jeans could be seen to be not faded but tailored pale blue denim, and her finely finished workshirt, sleeves rolled, came from a lady's shop not the Army-Navy.

"Watch the storeroom steps up into the kitchen, they're dark."

The mail train whistled three-and-one-third miles off. As Hind went to the house, she jumped out over the threshold, scampered to a flowerbed, retrieved a trowel standing in the earth, said to Hind, "Don't tell," and trotted back into the dark storeroom out of sight. The train whistled again.

New dark imitation wood paneled the kitchen, even the eye-level oven. Screwed to the floor in front of a Breakfast Bar, stood leather-seated, revolving stools. Almost everything was changed.

But the Abyssinian cat came slowly to Hind and looked up and made a sociable complaint and turned away and walked to the radiator. Then it jumped to the window sill, where it sat parallel to the window, head turned, looking up at the jay's nest in the fork of the rhododendron that at two or three points grew against the pane.

"No," Hind answered the woman, "I came from the city." She put English muffins into the Auto-Broil. She didn't seem to care that he'd known this place. "I modeled in the city but I'm small-town, there's a city noise that I hear that the real city person doesn't. One night I couldn't sleep because the electric clock on the wall kept quietly rattling, it wasn't even subways, just a shake-shake all through the city. Also there's no dew in the city, do you know there's no dew?"

"Yes, there is," said Hind, taking up his coffee cup.

"No there is not," said the young woman. "Except what my husband calls dewy-eyed liberals." She didn't laugh.

"But there is, there has to be, it's a matter of warmth and moisture in the air, and there's air everywhere."

"I'm sorry but I think that's wrong, about dew. But my husband wouldn't live in the city. He'll come in swinging three or four big trout, ravenous." She looked at Hind's legs and said evenly, "He's pretty big, too," but her meaning wasn't plain.

She fried some eggs.

Dewey Wood spoke of the city noise only "her frequent citizens" hear. This girl said precisely the opposite, then spoke of dew. "My husband contributes commentaries to the city papers—on nature and monuments—because I take creative nonfiction at the air base—but they tell him he's either too brief or too long. But I don't believe them, so I comb the city papers looking for his things."

Dewey Wood sent material in. And Hind had found the hook in the ironwood, heard the kid's voice as he ran to look at the well-cover, heard her again as he was finding no clue on the well-cover, then found himself strangely asked in—attracted in—for rest and refreshment. And now the hints of—that is, *about*—Dewey Wood. (Always, as the guardian often urged, distinguish among the prepositional objective, the partitive, and the possessive, when using "of.")

"What," asked Hind, growing suddenly tired, "what are your husband's little articles about?"

"Mainly we all come from nature and return to it, the government shouldn't sneak into a man's house (which is his castle)and take his money. He works me to the bone. Feel my muscle."

"If he keeps his money in his home, he's crazy to begin with," said Hind, and immediately knew he'd said not what he meant to but something more profound.

He hoped this childlike wife would say something like "Dewey Wood's my uncle's brother," or "There was a tall old woman out by the pond last week, but she would have come up only to your shoulder."

"You ate up my Goldenfield eggs fast enough. Our cat takes a dog food called Dash—would you like some frozen waffles?"

Hind yawned. "I got up too early this morning." The golf course was gone—as far as a clue that has now become another clue.

"You could lie down," said the young woman. "But gee, when you finish your waffles, you better go. My husband could get mad coming in seeing you sitting around. You should come here during the working day if you want to revisit old haunts."

"What did you say about your electric clock in the city?"

"I don't remember. Was it that there was a—" she looked to the ceiling offering up a frown and a small blessed smile, then smiled at Hind with lips pouted forward, nonfictional night scholar—"tempo, you know, like what I cook with, the seasoning they sell, there was a tempo I just couldn't get *with*, and which was audible... only to the city's...mmm what was it?...the city's frequent citizens, yes frequent citizens, frequent citizens."

Hind controlled himself. "Thank you. You don't have to say any more. I'll go quietly. I like your cat, where did you get it?"

"He's a stray, we prefer strays, more intelligent."

Why didn't she admit they'd inherited the cat from the Laurels? Maybe she didn't know.

Well, she had all but quoted Dewey Wood; and the necessary fluids were coming together ounce by ounce to compound a solution. To be an instrument in the operative sequence whose messenger or agent the tall old woman was, maybe this young wife knew of Hind in advance; what mattered was that she had spoken words which he had been drawn to the Sills and thence in order to receive.

How big was her husband, with his fish slung on a gut line?

Hind had wanted to cheer Ash up. Yet "of force" Peg and Ash had been taken and comprised by the new clue Dewey Wood, the clue they had led Hind to.

But surely Ash and Peg couldn't be mere means; Hind must drive back to them and spend more time with Ash. A person, an end in itself. Now then: which was clue number two: what he'd got from the old woman, or this plus what he'd got from Peg? If the former, then Peg's was three. You had to lock into your own logic— the hook in the wood, the voice above the well-cover, the wife alone in the forest who spoke the language of Dewey Wood. Locking logic: therefore, "of force" (as the guardian used to open the climax of his proofs), the trail must be ruled by an economy: yet now, from the site of the kidnap, Hind was in effect backtracking: for the distance between the Sills and here was so short when set against the almost unvarying distance and direction from the city, that the whole jaunt from and to the city was just a round trip or at best two long legs of an expensive

draftsman's compass locked closed: all of which meant—
which Hind exquisitely delayed stating to himself—that
unless the old woman was gratuitously persecuting him,
and/or (as Maddy said) unless the kidnapers were on the
move, and/or unless he was scheduled to pick up a *thing*
at each clue-stop, the trail wasn't purely geographical if
geographical at all.

Well, at this point it had to be Dewey Wood, though
perhaps as just now the indicated place turned upon a
person, so in this new clue the person could present a
place; and there indeed, a week or two or three weeks
inward to the slow press of city summer, there indeed *was*
the old boy, right where you hoped.

Naked, leaning against the resinous Finnish wall under the ledge where, in front of the big window, stood the
Magic Oven Thermometer at 180° F; he saved his towel
by sitting bare skin to the built-in bench, and left greasy
puddles where his buttocks had been and below on the
footrest over which he leaned now and then; he was almost too friendly, his thin white hair stood up in the
heat, his pot was larger, the wrinkles at the groin more
strained—imagining sauna controlled weight.

If here Hind was back in the familiar air of the sauna,
with the gym two rooms away and the pool and rubbing
rooms and lockers—in short, the Fieldston Hotel Health
Club—why not have skipped that second jump from city
to Sill to birch to well to delicate fernlike wife leaning
from the storeroom doorway? Why not have skipped all
that and simply gone uptown for the usual workout: thus,
Dewey. Yet if the trail's course wasn't exactly spatial,
then apparently Dewey had to take his *turn*.

But was that wife merely a conveyor of information?
Looking through the window of the sauna, judging
from the pool of sweat that DW had spent about fifteen
minutes, and recalling a certain pathetic ignorance in

the pretty child-wife, scatterbrained in her paneled new kitchen, Hind wondered if she was in danger. He didn't even get her name. Had he infected the air of the house so the husband, come home swinging his fish, would know right off?

Hind watched the papers for two weeks for violent crimes. The woman had seemed happy.

The crack in one sauna window made Hind think of Ashley, their car crash, the useful hours at the Sills.

Hind was listening carefully to Dewey Wood these days, not just getting another "Naked Voice" tape for the insatiable FM station. But all DW could talk about was Oliver Plane, whom DW knew through Hind.

Ol decided to teach summer school to pay off last winter's Spur-of-the-Moment Plan Aruba trip.

Wood said to Hind, "He's your buddy, you should do something about him."

"I took time to read two sets of term papers for him year before last and I think he'd have lost his job otherwise."

"He comes here once in a week," continued Dewey Wood, "but he's practically given up going to class. Says it's all right so long as they know they're getting their right credits."

"But he's got to go to class," said Hind, "he's the teacher."

Hind closed his locker, and he and Dewey went toward the sun room and the gym.

"But listen," said Dewey. And Hind had been expecting the question for several days. "How's the wife?"

*iv*

Art Courage, who by producing "industrials" supplement-
ed his wife's yearly blue-chip dividends, grabbed Dewey's
far shoulder as the Sousa waltz ended, and swung Dewey backward as Hind was thinking how to reply about
Sylvia without letting Dewey know Sylvia had moved.
Then Courage spoke not to old Dewey, who was little
more than a decade older than Art, but to Hind: "Jack the
beanstalk, when you taping me on 'Naked Voice,' I talk
any accent you want, running routines—haven't seen you
work out it must be a month—what, did you go get a job
for a living for a change?" Art shook hands with himself
and inspected a bicep.

A voice called from the inner complex, "He ought to
tape you right across your loud mouth."

Art's body had worn well, and was now done to a
turn, a careful work of aging—distinct, strong, shaped,
the thigh muscles almost too leanly strung. As Art
spoke of it, Hind detected three themes delicately
poised: painful training, wanton appetite, hereditary
invulnerability. Art shifted his eyeballs hungrily and
his bald top gave his broad face an even brighter force.

At the end of an aisle a naked member watched
through the crenate perforations of an open locker door,
then began to pull on a crochet-mesh T-shirt.

Art Courage said to Dewey Wood, giving a one-arm
hug, "I've just been to Miami Beach, and I'm going again
in three weeks, wanta come?"

"No one's ever invited me," said Dewey, "yes, I might." He was capable of taking Art seriously, and Art was suddenly not sure.

"I got a friend who keeps a twenty-five-thousand-a-year three-bathroom tree-house." Courage strode ahead on flapping sandals, airing his hard, knowledgeable laugh, which was answered by a lighter one from the sun room—Greenspan, Junior, an assistant manager. Art looked at someone in the Resting Room and said, "What are you eating, fella?" and then said, turning off toward the gym, "a chicken sandwich. Add girls and we could live here full-time."

Greenspan, Junior, in shirt and tie, stood in front of the sun tubes, getting it on his face and the backs of his turned hands, snapping fingers to the "Dearly beloved, how clearly I see" fox trot, and with programed hesitation turning one hundred and eighty degrees left right left having the ultraviolet from ear to ear.

Dewey wagged his head. "Art's coming here twenty-nine years, he never up to now asked me to go to Florida with him, never gave me a ticket to one of these big company shows he puts on in hotels and then sometimes they have a twelve-week run on the road. Not that I could go to Florida. Art's doing French sit-ups at a fifty-degree tilt flat out in the air with only feet under the bar and his calves against the leather wedge, you should see him at his age inviting everybody to come onto the tilt board and try."

"I have," said Hind, who tried to interpret these references to Art. Was Art Dewey's way of saying Florida? Did the new trail-blaze point to Florida? Yet it was Art who brought Florida up.

In the blue-and-silver gym Hind and Dewey looked in the mirrors directly across the width of the room. The ads were almost right to call the gym fully mirrored; mirrors were missing only from the cobalt-blue cork that sealed the ceiling and the cobalt-blue carpet covering the floor mirror to mirror. In spots the cork had broken down to a kind of lichen. A gym without a bare shiny floor wasn't a real gym—a gym floor made you think of black leather knee-guards, and the thundering run down-court knowing you'll be caught going up but hoping you can swerve and hook or fade off and set, and belonging to the bright-finished boards that hold the cups of your sneaker soles and bang the ball back not quite obediently at your hand.

The midafternoon group was significantly larger than usual: thirty-eight, including the two brawny Cubans vacuuming, and the supervisor himself, Honey Gulden, the Golden Superguy, but excluding Frequent Simmons, the air-conditioning servicer. He had repaired the unit and now closed the silver panel as Dewey said hello.

Art Courage had made his circuit of the seventy-by-forty room, greeting those he customarily spoke to. He now said to Frequent Simmons, "Out of my way, peasant," and standing on his hands he backed up to lean his heels on the panel. "Best in the world," he groaned and his face blew dark. Simmons as he left said, "Your eyes are bleeding."

Still upside down, Art Courage called his cronies around—a saloon owner, a senior chorus boy in elastic leopard, a travel agent named Pool who lived in the Fieldston when not actually traveling, and a plumbing contractor who was humming a combo's version of the Bach Pastorale in F coming out of the speaker. (FHHC never played vocals.) He was told to shut up by Art Courage, who then told a long story about a bald man who stole his friends' nose hairs to make a collection for a scalp transplant.

It was difficult not to hear Art Courage. The contractor absent-mindedly hummed the Bach pastorale again, and

Art Courage said, "Shelly shut up." Hind could shut Art Courage off completely, it depended on the exercise Hind was doing. If Art kept on about Florida and brought Dewey in again, Art would have to be seriously considered as another evidential springboard for the quest.

"About Sylvia," said Dewey Wood, starting his daily four hundred waist turns with a forty-pound bar across his shoulders. He always did them in this spot near Honey's desk. In fact, he did all his sets in this spot. Like Oliver Plane's students, who if late would even creep in front of him in order to avoid taking a new desk.

"Did you hear," said Hind, "the son who disappeared from college and the police think was abducted, the father upstate sold his electric appliance store and is devoting all his time and money to finding his son. The kid was going to graduate last month, a star chemist." Hind had been waiting days and days for Dewey Wood to divest himself of whatever it was Hind was intended to get from him. No new word from the old, the tall old, woman yet either.

"I heard about it several times on that round-the-clock instant-news station," said Dewey (and whispered to himself, "*Ten* and two, and *eleven* and two"), "but about Sylvia, I saw her in my Superette and she asked if I'd seen you—as if you were living apart. What does it mean? You're such a sweet couple, and little May with long legs for a five-year-old and a face to make the birds sing. I couldn't understand Sylvia's question."

"She simply meant what she asked," said Hind, moving to the dumbbell racks. He knew Dewey was rooted to that spot for the full four hundred at least. The old man's interest in people was too receptive and gentle; all you told him turned to sugar in his reply. Now Honey was after him, and DW was nodding fast and puckering his eyebrows, though his old blue eyes were bland.

Honey Gulden, elevating a T-shirt-sleeved bicep as big as his neck, held up to Dewey Wood a new kind of vitamin E. (How can there be a new kind?) Hind must save Dewey from himself; walk him home and talk him off the vitamin kick. It did not agree, you would think, with Dewey's fatalistically sweet view of sulphur dioxide and anti-diesel-fuel catalytic mufflers...and then rattling good helicops touring your lungs as you tried to think in midtown traffic congestion. Hind would save Dewey from himself, one day D would find himself cheated by his few friends and his city; and meanwhile Dewey, who spent all but a week of the summer in the city, was saying, "Pollen or pollution, it's in the air, what you going to do?" He too lived in an old house, the next street up from Hind's undertaker's, and they couldn't install air-conditioning except by rewiring an entire side, and Dewey was only a tenant of a floor, not the owner of anything.

In a minute Hind would return to Dewey, who would have forgotten Sylvia. Hind was thinking now that the clue-carriers didn't necessarily know they were. Indeed, what old Wood evoked from others might be his means of being Hind's clue; there needn't be a conscious message, much less direct links to that wife in her modern forest kitchen in the north country, or to the Sills.

Honey saw Hind's unfriendly eye on him, for he turned from Dewey and said to the whole gym, "Jack Hind's got a good thing going, watch him work. Jackie, I looked up your chart-card, you're getting up to a hundred-twenty press by Christmas time, keep up your high protein diet like Honey told you, stay off junk foods, and what if I give you some of my nice wheat germ oil, unique with me, by Christmas you see the difference." Honey Gulden represented a Santos-Dumont subsidiary health products firm, but surely the words here today had nothing to do with the Orientals; Hind had never seen them again despite having shadowed the subway station where the torn map was. Hind often listened dutifully to the Golden Superguy with the vast chest, because he saw that Honey admired, even apprehensively despised, Hind's six feet six and three-quarter inches.

"I'll stick with real food," said Hind, straightening up to start his curls.

"That's all in the mind," said Honey; "*real* food, sure—but supplements, supplements." He turned to the gym: "Am I right, fellows?" and back came ironic, gasp-punctuated applause, "You're always right, Honey," and Honey said, "Supplements, say after me, supplements," and back it came, "*Supp*lements."

"And you guys don't leave your weights lying around, you put them in the rack when you're finished like you know I told you."

His bowlegged walk inspecting the room made a little stumping rhythm to go with the, or perhaps in response to a, four-six-time pizzicato arrangement of a Stephen Foster coming from the speaker. Honey said to himself, "You take vitamin E, it'll soak up all that good whisky you drank last night."

He stopped behind a young man and made faces to others in the room who happened to be looking. The young man wasn't using weights; he merely, arms out to the side, slowly and as if in trance rose to toes and subsided, rose and subsided, like a dreaming diver. Honey turned from him and kept his voice respectfully low, saying, "You'll never get rid of your gut like that, young fellow, look at me, I'm fifty-nine, look at me." He had been five-eight and two hundred at twenty, and hadn't changed. Still an ad model, now a widower, still a mechanic who said he could and would take any engine apart, once a national wrestler (four thousand bouts, less than twenty losses), now author of his own bungalow on Mount Mary three hundred miles north, and a quality paperback called *The Sane Body*.

He was in front of a large, hairy, round-shouldered man trying to breathe his way through a set of upright rows with a fifty-pound barbell, and, taking it, Honey said quietly, "Let Honey show you."

Hind lay down on a bench near Dewey to do some presses. Dewey hummed and for a moment or two no one was talking. Honey Gulden had gone back to his desk, his newspaper crackled. There were emanations of effort, friction along black leatherette, fruitful pain strained through vocal cords, and gasps and the clink of forty-pound dumbbells Art Courage brought together straight-arm over his head.

The music, the very same that above for eleven floors regular Fieldston Hotel residents received, brought dreams of conquest, unexpected recollections of power—cathode images (bound for pink islands) of one saried stewardess lowering to your lap your sectored (Santos-Dumont-wrapped) dinner tray, and one wound in a dark purple kimono (with light snapshot patches designed here and there) lowering the movie screen—and of course your black stewardess in a white body stocking flicking on your first-run film courtesy Cinema of the Air.

Dewey was saying he had missed Hind here Sunday, the Sunday papers weren't the same without him—as if in allusion to Dewey's thoughtlets occasionally published in a Sunday supplement, or to Hind's kidnap search, perhaps a public event though never yet told to Dewey. And Hind, recalling Sylvia's towel left on the pier the day he followed the Orientals, said something about having likewise missed Dewey here at the Fieldston, though he knew DW seldom came on Sunday. Hind hadn't been to the pier for going on two months. Hind had been meaning to visit poor Ivy Bowles, whose chest still ailed her.

Someone said, "Honey, I got to work on my midsection," and Honey said, "We all got to work on our midsection." And more loudly, "Well, fellows, Honey's going out to have his lunch"; Art Courage called out, "So long, darling," and Honey answered, "Salad State here I come."

Hind used the forward weight of his barbell to help him sit up; he rose and replaced it slanted in the rack sockets.

"No," said Dewey, as if he had been talking to Hind—Dewey must be getting into his three hundreds by now—"you look out Oliver Plane don't lose his position at the university. Last time I saw him here he wouldn't talk to me, called me an old infant, lay on the slant board where he usually does dumbell presses and just read a Bantam book of sports statistics in his shorts and athletic socks, and wouldn't move when Laurey Sears asked him to. Well, I said something and Ollie says, "They don't need me at the college, don't even miss me, you could send in a substitute and no one would know. And I said wait till your pal Jack hears, and he turned away from me and wouldn't stop reading, or answer when I said what you reading—it was a book with plates of birds and a blank paper dust jacket."

When would Dewey make good with a clue? Laurey Sears? No connection—came to the Fieldston Saturdays, always praising the wife, shoveled gravel off barges out at the marine basin; through his union and his seniority had a ten-thousand-dollar-eight-month guarantee from the outfit he worked for: his name's kinship to Hershey's father's and his job's nearness to Santos-Dumont couldn't be other than an irrelevant lure from the main trail.

Dewey nodded to the old man in the corner pushing his belly against the vibrating belt to keep it from flapping—exercise done *to* you, passive; the man came twice a week and made a day of it—massage, swim, shoeshine, shave, a few light sets selected for him by Honey, who also had him do dead hangs from the high bar to take pressure off his disc; the man would hang for quite a time, watching himself.

Buck Field said he wouldn't go inside a health club, the idea was all wrong, the open city air was what was needed. Doing push-ups at the pier during time out from his gift shop, Buck's triceps above his oddly small and fragile-looking elbows seemed almost as developed as the guardian's. If he were here today, the guardian would scoff at the Fieldston and these exercises, indoor, outdoor, all the same, and he would say, "Use muscles to compete with somebody, or to build a cold frame for your early lettuce, but great Scott, man! use your talents, that's the thing, even if they lead you far afield. Philology, linguistics!—now that's what I'd do if I'd it to do over, make a study of the possessive case on historical principles." But who would want to turn into that prig Red Grimes, who was always kidding the young Hind? The guardian unsuccessfully tried to discuss with Grimes Grimes' well-known language studies. Hind would prove to the guardian's memory the need for the Laurel quest. The guardian liked to discuss with young people their "approach." But that word meant "coming near," and often what the guardian meant entailed being "already there." Which reversed Sylvia's famous "approaching" motor that she thought was getting up power to move out of the picture she had suddenly started to understand, the string bean and the rest of the salad, when in fact the motor was a car really approaching. "I can talk to you about the string bean," she said, "and you take it as it should be taken—seriously, but not too." This was what she said to him as their plane was getting up into the air headed for America, the day the guardian died. But Sylvia wasn't perfectly straight with Hind to say he exploited an overgrown wish to shepherd others.

Dewey wasn't in the gym, and Hind had forgotten what the date was. He saw himself in three mirrors, and saw repeated twice the sad man with round shoulders that made him look like a tired green heron; he did waist-and-shoulder twists with a thirty-pound bar fixed against the back of his neck by the pressure his arms and wrists and hands vinelike applied at the ends. A very fat, naked-looking boy with red hair did squats with a fifty-pound barbell, his heels on a leather-covered strip-rest. Art Courage, Pool, and the others—and now two others, who filed past Hind toward Art's group—stood, sat, or lay at various distances, moving arms and legs in various directions: from one angle you could look into the mirror only through a moving pattern.

Hind must go to Dewey, it might be just now that DW was going to reveal whatever it was going to be his to reveal. A heavy-set singer in a hooded sweatshirt with sleeves ripped out was talking about the Oriental "who-ers" and relating their commerce in Saigon to how the Vietcong helped balance the Chinese dragon's payments with West Germany. The visiting Coast Guard Lieu-tenant-Commander in wheat-colored Norse minims said, "We gon' stay de cauhce, Mao Mao ain't gon' confisti-cate Vietnam over *dis* rebel's dead body!" You smelled no sweat; the sweet flowers you smelled were not pow-der from the locker room but the spray injected through the air-conditioning inlet grille. Limbs moved toward and away from each other. Hind looked far into the mir-ror and couldn't tell how far the men all were, one from another. The chorus boy, who was flying off tonight to do a cigarette commercial deep in the Mount Mary for-ests, knelt straining under the branching steel pull-down arms–like giant bicycle handlebars. Flesh and silver limbs and trunks moved rooted between cobalt-blue sward and cobalt-blue cork above. Hind thought if he looked through the hands and arms and legs mixing, and saw all of them again and again in mirror after mirror in one of the fully mirrored walls, till they were too far away to see–and himself too far away, too–they might turn into a second picture the way the Sunday-school Jesus-puzzle picture did, that the guardian forbade. You looked, and maybe all you saw was abstract landscape rather like the ruined subway map, with no perspective to speak of, just flat, waving black and white; then, what Maddy Beecher and Cassia were crowing about, and ridiculing you for not perceiving, came clear: in the whole tangle was Christ looking out, the pale, rather northern Christ–but not exactly looking out of: indeed, rather, the tangle *was* Christ. And when Hind clapped his hands and said to Maddy and Cassia of course he saw, and thought he had seen all along, Cassia–even then beginning to feel a change in her limbs and to acquire slowly, so slowly, the knobby swellings and strangely beaten elongations in arms and legs, crawled laughing to him–she was fourteen or fifteen–and hugged his long legs and put her face between his high knees hugging his legs and cried out, "You're faking, you're faking, you don't really see it!" Sylvia said it was hard to forget perspective and see merely flat. (This morning Hind let the phone ring eleven times, waited, then phoned Smith to discover that Sylvia's father had been on the line: virtually in your flat, then suddenly with the slide of a tiny button, no longer in your flat but in the one downtown full of Smith switchboards.) Far away in a mirror's mirror's mirror there was, he thought, a flat scene containing these exercising men–Arthur T. Courage, in his blue-and-red singlet, Pool in his gray Bermudas with the slit legs, and the others, including Hind himself. But it was too far away really to make out.

Dewey might not have *gone* to the sauna today. Perhaps he was looking to meet someone like the old woman—like?—connected with the case, though if D was consciously *in*, he was certainly being used—or, as he himself would gently say, "utilized," by the group. He was so easy to take in.

Hind walked toward the other door by Citrus City Juicearama; he swiveled and ducked at the intersection of arcs created by the sad man's stiff, turning arms and those of the far boy, or rather, his elbows. Get caught in the two rhythms, get clobbered. Hind was moving in a foreign forest gnarled and haired, its distances unmistakably thin. He would stop coming to the Fieldston as soon as it was no longer useful to his search for Hershey Laurel. Not that he had joined the FHHC with anything more in mind than working out. Either the sad man or the fat boy smelled of mentholated camphor and eucalyptus.

Hind wanted the sauna for himself, the embracing burden of heat that made your skin set cold by contrast to the already roused heat inside you.

"That is what I'm here for," said a voice, not Dewey's, in the sun room. A small, hairy man was talking to another man who looked just like him. "I wouldn't ask her to marry me till I have a body."

"Playing it safe," said Hind, but the speaker didn't turn. The bell tolled, and both men promptly turned their backs to the sun tubes. "I got her and her sister working out, too, swim class, phys ed theory, light weights."

But Dewey wasn't in the sauna. Hind hurried skidding over wet tiles to the pool balcony, but Dewey was nowhere. Repassing the sauna, Hind saw only a wet, white-haired old back running in place to the pervasive vibraphone air, and the short bull of a German sitting eyes closed shaving himself with the oily moisture sapped out of his face.

Hind did not shower, he felt awful dressing. He took Dewey's route home and then called on him. But he found only a note from Dewey: "Plane looked for you at FHHC." But this wasn't possible, unless Oliver had looked when Hind was looking and in a sequence exactly designed to miss Jack. Dewey had left a note to Hind here, apparently because he didn't have time to go to the undertaker's and up three and a half flights, and assumed Hind would stop by to see him—forgetting that lately Hind had seen almost nothing of him.

Well, the telephone answering service knew all.

"Smitty, anyone call?"

"There's no Smitty here, this is Smith Answering, who you want?"

"Whoever you are. Jack Hind. Any calls for me?"

Not many. Another from Sylvia, and one from the student of Oliver Plane's whose autobiography Hind had corrected once in a batch of papers Oliver had asked him to do. And a call from Brother, Incorporated, asking him to phone back: Hind didn't have to, he knew they hoped he'd reconsider his resignation, the child Julio Loggia he'd been bicycling with once a week was in a bad way, father flown the coop, mother indifferent, they'd be moved soon by area redevelopment, middle-income housing going up, their tenement coming down. And a call from Maddy Beecher.

Sylvia wouldn't say anything about his giving up Brother, only about his signing on in the first place, or his motives therefor. "And," she had added when she phoned that April night before the old woman's first message, "What's Berry Brown's girl to you, you said you just met him and suddenly you're his welfare agent." Hind tried to get Berry Brown's girl a job in Oliver's university's college's cafeteria, but then Oliver forgot to ask. One day when Berry hung around one of Knott's areaways hoping to make fifty cents for some pretty broom-work, Hind gave him two passes to the Fieldston. A basketball team once stayed at the Fieldston, so the health club had had Negroes (colored, blacks) now and then, if not exactly warbling in the showers. But Berry worried not about his skin but the state of his clothes, though he wouldn't wear them while working out and he did say he had athletic gear.

Sylvia would have something to say about Hind's solicitude for Ivy Bowles, except Syl didn't know about Ivy, knew almost nothing about the pier—took May to the park and to Play School.

Now from what Ashley Sill had said, Sylvia had known Hind was going to the golf-course-country-club-complex. But could she possibly be in touch with the old woman? Better not ask; else he'd have to see Sylvia and listen to her. Wait till the Laurel thing was off his plate, in the bag, and, like late-night news, given the final wrap-up. Then again one morning go downstairs, walk around the block, and cross the avenue to Sylvia.

You got told everywhere you turned that the moral and hence difficult was at home, here, near, dear, watching up for you even if tired hounded lost you came sliding, skating, or rolling home late in the game: whereas the venture away from home, and block, and familiar limbs, wasn't the truly difficult, and was hence a dodge out of sight in what they called a general direction: in better words, you're married, sweet high boy—and what do you care about some kid napped (at, say, three to one) along some trail, backtrack, or home stretch, two-, three-, or four-year-old? What do you *really* care so far gone from you and yours that it's (like) not your response, boy, not your move, play, kick, ball, bag, pasture-to-patrol nor job-in-terms-of-function?

And he might hold May high and so tight she would squeak and try to laugh, and her legs around him would drop to the side and he'd know he squeezed too hard. She was as tactful at five as little Rain was independent, waving hungry car grilles to slow down when she and her granddad were caught halfway across with the light turned red, he with his Sears Roebuck towel-stand-like alumi-num-and-steel "walker" that he lifted ahead foot by foot.

What would Sylvia say of Hind's present solicitude for Ivy Bowles, if Syl knew that his preoccupation with the Orientals the day Ivy fell in kept him from taking his proper role, duty, job, function as the senior lifesaver present?

Phone Sylvia now, and she'd try to trick him away from the kidnap; judging from what Ash had said, Sylvia knew something. The barbell jungle with its distances and its independences and its feeling that he Hind was background like everybody else had confused him too.

All he knew was that the track led through Dewey Wood, and the next information had to be there. If Oliver Plane needed help, or for that matter if Maddy wanted Hind to befriend and influence the stray English guy John Plante, that had to wait.

How old was Hershey Laurel now? Why did Hind give up the kidnap? He couldn't blame that on Sylvia or even on the guardian's death. One day Hind simply did something else. He had given in some tapes to the listen-er-sponsored radio station, and they had been accepted, and next thing "Naked Voice" was eating up all his time. Why did he stop following Hershey Laurel one day?

Ivy needed a sauna's dry heat, if her heart could stand it. But how install in a one-room flatlet even a twiglessly ersatz mini-sauna? For under twenty bucks you could buy a plug-in portable individual, with sauna face-mask an optional extra.

In a dream during the night Hind saw pale nodes of semen dot the breathing lungs of someone, perhaps Ivy, and he couldn't drive away from his dream the seeping Bach Pastorale in F from the Fieldston. Hind wanted to get into the lung to wipe it clear. But Sylvia let down her brown hair so he and she and May were in her hair and laughing, and the guardian stalked up and down outside Rolleiflexing still lifes for the annual summer treasure hunt. Through Sylvia's hair Hind cried to his guardian, "She's my wife, but don't get the wrong idea I promise"— to which the guardian replied, "The *wife of Hind*: with an event as active as 'wife' be sure not to confuse object of preposition with possessive." And Hind called, "She's part of me, but she'll never own me, I promise—what's more, I'd like you to meet my little May whom you died too soon to meet and who looks like neither my wife nor me." Through Sylvia's hair Hind saw the guardian approaching with a pilot can of new men's and women's hair-spray Fix held at arm's length: "—that is, at the length *possessed by* the arm," said Hind, but Sylvia said, "Don't be devious, we are being attacked," but the guardian said, contemplatively, "Get your glamour right to begin with— and chief among your duties will be to understand the possessive case, and principally under *this* heading the word 'of,'" upon which May embraced Hind's leg and said, "What if he never finds us? Does the game go on?"

May often asked about the guardian, thrice-told facts of childhood, she would make a good, even dangerous family historian one day.

Waiting for the alarm clock to go off he woke up. The white brick across the street was flat and dull, no sun yet, the clock stopped, ditto the wristwatch on his wrist.

Hind stood at the window: Heather Fordham, diagonally across in her window, looked as far right as she could; lights were on in the first two floors of the ad studio, someone was working in back out of sight, but among the stools and tilted boards and piles of paper left balanced here and there, nobody could be seen—drawing all night, raking it in.

He phoned for the time but got a busy signal, he'd called the wrong number—his own. He phoned again. Five-eleven. Mr. Fordham would be coming down the street now.

The thing was, to be *with* Dewey today, if possible at all times. There would be, plainly, no further word from the old woman till Hind was in possession of Dewey's clue. Dewey might be up now and down at the Mitropoulos Always Open Coffee Cup opposite the Rivervale luxury middle-income complex. He breathed badly in this weather and had two cups of Mr. Mitropoulos's rough, salt-mellowed coffee first thing to clear his tubes. And later on he'd take an extra ten or eleven minutes in the sauna, his heart was still strong. Dewey wouldn't breakfast at home, he liked talking to the German butcher-twins, the tailor, the Czech TV man who all but lived in his store, the other Mitropoulos regulars.

When Hind was ready to go out he went back to the window. Reflected in a window diagonally across the street and to Hind's left was Rain's grandfather's milk carton on its ledge. The ad studio's big delivery door had been run up and the ramp brought out and put down flush with the platform. A beige Chevy Impala convertible (last week a Plymouth Barracuda) now appeared from inside where the great photography room was, and rolled bigly down the ramp. The assistant who had helped shove the heifer in the main door weeks ago parked the Impala across the studio driveway. He ran back up the ramp, and the door ground down. Hind heard his picture ticking away by his ear. Across the outside upper half of the lower window there was a strip of delicately laid soot unreachable because of the broken sash the undertaker couldn't get anyone to fix.

Mrs. Fordham wasn't watching now. She had trained her philodendron to frame the whole window.

When Hind entered the Always at five-thirty-five A.M., Dewey had a segment of chocolate-iced whole-wheat doughnut in his mouth and was chuckling at something someone had said.

Four other men sat along the counter, the Greek dropped an aluminum ring onto his griddle and dished in a Western.

Even years before his wife untimely died, Dewey Wood had said to himself and others that he'd asked entirely too much of life, had got more than he deserved, and now should damn well take what happened. He went further; he embraced what *would* happen, and from this vantage looked calmly back. Ivy Bowles, who had lived on the same street with him for three decades, said, "You're out of your bird, if you ask me." That was when he had just coughed up a smile after almost fainting from the exhaust fumes of a bus he and Ivy had missed, and had said, "Even that sweet smell—it *is* kind of sweet, you know—is one of the facts of life. Live somewhere else, face other hazards." To Heather and Phyllis, Ivy said the same thing: "Out of his bird, out of his tree."

As if continuing yesterday's talk, Dewey swallowed fast, squeezing his eyes shut, and said, "But if you phoned Oliver Plane I bet you didn't find him home. Me, I can't seem to miss him. Went out for a walk through Rivervale Complex last night—"

Under giant white light globes on the end of cement stalks, and under the twenty-story dwelling cabinets themselves, neatly bulking on comparatively tiny pyramidal pier-legs—

"and the green grass they laid between the buildings shone so, they might have just spread a spanking coat of paint, I couldn't describe it in words. Well, so no wonder the guards got mad chasing kids off it, they'd ruin it—"

Little Hershey (how tall now?) once had upwards of two dryp-dri acres to run in, and if those were not so pure as these delivered lawns ordered by the rood from an architect's planning board (and washed at night by lights from his lighting legend), and if moreover Hershey's acres in midsummer were dried and turning while these Rivervale grasses in walk-to-walk plots roto-sprinkled themselves by vegetal computer, water shortage or not, Hershey's lawns were greener in spring, and after sundown were dark—

"Mitropoulos, what happened to my second coffee? And I'm passing in along one of the arcades under the north side of the south building, and I was turning left at the end when I saw some awful big children playing in the concrete abstracts they have in the playground—very thought-provoking for kids to play in—"

This strangely warm last December, the puzzled sycamores may have felt it time to bud again: the seasons may be changing, so to speak—maybe as if to keep pace, up, in tune with, the bird-bewildering megalopolitan habitat-redefinition which that discussion station discussed one night from midnight till dawn. (Consider the poor "accidental" yellow-nosed albatross seen off one of the city beaches, confused.) Which of Dewey's words were leading toward Hershey Laurel? Dewey may not know, any more than did the fisherman's charming forest wife—

"But when I got closer, Jacko, it was Oliver Plane and a girl I've met called Cherry O'Dell—a 'pupil emeritus' he calls her—she has long legs and short skirts, and come to think of it, long hair and a short nose—"

Who once, in bed beside Oliver, addressed Hind as *Mister Hind*, and Oliver as *Doctor Plane*—vegetal reputer, digital supposer—

"They were playing—no kidding, *playing!*—inside those stomach sculptures on stilts, and Plane climbed over into the metal box perched on the cement crescent, and he said, 'If you see Hind, say I need him to hold my job'—and Cherry laughed and stuck her leg out a hole at me and said, 'He's stopped going to class, he gave a four-week assignment and said he didn't want to see the students again and never goes to class now but some of them forget his plan and come to class or to his office anyway—and phone him—it's a hoot'—that's just what she said," Dewey continued. "Now I like Ollie, 'cause I like people, just like I like this city; but how much freedom can you give students?"

After bio class Plane told poor Dr. Skoldberg the chlorophyll show was corny—but carefully within Hind's hearing; and later Oliver said to Jack in the john, "I knew you'd come along after me and apologize for me to old Skoldy; I bet you almost made it seem your fault."

"But a brilliant boy, Oliver Plane, he has his doctorate," said Dewey, backing up off his stool, "and the university's up to a hundred and some thousand students now. If young Dr. Plane doesn't keep his office hours, someone will have to relieve him of them."

Dewey sensed, but only sensed, the elliptical nature of his thought, and snickered modestly. But Hind's guardian, somewhere in Hind's mind, perhaps hidden by an objective, said, astonished, "*Of–of*? You can allow him to use '*of*' thus?!"

"Everybody's gone wild in this part of town, Jack, wild as...: why, three times last week I saw the same group of young adults roller-skating: once as I came out of the Fieldston (and barely could notice them because Honey Gulden stood there on the hotel steps at the end of his lunch hour taking the air and asked me did I need more protein candy, his records indicated I was out if I was taking the stuff regularly)—that first time the roller skaters were between buses, running down one, being run down by the other; then the second time was next day, downtown: they stopped for a light and the leader was pointing like at landmarks, but I'm sure it wasn't a regular Museum of the City tour; then next day when I came out of the movies they passed by again, tall every last one, though not tall like you. Seems everybody's *playing*, though these skaters were playing pretty seriously."

If someone didn't stick with Dewey Wood, he would one day be taken into camp for all he had. How it had not happened so far, Hind didn't understand, look at Henry Amondson just walking along a street over in the Heights and an Oriental who said he was a doctor asked subway directions, told old Amondson he looked peaked, and asked if he could feel his heart; and old Amondson was the last man to let himself be felt by anybody, but he let this Oriental doctor do it, and the doctor recommended vitamin E and thanked him for the directions, and when Amondson got home he found his wallet missing with thirty-eight dollars and his identification. Dewey Wood talked to anyone. The kidnap plot limited the time Hind had for DW.

Dewey was walking to the door, Hind got up and followed.

Hoping Dewey wouldn't make anything of the fact that Hind was leaving coffee and half an egg salad sandwich, Hind quickly asked, "What about children? Don't they skate? Actually they don't seem to nowadays."

As Hind and Dewey left Mitropoulos's Always Open, the quiet tailor, who hadn't seemed to listen, added, "They don't play stoopball around here because ain't no more stoops."

Or would the Dewey clue come from a go-between from whom it was to be elicited by a remark of Hind's in response itself to something Dewey said? Hind could think for a second that everyone around him near and far knew the answer to the Laurel kidnap, and no one was telling him—as if in those highly original hide-and-seek-and-destroy games that Cassia Meaning thought up for rainy days, yes, he was "it," compelled to look, threatened not merely with failing to find but with being attacked by a Cassia albeit inaccurately wielding his guardian's wooden applause clacker from English soccer matches.

Hind was aware of nodding as they bought papers from the blind auburn-haired Negro who sat grinning inside his box and offered a huge, long-fingered palm for the money. Dewey was saying he'd pay a call on Ivy Bowles after supper—and now, as they turned south, Dewey said, "Before long they'll black out that Connecticut kidnap, that's what they do in a case like that. I see it's in today's city edition: no news from the kidnapers, so you don't know about money, motive, or method." He chuckled at himself. He thought he spoke economically.

"Did *I* mention the case to you?" Hind asked.

"Yes, yesterday at the gym. But I had it on the news, you see, so I knew of it."

You had to ask—and here (a renewable kidnap!) he was asking all over again, as if Hershey were six or seven years younger, and the search only beginning—will child be killed if ransom not paid? if not paid *on time*? (Can you pay a ransom on an installment plan? The well of your own vagrant muse echoed up the information that "on time" means "promptly.") But then, if ransom not paid or if paid late will child survive maimed or unspeakably influenced? Or will child be killed, maimed, or unspeakably influenced even if ransom *is* paid? But what if the ransom is paid and the child alive is *kept*?

"Laurel's wife's brief disappearance," said Hind as he and Dewey turned at the butcher's corner into Dewey's street—

"Laurel's wife's?"

"Nothing, I was thinking of something else."

"Someone *else* disappear?"

Sears Laurel, totally alone there in the house in the trees talking to police and later to Hind, had said of Shirley, "She doesn't *have* accidents. It's quite possible she was bypassing police and tracking the case herself, she imagines she's one of these strong women, I let her think it. Quite possible, too, that she kidnaped the boy herself as a preparation for getting rid of me."

"'Rid of'?" the police had asked.

"I could even see her having the mad gall to ask ransom, then use it to take care of herself and the kid till suddenly after a while she turns up with a tale of how she stumbled into some trap and was held *with* Hershey, but at last tricked her captors." But by the time Sears gave Hind the retelling, Shirley had turned up, returned, then left publicly, and if Hershey had not turned up, it was public news that he was in any case the child of a marriage on the rocks.

And Sylvia could say he imagined too much!

What happens to child if no ransom asked? And what if, then, the child is simply held, simply kept?

The child grows up.

Hind caught Dewey quietly reporting what he was reading in his paper.

"Have you a piece in today?" That could be the clue's vehicle.

"They're holding seven of mine—no word, no money, but they're holding them."

Hind and Dewey sat for a while reading in the living room of Dewey's apartment, and. Dewey's music station kept being taken over by a discussion station in which people telephoned in and the commentator ranged smoothly over many topics, saying "We could toss that back and forth all night."

"The music station is being jammed," said Dewey.

Hind was keeping an eye across the street on Ivy Bowles' window shade, still down. Was she recuperating normally? It was three months since she fell into the river (the drink, the soup) luckily in the presence of the regulars, so she could be saved. Hind must look in on her, she probably thought it odd. Two cycles of gongs for the half-hour had already come from The Good Shepherd in Hind's street a block south; Ivy—up to when she fell sick—attended that church, but didn't like the new minister's turning it into a welfare center, i.e., a high-priced day school for difficult and handicapped kids ("Nuts every last one, even the duds who can walk and talk and aren't walleyed twitchers dress like animals and are sometimes fighting with their guitars").

"Jack," Dewey said from the bathroom where he was filling the imitation Roman lachrymatory he used for flowers, "I want you to listen to what I'm going to say."

This was to be it, twenty feet away and hidden, and against the mild interference of cold running water, the tears of bereaved friends, deep-welled somewhere in the city.

"You're a busy man, you wouldn't spend so much time with me unless something was wrong, and I think I know what it is—

The moan at the faucet's root was just like Hind's which the undertaker always vowed to fix.

"You'd be in and out of, up- or downstate taping for 'Naked Voice,' or helping someone or clipping relevant periodical articles to send friends—you wouldn't hang around here—I meant to ask when we met at Fieldston, but didn't know the right question to put since it's pretty personal." The water stopped. Dewey was just standing in there in the bathroom talking.

"Sylvia's what I'm getting at. I ran into her at my Superette—we were in the six-items-or-less express line, she was in a hurry and asked if I knew you well, and I said yes, and she said you weren't living together."

"She lives quite close by." Was the tall old woman's name also Sylvia? "Let's not talk about me. Give me something I can use."

It was raining, and Ivy Bowles stood at her window looking across at Dewey's. Hind waved, and she drew the shade down. Her eyes were not the best. A long green mover's truck rolled through the block. Though Ivy's shade was down Hind would perfectly well imagine her in that room, she couldn't get away from him: she had on shorts and a heavy tennis cable-stitch, she walked barefoot, against the orders of the health plan doctor who was also Hind's and Syl's and May's—walked across her pile-less orange-brown six-by-seven Khira with the tiny golden accident in a corner which in reality was the Persian weaver's signature; yes, walking to her TV, flicking her selector round to a channel with lots of talk, returning to her sectioned health chair that you felt must have been design-broken in several places yet held together by loose ligaments; swigging her cough codeine, and resuming the latest square of the deep green afghan she had started for a baby but now was extending and intending for her ninety-year-old half-sister in the nursing home. Hind saw all this, in spite of her attempt to keep out intrusive minds. "And so," Dewey was saying, now in the room, "I'll give you an iron-clad guarantee your life won't be simpler without your wife and little one." Dewey was pretending to run through his newspaper. Hind felt his own role, part, assignment, relation, intervalence, interception, in all this was not worth weighing; the fact—to answer Dewey's question—was that Hershey had to be saved; if, moreover, Hind puzzled often over effects in him himself of his ministrations to others, still those ministrations in themselves were good.

"Marriage is too good for me," said Hind.

"Marriage," said Dewey, "is an area where the air is clear and wise and your ground is nicely enclosed on many sides by perennial borders and neat trees and habitual greenhouses, and spread brightly with end-to-end grass." A rejected unquote.

Hind thought Dewey would give up the clue without knowing. But the clue would come at the Fieldston Hotel Health Club, where they usually met, where Greenspan would in another couple of hours be whistling the head of his imaginary 4 wood through an ideal alignment halfway between the mirrors on the blue rug, when he ought to be out at the front desk just before opening time checking which memberships were scheduled to expire within the next week. "Marriage," said Hind, "should not be talked of so much."

"Take you, though, for instance," said Dewey, looking above Hind's head to the Dürer St. Sebastian Hind knew was there; "you spend your worries on a funny guy like Plane, when your family need you. You correct themes for him when he drops by the wayside."

The kindergarten teacher who used her many attention-getting devices even when the children were murmuringly absorbed in their work had phoned Sylvia that May's latest "crayon" was unerringly a high-pitched red-belled male member sprung up out of a thicket of brown flames.

"I haven't seen Oliver Plane in weeks, for God's sake," said Hind.

"Have it your way."

Dewey would not keep on the subject. Hind went.

Why had not Hind continued and at last possessed the kidnap six going on seven years ago? No hidden reason existed. He had simply, very simply stopped looking.

But this time he knew there was no way but through. It was a way no doubt no finer and bigger and more final than Ashley Sill's way (as Hind envisioned it) along an eighteen-hole tunnel fed onward only by the moment of one's wish to act. Maybe at the far side of the continent, or another continent, maybe quite close to home, the boy, or the boy's whereabouts, or at least the truth about the boy, would be found. And since the old woman moved too slickly and strangely, left too much up to Hind, for him to believe she merely wanted the quarry hunted up and down, Hind must conclude that he himself was being drawn into danger.

Smitty said Madison Beecher phoned at nine—just a few minutes ago—to remind about John Plante's film at two tomorrow.

"I thought its preview was today!"

Smitty was merely breathing at the other end of the cord. Hind hung up. He needn't phone Maddy, what was the point, Hind would probably go, if only because of Plante's link with the strange roller skating that was going on.

Dewey recurred to Oliver Plane so often. Why? Hind should find out what Oliver had decided. You had to hold D on the subject.

He'd ask why the undertaker wasn't having any funerals—people weren't dying, was the answer; and why was background noise rising and thickening on "Naked Voice"? But then Dewey slipped back to Oliver, as if he were Dewey's old friend, not Hind's, and back—when?— to "Naked Voice": "Yes," said Dew at the Fieldston once, "that was fine, that interview with your old friend Christy Amondson who dropped out of sight; but the grate of the roller skates as you skated along and the humming and honking of the automobiles got hold of your voice and I couldn't hear the one without the other."

Then again Oliver. Or, briefly and ill-advisedly, the subject of Sylvia and May.

Hind phoned Sylvia at her office. After a remark or two had been exchanged, Hind was silent.

"Are you still there?"

"Yes," he said and nodded, he was still there.

"I don't care if you keep on after the Laurel child, don't you see?"

"Who told you I was on the kidnap again?"

"Many people know. I don't care about it, don't you see? I just want you here. It occurred to me last night."

"But you hated my interest in the case."

"And *you*, eight months ago, very much left *me*."

"You hated my compassion."

"I wouldn't say that. You were always a pushover, but I'm afraid now you're going to be cut down. I believe I knew that woman's voice on the phone. Don't laugh, but all I recall is that at the time we heard her voice—it might have been years ago—I had my cheek against yours, I swear I did; and to me her voice was quite far away though distinctive. What I don't know about the kidnap this time around might not matter if I'm right about this woman's voice."

"I only want to find out exactly what she said, confine yourself—"

"All she said was to phone the Sills that you were coming. And when I said why should I, she hung up. At first I thought it must be some aged nut you'd kindly acquired who, like some others, thought she had the right to oversee your life. Then I began to recall her voice."

"Well," said Hind, "you don't know her?"

"She knows us. Does it give you a kick to be sent by a strange old lady on a search for a four-year-old who if he's alive won't look like himself any more?"

"Who will look?" said Hind.

"His parents are dead," said Sylvia.

"Therefore someone else must look."

"No: therefore what would become of the boy if he *were* found?"

"But he has been lost (mislaid, taken away). He doesn't know who he is."

"Maybe. But what about you? You do know that whatever your name is, you're a husband and a father."

"A bad one," said Hind. "But the point is Hershey Laurel, not me."

"What happens when you catch up with Hershey?"

"Then the task is done. And he is free."

"What? then you'll come home again? Listen, years ago you simply turned away from those Laurels. The parents were dead by then, you turned away from the whole idea of the case. You didn't give up the search because I told you to, though I did; and it wasn't your guardian dying either, nor the police saying lay off. One week suddenly you were doing something else. You talked of taking up the guardian's land for a wildlife sanctuary but your ignorance of birds and animals was about as great as his knowledge of botany, you know what I mean if I don't express myself exactly. But then you gave that all up and went to work here, as I hoped you were going to. But the point is you gave up on the Laurel. Why go back now?"

Hind hung up. He had begun the phone call, and now he finished it off.

He was not committed to Plante's film, as Maddy said *he* was. Maddy had perhaps put some money into it. But whoever heard of previewing a film in the early afternoon in an abandoned classroom on the second floor of an office building downtown? Better to stay close to Dewey his whole time at the Fieldston.

If he could tell Sylvia! No matter what she already knew. Even if she in her way knew everything that he in his way was going to tell. But how did you? He must tell somebody. He would tell how each alarming diversion, as you retreated from it and looked back, began to be alive and independent, a subcounterplot thriving in a style its very own. To a true friend this is what, in somewhat revised words, he could say.

But who to tell? What happened to the three couples he and Sylvia, and then he, had listened to and given understanding to and lent money to, and, in detail, two cases to one, urged against divorce though for separation? Woody and Daphne Grew had already behaved toward him in such a way as to show that separated from Syl Hind was so different he even seemed to them a risk to have around, an unnecessarily imported potential blight. But the Grews' break-up was ancient history.

Tell? Suddenly now did he have not a friend? Tell? He could not, years ago, tell the guardian about the smoking and nonbreathing exercises and the nonbreathing head and elbow stands—three times as hard as what Art Courage did, five times—for he'd have had to confess to the guardian that the stands and other exercises were done to stunt or even shrink. The wonderful profile was always telling someone how if it *could* be done, he would see that young Jack should be faced by no impediments to his free growth. The guardian told the fifth-grade teacher young Hind was not to be made to play a tree in her production of her very own *A Modern Masque of Joy*; Hind had got used to the part, and liked the swaying protectiveness he imagined he conveyed in what Miss Grove called the warm pocket down left. And just when Hind, in bed at night, was commenting on his guardian's meaning of "free growth"–"He doesn't mean physique, he means the whole man"–another voice, probably Hind's too, said, "And without your great height what handicap in God's green earth would you possess? And if your height is publicity, it is strength as well." Then all his minds ran off speedily flank to flank. If you trained regularly with the weights you could lose five pounds in a week just by stopping. It went out of your shoulders; and your leg-roots turned soft. Art Courage talked of such potentialities. "Why, I could–" And if he did all he said, still his claims often made of the near future a present to the past: "And I can still do my midnight push-ups like I used to, as many as any girl wants, and I'm old enough to be your father. At my age last birthday, you'll have a good head of skin is what you'll have."

But the Polish doctor Grynberg said to Art, "You're old enough to be Jack's father, but you aren't a father. You make love but no babies."

"That's me, Doctor, you give beautiful diagnoses: lover but not a father, so I'm still pressing two-twenty flat on my back."

"You ain't got no kids?" said the lieutenant-commander.

"I *pay* not to," said Art, picking up his hand-sponges and reaching for a bar.

"He got a rich wife to pay," said Honey Gulden, returning from lunch. Four elderly men went to him immediately and stood around his desk ordering vitamins.

Dewey would not participate in this sort of threatening talk. It even seemed to test his bland benevolence, for he frowned at Art, whose views may have intruded through the dream melodies and the cobalt-blue-carpeted light to bother Dewey's peace.

But he joined much of the talk that was to be had. In fact, Dewey had been the principal interlocutor of old Mr. Bay, the final appearance he made. "You wouldn't have believed he was changing before your eyes, Jack. A metamorphosis, I called it." Dewey came back to the incident so often Hind scanned it for the destined clue. "I was aware," said Dewey, "that old Bay was talking even more fluently though more softly than usual there in the sauna, and the oven thermometer said one-ninety-one, which is only a bit high. He didn't lose pace or confidence, he was telling a long story. Later no one knew how long he'd been in the sauna, ten minutes is maximal at his age, oldest active member. Story was, his son-in-law had done overhand pull-ups on the high bar at some gym and perfected the rhythm, head back and forth on the way up and down, one two one two. But on the way down, thinking back to the lyrics of the tune they piped in— 'Land, lots of land, under starry skies above, Don't fence me in'—his son-in-law forgot to draw back his head and cracked his jaw in two places. And after he went home he discerned that the nerves in his upper teeth weren't working. And he'd gone to this gym at first only to get away from the lunchtime madhouse and for exercises to help his golf. But old Bay, sweating his heart out with me in the sauna and making a puddle on the wood because he hates to waste a towel, began to use words I never heard. And thought he was kidding until just before his shoulders, well, they slumped forward and he fell back, he was saying some language that must have swum out of the Finnish paneling—mixed with real words—like 'gla lala rooroo aal, aal rooroo lala gla.' I'd been bored and it was just the two of us there in the sauna, and I was going to leave, I'd had my time and also two lights were out so it wasn't easy to read the paper. But you can bet old Bay was lucky I didn't leave him to pass out alone."

Two glistening, loose-skinned old men in an enchanted cabinet with an oven thermometer and two long, thick, radio-station windowpanes.

"Bay didn't know he'd begun speaking gibberish. He kept squinting around at the oven thermometer, which perhaps he took at last for a clock—and it didn't change. He said if he could just sweat himself free of a pound of liquid a day there in the sauna, he might live forever. If he'd held out longer I'd have had to stay listening, and the heat might have killed me instead of him. For the sake of compassion."

Alone in the sauna, alone in the gym (as you could be when the club opened its basement operation at ten A.M.)—be then a member of the mirrors and the blue insulated ceiling, disappear into the walls and the steel and leather gear and the clouded chrome plate, be soothed away by muted saxophones and audio-rounded strings, remember the old Hit Parade and count your sets of pulls and presses, for at a certain number of sets achieved, you find yourself suddenly through to a now spaceless condition in which you can't be bugged, not even later by the old women at the pool's shallow end who swim across very slowly, thus destroying the pool's length, who wait till your chugging feet chop you, and your closed fingers and unarched spine and proud coordination have drawn you, twenty yards only to run your neat hand aground on a soft, unwarning shoulder or broadside just as you are planning to knife that same left hand across in front of your forehead, thus flip-turning you to punctuate your lap, all with an apparent skill your crawl does not have no matter how smoothly you picture yourself as you swim your lane all alone as only a swimmer is, and fancy no other coordinate waits to locate you.

If you arrived at the Fieldston early enough, you weren't interfered with by people.

On the other hand, pale Ash and handy Peg, having at an interval of a couple of years trapped each other (first she him into, then he her in, wedlock), found it wasn't so bad. Each wanted the other for the wrong reasons (if even so many as to be plural); yet they learned to breathe together in the same mansion, even if Ash had stopped writing poems for a long time (and had only this summer started again slowly, carefully). She gave him a black eye one night in her sleep, cried out in her dream and threw a determined hand into his face.

Hind had wanted Sylvia to depend on him, but it seemed her idea differed. She was not trapped, her life could not be taken by no matter how tricky a man. Which hardly meant she didn't want to give up work. He had all the materials for understanding Sylvia, but he hadn't quite gotten down to it.

The Laurel clue Dewey carried might hurt him if he carried it too long or to the wrong receiver. Ivy Bowles borrowed Dewey's loose-leaf notes from two sessions of the phil survey they took at the library, and threw them out by mistake when she suddenly saw the sanitation truck outside in the street and rushed everything in sight into her wicker wastebasket; she had copied Dewey's notes, but now he had to copy from her. Whoever planted the Laurel clue in Dewey impressed him into a responsibility he should not at his age and diminishing height have had to enter, even unknowingly. Oliver Plane took an incomplete set of *The Golden Bough* welcome from Dewey, and later told DW the loan had become an acquisition, Ol knew Dew would never read the dark green buckrams, so why should D have them in the house, and Dewey nodded puzzled agreement.

Four men Hind had lined up for "Naked Voice" had had, to their irritation, to be postponed. Then came a note in familiar handwriting stuck in the crenate mailbox panel: "You make slow regress." If from the old woman, it was a new departure toward the cryptic.

Hind let Smith Answering–more economical–take all calls and provide a summary breakdown late in the evening. Sylvia, Brother, Madison Beecher, Oliver Plane, the station about "Naked Voice," even a call from May in person, then encore Sylvia.

For a week the afternoons were not free of thunder, and ugly veins of lightning darkened the sky, river-forks defined dark deltas.

Hind wished his life could broaden again, but knew this wasn't possible until, to put it simply, Hershey Laurel was found.

In the middle of an afternoon, Hind could hear only the electric, boiling Ow Wow Wow of the emergency truck pulling past. The great deal he saw and heard seemed to take him into the narrowest of scopes. He had not seen Bee Bee Barker's political crowd in two months. Beside the Fieldston stood a slight girl like a younger Cassia Meaning, and she had on her right leg a fat cast colored all over with wildflowers so her leg itself seemed to have been turned into a papier-mâché bouquet alive and tangled. A child with a large unwrapped chocolate bar in one hand stood on the hotel steps tossing and tossing her beanbag. Late one dense dark afternoon when the rain would not come and men left their desks early and filled the taverns, Hind saw the well-known band of skaters led by a man who fitted John Plante's description; it was a month since Maddy left a message with Smith Answering that he had to discuss with Hind the threat posed by Plante's friend. Hind saw only poor Dewey Wood, put upon, a dangerous clue encysting itself in the stomach he was trying to reduce. In the Fieldston shower Hind saw that his devotion stripped the city of its name and placed him in an enclosure closed from rapid transit under the earth and choppers rattling above it, from the Mayoral candidate racing by on foot and a group of green and yellow long legs interrupting traffic to sing in their distant, thin sopranos to a K.P.E. Bach Fugue-a-rooney the news (designed by an ad firm) that this here (and they named the city over and over) was a love city. Yet Hind's enclosure, though imaginable as time, was more like space—say, a Santos-Dumont Sisters fortified bubble-top within which anything could be preserved. Dewey Wood's summer was now plainly passing, and the clue might be assimilating itself into his system. One day Hind and Dewey worked out early before anyone else arrived. Dewey had the Salvation Army coming for his old clothes in the afternoon. At last, watching Dewey's waist-turns, Hind felt that that clear ground of evidence and choice was no less than what he stood on; and that the chrome and cobalt-blue clearing had the answer in its very emptiness and in the ozone provided by Frequent Simmons' air conditioner; and that Hind himself would not at last possess but be part of the clue. After the rain one afternoon, some of the air pollution had been laid, and in the air a refreshing gap stood, like the waking aftermath of a dream. Maybe—and the idea made Hind's heart, as when he stood in the shallow end of the Fieldston pool after sixteen laps, go snap snap against his chest—maybe it wasn't he who would finish the Laurel case. Frequent Simmons had made a full check of the air conditioner's motor before going to Mount Mary with family for his two-week vacation, and the machine worked too well. There was almost a wind, and the gym's autumnal air made the sauna a new kind of relief.

Oliver Plane had not been seen; Hind must check on the poor joker; to save to pay for last winter's vacation, OP had now let himself be signed to teach all three summer sessions. Hind knew Ol would need help before the season ended. The Laurel case took you away from your friends. He needed a stamp for his letter to Sylvia.

Thursday Hind thought he saw the old woman at the shadowy counter of the pizza place Oliver sometimes took his girls to, a hole in the wall, nothing more; but Dewey hadn't answered his phone, which meant he had gone to the FHHC alone, so Hind was in too great a hurry to stop to peer into the pizza place to see.

They were all there, the gym was live. The slow toe-riser doubled up his standing twists with Yoga eye rolls. Art Courage stood on his hands up against the air conditioner telling his story in an undertone. Dewey was panting against a mirror, smiling at Greenspan, Junior, who was chatting wittily to him to indicate to the prospective member in a luminous gray silk he was showing around that management and members, old and young, were a team (family, flock) fathered in the common interest of working out. Greenspan, Junior, took his prospect off to the shoulder press/deep kneebend frame, and as Hind started for Dewey, Minerva's voice on the intercom broke off the music calling Dewey to the phone.

He had been difficult for days. He would speak only of waist-work, spot reducing, his fear he couldn't keep "the weight" down; and he eyed almost resentfully Honey G., who at his desk examined his face reverently in a mirror and chewed his own S-D vita-gum to a Mozart third-movement minuet—"I'm down to coffee, slice of dry rye toast, no lunch, steak and fresh grass without dressing for dinner, and two Scotches to get off to sleep." But Honey that time had been listening; he looked at DW in the mirror and said sternly under his dark eyebrows, "But you put some of your friend's green tomato preserve on that toast, *didn't* you, Dewey, boy," and D couldn't tell how Honey knew.

Yet Dewey's sad preoccupation was not with weight. If the clue, what?

You saw hairy limbs across cobalt-blue carpet and tangled in the inter-altered glass angles so that to trace the lines of sight from oneself to only, say, two or three others and back again would make a web so good you could bounce somebody in it. Greenspan, Junior, was at the fruit juice doorway pointing down the mirrored wall toward Honey Gulden's desk. At various points the gym could seem very long, this perspective might lead to a sale, the glossy gray prospect blinked and bobbed his head.

A languidly slouching youth with a slanted cut of hair staggered lower and lower from temple to jaw-hinge and over nape snapped magically into exercise. Honey called to someone, "*I* never promised to make you Mister Universe."

Art Courage grabbed the elbow of the long-haired youth, who could not know Hind knew him as one of the two who had pushed the heifer into the ad studio two or three months ago.

Art said, "You think you kids downtown got all the sweet stuff, listen to this."

Pyne, the now bearded saloon owner, suddenly squatted in front of their bench and ripped his elastic leopard skin up the buttock-parting; he raised up quickly and the elderly chorus boy Bill Post, an étude in sunset or sunrise rose, snickered and put his finger in the slit but obviously did not wish to interrupt Art Courage. There were thirty-eight men in the gym, including Honey Gulden, who now took from his bottom drawer two rubber breasts which he placed under his green T-shirt and wore around the room, saying, "My three married daughters got nothing like these," and stopped at Art's bench to hear what Hind was already unwillingly hearing while Dewey tried to explain.

He said to Hind, "I had it last night almost, I feel like a simp, and now it just almost came back as I was lying down to do those ladies' hip-turns, but now—"

"Absolutely not," said Art Courage to one of his group, "we'll go on the road like a legitimate theatrical show, I don't go myself, but the show goes, and I don't do three-day stands even for suck-truck outfits, and this isn't vacuum cleaners, dar ling, or candy bars, this is the Santos-Dumont annual, with a twenty-piece ensemble, which is an industrial you figure to run ten fifteen cities coast to—"

"—because you're a sympathetic animal, Jack Hind, the most sympathetic I know, and you've shown your concern for my modest career as popular *philosophe*—only ten things actually in print—and you may have forgotten but you said to Oliver once that you hoped to collect my sayings sometime into a pint-sized—"

"Part slick, part slap, not a single mention of Santos-Dumont products, that's how the Sisters want it: the girls do ex*quis*ite routines with the best original material you're going to see in any show in or out of a mid-town ballroom, plus incredible slapstick but intentionally corny, so bad it's good, there's three Norway spruce trees swing on with barkey trunks"—Art slipped his tongue tip out and ran it over his upper lip—"fitted tight as a mermaid's behind. But then two giant two-girl sheep come out into this country scene with Japanese paper sunflowers in five colors and a brown neon hill that shifts back and forth, and the sheep sing loud, then fall over each other until one of the rear gals pretends to rip a leg, and out comes her own leg just the calf, like a broken—"

"Last night and this morning I experienced two things I must tell you about, Jack, one not nice at all, one just wonderful but—"

Honey Gulden began to sneeze and couldn't stop, like the bus driver Hind had driven with last week who had

had finally to stop. Honey put a quick howl on top of each sneeze. One of the Cubans snaked in his great ribbed vacuum hose and switched on.

Sounds came together, background forth, foreground back.

"–though I can imagine what making a study of your kidnap must entail," said Dewey. Had Sylvia told? Was Dewey on the inside after all?

"Pipe down, peasant," called Art, "I'm approaching my climax, dear, you're distracting me, and I've got more money than you. So go sit under some other hill."

Dewey lowered his head and his tone: "I got a nasty note, Jack, this morning, unmailed; and I want to ask your opinion. You don't mind that I tell you, for anyone knows you're a man of sympathy." Dewey tilted his head, making a note of the phrase. They lifted their feet for the vacuum.

Art said, "There it is, they're singing, it's the Art Courage Country Put-on, a benefit gala for the greater glow of Santos-Dumont: my shepherd chicks in the chorus line got tailored rags, and the two giant, two-girl sheep sing; and, guys, it ought to be four girls' voices, but it seems more like three and a half, but then one sheep stumbles, the one that was moving around not following the chalk marks; the other sheep has been rooted to the spot right in front of the Japanese Norway spruce, and just as the first sheep trips and falls onto a trap, instead of three and a half voices you have four, and the fourth is unmistakably either male or the world's bulliest dyke: and me in the wing thinking there goes Philly, Chicago, Dallas, Houston, St. Louis, Seattle, the whole West Coast: but look at the laminated ID's popping in the front rows, yes all through the house: those gentlemen in the seats out there full of Cornish hen are breaking up, down, and around they think what I'm giving them is so rich and true–from my right wing I see a little guy in the second row jump up and down in his seat and clap his hands, then jump into the aisle and hold his hands like he's praying, whip out a bandanna, wipe away the tears he's laughing so hard, I didn't believe–"

"–the nasty note, Jack, if you're listening, said–hold it, Art confuses me–that nasty note upset me so I forgot my aphorism that had come together in my mind. The note said, in female writing almost like Ivy's–but do you see Ivy sending one like this even with her poor recuperation and her snapping at me when I drop in to ask if I can shop for her–the hand had a care and a roundness that stamps it as a woman's–and it said, 'Why do you waste your last days playing wise old Confucius? You're very ordinary and will keep on getting rejection slips from the newspapers.' Ah! That about Confucius reminds me, my saying which I dropped into the box just before the twelve-ten pick-up today, struck me last evening, and was worth waiting for, I think it's been building for several weeks: here goes, Jack, I've got it now, the Confucius reminds me–how do you like that, I remind myself! It goes, 'We are all of us trees and the chlorophyll we are helpless not to magically create leaves us powerfully what we are–belligerent beech, peaceful olive, western willow, oriental plane.' I'm sorry, but isn't that beautiful?"

"This was the most original industrial I ever conceived, when we got them out of the sheep, the fag had a hard-on and she was interested, he'd been doing something to her in the sheep–"

You couldn't ignore Art's tale, it was probably too important; but here at last was Dewey coming across!

"So I wish you'd come have a dinner with me at my home tonight, Jack, I went out shopping to the Superette for it early this morning. And if you come I'll show you a letter I had from a lady who lives up just south of Mount

Mary in the woods and read two of my truisms reprinted in some Boston house organ, and she, that is, her—"

Confucius was the Orientals who led to Maddy and precipitated the deepening search. And the giveaway was chlorophyll: for *Phil*, the druggist, chewed green Clorets chewing gum—which he cruelly gave to poor Phyllis's eleven-year-old pink-white Boston bull. And Phil and Phyllis went on vacation tomorrow.

Cabs weren't easy at five-thirty, subway was too far to walk: bus, then.

"Hey, Jack Hind, you didn't fill in your chart-card, you're suppose to press a hundred twenty by Christmas, didn't you have some capsules coming, some of Honey's new E or the special pasteurized wheat germ oil?"

A hundred viols and soft, malleable brasses and a field of green, sunny, swaying woodwinds broke gently upon one another, a hand was shuffling them like gold in a bag, they moved like the liquid colors in the new corner-bar's hypnotic beer-ad, with wanton capillarity: the instruments were getting ready to leave the introduction and move onto a plain harmonic track: the music hunted for the opening, and rolled through all the hotel speakers, upstairs and down, from the long chlorine pool and the contiguous massage rooms with their violet dusk, up five, six, eleven, twenty-two flights to the coeducational solarium, hall above hall, suite above suite.

Dewey called from the fruit-juice door. Art Courage called, "You left your towel, dear." A sign said, IT'S YOUR CLUB.

Two men stood with backs to the sun tubes, hands raised like the downtown mystic who ended his performance thus, exhibiting all-love.

Barbell jungle jingled far off, the voices nearly contained by acoustic design. Greenspan, Junior, was saying to a prospect, "And upstairs the female members are doing their sets to the exact same music."

And Hind a misbegotten giant gymnosperm. The guardian, ever tracking the movement of Hind's heart, said, "Get your roots right, and rich vocabularies open to you. '*Gymno*' is Greek for what, my friend? forget the Late Latin descendant, what is the Greek? think of the words that have this prefix!"

Someone in a far corner of the gym had fallen asleep head down on a leather sit-up board at the fifty-degree position; Hind should go back. The guy should be waked, he might pass out.

If Hind did not reach Phil soon enough, Phil might misuse his clue.

Would he know it *as* a clue? Would he turn out to be as outside the central line of lure and search, search and—as was poor, pleasant Dewey?

Hind's sides were sticky as drying soap. Chlorine salt and assorted sweat and cologne replaced the chill currents of the gym. Honey's vaunted short body would have a cold tomorrow.

The conspiracy was simpler than the shifting perspectives of the gym. Hind stole a wet towel.

And this suspicion of a root simplicity the plot threatened to solve itself into recalled Hind's first and later views on how the Laurel marriage touched the criminal act of Hershey's abduction. Shirley told Hind, "I never wanted the country and he knew it but kept insisting Hersh would have room to play and air to breathe—room, yes; kids to play with, no—but frankly Sears wanted the country for himself." So, first, Hind saw Shirley's wish to pursue the kidnap all on her own as evidence that the marriage was a disaster; saw her visit to the land-poor farmer, wall-builder, and firewood supplier Ken Love at the close of that disastrous weekend as further evidence of the same. Yet later Hind learned that Shirley merely liked Ken Love, merely happened to stop to have a talk with him; and when Sears came for her after being phoned by Mrs. Beulah Love, who thought Shirley wasn't quite right, Sears not only saw that Shirley was lucid but suspected she more than liked Love; and when he told this to Hind, whom he took for a plainclothesman or a detective, Hind believed.

At Phil's Neighborhood Drug, Hind stopped racing, took a deep breath. Phil pretended he had a stamp machine behind the counter, you had to ask for stamps and hand over a quarter for your four fives. "That's all the machine's got, fives," said Phil.

"Phil," said Hind, "why don't you stop that. There's no machine and we all know it; you buy your sheets at the post office and take a penny on every five-center, you with a summer house on a mountain lake."

"Now that," said Phil, "is exactly what your old friend says to me—Ollie Plane, he always says that." In fact, Hind had got the idea from Oliver. "But he's not really an adult, I'm surprised *you* go in for allegations like this. As for Oliver Plane, I'm a drug store psychologist and I say there's a child inside Oliver trying to get out. I gave him some pills to slow him down yesterday afternoon, there's a kid trying to come out in Ollie Plane, and it's just about to, violently."

But the rich speed with which Phil had ignorantly given up his clue and turned Hind on course to OP, whom Dewey had been calling and calling Hind's attention to for days, though OP was not DW's clue, caused Hind to leave the four brown national-park commemoratives on Phil's counter. Walking swiftly out Hind recalled the smell of Phil's gum, sweeter than the wintergreen Cassia Meaning used to have a supply of.

Oliver and his girls took tea at Pizza Valley, a white-tiled corridor sandwiched between Foam Rubber City and

U-Copy Photostat. Oliver had let his Gulden diet go and was back eating what Honey called "junk foods." Hind leaned on the sidewalk to-go counter by the great oven, looking hopefully down the counter to the last shadowy stools, taking in peppery smells of tomato crust which brought to the tongue faint drynesses of bread dust.

Hind did not find OP there, nor at the all-men clam house over the river where the men talked about hepatitis, nor at his apartment, nor at the restaurant pay-phone OP came down to in his slippers some mornings if he didn't want to call within hearing of the girl who'd stayed overnight. Nor was he at college, though Hind's inquiries had to be discreet, he wanted not to jeopardize the poor bastard's job.

But when he found Oliver Plane at home with an emeritus student friend, and it was six or seven days after Dewey's and Phil's clues, Oliver said he would go on vacation earlier than planned, and would Hind help out at college, didn't he have a backlog of "Naked Voice" broadcast tapes?

"I *have* to go," said Plane. "I can't face those creatures for the time being. They don't know enough yet, and they want to know what I know. And they write so ambiguously it's like a plot to mislead me. 'College life,' writes one young authority on the sociological impact of physiotherapy, 'will effect new experiences which will find its source in previous learning, induction, deduction, reduction, abduction, and others, and I am about to embark on the phase of life that will bring "useless" knowledge to a broader understanding. These will be, to my beneficiary, new insights into deep, future horizons, which I will encounter after my college career is complete. My knowledge will be greatly enhanced and by this, I will be able to see my way clear of new obstacles. There will be a new conception of reality without disbursing the intellect to avoiding the past.' Unquote," said Ol, "the future grinningly and benevolently breaking the fine surfaces of the present. What can my students do for *me*?"

"You'll lose your job unless someone helps you out." *Abduction* and *embark* might well be giveaways. Who was the author?

"Just for a few days," said Ol.

"Of course," said Hind.

"The information is all out at the college."

"Out? Released?"

"No: *there*, I left it all there, books, notes, syllabi, letters, cards."

In the very old days—along the past's horizon—Oliver Plane kept a spare set of books at home on the Heights. He couldn't be bothered to carry things home, and he liked people to think he didn't do any homework.

Hind looked around. That was only half-true now, for there was nothing here. Ol's long railroad flat had a couple of empty bookcases and a rich Spanish spread, ornately green and black-and-blue, over a bedless mattress. There was a ragged gap where a wall had been, and on the now visible far wall a geologic survey map of Mount Mary Hind had meant long ago to look at that had been on the wall that had disappeared. There was so little here that everything might be evidence.

He was told by Oliver that he could get in touch with him at a motel near Mount Mary. "With Hind holding down the home front—" he looked up from his duffel bag, grinned at his girlfriend, and didn't finish his sentence.

On the Monday, Hind did not renew his membership at FHHC.

When he had a moment he was going to reconstruct Plane's flat as he had seen it, and recreate the way the girl looked.

If you wanted to save a friend, you (as Dewey Wood had published) "save only in the ways offered you."

"Dr. Plane," the girl with turquoise eye-liner said to Hind his third day subbing for Ol, "this is the first time I've been able to catch you in your office. I did make your lecture yesterday but it was the first time and I want to explain about not coming. It isn't that I'm not motivated. But this summer session has defined itself pretty much in terms of some crucial interference in terms of some organizational problems. Say, I've just got an idea, would you like to be one of our advisers? Do you mind if I sit down?"

"I'm not Dr. Plane," said Hind as he waved her down, ending his sweep neatly by catching hold of the corner of the desk.

"Oh, *Mis*ter Plane, sorry." She put her hand on top of his, sitting down and moved it only very slowly and frictionally away to what seemed now, to be an activist bargaining position a few inches along. "I'm Holly Roebuck."

"Did you write a paper on the social impact of physiotherapy?"

At the doorless entrance to Hind's ceilingless cubicle a boy with an olive-green attaché case frowned. "Plane?"

"I'm subbing for him," said Hind. "My name's Hind."

"No," replied Holly, "but I know something about O.T."

*V*

Anything might—she used it twice in her sentence—
"relate," and soon. Plane promised that all necessaries
were here at college. The Dewey phase shouldn't have
carried so far into the summer. Midsummer flew by
the boards. In Julio Loggia's block crowded fire escapes
and their old glimmering pillows murmured above
the street lamps all night. Julio was demanding equal
time with "Naked Voice" tapes and a number of Hind's
acquaintances whose names he had somehow obtained.
Maybe he knew someone at Smith Answering. Hind
had given him more time at the beginning last year, but
now he was able to cite to Julio the Brother, Inc. "one-
encounter-per-week" norm. Hind had to school himself
not to let pity force thought onto the Loggia situation:
Julio griping that there was too much food around the
house, that his mother spent all their relief on blue
bargain fowl and half-gallon party tubs of peanut butter
that simply made him and his little sister fat, there was
never money for anything else, did Hind have the price
of a down payment on a tennis racket, two colored kids
practiced tennis up against the handball walls.

When Hind wound up the Laurel case he would unerringly give equal time elsewhere. Sylvia would never have
been able to limit her own interest in Dewey's talk as had
Hind. Instead of watching for that one destined exit, or,
if you will, hunting as it were a haunted golf links for the
overgrown and now un-flagged hole which you obviously must first find in order to play into and thus earn the
right to pass under the broken birch, over the hidden

twin-two-by-four'd creek to the new (men's) tee, instead (indeed) of sidestepping Dewey's standing tales of his dead wife or his doctor's search once in Dewey's eye long ago and what he incidentally found, Sylvia would have dwelt on whatever Dewey dwelt on and she would hence have lost the Laurel kid. Hind's method was a secret dearer than the actual whereabouts of Hershey, and to the ordinary person more puzzling. It was like the guardian's overriding theme for each annual summer treasure hunt. Like the portly Jap tenant's dedication to his own survival as man of leisure. Or like a dive in the old days. Echoes along the pool tile, the faded white enamels complete everywhere you looked except for one chipped gray half-unit four inches above the water-line halfway up the pool (or down), and Hind would let his mind go to it as he stood for a moment at the base of the board feeling his left heel rub the harsh cocoa matting, asking himself why they never re-enameled that gray patch of undercement, wondering then (though never later away from the pool)how on earth the electrician got to the light fixtures along the middle of the pool ceiling guarded by black wire sieves like deepfry baskets.

Siggofreddo Morales shrugging symmetrically and giving a calm smile. "In the air you ain't got that much time. You did all your thinking before you came on the board, before you got to the pool, buddy. Your body is all set. In between the two halfs of your twist, why, when you're flipping, you don't suddenly think whether to do it, you don't think up there in a tenth of a second maybe I do the full twist before I snap my knees up, or maybe I don't snap my knees at all, maybe *no* somersault, just one full twist that I try to make it *look* arched all through, very hard, buddy. With your height–" brown smile, bad front teeth, Dentyne breath like–"your flips could look great, snap-coil, snap-unwind, *buddy*!" His one-fifty dead lifts at the Y each afternoon (while his kid brother in jeans killed time by struggling with so much hip swing it looked lateral all the way across the hand-over-hand rungs) had trained Siggo's shoulders back.

Think through, then forget, and be your thought. When Hind had a moment free of these students of Plane's and of the kidnap, he was going to think about Siggofreddo and his fate: it was quite a tale, though not for now. Hind would tell it to young Edison Beecher if that child would for once not insist on being the storyteller.

"Because," said Holly Roebuck, "I wouldn't want you to think I wasn't properly motivated or wasn't coming because I didn't like your teaching plan."

"I haven't submitted a teaching plan," said Hind; "how do I know what I'm doing from one week to the next?"

The tip of her tongue was out. Why? Hind would want to question her, perhaps in her organization's office, perhaps back at the undertaker's. Was the tip of Miss Roebuck's tongue inviting a connection, through Sears Roebuck, with *the* Sears?

The boy with the olive-green attaché case put it down on the new blue too electric carpet that ran through cubicle after cubicle. He said, "How could you know Hind's teaching if you didn't come to class?"

"I know he's good," said Holly, tossing her head and its brittly final backcombed bell of black hair, but not looking at the boy. Her fingers tapped the knuckles of Hind's forgotten hand once, authoritatively. "*Very* good. The motivation counts for so much that you could say the teacher practically *creates* the student."

Holly rose, her white A-cut shift fell into place over her belly. Above her head the grilled vent divulged more sounds (now faintly sardonic) like those Hind had heard at the beginning of the hour: "If at first you don't succeed, try..." The speaker must have moved from the vent at his end.

Everyone said this new, designedly temporary building to which they kept adding entresols and full floors, was complex in the relations among its levels. There was joking talk among the glass cubicles about the new synthetic carpet's voltage and its possible sources.

Holly was leaving. She looked up at the vent, smiled at Hind and clasped his wrist: "Canned background puts you in perspective."

"Please," said the boy who was standing waiting.

In the aisle outside his cubicle she nodded to Hind over the top of the milky glass partition: "If you want to be our adviser, you have our number. You don't have to get in touch with *me* by sending messages through fancy grillework."

The crenate grille of his postbox. The old woman's notes.

But the boy with the olive-green attaché case was saying—just as out of the grillework vent came the words "sheep look up and are not fed"—"There are now, I believe, two groups on campus who believe that interadministration communicatioids are being fed through some of the newer vent systems. I suspect that's what she meant, but who knows?"

Hind looked at the vent again but a sound like the mere echo of a drone was all he caught, then feet and a large, soft, distant murmur—the end of the hour.

"Your time is valuable," said the boy with the olive-green attaché case, "and I happen to think mine is, too."

An elderly man with a high, blond briefcase appeared in the cubicle opening grinning at Hind. Was he onto Plane's stratagem? knew Hind from somewhere? But he could not have known Hind unless either Plane had told about the substituting or this man was part of the sequence that would produce a solution, sift the Laurel riddle's evidence, recapture the boy Hershey's sweet private freedom. The man kept grinning and, as if in complicity with Hind, shook his head and chuckled. He was just being friendly. "Seen the new methodology in the department office?" He thought Hind belonged.

"I haven't been in there," said Hind, nodding and bringing up a smile. On the other hand this was summer session (or, one of the three summer sessions designed now to make full use of the plant); regular staff mingled with temporary.

"Well, go see," whispered the elderly man, grinning, and passed on.

To the boy, Hind said, "My time isn't valuable in itself. Its value is only in what students make it into." He felt he should have smiled, but he couldn't.

"I merely want a statement. (Say, that last remark could be taken a couple of ways, wouldn't you say?) A statement for our paper. It was to come from Oliver Plane, but it can come from you. Perhaps you have more to say. It's simply this. What do you think this new temporary class-and-office building will do for campus *ambiance*?" He paused, and seemed embarrassed for Hind that Hind did not have an answer. "I mean, in terms of—"

Would the next clue come from Hind himself? The analogies were too many.

"Or is it just too much?" said the boy coldly, hopefully. He would probably have heard about Plane's harsh wit, absorbent, all-purpose, totally versatile. And was now hoping for a quotable slam from this tall tan considerable person.

But what new standards of relevance might occur? Hind had thought he knew them. When you walked with delicate acceleration one two three (in Hind's case severely limiting length of pace), the third a nearly running hop, to that mysterious limit of the diving board which, though still laid with (carefully prewetted) clinging, abrasive, familiar cocoa mat, turned your weight so nobly upon itself and was so subtly passive—the bolt at the root and making you think of the board lever as something else—you shouldn't deliberate, weigh, think. Or then wonder how from up up there in the still volume of the softly echoing long tile room (the one genuinely dangerous and unexpected place in all the buildings of his old prep school), the chlorine green below turned a dry olive pale. At that angle, above. You planned ahead, cultured your body, bred your cooperating trapezius, deltoid, and pectoral to know a feeling of composition, and then your will and memory you trained to find it again and again: then you didn't think, you tried to be your thought: you didn't think, say, of your guardian sizing you up affectionately one summer afternoon as you hiked in from your tree house back on the pine slope from which through field glasses you could see stray gulls sway above the town dump, and where, though he pretended not to know exactly where your tree house was, the guardian would wander late in the summer looking for snapshot spots for the annual treasure hunt clues; you didn't think, in the middle of a held, supple twist, about his loving look at you up and down and his dutiful words when you tramped lankily up to him by the old lodge: "'Badly cut but strongly sewn'—Gogol, isn't it?"—at the top of your dive (on your back) you did not think thus, no matter what your faithful guardian said ("In the quarter-mile I rethought and lived each damned pace, the questioning and concentrating took my mind off the pain I was inflicting on my legs and lungs")—the four-forty, you had to tell your guardian, might be after all different from the dive.

But the dive was like the Laurel quest, and that special mode of prethought right for both.

"–which is why," the boy with the olive-green attaché case was saying, "I appreciate your bothering to listen: I had a teacher once–'*had*'?"–he widened his mouth sardonically–"to whom I said once, 'You don't let me get close to you, Mr. Crooks,' and he came back like he prepared the speech iambically, 'What makes you think I want you to?'–which is O.K. you know, in itself, but it's the saying that matters, you could say that to me in a way that would be satisfactory, but he had it ready, or *it* had *him*, which means that in terms of my definition of a comeback–hey, this is new, I never thought of it before–well, it wasn't a comeback, if you see, a comeback is spontaneous."

Hind had not answered the initial query. The boy now used only last names when addressing teachers, in order simply to be more direct.

"Well," said the boy, "thank you for your time. I enjoyed talking to you. You're a born listener, Dr. Hind. I liked this. What you teaching the Fall term?"

"Nothing," said Hind, and smiled.

"That's good, too," said the boy. "You get to be a captive of your audience, or something. *I know*."

Three days later Hind received in his mailbox a form at the top of which the boy requested a "statement" on "the matter we agreed on."

Above the Department Coffee Urn, at which Hind was not yet sure enough of either his identity or his anonymity to stop, he caught (stole, had) a glimpse of a tiny Dürer print. But passing through to the mail room to Ol's box, Hind had only time to see in the print massed hatchings like foliage. (Early Dürer or hasty Hind!) A letter came from Plane for Hind care of Plane. A book salesman from Boston left his engraved card in a tiny, invitation envelope. Final exam copy to be in in two weeks to ensure time for dittoing. Joint articulation committee to meet in special session. The elderly man winked and grinned and bobbed his head at Hind, and said, "Good morning, Member," but when Hind at last asked what indeed was the novelty in the departmental office that the man had alluded to in passing the day the boy with the olive-green attaché case had been in, the man merely turned his snicker up to a jolly, hysterical guffaw and pinched Hind's neck. The man appeared one day as Hind was just off to class and asked him to sign a petition demanding that three Liberian grad students be bailed out of a jail in a town identified only as Plotsburg; and Hind signed "Oliver S. Plane," and the man went away grinning over his shoulder at Hind.

Ol's almost illegibly scribbled letter from Mount Mary said, "You could have rested on your laurels. You needn't have subbed for me. The courses run manual *or* automatic. I left my people two impossibly long syllabi, one required, one optional. My people kept coming before you arrived and they will after you leave." These last few years, Oliver had changed. If his (possibly unaware) connection with the kidnap revival was all that could make him matter just now, Hind could see the time coming when OSP would have to be studied in depth quite independently of Hershey Laurel.

It was true, these students had kept coming even after Plane had stopped. But before Hind had turned up to supply the gap, no colleague, janitor, greenskeeper, or random clerk or dean had noted the two unmanned rooms, each occupied by a class quietly discussing. Nor had these summer students themselves reported Plane to any central offices or office.

Now here were multiple choices, strewn among seeming layers and layers of other people and ranks of function, inner and outer Temporaries, the new high-rise blue-brick Topless Tower Number Two, and at West Barrier Hind's ever-rising shed.

Stalking rather shyly to the greenboard to write something clearly upon it for his students to copy, Hind wondered if this part of the search forced him into the open: should he come out and ask Plane's pupils if they knew a certain name, or hypothetically what they'd do if confronted with, so to say, what Hind found himself confronted with? (And "confrontation" was a favorite with them.) Or he might chalk "Laurel" up, and tell them to compose relevant variations upon it for forty-five minutes. Not that he wasn't glad to guard Plane's position, meanwhile trusting that OSP would see the risk he ran with his professional life and return from Mount Mary.

Hind told Holly after class he regretted that in the brief time allotted him he could not contrive to know his students (in her words) "as people." To which she replied that it was important for him to know only the few who mattered. She touched his gray and brown silk tie, and as she did he became aware of its hotness at his perspiring neck.

One afternoon he went with Holly and two other girls in Holly's convertible Impala to the beach. They were plainly most concerned to see him in his trunks. (Holly said she liked to look up to her teachers.) He could make nothing of what the girls said, nothing to do with Hershey Laurel. He watched a war ostensibly waged a hundred yards up in the soft, offshore breeze: like triangles backing, Indian fighter-kites leashed by regulation abrasive cord hung out above the breakers, and the idea was to saw your friend's cord and snap his kite off. Holly told Hind confidentially, when her friends were screaming in the low surf, that in a day or so he'd be contacted about the advisory position her organization believed they could fit him into.

The beach held no answer, surf approaching on one front, parkway cars humming on the other. Hind now saw that this clue—roughly, number five of the revived kidnap—must occur on the campus grounds. Must come in among the simple building shapes, in the sticks of chalk that broke in his fingers as he addressed the greenboard with a flourish. But how did you keep your mind both on helping Oliver and pursuing Hershey, when undeniably the students were people, mere and fully.

As he left home in the morning, Hind read all that had come into his crenate-grilled mailbox, for he could never tell when the old woman or her agents might call again. He read the undertaker's mail misdelivered to himself. It often offered information he could not use. Champion San-O-Spray ("First in Fluids") could do many things: on the handout a giant clothespin cut through the words WHENEVER ODOR IS A PROBLEM... (the three elliptical dots dripped very precisely): San-O-Spray nips "post-mortem odors" and ought to be used to counteract "skin slip, tissue gas, ulcerated areas, gangrene, bed sores," effects of drowning, burning, maggots. Sears and Shirley Laurel received minimally effective care prior to cremation.

Hind was asked in another circular to buy Champion Embalmer's Surgical Soap (with hexachlorophene). Was the undertaker himself an agent of the kidnap revival? But he didn't react significantly when Hind gave him some of the misdirected mail. The trade embalmer at the union center now did Hind's undertaker's preparations for him. As for the hearse, you didn't bother to own it if you were a small undertaker; you let the Rent-A people have the worry, while you supplied merely your own silverized plaquettes for the second window on either side.

Business got good one humid weekend when American Legionnaires were all over the city shooting water pistols, and the undertaker had (as he said) a double-header, occupying both first- and second-floor parlors (a duplex funeral, a double-play); the smell of packed lilies and (albeit deodorized)carnations choking one another passed not only up to Hind's fourth-floor landing but under his door. Ivy's burglar got into her apartment the same weekend by blowing cigarette smoke under the door so she would infer fire and open up, but (so she told Dewey) she opened up because she smelled someone smoking a cigarette on her landing blocking her fresh air. The burglar girl—"I knew it, I knew it, I knew it! Think about a hippie busting into your place and it's bound to happen"—examined the afghan and took it, among other things.

From a northern island, a card from May in Sylvia's hand: "Dear Daddy, A bell rings at night when the fishermen come home. Tell Rain I can bait my own hook. Mommy says come here and see us. I love you. Love from everybody. May." He saw rocks, a landing, a boatless mooring, a sunspot on ruffled, unreasonably blue water: this was merely *near* where they were.

Everything might count, though anything that did must stem from or toward Oliver's college. (Ol was "staying" close to Sylvia's island.) On subway and bus, then bus and subway, approaching college, receding from it, you saw girls with slanted, petal-lensed sunglasses propped (floating, clamped) on high nests of backcomb. Even on days when the sky's normally jaundiced blue turned to heavy, distant, wintry cerulean (deeper and bluer even than Dr. Skoldberg's Sea Holly found, photographed, but not—God forbid!—snatched from an English beach thirty Julys ago) unfiltered even by the finest depths of industrial film, these girls (often students of Hind's) kept their glasses up like resting weapons or as if over other auxiliary eyes under the fragile hair.

In class one morning he alluded to certain circumstances of his quest—a legitimate illustration of his theme that science and art seek each other but because the aim of each is to appropriate the other the aims of the quest are ever misrepresented, rationalized, and swaddled in camouflage: "as when," said Hind (hoping to evoke something from anyone in the room who was in fact involved in the kidnap clue relay—yet moving covertly, true to the guardian's idea that teachers must efface their own histories from official discourse to pupils) as when a city-weary citizen seeks for his family a home in the country, a rural seat" (a simple lair) "ostensibly to give his child fresh green air and hills to run up and down, but really because he wants the country for himself."

Above Hind's PA system box a vent said, "Let me tell you about my first divorce and why my wife's doctor urged her to forgo alimony. Soon afterward I got into *this* game." The speaker moved away from his vent and his students suddenly laughed.

But as Hind proceeded to balance his veiled allusion to Sears Laurel with one to Shirley, a picture image in his head turned his words to barely murmured air, and the allusion to Shirley dissipated itself in the coincidence of two images: this morning, after racing for the bus and catching only its parting fumes and the huge laughing face of an overgrown child observing his frustration from the bus's back window, he discovered that right by the bus stop (he had never had to wait for this bus) was a marvelous candy store window: you bowed under the awning's fringe and stood close to the glass to watch the tilted and often open gilt gift boxes of chocolates, your eye shooting around, finding lines of triangulation in the ulterior disposition of boxes, half-catching in the glass the variously bare legs accumulating behind you at the bus stop, and then feeling the mouth-watering tickle in your eye as the iris shuttered inward and the pupil saw itself in the window glass, itself and its possessor there hunched under the upward-slanting awning: but here in class, thinking to draw some facial slip or token tic from a person included in this phase of his quest, he found himself drawn (aborted, shorted) from the Shirley allusion to the silent kinship between himself there at the chocolate window and the man in Boston seven years ago as described to Hind by the Lynnfield, Massachusetts, girl whom the police ultimately declined to locate: the olive-skinned lame girl in the fifth row was asking about "the dichotomy of Man" and he wanted to nab her on the misuse of "of" but had here first to finish, to finish (as if it were one of these new teacher-dreams he'd been having lately in which the pupillary fauna greeted him in class with "Good morning, Member," and he then gave each eager beanie-beaned hand a piece of himself until there was nothing visible left), yes finish his unexpected kinship with the man: the man whom that girl in Boston swore she saw with the crucial (Finnish-import) heather-green blanket (intended but way too big for the Laurel kidnapee), swore she saw pass out of Jordan Marsh (first pause at the pastry counter for something fancy), stop down Washington Street to stare into Black Magic's awninged bay casement at tilted coffers of chocolates—his eye variously exploring the caskets of brown candy now and then suddenly refined into bright gold nuggets—look fore and aft, hither and yon, as if to establish perspective lines and distance planes, an eye rhythm possibly caught from the lightly longly centrally swaying metronomous spring stalk with a giant menacing master candy shaped like a Hershey kiss, a great manufactured teardrop, a broad-based sack goldblooming topheavily above.

"Dichotomy *of* Man?" Hind asked. "Do you mean 'pertaining to' or 'belonging to'? And I wonder how easily the phrase came to your tongue."

"Not *so* easily," the lame girl said, staring at her ring binder and idly sweeping her ballpoint back and forth in one spot so she seemed to be drawing the plumage of some bird of paradise. She had heather-gray-brown hair cut short. "It didn't occur to me before."

"The 'of' is ambiguous, do you see?"

She shrugged her thin (her pathetic) shoulders, and her words sounded glum. "To you but not to me. Can you make a blanket judgment like that? I mean, how would *you* say 'dichotomy of man'? You made a blanket judgment. Can you make a blanket judgment like that, Mr. Plane? For all intensive purposes, the 'dichotomy of man' just means he's split."

Had he *spoken* words about the heather-green blanket? Surely no.

Did she think *he* was Plane—he'd merely introduced himself as Plane's temporary replacement, though not by name. Or did she think any and all who taught this section were called Plane?

In the vent above and behind, students' feet moved. Hind looked at the clock embedded in the wall at the far end of the long room. His class was over and he had a less obvious and therefore perhaps more likely lead now: the lame girl, Miss Rosenblum—*Mrs.*? like Holly's friend at the beach whom Hind had seen bending over a drinking fountain in the memorial library trying to float her contacts in?—no; Miss Rosenblum, with young bosom under a white man's shirt, with narrow nose and large hazel-violet eyes, moved slowly toward the lectern. Her lime-painted legs glimmered. But Grunewald, the loner who in his starchy cord suit always sat bobbing his crossed leg as if to keep time at the end of the front row farthest from the door and shook his head from time to time as he bent to remove or return papers from or to his black attaché case, and whenever Hind dropped a name nodded and smiled, was ahead of Miss Rosenblum, whose neck as she came near had an unwashed, olive sheen.

"I really must see you," Grunewald said; "it's about this class."

"Then see me," said Hind. Miss R stopped; were her eyes more violet than hazel? She limped past the lectern.

Hind was about to speak, but Grunewald, who had been unprepared before because he had been unable to get the assignment since he knew none of his classmates, now went on, in an eerily querying tone, "I believe faculty personnel are sometimes given to Aesopian language?" Rosenblum limped away, a boy held the door for her, "a warped slip" (as the guardian would say) "of wilderness," *virga lauri* (in Hind's arms which wished protectively to rise, and in the beginnings of a tepid sweat ringing his neck, was she a new genitive invitation?) her name seemed to be Laura, nostalgia's muse, the mind's warm hurry, he would check Plane's grade book, Rosenblum. How had she called Hind Plane? She had known Oliver.

"In case you missed my insinuation"–Grunewald accompanied his words with a tone of ambiguous joshing too theatrically subtle for him to bring off–"I think I heard Aesopian liberal-left lingo in what you said about sex vis-à-vis art."

Holly came through the door against the crowd of departing students. She was obviously looking for Hind, who said to Grunewald, "Yeah, every artist has to have a sex."

"That is," Grunewald droned, making an intrepidly transitional resumption, "you implied that freer views of sex were conditions for a great art here in these United States."

"I said, 'sexual love,' Mr. Grunewald," said Hind.

Grunewald brightened: "You know my name!" (He was implying, and wrongly, "You *like* me!")

"I'll see you during office hours Friday."

But Hind could not bypass Holly to the door.

"I'm taking you to organizational HQ," she said, her white shift shorter today, her body browner, her hair a no more natural but distinctly more complex bronze umber– ostensibly a person irrelevant to the Laurels.

Rosenblum, at her slow limp, could by now be in a dozen places on campus.

Grunewald called, "Didn't that perennial favorite Hawthorne grow up among the puritanical American people? What about that now?"

"He doesn't matter," said Holly, taking Hind's elbow.

Grunewald had had in the hand he rested on Hind's lectern an official university staff-issue pencil with the motto "Think and Suggest." He hung around the Humanities Department.

Rosenblum was nowhere Hind looked. "Here," said Holly, as they eventually turned down into a subbasement passage, and she stopped at a Dutch door, the bottom open, the closed top bearing a stenciled "CDNV."

"Congress of Demonstrative Non-Violence," she said, backing magically under and through.

"Pop can't see you today, but he has just given me word to pass on to you. At the demonstration Friday it will be necessary for you, as a temporary adviser, to keep an eye out for certain people we happen to know are secretly observing CDNV hoping to nail us. They say we've been ideologically kidnaped—get that, kidnaped!—by a front group and there's simply no telling what it may do, subvert our work, force us underground, even bring about academic expulsions which of course would be chalked up to poor grades or some other para-standard. You'll be told Friday what kind of person or persons to watch for. His theme is, after Lao-Tze, 'Why are the people so restless? Because there is so much government.'"

Typing and voices faded through the pale-green soundboard that sectioned this from the next student office up the passage. Under a grilled vent was taped a pastoral ad: zebra-striped car in foreground, neat-muscled zebra pony in background against dense high bush further back. A great exclamation mark snipped from a glossy dripped elegantly beside the ad. Stripes began to merge.

Through the vent dimly "—the milk white heifer stands for the poet's girl, that's what the seer of the night says..."

"The long and the short of it is, Pop's interested in you, thanks to my build-up," said Holly. "He has so much to do, he has to create and run off a leaflet for Friday, he may or may not contact you—"

"—heifer" (loudly and angrily from the vent) "is a *Christ* figure, according to Doctor mmmmm—"

"may or may not contact you," Holly raised her voice, staring calmly at the vent, "before the demonstration Friday."

Which that very afternoon was proved to have been true.

As Hind passed through the central campus Plazette short-cutting to the subway bus, he was reflecting why in the spaciously appointed Humanities Department office neither colleagues nor secretaries wondered who he was, and he was seeing the cinereally softened mid-city profile ten land miles away and above it a detached bomber which now tipped in the westering sun so that, as if a flowering link (no, a new season on a remote star) in the one dynaflow of the plane's process, a tiny silver fire exploded silently above and ahead of the snowy tracks of its exhaust.

A yellow bulldozer swung vigilantly into the Plazette from south to north, blade high, and a voice above the general mutter called at Hind's elbow, "Hey, Dr. Hind alias Plane." And Hind stuck his left arm straight out to the side to keep the voice from stepping into the bulldozer's path but thus put his elbow into the face the voice belonged to, which if it had been Ivy's face, would promptly have bitten his funny bone.

"Like a blind handshake," said Larry Poplar, as this short, chunky, pallid, broad-brimmed, mustachioed, booted, attaché-case-toting person now introduced himself.

"You know me," said Hind. Poplar frowned, and grabbed Hind's tricep, and made a snickering sound not through his nose but apparently by putting the back of his tongue against the roof of his mouth.

"Do we talk here–" nodding to one of the single-stemmed transparent benches–"or in my car?"

This was Pop, apostle of student power. Three buttons decorated the left breast pocket of his jean jacket. One said, STUDENT POWER; another, BELLY: the third, BUTTON. Suspended from blue and yellow Indian beads, his black iron cross danced against his chest.

"So," he said, "you're doing another man's work, eh?"

"That would be impossible. I do my own. Oliver Plane can't be truly replaced."

"You're pretty generous. *Too* generous. Why?" (Why *too*? or why *so*?)

"It's not generosity. I get something out of it."

"Oh I bet you do," said Larry Poplar, "a big tall guy like you. My cousin Laura's in your class. A little erotic graft."

"Surely not Laura Rosenblum. I've been especially struck by her, I'm going to know her better."

"Summer students take the course, not the man. But nowadays that's the case with all of us except the ones who get lucky at registration."

Pop stopped at an emerald Mustang convertible, then blew air out of his lips ironically, and said, "You thought you were traveling in style." They moved to the next car, a much-hammered blue-gray gray-blue machine with a sticker on the rear bumper that said, BUMPER STICKER.

"Fifth-hand 'sixty Falcon. Your funeral. I got this slot in the faculty lot by posing (with his assistance, of course) as an assistant professor who happens to be a nondriver but enabled me to get the decal he was entitled to. Do students, will students, can students, get college parking facilities, and half of them with better-looking cars than their own teachers? Not a chance!"

Larry drove as if on tiny booster rockets, but this tempo of jerk-accelerated follow-through-coast was due less to some deliberate dynamode than to sounds around him. A truck backfire jerked Larry's pedal foot down and Hind's head back. The truck passed on the right, the driver staring at Larry, and when it backfired wildly in Larry's face (as if to say get into the right lane) he again jammed the gas, and Hind's head again fell back. Ashley Sill's Desert Wagon had experimental head rests in case of whiplash.

"I got to get head rests," said Pop. "But about my cousin. You should listen to her, she's an independent, I can't get her into CDNV, she'll give you a lead or two if you listen to her in class, she's an original, with her trick leg. You guys have inside tracks on a lot of stuff."

"What kind of lead?"

"New light on your area, field, or special interest. With students you never know when a spontaneous insight may relate to your research. And yeah, what *are* you up to—I mean, in terms of background? Do you think the university is a place where things are remembered, the past recaptured?"

"What leads am I going to get from Laura Rosenblum?" Hind asked. She was surely part of the CDNV and very likely of its no doubt unwitting role (agency, finger) in the Laurel case.

"Let's talk in terms of Friday and our root rationale. This quasi demonstration will look like a student power-play around left end. But in fact we mean to expose those who are shadowing us and hoping to subvert the movement; Holly has told you all that you need to know. What I want you to do is at the q-d look for an older visitor or visitors; at least one will be posing as a faculty member and may be wearing a green-on-gray seersucker suit. That is all we know. It is interesting to me that you agreed so precipitately to the proposition passed on by Holly. But very tall guys in my experience come either very cunning or very simple. Others, of whom of course you don't know, will also be surveilling the demonstration. We need all the men we can get. You'll be notified about a poetry reading later. This term our entire secretarial staff is in Spain on an incredibly banal sell-out live-in-a-family summer language program. They gave us no warning. Europe is how you have her. I had Europe last summer. Maybe I kissed no girl on the roof of Milan Cathedral, but I found what I discovered I was looking for unbeknownst to myself, on a prohibited pier in Ostend, a night in August—rainy to be exact."

Hind wouldn't be in those profound, oxblood-bright boots for all the suburban security jammed into the expressway's outgoing lanes which Pop was now passing so fast on this in going side. "I was in reality looking for myself." Pop stared at Hind steadily for four and a half seconds. "I stood on the pier looking out and wondering exactly what country I was looking toward but then it came to me. I was really looking for myself and there I was looking at myself looking out to sea. Well, it came to me then. Student power. *Student power.* Self-rising power if there be a self to rise it. And I say to you, whoever you really are, once you've seen this you bear always the burden of its sight. And, as Laura says, you can't unsee it." (Unquote John Hind.)

*"Whoever I am?"*

"A figure of speech. I know next to nothing of your background."

Hind wished to correct Pop's phrase "its sight," but wished to rouse his suspicions no further. But not knowing the relative validities of Holly's Roebuck-Sears, Laura's blanket-blanket, and Larry's Laura links, Hind had to play someone else's game in order to have his own.

"I'd like to know more about your program for student power. I certainly believe that students need some *kinds* of power."

"I anticipated you would want to watch our plans."

"Why can't you get your cousin Laura to join?"

"Actually she's of no significance in the movement." Finding himself too close to the microbus in front, Pop absentmindedly swerved left around it without checking either of his rear-vision mirrors. "She is of *personal* significance to me."

"The movement toward student power. O.K. But power to do what?"

"You persist," said Larry. "Oh, say, power to Minox-photograph a faculty member's greenboard diagrams of, say, how to unlearn Renaissance perspective."

*Hind's* greenboard! So this was one of their methods: that he, Hind, should effectively act this stage of the kidnap by having the power to find the truth in *their* reflections of *him!* "My class is open," said Hind, lest Pop think the point had not taken. "But again, power to do what?" Hind hoped a mask of stern inquisitiveness would barely suggest the sincere concern simulated beneath.

"Power to *be*. To be considered, to be known, not lost. Hence, power in other sectors, areas, complexes."

"Power over tenure?"

"Faculty tenure? Who *are* you, one of Groveland Cleaver's plants?"

"Tenure generally," said Hind. As President of the Student Senate, Cleaver sought to modify demands for a student voice in teacher tenure.

Unaccountably Pop goosed the car to fifty-five and the front end shivered.

"What you want me to say? Student tenure? I'll say it then: student tenure."

"What do they want to hold onto?"

"Power to stay on as long as desired."

"Desired by whom?"

"I'm sorry," said Larry, emerging from the interborough tunnel's simplicity to the great tower-shadowed floor of the mid-city by Hind's Sunday handball courts. "I detect Aesopian diversionism here. I'm sorry. There's a lot of good in you. Your chance to prove your relevance to us will be Friday, of course."

Two cars behind were honking as Hind got out; and (like a Russian celebrity applauding himself, like Berry Brown joyfully jumping into the river after Ivy Bowles, like the guardian that summer night of the farewell party going out into the sea to swim only after everyone else had come in out of the water and when the nefarious, fully primed Jap was chanting his plagiarized "Green, green, how I love you, green") Pop thrice pressed his Roaring Twenties "AH-OOO-GAH" horn, and an old Negro messenger, shoulders rounded over his portfolio, stopped halfway across without looking either way and went back to the curb from which he'd come.

"Six-volt horn, paid by deductible contributions to CDNV, ten dollars fifty cents at Sears! Now *there's* some evidence you might use against us."

Pop gassed his Falcon and was pressed back against his seat, and this made him, pulling away, look like a little old man barely governing his newfangled contraption. Pop reached the light as it went red, but sneaked screeching round the corner ahead of a gunning, honking front of cars going south.

How the guardian loved in the old days to drive from college town to college town seeking opportunities to give advice, brooking no distractive noise in the car, no talk, no radio (there was none to play), swiftly cornering a town-square war monument, a proud driver overshifting, seldom braking.

A blue whirlybird rattled straight across the yellow sky.

Laura, Pop, Holly, CDNV, the college, the vents, Hind's expanding office-and-classroom shed with the crane pivoting outside the window—and possibly even Oliver Plane's railroad flat—would all somehow bespeak the relevance of this stage to the kidnap revival.

Carmen La Grange blinked out of the television cool in which he had sat all through the heavy summer day. The undertaker's new air conditioner whirred; on a low table at the far end of the room Mrs. Knott's cat dozed before the TV as if at a cozy window.

"Your wife's letter got delivered to us," said Carmen, pointing to the undertaker's desk—Sylvia's high, art-school hand among the circulars. Everybody needed Hind. Laura Rosenblum's game leg was the left, Cassia Meaning's the right.

When he left on Friday for school, thinking about his lecture, about the guardian's perhaps lifelong obsession with misuses of the possessive "of," about the upcoming conference with lonely Grunewald, and about who could be the "old friend of his father" Smith Answering said had called, he still had not opened Sylvia's note, though he carried it with him.

Grunewald missed class but then was waiting for Hind in what Plane called the Hall of Cubicles. In a crisp cord suit and standing richly in shoe-backed English sandals that all but hid glistening white socks, Grunewald was looking over the milky glass into Hind's nook.

There, as it turned out, Larry Poplar sat with a boot up on the desk. He lowered it to the blue electroacrylic rug, dropped an elbow on the edge of the desk, and in welcome all but nodded Hind to the straight-backed conference chair. "There anything you want to be refreshed on before the q-d?"

"Get out, Mr. Poplar," said Hind as Pop tried to murmur "Quasi demonstration." Hind nodded to Grunewald, who nodded formally to Pop, who rose.

Larry squinted at Hind and at Grunewald, tilting his head, then coolly reached down for his attaché case without looking at it, but had to reach a long way because it had fallen on its side. Softly he said to Hind, "Oh, I get it. One of GC's plants?" He must mean Grunewald was one of Groveland Cleaver's men.

Hind nodded abruptly, just to get Pop out, who said as he went, "You've got a date with Laura, don't forget yours with me." Laura? Hind had no date with Laura.

In this floor's corporate honeycomb of cubicles, there was also a widthwise vestibule where students must wait till their conference numbers came up—voices reached you depending on distance, direction, volume, height of projection, and amount (if any) of interference from the green-grilled vents.

Grunewald was requesting a definition of a C plus, again with menacing earnestness elucidating his lovingly possessed complex qualification that of course it was not basically the grade he cared about. The only time Hind had seen him even address another student had been to show a paper Hind had handed back. That time, Grunewald got only a curt nod. He was eccentrically well dressed, his costume so formally full that Hind was extra careful in his lecture.

But now Hind was reading the least impressive passage of Grunewald's essay and discovering a dense scent
of violets he thought must come from the head whose
shape his eye's far corner barely embraced, and this had
to be Laura. Grunewald kept interrupting Hind's reading
with "But I am a conservative, Mr. Plane, I mean Hind."
And Hind silently continued: "A case in point is John
Dos Passos's latest book, *Occasions and Protests*. John is
considered by many, including Jean-Paul Sartra and off-
shoots of his ilk, to be the best American writer of the
twentieth century—my century. But merely because John
leans toward the conservative rather than the liberal-left
light, British novelist John (an ironic coincidence that it
is another John) Quill condemns the book. I personally
dissent with the opinions of the muckrakers, but I still
revere the talent of Frank Norris: criticism must be free
of overmuch political prejudice."

The head of Laura had gone away, perhaps to the Waiting Vestibule, though Hind would never have enforced
the rule. Hind was explaining the difference between the
"of" after "talent" and the "of" after "free." Running out
of viable comments and wishing to lower the grade, Hind
asked Grunewald for the time, then proceeded to read
the closing paragraph aloud: "'I must end this monograph
on a sad note. Dr. Plane, I don't like to discuss religion or
sex—'"

"I'm sorry," said Grunewald, "Dr. Plane—I mean Dr.
Hind, I meant to revise the name."

"'—for to discuss it is to get personal. But'—dot dot dot—
'no, Dr., and I quote your class comment of a fortnight
ago: 'freer views of pornography and sexual love' will, I
dissent, not help solve the great, and I may add grating,
art problem in the United States. Did not the highly
proper Victorians raise Dickens and Tennyson? Didn't
those perennially fruitful chestnuts Hawthorne and

Edward Taylor grow in puritanical soil? Yes, Mr. Hind, *vive* the right to dissent! but not from G-d. For the right to rebel-rouse and to grow an unweeded garden of bastard hybrids aren't necessary'" (The reigning miscegenative metaphor horrid: but on what playground could you meet Grunewald except verb-subject agreement or dissonant contractions?) "Mr. Grunewald, this is nearly insane."

"Insane!" Grunewald stood up.

"I should have failed you. Compassion and curiosity about your use of the possessive case deluded me."

"You *have* failed me, Hind, Plane, whoever you are. You *have* failed me in terms of relationships."

"To make any sense of your essay, one must pick and choose almost as if what you've submitted were a sort of jumbled vocab from which one might assemble almost anything."

Furthermore, the essay was bizarrely irrelevant to the kidnap revival.

"I'm sorry to have to say this," said Grunewald, as the head of Laura–Hind looked right at her–again appeared above the partition, "but Dr. Hind, my fellow students are not following you in class. The major part of them won't be blunt enough to come out and tell you that your notes on Nietzsche's *The Genealogy of Morals*–the Bad Air passage particularly–didn't come out clear at all, and you tend to snatch up from a student's answer just what you can use rather than deal in terms of the response as an organic whole. I tell you this for your own good. I am privy to their sentiments. Speaking on behalf of my fellow students, you don't get across."

"You represent the students, do you?"

Laura's head disappeared below the edge and her shadow sank slowly down below where the milk glass ended and out of sight below the lower, green-steel base section. She was sitting in the aisle. He'd have to help her up.

"They're my fellow students," said Grunewald.

"And you are their hypocrite. You have almost no contact with the others in that class. I've never seen you speak to one of your so-called fellow students. I don't see that we have anything more to talk about. Come back when you've cleaned up that essay." Hind opened the envelope he'd found on Plane's desk and noted the time and place of the poetry reading Pop had warned him of.

"But," said Grunewald, appearing to try slowly to understand, "I cut my job at the Ivy Haberdasher today in order to have a good hour or two with you, go over what's been happening in class this term, what Mr. Plane did the day I cut, ekcetra. I've only had twelve minutes." He whipped his gold wrist band up as if for protection, and Hind noted the miniature transistor at his belt next to the leatherette pen-and-pencil case. "And my employer had to take delivery on a large shipment of CPO jackets this morning all by himself. You don't know what *our* problems *are*, Professor: you're so far above them, Vietnam, one's future, marriage and the family, crisis in suburbia, job application, the Bomb. You haven't a clue—" Grunewald talked on. Laura had Cassia Meaning's face. The question was whether Laura was a means of indicating CDNV, or Pop a means of indicating Laura. This became (as Grunewald now again said) "crucial," because the quasi demonstration was on in a matter of minutes. Hind had forgotten to wind the clock at home and when he had waked promptly at quarter to seven the clock had in fact been stopped at yesterday's quarter to seven and after breakfast and a review of unused "Naked Voice" tapes he had glanced at it and thought it said twenty-five to nine when indeed the hour was much later.

Grunewald was looking in over the glass as Laura sat diffidently down. "I bet she doesn't get short shift like me."

"I bet she doesn't," said Hind without looking directly at Grunewald.

Grunewald muttered some more as Hind carefully began his unscheduled conference with Laura.

"I'm glad you brought your paper." Large eyes, long narrow tense mouth.

"Otherwise we'd have had nothing to talk about? Quote unquote?"

"Unquote whom?" (But she was smiling, happy to be here.)

"The other man who taught our class."

"Mr. Plane, that is."

"If you say so. I'm beginning to wonder."

"You think he wasn't Mr. Plane?"

"I heard a lot of things."

"From your cousin Larry Poplar?"

"You might say so. You're a real quizzer, aren't you? Whoever that prof was I liked him. He didn't stick to the point, exactly; but he knew his beans. And he was ruthless." Laura's violet eyes were watering.

"Let's look at your theme." Perhaps in her revisions.

"How come you're substituting for him?"

"He's a friend, an old old friend. I'm helping him out. He's not well."

"So where's he recuperating?"

"At home, of course."

"I didn't get any answer when I called."

Why phone Oliver? To see if he had put Hind onto the college clue or clues?

"Look, Laura," Hind pointed to a sentence, "pull your chair around."

She seemed to doubt him. So did her cousin Pop. Yet was their doubt precisely the means the tall old woman used to employ them? and was the point just that Hind must convincingly identify himself to them? Or, as he had thought, was the point of any dropped clue unknown to the dropper, the blanket reference merely a new lead that came onto Laura's tongue through prior, perhaps never-to-be-known, forces?

"Look over here: your pluperfect has been taken over by your past tense, and over there your conditional too. And you use 'of' ambiguously, don't you."

She stared at the page and very very slowly nodded. "You giving the final or your friend?" Was this as irrelevant as the question of the rather suspicious fellow in the back row of Holly's class, who stuck up his hand in the middle of Hind's discussion of Dürer's surface and asked how to get to emergency exit B?

"I don't know yet." Her arms seemed as fragile as May's. In Laura's life, someplace deep in its motion, was a finer clue, a different kind this time. And so he must find her secret.

Yet Holly Roebuck's invitation must mean that Laura's depths would be entered only at the level of, in the total context of, in terms of, Pop's CDNV q-d now only minutes away.

Well, Hind would take her to the Plazette, stick with her while looking for the green-on-gray seersucker, then take her home for dinner at the undertaker's.

"This possessive case perspective really sends you up, doesn't it." Her left foot moved back and her right toe sneaked behind it.

"But wait—" Hind touched her wrist and she looked up with eyelids half-lowered either languid or sad, not stupid, and perhaps because she sensed herself being, inevitably, used. "The possessive problem has almost nothing to do with the case of perspective."

She smiled. "And what do *they* have to do with Humanities 5A?"

"If I get the time I'm going to lecture on that. On the relation between ambiguous language and the need to unlearn perspective in order to see things flat, as they are on canvas and really to the eye. It's so hard to unsee, that we assume we oughtn't to try. But you came here to discuss your paper on urban ecology."

"Not exactly. I was talking with my cousin, who I don't always believe what he says, and from what *he* said I thought I should see you." She wasn't smiling any more but she had something in her eyes. "I can't *unsee* you, can I?" (She was delicate-chested.) "Any more than I can unsee myself or unsee the subway or unhear sounds through three walls of our apartment." Was she drifting into autobiographical irrelevance? Someday there would be time for that. "It's a beautiful high-rise, the Ironwood Arms—"

"Ironwood? *What* did your cousin say that brought you here?"

"—with palms on top and an official-length pool and sauna under the basement, but through one wall—"

"—of the sauna? do you hear things from or in the sauna?"

"Oh no, I never went near it, what good's a sauna to me? I swim, for my leg."

"But Cousin Larry?"

"Through one wall you hear every five minutes Mr. Trellis's musical clock he brought home from his European tour where he lost his wife, or she lost him; through another wall Mr. and Mrs. Sundeen sunk deep in their matching wing chairs—"

"You've seen the chairs?"

"Believe me, I don't have to. Everybody in Ironwood Arms is the same. Same corner couches, same secret-compartment bed-headboards—but the Sundeens arguing, and flipping the TV channel so fast you'd think they had two remote selectors instead of one. But I think sometimes they're not yelling at each other but at the channel. The only thing keeps them both quiet is the last four holes of the golf Saturday and Sunday. Mr. Sundeen says, like, 'He swings from left to right to allow for the little hook and the woods.'"

Distinguish between accident and necessity.

"But Cousin Larry?"

"I thought you wanted to hear about where I live. I didn't tell you the third wall. Two brothers, their parents hate them, they scaled the Ironwood Arms one Sunday, it was in the newspaper, didn't you see it? They were interviewed in the Golden Penthouse on the top."

"It's late, I'm afraid. I have to go across campus. Would you like to limp along–*come* along–" Just when he wanted exactly to keep her–and thus combine her possibility with Larry's and the demonstration's–you said–had said–"limp."

"My cousin said you said quote unquote, 'I've been specially struck by her, I'm going to know her better.' Today we didn't even talk about my paper. And you didn't let me finish about my neighbors at Ironwood Arms, the third wall–."

She was up, at, and through the cubicle entrance.

"Wait, I'm with you." The third wall, it was the third wall, Ken Love's but partially erected third wall, Beulah's phrase, Ken's desire, Shirley's device, Sears' resisted possession.

"You don't want me to know you, you don't want to know *me*." Laura spoke above the milk glass partition. "I'm sorry I bored you telling you what I overheard through the three walls. Obviously you gotta have a special appointment for a conference with you. I don't have the patience to be your student." Student *of* you. Meaning what? "The other prof was different."

"Laura dear, wait!" But the elderly colleague with the blond briefcase stood frowning and said, "Hi, can I help? She seemed a most unhappy kid. Ah well, if the Student cannot receive what we offer him, we must modify our offerings or risk failure, nay, impotence."

"The third wall," said Hind. "Behind the third wall."

"Coming to the cafeteria, Member?"

Outside, Laura was already out of sight. Did time periodically pause for others but not for Hind?

But when he caught sight around the corner of Holly Roebuck remonstrating with Laura, he felt there was plenty of time.

When they saw him they separated and Hind followed Laura. Glancing at her watch she began to move faster, almost a run, with a wonderfully animal difference he had never seen before. But she was moving into the Old College, the buildings phased for the President's trimesterly (triwesterly?) demolitions—and therefore Hind was being drawn off the direct route to the demonstration. But now at a key fork in the asphalt path at which an Oriental girl and an occidental boy were Frisbeeing their green plastic plate with a good dreamy float back and forth, and ten miles off the mid-city profile received the noon summer sun softened by a number two haze as if a billion bees had sprung a billion delicate laurel filaments, throwing out a full atmosphere of pollen dust, and far to Hind's right among smudgy shouts an amplified voice at the Plazette went "One, two, three, four, five," he had lost Laura. She could have gone right, thus toward the demonstration, or left, toward the new athletic building, where she took Girls' Scuba Diving for credit. The Frisbee-ers looked at him apprehensively. Classes would let out in a second and a thousand kids would come into this network of asphalt paths set upon a mass of forbidden grass. Pop probably didn't know of the kidnap, merely felt (like so many other students in other ways) that he'd been taken and put to strange use, wondered how the hell he could get to see his teachers when he must take a numbered card and wait standing in an electri-carpeted, noise-damped corridor, when he had to line up for an hour at Registration Center and like the blond teeny b. already weeping in nervous expectation to be at last told that the course he wanted was filled up, and when looking at all his quote unquote horizons he saw furious competition (from his Generation!), saw also his personalized and chem-sprayed roots, saw wild super-roads jammed, crawling, fully mobilized with mile-a-minute mobile homes whoosh homes whoosh homes. How could Oliver not feel these were his people, who needed him? Pop and all the rest were like the soccer teammates years ago whom Hind protected from deep in the fullback slot. And all Pop could poorly do was act out what little he felt was his own of the tape-script pregiven him—no more his own man than was Maddy Beecher: and remembering the Santos-Dumont Sisters Juxtaposition Division panel truck seen on campus twenty-four hours ago in a normally pedestrian path driven through only by the President's cab, Hind, at the Frisbeeing fork puzzling where Laura would have gone, looked in the direction of S-D (less than two miles to the south-southwest) as if some long S-D eye could burn through this old red-tiled, stucco-corniced Humanities wing from the Thirties, which blocked his view (done in Temporary Spanish, and, strangely, housing the A-to-J lecture rank of the Spanish Department night session). If Pop was telling the truth, Hind owed him the introductory allegiance asked and offered. According to the subway change booth man, Newton said an effective—here, the kidnap revivalist or revivalists—can act only in terms of the powers of what receives its action: and only Hind here could help Pop (and/or Laura) receive.

"If you receive, Hindie, you reverse off to Lief." That dim oral pasture of the past could never lose itself in the beeping, cross-communicating stretches of Hind's mind. Trying very simply to hold onto his old body, poor old Buddy Bourne tried too hard to clean two hundred fifty pounds on a day when he was hung over and as a result henceforth walks as if perpetually in a football huddle.

Given the Pop situation, this was what Sylvia would want Hind to do. He now broke into a run and cut between the Frisbee-ers, and to protect his neck he had to grab the green dish in mid-float, and first darting, dodging, loping with slow-stretching speed down a side path he to save time hurdled the warning chain onto grass taking the shortest way to the demonstration with the Frisbee saucer tucked along his right (lately unexercised) flexor muscles like a two-dimensional football.

Bells rang behind him, classes were out.

In the Plazette Holly pinched his arm and smiled up at him, then passed back into the crowd. Students pushed by at his chest level. His height was making him less noticeable, instead of more; and this would help him to do what he had to do.

Larry Poplar, on a low platform so he stood at about Hind's height, called for student power. He spoke with the authority of a series of rhetorically parallel sentences, naming, though with the pathetic poverty of the bureauclinically vague labels that were all he had to work with, the official places student power must invade.

"We must, will, shall, assert student power in the Cross-Disciplinate Planners Council. We must, will, shall, assert student power in the Inter-Departmental Tenure-Perspective Board and on the President's Task Force Regarding Make-Up Examinational Formats."

Nowhere could Hind make out Holly in the mixing mob, the stirring students, the breathing body; and nowhere Laura. But he could not make out a single eye turned toward him despite his height. No one knew he was hunting Holly, Laura, Pop's alleged seersucker green-on-gray, or, in effect, Hershey. As his eyes searched, Hind as if *with* them recalled the front window of the lead subway car the Saturdays of the children's concerts the guardian sent him to: your hands and shoulders behind you (the compartmented motorman an isolated authority on your right) as you let the train prove for you the dark-lit, loud, city-made earth of the rapid tube like—oh yes, so like—a pneumatic message (receipt? change?) in the Boston or New York department stores where the guardian took child Hind on shopping trips whose aim was to buy in one two-hour go Christmas presents for every person the guardian wished to remember. But return to the point, while Poplar talks. Those Saturdays in the lead subway car your eye (if you were not being badgered by kids who wanted to get where you were) saw nothing to prove it part of anything else, for it couldn't see your arms or legs, much less mouth or ears or forehead (unless with that mouth-watering turn of the inward-shuttering iris your pupil saw itself and you, smudged in the glass). Sylvia believed Hind wanted to feel this disembodiment. She knew too much, but knew it crudely. You were adopted; you owed your guardian immense gratitude; if you could disembody, then no one (including yourself) could possess a lien on you or your future. Unquote Sylvia.

New masses filled the Plazette and kept moving, always moving—diagonads and zigzags and elusive curls—snatching phrases of Larry's quasi-demonstration-address, but mostly just passing through headed to or from cafeterias or distant unoccupied single-stemmed fiberglass benches, parasols up flashing their strawberry cross-sections, daisies, op-dots, or damplashed Cyclop eyes.

"Let's look at the history of the problem," said Pop. "How did our classrooms come to receive these phlegmatic predators, these genteel pneumatic prof-ettes, not searchers but researchers? Faculty and Administers, they ask me what do we—you and me—want to hold onto that we can't." Holly pushed past Hind staring radiantly into his face, and Hind captured her hand just as Larry spotted them. Holly moved away. Many on the Plazette's north side were leaving for the cafeteria and vanishing points academic. Somebody said, "Can't the Joint Deans think up better Free-Hour entertainment than this?"

Pop repeated, "I ask you how dare the Authority hire and fire? how dare it remove the few bristling young men who matter? Are we going to bear our imminent powerlessness? Need it be ever thus? We might rest upon laurels could we find any. Ha! But soon our rose will bloom again, self-rising up the trellis of our discontent, and in ultimate terms over the wall which our two enemy forces, Faculty and Authority, have builded against our tendencies."

Larry was looking again at Holly, it was easier to see her, the crowd thinned: yet he was looking not exactly at her but toward a cluster of people of which she was a part.

Rest on Laurels (rest!), rose, bloom, trellis, third force, wall! Pop simply could not know how Hind's heart answered.

"Are we going to bear our imminent powerlessness?" A tactically too long pause faintly crackled through the electronic throat into which Pop continued audibly to breathe.

"Please, sir, could I have our Wham-O back?" said the Oriental girl smiling with intolerable good humor. "My friend's an exchange student and you're a professor and like he was scared to ask you for it back." She giggled.

But there Laura was! In the group Pop was looking at. Laura, turning from Larry to look at an argument Holly was having with the young man with the olive-green attaché case who had interviewed Hind and subsequently been spotted lurking in one of the Underway corridors where the CDNV office was located.

"The roots of a university's virtue and potency are its students. And there are those among us this very moment who would overthrow the work by which CDNV... works for a new balance of power." Power's balance.

Holly said, "Will you leave me alone, once and for all alone?"

"My Frisbee."

"–among us one who has planted himself here ostensibly as a faculty member when in reality he is working–"

Hind would kill two birds, Laura was now aware of him, Plane might well be exposed if Hind were, and Holly was now in effect being molested by the olive-green attaché case; in the now bright yellow heavens there was for a series of moments a steel-hued blinking (like TV interference, a new daytime brand of northern lights, or the flickering corps of Santos-Dumont remote control service copters running a stretch of sky less thickly hazed): a diversionary maneuver was called for.

"He's got my Frisbee!"

"Hands off her," said Hind, striding to the group. But the young man's hands were not on Holly, he was merely talking to her.

"The man *I* mean, of course," called Larry Poplar, "is the tall man yonder. His name is Plane and he is posing as a–"

"I'm sorry," said Laura, as he caught and held her eye, "I didn't mean to be crazy this morning. Actually Larry's been bugging me. He likes me."

"Let's get out of here," said Hind, and taking her wrist managed to move with remarkable rapidity away and off to the exit well that was centered beneath the new reinforced concrete umbrella whose hyperparaboloid structure provided the Meditation Shelter and Underway. He was looking at himself pursuing the kidnap for years. The child is getting older, the kidnapers themselves are getting on, the usual key alterations take place, school, new sports, summer jobs, new fields. Then one day the boy—the budding hero Hind was to save, his hair now long now short but ever the heather shade inherited from Sears—gets married. So where does that put Hind? Well, still chasing, if the chase isn't over. Here the boy's carried off a girl; she's from, it happens, the very urban village the kidnapers once holed up in: same low, lucidly disposed shopping center, same new A-frame Episcopal (that seems to leave the rest of some conventional church under the brilliant turf), same new Industrial Park occupied by—what does Hind do? Walk into her clear kitchen where she's leaning agilely against her push-button range confronting a Penguin recipe, and tell her, "Your husband Hershey Laurel is a kidnapee!" Yes indeed: when ultimately hunted down (or up), what shape is your quarry in?

And as he tailed Laura hastily into the first curve of the well spiral knowing again that the kidnapers had been after neither ransom nor blood, he looked back and could see strolling forth from the edifice-framed flat backdrop of the now much less crowded Plazette toward this exit well, as if acknowledging his upward progress, none other than the tall, dark-eyed, white-haired, long-limbed messenger woman in a spanking crisp green-on-gray seersucker, her skirt amply below the knee.

Well, the new-dimensional action was now his. Let the old girl follow *him*, and as his hand reached down not quite far enough to touch Laura's gentle shoulder, he thought that maybe the old woman had in fact or effect never been ahead of him, but behind, and that ahead of him had always been some subtle space.

There was not much conversation in the cab to the subway; nor in the subway itself (which was too loud for Hind to do more than merely point through the (then) elevated's unholy racket toward Bella Church's green-tarpaper and her doughty yard and this outlying maimed branch of that great mid-city department store where a certain tall man (a subway-token-size mole on his upper lip the color of the Black Magic chocolates he admired in Boston) had bought two identical bean-bags seven going on eight years ago); nor did Hind and Laura talk much on the platform passing up to local level (though Hind, imagining Laura might know what the Orientals had written, did pause to show her the new (however) utterly delaminated map with (yet) multifarious hints of quests, chronicle, psychic distance, and urban idyl).

At the undertaker's street's intersection with the fuming, turgid northbound avenue, a great pink-stemmed herring gull stood lost upon the centrally hung traffic light. Hind pointed it out, and Laura seemed to shake her head. If the ancient salt couldn't penetrate the city's fly ash and sulphur and its colorless skins and flesh of divinely deodorized carbons, these kids could at least know they lived in the uncast shadow of the ocean. Yet they'd skip off to France or bus to a pine cabin or a crowded mountain lake. Yes, where was this sea in their lives? And even like Holly and the kite-men they might go to the beach, tan their bodies or wage aerial war, yet never feel that old scalp-stinging salt thing as more than a spumy, turquoise strip of dramatic furnishing defined by red-letter undertow warnings or a beachboy's thermometer. When Hind's late guardian swam the waves he all but drank them—like Hind he would twist and flip under

the water as if doing slow-motion dives, and would sometimes seem as if he was never coming out, and the child
Hind would stand shivering on a slope of the guardian's
private sand and call to him to come out.

The white-haired undertaker's black jacket hung folded over his white-sleeved arm; he was looking up and
down his street and chatting with Heather Fordham,
whose head was turbaned in a white towel. At sixty he was
in as good shape as the guardian at fifty. Beside Heather
was little Rain holding the Knotts' cat on its extensible
leash. A car parked in front pulled out and Carmen La
Branche appeared instantly from the business entrance,
trotted to where Hind and Laura stood, and swung the
undertaker's blue Boa out and (barely two feet from the
line of parked cars) backed her seemingly in one shot to
the newly vacated space. The undertaker got in, Heather
and Rain waited between two cars for a cab to whisk by
and then crossed the street to the Fordhams' side, and
Rain called, "Hi, Jack, Heather brought me from Play
School. How's May?"

"She wrote me to tell you she can bait her own hook,"
Hind called back. Laura smiled, Rain's small, busybody
voice enjoying the distance came again from across the
street: "We don't have fishing at Play School." Laura
brushed him as they walked; he shortened his pace,
addressing Rain: "She leaves her own *special* hook in a *tree*
overnight, isn't that funny?" No rise out of Laura.

"Yeah," said Rain almost inaudibly from the other side
of the street.

Heather Fordham said nothing and didn't look.
Probably because of Laura.

The undertaker had his motor running, was staring
straight out the windshield, and was apparently listening
to the helicopter traffic report. Without looking at Hind
he said, quite low, "How they hangin'?" He wouldn't have
said that in the presence of Sylvia.

The right answer, vegetable, arboreal, was two in a bunch, but Hind said, "The ceiling man still hadn't come as of early this morning. Did he come today? I left my upstairs key with Carmen."

"I may have to come up there and plaster it myself," said the undertaker quietly, grinning at Laura, who shifted her weight and again brushed Hind. "Haven't seen a stiff since middle of June," he said. "But you do all right for yourself."

In the crenate-grilled mailbox there was an envelope from Oliver postmarked a rather long four days ago "Mount Mary Station" (the train had in fact been discontinued two years ago, everyone flew up or came by car): Hind sent Laura up the stairs ahead of him and had a look at the note: "Forgot one stray term paper in flat. Should be on mattress under geologic survey map that used to be on the wall I and Mad's friend tore down."

The dishes in the rack were dusty. Laura remained ambiguous: she examined May's fiery crayon original in the kitchen, yet gave also the feeling that she was indifferent and tentative; looked at all the plants Sylvia had left, yet let her eyes seem to keep moving in some complicated circuit that would end upon an event, a surprise, a means of leading Hind in at last to the heart of the revived kidnap.

"No air conditioner?"

"House is eighty years old," said Hind. "You'd have to put money into rewiring and the place is only rented—"

"A whole top floor," Laura cut in, stepping urgently to the living room window, the back side of the apartment. She would be seeing six backyards, three from Hind's undertaker's street, three from the one a block south. There would be a woman playing her guitar beside a large brazier on wheels; there would be a man—it was just time—cautiously holding open the lid of a large box in which there were some restless, broken-winged pigeons; there would be a woman—it might be too late—helping her husband erect a complex canvas roof-and-pipe-support system, they'd been at it for several days.

The phone began to ring.

"Leave it," said Hind.

"How can you stand to?"

"My answering service picks it up after it rings eleven times. Then I get the full breakdown later tonight."

"If I could have my own place, I'd live in a quiet section like this with far-out gift-shops and antique brass beds on the sidewalk in front of the antique shops. I'd live in a quiet brownstone on the top floor like this, and people would come to see me, not like seven point two miles out the expressway and you need a map to tell which high-rise is yours even though you live in it with your own parents."

Another lame duck like Julio Loggia? "You feel trapped?"

"You have almost as many records as my mother." The kids didn't call them LP's any more. "She's appreciating fugues and concerti all the time, it's fantastic, I mean literally, she takes a course in the adult program but they don't have listening rooms for the adult ed so she has to listen at home on our stereo. I love the listening room. The old man I have in Music Five that they can't retire because of a technicality that he talks about a lot but never explains exactly what it is says listening in solitude is one of the essential luxuries in the kind of society The Enemy is breeding, he says. It's a chance to get away from home and kicking the ball around in class, where everybody gets a chance—and home is an acoustic hell, if there is a hell—but look at the vents also, not only in the new buildings but in the old—I heard a voice coming from a vent in the ladies' john last week, the vent's connected to the number two capacity lecture room two floors up: this professor was saying in a low, low voice, so low I thought he must have slowed up his rpm, 'Significant intercourse demands flexibility,' then a pause for note-taking, and I didn't hear a peep out of his students and I wondered if he was alone up there. Now what course could that be?"

Laura picked up a pink-and-white Ravel and read the jacket's back. "This is a radio announcer's godsend. My father took a course in TV servicing because he doesn't like people coming into our house, and we have such a big screen there's always something, or *was* always something, wrong with it, and now my father is taking another course in TV servicing, a refresher even though he just finished the first. So he services our TV's, the baby portable in the kitchen too, while my mother is playing Ravel's"–Laura looked at Hind with an utter neutrality that challenged and even alarmed him, she was getting ready to say something important–"Ravel's what-you-m' call-it, taking notes on the rhythmic themes, while my father watches everything on TV (he feels that now he fixes it he has a right to look at anything, he doesn't feel guilty any more, which is kind of sweet); he keeps his sound from interfering with my mother's by using like little plug earphones, but he gets overexcited and makes his own noise which he probably can't hear. I think I'd like a nice job in a museum, walking on cool marble with rubber-soled flats."

"You have a little brother? a little sister?" asked Hind.

Laura turned from a ceiling-high bookcase and walked right up to Hind. Anything to bring her to the point, even if "little brother" could never mean exactly to her a heather-gray-brown-haired child in midget Levis (better than the oversized Bermudas one pier mother put her four-year-old in) and clasping a greasy beanbag like a weapon how many years ago and where?

"They stopped after me," said Laura. "Not because of my leg, it's not hereditary, it happened later. It's that my mother always believed in the population explosion."

"Even in 'forty-seven, so soon after the war?"

"Who knows? I was born in 'forty-eight. She wasn't taking courses then, but..." Laura smiled rather shyly, he thought. "Questions, questions," she said quietly, and sat down. "Well, what else? You've got a green thumb. I can't see the other teacher your friend keeping plants in his apartment."

"Who knows," said Hind, "maybe he has a house and garden. How do you know he lives in an apartment?"

She reached out and picked off the rugless floor the small solid-state tape recorder. Sylvia phoned the rug people in June and told them to take Hind's rugs for summer cleaning and storage.

Laura flipped up the plastic lid, put it on the floor, rested a hand on the spools.

"Well, then," she said. "What's happening?"

What did her question cover? Plane, apartment, house, garden, Hind's green thumb? or that she knew what he knew?

"I mean, you brought me here for something more."

"Wait," said Hind, raising his hand in the most-easy-going, lovely, mild-as-love way (if also a bit too like a one-arm half of the famous drug-prophet's welcome designed to disarm riot police or defensive civilians), "remember your third wall? I have a third wall too. I didn't mean not to make friends earlier today, I was just in a rush to make the demonstration."

"No," said Laura. "I meant something besides the sex thing. You must think I thought the sex was ulterior and the something more was the trick to get me up here. But I figured vice versa, and I think you really did too. I put a high value on myself, I don't go to bed out of pity. Larry said pity could grow into something more, that's no way to make it. A lame leg has a crazy attraction for faculty members. No, really, what I meant was, what's the sex bit hiding, what do you really want? Didn't we come up here to make it?"

If he smiled, as in Plane's class, he might, even in his own darkness, lure the speaker on and on to discover what neither of them had known. If in a rain-threatened game, the home team is behind, then the top half of the fifth inning isn't enough to make the game complete, you need the bottom half.

"You got all excited in class about what I said, but I said 'blanket judgment' *again* because I didn't know what to say. I liked you in class; and I liked your friend and I thought if he liked you you might be pretty good. But don't give me this third wall. That was just about the parents of the boys who climbed Ironwood Arms. The parents got so mad at the kids they decided after all not to get a legal separation, what a hoot."

Laura led him in a direction in spite of her disclaimers. She was as delicate in her movements as she was seemingly frank in her words. The way she smoothly saved her affection for what might be the right time—that is, apparently to underline the information when she finally brought it out—the way she made prickly references to Sylvia's green mittens all alone on a shelf of a bedroom closet—these moves caused this enveloping interlude (that was all it could possibly be in the kidnap context) to carry that minor menace of apparent reality that seems to guarantee the best of fantasies.

In his reconstructions of the broken-leg episode, Hind erased the left-winger's dreadful fracture and the dreamy selfishness displayed by de Forrest in getting possession of the ball and starting to dribble upfield even though the stricken winger was howling on the ground: but to guarantee the fantasy, Hind imagined that the winger had intentionally tripped up and broken the ankle of de Forrest, and Hind had punched the winger in the nose and broken it.

Hind could not separate the secret Laura would betray and her elbow's vulnerable dimple, her prospectively tedious background and that other background from which he waited for the new clue to emerge from merged worm-tracklike intricacies like the Apocalyptic incisions of the guardian's early Dürer in which distance only intermittently strives to be other than the horses or leaf-winged monsters or dark-angelic persons above or below whom it occurs as a tidal river or a silent town. The guardian did not really like Dürer, though he felt Hind should know about him: the guardian preferred the decorous fitnesses and limpidities of the Italians of that day, say the Naples *Aesop* of 1485; but what would he do with the ornate puzzle of priorities Laura was inadvertently hatching and crosshatching here and now?

Now, *one* way might be deviously through the quote unquote homework phrase of the subway change booth man with the hair impaled in his wrinkling forehead. Hind had hoped, at the moment when Pop had perhaps unintentionally revealed that his organization was Minox-photographing Hind's green-board schemes, that ordinary behavior patterns—for instance, being close to Laura—could elicit in *others'* reflections of *him* the clue that would grow goldenly and miraculously into the lost child Hershey. But ordinary behavior patterns would not do. Possibly the old woman's measures changed; possibly it was in the greater pattern's interest that Hind's own measures needed to change.

Laura wanted to know what he saw in the picture on the wall toward which the foot of the bed pointed, she

didn't like religious art–"Augustinerkirche altarpiece"–
"Sounds expensive, when I go to Europe I'm going to get
to know the *people*"–"It may be religious but there are
interesting *human* figures to examine in it"–"Sounds like
it would take years to understand, and who has the time?
what's the idea of *that* part?"–"*St. Vitus Healing a Man
Possessed*"–"St. *Vi*tus! He couldn't even heal himself!" No.

The bold thing would be to tell her of the kidnap. She
was not the kind of girl to be willingly used in a plot like
this; her knowledge of Hershey, of the whole bit, might
well have come into her like some unnoticed, unresisted,
subocular effluent, so she was possessed *of* by being
possessed *by* the shrouded, running tale.

He was sorry for her that she could not be sufficiently
in control of this event to recognize in him more than
a somewhat older man to make love to, maybe a kook
(for she asked again what he was looking for), maybe a
klutz (though she said she liked him). Her sudden soft,
researches kept him from getting off the bed, first to
answer a knock on the door (just as well, for it was the
undertaker muttering as the steps went back down after
no one had answered the three batches of knocks on the
unlocked door which the undertaker had his own and
Hind's extra key to in any case), and a while later when
the record needed changing. When she did let him out of
her hands, he padded through the hot apartment over the
rustling soot of the bare boards and barely thinking put
on Ravel's astonishing Piano Concerto for the Left Hand
which Laura had been handling in its pink and white
jacket more than an hour before.

Laura's near leg was raised when he came back. She
had said she liked his height. She was larger naked than
in the fancifully short skirt she had had on, but she was
none the more in danger of seeming strong. But then,
turning to him as he came to the edge of the bed (and

wondered if the top floor ad people across the way saw under the shade), she said, "Larry called me a nympho."

"Oh no," said Hind reassuringly. Nothing there. But what had been primed into her about the green-on-gray old woman with the literate white bun and the well-bred dark eyes and long legs? He again made up his mind to bare the kidnap, or part of it, to Laura, then study her reaction.

"Well, Larry was foolish to say that," said Hind and pressed his eyelid gently against Laura's moving mouth.

"And if I was pregnant with Larry—which isn't possible, by the way—do you think he'd, I mean, do the right thing?"

She mumbled again as Hind's closed eye came against her lips. He said, "I doubt he would. He doesn't want the responsibility of another person."

"Not *marry*—I mean, pay a doctor. Get rid. It isn't because of my leg. This isn't hereditary, feel it right here—" a narrowing under the knee, the sense of some usual substance gone, not like what Hind had thought the broken winger's leg would feel like with the fresh edge of bone aiming through, as the guardian ran onto the field saying, "It was not Jack's fault!"

"I had what my father used to call 'a touch of polio.' He was embarrassed by my leg. Also, though, he became an anti-inoculation nut because he said my polio came from a dirty needle."

Then, "Oh," continued Laura, agreeably seeing what Hind wished, and together they shifted her gently. "He made me kiss him in that office of his. He couldn't even get the joint deans to give him a secondhand typewriter. Well, he shook all over and he stepped on me. And he started to pick me up, he was getting his arm in behind my knees—feel there—" she was giggling, pulling his hand down, but she let go when the hand went inside her thigh—"now being picked up by you would have been an experience, I can see that, but when Larry got me up—"

"You're scarcely heavier than a child," said Hind, trying to intrude the Laurel case.

"I said to him, 'You got no place to put me.' There was the little typewriter table under the car poster, but no typewriter. Larry called me a hypocritical nympho, which is too complex for me to figure out, though it meant mainly he was mad I liked *some* person but not him—and probably a faculty member, because he knew that my disability, my problem, is attractive to certain faculty members. But a *nympho!* How does that grab you?"

"Promiscuity isn't properly understood," said Hind, and laughter pulsed in his stomach, and Laura went, "Hmmm," as if doubtfully noting a diagnostic clue.

"I can tell you about a woman, Laura, who probably was called a nympho by certain people in the rural neighborhood to which she and her husband and child moved. Yet, as is almost always the case, she just wanted to be loved. It was insecurity, not some maniacal burn in the loin."

"Yeah, well. That's going a bit far. It's more than insecurity. It's hot all right. You head there and you can't turn back but you got to be pulled through. Inside out. Say, a hospital bed could be interesting, my grandfather had one that cost two hundred dollars, all the basic hospital positions. Think—"

"This woman ended tragically and mysteriously in a European hospital. Her husband never quite got to a hospital. This was five years ago."

"You must have been very young then."

An effective acts according to the powers of that which receives its action, not according to its own. But what, then, *are* its own, apart from those of what it acts upon?

Laura said, "There's a gold lamé bag on the shelf of that empty closet."

"It's my wife's," Hind said. The word came as inevitably as "limp" earlier, or as clues in the old woman's pattern.

"Well, I wasn't going to take it." Laura was almost weirdly casual over the sharp things, the "limp along," his quasi abduction of her at the q-d, and now revealing Sylvia.

Laura got her elbows above his shoulders. "You've been talking so much you have to pay a penalty and do something special." Her upper body became, from its inside, a means of malleably palpating his own, and she was more deeply still a "warped slip of wilderness" through which the guardian brusquely said that Shakespeare's phrase applied to a man not a girl, strictly speaking—but this wild slip here two warm hours after they'd first lain down (he with almost classically ulterior ends) was now instinctively turning him slowly away from the story he wanted to use on her, turning him into a new brand of lively vegetable that less and less clearly heard the voice of that other lame girl now probably in England, his beloved childhood tormentress Cassia Meaning, saying to a young gentleman vicar years ago on the Heights, "Father, thy rod and thy vicarious staff are not at bottom a question mark to *me*."

He and Laura were growing together, which was not what he'd planned, though they might well be growing toward a dark golden light like some exotic cornucopial swollen-noded Touch-Me-Not the guardian would mention pedantically to old Skoldberg.

"Hold it," said Hind huskily. "I want you to know about this. I think I'll go nuts if I don't tell someone, I doubt if even my wife knows very much even though years ago it came between us. Listen, there once was a family—call them Laurel, the father Sears, the mother Shirley, the baby boy Hershey. They lived in the city, but Sears, who was eleven years older than Shirley (which is probably irrelevant), thought he'd die if he had to stay in the city noise and bad air—"

"Nietzsche's 'bad air'?"

"Of course not. Well maybe, at that. But plain bad air, sulphur, carbon, particulates, photochemical smodge. All these he thought bad for Hershey. And at this critical time, Sears, a clever but somewhat detached advertising account man who through ignoring the possibilities of policy power in his firm had charmed both factions into wishing him out of the way, found it feasible to be moved to a brand new branch office of his firm in a city a couple of hundred miles north—"

Laura whispering into Hind's ear "—which shall be nameless."

"But this similar city, I mean *smaller* city, was not better. And so Sears thought he would try to build himself a house in a certain rural area, when miraculously a house somewhat larger than what he wanted became available and he took it, in effect without consulting Shirley. He thought he prospered as head man of the branch, got some German accounts and a blossoming young paintbrush concern that had a special new method of holding the paint and then a few little electronic firms in the suburbs that began to boom about the time he got them: anyway his branch grew quickly into a kind of competition with the central office in the larger city. Sears was able to step back—but this isn't my point, you distract me—and let two ambitious younger men do all the new media plans, in fact just about all *his* work, while he would commute only two or three days a week for the unavoidable lunch or dinner or presentation. Which meant he could live most of the time in the house in the country, which of course was much much nearer the second, smaller city than the first, bigger one."

"Of course," murmured Laura. Ironically?

"He wasn't rich, but he was well off. But his wife Shirley was restless, she didn't understand him, and he thought she didn't understand the country, though you know she began to make all kinds of things for herself—a combination bunk-bed clothes-commode for Hershey, a Heathkit tape recorder though there was nothing she wanted to record. She seems to have hated the country; that's what Sears told me. On the other hand, almost immediately people they didn't know even existed began to appear out of the hills and the side roads that connected to the road up the mountain or the road to the lake—a writer who for a fee took shooting parties on his land in the Fall, a semiretired general who worked by phone as a freelance industrial adviser on missile batteries; then there was a former adman who had become a corporate head-hunter 'placing' top execs and was planning to buy a plane, which would have made things even easier for Sears. So there was social life. But still Shirley lacked something."

"She was bored," said Laura, who moving again again threatened Hind's secret control over the tale.

"She told him he was home too much, and soon this remark grew in his mind to mean she wanted him out of the way. He bought her books on wildflower landscaping and butterfly gardens and didn't understand that she was interested in flowers to begin with but resented his enthusiasm."

"See? I was right," murmured Laura. Half asleep?

"There was a rather land-poor Jack-of-many-trades named Ken who lived on a road that except in summer was deserted. He had two Jerseys and two huge Holsteins, and corn and strawberries, and firewood, and he and his sons worked part-time for the township resurfacing and snowplowing, and he even was said to have had something to do with the selling and buying of the Laurel house. In the early spring Sears took his advice on what to do before painting the house, and Ken would appear sometimes on the way from one job to another to stand in the drive watching Sears calk under the shingles and bang some in that had loosened. And I believe Sears would look down from his high ladder to catch Ken watching Shirley in the flowerbed. I'm putting in too much that's not relevant."

"It's not relevant to me, I'll tell you that."

"One day Hershey the little boy was kidnaped."

"That was sudden."

"Did you hear what I said?"

"Don't you like me any more after we've made it?"

"But wait, Laura," in a low voice, wheedling, "I want you to respond: this whole bit is to evoke from you a—you're a woman, *you* figure why Shirley waited for Sears to come home and then left and didn't return for three days even though she knew she'd come under suspicion, and Sears stayed right there at the house, the police in and out, he even did a few odd jobs, you know, stayed near home in case."

Laura raised her head from his chest and he turned his head to catch her eye.

"Come on," she said, "you stalling?"

"I'll skip ahead," said Hind. "When *I* came on the scene—"

"I didn't mean that kind of stalling."

"It was a long while later but still long before my old lady got involved—"

"Your mother?"

"No." Just a thought: did Laura know the major involvement of the tall white-haired black-eyed—

"Oh your *wife*–you talk old-fashioned."

"Not my wife either. Someone else. It doesn't matter."

"You're always saying that. What the hell does?"

"Shirley, at that somewhat later time, had just gone to Europe, I ascertained–it was the last time the police consented to help me, and I gather the eve of Joe Praid's advent who I later learned had been assigned to phase the case out. I ascertained there were no more living relatives. Sears was in Baltimore personally rechecking a prescription Peoples Drug filled for a tall man who couldn't be traced, who had a mole on his upper lip and a bag of Black Magic candies and it seems had forged, but we now know invented, the doctor's signature on the prescription. But then Sears, I believe, found the clue he thought Shirley had found before him, and when I got to Baltimore an old friend named Lief Lund who was a Reserve JG on a drydocked weather ship and had nothing to do most days except keep an eye on some colored welders thought to be taking bets, found out for me that the police knew that Sears had followed Shirley to Europe and I tried not to believe that he might have followed her merely as one stumped competitor follows another in a treasure hunt."

"Maybe Sears gave up and just wanted Shirley."

"When there was no evidence Hershey wasn't alive? and some fairly consistent evidence that a tall man might be involved as kidnaper?"

"There wasn't evidence Hershey *was* alive."

"Wait, wait–"

"Don't you like me any more?"

"Yes, yes," whispered.

"Well," Laura was saying, "why do you tell me this stuff with the names changed to protect the innocent–names are changing all over the place, I don't know if the woman who made the error registering me at registration for a special private tutorial with a nonexistent professor is the one at the same desk now or someone else, I don't know if you're Hind or Plane, but I thought I knew Plane pretty well, and my phys ed prof calls me Laurie, a girl I don't even know calls me Rosie, Larry calls me Law (no one ever called me that before), and the dressed-up Grunewald kid called me Miss Rosenblum when he approached me two days ago to ask me for your notes, I don't even know the guy–"

"*My* notes!"

"Notes of your class. And our doorman calls me Laura. Even my father forgot my mother's name, he asked her a question and she thought he stopped when really he paused and she began to answer but then when he suddenly remembered her name he butted in with 'Miriam'–so do you want me to say something like I sympathize with this quasi-imaginary Sears–"

"No, no–"

"And like annihilate Shirley because she loved someone else for a while–what, is this some teaching strategy like in Ed? You and my third wall, you meant something by my third wall, the kid who's following Holly around that she really likes told her you were an anti-CDNV plant–"

"No, this really happened, and I'm the guy that tried to find the truth."

Laura rose back on her knees. The late-afternoon dark of the room was dropping into something denser, though twilight would be long. Hind put his hand on Laura's stomach.

She said, "All I wanted was a nice time, no complexity, no nothing, you're telling me about your wife and kid, or if it isn't that, you're playing some trick on me. Go back to your wife–"

"*Sharing* it with you, it's been part of my life—"

"Don't share. If you keep throwing me this fantastic stuff I'll really have something to say to you."

"I'm not exactly sharing the kidnap search."

"So why'd you do it?"

"Because it had to be done. Someone had to find Hershey Laurel."

"But why you telling me all about it? I'm just temporary around here. You're not telling all this just because you want a relationship. What if you do want a relationship? Then you should be ashamed at your age, you went to schoool with Professor Plane, if *you're* not Plane. Add a few years you're twice my age, and you pretend you want to get serious. Well, get serious with Sylvia."

"*Someone*, you see, had to maintain the search, else it would simply be transmuted—"

"Whaa?"

"Into statistics, or (until people soon forgot) tragedy, or indeed into a standing procedure of perfunctory surveillance."

"You go find your wife, not that kid. And how come you're giving up all this time to Oliver Plane, and what's this about depth-perspective got to do with your major field, much less with what Plane was doing in lecture when *he* disappeared?"

"Everything! Take Dürer's *Bearing of the Cross*: all the tricks that lure us into seeing the central foliage-like mêlée as a delicate adjustment of distances so that even homely Veronica gazing at and kneeling near the laden Jesus appears in a slightly more forward plane, lure us also to forget that this is an exquisitely jumbled flat surface cut by an unhappily married man upon a block of wood or in the engraving on the same theme cut by a growing man's mushroom-handled burin—and just as,

until you, like ostensibly immortal Dürer—wait a second—
yes—can see the beautiful object apart from the alluring
illusions it seems to have—until then, you can't see his
human achievement, so also—"

"But it's just a woodcut. And I've got to go. Tonight's
my father's night to cook out on the balcony, I said I'd be
home."

"—*so also* you must see Hershey's kidnap in its flat
reality. The parents' disappearance from the scene makes
my point the more incisively. For the essence was and is
that another person (with or without aid) came and put
his or her hands on Hershey and *took* him from one life
into another. Do you see? That is the thing in itself, like
the cut surface of a piece of wood."

Laura had on her golden panties and now pulled up her
pitiable (if pilot) miniskirt. She paused. "The woodcut's
fresh today but the original wood is probably no good
any more. Oh—" she zipped up—"that's your business."
She turned her skirt around so the zipper was at the back.

She was going to have other things to say to him. This
she had admitted.

The relaxation which Hind plunged them both into
through staying off the Laurel topic was as sweet as his
narrative ruse had been painful to them both.

He resented having to use Laura.

He had a little dream from which he woke up he
thought into the first afternoon with Laura but which he
sluggishly came to see was the fourth or fifth. She was
going to tell her dream too, but eventually they never
got to it. He was dreaming his way, he thought, back to
Ashley Sill's or the Fieldston, but he was sure only that
he walked in a sparse windy stand of nonetheless thick,
high trees: I measured the stand, then I was electrically
pruning the tops the way Siggofreddo Morales did for
the guardian in the old days; I pasted my silvicultural
sheepskin on one trunk: and among the swaying ack-ack-

ack of the trees' bodies I saw myself as guardian of trees, yet tragically temporary, for now I see tattooed on my various parts prices: for my right leg, an Indian canoe; for my left arm, a copy of the Britannica. And so on, until, becoming fascinated with my body I looked at it more closely and saw something terribly interesting.

But when Laura did not ask what, Hind woke up all over again and found he'd been still within a dream telling the tree dream to her. Which raised another issue almost as interesting as the "terribly interesting" thing he in his dream had told Laura he'd dreamed he saw.

She would indeed have more to say to him, but he mustn't go too hard at her, the undergrowths were going to yield now not a mere clue but a turning, even an end. And from Laura Rosenblum's first powerful reaction you had to suspect that the *place* of the clue (if the clue had one) would in some sense be near the cool, clear island where Syl and May were summering.

He was going to have to leave Ol with a raft of student papers (a draft, a rift—as there surely now would be between Ol and him in spite of all he'd done for Ol): but you couldn't be so descendingly generous as to do all a man's work for him; and Hind had again found an opening through the now slag-thick, sea-dense, reverend mugginess of the August heat, toward the case's last, inner darkness where he could prove to Sylvia he wasn't nuts and Hershey Laurel existed trapped.

"Where's Plane?" a young man asked, standing in the cubicle entrance.

"I'm subbing for him," said Hind pleasantly, pivoting Plane's chair.

"O.K., then," said the student, "so long as I know where I am." He put before Hind a dark green attaché case and clicked the end buttons.

Hind was short on time. "Your name?"

"Max May—I mean—"

"Is it?"

"It is," said the young man, ignoring his own momentary discomfiture and placing before Hind a blue plastic clip-folder. "It could be called fiction. Would you read it and give me an opinion?"

"Sure, have a look tonight."

The boy's thanks came only in a shy nod. Hind loved this job for a second. Maybe Laura would be willing to read the blue clip-folder.

"This is a work of reflection," said May, bending to sit—but Hind's quick hand caught him halfway, "Not now, sorry; these aren't my office hours. I have to meet—"

"In the interdepartmental file it says these are your office hours."

"Plane's, not mine. So if you'll leave your manuscript—"

"It is a work of reflection to be judged only by the habits of its inner organism: it is self-contained: it is in a way untouchable: you won't understand it by checking it against outside reality, for instance against that crane and bulldozer, or against psychological laws like those that obtain between Man and Woman, teacher-student."

"I will as soon as I can. Have I seen you before?"

The boy snickered resignedly to himself. "You'll see that I take a dim view of human nature. I'll tell you about Plane someday."

"O.K.," said Hind—a phrase the guardian abhorred—and rose.

"Jesus," said the boy, stepping back, measuring Hind. "Well, have fun with it, it grows on you."

"O.K.," said Hind, locking a batch of themes in OP's briefcase, then laying the briefcase on its side in the green steel bookcase.

"I got a conference to make," said the boy, who seemed to be getting younger and younger in tone, maybe just more relaxed. "You and I have something in common."

"Another time," said Hind, catching sight of the book salesman smiling over the milk-glass partition. The man held up his gold wristwatch and eagerly nodded his head, eyebrows hopefully raised.

"I've been a sub too," Max May said. "It's my client who's really registered for Plane's course. He needs just three credits, but he got a job in TV animation that's too good to—"

"If you won't go, I will," said Hind, grabbing his newspaper, leaving the cubicle, sidestepping the stammering book salesman—bracing his right hand on the inside end wall of the Hall of Cubicles in order then to expedite his right turn into the Waiting Vestibule whose carpeted length he devoured (negotiated, crossed) in three great skip-swing strides far too long and reckless for a dive approach—he'd have been ten feet up the pool before even going into his dive, a comic trick he had once abortively learned and forgot he could do far better than any competitive dive.

Laura said if he pushed her further she might really have something to say to him. She asked him to visit the pool after the midafternoon Scuba session but he preferred the undertaker's. Before the class two days ago she had been talking to Larry Poplar, who kept looking at Hind. Then after class she said she could not hand in her paper on the metaphor after all, she would give him a late revision—and in a lower voice, with Grunewald hovering near nervously flapping a fat green plastic ring binder, she had said, "Shall I deliver the goods at your place," and Hind had said, "Yes, and I'll call you."

But instead he had now flashed Plane's laminated ID to the policeman and was now in one of the pool's doorways being asked to step aside by two girls, while at the far shallow end, where Laura could be seen reaching and scissoring across in a creditably unvertical ladies' breast stroke, a short broad man with a neck like the late Buddy Bourne's in a T-shirt that said COLLEGE T-SHIRT on the back, lugged away two gray tanks and masks with yellow hoses. So many distinct cadences of wave disturbed the green-tiled water. Hind passed three suddenly silent girls sitting tight together along the base of the one-meter board. When Hind stood above Laura, who had finished her lap and was gently treading water and looking at him with the composure of one who has already been swimming, she said, "Do a dive."

"How do you know I can?"

"Dr. Plane told me once you were the diver on the school team."

"Where did he say this?"

"Go on."

The girls made way pretending to continue their conversation. They were ready to show deference if it seemed called for, they didn't know who he was, grad students over thirty went home or to the library—or did those girls think *anything*?

Laura was a mile away, and for a second, as he kneaded (contracted, gripped) his toes on the harsh cocoa matting, he wanted to get to her instantly, which would mean doing a Julio Loggia (that overweight thirteen-year-old), rushing his approach, hitting the end of the board leaning, departing at an aeronautical forty-five degrees and landing a respectable broad (or as the guardian said, "long") jump from the board. Instead, for you didn't embarrass your friends, Hind did not risk a statuesque compulsory like a front or a half twist but took a severe high hop on his third stride, took the board straight up with his approach motion to carry him outward, and in an echoing wash of silence so vast he would hear above the board's quivering recoil the guardian's heartbeat, he tucked into a one-and-a-half so snappily he could have made two and so he sloshed his calves over and ruined his entry axis. But then swam twenty-odd yards under water, to tickle Laura's leg self-depreciatingly as he came up.

"You're *really* good. You're a ringer."

"They probably thought down there by the board, 'A six-foot-seven-legged maniac one-and-a-half with a slap-splash—"

"It was great," Laura broke in quietly. His hand was on her unified buttocks, he and she faintly rocking in the remains of his entry wake.

There are so many other mysteries in a person besides the one we use him for. Why not settle for those rather than this? Skip the prospect of Laura's calculated or incalculable response to his provocations. Forget the kidnap commitment and spirit Laura over the seas to Naples, Brindisi, Cracow, to the eerie postwar replica Warsaw that he and Sylvia had seen when he cared only for the Laurel track. Yet if Laura could fully understand how she was being used, she would gladly agree to have been a clean-cut illustration of Dewey Wood's twice-rejected "You keep your friend only by imposing on him or her." The thought that Laura's link with the kidnap was so dim as to be unusable had occurred to Hind on seeing her with Larry two days ago before class. This stage of the kidnap revival was lasting too long.

The plastic water changed her leg, it seemed as usable as the other one. "I owe you that paper on the metaphor. Hey, those kids are watching. Plane said he didn't like pools, he wouldn't come swimming here."

With her? Had there been a thing with OP? And if so, was it a means of briefing her?

"You said tonight you'd give me the revision."

"Yeah, you went pretty far in class, as I said."

"That first afternoon you said if I pushed you too far you'd *really* have something to say to me."

"Faculty playing around with students." She pushed off and went under, and following her he caught in her face so close and even touching his but separated by the substance they tangled in, the mild buoyant hysteria of knowing no Scuba tank held her breath for her.

She was saying again—and he was losing her as she said—"I'll get that late paper to you. I'm sorry it's late."

"It doesn't matter," Hind said.

"Oh but you're the teacher."

No one knew him, not even the colleague whom he'd caught standing at Plane's desk staring at Plane's student IBM cards (but whom he Hind was at least known to as Oliver Plane).

"And you got a wife and child to support marking our themes. Plane never handed any back."

Holly and the boy with the olive-green attaché case watched from the stainless-steel-railed balcony.

What exactly had Hind said in class? He said good-bye now to Laura, and he backstroked down the pool toward the diving board gossips appearing to look toward each hand as it reached with bent wrist but keeping an eye on the balcony, from where indeed Holly was having words with Laura.

He treated himself to a cab, for he had reached a state in which he must be clear for whatever Laura was going to say; and if he took the subway home—first elevated, then, after the two separate bread smells, approaching the river and slipping, almost dragged, down into the first two jaundiced stations in the factory area, the first containing the unmarked billboard advertising "FUDG-

ICIDE INSTANT HOME FRAPPÉ BLASTS—Justpress-
buttonandfoamitintomilk," the second the stop for the
paintbrush plant Maddy had an interest in (the boss's Naked Voice saying, "See, this man over here quickly jams a
bunch of bristles onto this set of overlapping cutters that
split each bristle-end into two or three tiny fishhooks to
hold the paint, but wait till you see what we do at the end
what nobody else does that one more thing to these tiny
hooks")—Hind would have been enticed into themes as
irrelevant as whether or not in this city that Mad Beecher
said had lost its name, there was a connection between
the one hundred forty-four laborers who wash down six
thousand subway cars every ten to fifteen days and the
one hundred forty-four laborers of the one-hundred-six-
ty-nine-strong Maintenance of Way Department's Track
Cleaning Program.

Like one of the undertaker's Rent-A-Hearse chauf-
feurs—if in fact the undertaker had any more funerals—
Hind's cabbie said hardly a word on the same five-dollar
ride Larry Poplar had given Hind free how many contact
hours ago in Larry's peri-military twenty-four-hun-
dred-hour-timetabling adopted from Italian railways.
Heavy rain began to come down more honestly than
Hind had seen it all summer—not merely a sinister, disingenuous change from dark humidity to moving wet.
("Drenched?" the guardian had asked. "How on God's
green earth can you say the sun *drenched* you?") For seventy-five yards along the expressway where they were
adding a lane and in one swoop laying a sewer annex,
they had shored up with pretty casually spaced timbers
eight feet of the great cemetery's boundary bank which
they had cut right up to, and which they evidently feared
might cave in toward, the expressway. He fell asleep for a
moment, lulled by the heavy wash that slimed the windshield, and he and Sylvia were being shown by Lyons's
California brother-in-law into a gray field of succulent

high gray stalks that buzzed—and, if as you passed you turned to one of them, nodded—and the brother in-law said, "Ever since sixteen-thirty the Lyons grew beans on these stalks but I've won poor Elmer over to California Golden Retrievals." But Hind came awake startled not by the cab braking but by recalling that Laura not Sylvia was the relevant element at this point, at least for the next few hours. If May and Sylvia had rain up on the island— which doubtless they wouldn't mind fishing for stripers in, May in her dark blue vinyl slicker and hat which Buck Field gave Sylvia a special on—it would be dryer rain than this on the expressway as the cab passed down to the toll booths before the mouth of the interborough tunnel.

In the undertaker's street the sycamores and the ailanthus were dark wet, the air still had in it the downpour that had just stopped, stopped an hour too soon. Dark humidity made him think of bedtime as, stepping from the cab, he looked up to Good Queen Rain's fourth floor and received her wave from where she watched with her electric candle by her cheek and the hot needle bright in the clear glass flame, unseen elbows on her sill, cheeks resting on fists. Hind felt he was the only moving thing in the street. Far through the business door at the other end of the front room, the pale face of the TV shone, no doubt for Carmen and the old men. One of the Old Chestnuts had lined up three orange-red persimmons on his stone window-ledge. The dream in the cab hadn't been long enough to yield that feeling of sinal rinse he could almost always wake up to in his childhood naps in summer, often hearing as he woke the guardian's busy step.

Swimming away from Laura he had felt, as several weeks before when he drove from the Sills' to the kidnap site, that he in fact already possessed the clue he went in search of. Well, she was taking him to a reading tonight. He was dripping with sweat, he would take a couple of showers before she came.

Like cattle (like sheep, like kindergartners) Laura's class two days ago wrote down his commonplaces, and Laura stopped and was the only face looking at him and the only face he cared about. "I hoped you would come to see, in your reading and now in the paper you are handing in today, that all ideas spring from assumed metaphors—for instance, Nietzsche's septic equation by which *freedom* is in fact feloniously rooted in a cheap class determinism by which he seeks to incarcerate our natural notions of love, help, intelligent self-sacrifice, and that mysterious penetration through ourselves to others. You have, I hope, found that no matter how much faith you have in them, these major medi-phors break down" (or up). "I wanted you to find this out in, as my assignment put it, a metaphor, a likeness, that matters to you. Do you see then how intricately flimsy it all was? The river is not singing, any more than it's watching you, any more than its valley *enjoys* clement weather. And the vent behind me is a vent." And Hershey is just one kid.

The short-haired blonde sitting with her long-haired brunet boyfriend in a back row nodded bemused, while he shook his head sternly.

"Did I ask too much," Hind had continued, "asking you to see that in the end your work tottered because in that likeness of yours you exaggerated your own importance?"

Though just when Laura's blankness had become a frown he heard in his inner ear the guardian urging him to mend his language, still Hind was offering Plane's pupils a tantalizing exposition of—

"Remember the slide we had on the screen? Imagine yourself a cat—let's say, a tan Abyssinian—" Laura blinked as if she were gulping with her eyes—"a tan Abyssinian cat watching the pale bright almost flat scene of your TV. And this, lest we let our pitifully man-centered conditioning take over, is always one thing at least that we ought to see, when—and here I come back to the

slide—when we see de Staël's *Agrigento*, an exact arrangement of rough-hewn two-dimensional shapes devoid of
depth. The yellow triangle's sides are not mainly road
banks bound for some vanishing horizontal point, for
that road, if it truly existed, would not truly vanish; but
rather they're not a perspective recession at all, but an
oblique triangle of pigment. To see thus is not to see a
less human scene but to find a more human act—de Staël,
the strong doomed man using thinner and thinner paint
and now, what?, less than two years from suicide, covering a surface the way a...the way a teacher—" well-dressed
Webster Grunewald hated the blind man near him who
tapped his three-register Braille-Rite so fast he got ahead
of Hind, who in the other, professionally unengaged eye
of his mind wondered if the blind man knew, or even
dictated, what was coming, as Grunewald looked at the
blind man—"the way a teacher covers a class period."

He combined pedagogy with neat leads to Laura:
"Where is a past, from today or from here? If, like me, you
are thinking of an object—say, a wall—" Laura looked back
at the clock in the far wall—"which recalls another wall,
and then, say, a third wall of, say, seven or eight years
back, can you seriously maintain that the third wall is
distinctly near or far, the three walls plainly foreground
or background? Or must you not see faithfully that in one
extent a roadlike shape such as perspective lines might
give, receding to a magic horizon, yet also and mainly a
triangulation of moments, is very like our arrangement
of past and present, and the top of de Staël's triangle is
as near as our temporal fore-area is far! The best reality
is what we're not invited to see ourselves in the center
of, just as the best language is not an invitation to find
ourselves drawn to the life at its center."

And the dead guardian's voice replied, "Then why
your faithful habit of releasing triune verbal extensions

of your private insights? Why see the subway elevated track as, quote unquote, 'lattices, ladders, grilles,' the first essentially domestic or even rural or floral, the second vertical and associated with feet, the third essentially very small in the scale suggested? why trap a poor simple golf course in words like quote unquote 'moon-drenched, moon-rinsed, lunaroid'? why the falsely athletic and musical in words denoting your damned radio station's activities—'keep pace, up, in tune with'—not to mention the degenerate parallelism; and then, alas, Pop's thrice honking his ludicrous horn as if in answer to the honks behind him you associate with a Russian celebrity, an irrational Negro, and your own man asserting his—what shall I say?—aqua-privacy!"

And as the radius second hand on the far wall swept through its last infinities of segments, and Hind was tempted to drop a gnomic grenade in Laura's lap, a familiar voice, as if on a helicopter-mounted zoom lens (and it made him shoot out his left arm), appeared in the vent saying, "Is it possible to doubt who Ovid's heifer is?" and reciting:

> Came and lit on the ground, chattering, clacking away.
> Thrice, with a petulant beak, it pecked at the breast of
>     the heifer,
> Carried away in its mouth tufts of the snowiest hair.
> After a while, so it seemed, the heifer rose and
>     departed,
> Bearing the mark of a bruise dark on the white of her
>     breast,
> Saw, far off, other bulls, happily grazing together—

which these poor simple students were frantically transcribing into their ring binders, all except Laura, who watched Hind—

"Saw, and hurried her course, and joined these new-found companions–"

And as the buzzer sounded and behind and in front students' feet scraped and books smacked the floor, he said hastily, "What happened to Beulah Love's red-haired sister, whom Ken told Shirley and reluctant Sears he'd like to bunk in at the Laurels' in order to escape? Your papers, please." As she reached the lectern, Grunewald asked about the permissible noise level of the blind man's Braille-Rite's interference, and instead of adding her paper to the strewn pile Laura turned away.

The bells of the Good Shepherd kept ringing and ringing; Hind's phone went and he decided to take this one himself rather than wait for Smitty to pick it up at the office, and it was Ivy Bowles to explain that since she still belonged to Good Shepherd (though she was seriously thinking of transferring her letter), she felt responsible for what was going on there right now, she had heard from Dewey who had had it from Phyllis, who was just back from Mount Mary, that three of the retarded problem boys at the special school the minister had started had fooled with the electric governor and the bells wouldn't stop–"I thought it was me at first!"

Laura appeared that night with a manila envelope, her late-late revision.

"Don't look at it now." She hugged his waist and rubbed her ear on his chest, and he felt too tall, she moved a hand down the back of his thigh. "I'm sorry," she said. For him? (Insufferable.) About everything? (Conceivable.) And she wasn't exactly the compassionate sort, if he could ever finish the kidnap and come back to her and know her fully, he might well begin here, her need of compassion, indeed a strange phrase redolent of the guardian's preoccupations, a phrase he might well have had a hand in, smelling of the huge green-tinged Italian lemons he liked. "The tragic point is," said the guardian, "you can turn away from your real nature."

Laura sat on the living room daybed. She reached for Hind's hands, but he turned and picked her manila envelope off Sylvia's abandoned onyx coffee table. He took it to the study. When he switched on his worktable lamp and glanced out the window he found staring up at him from way down below across the street the advertising girl, the motorcycle maid (who'd graduated from lightweight Sabre to a 250cc Austrian bike with white fiberglass saddlebags), the vinyl virgin motomorph (who'd reversed her outfit to white-striped black). He kept looking, so so did she. He turned his light out.

"All right," Laura called, "what do *you* get out of hunting for this lost kid Hershey Laurel?"

But if you had to ask, then you couldn't be really answered. Yet Laura touched him anew in old ways, made him for the millionth time fear the narrowness of his Laurel commitment, touched him in his most minor memories: Doc Skoldberg and his tall, squinting, adoring Jewish wife dropped in (literally from the mountain) one summer day nearly on the eve of the guardian's treasure hunt and hoped to stay the night but weren't asked, though the guardian promptly directed them to the two converging roads (a state route and a township gravel) that would unerringly lead (in those premotel days) to Echo Inn: and Doc Skoldberg, oversensitive certainly when former pupils he was fond of were concerned, was happy to talk about cornucopial Touch-Me-Nots but reacted unfavorably upon being shown the guardian's *Capsella bursa-pastoris* with its triangular pods and tiny white blossoms: "Shepherd's purse is just an ordinary weed, of course. The last thing I'd bring in from England." Though for the guardian perhaps it had associations.

"But you're a hell of a shepherd," Laura had said three or four nights ago reaching a very thin, bare arm out to take a Lark from the bedside bureau where the clock stood stopped. "Instead of looking for the Laurel kidnap, you should look after your wife Sylvia, I found some of her book-jacket and clothes-design doodlings on some cards behind the spices."

That had been only the second time Laura mentioned Sylvia.

Now, turning away from his dark study window and the ad girl in its lower corner staring at him with her hands on the handlebars and standing near the new tree Knott told the schnauzer-walkers to keep clear of, Hind concluded that Laura was preoccupied with Sylvia for some reason.

Laura had not asked for more of the kidnap. She seemed to think he would tell her more if he wanted to. Maybe she thought he only told her about it when they were in bed. She was neither more distant nor more interested in him now that some measure of the Laurel tale existed between them, she neither took for granted that he told her something about Sears' search for Hershey and about the apparent characteristics of the person or persons who had taken Hershey, nor showed curiosity about his own concern with the boy's recovery. She was being used as clue-bearer, yet had known really nothing about the case the clues led to.

Nor had she objected to a night with Hind in Oliver Plane's apartment: Oliver's neatly tagged key which Hind discovered in the cubicle at college turned out to be unnecessary, for the flat was open, the long wedge-bar for the police lock lay strangely across the other end of the long hall like an old-time stickball stick waiting for a thrown and now rolling ball to hit it, bounce up, and be snatched by the defending batter. Laura had not minded spending the night on another strange and not very clean bed. She had a sense of where everything was, seemed almost to know that there was part of a carton of Larks and some orange-flavor child vitamins under the kitchen sink. But he was looking for something else, that term paper, and then he nearly slid off by accident on a loose skate.

But Laura didn't like it when the janitor came as they were leaving in the morning, and said, "We ain't showing this till tomorrow. The tenant went away, some friend of his got to come take his stuff and pay his rent."

"This *is* still Oliver Plane's apartment?"

"Of course it is," Laura had said, moving down the stairs.

The vinyl virgin shrugged, and straddled her bike.

"I said what do *you* get out of this lost kid Hershey Laurel?" Hind did not answer, and Laura said softly, "What you doing in a dark room?"

She was not excited about the poetry reading at The Dive, she knew some people who would be there. If only Hind could draw her into that broken dream to finish telling her the terribly interesting thing he saw on his body. Pop had invited Hind before Pop's abortive and unsuccessful exposure of Hind in the Plazette. Presumably, in (as vent voices liked to say) the larger context, the poetry reading would signify in terms of Laura's presence: as if her presence (her lean lap, the fine forward-hunch of her vulnerable shoulder blades) were like Child Hershey's beanbag, suddenly appearing at a table in the drafty junk shop flipped back and forth to the sound of clinking crockery and in the intense hesitations gapped into the projective breath line of the verse-reciter, flipped back and forth with hysterical rapidity by two kids ignoring the reading; *or*, like (in poor Grunewald's exalted phrase—who incidentally seemed to like Laura Rosenblum and to sense her link with Hind) a catalyst, not in G's misuse, but exactly an active agent that in the train of its action yet remains unchanged or is uninvolved.

But Laura wasn't like anything, and this stage of the revived kidnap had gone on too long. What would Laura be like in a life untouched by the Laurel kidnap plot? Could he ever find out?

"I never went to a reading until last month," she said in the subway as the train remained at the stop, the generator pulsed like an insect, and the doors didn't close. "And after, I thought I wouldn't go again. I can't listen to a poem I didn't already read. And you can't help looking at the people, they're acting like a funeral except once suddenly this girl burst into the old radiant smile and there's an older guy your age from Texas who right during the readings is creeping from table to table lining up poems for his review called *The Far In*, he prints it on a ditto, that's all it is; the kids listening, every line wakes up a different part of someone's body: a word in line one, a neck breaks; a beat in line two, a chest comes out in a big breath; a rhyme in the third, the hands come together, like this, like the ribs of your skull after a concussion, that's what one of the brothers who climbed Ironwood Arms told me, he got concussed when he fell off the kitchen ladder."

Here again: approaching the poetry reading, approaching the kidnap: Sears Laurel—and Hind had not told Laura this—suffered a concussion the Sunday in Paris he had been diverted from Hershey to Shirley and had suddenly decided she was better than nothing, and in any case a kid eventually leaves you, while your wife—and he would see if the news was true she was arriving from Norway.

"But you ought to listen to the poem, don't snoop on others' responses."

"The poem I can read, the people I may not see again: the poem is like a background to them."

She knew some people who were supposed to be at the reading, but she didn't say they were associated with Poplar. It was as important for Hind not to know too much about her as it was for her not to know very much about the kidnap revival she was entailed in: if indeed she knew anything more than phrases she was supposed to drop at the right times.

A poem had finished, standees leaned against the wall, strangely a table in a smoky corner was vacant and an old woman in some kind of pale body stocking beckoned them to it, she had a hard gold wig, belled and banged. Spotlit, the poet was trying to put down a heckler off in the dark. "But listen to me!" "I already *have* listened!" They were emphasizing almost every other word.

"You're *ha*ving us *all on*," the heckler said. "You *can't* be *known* by *things*. How-can-a-set-of-*stars mill*ions-of-years-*off know* me?"

"Precisely!" called the poet, "that's what I *want* asked. You *are* known in a way *by things. How? a*ny type of thing? and *how* are you, in what *modes*, in what *terms* are *you* your*self* known by a *berry* on a *sprig* or a *space* full of *par*ticles? If a *gal*axy lacks a sense of humor, so do *a*nimals, the contour of *hills* you watch."

"But," said the heckler, "you *assume* what I question, you don't *answer* my question."

"*I* don't have to defend the poem," said the poet. "Anyway, I didn't write it. But it's a *great* poem."

But Laura, after Hind had turned his chair to face the reciter, had gone off.

And so had the air conditioner, probably because of city water rulings.

Laura had not gone far. A new young man had seated himself on the low platform in the old bentwood drug store chair and, as he shuffled his pages, he said, sheepishly, "Look out."

At that simple smoky moment of onsight, the poet-aster's tired flowers and Hind's own plainly exasperated Laura loomed no farther or closer than the name "Sylvia" or its distant possessor or the flexible vent-to-vent inter-course through that perhaps now darkening Cubic Cam-pus some eight miles off. As if like little Miss Manikin in the show at the Hotel Fieldston's Mont Blanc Room who through Yoga and instant self-absorption switched into trances of perfect rigidity or of programed robette jerk-walk, so also Hind now could make parts and whole of a picture become simple surface, be as two-dimensional as the Sunday school Jesus-riddle had been until his eye had simply relaxed into understanding. Even then he had thought, What I first saw is also there. But at last, when he and the puzzle had clicked and instead of relying on faith in what he couldn't see (and Cassia Meaning *could*) he actually saw the Jesus, who looked like the sickly man with bad breath who worked at the Heights branch of the Public Library shelving books and looking longingly at people, Hind was afraid to say to Cassia, "But still, what you first see before you see the face, is *also* there, you can't deny that—and I bet you couldn't go back to seeing what you first saw." For if he said that, she would again accuse him of not having really seen the face. He couldn't bear her smiling doubt; it was not intimate. However, when he sent her for a Christmas joke years later the old puzzle with the head outlined in ballpoint—to prove he did see—he added the long-rankling challenge: "O.K., now can *you* see the picture with*out* seeing Jesus?" that black-and-white Jesus she as a kid so graspingly imagined he could not see. He would like to show Sylvia that that strangely familiar flatness theory she had almost tanta-lized him with could indeed be applied to this Hershey Laurel case she hated. Did she begin to know that she was his new step? He'd fly to Mount Mary Station and drive a hired car to the coast. And leave a note to Oliver that a

City Marshal was seeing to that flat of his with its dere-
lict bags of clean laundromat laundry which OSP used instead of bureaus, and the three king-size mattresses and
the piles of someone else's *Architectural Forum*, OSP didn't
subscribe.

Hind had first to connect the term paper with the
new step. He was impatient steadily climbing the
marble stairs. The undertaker would never install air
conditioning in the top-floor apartment, he could get
much more rent than Hind was paying. But eventually
the undertaker would get the plasterer to come, he knew
how to joke him—"You're in the plastering business, I'm
in the planting business."

Hind knew the next stop had to be Sylvia—Laura's
insistence, and Sylvia's coincidental nearness to OSP,
"and ekcetra" (as Grunewald would say)—and so here it
seemed almost supererogatory, if not exactly absurd, to
stalk that waiting envelope probably no different from
the other papers in the same batch—he hadn't touched
them yet. He was neither like Plane, who rarely read
student papers, nor the older man now circulating a new
Plotsburg protest, who appended pages of exegesis to
each theme.

You told yourself one day you'd come back and revive
relations with, come to know, really get to, all those
"kids" (as the joint articulation chairman called them),
those who nagged you, those who loved you, those who
napped now and then in the formal intimacies of your
classroom but in whom you had faith.

The long-haired boy began with an epigraph ascribed
to The Unknown Student: "Beside my mulberry bush I
push away the housing blocks and create green-fringed
hills. Here alone can I dance with trees and become one
with them." Grunewald, in a P.S., requested an explana-
tion of why Hind had not elected to use Senate President

Groveland Cleaver's recommended Student-to-Teacher Course-Evaluation Questionnaire In Depth, didn't he care what students thought of him "and/or" Plane?

It was harder to catch the relevant parts of Laura's performance. "This is, like me, more than what you asked for, yet probably also less; for I want not simply to give my new, revised metaphor but also to interpolate on you." O.K., O.K., the difficulty of the assignment, the laboring preamble. "But the paper and then my comments on you will interlard so homogienically that it will be like scary TV ads that seem actual continuations of the programs whose parts they follow. You're being shown the way west complete with bonnets and prairie schooners: then CUT: you see cows and cowboys in the smoky setting sun but it isn't the drama any more, it's a cigarette. You're a good-looking crook being chased by a mad cop along the coast highway: CUT: there's an independent tire rolling down a ravine, bouncing on, but it's not the drama any more, it's an ad. The two come together. So also in this paper." O.K., O.K., Laura, difference between captive audience and captivated. Still not sure about interaction between, interrelationship of, perspective and metaphor, Aristotle and the masters of metaphor, like saying something is like something is pretty hard to do, no? O.K., O.K. More relevant now: "I have followed all this—and you—because I did not want to fail whomever's course this was and/or is. But I firmly believe you ask too much....

"Mr. Hind, have you too had intimations someone started to search for you but has now stopped?"..."Your own private kidnap inspired me to":

yes, a child is abducted by a man and a woman in a late-model hardtop convertebrate, Laura; but didn't *I* supply you with that detail? "A considerable sum of cash is asked"—but for heaven's sake this isn't the Laurel—"but

to protect themselves the man and woman pretend to ask
for half now (down), the rest to come in monthly installments." But before the apparent down (which would have
been the final) payment can be met, Laura, if I may ex-
trapolate from your term paper, the vivid forceful woman persuades the tall clever man to keep the child and
forgo down payment as *well* as time installments. "Call
the kidnapers Sylvia and Jack, Mr. Hind, call the kid
May." Sylvia again. "Or call the kidnapers other names:
the facts don't matter, it's the *idea*. The point, though, is
this: how like our own life is this event! Before we can
even wake up into our strength, we are transferred, injured, stunted into a new scene we aren't familiar with.
Later we are made objects and priced." Generality, Laura:
or is the general meant to marshal a smoke screen to hide
the simple particulars, for instance associating himself
and Syl in such a reversed—"Just think how our life is like
a kidnap: the black man, literally abducted to this country, has his manhood—if he isn't lucky—bled out of him
before he learns his true identity; maybe he resigns from
society, maybe he has love left." (Berry Brown, the pier.)
"The child can't reach his parents, who are half in the bag
before dinner, and so must invent his own bedtime story." (Edison Beecher and Maddy, though not Flo, who is a
devout cook.)" There he is in his bedroom, a prisoner. Or
look at marriage: safety at the price of mutilation." (Very
possibly Ash and Peg.) (Who kidnaps whom?) "Or look at
what *you* look like and sound like—find an empty bottle
to blow across the top of that tells you what you want to
hear, and then you'll keep coming back to that bottle for
the same reassurance, and you'll also find a person who
sees you as you like to see yourself, and you'll fall into an
identity that works—" (Not so fast, mirrors are "in" these
days, all the mutually mirrored FHHC members merging
with each other's hopes in the blued, faintly elongated,
faintly intimatized gym mirrors—in them Hind alone came

off badly, but his accentuated narrowness reminded him that, mirrored, he could multiply and thus be more numerous in the FHHC gym where he watched and heard.) Just out of college Hind would bicker emptily with the guardian and not know how it started or what the point would turn out to be: "Damn it, Jack, there is such a thing as inborn character, however true all our liberal views are of the terrible ambiguous collaboration between circumstance and genes. Yes, character. But the pitiable point is, you can turn away from your real nature." But "Circumstance controls that chosen turn," he the adopted son retorted to his guardian, "circumstance." "Nothing doing. Circumstance is only one parent, and a spectator-parent at that. No, character is there from the start. The trick is knowing who you are." (The day angry Mr. Amondson had his wallet with all his identification pick-pocketed by the friendly Oriental, he'd been looking all over the Heights for his son Christy, listening for Christy's skates, listening up Remsen and down Hicks—but that's another tale made of forgotten, irrelevant names:) Laura was back on her parents. "But you had some idea you would take me away from all that. Which was generous of you, Mr. Hind. But I don't need it. If there's any kidnaping to be done to me, I for one will do it myself." No, no, irrelevant again. "But being kidnaped is par for the course. Look at what they've built up around us, they're trying to break us." He wanted to skip this obviously irrelevant passage but the words seemed attractive simply in themselves, their shapes, associations. "A city turned to glass, and on a hill a glass campus of blocks inside which you see dark banks of students and the lighter planes of the green slate blackboards. But then the word is published abroad, the slanting green of that slate colors all the outside surfaces of the university and the slate green spreads out on the city till at last the city is made of the green blackboard slate and younger generations screech their white chalks all over the green, drawing people and trees and lewd double meanings that have nothing to do with real sex; and our real teacher, Dr. Plane, is going all over taking down graffiti." Hysteria, some daydream, though rooted in her real agony. Someday come back to these students, and with nothing else in mind. "You've enough to do for your wife Sylvia without making a hobby out of brainwashing us."

Air pollution woke you up in the morning with an aching dryness in the front of the upper gums. But Laura was wrong (or misinformed, or fishing for information) when she complained that he reduced his job and those entailed in it, to one weird hang-up she had wondered about but now thought either didn't matter or did to the wrong people like the Inter-Disciplinate Council or the CIA—she couldn't trust him. He couldn't of course ask her point-blank how she could even hope to guess how wholly he embraced those entailed in the Hershey hunt, the Laurel Labyrinth, the—

Indeed the truth was that his participation in these people created the Hershey hunt, and Hershey followed from Hind's part in others, how could it be else? Consider, for example: (1) Hind's concern for the sunbathers at the pier—hence naturally he would care for the Laurel case, and hence likewise he was destined to overhear the pier's Oriental visitors, whether or not sent by the white-haired old woman; (2) Hind's strange likeness to and intimate interest in poor supervisory Maddy Beecher, old friend who like Hind busies himself to help, and like Hind made the public possibility his field, yet who the exact reverse of Hind did not by pursuing one end touch strongly *all* but rather in trying to do everything (design, production, PR, administral policification, pedagogy, social work, patronage) ended with the mere *one* disembodied job paid in hugely inverse proportion to its definiteness; (3) Hind's physical link to Ash Sill, their ears, to remind Hind that he listened totally for the needs of the many (hence the one, Hershey Laurel) to protect People from becoming Objects, to indeed defoliate with helpless, irresistible compassion the jungular assimilations in which the perishable Person more and more was lost; (4) the significance of Dewey Wood—for instance, his "You can't have your pie and eat it too": (he could think the change from cake to pie deepened the proverb) yet his mind sounded not deep but bland, and charitable resignations that had made Hind like Dewey turned thin and flat: so—and here it came—suppose you revolve the chamber (whether the pistol is to be aimed at you or something else) and translate instead: "You can't have your pie with*out* eating it"; (5) how Hind's aid to Ol opened Hind's arms to all those college kids, simultaneously moving Hind up (down, through) to the Laurel answer.

Smith Answering would type and send him to Sylvia's a list of calls and messages. "So, Mr. Hind, I conclude—" (but Laura was compromising her usefulness letting herself drift into criticisms of him) good, you shuttle partway, take that small airline the rest of the way to the foot of Mount Mary, hire a Chevy and cut to the coast, forty-odd miles—"conclude, Mr. Hind, that you asked too much of us in class, roped us in but then after we did the theme told us we were crazy. But—and I bet I speak for the rest of the class, though I may not know them—you didn't at first *plan* to undercut the assignment: the truth is, you changed your mind about it. More shocking still—" *you*, Laura? *YOU!* shocked cocked, you hypocrite!—"you did not convince me your mind would stay changed: you try to make us unsee degrees of depth in Dürer's *Flight into Egypt* so we can see truly the quote unquote ultimate topography scratched by the man's hand in a wood block that remains a wood block. Yet the picture's story"—Sylvia might have someone up there, a guy, even a girl, anyone, Hind would have to reconnoiter, he didn't even know which place on the island she had this summer–"big Joseph tramping through the trees leading the ass and apparently a wavy-horned, surely not casually wandering, cow (the church?) past a fork-staked pen and onto a small bridge–and as he sets his big left foot down looking back at Mary to see if she's all right–or even, still there–well, you couldn't begin even to *tell* us this story if Dürer's modeling and depth and perspective did not make you see what you dare to dismiss as illusion. What are you trying to do, break us? What good is it to say, Unsee all this and even if you have to dilate your eye to do it see only surface sections of hatchings and blanks."

It was earlier than he expected when he arrived, and the light had lasted longer, he hadn't been paying attention lately to the times of dusk. And Sylvia and May were barely moving in the boat in the bay, he saw them from the so-called ferry, just an old greasy-beamed scalloper retired from active duty.

"And I would add, though this will probably lower my mark with you, that I can be just as truly there in that German forest that masquerades as the borderland near Egypt, near those peering trees and that reptile palm, as can Dürer himself who has hooked his initials on a woody root. You change back and forth, Mr. Hind, because you don't know yourself. You say it's all background–us too–there is no foreground, we are part of a flat design. Maybe you want to disappear into your background. But I see myself *against* mine. I'm here, and behind me at opposite corners of this long living room–" Long Corners, four miles from the Laurels' and the Loves'–"my mother with her stereo earplugs and my plump father with his new TV earphones monitoring for audio flaws, catch each other's eyes and split my kidnaped silence between them–and there *is* space between us, and each has his own perspective."

Now it was again becoming personally (particularly, irrelevantly) Laura-1, and thus extra-Sylvioid. I have to leave you, Laura dear, clue-bearer (-bearess, honey-cluebear) an excellent bedtime end doomed to be my momentary means: dear Laura, the gulls are calling and I am trying to pay the highest heed to Sylvia's bedtime documentary to May, who is less sleepy in her bunk than I in this wicker thing nearby. For, dear Laura, I have, intend, and hate like hell to leave your Hershey-hazel eyes, your legs, your neck, your bitten nails, your floating ribs, your hair, and the chance to draw you into that *somnium interruptum* to tell how I looked at my form and saw a terribly interesting thing, saw it exfoliating and turning to a horny green bud.

The child I pursue gets older, Laura; the kidnapers themselves are getting on. If it's any consolation I'm going to try to use Sylvia as I used you. But again for a decent (docent, demi-) end: namely, the recovery, salvage, rehabilitation of Child Hershey, that closed case. Next stop: Sylvia. Then maybe Long Corners maybe via wherever Syl first says to, hints to, go.

You will hear from me. In class you will discuss my absence.

You never know when a demanding memory may turn up (over, on).

May, once upon a time.

Hind's height, say.

And may require extrapolation like a statistic, or extraction like a tonsil.

"Vanilla for your ice cream cone comes from a bean on a plant. And once upon a time they thought it was magic medicine—once upon a time, before tractors and billboards. But I know that with you—and now you suddenly know numbers—it's 'Three years ago Christmas' or 'When Daddy was only six years old,' which you're going to be this month, so isn't it great that sleepy Daddy came up to be with us and maybe stay for your birthday cake next week? I know with you it's the event, not the fairy story, and Daddy's always been a better gossip than I, I have a hard time recalling what who said about who, though *my* thoughts are full of things too: but imagine at five going on six such a taste for family fact. You caught me—May?—on a story last night, are you too sleepy to remember how you caught me? One I'd told before, about Daddy's Daddy's treasure hunts; they had practically stopped by the time Daddy and I met, and your Granddad thought he'd keep having them for local year-round children who lived there in the country, you said you wouldn't like the country all year, remember?, because of the big orange crêpe poppy you saw at Buck Field's shop that Oliver forgot and didn't bring you. But one day when you were wheezing on the smelly elevated subway just before spring came you weren't sure, but maybe that was because Eddy Beecher was trying over the noise of the train to teach you negative numbers the way he learned at the school Daddy wants you to go to, you were only four years old then in the subway elevated, Eddy four years older bragging about an océanographic scavenger-beamer toy clamped to his bed. But Daddy is right, *my* Daddy, you can't bring up a kid like a plant—Granddad had to keep holding his treasure hunt every year if only for local kids, he loved giving out the envelopes on the morning, and the kids bustling away among the trees so not to be seen by each other when they decided where the first clue was telling them to go. Know what a clue is? (I bet you don't.) By the time I met Daddy, only a few parents cared, it was always anyway not the treasure but the hunt to keep the kids busy a whole day, Granddad put out two dozen black lunchboxes in two rows like—on the trestle table by the well; by then, when Daddy and I met, there were new Inter-Township Activities (as Ford Free, the Selectman in Charge of Health and Heritage for Children, called them) and the treasure—the autographed baseballs, the honey-leather Quoddy moccasins, the soccer shinguards, and books on white rhinos and Arabian antelopes and English wildflowers, the knife with the hartshorn handle, but nothing as nice as the paper cutouts Daddy bought me in the Polish castle—well, all this didn't seem enough in return for giving up a day at the brand new town pool with the high board Daddy said was too stiff, or giving up practice at Little League Park— May?—and instead do all that hunting in bogs and bushes and big old trees and dark holes right through to China, to boot. In fact, one little boy showed up for the hunt in his baseball uniform, but Granddad didn't know that the little boy had said after breakfast that he wasn't going on the treasure hunt, he had to try out for left field that day, and he got into his uniform (you remembered I forgot), went out to his bike but his father caught him and told him he *was* going to Granddad's annual treasure hunt because if he played it right he might be able to get him into college someday, even fork up a scholarship, which you don't understand, all if he liked him, it all depended if he liked you, this father said. And the little boy said, 'I don't want to go to college,' and his father said, '*Don't—*' May? you asleep? don't shake your head, you can't kid me you're resting your eyes again. Who'll fall asleep quicker, you in bed or Daddy with *his* eyes closed in the wicker chair?—the little boy said, 'I don't want to go to college,' and the father said, 'Don't ever say that to me again, what a dreadful thing to say!' May? So he was almost the only kid at the treasure hunt and the guardian, Granddad, felt almost like just awarding the prizes and calling off the hunt. May?" June, July, Jack. Asleep. Alone. But silent words are faster, brighter, though not colorfast.

*Vanity*, a nasty sound and not a fair summary. But vanity, my vanity, is at issue. You over there in my landlord's wicker chair with May's sand in the cushion were staring at me as if you'd never seen me before, but I was so vivid you dozed off. But I'm really quite eloquent when I don't have to speak. I'll wake you up to go to bed; want to touch you. And will you stay to breakfast? And which meal (tomorrow?) will be your last here? *You* won't stay for May's birthday. Clear weather tomorrow night, you'll be off, we'll spot the high-frequency beacon on top of Mount Mary. However, have I done a good job, have I? Creative Playthings, Inc., says that "These are the critical years." May doesn't have hovering over her one of those perspectival bed-anchored seascape stabiles like Eddy Beecher's of course. You're tired. You, let us say, have temporarily broken stride to come see wife and daughter. Or kill two needs with one scene? You went for the local phone book and didn't find what you wanted: we aren't in the Mount Mary area, is there a contact on Mount Mary? Your worn, shaggy-haired frankness hides ingenious desire. How tangled it seems, though I've been of course out of touch the last many months with your new search. You're an historian of long-unheard-from corners. So you've learned to see pictures flat you said to me as you were hauling the skiff up tonight, you've learned to see pictures flat: but how serious did you think I was the night—the day—I told you what my friend the friend of Maddy's had been saying to me? We'd begun merely on some snaps I'd had developed up in the country at Giant. Most men would ask about the guy himself, Maddy's friend, where did he know me and so forth: but *you*: you cared for his theory which isn't his own really, which is over my head, he heard someone speak of it at the Royal College; and you cared about some people he's supposed to know whom I do not know and neither I bet do you, you don't even know their names, people who roller-skate and snoop in other people's incinerator traps. Or: how is your old friend—"No," the guardian chaffs (chafes?) shy me, chides me; "speak univocally, Sylvia, univocally, you let double intentions lurk side by side in words where they're not wanted, or better said, *in which* they're not wanted," then his familiar refrain, our no-deposit Babel-ling multi-tongue—well, by "old friend" let me mean "elderly"—and how *is*, I mean, Dewey Wood? he'll hold up a Superette line five minutes to discuss with Captain Kidd the enlargements of his tinted grandchildren hanging from a Chap-ans Lip Balm placard above the register, until Captain Kidd pivots on the hip-length leg his policy did not after all cover and tilting his head at the basket-jam of irked customers says to Dewey, "Le'stalk when I got time." And you, who are supposed to love the world whole, give one last heavy lurch back with the bow of my landlord's skiff, so the old thing is now safely on the pebbles, and you look up at me and ask too quickly, "What *about* Dewey Wood? I've barely had time for him this summer." I thought you wanted to find a way to take my hand, not that this would change things. Or: how are Maddy and Flo? I ask, soaping May's golden arms ("Dial-A-Child")and salty hair so easy to bathe because she is charmed by your squatting presence at the tub edge, a hungry monster hesitating to reach into a nest—but one of your several forms and made by *my* mind, not May's, who cannot understand your great height except as a grownup's. You'd rather help anyone than us. Rather yield a real find for "Naked Voice" than have to hear the *true* story of one of your lame ducks. You want to help, help. And you'd sooner develop Hershey Schmershey than look fairly at yourself, as I told you you should for your own peace of mind. For instance, you know where the Hinds are buried—where they "are," as Thea Dover would say; and you know the guardian was their friend. But you don't care. Sure if all the tale did come out, how who happened when, nothing would no doubt be meaningfully solved; yes agreed, knowing the past is like getting married, doesn't change your hang-up. "Maddy and Flo?" you morosely say; "I use them, do you see, I just use them, especially Maddy," as if also it were my fault. I seldom found apt words—much less the key to your guardian's word challenges at lunch on the yellow screen porch. Professor Grimes tolerated their frivolity, while at the same time he would not be trapped into arguing his serious philology with your amateur guardian, who said, "What word—let's stump little Sylvia—" little only by contrast to you, though (strangely?) your guardian stood well over six feet—"what word combines travel expenses with last unction?" I bent for a considerable mouthful of the nutmeg spinach ring—the guardian's eye on me, my mouth safely full remembering how Mama caught me nibbling nutmeg when I was tiny—but the guardian kidding me as I munched, "She really knows but doesn't want to seem too—" But I did not, and I did not think the game of any importance, and Professor Grimes, with our beach sand still in his eyebrows, didn't know the answer either. Nor, as lunch passed, did he really want to discuss his Sound Spectrograph, either the guardian's general invitation—"It's fearful to think what the spectrograph may tell us about human speech"—or your sharp uncertainty—"Let's see: you would break voices into a gibberish of frequencies in order to penetrate—" But Professor Red Grimes went "Whee!" as dessert appeared, I had delivered a platter of vanilla ice cream piled as the guardian liked it, roughly, richly, in trowel-scoops, the specks of vanilla like dark sand, and Grimes did not even treat your query like, say, a student who'd bristled into class without actually doing the day's lesson. As for me your guardian was only once or twice anything but courteous, though so watchful of my every turn that I was in school taking an exam, with you yourself the good grade I may have wanted but doubted I'd get. I hear him: "I don't own Jack, but he's virtually my own son and I cannot help feeling that I give him away to you. Thus, you become the person who must be able to receive him. Do you see?" Wow! Why not! Of course I saw! And more clearly than I saw the point of debating the psychomorphology of the linguistic contamination "irregardless" or prescriptive versus descriptive lexidermy, or how to say "banal." More clearly though not conclusively I saw your four hands: how you caught his gauche habit of leaving one hand behind when using the other: I saw this when you jockeyed each other in that skylit country squash court that Daddy said you couldn't build today for less than a hundred thousand, what with the springy end-on wood of the front wall, but now abandoned by you to trunks and paddle tennis racquets and tangled unidentifiable nets and the chipmunks along the high corners near the broken skylight—left hand left in a funny awkward reach, or thrust in the middle of a right-hand stroke as if independently afraid to think itself into a relaxed place back by the side: he did it, and you did it, and I caught a hint of it tonight when you first reached your right out to grab under the ridge inside the skiff's bow, your left hung out as if to balance—and (or for) your guardian did the same: yet his left scooping up ice cream that summer day at lunch, with Red Grimes sighing blandly refusing to reply to your irked word "gibberish," was near your right that rested palm down on the table by the creamy platter, when I saw, for I study hands (not palms), a thing I had not seen: each showed an abnormally high bone bump an inch behind the knuckle as if (and also on your guardian's right and your left, I later saw) you'd broken your hands:

and yet I knew that was not what had happened, they simply were that way. I see and feel and at special times hear hands clearly. How well can you asleep in my landlord's wicker chair's network recall when you and I on the day of your guardian's death sat in that great Heathrow waiting room and I told you about my billboard with the mobilized string bean, and you seemed to listen but were getting, in a word, teed off at the man using my ashtray, and I don't know if you were listening to me, I barely listened to myself I was worried so how your guardian's death hit you, especially as there you were, chasing a hunch so scarce I never wrote Daddy why we were really in Europe: and I was wondering would you feel guilty to be caught by the guardian's death in such an act? looking for an obscure kidnap victim? And then you turned in your seat in the waiting room, so determined to turn your back or almost your back to the man who irritated you with his cigarette that you got into a perilous position one half of your backside off the leather bench—it was a leather bench—and you said, "Sometimes I think a day will come when all the right people have died and I am alone on the earth. Did you ever have that feeling?" I'd have asked if you meant that all other people as well would have gone; but you were not in a state to be taken seriously in that way. Nor I (that summer day on the porch at lunch the clock ringing two barely in range of the waves a mile off coming in upon the guardian's beach) to take him less than too seriously when he puzzled my hands with his word-game reminding me of the word I couldn't come up with, so that I in a menaced pause ignorant of the answer word (travel expenses, last unction) could think only that I hadn't had that grounding in Latin that he said was indispensable and I could not move my hands from their dead, clammily dismembered embarrassment there by the platter of faintly dark-speckled big vanilla hunks that, the way they melted, Mama would have thought a poor substitute for a good lengthwise cut of a three-flavor Family Brick and you could return for more if you—handed round the helpings dug from the huge-looking chunks by the guardian, but even with hands occupied couldn't come up with—

"Viaticum!" at last cried Grimes the no longer red-haired perhaps in part to end my dumbness but also in the voice of one who went along with the guardian's game so gaily you wouldn't forget who he was, I've seen this kind of thing before—Jim Lowe Cedric worked two years for Burroughs in Italy, got so good at bridge I guess that when I saw him again wearing tighter trousers and perforated shoes he was talking of picking up master points; he played poker then one Sunday night with us and lost loudly and lightly and asked Daddy twice too often if a flush beat a full boat, as if poker were a gag, which the stakes were to Jim. Yet also a person will think you're brooding on him when you hardly are: and so the guardian appeared in the kitchen after lunch as I was turning on the FM with wet hands: and he said, "'Viaticum'—used to confuse it with 'Vatican' but I'd never have admitted it as a testy adolescent at my father's cutthroat table": etcetera, as bad (the guardian said) as looking at a big "X" with "I-N-G" after it painted on a California street and not knowing it meant CROSSING: "Thea Dover and I," said the guardian, "howled at little Jack that day for asking idly what the four letters meant, he was a daydreamer then. But I was thinking one day just exactly about this word 'viaticum,' and not as ink or sound or what Dr. Grimes would diagnose as, in part, a voiced labiodental fricative, but as a warning to me not to get so used to living that one day I'd die without providing for someone to keep an eye on Jack. Left unadvised he would give away time, money, and more patience than a man should have, to anyone who went to him in or even out of trouble. I thought of a cousin of mine, my age; we would have to have a reconciliation, for this cousin disowned me when I adopted Jack, possibly because Jack would inherit, possibly because of something more personal, more dangerous." But then the guardian faded, though he couldn't walk out in mid-conversation or go to the radio and ask me what I wanted while I did the dishes, or (because of his grounding in Latin?) offer to help with the dishes. And so he said, "You know, someone older, to keep an eye on him." I could see, he hoped, that quote unquote "viaticum" and any other word wasn't a fetish with him, although—now moving toward the swinging door—"Your favorite word—" "What?" I asked, "*My*–?" "Your word 'Wow' is perhaps no more than what Grimes would call it—a voiced labiovelar glide." He smiled, winked, and wetly clucked his tongue, I wondered when I'd start calling him "Fossy." Later I heard him getting angry at his guest Grimes, who I gathered preferred not to discuss his specialty (speciality?), and was glad the squash court was too hot to use, and hoped to just pass relaxed talk back and forth, stroll to the beach, get genteelly canned before dinner, and afterward slightly boss-eyed read Housman aloud poorly. "Wow"?

Viaticum, viaduct, vis-à-vis—words, Laurels, ho and hum, well I have a mystery too, and not merely the bill-board and what it meant to a ten-year-old nymph un-expectedly at sea the day the wedding Chevy—a *Chevy, yes!* sporting a sailor's hash-marked arm—all but ran me down—but a mystery about you and my father, both of whom are, as Thea Dover nostalgically said of your guardian, "So many different men." If I said—assuming you were awake in my wicker chair, which you're not—that I saw parts of Daddy in you, you might well try to weigh my words in the scale of your kidnap investiga-tion; yet, for all that madness, where am I in your kidnap investigation? Yet it wasn't merely May and the nearness of Mount Mary that brought you over here to the coast.

You like my kidney beans, or am I a silly cow vis-à-vis the fact that like the millions of other American husband chefs you can roll your own omelet and sauce your own salmon much less bake your own beans, small pea, big red kidney, large yellow eye, dark brown sugar (not brownulated but thick and crumbly with an after-stickiness), ketchup, and a suspicion of English mustard, yes I am a silly cow: did you come up to see merely me, am I an end in myself, yet can you be an end in yourself?—do I steal an unquote from your guardian or my nice man in the subway change booth who tells me what he's learning in his night course, that there are no such things as ends in themselves. I have a mystery too, and not merely what my relations once were with the middle-aged, ravishing Staghorn in his attic across the valley with whom I did joint sketches he a stroke I the next he the next stroke and so on, and who Daddy poor Daddy was grateful to for living so near us, when Staghorn hadn't chosen that big house to be near us but only because he wanted to be in a village at a considerable distance from the college, where he loathly but uniquely taught, the college in whose town Daddy worked, the coed institution not (as I told Thea) to be confused with the girls' college where *I* went quite far away (for as Maddy Beecher said vis-à-vis the beautiful IBM operator, You don't shit where you eat). Not Staghorn was, is, my mystery (though I did come to him), nor is the Gypsy Woman, wherever she be now and however old:

Visceral her performance assuredly was, and totally convincing, wrote a reviewer visiting from our so-called and much despised brother-college seventeen point three miles off over the state line and two small purple mountains, who happily confessed he wasn't familiar with the German original our college's play was dramatized from and would like to suggest, he said, that he was thereby better equipped to respond thereto—the Gypsy Woman was with him the last night when with her feet darting out like a dancer and her too muscular calves in Lincoln green rehearsal tights from her senior (transfer) year at High School of Music and Art, she came pounding down our hall intent on seeing not me—I was back in the auditorium building looking for her—but (and taking to a cast blast) Aster the Student Reviewer at our own college who had called my Gypsy Woman wholly persuasive in the newly expanded role, and I thrilled to every printed word, saying to myself I *know* her, feeling also I barely guessed what: privately she told tales of her travels, though never exactly of her background, and though funny they were not greeted with laughter, though with alarmed attention. There was serious, sunlamp-pink Aster (who wore tailored suits there at college deep in the country), and there was the elegant, blue-haired gent whose constant visits to the college from his nearby estate were purely social, I thought, till I found out he had always wanted to be asked to lecture on the history of gambling, and he would say of the Gypsy Woman after one of her stories, "Where does she dig up this wonderful stuff?" Viscerally speaking, as Maddy said that long night much of which I spent with him and John Plante in my smoky apartment that didn't seem to get less so with the windows open, viscerally speaking I have my own mystery which you cannot understand, though Daddy could understand it even though I'll never tell him for he is part of it but he is so unlike you that I wouldn't call attention to the differences by explaining to him the mystery, it is so simply silly in words, but so hard beyond words: so smoothly Mama said one day, "You couldn't hardly have picked a fellow more different than your father, Jack Hind's almost the spitting opposite, might's well be the other side of the street without my glasses." If I had, say, Flo Beecher's soft blond patience—not to mention societal tenderness radiantly eyeing dressed-up colored kids on the bus and (give her credit) dying to get her hands on them, and if I had John Plante's eye, why maybe then I would study you: not your knee that you barked beaching my skiff or the long olive shorts you wore up on the plane, or the perma-seem twist-curl of the hair over the left temple by which I tell that you haven't shampooed your hair in a while, an almost greasy cowlick your guardian foster father had all gray in the same exact place: not all that, and I know all that anyhow, or without knowing it: no, in order to know why you look like your faster fother (some grafted sympathy?), and why in heaven's name you picked that little boy with the fictional name to pursue for God knows only how long—your talk of how everyone forgot the case, and what forces would seek the truth about him if you didn't, namely none. It isn't like a hobby, yet it isn't true work either. Yet "Naked Voice," which really got a name among ordinary people and sociologues and even dialect scholars and even the Love Folk, it's a little thing on your heart, even when listeners react like they do to any documentary nowadays, only with yours more so thinking you have some editorial scent when I for one know your editing is not to edit. Basically in terms of what you actually do: you let the guinea pig talk. Daddy's good at that, though like you usually with strangers. If the stranger wants to talk Daddy will hear him with the beginning of a smile on his mouth for sometimes an hour on end, even when the person is half the time looking not at him but handling paisley button-downs or half-pigskin driving gloves and in the end doesn't want to buy and never did. The billboard etcetra was not separate from Daddy, in a way he was its end, the string bean mobilized there on that flat garish oblong only led me to him, the new him, and suddenly there he was, puffing round the bend. But I did not say to him that thing. And we've all gotten along without my having said it to him. I was no stranger. Strangers talk to Daddy. Where is the billboard? Its nine-by-fourteen window against the thick, poor growths of birch and scrub oak fifty feet back of it has now been repeeled, repasted, year upon year. There was our house at the north end of the village (with the high ramshackle barn Daddy could never quite bring himself to sell for the two hundred dollars the timbers were worth, and didn't have the nerve considering its state to advertise for winter boat storage); and on the road northeast from our place was the billboard. Before that morning of the wedding Chevy, I had the billboard, and I had our deep yellow house with the white trim (Was the *house* deep or the *yellow*? asks the guardian, well grounded in Latin, from the grave if he had one, which he did not), and I had the road to the town where Daddy worked, and then the lake at the far end where until years later not only couldn't you drive because it was private, but there were two flashing green canoes, I always see them. Yet after the billboard I remember distance: like: two miles northeast from house to billboard; from the village the other way eleven miles to the college town where Daddy worked; three-plus miles past there to the long lake at the southwest end of which was Amondson's rickety dock and on a rise their brick house that was empty seven months a year, as fine a red as my maple on October fifteenth. I came to know that in summers behind the house Mr. Amondson hoed in and weeded out his steady gripe against a son and wife who had absorbing interests of their own, and against the land itself because he always put in too much lettuce and cukes and crunchy New Zealand spinach, though there wasn't any difficulty eating up the radishes, he ate them all himself. Christy did a lot of eating too (barbecue corn, which Mr. Amondson did not grow, and plates of crusted, flattening piles of brown pea beans), and about killed his father by roller-skating the country roads around as if it were Remsen Street or Garden Place, and (unquote Mr. A:) "reacting negatively" to his father's ingenious canoe tests modeled after those given at a nearby camp, to which in despair one July he did send Christy so that Christy, as it fell out, could overnight become an absolutely inhuman badminton player (grew four inches that summer bouncing on the balls of his feet near the high net waiting to kill anything that got too close). I don't try the impossible, and it's not worthwhile looking, like your guardian, for primitive motifs in my flat designs for wrapping paper much less in my book jackets—though maybe you were right I should have tried to go beyond the—men in my life—should have committed myself to, "committed," an ugly word of crime or lunacy—men at two A.M. three four five in my smoky Hindless flat disqualifying each other: "*You* have to call that a ghetto situation because," says John Plante to Maddy Beecher, "you're committed to those terms"—irked that Maddy called him Jack and Johnny—and just before scrambled eggs, which I knew May would smell and wake up, Maddy disqualifying John Plante, "*You* have to conclude the Family quote unquote is finished as a viable socio-entity because you're committed to your polyamorous roller tribe, so you can't even so to speak let me into court." Occupying, taking over, stealing me and my flat while I shook too much chervil into the eggs, pretty to see, and hoped the humming hub of a reconditioned humidifier in May's room to compensate for the radiators would drown out the Plante-Beecher differences. They wolfed their eggs and suddenly went, Maddy as usual half-seriously saying to Plante, "If that kid you brought up with the girl weren't so committed to something or other he wouldn't snub me in my own house and sniff around the incinerator as if he hoped to find Billy Jim Hargis Christian Crusade literature or my indoor golf instructions"—I hardly gave a thought to the perspective idea you later picked up that Plante had—half-seriously was almost all Maddy was willing to speak to Plante that night (men have some-

times impenetrable friendly conflicts), and even I could
see he wanted to take off the gloves (*put on*?), he wanted
to say something personal to Plante and wouldn't even
alone without me, was dumb with admiration (now I
think of it) when Plante aired *his* English friend's perspective theory which was part of his plan to switch from
architecture to sculpture from uptown to downtown
from war to peace and to his friends who all live together
near Chinatown and who Love. But I learned perspective
and know it exists: I see it and can make it and know it
can't be avoided. What do his friends who Love talk to
each other? Would you really wish what they claim? Isn't
there something you don't tell no one: the guardian, Daddy, you—old Staghorn asking me at the age of nearly sixteen if I had ever been bedded—Jim Commons, who misunderstood that I had no resistance at all to the idea of
his flat on the Heights but resistance to everything else,
every planned improvisation, he misunderstood my ruse
about having bad cramp, so at last I had to simply say, "I
don't *want* to stay over." I could wish the guardian had
told me, in confidence of course, some more of the truth
about you: for then I could have—told you immediately
and you would know: yet I know well all you've said,
dates, ages, grades, games, faces, hands, better than you
think, I've plotted monogrammed cobwebs casually left
by you: if I were someone else, and if I were you, I would
have tried to track down your parentage beyond the family facts of who they were, you never broke down and explained why you didn't undertake such an investigation,
what with your techniques, equipment, contacts, money,
time to sift the evidence. The guardian was, I believe, on
the point of giving me something before we sailed. You're
so great a gossipy God knowing all about others, either
you know about your own past and won't tell, or simply
don't want to know—but think of May, she'll want to
know. But I have my own mystery, nothing about per-

spective, nor do I mean the billboard revelation—nor even the lost ring I never told you of, that you gave me. I took it off to wash dishes, you were coming to take me away to the Cape for the weekend. The water wouldn't run hot, but then suddenly it did as the door went: it was you: I turned the sink drain so it caught and dropped and plugged the sinkhole, and I couldn't decide whether to answer the buzzer (you're not patient) or squeeze some Green Magic into the water. Well, I did both but neither: I did run out into the living room and through the hall to the door, but first, without squeezing any *in* the sink I grabbed the detergent and as I went out registered another sound, a prickly rustle as I left the sink but never thought what was it. There *you* were, or rather six Sweetheart Roses, you held them around the edge of the door as I pulled it open, but we were going to the country where flowers grow: without looking at who was on the other side of the door I dashed back to the sink clutching my Green Magic and I squeezed some in and heard feet and then thought what if—Christ it could have been the tall Chinese grad student who'd stood across the street when I came out twice that week, not that I'm like that about Orientals despite their masked skin but: then you said, "I'll do those," and I went to the bedroom to finish packing. When you put a handful of silver into the cutlery slot of my drying rack, I was coming out of my room, and when I put down my bag by the bookcase in the foyer you loomed up with a crackling brown-paper bag of four days' trash garbage for the hall incinerator. Walking to the kitchen to see if you'd—I could visualize the ring sitting on the sink edge by the detergent, and I recalled the rustling sound just as I'd got to the threshold, and I hoped it wasn't too late to restore that full trash bag to the waste can, I turned toward the room you'd passed through, and I heard the incinerator trap bang. And suddenly you were back, you took a book from a table and said, "Put this in too, eh?" My hands clammy with fear for the ring I got ready to go, we were wonderfully alone, and there passed into my mind the theory that my figure was a sort of hourglass figure. If by then I had already moved into the older bigger apartment without the incinerator, I'd still have the ring now.

Viscerally speaking, of course, droned Maddy, half-drunk with tiredness trying to interrupt Plante, viscerally speaking, where does your pal with the long hair and the Nazi cross on his breast get off nosing around my incinerator when I'm his host: but Johnny was talking to me and merely said it didn't have to be a Nazi cross, and Maddy went out to the kitchen, the dumb-waiter door so thick with old paint you wanted to chip it, and he was muttering quite loud, "No incinerator, what kind of building is this with only a dumb-waiter? Answer? An old building:" and as he opened the old door and began with that ancient rumbling from down below to haul on the filthy dumb-waiter rope, I couldn't listen to Plante and, wondering if you emptied your trash properly at the undertaker's, who of course has no incinerator in that old brownstone, I recalled Daddy, or rather the back of his head which in reality it would have been impossible to see with the trunk lid up, for the sight was him driving the trash to the dump Saturday afternoon, the two cans and the high yellow plastic kitchen wastebasket wedged in the open trunk, so you of course couldn't see the back of his head, though I could in my mind's eye then as Maddy began to load my dumb-waiter with a brown Superette bag of bottles, bitching about his incinerator. Daddy and I took the trash to the dump through the rich trees on an October afternoon, and the old bluenose in possession of that soupcan-strewn hill told me this was but one of five jobs he held down in his retirement, he named them on his swollen fingers, and no one was permitted to take anything away from the dump except him. The weekend that began by our losing my silver ring I let myself feel guilty for going up to the country but not going to see Daddy (and Mama). He'd never have said, "He's abnormally tall—for you," or "He's city, you're not," any more than he'd have said, untruly, "Jack Hind's sort of upper class, bet that's high society where he was raised by his foster father." Daddy's objections to you were as indirectly put as my question and his answer would have been had they ever been exchanged that day at the billboard after the wedding Chevy whisked away honking. Under hill and under dell, I know myself. In the end I am—am I?—not city—must shampoo my own rug, wax-wash my own floors: not Shirley Laurel hiring one of the Love kids to do housework, for which Beulah despised Shirley, a city softie, shirker, amoral, who did only her own cashmere sweaters, of which she had twenty-three-odd monogrammed, all of which she hand-washed, sandwich-toweled, and strung along the line one end of which was tied around that tree you got so warm about: in those days before the Welcome Wagon brought a new threat greater than the one of isolation, Shirley's compensatory late-night ceramics were accompanied by her radio beamed there in the woods to far peculiar all-night conversations, Long John and life in the Elsewhere. I was by then of the city, your city, which you said tonight looks less to be that old bag of dramatic dilemmas with its old geographical name, and more and more a less and less distinct coastal density marked by ever-rise edifices—seal-tight see-through solid-state tubeless dead-end-tubey vertical message units. There was a *true* question I didn't ask Daddy—as opposed to what you in your driven delirium emergency might have: I, yes, unlike you, did not look at that mobile bean and plead with Great Know-It-All prosperously expanding His Royal Space—to tell why bean and tractor and the rest were unassorted distance-wise, and tell why there was a flat billboard without perspective which was always mere illusion anyway. I must start again. That wasn't the sort of thing I'd have asked Daddy then if I'd asked. Not that I was ever in front of him afraid to be a fool, as I *could* feel (and in a word sexually) approaching an intersection-turn having the right of way and being observed by an eligible male driver through his windshield, waiting for me to do whatever I'm going to do, watching me with a maleness quite tense considering the distance, the metal, the shatterproof glass. At first after Daddy taught me (all but backing in, which I taught myself and then you taught me), I would always turn off the radio approaching an intersection-turn and being watched by waiting male motorists. You don't want to make a blooper in front of a man—for the sake of grace, not so much to win—and nowadays they'll watch like cats; but I don't want to win some heterographic completion, to win at all, or lose, yet most not to make a little fool of my country self, or to be so made, as by Jim E.'s buddy whose interest in me was I suspect something fairly peculiar between him and Jim: yet more than to be made, to make: the Hit Parade (poignantly and electrically authoritative) zeroes in upon that day of my muffed bombshell delivered to Daddy that may not perhaps have been a gaffe for a kid of eight but: hearing the news that Sunday afternoon seemed like the announcer saying the night before, "Thirty seconds away from Number One," the week's Top Hit: but this was Sunday, but what was the hit Saturday December sixth, and did Joan Edwards sing "The White Cliffs of Dover" that had virtually slain my heart with yearning the last couple of weeks so that when I (thinking it would be on in three hours) did the supper dishes Saturday Mother asked me to please not hum it any more: but I, the next day, that Sunday afternoon, lying on my elbow with a stack of Mother's old *Delineators* and *Home Companions*, had that very kind of Hit Parade thrill to leave the steady serious radio and walk with a busybody's bustle downstairs, then past Mother and the guests' greetings—they should not be the first to learn—down cellar where Daddy they said had gone and where he—was just standing (what on earth was he up to, was he getting away from guests or Mama's hospitality?), and turned to me as I clambered down the wood steps to deliver my hot news: "The Japanese bombed Pearl Harbor, guess what?" having nothing to add after the misplaced lead question and he turned to me as if I had lied—though he didn't then ask, "What?"—and all I wanted was some thanks for producing this surprise, but he only said, "This time *we'll* get bombed." Herbie went to no war, for in the usual sense there was none, though Herbie refers to himself as a Korean veteran.

Vantage is the name of the game and Daddy was trapped there in the cellar and did not enjoy being flung that headline. On the other hand maybe it's relevant that Daddy never liked being brought the bed tray when down with flu, and always liked to read when eating but wasn't allowed to unless he beat Mama up for breakfast, which was hard on him because she didn't sleep exactly like a log. Here I am looking at you but thinking of Daddy, who said to you, "You seem to get into a lot of lines, communication media, rehabilitation, teaching, child welfare, what else?" "But they all lead," you said, "to one thing." "Social work? the man in the street?" "No, me." Daddy stayed off the topic of your money because your advantages embarrass him but not because he didn't have them (though he didn't), rather because he seldom used his own. Which you'd think were everything that happily seems to be seen in his calm, intentional face when in September he's pointing out to a returning student—considerable customer or just a sock-jock occasional (with a Christmas plus of gloves for father)—what changes had been made during summer school, the selected best-sellers in one long window next to some new Oxford shirt stripes, or getting rid of the phonograph records (no space, wrong tone, you got to let a kid play the record before he doesn't buy it)—that seems to be seen in Daddy's reluctance to persuade, to speak unless spoken to, his watchful attention to the young people, not in case of pilfering—he didn't care about the case of disappearing socks—but in order to regrasp the receding hand of the future, to listen—to "This 'Naked Voice,' Jack, for instance you come down to CCC—College Corner Clothier, if anyone wants to make a note of it—and you'll pick up the sound of the younger generation, they're returning to college from all the cities and the big towns, you'd be surprised—have to revise some of your ideas—and they can find anything they desire in my place, and I'm usually ahead of them, double-breasted sport coats came in and two fellows from Worcester didn't even know, but bought." In the hockey and dance programs he advertised "SPORTS AND MUFTI APPAREL for Ladies and Gentlemen," but he's no more salesmanlike than you, he wants to be asked to give his company and his opinion and his talents whatever they may have been. But hasn't a chance to for Mother finished planning her life after I completed college, there's no more space in her life for accident or help than there is in the kitchen for another of her "Wall Accents" like the forty-inch American eagle with the five gold stars stuck in the wood paneling above. Herbie followed the stock market from Boston to New York, his narrow, soft face betraying only the tic-tic at the jaw's long corner, but more in dirty jokes he told like the terrible mustard speedway when he was eighteen and I was nauseated, no man who calls it the mustard speedway really likes women—and since he claimed to me he feared Daddy might one day shift from his steady four-and-a-half percent savings with the Co-op to the wrong kind of growth stock, Herbie didn't pass Daddy any tips. Daddy was given a tour of the Exchange and of Herbie's firm's offices. Daddy asked you, "Why do you take on these underprivileged kids, your private help isn't barely a speck on the horizon, I'm not exactly saying let them help themselves but isn't your work private handout charity when...?" "What?" "When what's needed..." "Is a program?" "Yeah, if you see what I mean." To which you replied, "You're sounding quite left." But all he ever said against the grain was once, and no question mark, "He's too tall, isn't he." But was sort of proud of what you do. I told him more neutrally than you deserved how you'd listen to our so-called friends for any number of hours tell the holy ins and outs of why they wanted, and ah then did not want, divorces; or worse—in a word, Bee Bee Barker, with the handsome flat, waxy face maybe to some tastes unfeminine but terribly female, calling every third man she mentioned a Fascist, at last breaking down in front of you saying she'd lied to you for months (though, she said, what difference could it make, the man in question was a Fascist cop-out do-gooder), lied to you on that couch for months, for she didn't really want to be married she wanted only to live with (attached to, hold in her protecting arms) the dearest, most mixed-up *un*dyky kid we'd ever seen who resisted and resisted Bee Bee though Bee Bee had touched her and knew she wanted to be touched and knew much better that she needed Bee Bee to cook for and be organized by whereas despite Bee Bee this kid wouldn't walk out on her fat blue-eyed father although he invited an industrial psychologist on the make to come to dinner and unbeknownst to the kid herself sound her out—Bee Bee explaining in grateful detail all night to you, for I had at last soon after her third drink gone to bed, though I listened in, how this kid was tiny and her skin was smooth as olive oil and she could be very aware and also quite funny when she, if she *would* only, let herself go, and had to instead do dinners for her father's Fascist partners, her father lived near Maddy and Flo Beecher but Maddy and Flo hadn't met exquisite Marina yet but would. "He feels," said Daddy of you to someone, "he's especially lucky, and wants to help others as a result. Anyhow he's probably got his tape recorder under the settee capturing the neurotic city." Neither of these remarks is, or was, true of you asleep here. You were too tolerant when Bee Bee got hold of herself and said, "This is not an age of marriage: it's a newly communal psychocyclorama, we're all of us the scene together, we're brothers, our life together is a continuum you can't cut off with apartment walls and baby-sitters' schedules, if two people stop living together this doesn't break the social continuum, it feeds it, we're all brothers shaking each other up, prying upon each other's life, and wedlock is out." She never inquired how things went with Jack. Or me. She didn't cry again that night, but twice gruffly sent me into the kitchen: "Hit me again, honey" out of an unmagical cough of smoke, and when I came back and handed her her rum on the rocks she held my wrist the second time and looked up from the couch and said, "Honey!" She was tougher than true. Yet truer than John Plante, who never phoned again. Yet truer than my Gypsy Woman, who it turned out had never personally met the polite Italian pair she stayed with on the green campus of my college who in fact knew (in a way) socially the couple the Gypsy Woman said had asked her to look the Italians up on her passage through New England to Montreal, and she did, and almost uninvited stayed with them for (as it fell out) the period of rehearsals and the ten-night run, one might have thought she turned up just to be in the play, and did she foresee how extra hospitable the Italians would be? And so persuasive in the role was she that I caught myself calling her Gypsy Woman, and thought of her so when later we knew each other elsewhere: yet when those Italians years later ran into the Smiths from whom the Gypsy Woman had come to them, the Smiths could recall only running into her at a PTA-sponsored Round Robin Spelling Bee somewhere in Mass., Somethingfield: but her gossamer credentials could not be confused with her performance—was anyone even sure that she was fairly picked for the part over enrolled students? over, for instance, the skinny, huge-breasted one who did old people so well and would have played the Gypsy Woman in her two haunting appearances old? But *my* Gypsy Woman appeared at college, enchanted the Turin economist's wife (herself no less than a thirty-year-old retired archaeologist), though failed to enchant the man himself; was to be seen that warm November tramping the nearby hill in her luminous metal-green kerchief that made her nose Savonarolan, and was the hit of the run as the Gypsy Woman played by her I gathered later younger than written, though not very young; and made friends with me. I told you a piece of it in order not to tell you all. When I considered telling you, once when we were swapping secrets, I caught myself thinking of Daddy, who is part of the background I know I partly am. And you. You I could tell it to no more than I could Daddy: though your reactions would appear to differ, Daddy closing his eyes (raising eyebrows, giving away his hand), but you responding too wisely, warmly, and well to be intimate. With. You would underneath not even be so startled as you'd seem. Yet would fear to show the square old male thing you've always wrongly imagined would fit your huge holy supersympasocial hand. So I told you and Daddy some of it but not all of it, as the kidnapers must have little Hershey. Side by side, even overlapping, you and Daddy were listening to my every syllable about the Gypsy Woman, or so it seemed when really I told you separately, so maybe in some bypass language I mouthed but couldn't understand, the Gypsy Woman's prospect of Personatic Flow was true, you and Daddy overlapping. Told her childhood tales so strangely and briefly I felt

taken right away from her and from wherever one happened to be—and I listened to her tell stories in at least
three different places—taken so very far away that when
the tale was done you had a funny new look back upon
the life we all live. The Tall Platinum Mother—not a story
for May—lived in a dark charming city where rents were
never heard of, faintly central European, heavy stone
bridges over a slow amber river, men in long punts—but
beyond even this: and this Tall Platinum Mother one
bright morn came into the child's room where she was
watching her dolls dance a dance her mother had choreo-
graphed: and from behind her back the mother brought
three pictures, each of a handsome man: and she said to
the little girl, my Gypsy-to-be, "Which of these will you
choose to be your father?" And the little girl saw that two
of the men had light hair like her mother and one very
dark, and she could hardly believe that she was actually
going to pick out a father and touched the dark man and
found herself screaming with giggles: and her Tall Platinum Mother, picking her up off the floor though she
wanted now to go back to her dancing dolls who needed
her attention, kissed her lips, leaving a slight candy taste,
and said, "You have chosen and so it shall be." And indeed the dark man became the little girl's father soon afterward. Or was it really the Gypsy Woman's own mother's flat near the San Diego marine base? I turned up in
three or four locations as if on purpose to hear her tell
stories, so you might have thought I in some eerie style
was trailing her, or she forcing me to. You may go ahead
and tell me I like a story a bit too much, something silly in
me. But I like a tale never better than the teller—poor
Eddy Beecher, frightfully bright yet unbeknownst to him
well shy of genius, listens and listens to the stories he
reads, trying to sense which figure is the *real* teller of
the—which of the characters locked into the series, and
then, and then, but lo tally-ho and behold what should

the Black Prince begin to think as his couriers one by one came back from the Far and Long Corners of the Earth: only think how close you and I have been recently: from you to me has been a block south and then east across that wide, black avenue with the Police Emergency Service trucks running wild down the middle: And once a few weeks back there was a car—got puzzled because after it thought it couldn't, due to me, turn wide left into the avenue and then elected to corner close to sneak-and-run tight left between me and the curb where the grizzled Sabrett man under his blue and orange umbrella stood weekdays at noon, May broke from my hand and skipped the rest of the avenue's width so fast the car didn't think to brake until she was already past and shaking the grizzled granddad's hand through sauerkraut steam. The driver had at first looked hard at me—because you're seen for that transportational instant and no longer and will never be seen again and will never make a demand on him or his alternator bearings, you become takeable and are eye-fucked whiskily. Would Daddy have let you take me away if he had known you would desert me five years later? But I had deserted Daddy years before, and my heart belongs to Hind. Perhaps now asleep you hear my thought more plainly than when awake, so I wouldn't have to come out and say it. You take my thoughts.

Vandal, you traded what, I ask, what, in for your five beans, Jack? (May gives only polite interest to that tale.) I traded my greasy Kahlil Gibran for my association with the Gypsy Woman, who made such a quick theatrical mark at college then disappeared except to me, to whom she often gave analytic ultimata, like, that I didn't know enough about motivation, she didn't understand at first I wasn't going out for theater, I had to explain three times that I wouldn't be an actress if you held a white slave Shanghai over my dead body: you, she said close to my face, you are many of those people out there in your world and you must learn *how* you are: which, the famous night I stayed with her in the city, she (with much vis-à-vis, her pet word) resumed as if I had never heard the spiel before (she would have fit in well in the dance or drama department at college, which is not to say she was not magnetic), she imagined much later that I had come to the city, when I came, to get into an acting workshop, and would not believe me almost when I said it was design I was in: and murmured *as* if (but maybe not) facetiously, "But is it *tac*tile design?" getting up and walking around behind me, when suddenly I saw her lighted butt like a fuse on the arm of the upholstered chair she had sprung out of and I jumped forward to snatch it off and she said, "I hardly had a chance to touch you, for Cripesake," after which she talked to me her theory of Personatic Flow— "You hold onto your self like integrity, but what is this Person of yours in terms of permanent—?" I vainly hoped she would tell a story. Yet through the haze of laziness I saw her come, and was neither willing nor unwilling, which is bad, though I think I was not like the slim, quiet, SayBrooks Brother marriageable party-snatch Buck told me he took home who mustered little more than the passive poise of a spread-eagled martyr and, in a word, looked away while Buck had him. But my laziness made your guardian, your beloved guardian, judge me ignorant, which naturally I am, but:

"Vanish," his gray eyes seemed to say at first, for I wasn't able to discuss with him technical dumb-dumb like silk screen photo transplants that make the ashy gray and white maze of the document face look like Auschwitz; or design materials—for I simply knew them and that was it and I hoped to get him to tell tales about his father the scientist James Foster or about himself when at the time of the Crash he was painting in the Czech Ta-tras: but after the subject of Me the Professional wore thin we examined in depth my ignorance of English wars and English gardens, the origins of smoking, Dürer's *Melancholy*, the achievement of Dürer (the derivation of *achievement*?): did I know Dürer had a collector's passion for American aboriginal spears? what about his apparent marital misery vis-à-vis the rich Pirckheimer friendship, what was the evidence? did I know the portrait of Dürer's dad that...? seemed to find itself separate from both background and...? foreground? didn't Panofsky—yes he did of course—say. And this was true, and as plastic a riddle as: "the portrait drawing of Dürer the Elder is like the portrait drawing of Dürer the Younger," quote unquote somewhere, but look at the "of" there, does it mean "by" or does it mean "depicting"? even allowing that the things in question might have been *self*-portraits:

"Vanish," he was no longer saying at the end of the meal, you told me later he was more concerned to make a hit with me than I with him, and may not have heard a thing I said: I'm glad we never saw him dead, for he was good to look at alive: not knowing a fine old phoneme from a glosseme from a cognate wasn't what made me so dreadful in the guardian's eyes, or even not being well grounded in Latin: he chaffed (chafed?) me on my poor joke when I said I think in complete sentences but not in complete thoughts, but I do know that a phoneme is a family even if a home isn't always a house: I was taking his notable beanstalk away from him leaving instead two of us rather than—but was it my fault if this orphan now here tonight before me with his long legs out straight like the frame poles the Indians in my book trucked their belongings on, two beams, booms, poles, dragging in the continental turf mile upon mile—if this or that orphan chose me, was it my fault? But I wouldn't ask the guardian, any more than I'd ask Daddy the big question the day of the billboard revelation after the car nearly cut me down by the giant string bean and he came up crying,

"Sylvie, Sylvie," and in his panting his voice broke, he
was running up as if he'd been in a mismatched race with
the Chevy that was ignorantly buzzing berserk careening
into and down out of the picture, I couldn't ask him the
question because he was so afraid for me and as it turned
out all I suddenly wanted to do was blindly hold and kiss
the way May at three weeks mistook Jack your proffered
cheek for the bottle when she'd just been changed before
a feed: for she didn't see. And I was willing then not
to ask the embracing question of Daddy, not a madly
penetrating question but then it mattered and now
is too late, and if I should say to my lean dry old Dad
now, "Did you feel you had made a choice of me when
first I was born?" "Did you feel I was your daughter?" a
foolish question would have drawn from him a foolish
yes, but words he and Mama once exchanged that
could never now be unquoted had made such questions
important to my edible nymphhood. And how could I?–
well I couldn't–have shown him the, in a word, family
connection between my query and that billboard. How
show you why on that day in Heathrow Airport waiting
room I wasn't just making talk to take your mind off the
guardian dying–or off that hand threatening our ashtray:
I had seen a link between that old billboard and this new
shimmering event of the guardian's death in 1959 that
might change us and help us, for where the kidnap hunt
would lead (and you seemed then to give it up) seemed
much less human than where abandoning it might lead.
And at the moment when Hind you looked at last straight
into the face of that cigarette-ash man and first saw
the bony girl he was with, there in Heathrow Airport,
London, I thought it doesn't exactly matter if we don't
have children of our own, or even children, for–and then
I forgot *why* it didn't matter, but the girl was snickering
and Jack you pulled yourself up enough not merely to
introduce her to me, Cassia Meaning, of woodblock-chute

and Saturday afternoon fame, but not to tell why we were now flying back but only where we'd been, and the flaxen Henry, Robin, or Adrian she was with asked with severe enthusiasm rapidly, "Did you have trouble getting Polish visas?" To capture England and America in a word, I like English girls and some American men, I think. I thought, If he liked Cassia a semi-cripple so much, how could he like me, she looks so different—not only her illness that had swelled her joints and cramped her stilts even in their salad days playing doctor in Jack's room when they came home from the junior concert, but how many rainy Saturdays in one season? Not only her disease but her basic build and her type of face, of beauty: where I am strong and pretty tall, well, not stunted, five-four, she is— and where I'm light brown of hair and hazel of eye, she is— and where (unlike Daddy) I'm full, though not fat, in the face, and friendly and shy, she's—hard and narrow from cheek to cheek, dark-bunned and skim-milk-skinned and cold-blue-eyed, slight and in a word short to begin with and bodily weak so to compensate she adopts an edge, looked hastily at me in Heathrow and said to Jack, "She's quite unexpected, Jackie, who'd have envisioned for you a strapping creamy little Miss Mount Mary of nineteen let-us-say-fifty-four?" And then she addressed me mockingly: "So you think you're an authority on Jack Hind." Why didn't I accept my advantage? Because I thought if he liked her as much as I knew, and he knows, he did, what does that make me? Yet here am I years later her friend. A book title, *Cassia Meaning's London*, was the way one of her recurrent dreams haunted her view of herself. And at the dream publisher's dream cocktail party in the cobbled garden of a hired pub south of the river, she would look up from autographing copies for variously knuckled anonymous hands thrust at her from every side, and she would see, like her childhood cat's cradles, the masts and woven rigging of cutters and merchant schooners tied up generations ago at the Isle of Dogs. *Cassia Meaning's London*, the painfully overkeen knowledge of an adopted city: in it she would put nothing like Sweeney Todd's barbarous barbershop. But she could if she wanted. (Her letters turn the very leaves in Green Park green, the distances into warm courses of activity and people.) She had known John Plante's crowd, but also saw an older man, a banker-ornithologist for one (who wouldn't take her on an expedition to Bulgaria); but to you and me she wrote about another sort, a sleek Scots orientalist who married a girl from Cincinnati and went into Labour politics, or a Tory minister's personal secretary, or a UN economist, or a baronet publisher: her book, which would never be written (because it never could be written without misappropriating people she liked and loved), would itself be like London—a city where every occasion, person, kind of change was possible. Her pals back here (whom she seemed to keep separate, she did it in the old days when she made you miserable), Baltimore, Los Angeles, Boston, Cincinnati, New York, may have thought they saw her London through their own eyes, and may only, in the end, have seen her, not her city. Did they think, like us, that she was going out of her mind in order to make and remake this city hers? You'd have married her I know, and even hopelessly persisted if she had not started to be nice to you after she said no. Am I as unlike her as, perhaps, you are unlike Daddy? If I had been a lame duck, as Cassia only literally was and is, I could see our marriage: but was the point about me something else? The phrase sounds like your Anglophone guardian, who, *noblesse oblige*, thought your interest in the Siggofreddo Morales lame-duck case appropriate, in which he felt he distantly participated through having seen that famous diver long before his fall defeat you in dual and championship meets three years running. The guardian cheeped his well-grounded lips in mild contempt when I insincerely asked what was the status of Puerto Ricans in the U.S., did they have to have—

"*Visa! Vis—*" "O.K., O.K.," I said, a phrase he did not like. You winced to hear him call the Morales "an old Puerto Rican family," as if citing Christy Amondson's mother's Heights credentials' entitling her to be on the Tree Lighting Committee's Musical Subcomm. But you half-guessed your view to be as narrow as his; you called Siggo your friend, the athletically gifted, pathetically underpatronized Siggo—yet not even this, for the father could have paid Siggofreddo's Yale bills even if they did live in what Maddy says was once ghetto just below the brink of the Heights—Puerto Ricans rather feared by Thea Dover in the old days when you were young and she aimed to be your mother; much feared as waylayers of private school kids who got out later than public kids, some of whom on split session had the afternoon off anyway; "much feared" (though even then Engleman Deal said, "The Catholic Church keeps them from getting out of their depth," and Cassia Meaning handled them with her tongue all but once); much feared once, they have become largely O.K., at least as objects of fallow feeling: Mr. Morales seldom swept his ghastly-bright grocery he later renamed Morales Supermart, on the corner a block below the number two Episcopalian whose pastor marches and is now known to be manipulating his radically youthful congregation: but Sundays Los Morales went under the river and clear uptown near my hospital to that evangelical hole-in-the-wall part Puerto Rican, mostly Cuban even then, which (Judge Deal was eager to hear—for he'd vacationed down there and knew the people and how Hondurans label the islanders "Caribbeans") did not welcome regular American Negroes: you went with them once, which the guardian approved of: I can imagine father and son, their cornets alligator-cased and their slim-brim black fedoras as if balanced, and Siggofreddo's sisters with starched linen hatlets, knees together, ankles crossed, necks and ankles braceleted, maple sugar arms soft from fresh-ironed sleeveless armholes. Your tape of the racket that was made there uptown came on like the instruments themselves were high and being caught in the flesh for an airline spot ad for cheaper Virgin islands— "irrepressible people," said Judge Deal. I took a different city walk each Sunday and came to know the parts far better than your Heights folk (except you) and wrote it all to Daddy Monday night. Put him in the picture was what I was supposed to do: did "Beatnik" get overnight from the West Coast to the East? and did it mean they were glad to be losers or merely made an official thing of what was being forced by implication on them? there didn't seem to be any Beatniks around the college, Daddy said, but then again there weren't any colored people either except two wild African gentlemen who dressed native even when attending graduate classes in agronomy and had bought shoes and socks at CCC. Daddy wanted to hear everything else too, even old stuff long before I met you. The background to the Morales case, Siggo's terrible accident, his new life—what anyone knew of it, his falling out with you. Police brutality? I saw it only once but Daddy wanted me to comment on the occurrences you could read about in the paper that happened near you in the city; and then all those smooth people you listened to, and helped, and surrendered to, and gave our flat to so the day I had to lend you my key and you gave *it* to Ashley Sill when you met for lunch, I of course (for there was a funeral on and I couldn't go through the parlor to the stairs) had to ring my own buzzer downstairs then ring again upstairs and be let in by a highly conditional Ashley seeming to lean vaguely back upon great high showers of a Schumann symphony who greeted me by asking if you had a Britannica; and take Bee Bee, whom I edited for home consumption but who has her considerable place in my later letters home: Bee Bee? Why, I think you chose your kidnap partly to find a way of not contemplating what so keenly depressed you: for instance, Bee Bee turning obscure losses and alarms into something else, translaboring something close into something foreign and unnatural, losing each new chance of simple ease for, instead, an easy answer that merely tipped Bee Bee half-meaningly into another parallel course, saying to you at three A.M. (so I finally jumped out of bed and went in and kicked her out), "To have been Alexandra Sokolovskaya converting that marvelous thick-haired boy Bronstein in Shvigorsky's garden, feeling him develop in opposition to me; to possess his mind in order then to be his servant, his possessed–*that* could have made a life, knowing that the marriage angle was a minor expedience and one day either of us might be made expendable by a new turn, a weakness–*there* would have been a relation in terms of honor, strength–" "But Trotsky *left* her!" you interrupt as I appear and do my own interrupting. Bee Bee had terrible faith in fidelity. I think you kissed her at the guardian's beach party, something shut her up for several minutes until she objected to the folk song but she was quiet when the Jap tenant chanted those crummy poems of someone else's. But Bee Bee's a friend, as are not the majority of those who came for comfort: what of a girl who married an older man who is now leaving her for an older woman? (but, unquote guardian, older than he or merely she?) what of a guy who subjects us to a close oral analysis of his wife's vagina–let them divorce, and more, let him divorce us from him, couples and couples whose city savvy would scorn my fear of the simple fatigue of afteryears with one man starting fresh with another, and scorn too the folk odds behind my unspoken quote from Daddy, "Chances are against improving two pair." Daddy seldom ventured south to see this vigorous intermeaning process—

Via thick-crayoned major routes and the newest by-passes, he would come down to visit me and later us, but it would be an occasion and though he'd sit with us most of the time on such a weekend he would always have two or three museums or galleries to go to that Staghorn, who came down even less often, had told him he must see and report on. And Daddy would have to take us out to a most uncity wholesome hostelry that served a free cherry liqueur and, as Daddy pointed out each time, had a nice relish tray. I am not sure that we welcomed him well enough or that he was capable of receiving our welcome; certainly I could find myself feeling while he was down that I'd prefer to have him and Jack separately. Together in that bare but not barren room of my gradually altering railroad flat that I insisted we live in against the guardian's gentle demands and back to which May and I moved five years later (and which was the only address Grimes had for us when he phoned six weeks ago), you and Daddy and I sat on mattresses, the bareness at least clean, softened only by a selection of rich spreads, one the wedding present from Thea Dover, a maze for if you started by looking hard you would find a riddling fabric, but if you first glanced only casually you might see among others the infamous Myrrha three-fourths embarked into her new green quiet self, turning into the strong scanty spiny healing shrub, her bitter lovely lust-filled cheeks narrowing into leafy silence, into Myrrh, and elsewhere, in the middle of the spread just where Daddy was uncomfortably sitting I knew were tangled and simultaneous the snow-white bull with the black mark in his forehead, the Queen Pasiphae, the maple heifer she turned into (and turned into life), and, mingled with these beginnings, the end (or *an* end), namely, the terrible, infant, unmanageable minotaur: you and Daddy and I sipping brandy and at last, to his relief, abandoning your postmortem of the Series broadcast Daddy had come in at the end of, and the key difference between run-and-hit and hit-and-run, and you went sentimental when May came out for her ten o'clock bottle, a twisting six-week-old body struggling to see what it was to be awake, seeking again and again the vague room, and newly strong in the neck (so when earlier Daddy had taken her from you without supporting the head it had tipped but as if May were merely surveying my old white wedding-cake cornices)—I came back from the kitchen, Daddy was staring at you, you sloshing brandy, I sat above you in the Harvard chair the guardian had determined to give us, and May was smiling impenetrable smiles right through you that nonetheless were seeming now more than mere digestive highs—you said, "The worst I can imagine is to die before she gets old enough to know who it is that has died, do you know what I mean?" Daddy liked that, I saw he did, and he merely said, "Hey, she'll be *burying* us," he liked you more than he had before, though he said you had a self-satisfied reckless streak underneath—Daddy can be subtle too even if at CCC fitting black feet under the altar-like display niche for Bostonian Shoes he imagines that back home Africans don't wear socks. And he was moved to tell about teaching me poker and how like him I was at it—"Hey, like life, part skill, part luck." He often wanted to tell you of me, though I felt he wanted to cast you as a bystander fascinated but not by virtue of husbandry, maybe as the well-known Naked Voicer, and this because in part he believed that—

Via, perhaps, Mama's dryly slowed-down remark that I could not have picked a man less like Dad than Jack Hind, and in my promiscuous memory hangs suddenly, steel-heeled, the Brannock shoe-size measurer on a hook inside the Bostonian altar snugly set into a CCC wall. Lucky you knew some poker, even if ours was only Sunday night, pretending we didn't know the odds when to drop, and with our wrists upon the green baize we could turn into such sharps for five hours that I wouldn't have thought of those faces and hands as belonging to people with last names. By then, when my parents were into my teens much had passed live between them that need not be said again but unluckily couldn't be unsaid. At the poker table, filled up by Staghorn and Herbie and others, our words occurred within the given hand, which itself might overwhelm Staghorn who under his hoary eyebrows said almost nothing for he was not instinctively good at cards and had to think. Mama might murmur, she would never look at Daddy, there were few misunderstood words now, it was as if growing stronger I had grown out of the old abandoned words my parents spoke long ago: like, "−when Daddy made you grow inside me−" "Well, it wasn't *my* choice, I can tell you," Daddy meaning merely, I supposed, that I happened to happen, though in the next words meaning more: "Your mother and I just got mad that night," never guessing on that day he said it that a seven-year-old Sylvia who didn't yet understand about her older brother Herb could take amiss words so easily said. A seven-year-old can't apply, as I now do, Daddy's other frequent words to the act that preceded− or, to be guardian-clear, began−me: words spoken that lonely World Series day as he sat uncomfortably upright on a mattress covered with narrative vegetation, his hand flat down pointing by chance to the corner where male and female palm trees (if you could pick them out of the tangle) bowed seminally toward each other to make a mating bridge, and high behind him my muddy silk screen print from art school days: "Like life, part skill part": if there's skill it belongs to Jim Sperm, who according to the hospital obstetrician cannot possibly achieve the egg in or even not in, or out of, time, for lack of speed or staying power: which raises again a riddle almost as nice as the arrival tonight of you asleep in the wicker chair (so I, sitting at the foot of May's bed, make the waking apex of a two-thirds sleeping triangle), and what on God's green earth possessed me to be possessed by you, who're you dreaming about right now? But part skill. So my turning energies tell me what words to use but my returning words tell me what I can't help: He is lurking in pressed discount khakis, belt in the back, part hidden in the bottom boughs of my fat sugar maple, narrow head above the lowmost long deep-bending bough, and since he seems grown right in among the leaves (that are halfway between first turn and Fall bloom), he looks taller than he is; I think he lets me guess he's looking at me when really he's not; once again, annually, his wife has not sensed his autumn gloom except as some prospect of a new season at the College Corner Clothier eleven miles from this maple and this growing village; she cannot guess the gap in which he moves that is marked off by extremes he can't resort to: he is and was neither in a city knowing his brains, stamina, and looks are being crash-tested in soundproof phone duels and at the bronze base of some fragile office mountain with on the gusty corner his newsstand where he spends five or six dollars a week and plots practically his complex route home after work: *Nor*, truly a yeoman sawing and fencing, turning over the sticky hunks of spring ground, moving a few animals, measuring sap; yet not writing delicious books about paradoxical otters ferally trotting out of view at the far loop of, say, the Laurels' lily (-padded) pond, but not engaging in nature walks either, where one sort of silence was from which at a fence a mile off the hysterical bark of Staghorn's stark white setter seems as endlessly remote as the sudden probe of a jet which then went back into the nowhere it came from: no, this neighbor of Staghorn's in his discount khakis is neither city nor deep country; nor does he own the CCC, though he's glad to be only a nine-to-fiver in that college town where even I had little traffic even during the painful high school months and months. This man could not, despite my suspicions, be you. He's my father. Not being *chosen* by Daddy meant less than the plainness of his saying it. For at seven, what did I think about having kids? Storks risky, what if they changed their mind, altered course, ran foul of Hurricane Elmer, left you—one, me—on the house next door, which would make me the girl next—nor, as in your nightmare, was I slimily awash in a pelican's ladle jaw, though for a time before I was six or seven I thought that, in Mama's special disease-vocab, babies were rectally evacuated. But I thought something else which oddly it is a relief to know you felt too: you were holding my hand in bed and being funny, and you gave me almost my own words from when I was seven (though you called the thought a, what?, a flaw in the evolution of your impulses) that as a tall wondering child you concluded that in a household daily way the love lived by two people was, just in and by itself, marked by interludes of coming to life inside the woman, it was as if she could only grow a child if she was happy, it was the happiness that made the being come and grow, and you couldn't force it or stop it: This echo of myself in you then reconvinced me, sentimentalist that unbeknownst to you I am, to try and win you. And—or for—I couldn't imagine Daddy putting that as you put it. Not that he'd have used marriage manual terms though he did speak of "deriving satisfaction," but he meant deriving it from your chosen lines of work, not (as in a manual) via intercourse cum fore- and/or afterplay. Words form my calico thoughts, my jim-jam thoughts don't choose my words. Well, though not grounded in Latin, he did tell me the old stories, and very well: the dark-skinned Egyptian maid transposed into an acacia tree because she wouldn't give herself to the Holy Warrior of the North; the old hag become a lovely girl because the knight made good his vow to marry her; the golden goose that laid the plain egg; bitchy witches, head-hunting step-mothers, chocolate cottages, possessive giants—I heard through politely Mama's cozy readings of Thornton Burgess's animal chat but asked Daddy for what I really needed, say to begin and end with, all of Grimm over and over, for which Daddy defended me against Mama's charge that I would have bad dreams. No, I derived satisfaction youmaycallit. Went off to sleep gorged by the most threatening nighttime and woodland changes, or by the sweet, sweet almond tree of which the beautiful, pious wife at long last blessedly with child ate too much when she was seven months gone and when in time the child as white as snow and as red as blood was born, the woman died happy and was buried under that tree. Did Daddy bore me ever? Did his Grimm fail to scare me (as Dr. James' lekturanalab of one of them scared me) because they came wrapped warmly in Daddy's voice? Bored me only when he would tell me to have a more scintillating life than his. A parent can tune at you as if it might just jam you. Surely each being possesses his own flair for boring others, a topic or a certain minor repetition, a tic or tock, or something in between that he is scarcely aware of except sometimes to be vaguely proud of—how the parent will repeat if he assumes we didn't see: the guardian your guardian never knowing how pellucidly suspended in Hind your large bright eye he was when he said to you first of all all that about not needing to make a mark or be known, and second about the fully satisfying science of words: which you knew was for some partly unconsidered reason his fatherly desire for you. Like Mama deeply seeing in me a future RN of all things because—her father had hoped to be a surgeon and her favorite sister Jemmy was a hard-working OB who kept on her feet the full term of her third pregnancy and gave up only to go into labor, literally into the labor room where she'd done so much of her work those nine months. The labor room, one of four, of that small new hospital on a hill above a tidal river in the middle of that town at this instant fifty miles from May's bed. Jemmy would have laughed out loud if her husband, like you, had come to be with her during. You were high above my bed until it got bad, and then I forgot you, you were looking at me and talking to me you later said, but with an hour to go I was wholly taken up by May coming down. You there high-courteously timing contractions, you there curiously listening to my anesthetic you-aimed obscenities. Magically tall, holding the gold-speckled thermos top of your coffee, and more remote than you let on. Yet Jack to your guardian too courteous you often were too, and once he divined he was boring you: "If I had it to do over again I'd be a *real* philologist, you know"—he might just have appreciated a blunt retort from you rather than evasive praise—it was one of those smoky vinous Sunday noontides, your guardian fresh from his round trip over the old bridge, his friend the vicar fresh from church right down the street, and in those words the guardian I know was speaking secretly to me—even then, unbeknownst to him himself, preparing to one day come near saying something very important to me though he was never possessed by indiscretion—

Visions of something reached up to me out of his flat sharp voice, he did say something but stopped—with a question: "Did you know how well I knew Jack's mother?"—stopped so I thought he had meant to go on: 'twas then I thought, He adopted Jack not because the *couple* had been friends but because *she* was someone special: and he except for the first four or five weeks did not even take on a nurse, being a man of leisure and determined—to wash your skull and foster your beloved bones, though Thea cut your nails and diagnosed your spots as mosquito bites (not ECHO virus devoutly discovered by your guardian in a baby book). You were too young to know those parents your guardian took you from bequeathed, but I in my mind as in your wicker chair you dream opposite me return you to that turning point to make of you whose chosen child? as you sleep tired in my landlord's wicker chair. Thea Dover of the sweet-spun cornsilk hair that now turns not white or gray or silver but simply a milder less pretty tone, moved in at last when she saw she couldn't make your guardian invite her: for he knew that her able touch upon you came nonetheless to a pretext: she wanted him. Yet knew how to ease him years after, when during your brief postgrad decline he would say to you things not unlike what Mr. Morales said when you paid that charity visit after Siggofreddo's disaster: "In college he was my son: back home from college sitting around all day with *his* mind (and not even playing his records) he's someone else, like they just took the real Siggofreddo and sent him someplace else." You said that by being a woman to your guardian Thea Dover had been in a way (in a word) a mother to you, but she would shrug incredulously if told. And she didn't last. He kicked her out the summer she moved in, he said he was too conventional to run a household like that. But they were more than friends afterward, and she was in bed with him off and on right to the end. Divorced for years, she has been like a widow since he died. Sometimes to look at them taking a walk up his beach you'd think, Neither of them has anything to do. You would think he'd have married her if only on your behalf. She's glad you want to make it into a public wildlife sanctuary. She belongs to the Trillium Club. But Grimes the bastard (gastropod?) I'll swear used your guardian just for a vacation pad, could wow your guardian with language lore when he felt like it, and. At the end of that summer, at the end even of that special lunch Daddy came to, the guardian had changed his view of Grimes and, you thought, of Grimes' field, which (at least from a distance) had, you thought, meant so much to your guardian, had been (you said, with this acuteness you flick off and on), a future he secretly counted on and persistently speculated about. Your guardian quoted a book of Grimes' on, I believe, sound clusters. Grimes pretended modesty but *I* know was bored and impatient as if how can *he Grimes*, the authority (chortle chortle), begin to explain to your guardian layman the roots of Potawatomi phonemics in the history of modern American linguistic search? But then it happened, it was the day Daddy drove fifty-odd miles over to see your guardian and don't think Daddy's presence didn't make its mark. He watched me inquiringly when I got up to clear off and for a second I was afraid he'd try to help. Grimes was saying, "Linguistics is a game I play professionally eleven months a year, but" (chortle chortle) "not to be taken seriously," at which I'm glad to say you dropped your usual interested tolerance of even bastards like Grimes and said, "God you don't believe that, you've bet your life on your work," to which the man retorted in a tittering uncontesting murmur, *"Bet my life, bet my life*?" But even this came too near being a tangent to suit your guardian, who pressed Grimes to explain (though they had not, in my opinion, been talking about) "juncture," what it had to do with the nature and function of the phoneme or the hairy-tailed allomorph, I forget, Grimes had produced a monograph on juncture but the guardian, though he had read it, wasn't just sure how to answer the question that he had (therefore) just posed: Grimes first said he wasn't interested in juncture any more, then said wearily, "I suppose you know Bloch's nineteen forty-eight article in *Language*? Your answer's there, or did you merely ask what 'juncture' the term means? The point about 'juncture' is the pauses that tell whether we're saying, say, 'I name' or 'An aim'—you've"—Grimes blandly looked us over as he reached for the jade cigarette box, the guardian stocked the Russian ones with the long mouth-piece—"Every schoolboy plays games with these sort of syllabic phrasings, take the title of Feydeau's farce Englished, *A Flea in Your Ear*"—("Englished!" incredulously from the end of the table)—"how the sense changes if you, heh, well there's prepausal juncture, sounds dirty but it's amusing and not essentially heavy work, *if* you know what I mean—but Fossy you *dooo*," ended Grimes on a wheedling alto smile. "But," said the guardian like a solemn soph, "you admit meaning to your province." "*But, no,*" said Red Grimes with slow, capricious pace smiling at of all people Daddy, who dropped his eyes to the last two oil-slick peas of the Green and Gold Salad I'd made specially for him, "*I don't.*" "But how *can* you not?" said the guardian. "Noop," trebled Red Grimes quietly, looking saintlike upward then winking at Daddy, "we simply describe what happens, we"—as if "they" had white coats and graduated beakers—"we arrive at operational descriptions, whereas what the words at this juncture (I mean this time) *mean* matters no more to me than, say, a wife to you—or to me, for that matter." "We differ there, Red: you see simply marriage, I monogamy." "What's with monogamy," I whispered. "It's a price," the guardian continued—"so your view of it, Red, varies with what the paramarital advantages are. But today, when everywhere English is debased by scientistic pretension, bureauclinical ego, proud casual incorrectness, governmental—" "*In*correctness?" pronounced Red Grimes in a way that proved to me he was no friend of your guardian, who now hurriedly said, "Don't let me finish—I mean *let* me finish—there is no standard English or even American English in your view, but switch on the radio, the announcer announces a 'really nice number'—why, when I was up at Oxford—" "'Nice,'" said Red Grimes, leavening the difference for us laymen and women, "means what people say it means. You want to go back: well then, go way back to what it meant to Jefferson—or Marvell if you like him better (though they were both roughly, I believe, in your social stratum)—hell, go back to Indo-European, ask Adam the relevant negative derivative, he'll tell you 'nice' must mean 'not cutting'—and let's change the subject, Fossy." "But," said the guardian, "I suppose you condone the double negative?" "It's logical in French and Spanish, why not English, and we're drifting toward it anyhow, which is logic, too." "You would argue," countered the guardian forking a spot of his salad mustard out into a star, "a black disadvantaged man in Los Angeles isn't wrong to say 'hisn' instead of 'his,' but great Scott! which society do you want him to break into—which books do you want him to be able to read—?" "'Hisn'," said prim Red Grimes, "I'm glad to report, is a possessive pronoun and thus more precisely usable than 'his,' which can be a possessive adjective as well, 'his son, his X ray, his funeral' "—which made you look hard at Grimes suddenly. "But," said the guardian, "you called drift logical, which means you abide the great nescient majority—" "Speak English, Fossy"—"yet if polled (say, by Jack's old friend's organization, what's his name, Lief Lund) they'd eliminate you just-like-that, put you out of business, what do they care about linguistics, yet in actual fact you are year after year allowed by this society to pursue your research—" "But all this has nothing to do with me," sighed Grimes, "whether one language is better than another (nonsense, they're all equally equal), whether German is fouled by the uses to which it has been put (which by the way to me make it all the more fascinating), I'm off in a corner eating Christmas pie, a moral luxury (it and me), but thank God at least I don't tamper with the living lang—" "You will *kill* it, you and your—" "—*tamper* with the living tongue in terms of canons of right or wrong set by upper class...intellectuals." Ice cream?, I asked (ungrounded in Latin the Queen of Tongues though I learned *sic* and *ibid.* in graphics). "This vanilla is real vanilla," said Daddy. You said, "It comes from a good place." The guardian, you said later, knew that Grimes instead of upper-class intellectuals had almost said, "Upper-class dilettantes," but when the guardian bolted now from the table back off the porch into the living room, it wasn't a summer exit but that he had to get hold of a book, we heard him looking under papers. Grimes said, "Vanilla comes from a good place," and snickered, and then said to Daddy, "Every man's language is his own. What do *you* do, Mr....?" "You were pretty rough on him," you said almost genially; "after all he's not a specialist." Before Daddy could answer, the guardian said, "Great Scott!" inside; so there was more to come, stay marooned to your set, there's more to come. Which is how you plugged Siggofreddo to his sad father: more to come: the best is yet to be: you can't dive all your life, coaches get bored (take Buddy Bourne), and as for Siggo needlessly leaving Yale, why, too many kids go to college. Today. Siggofreddo will end up. On someone's feet. The Holy Central Evangelical Church of Jesus they all trekked up to Sundays with their instruments was evangelical in acoustics but private in temper. It was near the urine-toned pedestrian underpass chalked by kids and blackened by railroad grime that I went through later when I was carrying May and had enrolled in the childbirth class, classes for everything. But miles away from where they went Sundays, Mr. Morales's Supermart on the edge of the Heights might have misled one with the green horse bananas in the window which Thea Dover, on the way to confer with her upholsterer, once pointed out to me as the kind the people "down there" especially like: you'd need a knife: but in fact Morales netted close to ten thousand by your snoop-figuring and could in those days have met the tab Siggofreddo's college scholarship paid. The neighborhood packed the window sills and crouched on the fire escapes when he appeared on the corner having won the interscholastic, you described to me every optional he did, though maybe they skip my mind, and his father and brother went all the way to the nationals, which Sig-gofreddo should have won. But it wasn't long before he lost everything, though if he'd played it right he would have kept, if not the scholarship, at least his standing: but according to you he felt an imposter at that college now that he wasn't any longer the diver they had snatched from several competing coaches, as if now that he couldn't dive any more his passport—

Visitors came from all over to recruit him, but he went to Yale, and after the accident he let his grades go and Yale let *him* go, and though if he lost his scholarship lots of other fellows were in the same boat they weren't really in the same boat going back to Old Lyme, New Orleans, San Francisco, wantonly transferring. He didn't want your help. He'd plenty of other jailers. You cast him as a hero he said he wasn't, and wanted no more to do with you but then said that if you and he weren't entirely from different scenes (which he'd give you the benefit), you and he anyway had never known each other; but the worst scene was seven eight years later and revealed more than the actual accident in the pool, seen not by you but by your friend the well-padded though not fat Yaley Oliver, who wrote an unfinished though gradually published poem on Siggofreddo's accident, or at first about it which Staghorn called mere "expression"—vis-à-vis Staghorn's own elusive art pursued among heartbreaking dispersals of energy disbursed to mild nice classrooms of literature students. But I was more than mere expression, he said, lowering thick eyelids, and I was then how old—

"Visit me," he said, white-browed, parental, professid-ual, informal. He took me into our downstairs bathroom, something in my eye, closed the door, his tobaccoey warm breath murmuring as he rolled my lid back, "Your deal" said my mother from the dining room. When you've tried too hard to look up to your father your heart finds a habit: Staghorn was forty-five, he pointed out to me when I was telling him my growing pains that I'd never see fifteen again. Daddy wanted me to go to Staghorn. You drew from Daddy's remark about the Hungarian uncle-niece piano duo, the Pro Arte wind sextet, Richard Dyer-Bennet, and the Metropolitan tenor, the idea that Daddy and I went to concerts and other college functions as a rule when I was a high schooler and living at home. Indeed CCC handled fifty tickets for the Dance Group Annual. But at first I cared not much for that college of his, even including and beyond the time of my string bean Vistavision, and then, when I'd begun to change fast I for one cared even less for concert series and itinerant lithographs and wanted and waited to go quite far away. Daddy and Staghorn knew this and encouraged my visits to Staghorn's place over the little valley. Daddy trusted Staghorn would do what? Well, he was right to trust him, though if he had understood what I meant then, there'd have been no more Sunday poker involving Staghorn; or if Mama had been able at visiting hours to look in Staghorn's attic window and no less than four other rooms of his house in my sixteenth and seventeenth years. Part of my eighteenth, too. "Have you ever...*known* an older man?" the Gypsy Woman said to me one night quite early in our relation, and when I said, "Yes, I have," with, in my eyes, a direct inquiry as if I expected her to ask if he had tangly white eyebrows, and painted three major motifs over and over, and still climbed maple trees, and once beat up a supermarket manager he caught shooting woodcock on his land, the Gypsy Woman ignored my abrupt "yes" and continued to speak to her long lovely hand, "Every girl needs this, so few realize it, there is an abandon possible with a much older man in terms of a peace, in terms of strange lines of suggestive connections to in a sense other experiences, people; and you are not sometimes possessed quite so viciously...but you will learn, Sylvia, you will—" earn the desire, my mind arched, yes I had already earned the desire, not to tell Staghorn to the Gypsy Woman or to you, much less to Daddy, who I once thought of one Sunday noon as Staghorn was taking me very slowly and my open mouth was in the crook of his right arm and I opened my eyes to his bright north window, uncurtained like every other window in that house, and his gilded banjo clock downstairs had been striking for a long time and I half-heard Mama and Papa year in year out bickering over how often to wind ours, the big chiming wedding present on the mantel, and the freckles on Staghorn's arms were like those on Daddy's hand, and I closed my eyes and sucked and wondered, Seventeen divides into forty-some how often?, which was another way of stating my mystery, for I too, my sleeping husband, have a mystery—such is given not only to you, with whom it has been so much more congested to live than it was to simply be with weathered Staghorn. When from Florence you were phoning the hotel the Laurels had stayed in in Pisa, I mailed Staghorn a fairly silly postcard of the outside of the Uffizi, which caught the colonnades a bit too murkily, and trying to say something amusing wrote that the Andrea del Sartos were quite unexpected after Browning's Andrea. Such would have fooled Thea Dover or even your guardian but I doubt Staghorn, who may well have smilingly groaned on receiving it and said, "There she goes again, saying what she thinks I want to hear, but damn her let her be herself," to which Daddy (though never during an actual game Sunday night) may modestly add, "It's a mistake to try to bluff a bad player, a big winner, or a heavy loser." And I heard later that Staghorn had disliked Florence the two days he'd spent there years ago, I think he wasn't jealous of you, he scared me he was sometimes so disinterested especially about his own work, thirty pieces of which were always, as he said, resisting the finishing touch. The talk was not frivolous with Staghorn, though when he got personal he was never clumsy, he was civil and light and brief—"Oh God"—taking my hand as we climbed the hill toward the house—"Oh God"—a groaning, a laugh—"you see beside you a man—that's what you've had, Sylvia—a man who will want you even after he abandons you. I've used you. Someday soon I'll send you away." And because Staghorn was not in the Art Department the Art Department, so Daddy said, did not bother to ask him to show his work, and Staghorn both knew how plainly distinct his work was and refused ever to propose that he have that exhibition. Daddy prepared topics when Staghorn was coming over. Daddy didn't see how gentle my Staghorn was.

"'Visceral'!" He'd have laughed in the face of Maddy for saying the word as he or the student reviewer did, for—yet he would not have gone out of his way to destroy your guardian's tiny thick oils that hung in the apartment on the Heights and like your guardian were much admired, if not like him much loved. Since on the first savory Sunday noontide (the radiator a bit high steaming the aroma of postchurch Fritos and sherry and old fashioneds, though only three there had *gone* to church) you took for granted they'd all like me as much as you loved me, you barely saw just how I was being looked over, Heights style. Though not looked at, any more than Daddy looked *at you* when you met: looked at secretly by the guardian who maintained a roving conversation with his old friend the perennially bachelor-blooming, russet-cheeked vicar (who had been invited like most of the others only yesterday, when it was learned that you were bringing me)—looked at so openly by handsome, round-shouldered skinny Thea Dover that her brittle bluffness was only one more secrecy, she didn't let much out: no, she had known your guardian indeed before you were born and your parents died and the only grandparent you had left even at your so minimum age lived in an annuity commune a stone's throw south of San Francisco and thus Thea spoke on through three daiquiris she had had the guardian mix specially for her, how she had done as much for you at first as your guardian would allow: Thea Dover took me through your young life crisis by crisis, as if she'd been present through it all—like the policeman's visit when you and your friend had cracked a window playing stickball and your friend had then got so excited he simply threw straight at another window in the house and broke it too (and the house swallowed up the ball then), the frequent visits of the Puerto Rican diver Thea thought it was so wise of you to be good to, even though—but Thea's own

Vanishing point, to whom she looked and to whom her talk all pointed was the guardian as he argued a couple of hobbies with the vicar his friend (whose church he would never attend except compulsory funerals), and they went to his *Field Guide to the Shells* (which I later bought half-curiously for myself and Daddy found dry) and they discussed how much you'd have to pay for a Precious Wentletrap here in the city, could you go as low as five dollars at the shop way uptown, that was a dangerous area, and the vicar was soon bound for the renowned shell beach in the Keys, while Thea Dover continued to discuss you and her and the guardian merely as a kind of formal welcome to me or as if I had come under the river not merely to appear—but also to interview Thea Dover, a lady well known on the Heights and of a terrifyingly old family, or so the tall rocking organist in the red corduroy jacket confided to me when Thea D. took her little glass over to the guardian who then momentarily stared (then pleasantly raised his eyebrows) at me (so I felt I was standing up for Daddy) and the guardian was persuaded by Thea to go with her and her glass into the great old kitchen to make her a new batch of daiquiris. Also there: (a) a middle-aged man in khaki shirt and beige velvet pants and a copper earring, who swung his gaze but paused a crude second too long on me not to have to express a feeling, it was an accustomed charmer's quick stiff half-nod that passed for either formal or intimate, he knew we might have once been introduced, the Simp: like a driver's safe glance at pedestrian me; (b) a case worker with an olive shirt with a white stiff collar and a tie pin and a prep school drawl joking about how his Puerto Rican clients across the river hated him but put up with him; (c) Maddy Beecher, my initial encounter with same, who was drinking Nina pale dry and promised me (twice) a Heights tour concentrating on landmarks of your athletic, criminal, and festival childhood, which he then sheepishly retracted saying you were so painfully sentimental you would never have snitched a licorice twist (be it red or black) or a Clark bar or a pink rubber punchball from the shop you all patronized, because you'd think you were depriving the proprietor's spoiled fat proprietary son of a college degree, so said this Maddy Beecher of whom that first time I wasn't at all sure; and (d) a tall pale blond girl called Charley who had a tartan wool that came to mid-calf and who asked me if I liked having my own apartment and if I liked dogs and if I knew Lief Lund, said there was a boy over there listening to Van, who Maddy said was supposed to have known Lief Lund, but when I said I for one didn't know any Lief Lund, Charley said, playing with the silver daisy at her neckline, "God, he married a gal I came out with" and then she said I must come out to the Island, did I play golf, her mother found some mysterious brown thrashers at the country club and her father got mad when they went "Smack smack" as he was chipping up and all her nonplaying (member) mother could do was keep the glasses on the silly birds: and Charley (as if intimately, but merely intimating her own in-ness and my not-ness) said, "Tell me what you think of Jackie." She loved my olive sack which she called "shift" and was flattering me when she said I had been to art school: you came over and planted a kiss on me, which startled me in that it seemed to announce something that had to do simply with you not me (though Daddy would simply have approved, or as much as a father can). But the discussion of Mattioli's *Commentaires* (which I later looked up, Lyons, 1579, to get into the guardian's good book) made me feel at home God knows why, and then verbal doublets, then Cuban tree snail shells (which made Thea turn away from you and from telling you you were crazy to take a trip behind the Iron Curtain, Judge Deal was coming in any minute and after a report of unsavory elements encountered on the street on his way over to the guardian's would tell you the same damn thing about the Iron Curtain), and she said loudly at the guardian, "Don't talk to me about Cuba, sweetie": it turned out there was a buffet and everyone stayed to lunch, and after, once, the guardian and the vicar (who everyone called "Van") started arguing loudly about the family link between the Common Atlantic Sundial and the Noble Wentletrap and everyone else piped down, Thea Dover, who had been speaking about the similarities between you and your guardian, paused and murmured to me, "*Sthenorytis pernobilis* is what matters to *him*, but they're *ab*solutely stunning. A pearly cream spiral with the tiniest outside ribs like ribs along a sailboat's gunwale, well no nothing like that but so beautiful not even the Japs could imitate it in synthetic rice paper-mâché, if he only knew how beautiful"—she was in love with the guardian, I thought, and her voice was turning lower and harder—"I don't care what the Latin is, Sylvia, or what Wentletrap means—it means 'spiral staircase' in German, doesn't it?—" but then Judge Deal arrived nodding generally, and we moved in to the sideboard in the dining room, Thea Dover (herself one of the invited) trying to act as hostess, explaining that the man with the earring had twice almost crewed in the America's Cup trials, then telling Charley to get a serving spoon from the pantry counter, but I was way ahead of Charley and as Thea stuck my spoon into the guardian's tureen of chicken spaghetti and I was accepted here in part just because I *was* here, she said, with a slight drooping of eyelids "Jack advises me that you're wonderfully healthy." Which came back to me in Heathrow Airport waiting room when I stacked myself against your wasted, witty, fever-edged Cassia and wondered if you had, in a word, taken me for someone else. I tried to be hostess to my father that summer day at the guardian's shore estate when Grimes the bastard seemed to let the guardian defeat himself rushing off the screen porch which was just then getting darker though it was only two P.M., rushing back then to read from a paperback called *Let Your Lingo Be*: "Hear this, Red, quote, 'But authors like Dos Passos or James are of course atypical in language as equally in content, which *per se* disqualifies them as models for typical, normal usage. Wouldn't it be nice if one talked like great literature in one's daily intercourse? But—and here comes a complex point—Saussure's distinction between *parole* and *langue* must not be taken to mean that they are not *wholly* not both on an equal level.'" "Noop, noop, noop," Grimes trebled, "a dead horse Fossy, just a dead horse my boy. Now Leonard *Bloomfield* couldn't write like that if he tried, I'm an old Bloomfieldian and always was, Bloomfield built on Saussure—" "*I* know, *I* know," faintly from the guardian—"The whole idea of patterns of contrastive features contained in impersonal *langue* stimulated Leonard to pursue his own lead and complete the line that began with Grimm and passed through the neogrammarians: Bloomfield finally establishes linguistics as a descriptive science: he writes a bit better than that chap you so gleefully read from; in fact, Leonard Bloomfield is to his science sometimes what some of the great English scholars are to their studies, say Kerr to medieval studies, a great, great summarist, his simplicity–" "– whose?" came faintly from the guardian–"digests" said Red, "with uncanny right-headedness and wholeness just the elements of what needs to be said and implied– *sound* changes occur systematically, and *meaning* remains a nonlinguistic factor: from which follow the uprooting of false derivations and the disposal of apparent contradictions in correspondence classes, and indeed all good things, Fossy, all good things. Even, heh heh, *va-nil-la*."

"Vanilla?" said the guardian. "You're changing the subject pretending to be polite to the others." "Oh," said Daddy, "I'm enjoying every bit of this even as a layman." The guardian started strong and ended unsure: "I don't think your Leonard Bloomfield says exactly that about meaning, the meanings of words...he's a bigger man... than you say." "Oh Fossy *he* would have dismissed your wish to set up absolute standards of correctness," Grimes went on. "Yet," said the guardian, "when you throw out all norms of correctness you simply erect another norm." But then he was unable to follow up his thought in the pause Grimes seemed to dictate, create, smooth out like a piece of wrapping tissue, and you my darling came in, thinking (you later said) that before long you and I'd be sailing Europewards and you didn't want unpleasantness these last few days: "Mr. Grimes, tell us where the word 'ramshackle' comes from." "Oh," he said, heh-heh-ing, "it is either a back formation from 'ransack' or–" "You may well take your insulated view," said the guardian, "in your academic oasis, your pastoral retreat, your" "Or in yours, Foster," said Grimes, "where I presently am–" "*Now* am," said the guardian, "'presently' means 'soon,' in *spite* of usage." "Well, in terms of our continuing friendship," said Grimes, "I'm sorry: for 'presently' is what people say it is, and you haven't got your ear to the ground." (However well grounded!) "Oh," said the guardian wearily then, "maybe you're right," and looked abruptly at his most guestlike guest, Daddy, and put on a smile even though you could tell he didn't want to change the subject even for Daddy. Yet, wanting to move it from the foreground, I remembered the coffee water boiling and said so, getting up, and the guardian said, "Oh maybe you're right, well, if I had it to do over again I'd go into linguistics, yes I would, and"—frowning upon Red Grimes—"make a study of 'of' or go back to a couple of the grand masters you people discount today—that German etymologist Pott and his organic life-cycles in language, and dear old Schleicher and his genetic genealogies." But Red Grimes missed the transitional mood and laboriously sniped back, "Your 'of' thing's been done to death, syntax-wise, phonological, it's all implicit in what Jesperson said about encroachments upon the genitive; but what would you have done if you *could* have? I mean seriously." "But," said the guardian—and I rose, but did not move away—"*look* at 'of': *have* you ever? Forget your structural linguagraphs and your glossematics, hell I'm just a dilettante—" "Oh," returned Grimes, "you betray your own principles. Fossy, you're not at all like that in lots of sorts of kinds of ways: at being a father, for instance, oh I know a thing or two about you." "Well, I'm a dilettante, but a few things I do know—" "Wait," said Grimes. "No," said the guardian, "*you* wait, the host has a right to a hearing, someone I think said the host wants to be thanked, which is, as you'd say, the point about the host—and you listen to me, or I'll smash you." Which the guardian could have done perfectly even without all his manual work every day or his skill as a boxer and his afternoon run with the little black dog. "I have watched English decay, advertisers change our spelling, the cold war change our clichés to terrifying blandnesses no one seems to hear as keenly as I do, and I keep badgering editors, including Harvard people I was once on speaking terms with, and meanwhile people like you keep saying change is irresistible, whatever is said is right, is A-O.K.—and worst, that you merely describe what's happening when in fact you scoundrels influence and prescribe; and by the way, a man can't live his *life* as if he were *describing* what drifts upon him, he must both resist change and determine it. If I, quote unquote gear my evaluational level to a broader scope I hope to experience motivation. Hyphenated couples disappear into the dark tunnel of usage, Red, and emerge joined and de-hyphenated without once asking my advice. In some terrible manner these repugnant tics in the face of my language will be on hand when our culture ultimately switches off. And you, Red, and your school will be immanent upon that scene however really far away you're performing your self-consistent calculus." "That's Hjelmslev, of course," said Red Grimes, "Copenhagen." "All right," said the guardian, "whatever you say." When I came back with the coffee tray, Grimes was demurring, "Oh no no no, Sylvia's father doesn't want to hear about glossematics." Whereupon you Jack startled your guardian by saying, "Something will come of it—but Mr. Grimes won't be involved: the generative grammarians with their surface signals cluing their deep structures are going someday to meet the Freudians and parapsychologists at some cross-river deep down in the future. But not Mr. Grimes." And the guardian said, "Well, listen to these '*ofs*'—'The Birth of the Blues,' for instance, 'dictatorship of the proletariat'—perhaps I'm almost sorry I didn't go further left twenty-five years ago, perhaps I'm *not* sorry. But the phrase betrays: dictatorship *by* the people? *over* the people? leave the phrase vague and you wake up one day to find it's tricked you, do you see?" "*You're* off the subject," murmured Red Grimes, but my Daddy "saw" and tried to encourage, and nodded at your guardian, who said, "See the paradox?" They all did. "You see, if you could phrase my thoughts on 'of' better, you'd find a prophecy in your hand probably. I've gone as far as my equipment could take me. Oh Red, to be taken over by the thing you thought *you* were adopting and possessing! I tried always to be free. And mind you—" he got up, walked to the porch's upstage doorway, and stood with his back to us musing (as Grimes murmured, "You're a nice nice man, Fossy"), and then the guardian's words, projected away from us into the living room, were either simple or hopelessly deep, I didn't know which: "I succeeded within limits—though I had leisure, of course."

Visions of past and future possibility swarmed in the figure of that strong dejected back fixed in the door leading off the porch to the room where he'd been rummaging: a future of your fruitlessly trying to both please him and step apart from him, use your freedom but not as a rebuke; and a lodged past uniting him with Grimes in college, or Grimes with his own New Jersey brother's Shell station located like others by local ordinance on the outskirts of town, uniting far and near queries, some of them logical refiners of that past (like did you travel with your guardian to every state of the union, did he attend to your schooling, did you love him, he you?), some of them dangerous dislodgers of that past (like what was between your guardian and your lawful parents, did you and your guardian ever have a showdown like this disguised one on the porch which Grimes did not realize turned a long corner in his friendship with your guardian, and if you did not have showdowns (for you were strangely good to your guardian) what instead?) and simultaneous also were rushing pasts and futures in which Daddy stood both strong and disseminated. For never between you and me—no, I mean me and Daddy—the biweekly showdowns rumored, overheard, and on occasion by me witnessed, between Daphne House and *her* father:

"You know very well you're going all the way with that squirt—he's only a kid!" "But not often enough, not often enough." "Don't you care about your*self*?" "Exactly." "Where is the Daphne who used to walk with me past the elms on the Common and watch the squirrels?" "Father, she has given herself to another." "I bet *Syl*via's still a virgin." "Try her." Instead, for us—I mean me and Daddy—a gentle rhythm (as the unmagical young lecturer said pointing at the screen with his wand in the compulsory art history credit at art school) of untested moments, times when it wasn't good daughterly fear that stopped my tongue but a laziness that passed all understanding: and *my* true penalty, unlike Daphne's, whose father died in his forties one day after she had (she says) wished him dead and now feels clearly in her lungs and everywhere that things should never have been said, they were untrue—*my* penalty is that he lives, on, even quite well and handsome, and though he is bodily my chance at last to say what Godmaydamnme for not saying, I'm afraid I can't, afraid I won't, and even (though not much) afraid such Life Questions as the Billboard slant-bar Bean Question would stump his heart and make it stop. Bee Bee Barker after a night spent with your sympathy wouldn't hesitate to scowl at you and perversely—"So you want to make the world safe from kidnapers? In another society there wouldn't be big fortunes to hit for ransom, there wouldn't be these unsatisfied desires. You want to make the world safe from kidnapers—but think (for a change, think) how it simplifies the lives of the parents, especially of big families" (tired irony, nary a smile) "redistribution of"—

Antecedents, mother, father; rediffusion of fidelities, Bee Bee believes in a high degree of fidelity despite what she says and tries to do, and would be as shocked as you would be quietly surprised to hear what happened the night I woke up my eggs with more than a suspicion of chervil and Maddy investigated my dumb-waiter and I met John Plante, whom Maddy must earlier have told about you and your absence. But it was not five-thirty but four-thirty they left, my mistake, and May had a good two hours to go, maybe more with the humidifier burring near her bed: but I couldn't have arranged for Plante to stay without letting Maddy your old friend know. ("Speak univocally," says the guardian from the Heights.) But then came the knock, and after I made sure of Plante's black hair and green-and-black bandanna through the soiled frosted-glass panel, I flipped the knob and dislodged the police-lock brace from its socket and holding it like a formal staff I greeted Plante again, he whispering, "You're not surprised," a self-conscious courtesy I could have done without, for he and I both knew I was at the very least rather surprised. He made conversation for about twenty-five minutes and we played Bernstein's *Candide*. I couldn't tell you about this or about the lost ring any more than I could tell Daddy about the old abductor Staghorn or tell anyone about the Gypsy Woman, any more than you could tell your guardian about the Bowie knife with the hartshorn handle, a prize which a small delegation of defeated competitors thought had been unfairly awarded to you at the end of the nineteen forty-two treasure hunt. You could not listen all the way through when in London I told you this billboard revelation from an old folded corner of my nymphhood: for there in a Heathrow waiting room full of bare-legged campers in sandals you were irked by the cigarette man, surprised by Cassia Meaning, and trapped in the simple new knowledge that the guardian died: I sat there in England mulling irrelevantly, who now will correct my tenses in the kitchen? Who's gonna praise my snap beans done with mushroom and nutmeg? Not that I knew him long, but we did hold hands and make a promising start, we did talk. His hands complemented

Daddy's. His tapering long fingers led back to a bumpy strong coarseness; Daddy's shorter, stubby fingers led up to lonely knuckles and a back not hairy not pallid, of a delicacy you thought you saw through to the very hair muscles and sweat ducts. He was sensitive enough probably to receive my meaning of that series of awful instants looking at the billboard and beyond and behind, but I did not tell him. The meaning was this: No I do not know the meanings. You have to capture the event in itself. What happened was that Elmer Lyons's billboard (which Daddy said Elmer didn't want but his brother-in-law had had one of his own men design, and Elmer felt obligated) simply stood at that rise facing you if you were facing roughly north, with behind it what I'd always taken simply as part of the whole thing, namely the pines and down the hill some hardwoods and on the hill the far side of the little valley Staghorn's house and beyond it the familiar gray hills and the deserted white house on land next to Staghorn's that he was always saying he must buy to protect himself. I wasn't too happy on that day, Mama and Daddy had had a standoff, and the words would take at least two days to go away, and kissing him good-bye at the car I found myself thinking to prolong our kiss, and reaching for his hand while I kissed him, I had never reached for his hand like that before: and he drove away, for the day (I thought), and being unhappy I went off the other direction aimlessly on the road I regarded as my personal possession or preserve. A hot, tar road moving in the late-morning heat, soft to my sneakers with the superhumanly fat boy standing by his mailbox grinning, four hundred pounds and not bright, a fetal trick, and though we lived near them for years I never got his given name, he was ageless after a while. As I walked I was thinking of how my determined concentration hadn't been able to shake from my mother's face her mild smile as she sat at the kitchen table attacking and attacking

Daddy, revealing her own fierce engagement merely in forgetting to relinquish her yellow-knuckled grip on the pencil she'd been writing her market list with. It was something between her and Daddy, he was a bit polite perhaps. There was one big, piled cloud in the sky, I couldn't tell how far away it was. I took my usual walk and there were no cars—Staghorn (then *Mr.* Staghorn) would be finishing his morning's work in the attic before the air grew too hot, he was supposed to be living with someone, I remember those words. I turned a curve and then another, walking more and more slowly—up the rise the brown, glassy heat-shimmers looked cushy enough to slide on, rest on, go on forever: I heard a car way behind me slow down and disappear, perhaps a driveway, not gravel: and then a long time it seemed later I was at a rise thinking what my fifth grade teacher Miss Tree had said about Portuguese seafarers setting out to spread the Gospel and unexpectedly discovering new lands: and for only a few seconds surveying the green and brown and blue and feeling the approaching noon heat through my hair and on my neck and shoulders (I was wearing a green junior T-shirt Daddy had brought me from CCC with the college WILDCATS decal on my chest), I knew that Mama and Daddy arguing didn't matter, but then, all gathered together at once, the billboard revelation occurred: and then, though I wanted a word to finish what was happening to me, I couldn't: because the wedding Chevy, it seemed with almost no approaching noise, blew up on me from under the hill I had climbed and as I dived for the bushes hearing the road's sandy shoulder, and feeling the wind of that wild car on my legs, I heard out of it a happy scream; then Daddy was running to me. And he was just an older man.

"Vanished into thin air, you poor kid!" He was pulling things out of my T-shirt and my shorts and saying very quietly, "My God! My God!" and I was going to tell him what I'd seen. Which mattered. But instead replied to his questions how close had they come to me and who were they—questions that didn't matter, and belong in the same class as men's (and sometimes now even women's) godawful talk of automobile performance, cylinders, pick-up, alternator bearings, cars like talented relatives: when I should have said and now he'll never listen (since he thinks I'm grown up) or would never understand and anyway won't hear) as follows: I'd never thought the mobilized string bean human but I'd never exactly thought it wasn't. I'd never thought how far the flat billboard was from the gray hills, or from the hardwoods down the hill or from the near pines (whose needles in clusters of two and five Daddy once picked to show me)—all of which, with some of the bright flat sky, made a natural frame for the billboard I had till then thought so familiar. Nor had I thought that the grinning bean on its red tractor *saw* anything but *me*, when of course—stupid me!—I had a surrounding background, and so did each whitewashed guard post on the road's shoulder and each hairy red berry of the smooth sumac. Nothing belonged to me, I mistakenly thought, certainly not Ken or Ben or Jim whatever his name was down there in the little valley as he slowly parts the big bushes making his way in toward the stream he fishes. Yet, as my father was sprinting up to me, another kind of notion came: namely, what do I look like to, what *am* I to, that tough red pine, that familiar smooth sumac, the high old mostly denuded white pine? Did I fear or hope Daddy'd reply no less than, "No more than you are to those whitewashed guard posts or that ugly Lyons billboard." He didn't. But indeed as he petted me I for the first time thought the giant human-eyezed motoroid sunray-irised bean grabbing the small stalk it had been picked from or had picked itself from, ugly—and its sunray eyes that were designed like a tomato juice can Mama saved fat in, ugly. My father had turned around and driven back to have another go at Mama, and he had had it, and then had come walking after me and had been flattened against the cemetery hedge by the wedding Chevy that lost its can as it passed him. He touched me a lot there at the edge of the bright quiet soft tar road. But when Plante came back after putting Maddy in a cab you would have thought he'd be all business, charm, easiness, and touch; but for twenty-one minutes, twelve with me on his lap, and Bernstein's *Candide* as far away as May's humidifier, he spoke of the future, his firm's South African jobs, his disillusionment with curtain-wall high-rise and glittering office transparencies moving against the sky that struck him so when he first came from London, and then his decision to turn down a row-house project down south. He looked away most of the—hurry up and wait (unquote Herbie, U.S. Coast Guard), Plante's straight slack hair was so black it was blue, and he said, "You can't do the things you want to, see what isn't happening in Boston and what did at Lincoln Center which is no more a communal center than Aalto's TB sanatorium at Paimio and not as musical either: and they almost destroyed the Sydney opera house, they hate its site on the pier, it's all dangerously projective, you know huge-scale wings sticking up parked waiting for the angle to come back." Plante said he was taking the advice of his friend in Leeds and would blow his mind very cold in what he now saw had always been most alluring of all, the sculptural containments that would reflect his sculptor friend's theory about unseeing perspective, seeing—through the "mere real" (:quote)—the (unquote:) "flat face of truth," and it would take a short lifetime to work this into sculpture, which seems three-dimensional—and therefore his theory seemed too cerebral, but lucky for me I could sense there in his lap that cerebral or not his motor centers were operating properly, it was only a matter of time, I could hear his hands thinking whether to move now or not—two dimensions, three, I lay against his shoulder and silently wished us luck.

Vis-à-vis did Plante in all these thoughts of his think I had all day as well as all night, I wondered, Jack, what Daddy would think to come in and find me here with a stranger not earnestly turning each other in bed but in a black leather bucket trap here so dearly cuddled and lapped. I wondered, seeing the scene in depth, if Plante expected a less self-effacing response to his strange attack of words than my nod every twenty seconds and my hazel blink, and wondered if all this about seeing the world flat would lead into a backdrop of hot air—but it did not, and I was able to escape speaking and instead demonstrate my unique view many-sidedly. Or you could say Plante's perspectival (view-) point of origin met mine at last in a vanishing point that kept retreating till we could catch up and it held still and if it is possible I believe that up until Plante and I had the pleasure of so meeting, I seemed to flow back and forth, back and forth, into not hot air but warm rain, forth and forth, between, in a word, Daddy and you, which in a word is getting warmer and warmer in our request for my favorite mystery earlier alluded to: But after the lingual lunch that summer's day, Grimes and Daddy stood in the living room, and it had begun to rain, and to Daddy's remark that you couldn't control the elements and we probably shouldn't go monkeying with them, Grimes thought the rain would pass so he could "beach" it again, he stood telling Daddy about plus-fours he had worn at Harvard, the neat security they gave your legs (Rabelaisian monks welcome to their "visceral free swing," Grimes preferred to be snug), but Daddy, one-third proprietor of College Corner Clothier, didn't see he was being patronized, and I had dishes to do.

"Viands," the guardian said to me entering the kitchen, "you'd think such a rich-sounding word came from rich roots, say Old French for 'spitted venison' or Late Latin for 'blood sauce'"–"But *I* wouldn't think that," I said, and was glad he found a fondness I hadn't exactly seen was in my sharp words as I said them, not even, before that moment, *in me*, until he'd countered them affectionately, and made me turn from the grand wooden sink to attend to what he said. The guardian said, "Make him free. It's what I wanted, what perhaps I've had. But make him open himself to all influences and aspirations while you're abroad." I grinned, alas. Rather stiff, he was, formal, old-hat, like Judge Deal being shocked that we would think of going behind the Iron Curtain. (Together!)

"Jack," said the guardian to me, "I've a fear Jack'll trap himself in a job that isn't him. It isn't only this with friend Grimes, it's other reminders—old things about Jack—" but I said, "Professor Grimes is *not* your friend." "Of course he is." "Well, not in how he put you down." "I've known Grimes since—he was my generation at Harvard." "You *might* have known him but you don't now. You're too nice for him." The guardian ignored that: "Remember what I've said about Jack. I hope that you will marry. I could tell you a story about not marrying. And you would understand Jack even better than now, and so would he. But I don't lecture you." "Only," I jibed, "on Latin's usefulness, a good grounding—" and he kissed me smack (maybe misaimed) across the mouth, I didn't get chance to finish "grounding," much less pucker, he wasn't unaware of his appeal, you could see the flesh of his face was alive, I smelled not that comforting tone of almondy fixative you get in the (in my opinion) enlarged cheek pores of some men of that age but his aftershave, which unlike Daddy's was lemon, and under it a mildly rancid smell of growing. I wondered what he had meant. The "you" meant both of us—to get married. The "things" he "knew about Jack" I am willing to bet pertained to your kidnap search, though we never had proof that he knew; and I for one believe the guardian hoped you would desist—he asked us to look up in Cracow a man he had corresponded with since before the war, who had thought up and now hoped to see adopted a world language totally unlike Esperanto, but all we found was a young structural linguisticist in the Hotel Bristol nightclub, Warsaw, who had just joined the Party and did not know Grimes' work.

Vis-à-vis the guardian's not inanimate kiss dead center, I couldn't come up with anything and seemed merely to be awaiting a second and he turned too quickly and summarily pushed through the swinging door. Later, as they looked out a window at the rain, he and Red Grimes made up. And Red explained that it was a common error of students to confuse haplology and jamming, and there were some other words, like 'dissimulation'—and in a well- (and clean-) cushioned wicker chair Daddy dozed off to the sound of the rain, but woke suddenly when it let up at three-thirty, the clock rang. You phoned the man Praid long distance who had phoned you, and just before the guardian re-entered the living room in wet yellow slicker, you said, "You can't take my passport if I don't break the law," and I guess there was laughing at the other end of the cord, and as you hung up I asked the guardian if Thea had left these copies of *The Delineator* I'd found in a window seat and you asked your guardian, though it was early, if you should drive in to the airport to meet Thea and the vicar, both of whom fortunately by then I knew to speak to, which was only to say since that recent Sunday noontide in the city Thea calling for a serving spoon, Jim Commons preparing me not very well for what he may have envisioned as a premarital coup behind Jack's back—as the vicar told of his encounter with Conte (but which one in retrospect *was* Conte?) the gangster; while Judge Engleman Deal, after a huffy bout with Beecher about the new remote-beam, noncontact lie detectors soon to be ready for limited use, slipped some Irish into his coffee; and we all listened to the vicar, our feet on the red carpet in which a couple of Arab steeds reared like an arch augmented by the arcs of the two fierce horsemen's jumbo scimitars in mid-swing, you might have looked around for, prayer books, you would have felt it even without the vicar present: this was an undisturbable occasion this Sunday noontide and not susceptible to, say, Herbie's performances at the guardian's Sunday supper a few long months later when he got tight and loose, passed out his calling cards, recommended in depth two small airline stocks and an over-the-counter saxophone company (which indeed split as soon as the vicar bought it), and ended with an enduringly repetitive account of what he'd do if he had it to do again, and while the guardian kept saying, "But you're only twenty-nine, man, twenty-nine, I'm twice your age," Herbie persevered unlistening, "I'd go into space law: isn't that something? I'd go into space law." But the earlier Sunday noontide, my Heights debut, the closest we came to difficulty would have been due to me if it had occurred, Jim the social worker trying to take me over during dessert, "But sweetheart, if you call me a do-gooder, at least you concede it's good that I do, but you're tense here today, don't think I don't understand, look Uncle Engleman and Aunt Thea are as they are, they genuinely are fond of ESSO of New Jersey, genuinely moved by its, almost its venerable substance, they're literally dying for a chance to vote for Nixon over Johnson in 'sixty, and Uncle Engleman will say, 'Speaking pragmatically, Washington has become an African capital,' this is how they are"; and when I said is he really your uncle, Jim said of course not and went on talking me protectively into the ground ever smiling widely *while* talking so that his well-used dimples winked and his mouth kissed forward, and I was the outsider thus inexorably in need of his experienced, trained aid, which then coaccidentally the vicar brought with his tale thus sparing me the chance to clobber this creeping Jim: I very simply turned my head northeast and listened, like everyone else in the room except at first Commons: a strong, light, well-brewed voice with modulations and transitions to make even Eddy Beecher listen watchfully: you can recapture at least the spirit of the vicar Dr. White's tale (which Jim Commons immediately afterward called a "para-story," being beside the point): the vicar began ere Jim ceased muttering and whispering to me, so the tale had–"began by my remaining (of course alone) in the parish house half an hour longer than I regularly would on a Friday afternoon–indeed as we–I repeat, we–left, we met the first of the choirboys coming in for practice, but I get ahead of my story. I said 'we,' for I had a visitor and it was with him that I departed: he was what is commonly called, I think, a 'heavy.'" Dr. White's voice embraced us all, but his eyes stayed upon the guardian's–"This chap was wearing gray serge, double-breasted, not unclerical in fabric though designed quite signally for the secular arm: and he said to me, 'You'll christen a kid for us this afternoon?' the intonation just barely a query. 'It's right now,' said he, 'it's down the hill across Atlantic but–' then a pause both minatory and inveigling–'we'll pay,' he said, and said again as reflectively as such a man can, 'Yeah, we gonna pay you.' I had been quite formally invited, you'll have to admit, and I knew I had little choice at most. 'The old man'll pay,' my visitor said, and took my elbow; 'you better come along now.' In the street as I was about to bend down to get into the back seat of a fine old gray La Salle in mint condition, I restrained myself from greeting Cassia Meaning (then no more than fifteen) who was coming home (rather late it seemed to me) from school and who greeted me; I feared my compelling chauffeur might fancy I was hinting at my abduction, though in fact I did not myself see it as a bonafide abduction. I didn't, by the way, suspect then that he took me for a *Catholic* priest.

'O.K., Father,' he said, and soon we were pulling up in front of a brownstone in a run-down block about a fifteen-minute walk from the church. Though the house could have used our own mason for a face-lift, its interior was pretentiously prepossessing. A short, broad-shouldered gray-haired chap in a dark suit and silver tie opened the vestibule door; there was no postbox grille in the vestibule—this being still nominally a one-family house—so I could see no name. I passed into the low-lit entry hall and was facing the long carpeted stair, when the tall door to my right opened sufficiently for a second short broad-shouldered but portly gray-haired man in a dark suit and silver tie to ease himself through—sufficiently also for me to see beyond him into the well-lighted room itself and to see what was going on there. 'Hi, Father,' said he in a deep voice, and pointed upstairs, saying 'After you.' In the dim halls were gold-framed paintings of eighteenth- and nineteenth-century American gentlemen grouped round tables engaged in crucial discussions—documents, ventures, turning points. We didn't stop at the third floor but bore steadily on up the red-carpeted stair till I'd have sworn we'd climbed much higher than the building whose height, if not whose number of floors, I had thought not unusual leaving the La Salle—how high were we? how many brownstones (Puerto Rican rooming houses or Engleman's pile) go above four or five stories? was I in some subtly begun state of mesmerized lull? If so, maybe by the agency of the sounds that came to my ears, my escort wheezing behind me, not evidently having like me climbed Mount Mary's north side summer after summer—till we reached the destined room—at a height, I repeat, of which I could no longer be sure. But of course you must be yourself against all comers, in all situations however strange, for yourself is all you have to be. Well, in a sumptuous well-curtained room away from the street there waited a still older, ruddy man in a black double-breasted suit sipping a dark highball and chatting to two younger men who appeared to be his employees. Near him, holding the baby in a voluminous mantilla, was a girl surely no more than twenty, also in black. 'Go to it, Padre,' the older man said, motioning the girl to give me the baby, and she did. When I demurred, saying that he or the mother should hold the child till I was ready, he said, 'You go to it, Father, don't give us a mass, just the short form, you say me a mass later, right?' And the swaddled infant was shoveled into my arms, I performed my task, nothing was said about the English of my service, I got no reply when I requested the names of the parents and the beautiful, almondy-eyed child, but then his first two names *were* given me, James Angelo. Well, eventually I was ushered down the stairs again. As I turned to my chauffeur, who was waiting for me in the hall and nodded grimly, the door to the first-floor front room opened again with the same slow murmur of voices, and I saw again what I had seen before. One of the gray-haired men came out, and just before he handed me an envelope, saying, 'Thanks, Padre, anything we can do for you any time,' he closed and buttoned his double-breasted jacket, and just before he did that, as he was finding the inside button I saw part of a shoulder holster. As I crossed the threshold he detained me saying quietly but authoritatively, 'I really mean it, Father, you want some-body taken care of, you come down and see us, no kidding.' Then snapped his fingers at my chauffeur, my elbow was taken, and I was driven back to church, after which I went home, glad I had not acknowledged what I'd seen past the partly opened door to that ground-floor front room, unexceptionable as it may have been."

"Van?" called Charley the blonde from across the guardian's living room where she sat, and now swung out, on one revolving "buttock" of the mahogany two-holer duet bench, "what on earth *did* you see?" "Only a bronze-colored casket with flowers, and people were standing about drinking and I detected a laugh. And *that* is the area they call Puerto Rican." "But you're not a Catholic priest," said Charley a little too loudly, "they took you for an R.C." "I weighed my situation in depth and elected not to confess myself not in their sense a Catholic priest." "But *Van White*: we're Episcopalians first, Christian—" "I weighed the situation in depth and concluded that herewith the child was Christian, that was the crux." "But we're Episcopalian first, and we're Christian second," Charley said. Judge Deal was looking at my legs steadily, and the guardian, who had been looking me over as if he'd never quite got the idea of me before—I was appealing maybe because I was yours—said, "At times the lot of you seem closer to Catholicism than to Christianity." "But," said Thea Dover, "look at Jackie's Puerto Rican friends, *they're* Catholic, the Moraleses." At which the guardian shook his head with a hopeless smile— at me!—her irrelevance, I guess—and got up and went to a high bookcase. She saw this and persisted: "Jackie, you belong in this Peace Corps thing if it ever gets started. In Tarzania. Engleman, isn't there a Tarzania now?" "No," said Judge Deal.

Visions, some visceral, bound rarely (only French, I think) in paper, and looked on by the guardian (who had also a library in the country) as a revered possession, I imagined he was reaching for that German author I couldn't recall: in my college version the story stayed with me even though never in the German original by me read; stayed with me as, say, I have stayed with you: starring the Gypsy Woman (with whom, just one year after those college performances, I spent the night) and starring mainly the man whose head is cut down. I wanted indeed *not* to hunt up the tale, I'd so loved the play: wanted not to look *her* up again after that night a year later in her borrowed flat downtown, and it was easier wanting not to because I knew that at museum card counters or at a certain stainless-steel hole-in-the-wall she would be easy to find, she had not liked me later: in the A.M. she said to me like a doctor at a desk, "You were perhaps not in the mood to receive my confidences last night"–did she affect a faintly European accent, was it mingled with New York airs?–"if not," said she, "you made them lose their efficacy," like some faith healer: and I hardly knew if she meant her hands on passive me or merely, before, early in the evening, before we went to bed, her long talk on how she'd spent the summer thinking her intensive problems through and had now begun to attack various extensive, I waiting for a story and thinking how much extensile talk stands between people, she voicing her free-flo view of personality, undifferent reservoir, and from there our current selves go-flo into differing acts: and then, as I half-listened through the half-raised window to a couple of men horribly hollering and whistling for a taxi, I could imagine their cruel dimples, the bottom lip stretched against the bottom teeth, then they were running laughing, and the Gypsy Woman was suggesting that sexuality (which she called "sexuacity") was *like* this free-flowing inherently indefinite personality she envisioned: we were sexually many, just as we were personally many–sexually many forms and personally many potencies and ultimately it was possible only to live; possible to know ourselves merely to date, never wholly know (for by then we were officially dead). I for one would have thought sexuality part of: personacity. And I may not know anything about myself but I know what I am. In the morning, after labeling me an inadequate recipient of her bedtime confidences, she made me cinnamon instant and told me she hoped I'd have a baby–she said this again, "You must become pregnant," in her foreign off-cadence, aiming her crested, nearly connecting eyebrows at me, curling out her mouth. And when I asked Staghorn what getting pregnant by a woman would be, he began cunningly to describe the infant, and drew it with his water pencils in at least five colors, but didn't finish what he–it was a boy baby, two female minuses contra-spun forty-five degrees each to make a tilted plus, and far nicer than Maddy's Santos-Dumont pilot-project Boyoid doll now at last released that I hope May's excellent eyes won't see in some window, and will come in pink, yellow, and (what's expected to be biggest of the three) basic black. And I wondered if, after two years that he hadn't laid eyes on me, Staghorn, then fifty-two, still liked me. And I wondered–no, I didn't wonder really–if I in the same manner liked him. Then again my mystery came up in me, as I saw Staghorn make room and other speaking figures strangely approach, but my Daddy did neither, for he simply stood strong in foreground, backdrop, and deep middle-age, view-found by me in a pattern others may vie to see who can see quickest into, but I will not

Vie with any city sharp or sheep, any clever cripple, any kind giant, to be first to find Daddy, for there could never have been even a hunt, he is in me. I dream. Am I therefore asleep? Like you? Words come in me and I am strong and fluent. I had just sold two originals for seventy-five apiece to a gift producer, one a maze in blue and green, one in large paisleys–what objects they would go on, I didn't know, and he didn't, perhaps wouldn't, tell me. And I had heard from the boy I'd met at the penthouse barbecue that he'd been serious, about the jacket design (and hoped that if I did the job cleverly readers would not know the book by its cover), and half an hour later the old messenger with his dead cigar that smelled was at my door. So, that evening I had money, work, I had a date for a cocktail party, I'd found a zinc-lined dry sink for my hi-fi, and I was cooking three-quarters of a pound of virgin halibut I had walked all the way to and from the market for and I was thinking of its wet cobbles and the stockbrokers ambling by to the second-floor fishhouse on the corner where imperious Negro waiters wear epaulets and general's stars depending how long in grade, or so Herbie said when he took me there and they forgot my parsley: and as I was smelling the first broil of the halibut from my oven and wondering should I rinse the spinach despite what the plastic bag said, and hoping Daddy would come stay the weekend if he could get Saturday off, and was thinking that it was my city and I would make it, the phone went, I forgot the halibut thinking it was either Daddy or someone else, I picked up and it was Mr. Amondson coming right out of that black plastic receiver wanting me to go with Christy to a tea dance on the Heights. Where, to be sure, I met you, who dropped in politely and stayed on account of me though not to dance. Do I embarrass you dreaming as I fluff up these flattened spears of old green grass? I didn't want to get involved with the Amondsons in the city, old summer people where I lived but I was their equal in the city new as I was, which you and Maddy say has lost its name, you survey it in your melancholy charities, your surveils of vanishing evidence, your theoretic love.

And the gold lamé bag your guardian gave me for my first and only birthday with him I left in the closet at the undertaker's not by accident but as an evidence of me, nor did I take the spices, only the Penguin recipes. And gladly I leave you your free clients who came for counsel: the chronically pretty sapling thrice married seeking herself in an advanced degree who was passionately grateful for, she said, using you as a background to bounce ideational concepts off–grateful (I retorted) to herself; or the chronically cruddy young hubby (friend of a friend of someone else, who had gotten the idea that you possessed Guidance qualifications) for hours on end told the tale of how he chose and appropriated a girl quite opposite to his (in his description vital vivicious) mother; or that nice dull girl who I thought kept trying to aim her questions at me, so dull I can't just bring back what she was up to, but I will in a moment. But if you like these confessors, these needy, how could you have liked Cassia Meaning, who whatever else she bitchily is would never give you the benefit of her trouble, she and I alike there in our—Though I'd have been gracious, oh happy, to be saved by you, unlike the physically different though not indifferent Cassia fourteen and three-quarters that winter afternoon on a silent block of Smith Street slowly going home from Marie Verity's house and stopped east of Clinton by three Puerto Ricans her age who demanded her money, were sneered at, and according to team-plan were tugging her little drawstring calfskin sack, trying nose-to-nose intimidation, and bending her arm up behind her when your yell was heard a hundred yards away and your unusual run was seen by those toughs who according to Cassia may have thought that even laid end to end they could barely match your length, which was then, at just fifteen, how many famous inches more than seventy. But you had begun to run before seeing the situation though you were glad the punks, who had not had Eddy Beecher (then unthought of) explain to them how the (what is it?) rabbit can never reach the finish line and break the tape because of the infinity of divisions his racing legs face, scattered because of you: however all Cassia said was, "I suppose you phoned Marie and tracked me down. I'll thank you not to treat me like a missing person. As if I couldn't have finished this myself!" But her tongue would not have gotten her out of that jam without you. You'd have played your rebound another way if on the night I was with Plante in my widow-flat you'd happened in between four-thirty and five. You'd have been polite to me, implied my love life's my own, you love life too, you're making it or you're not, you don't fight your way into it and out of it, though maybe you worm: I know the whole hand; but skip your cozy odds. And so forth, would you have fought Plane?, yet would I have let you in, yet would you have needed me enough in the first place to come at four-thirty, five, five-fifteen, five-eighteen, five-twenty A.M.? I couldn't give you enough weakness to feed your moving jaws: "Only think," you are telling Bee Bee Barker as I undress in earshot, "only think of Trotsky's father farmer Bronstein—imagine a Jewish farmer, visiting his son Trotsky in Odessa prison, imagine what he'd wanted for his youngest son, what he may have thought looking at your wild-haired boy whose name was still Bronstein but who to farmer B may as well have been the Odessa jailer named Trotsky whom his son later adopted for a namesake, as be Lyova Bronstein the math prodigy." At which Bee Bee scoffed and went home, "liberal fiction, false depth, sentimental rapprochement, ahistoric." The guardian at some other hour and place comes flush up against this Bee Bee talk as if he was in the same room high above the undertaker's declining establishment, and in my (whore?) fancy observes (to, let's say, a Red Grimes genial and condescending), "Let them call such doctrinaire commitment a location of liberty within ideal limits, but great Scott!, Red, these kids have found in all that ideology just a simple *reductio*, you know that as well as—well almost as well as I." And Grimes' unmistakable thought at that moment sweeps smiling in off a great dry tide to penetrate another moment at which on the guardian's firelit beach I am thinking what to wear with his gold lamé bag, and the Oriental tenant (Jap? Chinese? Viet?) has just blown his bit of bad verse, his put-on sayings of his father (though if he was putting us on or his father, who knew?) and at last after a gentle snipe from the guardian the other side of the fire drying off, the Oriental tenant calls him a "wall-to-wall, ship-to-shore dilettante" but instantly covers the point with "one of the great ones." The guardian said to me, "What will I do without Jack? Though I haven't seen all that much of him the last few years." I said, as he took my hand, "My father thought he felt that way when Herbie went three thousand miles to college, and Herbie's adopted." Which perhaps I shouldn't have said so reassuringly: the guardian squeezed my hand politely, let go, and said, "Yes, Jack is adopted, but a very special sort of adopted son, you know." Then he took my hand and said, "*You* might make him feel differently about it, you know." Since I didn't get him, I hurried stupidly on with, "They couldn't have a baby and couldn't and couldn't: then almost as soon as Herbie came along, my mother got pregnant with me—well, nine months." The guardian said, "Funny, how one thing leads to another, your brother being adopted yet growing to be your father's son." He was absently walking off, down the steep shingle, he couldn't stay away from the water, it was like Ashley Sill turning up the hi-fi to drown us out: and the guardian said without looking back: "It can happen the other way around too," the guardian said it not tantalizingly (like Daddy speculating about a poker hand he already had guessed, or you kidding little Rain), but flatly, sadly, a deep truth that wouldn't seem to have much juice.

Vying with each other by that fire were the Oriental tenant's hoarse recorder improviding and Maddy's getinkling five-string banjo carrying anything that touched its stroke steadily ahead into the evening, like—perhaps nothing, and even kissing Bee Bee (maybe not exactly as she would have prescribed had she not been I guess skin-shy) in the dim thickness beyond the fiery area you must have like me noted that Maddy's folk song (which the Oriental tried poorly to noodle away from and failed) was the very tune that, stuffed unsuspecting into a big, visionary union orchestra, had come at us from three directions in the Silver Spring shopping center near Washington just two weeks before, as well as at the

similar center near Lynnfield, Mass., the week before that
and I wondered again if the guardian did after all know
how his adopted son was using the freedom which money
and care and love had intended—for if the guardian was
locked back in his remote libraries and gardens and his
unsolicited college advice project and correspondence
with newspapers and magazines, he also, in his son,
seemed a forever present sentinel hand. Flo Beecher
started singing, and Maddy and the fat Oriental did the
song all over again, which brought the guardian back out
of the black water—the girl is pregnant, her fellow goes
right down the street and ignores her, he has a new girl
with "gold and riches" the pregnant singer hasn't got,
and although at the shopping center two weeks before
a chorus of men and women that seemed to have been
electronically multiplied sang the refrain about the
deep grave and the wild goose grasses growing upon it,
Flo's space-isolated alto erased that other kidnaping
sound until Bee Bee and her sarcastic voice appeared
ahead of you out of the dark calling "Who knows 'Kevin
Barry' for Christ sake? In a society that wasn't like all
tyrannical societies sentimental, she'd either have the
child and the state would look after it, or she'd abort
and the state would look after that, too," as you followed
her into the light. But the guardian, with a towel around
his thick shoulders protested, "It's traditional Hudson
Valley, you find variants anywhere you look, it's a fine
fine traditional song and a fine familiar tune." Had he
a stake in it? something about it beyond a simple blue-
chip response to Bee Bee's nerves? or an interest like,
say, his privately printed thing on the Mount Mary (big
stud) variant of "Little Maddy Grove," the lovely, gutsy,
seduced, murdered adulterer? Bee Bee cracked open a
beer can and remarked, "I'll stand by what I said." Tired
words: yet again, as you said on the ship next week,
Shirley Laurel's verbatim to the cops: "I'll stand by what

I said." I could have helped if you'd included me more: I might have found a way to check deeper into the tall man carrying the Finnish-import blanket down Boston's Washington Street who stopped to stare at Black Magic chocolates until he apparently caught the witness in question watching him: I could have checked deeper into the witness, you told me only it was a girl named Lynn from Lynnfield who went away, you thought to Arizona, no private agency of those you at last broke down and went to would take you on, which Inspector Praid somewhat later with too-nice accuracy *fore*saw, the blanket-wrapper-label found on the floor of the Peoples Drug Store in Baltimore wasn't enough in itself or (and also therefore) to support the dim idea the druggist drew of, yes, a kid maybe five at the most in Levi's and a tall man sharing his Mounds bar with the kid who kept hold of something soft in his other hand, the druggist couldn't see, and near the tall man but maybe not with him (the druggist couldn't tell) a woman (any more than he could tell if the adults resembled Ken Love's brother and sister-in-law, whom the cops checked apologetically after the final instance of your being permitted to have any effect on the official investigation): and, too, I might have drawn more out of Sears on the "No comment" ransom answer— your view that Sears didn't believe the police nor they him on the issue of the mutual assurance that neither had ransom been asked nor a kidnap note received, may have been right: but Sears and Shirley had European leads of some kind: how? I could have gone after the woman's angle, couldn't I? But I ended up indiscriminately sight-seeing—the university in wind-swept, desolate Bari, an unilluminating chalk-walled church in Brindisi the day we took the car ferry to Patras, or in Cracow the loggias of Wawel castle courtyard, or, in the Jagiellonian, the gold chrono-globe on which the American continent like an unidentified foreign body was first shown, though I didn't believe the claim. And I ended up feeling close to you only when, as we walked from the Louvre toward the American embassy you told me news of the American student Sears had reportedly been pleading with near the Bois just before Sears was hit by the taxis and the American student had been overheard to say he had a date with a university girl in the cabaret review in Cracow, this was all: And shouldn't you have shared with the guardian your desire to find the stolen Hershey, if only, as it turned out, to restore him to: whom? he wanted to book our hotels for us; he said to me in one startling rush the morning we sailed, "I was always loved by the wrong women, and I'm lazy; but once I loved the right woman after she'd been taken by someone else. Don't get married without letting me know, will you?" As if he needed to be swiped then right away from the fact of our future, he started a little something with the sinister Grimes who had arrived in town for a committee meeting and with no reservations as yet had invited himself to the guardian's and felt obliged to see us off. "No," the guardian was saying, "'of' (whether or not meaning 'by') not merely as an object to be described but also as a possibility to be limited: descriptive prescription"–"Mmmm," went self-effacing Red. And this two-speed talk ran on after they'd gone ashore and were standing up against the barrier, the guardian more or less watching us where we were jammed in at the starboard rail, yet still talking to Grimes: so, like your own spirit that obeyed the guardian's but only by means of wild variations and departures on it, the guardian was all the more with us and loving us, his bright casual eyes shifting everywhere like Daddy's and his conversation silent far away from us like me talking right now to you, and I waved and he worked a hand out to wave back, his large longing eyes (which I know to be hazel-brown since my own are hazel-blue) made me think of yours. And as we began to move and the dock's shed then seemed so different from the ship, such a dangerous parallel, I found further down the dock an elderly dame as tall as the guardian almost, staring our way and I thought watching us but I couldn't tell, I felt in my pocket the crumpled telegram from Mama and Daddy and thought if they phoned this instant their voices so plain last night at six would already have become distant, and then the river was there straight away from our broadside and there was the harbor clearing and beyond it a mass of land in the late-morning haze; and, unquestionably embarked, I started crying because wrongly I thought it was so wonderful the world had arranged to send me to Europe. Which then, as you turned to shake the hands of a couple you knew, did not mean those Laurels so vivid to you not me, who now stand in mind behind no one but beside everyone else, but were, that sailing day, as inconceivable as Shirley dead and ashed and urned and returned C.O.D. from Paris, Sears dead and buried there, and Hershey growing older and bigger, shooting up, if not himself shot, smothered, knocked, or dismembered. And the Gypsy Woman's breath-of-an-accent came to—

Vienna itself in the real seemed to approve of me, and there I heard none of this continental tone meant to instruct by withholding all of the instruction except the distance. And you didn't know that at those curbs you'd seldom need to stick out an arm to save pedestrians from stepping into a car's path, nor would the tart trim cop either who watched for crossings against the light when he wasn't watching the ladies whose breasts and legs— the Gypsy Woman phoned the night before May and I came here to the island, as if doing me a favor, one of her memories lost and found: how about my book-jacket designing, editors were dogmatic she said, was I how was I, I was, my contacts in publishing, would I how could I, I would, and gave her Marina's poor overworked name who might know of something, "I would of course be interested less in any particular category than in anything that was Far In or Near In, any of the Para's," which, far from the bedtime tale she did not tell me the night that I spent with her and her pollen-possessed, hyperactive sinuses, reminded me of what she did go on about then, the manyness, the interpenetrations, which touched my life while also that Gypsy Woman had I knew no true right to touch my life in that way or even a right to those musical notions of Polypersonacity: yet now she faded into tired fact, was I interested in breathing cleaner air (oh yes), relieving respiratory allergies (sorry, my allergy was to mercury ointment which once at eleven to Daddy's fear and fury inflamed an already thigh-to-waist case of impetigo into wet welts worthy of punishment inflicted in the days of the unjust torments of Michael Kohlhaas—*that* was the name Kleist, the German author's name, gave him—who was climactically decapitated in the Gypsy Woman's sight on my college stage: who now across the years told me) she'd sell me a Selectronair that in its twenty-by-twenty-foot effective area could reduce pollen count 100 percent in an hour, bacteria 84.8 percent in two, and mold spores 98 percent in less than half. (Of an hour?) "I can't afford one," said I, which brought on a pause and then the operator saying our time was up, to which my Gypsy Woman said, "Of course it's up, we've been talking and talking, what do you expect? Hold on, I—Sylvia, I am in a pay phone near Spring Street terminal, here's my number, call me back"—I was irrelelevantly thinking how the last morning I'd seen her she'd told me to go make a baby—today she'd had my old number, for she could not now have found me in the book I thought, but—"and since you have a rich husband, what do you mean you can't afford a Selectronair, a Sele—" We were cut off. By me. Sele

Vie. "Compete. Compete with me," her words pass wishfully from me toward Jim E. the night of Daddy's

World Series afternoon visit, but he does *not* say them to Daddy. "Compete with me," the Gypsy Woman said that other night which is side by side with tonight and with the World Series night; "that way we meet, mix, like, become what of each other we can become of the manyness we can be part of," her Lincoln green tights lain shadow-neat down over the chair: but Jim E., though he doesn't accept the words Selectronair-borne from the Gypsy Woman through me, does take me back to the Gypsy Woman's role (and cadenza speeches) that college night, for I took him: yet he is at this point thinking only of Daddy's diffident remark, "Elmo Lincoln's nineteen-eighteen Tarzan was worth seeing," accompanied with a slight snickering breath and shake of the head. (Jim E:) "But it's dead camp, I mean it's a hoot, it's—" (Daddy:) "Well, it had appeal, you know, we were all younger, there was the war behind us." "But what a put-on." "You say...? A *put*-on?" "A *put*-on, simply." "I don't catch your meaning." "It puts us on, you on, me on, didn't you sense that?" "Kids me?" "And puts you onstage? inscene? upcountry? No? *Nicht wahr*?" "Well if 'camp' means 'bad' then I guess Elmo Lincoln as Tarzan saving the English girl from the city slicker with the *mus*tache—" "*and* the dirty black savage, let's not forget *him*!" "—wasn't a good show. But I did feel part of that story, I guess a lot of us did, Sylvia's mother cried—" "*Which* part?" "No, *feel part of—*" "Oh." "The lost kid, everyone feels that, and then him making out on his own showing his innate superiority to the apes that raised him and when he's found at last, why he's found him*self* al*ready*..." Jim E. saw that Daddy was fool enough to feel out on a limb, out of character flowing culturally along, and so Jim E. clapped. Daddy said, "I guess it was trash if you took it seriously." "Which," Godmayblessyou *you* Jack then said like dry ice, "which the brave vanguard subtly neither does nor does not." Jim E. had not found himself by then any more than he had in nineteen fifty-something when I took him to the Gypsy Woman's performance in *Michael Kohlhaas*. He talked and talked before curtain and likewise during both intermissions, to wit how a natty old dear with waved gray hair and a high-lapelled Edwardian jacket had picked him up hitching and then deviously, after asking if the boys played pinochle and shot crap at college and asking where he was going, wanted to know if Jim E. minded getting up to his destination this evening—in a word, namely, me—with a flat tire. When Jim E. brought it up yet again after the final curtain, I asked what he was so nagged about, was he afraid the old man had had him there on the front seat unbeknownst to him, and I lied that I had a cramp and had to go back to the House and to bed, for which he didn't ask me out again, but he sang occasionally at The State Line (in the wilds halfway between his college and mine) inside the circular bar to a mike and supported by a droopy piano drinker who had never heard of the subdominant but was good at switching keys: "Down with love, the root of all midnight blues"—the local dragsters paid aloof attention to the collegiourban words—"Take it back to the birds and the bees and the Viennese." But now Jim commutes to a suburban Bloomingdale's and sings some nights at The Good Guys Saloon, part-owned by Buck Fields; "I don't like men, Women I don't like too, But da da dee dee dee da dee dee da, I doo doo doo like you." He sang that right at me the night Buck made me come and have whale steak there, and in answer to those not very obscure lyrics I thought (to Jim E.), "Well don't look at *me*: *I* know which I am." Unchanged by Marriage and the Family, a Trip Abroad, the Learning Experience, or Sub-, Pre-, and Extra-Marrygold Situational Choices. "You think you can't," said Knott to Daddy under the undertaker's awning one day, "but—stomach, lower thigh—you just don't run out of places to stick yourself." Daddy said if he ever got diabetes he would bear in mind what Knott said, but as to synthetic insulin he guessed we were all coming to synthetic products: which got Knott mad, though not at Daddy, and Knott went on against Phil the druggist for some minutes as if Daddy, the springboard for the diatribe, weren't there, or were Phil. Which, given Daddy's kindness, may even have been part of what he meant when he once said to me, "I feel like I've got a door into the city, now you're here with Jack." One night that Daddy was with us, I wanted you like nothing but it put you off until I forced you, and a little later Daddy went to the john. Your hushed "*Come* on, Sylvia, for God's sake not tonight—" was so like Daddy's voice but not from the other room—from another time.

Vanishing point all very well in art school, but applied to human not easy to think about. The guardian was on the point of vanishing when we put down at Idlewild. Thea Dover had let it be known the body could be viewed at Fairchild's. (I'm going to wake you up, Jackie darling.) No flowers. A postcremation memorial at the guardian's, at *your*, at (if we wanted it) now *our*, apartment. The vicar had been asked by Thea to conduct a nonreligious reading of, to play a certain tape of (I'm going to wake you up): and Thea would not be persuaded to understand when, referred by her to Fairchild, you phoned still from Idlewild and ordered the guardian's casket closed: "But," she said, "I was with him when he died, and he looked—People want to see him." And how had we heard? She hadn't known how to reach us, had had half a dozen addresses for us, too many, and then had gotten our cable from London. The damn thing, you said a couple of days later, is you're made to feel you owe so much time to those who want to show you their pity. But Jack, no, they wanted *you*, not your pity, as if your remembering their names would guarantee their root to your guardian whom they loved: except Grimes, who may have wanted as much of the two libraries as he could get his hands on. My landlord's clock above the wicker chair has only its hour hand: I wish I could wake you with one air-swift thought. Thea got sternly tight, looked more haggard, stood on her skinny, feminine legs planted with toes out in the red carpet. "We were the very same age, give or take a few months," she said. "Did I discipline him?" nodding to you. "The way his guardian oversaw him and thought of his future I'd have felt like Mary scolding Jesus—not that Jack ever needed me. I'm sorry, I was interested in the other one, even if *his* great love was not me. Though I gather I was like her, am like her. Different backgrounds. We used to think of going to Europe and it was further then. I remember my great-aunt's family came in from New Jersey, stayed the night in a little hotel in what became the lower garment district, and next day stepped into a carriage and went to Europe. And Jack's guardian met her before she died and had long talks with her little Irish dressmaker who after my great-aunt died was snapped up by Daisy Deal, you know Judge Deal, Sylvia. She *ab*solutely refused to sew a certain shade of green thread, you know." And I trying for the eleventh time to take an interest in knitting. The lush labyrinthine spread Thea gave us had been a present to her from the guardian: why then did she give it to us, and what did her curious words mean: "Well, it stays in the family, in my possession, even more than if I kept it." They admired it one Saturday afternoon and the guardian had bought it for her there and then.

Viaticum. Daddy couldn't come to the memorial; Thea didn't ask, though you did mention it, and in answer—and all through the memorial—I pondered that Daddy had always said when the time came he wanted to go fast, so he wouldn't have time to be afraid: of the need to speak and act summarily, last wisdom, short words, a fully final, self-rising, prepossessed death scene panned and time-exposed to (last-wise) get us all in (even himself?). However, the guardian always wanted, and now was

denied, just these chances Daddy didn't want. So there
sat the vicar among forty-some friends of the guardian,
and though absent, Daddy was in all that happened
there, as in your voice so often, as in Staghorn's crook,
as elsewhere, which I confess silently to (dreaming)
you was what I thought I meant by my mystery when I
hazarded (an eighth of an inch ago on the landlord's clock
that's missing its minute hand) that I was the possessor
of a mystery too, you and your Laurels weren't the only
ones in this family. But now my mystery has relaxed
and spread. Here are the Gypsy Woman, Staghorn, John
Plante, you, Daddy, side by flank with, say, a Maddy
Beecher who long ago said that at a party he didn't dare
get drunk since he'd quote want to unquote all the, that
is, skin all the girls in the joint (which on faith I assumed
both did and could not include yours truly, and which
implied that should he so wish, no man or nothing could
stop him); and the six-years-subsequent Maddy Beecher,
who tries to get you to share his Sears Belt Massager and
mails friends Polaroids of himself in gross poses looking
gasping up from the lip of a flowered rain barrel into
which at a party (in the background) he had been sick,
or, gray-breasted in long Brooks trunks, entitled "The
Monster Awakened by the Sun": you all line up like days,
in front of me, serving me with my mind's process, fore
and back, here and there—all here. Well, yes, when the
Italian kid Julio Loggia and his pal were to come and live
with us for a while, I should not have walked out with May
but stayed and fought and hoped to keep your charities
at bay. That's what I hoped to have courage or wit to be
able to convey to you and also keep my cool, when we
ran into you coming out of Buck Field's shop, and May
captured your hand in both of hers, but all I could get
out was that Maddy and the Englishman had stayed one
night till after four yammering—and discomfited I filled a
pause with what I after all cared not a whit about, Plante's

Leeds-London friend's no doubt murkily reported antiperspective theory, which you in your unhappiness awkwardly picked up as a possible topic for conversation and instead of acting jealous you–(must wake up) May jumped around you and got hysterical and clubbed your leg the way little boys do and when I'd had it and grabbed her moist hand and pulled her along away from you, she said she hated me; so to please her instead of a cab we bused uptown, I stood holding the bag from Buck's with one hand and the steel loop with the other reading some virtuous remark of Thoreau's in one of the advertising spaces. Well, that's the perspective *I* see things from, if you wanted to know. Staghorn in the beginning only digressed upon my talent, in the main meditating upon my fifteen-and-three-quarter-year-old self; but at a later phase it wasn't a mere digression, he was intellectually serious, and did not understand that I liked pretty things, didn't want to paint, would leave art to–the proof, he was explaining one rainy afternoon in my seventeenth year, is in the cooperation of your eyes (my? lovely?): look at a doorpost, then the tree beyond, and–since it's winter– through the limbs to the white house beyond that. Your eyes can't focus on the doorpost and the tree at once, though they can on the doorpost and my initials MS cut in it: for your eye lines are like parallels envisioned in a perspective drawing and the spot they go to must be embraced in no more than one plane, however far or near; likewise there couldn't be two vanishing points from one perspectival vantage. And as Staghorn transfixed me but not as you did May in the tub, an unruly event occurred: a hair in his rich white eyebrow whipped free of its tangled bed and stuck up oblique like a daddy-long-leg. He asked, "Are you still with me? Sylvia?" But then at the same time, years nearer, he stands unique at my dingy city door, green eyes accusingly intimate and alone and cold and courtly. Dark blue home-pressed flannel, heavy green wool hunter's shirt, yellow plaid tie, he is down for a young friend's Thanksgiving show of big hoop-strip paintings you step into in order to see—endlessly—at a gallery with a good address: Staghorn doubts the idea but likes the young man. Three gifts for three-month-old May: a painting (motif category one), a mobile collapsible into one big manila envelope, and a Heinz baby tumbler. When he left he said, "Now I really feel I have given you away." Presumptuous. "Now you're on your own." Boring me. "Now I can face your father again." We shook hands and kissed, giggling.

Via Staghorn Daddy sent his love. And there you are, suddenly, there you have it. Wait long enough, as Beulah Love's horribly old father would, well, nearly but never quite say, and your words on their own will get together and say what's way deep down in you. But they've now merely assembled what I'd thought was my mystery, Jack: in a word, that Daddy waited in just about every man I ever wanted, because I took and went and put him there. Which you may not have known, when, like a good poker face, you indirectly asked him for my hand. But you are not like him, and my mystery deepens beyond me. The guardian's letter waiting for us in Brindisi, the last of the stops he knew for sure we would make, asked us to look up a grove of palms in Otranto eighty kilometers down the coast. "The poet Pontano has two palms, male and female, growing in Brindisi and Otranto, whose love was so pregnant they began to bear fruit pulped full of liquid honey." The guardian came through then with a juicy, though scholarly, bit about the male's erected leaves and his potent exhalations of pollen which made it from Brindisi to Otranto more easily than we thought *we* could, so we didn't go. A Greek philosopher, according to the guardian, claimed he saw a Garden of Eden painting in Naples where contrary to the Eve tradition indeed *male* palms bridge a river bending to tempt their females.

Which made sense to me thinking back to the day I spent straining to slog after you through Jordan Marsh. As now I strain not to follow my word-self, but to think a halt and settle for my first and long-possessed mystery—Daddy almost everywhere. But we are going to bed; and your eyes are open, and shut, and open. And shut. If I stop now: think what happened to Siggofreddo Morales, who you might say stopped. Yet you don't choose to stop—"Speak univocally, Sylvia," speaks the dead hand—yet could you choose? To, for instance, stop May after the point where I was effaced and had been given into the hands of the OB at the hospital? I could stop dilating no more than I can push away the possibly deformed darkness that you are in front of me, pressing me from behind. It takes over, the process, the birth, and I forgot my fear of leaving what was passing. If I trapped my daddy in you, what does that make me, and what was I thinking of, what did I do to you two? Amondson's huge unpicked pole beans going to seed, huge arthritic fingers scattered along a green bone. Get to the seed at last of anyone you know well, and you find it too is divisible: but maybe so because you yourself fancied it something else to start with. At your heart I find Daddy and me? But if I kidded myself you were very like my father, kidded myself I was carrying my father off from the shadow of our sugar maple into the shuttering size of your city monitored by your seven-league walk and your sensitive little solid-state portable tape recorder that at the real crunch did not work on Siggofreddo, kidded myself that your generous failures would be my birth-death gift of my father to myself in you, I nonetheless do not kid myself now: you aren't half the man he is, or was, and he's not half you either. But at one time when you were germinating in my jolly old *penetralia*, I had to sense, unclearly, that you were almost, and thus enough, my father. It wasn't so. Your eye is open. And shut. You smile as with a baby's toothless trust; or is it a man's unconcerned heat. If I then say, I married in you *not* my father, I married your difference, your background, your overdrive, why what have I said? Married people come to look like each other? Balls! (basket-, base-, squash) Some of them see in each other a facial future, and hence some marry future likeness. Now *you* know you often thought he looked like you, your guardian, didn't you? Yes, I am a clue, your instinct drew you well to me. But a clue to a deeper case, and believe me I'm no usual piece of cake from a simple supermix. I will try to drive Daddy out of you, for else what am I doing to you? *And* to Daddy. But what will I be doing to you if I do drive Daddy out of you? I see. Which is not to say I can bear your kidnap in which I was today just one touch on your roundtrip. You were disappointed when all I appeared to have gotten out of the pitcher's duel you took me to one blank gray April day, my first major league game, was that whereas the one umpire at the college game yelled "Strike" crisp and clean, the plate umpire here yelled "Steeee..." long and unfinished, or anyway said the "–rike" (if he said it) to those close to him–and you said, "What about the first-to-home-to-first twin killing, what about the outfield pickoff after the catch, what about the left fielder pretending that home run was catchable hoping the man who hit it would think he'd merely skied out and give up and run out of the base path?" "Steeee..." I'll never know if he finished the–

Visit my heart's memory, not my mind's, ungrounded as I am in Latin. But no, step please out of memory into: what else there is besides. On April fifth, according to you, you decided to come to me, and next day you were on the way but got trapped by an "invulnerable new clue." I was trapped by May inside me five going on six years before, and toward the end when I was about ready to leave the labor room you were more conscious of what was going on (coming off, down, on) than I, which put me in an unfair spot between outside and inside, and somewhere amidst May's down-and-out grinding certainty then seemingly independent of whether I pushed or—pant pant pant—did not, was a screaming silent thought I hope it's me and not the baby that he: you too were trapped that morning—box lunch or not—by this bested event not wholly started by you, and ended not even with, in attendance, your own stop-watch, of which you divested yourself in the doctor's dressing room in return for surgeon's PJ's and surgi-green convict's cap. I am not sure you learned enough that day—I must spurn profundity somehow, and we are going to bed—for your resumed kidnap smacks of your defeat at the hands of the injured Siggofreddo Morales, whose future you described to him as being open-ended yet in whose very (Latin?) self you proposed to intervene and who said, "Can't you see? Jack? Man? I don't remember *how* to dive, man, and I don't want to. You fall into another pitch and if it works, you going to stick it" (though in fact at that point he hadn't the slightest idea what "pitch" he was going for). "I scratched college when I scratched diving, can't you hear me, the know how goes with the nerve: *goes*, man. And you want to help me by sneaking me upstairs into your yesterday whether you think you are going to get me to go on a board again or be coach someplace or just puke my life into your portable tape, man, you're just a private school guy I used to beat in the dive and I don't need you now, catch?" You tried to catch onto the piece of him that had been *your* in, but there was a stump there now and anyway why *should* you give Siggofreddo an unsolicited hand? This went on. And my stomach rumbled, listening to you tell me, even if I contracted it and held my breath, I wanted lunch and you persisted—Siggofreddo was able to stand up quite easily to see you out, the vertebrae had set right and he stood because forced finally (and I could visualize it) to kick you out of his father's living room: "Look," you insisted, "I do understand, had a board accident too (remember?)–I got too close on a simple front and would have killed myself if I hadn't been overarched so all that hit on the way down was my chest and the cocoa mat brushed half the skin off, I didn't come near the end of the board for weeks after, I was hitting the end like a falling tree and entering the water ten feet out." "It was your fault," Siggofreddo according to you said, "I thought I never thought in the middle of a dive, but this time I thought first about like I once said to you in high school you don't think once you're into it and then I thought even if this is an exhibition what the hell am I doing an artistic dive that's not even in the book at least not the way I was doing it–and I stopped at the end of the board, I mean stopped to think when really my mind should have already stopped but I had kept going–I'm thinking, 'What am I doing this stiff layout gainer and a half to look like a mechanical pinwheel? that's like the Sands Beach Aquascape on a Friday night in August: so Hind go away, don't bother me."

Visionary foresight might have saved ungrounded me from your driven–deeeeriven!–love for, hunt for, possession by, others. But in the absence of foresight I will end what you have started and try and return you from your heights of trouble to become yourself–("Univocal, love, vanish, smack")–instead of like in the Gypsy Woman's play the horsedealer Kohlhaas committing incendiary mayhem flattening the landscape of eastern Germany losing his life at the block and thus in another sense his five kids but only after extracting justice for the material wrong done to him and his man and his horses by the Junker and, even more, only after the Gypsy Woman's threefold prophecy committed to a piece of paper given into Kohlhaas's possession had afforded him means to have one over the Elector of Brandenburg by swallowing that prophecy just before committing his neck to the axmen's red hand. But ending his life so cleanly left out those kids who having been kissed by Daddy at the place of execution were led away into the depths of another future by The Helping Hand. To be interned for the duration. Well, a poor foster father Red Grimes would make, who broke himself up telling the tale of one of the King Jameses locking up two newborns to see what language they'd begin speaking, which must therefore be man's original language, Tongue One. Thank God May wasn't deaf. Anyway everyone knows, who, ungrounded in Latin, has listened to your guardian that in the Garden of Eden the snake spoke French, Adam Danish modern—and God spoke Swedish, when he said to Adam to seal their pact, "Give me five." Drawn like you in over my head I find my mystery swells to join another. Beulah's practically disemboweled surviving father who lived with the Loves and didn't like his other daughter, Ken's sister-in-law, any more than Ken liked her (or him), no longer had his hearing, so may not have been able to control the weird winds on which his high-toned words came out of him toward you, who thought he might have a clue left somewhere inside him; but he had his eyes and maybe his mind, and he said to me one day while I waited for you to finish questioning Beulah about her childless sister, "Be'n't it the truth a party gets to talking round and round and 'fore he knows it his words be takin' over and he be sayin' things he didn't know, in words he didn't know was hisn." Not the Pick 'n' Pay, Stop 'n' Shop, Look 'n' Show Australian gent I got stuck with on the bus to Siena who was on his way around the world and used the phrase "permit of only one conclusion" three times at one Florentine traffic light who said, "All the words in this language end in vowels," as if this were unsanitary. "But," two months earlier on this side of the ocean Grimes is saying, "I thought what you wanted was to be a specialist." The guardian replies, "I thought so too until

I felt the desolate insignificance, the flat abstraction of what *you* do. Glossematics, indeed!" But Grimes said, "Go learn some Algonquin, then come back and talk to me, Fossy." Is my ignorance what skelters all these elements chip-foolish on a Sunday-night green baize before me for all my little world as if we were all approaching the end of a big pot in a thirty-or forty-hand game? Cassia Meaning, your old flame, who never met my parents, is nonetheless here, her beer schooner showing a three-master blue against the gold lager. Thea Dover, who likewise never came close to my parents and knows no poker, is telling none other than Red Grimes, and Staghorn and Plante and several Jims, that there are only thirty Javan rhinos left, eighty Cape mountain zebras, and a hundred pair of bald ibises, and she proposes to transport these to certain obscure Antarctic, African, and Australian last paradises, but Grimes is also telling a spectral Bee Bee that "wedlock" has nothing to do with Yale or Segal but comes from words meaning "pledge dance," while unbeknownst to her you have seen her hand but Daddy has seen you do it. If Daddy is everywhere and here, then everywhere and everyone are—

Viaticum up to my attic in words that inhabit my vocab but that I do not wholly possess: Staghorn had openers but probably won't bump, he saves his daring power for what he hates and what he loves. I eye him over my low two pair—has he no more than jacks?—and think of three pictures once newly hung downstairs near his doleful clock. His pictures he cares neither to sell nor to exhibit. He shakes his head darkly when I tell him he's got to have a show. Were a college colleague to risk fronting Staghorn's critical instinct by visiting Staghorn at his hermitage, Staghorn would be glad to hear truly discussed, but not with the truly timorous you-tic-my-tac-I'll-tack-your-toe that passes for charity or charm yet is only the basest hope, these paintings for instance recently done, two in oil mostly with the knife, the third in flat but not thin plastic paint deepened by growths of real live sand: at first glance the first is a façade-steep but fast-deepening slope of huddling harsh blue boulders and strong small surviving scrub fir bending green and brown up out of splits and dark pockets: this Nature watches you and makes little of you: which is what I'd have liked to tell the nice dull girl who, I now at last remember that night she bent your ear, said at least twice and maybe three times, "Jimbo was like my father but I didn't know how exactly; but now that after months I've figured how he resembles my father, I have this awful intuition I'm not interested in Jimbo any more, I mean in terms of the psychophysical. It's kind of a paradox, Jack." And you look tired and say, "No it isn't." And of canvas number two she might well also say paradox, if ever on a summer weekend she were to pass close enough to Staghorn's loud brook to feel the pull of his isolation and venture into his house and see in number two the billow-road flowing silently through a darkly glowing town, real houses tall-ly leaning into the road (as if old man Amondson had tentatively taken, say, Ken Love's tractor to their foundations), a church and a high-porched well-stacked general store: and on the other hand see the signal absence of people, shall I say of the people who said Staghorn was a champion lecher who dissected live beagles and otters in order to paint them with their own blood, and who was too stuck on himself to know how to get along with his fellow professors about whom if you couldn't say anything nice you better not say anything at all, for some said Staghorn was English born in Tijuana and thus had no citizenship and so what could you expect? and others, that he was born in Lapland in winter of a farmgirl and a marooned seaman part Texas mulatto part Oriental. Well, the hazy-glowing town with the billow-road was a town of man-made things, buildings and bikes, deep-angled dark thick telephone poles along the banks of the billow-road and a couple of rounded trucks deserted like the other things by the human and yet thus then free to observe some vanishing background of this town which unlike that well-quoted Oriental landscape (and maybe to Staghorn's dismay) would not let the artist-maker disappear into her, unfair since he had made that deserted town lovely, blue and gray-green and earth and all over it a changing finely-screening rose, a memory of dawn and dusk. The sort of town the Gypsy Woman's steps may sometimes have wandered into: the town deserted because of a muscular dystrophy fair under way on the outskirts, the Gypsy Woman tramping swiftly through the quiet town, being welcomed at the fair ground by a sharply competent ten-year-old girl who took her to be the (heretofore unmet) Mrs. Fern Bunker who had said she hoped to be able to come in costume and read palms—but where were the Gypsy Woman's peasant apron and Rumanian rings? the palms were read at twenty cents for one, thirty-five for two, and what she found in those sixty- or seventy-odd seamy-moist child palms so (she said) distressed her she elected to leave, with the take, even while, eager for *their* fortunes to be ransomed too, twelve seconds waited in line, most with mothers, and at the end of the line on the heels of rumors sweeping the fair, the resplendently embroidered true Mrs. Bunker determined to expose the false palmist. Which Staghorn relished when I told him. Not as he did me—but look at these two oils so alien to the twosome sketches he and I in jointly alternating strokes composed, and move to the third picture yet look back, you feel, I feel, one feels, the ugly scrub fir and monumental rocks and the shapes of that dream town drawn into another life parallel and grown abstract, until as I turned to see the third of Staghorn's essential trio I felt I was losing surfaces but, against my selfish fears, gaining the powers from which these surfaces derived and could now leave my Staghorn, these geometries had been there all along in me and in things and in his mind and paint, I'd felt them in me, like the early motions of your May in me, you saying, "The child's with us but a long way off, coming so slowly, coming wherever we go and however fast so long as you don't take too many subway steps." "A pregnant construction," snickered Red Grimes (when?), but did not see, like you, the slipperiness of his mere quip: for that construction, grounded am I or not in Latin, is where the verb's case shows not merely the verb's completed action (I learned that much) but the permanence of the result: yet how could May four months after birth be permanent with budding deciduous teeth? Staghorn's ravinescape and his townscape swim up again, but then sink into (though not back into)—the picture called "Sylvia Before Her Bath" is the third, but at *first* glance abstract, not the other way round: pale shapes grow from top to bottom, gray and brown and orange fields stand oval and triangular hither and hence in the same plane as the linked pale shapes, and would slowly begin to turn clockwise like objects torn round by some tired tornado but the linked pale ponds, mounds, limbs, hands will not let them yet. And then there *I* plainly am (though I could be many) humanly unmistakable, my odor abstract, my flesh freshly inanimate, the top pale blotch becomes my face cast up and back upon a brown and orange rug—hot stuff, however studiously my foreshortened head has been (as if with some old halo) built up via concentric circles beginning with the corner of my eye, hot stuff: and Staghorn can never know how I treasure his delineation but am in myself mere crass and getinkling thimble asking to be filled:

Vanity vanishes in a friendly tongue, shared tongue—wake-wake, Jack—as Daddy into you and into others, but then too as my Daddy-mystery into other unforeseen mysteries which, as when the breakfast TV show

"Today," mingling with our conversation and your smoke in May's nostrils as she handled her cereal, multiplied us into one substance and I wanted to tell you the Gypsy Woman's Osmotic Interport theory but it was too long a tale and I didn't, words towed me toward and give me, if not foresight, maybe—so, old hard perspectives (like when we met by Buck's, which I stupid boring cow though good goose now recall was not the first time I mentioned Plante's friend's perspective, it came up over my phone in April, fool that I—) vanish in new sweet (plain ungrounded) si-mul-ta-ne-ities of time place side-by-side-by-thing-by-thigh-by-calf-by

(Via) hand, you and others now then here there are in my altogether: and depth departs for the time being but no longer: and if I hereby temporarily embrace through you the stolen piece of Plante's friend's vision of flat, I also find fluent from me evidence that my fake Gypsy Woman, bra-less and in need of a wash, had something too and I cannot now say with a straight face, "I for one," I indeed find a tricky shiver on my stomach like the current of an approaching fingertip, as I reverse my position to: I may not know who I am, but I know a lot about myself. May and I will look at your barked shin in the morning, you will be capable of receiving our attentions; adolescent Cassia (whose figure let me add was never to grow into an hour-glass) would pore over your bruise-blue smudge and say, "I think it's going greeeen." An instant of content (tolled by Staghorn's clock downstairs which I took to be the gilt banjo clock topped by the acorn finial, but which when my eye moved from painting number three—me—to the indeed nontolling banjo, proved to come from a grandfather in the hall) arranges in my eye your face and the crook of Staghorn's arm and Plante's black mane through the swirling glass of the front door of my city widow-flat; and your guardian's hand and yours, and—what an old tramp my mind is, I've gone so far I may as well challenge Red Grimes to a hand of stud—and Sears Laurel about to step off the curb near the Bois, about to escape (unbeknownst to him) your intercontinental reach: as Grimes, grounded in Latin the Queen of Tongues, laps up vanilla ice cream one lunchtime when Daddy wasn't with us.

"Vanilla," I said on your guardian's summer porch. "Where does vanilla come from?" You looked blankly my way sensing I'd asked only in order to contribute something, you don't mind my shyness, I think you love it. "Ah, vanilla," hummed Red Grimes, "you know some Latin, Sylvia? No? I am happy to report that there is an etymological intimacy between, uh, Vanilla,' and the Latin for 'pod' or 'sheath,' to wit: 'vagina' or, properly, *vagi—*" "That's enough, Red," the guardian coldly interrupted, "what do you mean using language like that to Sylvia—" "I," I said, "was only thinking of where the flavor, the oil, the extract—" "He knew that but he thought he would fluster you with his little derivation." Well, Jack, if I intruded my Dad into you, whom did *you* intrude *your* charming, pathetic, handsome, stuffy guardian into? in his priggery at that moment of dessert I felt pricks of past possibility and past refusal and past derivations like salt and flour sift into a perpetual present of our joined despairs and puzzle-shadowed family fact—yes, who did your guardian become, as *my* father became others? and why will you not investigate your guardian? Daddy was glad Herbie made good money, but there Daddy stopped: "You mean to tell me you're going to spend your life manipulating money?" "O.K, O.K.," says Herb, "maybe I'm not quite my father's son, eh?" (Mama, intervening:) "Oh, Herbie!" (Herb:) "I believe in the integrity of an individual's career, if I was a teacher that's what I'd teach the younger generation, integrity." *Sic* Herbie: and you will find him. Bet he's unprincipled in bed, adopted bastard, though no short seller. (But I am not so sure the landlord's sandy hour hand has moved, nor of its size, for it's long, like you, and was it, is it, rather the landlord's minute hand? Jack, we're out of time, and only present, and spacewise my darling all fore-here, you give me length I give you breadth.) Yes, we're neither deep nor single, Plante and Gypsy Woman are right—about space and person and present time—and a vanishing point I have mysteriously become, and feel I have begun to finish what others had openers for: I look at May, the parted mouth whistling the prophecy of adult snores: I look at you, you who like a consolation to be treasured came wrapped in Daddy's voice, each long last breath before you wake now like a cutter's bow rising high then falling hard to crack the sea, if I were a poet, and not merely, as the guardian said, pure gold.

John Plante (for me, though he didn't mention me) if he was the one, Plante said maybe ask the Chinese micro-botanist from Washington who moved in with this crowd Plante lives with near Chinatown, Maddy's worried about Plante's vagueness lately, Plante asked Maddy if Maddy could see goldenrod growing out of the top of his head, where only a few weeks before Plante was at least talking about this sculpture he'd started in the middle of the air and was trying to get down to the ground." Then, when her room was growing lighter, Sylvia was saying, "Just before we left town Peg phoned to see if Ash was with you, he'd been angry over your visit and three days before simply got in the car and drove off to see you. But then she phoned that he was back, and she asked him if he wanted to speak to me." Also Sylvia was saying quietly at a time that was less light but still seemed later, "I met Dewey Wood, I think he knows we're living apart, he said a man named Courage was trying to get hold of you, had a show at some hotel and information he thought you'd want to tape." Then, in the wee hours (for time was flattened and fading as if to the sides of an emergency street of a zone that was in danger of being towed away), late night or early morn (for time had let go), Hind thought he had a dream which side by side he and Sylvia in a double air-berth way above an ocean, shared like a TV show aimed specially at plane passengers, woke to find his arm under her head asleep, wondered if the central substance of the apparent dream had after all been words she really spoke to him gossiping gently here in bed at intervals, for she watched the gogglebox an awful lot these days—this central substance the white-haired, dark-eyed old woman seersuckered but not in color though doubtless green-on-gray, telling an MC on a giveaway quiz that she liked to work with young people, felt in herself merely the gift to inspire others, had no settled home, stayed at Angel Mews Hotel when in New York because it was run by a retired English colonel; she found herself at present, in general, in the media and also a freelance child-rehabilitation consultant (in case anyone was listening); she focused on certain older forms of language therapy, *mutatis mutandis*; had never married, having carried the torch for a late cousin many fruitless years indeed even after he had somewhat fruitlessly given himself to another, though the gods knew these judgments (in this case hers) were easy to make in retrospect, and after the audience of female hands clapped after each new fact the MC got down to it at last and cried, "Tell me now, Miss Foster" (who had—why?—the guardian's name, for was Hind's sense of her kin to his sense of the guardian?), "for a Custom Poly-Purpose Laurelair Clearance Pod, tell me what is the connection between a small Mexican evergreen and the object-subject relationship in the feminine personal pronoun?, you have a twenty-five-second countdown on our Big Bad Clock": But the Old Woman knew, and over the Expectation Music was already speaking.

"How do you like your eggs these days?" Sylvia asked. Sun was hot off the landlord's copper fish mold above the stove. May and Sylvia had on white one-piece bathing suits. Sylvia held the icebox door open. "Baked beans from last night. You and your old man always liked them for breakfast." The ghost of a draft on his bare shoulders.

Brown feet on faded linoleum, scrub track at the screen door threshold flourishing either inward or outward as if the three white wood steps outside the door leading to a dirt path marked by shells and flanked by grass had been a preliminary or subsequent phase of washing and rinsing this kitchen floor, a job whose end could never be found. May brought her materials for a second-breakfast FUDGICIDE over to the table-cover at his left elbow in order to be right next to him. The tip of her tongue showing, she held the can at an angle and pressed the spout button releasing cocoa foam into the Bucksport Lions Club tumbler half full of milk. Early sun had cleared the dew from the screens. May did her own pony tail now. She turned to him holding a full glass to her lower lip and before she seriously and carefully drank, she said, "I love you." And after drinking she licked off her mustache and said, "I bait my own hook." Through the screen door you could see the pebble beach and on the water color-dissolving pools of platinum. The landing that ran out thirty feet was outside the frame of sight. So were the moorings. For a second Sylvia and May were watching him; then Sylvia turned to dish into her NO-STIK Free-Fry five fork-scrambled eggs, and a quick-flow of yellow stopped the pan's hiss.

"Wasn't it horrible, the missile silo that went up in Arkansas last week. Did I say last night that Grimes phoned before we left? He had the number from long ago, I gave him yours, he's a visiting curriculum adviser in Oliver's department this summer and thought he'd look him up, you must have introduced them once—the city seems so far away, Jack—but I bet he figured Oliver for a few new connections, snickered as if he had sinus. Oh—he asked if you made a good father."

Old Skoldberg told them—Maddy, Jack, Byron, the dangerous Oliver, and the other boys—that only the male seahorse can bear young.

You knew what Sylvia meant even if she wasn't always clear. She was less troublesome than these particles of possibility had been in her talk off and on in the night like broken comments on their bodies.

She said sometime last night that from here they could go in any direction, it was up to him, but that if as she guessed she was now herself unwittingly a lead or had in her a lead to the kidnap, she was afraid she could only be a truly useful clue to him if he just took it but didn't use it for something else. That remark's meaning, that held the power to discredit all he had done and even to defoliate as if they had never been there the terrible swift woods that traveled with him or under him from clue to clue, plunged him then again in the middle of the night into the middle of her (after all) considerate limbs losing himself in each fresh intersection.

"Oh, and Grimes asked if I knew the address of the Chapel of Laughter, a girl he asked about Oliver mentioned it, a girl in a gold Mini-Garment, the prefix old snickering Grimes said was ambiguously rooted in both *miniature* and *minimum*."

"I know of the place. It's been exposed in the house organ of some league of women's clubs as being orientally oriented, and as being influenced, and as being a front organization attracting many young people. Is Oliver there? I thought he was at Mount Mary. Oh I see, yes, of course, this was before you and May came up here."

Hind was wording slowly now. He'd have to watch his words, language the trap lured you away from plain description of what you were directly looking at. And was Sylvia's clue, assuming she had by now given it up, just this idea of not using a clue—or a person!—for something else? Well, what did "else" mean? Then Sylvia could point to all the people Hind had used for kidnap purposes. If so, then categorically she'd have to point to Oliver.

Yet first you had to review the night's take: Even if you'd never noted your own wife's violet mole among the other chocolate moles on her back, you had to take her word for it and Staghorn's, who might thereby be, as it were, a new knot on the rope, for who had had a violet birthmark on him but the one and only Hershey Laurel, advertised from helicasters and other radiomobile units for several days in the hunt's first flush. Then the venerable marm Rose Tree could mean *rhodon* and *dendron* (transliterated from Shirley Laurel's Greek glossary or the guardian's), therefore possibly the rhododendron outside the window whose sill the once-Laurel Abyssinian cat sat on.

"Tell me about Oliver." The eggs are chewed into plain frozen waffles. "Where'd you get your tan?"

And then there were para-visible particles you had to either acknowledge or not. Was the man Plante under the power of the Chinese microbotanist and was this C.mb's field botanical sex, for instance His and Her Laurels? And, given the other givens, was it not possible that Ash had found his way to this loft near Chinatown that grew ever more real to Hind as he considered all that poor Sylvia must now have against him for having used others narrowly? On top of which came Art, the dirty old swinger quite possibly seeking mere road publicity for his self-styled pasture-ized "industrial" put on for Santos-Dumont; yet might not Dewey's two-pronged confidence about the nasty note and the arboreal adage have been in truth juxtapointing to Art's familiar noise which Hind as usual jammed out but which at that moment among its Japanese-human Nor-spruce and its shepherd chicks with mere-maid behinds and its not quite all-girl sheep, and—reveling in the ripped hind leg—a human calf like the broken left-winger's, have been communicating to you something of value in terms of the Laurel lair? And now, was Grimes searching the Hall of Cubicles, the Waiting Vestibule, the Meditation Shelter and Underway, possibly classrooms, for the person Hind had stood in for? Which could mean that Grimes had seen Hind teaching Ol's class and withheld comment doubtless speculating what was the story behind the substitution or (if he had overheard a conference) behind the Plane impersonation. Was this news of Grimes a Sylvian relay thrown, through a Red

Grimes who no longer had any use for the guardian's boy Jack, right back to Plane?

How do you repossess a clue? If the recent sequence unversed itself you could find yourself back on the pier by Christmas, but you might have to act fast, for, as Ivy had furiously learned a week ago today, the pier was now promised by the city to the U.N. for its International School currently housed in a dirty brick the city wished to repossess uptown. It was the new nations that were to blame, Ivy told Charley the Pole, who pointed out that in the very same issue of the paper it told how an aboriginal student kidnaped a little, about-to-be-deported Indian girl from Sydney Airport—Art Courage is saying, "My old friend Sidney!"—just to point up Australian immigration policy. Ivy nodded: "It's the emerging nations." Charley nodded: "This student he's only an aboriginal."

Sylvia moved her hand close to Hind's. "What all did I say last night? It all just came out. I guess I'm boring. It must have been your magic touch that set me off. I may be only a wife, not a clue, but I'm…"

"But if you were, let's say, a clue, how could I do what you said before? how could I just take a clue without using it *for* something? It wouldn't be a clue, would it? How would I sit on the pier and just take, say, Buck Field? As a useless but charming but separate but equal gift like the antique Whitman Samplers in his shop? How do you just take a person without being led somewhere by him or her?" Hind looked over his shoulder. "Where is she? She didn't go through the kitchen door."

"She went out the front door. She plays with her doll baby carriage after breakfast."

"You know her well."

"Yes. Though we're quite different. She doesn't exactly daydream the way I do."

"You don't daydream."

"Lately I do."

"Syl, if I were to give up the kidnaping, I could assume that Hershey Laurel's dead—in which case the truth's of little moment; or if he's alive—and so almost eleven—and *if* he's unhappy with the kidnaper-parents, who else could I assume will make him happier? assuming you or I could even control who got him."

"I'd almost changed my mind, thinking that, well, your kidnap mattered at least because you put so much into it. But now you sound like you'd like to find a way of giving it up."

"But how can I finish the hunt un*less* I go from clue to clue, person to person, using each as a means to the next?"

"You're just using what I said as an excuse to do what you want to do."

"I can't stop over someone for stopping's sake as if the person were—"

face each ev'ry fac' like flying flak, for when a personnel bomb hits, its load of person will fac'-fac' like nothing you can funnel up to suction headquarters but rather you must (even the guardian in his old language would agree at least in the abstract) must let him or her, she or he, self-determine at the local level or base homelet—

"—the undertaker, take him for example, Syl: yesterday was Friday the thirteenth and at a meeting of the fourteen-thousand-member-strong National Funeral Directors Association of the United States, Incorporated (of which he is a member) and the eight-hundred-member-strong National Selected Morticians (of which he is not) he voted with the majority to endorse a revised code of ethics, the centerpiece of which is that the family must always be told item-by-item what a funeral is going to cost: he complains that in fact he's not trying to make a killing, it costs him $125 to open a grave plot, most of his expenses are fixed—"

"Is he a clue?"

"I don't know any more."

"*I* am a clue." Capricious. "Your instinct drew you well to me. Most ingenious thing you've done since you gave up the kidnap the first time."

"But you say if I use you for some end you won't be a clue any more."

"I'll turn into what you've used me as. It's up to you."

"You never talked for long last night—I didn't let you— but you talked a lot."

"Well there's a lot that's happened that I can only tell *you* about. And there's no law against a little affectionate conversation."

"As you said, it could go in any direction from here. What you said last night made it seem *all* rather than *any*. Staghorn, Ivy, Plante, Art Courage, even Mrs. Tree your old teacher, and why stop there?"

"She's not married."

"Stick to your point. If I give up the kidnap it has to be finished."

"If you give it up, it *will* be."

"Just giving it up doesn't finish it. You finish what you begin, or it goes on inside part of you."

"Finishing sounds like killing off. Sounds like your guardian's perpetual resolutions. And *say, you* didn't begin the kidnap."

A delicate run of feet nearer and nearer materialized into May, pigeon-toed on the threshold.

"Take me to the beach," she said to him, though the beach was only fifty yards away and she could easily be watched.

He got up. She reached for his hand and said to Sylvia, "I'm a teach Daddy how to fish."

"Not yet, let's wait an hour and all go out."

"No. I go myself." Then May was giving an imitation boo-hoo, rubbing her eye-sockets red. "I don't go with you." She was contemplating neither of them but the floor. "I go myself." The imitation was real.

Sylvia was carrying dishes to the sink. "She can't solve *her* case without *you*," she said, and Hind followed May out into the silent sun.

The beach pebbles shifted underfoot.

He was squatting at the water's edge. "Eddy goes under the water," said May. "His daddy bought him a black suit like Buck's, he can breathe under the water. I can hold my breath underwater, watch—"

He got her leg. "Too soon after breakfast; you'll get a cramp."

"I had my breakfast when you were sleeping, I watched you."

"You'll get a cramp," Hind said stupidly.

"I'll get a cramp," May said, and came around behind him. She tried to climb on his shoulders. "*You're too tall.*" She was giggling, kissing his back, licking. "Eddy showed me his air bottles. He carries it on his back on the rubber suit. He said he goes down as deep as a...fish. He can't, can he?" Her delicate forearm struck Hind's throat.

"Depends which fish. But a grown-up skin-diver if he's down for a long time has to take his time coming up, he may have to wait a while at two or three stages below the surface coming up, till he..."

"Till he gets the water out of his eyes," May giggled and got a strangle hold.

Again, time was letting go. He had to change his whole way. His words. His thought that two things might be alike, comparable. His kind of wholeness unlike the guardian's whole cloth of deep past and hereditary future, had to be reached via (vis-à-vis, in terms of, and/or re:) breeding a cocoa mite from magic ground. But Hind could not reverse precipitately. He would reverse. Sylvia was right. Like a turn for the better in a familiar tale. If you used people as mere means, you lost everything.

Take each person formerly a clue and ignore the Laurel utterly.

If any one was to be a true clue, any one could be so only by leading nowhere.

She had said, "Tell me about Oliver."

He wanted to be riding in an early-postwar Checker Cab with Sylvia down a real city under Christmas bulbs treed and banked and curtained and circleted and built, a city real by virtue of being full of folk he could do nothing for. Julio Loggia wasn't interested in pruning trees up in peasantville. Daphne House (Grew) Commons didn't go to the Dürer seminar Hind wangled her into but phoned her old friend Sylvia's foster brother Herbie who (and thank God (she said) he wasn't a creative person) found her something in his firm's research library getting back-quotations on stocks that didn't trade often, filing lush annual reports and Standard and Poor special services; she was studying L.S. and had attended a special libraries convention in Detroit where they had been shown the Ford River Rouge. And when Hind saw her and Herbie dancing one quiet summer midnight outdoors in the very middle of the city on the concrete covered in winter by the ice rink, she saw him above leaning on the wall at sidewalk level looking into the well where the table and dance floor were and waved and called, "Hi, Jack, come on down," with a new jollifying touch—and had, as he saw next week, become beamingly bullish. Hind held May's small ankle.

You should be able to see Oliver Plane perfectly separate from the kidnap, from Hershey Laurel, and the three beanbags and the tall man's lip mole which may well have been a spot of the Black Magics he loved so well. To use Oliver as an end not a means, you had to see him perfectly separate from the kidnap. And use words that found him simply, exactly.

Hind might say to Ol—to clear the air and the decks and the desk—I've given up the kidnaping.

Oliver shrugged.

Beginnings must be advertised or in any case marked.

Alert the Old Woman? Where?

How could you begin to thank Syl? But *when* would you?

Had Hind finished Oliver once and for all by fixing him in the length and breadth of the Hersheyscape Laurelscope?

Yet there was no spot to begin, now nor then.

The guardian knew the late father, Elder Plane, a very good internist practicing generally on the Heights and specifically on a group of old Heights folk from the Amondsons with their orthoneural complaints to the Whites with their gastrointestine disturbances, and the Beechers, the Meanings, the Deals went to him, even the rich Italian Presbyterians who had lived here only since 'thirty-eight. The feeling had always pleasantly been that if the guardian *were* ever to go to a doctor he would probably go to Elder Plane, to whom he certainly sent, each Christmas, his annual agnostic poem, melancholy in its encasing sea-march of coarse Homeric hexameters.

"Why did you say, 'Tell me about Oliver'?"

Elder Plane once said to Jack, "I knew your father. That's how I know your guardian." And Jack had said nothing.

Now if, estimating how you know Oliver, you said, "The distances and intersections then, across the city's veering grids, prefigured distances and intersections now," would that mean there had never been much opportunity to know Ol, near as you had been to him? How near? Three blocks on the Heights, three desks in Skoldy's bio, though nearer than that in the strangely convening and intimate way Oliver picked on Skold, attuned to Skoldy's every turn, even sympathetically responsive yet also pouncing on, fooling, defeating, making game of the old boy, blaring the premature baritone which de Forrest envied him—Hind had understood even then at thirteen Plane's very feeling but could never bring himself to tell Plane so and went only so far as to say No to the several schools of opinion on Ol's behavior: No to Lief Lund, who coldly called Skoldy's response simply not tough enough and Skoldy himself too soft to "handle the class" and said about his drubbing at Plane's hands (whom Lief did not like), "Tough!": No also to Maddy, who said, "Poor, poor guy, I could tell him how to cope" and pointed out that what Skoldy needed was a more flexible response: No also to de Forrest, who despised Hind for liking right fullback and whose father was renowned for having played an explosively ambipeditrous outside left on the record-eclipsing nineteen twenty-one soccer team—de Forrest had no sympathy for Skoldberg and felt that both he and Plane should be removed before they cast further shadows among the ancient and hollowed aims of our school: No too to Byron, who apologized when Hind queried him, and could—("We call plants green—"/ "We call plants green because they use..."/ "Because they use, because paradoxically they use green—"/ "Least!")— could only call it unfair to Skoldy but, well, Oliver was a terrific guy: but By knew Ol no more than did anyone else there then. To take all their responses and make of them for yourself one adequate one: was as hard as to combine the child in Oliver, the dew in the left-hander's wood, the pattern of empty air made by the undertaker's crenate bars, and, say, the probing energy of semi-sweet chocolate afume twenty-four hours a day from the plant (corollary and) next to both the name department store's branch doughnut and the (now according to rumor perhaps only) *semi*-permanent bite out of it, or, Bella Church's green-tarpaper-roofed establishment, she who had recently found a part-chewn dark bone of refined semi-sweet but unimprinted chocolate unburied near a sick, sick Boy, whereupon "well," said a spokesman for the chocolate people (overseen by branch and central offices and, if possible, by any larger holding firms within which the department store as a whole might belong), "without the whole piece we can only speculate, but this may have been a pilot bone from the lab."

Distances, intersections: three or four encounters at Lief's after-school blackjack sessions where six seven eight paid five times and a virgin triple, and Lief Lund dealt loudly and monotonously like an auctioneer, and had the deal too often (as his strident-voiced beautiful mother pointed out when she came into the high-ceilinged front room, tossed her floppy maroon felt on one lacquered point of a five-slat ladderback and was successfully gaped at by the more sophisticated of the players).

Distances, intersect: one tense afternoon, rain across the harbor and a fireboat whistling pointlessly as if it had programed for a festive marine progress that never came off, yes one tense afternoon at the Meanings' Cassia and Oliver, Maddy and Hind, played her brand of True Confession, and Jack and Mad each assumed the other had run into Ol and told him to come to Cassia's when in fact as they later learned she had broken down and phoned Ol herself, the only time to Hind's knowledge (then) she and Ol had been together like that.

Now if you were so systematic as to proceed now in reverse from Oliver to Dewey to Ash to Maddy to, from the university to FHHC to the golf course to S-D Sisters to the pier, still if you were to avoid using people as means you must negotiate without any end in mind, merely go to these persons and receive them, and think of the violence you once did them to take from them only what the Laurel kidnap had need of.

But why begin with that afternoon on the Heights years ago at Cassia Meaning's? In this Mount Mary rental car Hind could reconstruct that scene of adolescent recreation as he passed from one superroad halfway round a turning rotary into the next superroute feeling only a twinge as he veered away from yet another historic kidnap site—in this case Lynnfield—put it out of his mind and proceeded to recreate that rainy day, complete with the new tumescent prickle dreamy discomfortably sweet.

So what if Cassia was constant in her ruthlessness to young Jack Hind, he knew her well and there was something between them, her bones and his height, and his one disobedience of his guardian, who judged Cassia Meaning unhealthily too sharp by half and not a girl Jack would have much in common with, kindness to such people need not mean intimate after-school afternoons exposed to that child's tongue. It had started with the construction blocks when Jack was nine and Cassia not noticeably stricken, and if the guardian had known how to work it little arrogant Miss Meaning would have been discarded, but now her hold on Jack (unquote guardian) was out of hand, and—in any case there you were, hearing the fire-boats crying in the harbor rain and drinking Cassia's ice-cold cocoa malt and assuming that the

True Confession tale Oliver told was shared essentially
between you and Cassia, for Oliver was not in the group,
not knowledgeable either about Jesus-puzzles or block-
chutes for marbles. Or those family reshufflings Cassia,
you, and Maddy delighted in deadpan—you married the
Vicar to Mrs. Deal and gave them the Chinaman's son and
old Christy for children, or you married Cassia's mother
to James Commons III and gave them the Amondsons'
summer place and for a son Oliver, who knew none of
this, but that rainy afternoon told his shocking tale which
you dimly fancied had no meaning apart from the little
group (Cassia, yourself, and Maddy) of which Ol was not
a member.

"I wouldn't be telling this if I thought I was giving
away anything. But I'm not even as nice a guy as our
colored handyman de Bury, and I never was, see? And I
don't care about *your* True Confession, whether it's true
or you even tell it, I might stay to listen, I might not."
Ol turned and, with (Hind then thought) a college guy's
coolness, took a slug of his cocoa malt.

Cassia with a leg under her leaned back among the
cushions and was giving, Hind thought, a stare so simply
blank he couldn't understand it except as perhaps a mild
signal that at any rate they should politely hear this ag-
gressive newcomer whose independence was *well* known
(a dancing class dropout said to know where the Montague Street butcher got his black market beef, said also
to have left home one winter Sunday at the age of ten
officially disowning his parents in a brief note). Cassia
pretended to like rude guys Hind was thinking as Oliver
got into his True Confession; some of the Heights girls
thought they were after Plane, but it would be only up to
a point, for you never knew what Plane would say even
though he never said much that was bad. Cassia's stare
at this moment was something new, and seemed to Jack

Hind a gentle gap in her customary behavior; and he had the half-pitying desire to run his hands up to her bare hips and pull her over onto his chair; but it was her apartment and anyway she would call him (as at dancing class to which neither he nor she now went) a freak. She knew he wouldn't retaliate. He was under the impression that at a certain point, closer than most people knew, Cassia could be hurt. So he went easy on her, even though she told him he was slow.

"Furthermore," Ol was saying, "you can interrupt me. I couldn't care less. And you'll find that your interruptions will fit right into what I'm saying. My father heals the sick. They are successful sick, for I have banked twelve hundred in checks in a single week and that's O.K. It isn't that the spies across Atlantic Avenue don't come up into the Heights with their Caribbean tongue germs Lady Commons dreams of, or that the new young guy at the barber shop who just got shot out of the army with a bad leg couldn't get treated for a reasonable price by my dad. But they just don't come to him. You'd think we had an unlisted address. And like his address my father with his thing about vitamins is also too nice to exist. There was once a time when I wondered how his smile spread out. But I know people aren't like that inside, so I try not to be, see?"

Cassia was unnaturally calm, against the deep green corduroy pillows. Wasn't Oliver an ordinary showoff? Fireboats celebrated in the rainy harbor and outside in Grace Court you heard then the unmistakable echoing huge "Tock-Tock-Tock" which only Jim Commons of all the Heights kids could make like that, tongue on roof of mouth and loud as the genuinely phonemic click in Xhosa demonstrated to everyone's satisfaction by the black South African Flo had given a real African dinner for and was, Flo later said, terrifyingly honest.

But why (as you looked ahead through the unbreakable windshield of the Mount Mary rental car) did Oliver's True Confession turn up number one on the new, post-Sylvi-agenda. Why turn far back to that, and you really couldn't anyhow because that afternoon there was something you didn't know was between Oliver and Cassia that you found out soon afterward and that changed the proceedings of that rainy afternoon.

But if you contrived not to use people as means—but as ends in themselves!—if you let them grow to their natural height in front of you—and behind you if necessary—you received them as was. But you had to judge his True Confession, and that meant using it and him. You didn't know the simplest thing that afternoon the day before Christmas vacation, and even now, over twenty years later, it is hard to think directly upon the thing you didn't know. Or is it hard not to color in your every view of Ol with what you later learned about that rainy afternoon?

"I'm not talking about how I go through my father's patient files once a month for laughs, and he hates to admit it but he's scared what I might do. Or how I got onto the intercom the other day when he was in the john to tell de Bury's wife waiting in the examination room to remove every single stitch, the doctor would be in in a minute, and how mad she was when his smile dropped a foot when he came in. I got his voice to a 'T.'" Ol could bark out a startlingly hard voice for a thirteen- or fourteen-year-old.

Ol's trouble—but everyone knew this, and Thea had spoken of it—was that Elder Plane was too nice to be real, though not a provable hypocrite. Before Ol could grow up he had to fight his father, but his father wouldn't fight. Ol could yell at him from a squash court gallery and Dr. Plane would neatly slip the racing ball onto his racket halting the rally, pivot on his clean sneakers, look up and smile, "Hi, Ol, what is it, dear?"

"Let's take little Byron Bean, he'll do for your cute little game–" though Plane didn't look right at Cassia, only at (it seemed) the knee of the leg that was bent under her–"Byron, as Hind knows, will believe anything I say, though I don't know yet if he will *do* anything. Now Byron's mother, the *wid*ow Bean–" Ol paused to receive Cassia's warm titter–"she's fantastically old for his mother, ever seen her? she has, or had, in her possession an object that makes you think of the fetuses at the World's Fair or one of Skoldy's live relics. It's in a jar of alcohol, and she has this superstition that this thing in the jar means everyone is going to be kind to Byron. He's picked it up too but not because of the thing that was in the jar but because he thinks that because his father died people are thinking of him, like they all say in these letters he showed me that he received when his father died, 'We're thinking of you at this difficult time' they all say at the beginning, and 'Time heals all wounds' they say at the end; and Byron Bean believes that losing his dad means he gets a break, some people have encouraged the little shit to feel this, not mentioning names; well, I was there, see, a month ago looking over his stuff and then we had to talk to mother a while and out comes the jar. With the thing in it. 'All right, what is it? I'll bite,' I said, and she tells me it's a caul, the kind that–know what a caul is?"–Cassia nodded, she seemed humbled in Ol's presence, she didn't once drawl at him, "O.K., Mister, get to the meat"–"I'll tell you: it's the skin around, well *this* was the skin that part of Byron was born inside, a hood over his head made of skin, that's born on him, and his mother gets very serious, it's almost sacred, she says, nobody knows why but a caul is good luck and By is a good-luck child, she says, and so she's got to always keep that skin in that jar–old Skoldy would look at the floor and say through his nose, It's a membrane in which the fetus–' 'Whose skin *is* it?' I asked her then and there and Mrs. Bean said it was really Byron's *extra* skin."

Jim Commons's huge "Tock-Tock-Tock" had passed again in the street, and Hind remembered thinking Jim must be on his way to special choir practice with Christmas coming up, and must have come down this street to see his friend who went to Deerfield whom he didn't see much any more but who got him into a couple of the Christmas dances across the river.

"But," continued Ol, "I said how could it be his skin if he didn't have it on, and Mrs. Bean thought I was crazy and started talking to me like a child, 'It's really from me, you see,' she said, 'and it's the token—do you know what a token is, Oliver?—of the good things that are going to come to By-By, the nice people he's going to come in contact with and who will help him.' Well, she left it there, dark yellow like the French pancakes in your icebox—" Ol nodded at Cassia without looking at her. "But how was I going to get it away? We were back in Byron's room looking over his stuff, and he said I could take anything he had as a temporary gift, and I thanked him and chose the new briefcase his mother had given him as an advance Christmas present because she couldn't wait. Well, he was good, his mouth started to drop a foot and then he grinned and said O.K. but what did I need with a briefcase I never took books home from school, and I said I liked it but we better not let his mother see me leave with it, and it was only for a few days so I could get the feel of it. So we went to the kitchen to get a peanut butter and marshmallow sandwich and I left the briefcase in the alcove by the living room, and when she went upstairs and By did the plates and glasses I managed to put the jar tight into the bottom of By's briefcase, and then I said I had to go and whispered to By that I better go now in case, and then off I went with Byron's caul."

Passing a Howard Johnson below Lynnfield Hind could not decide to stop, then found it would be miles before the next unless he turned off the pike at the exit four miles down and either doubled back or struck off toward a town. To receive Oliver fairly tonight or tomorrow, or whenever he could get in touch with him, he should pull this ancient history out of sight, not that Hind had ever thought Cassia would want *him* in that way or even when she grew up be likely to marry at all, for she was going to be more sickly and crippled than less. Why had he these last few weeks been in effect saving Oliver from the sack?

When Ol drank off the last of his cocoa malt that afternoon years ago, he seemed to have altered; and he said, still without looking at Cassia, "Your icebox makes real good chocolate milk." Now he did look at her, long and cold, and she shifted and said mildly, "True Confession marches on. Beecher's next–"

"Would you blackmail any of us?" said Oliver, and tossed his hair out of his face and said craftily, "I am *not* finished my True Confession. Mrs. Bean thinks I got her souvenir and came and told my dad Tuesday night when he's faking he's got house calls so he doesn't have to go with my mother to hear the Philadelphia. And Mrs. Bean has Byron with her and she's appealing to Dad's pity, and he's trying to be sympathetic but he really wants to know how big is the caul and is it preserved in–so I tell my father and she to search my room and shrug my shoulders but as she's passing me I mumble, 'Maybe it got flushed out by error,' but when she turned at me with her little black box hat and veil stinking of perfume, she didn't know what to say. So there we are. I confess. I did it."

"Maddy," said Cassia.

"But," said Oliver Plane, "I really *didn't* have it. I got it cached."

"Where?" said Hind.

"You're quite warm right now," said Ol, as if to Cassia, who for the first time in Hind's seven-year observation of her had lost her independence, had gone a startled white—"and you might like to know how I *chose* where I hid it."

Cassia said, "We've had the story."

"That isn't all we've had," said Ol; "well, *some*body, not mentioning names, wanted that old caul and was ready to go all the way for it."

"You made your point," Cassia said, and Hind's shock was due simply to this bombshell—that there was key knowledge between Oliver and Cassia, and he Hind had no inkling of it, and he was smelling, for all his inborn kindness, the strong flesh of an alien.

"If the Beans want their caul back," Ol went on, "By-By's going to have to steal the three hairs from my father's head, I can't bear a sweet, sticky, weak guy like that, probably being the son of a doctor gave me a block against anemia and disease." He continued to look at Cassia Meaning, and Hind could barely resist putting his hand on her.

The Meanings' maid had come in with four Golden Delicious. "You mother said you eat an apple this afternoon."

"But Laurel I *like* apples."

"Give us a True Confession, Laurel," said Oliver, and Hind was amazed that Ol knew her.

"You a wise guy," said Laurel quietly and turned and scuffed slowly back toward the dining room door.

"I *know* I'm a wise guy," said Ol, bragging lamely.

She was in the dining room heading for the kitchen where she was doing the silver, and you could just hear her say, "It's all the same to me."

"Your Negro menial," said Oliver to Cassia.

"This True Confession," said Maddy, "concerns last year's Cinderella Ball."

"Which you are no doubt going to next week," said Oliver.

Hind said, "We're *both* taking Cassia next week."

"They don't work it that way with that dance," said OP.

"I've decided I don't want to go," said Cassia and got up and walked stiffly into the hall that led to the bedrooms and the bathroom.

Working south below that second Howard Johnson don't turn off to connect via bypass with the new, faster turnpike route to the city, but keep to the older parkway landscapes farther from the coast. Nothing in Oliver's now repeated and repeated True Confession had implied the precocious closeness with Cassia that Maddy one day simply came and told Hind of. At thirteen or so—and Cassia never cared what went on between him and starry-eyed, gardenia-necked, willowy Charley (née Charlotte)—even a second-best thing with a girl both veils and palpably thickens the feel of every thought that comes up, every plan you get ready to step into touched and excited by: (after Hind's Saturday overnight scout hike in Alpine) Charley's clear outdoor kisses in her parents' iron-barred backyard, her boxer wiggling around eating sooty snow; or Charley's forehead faintly smelling of Social Tea Biscuits against his cheek shuffling in Lief Lund's notorious and pent-up dark basement after a round-trip to Long Island with Charley's big brother to cut Christmas trees; or her willingness to stay out later than her father, frowning over his book (*Reveille in Washington*), wished; and her softness leaning against Hind at the Fox double-feature in whose dark, candy-wrapper-crunching enclosure safe from agony, ambition, loss, profit, you could enjoy the domesticity of the glasses she put on, or the tartan wool of her pinafore flickering up when there was a bright face on the screen, or the way she would promptly look at him if he looked at her and whisper only if he did—but after two pictures, a trailer, a March of Time, a cartoon, and a deeply satisfying Pathé News with Ed Herlihy, they came out into the afternoon light and the truck noise of that old avenue at its cobbled root near the bridge, Hind would think with such harsh new vigor of Cassia Meaning that he would lose Charley without a single strong Saxon trace until he felt with a sudden Cassiaward outrush (like breath, like life) that Charley had not reached for his arm. "Oh boff! you didn't go see *that* cruddy thing," Cassia would have said, if he had told her he had seen *Northwest Mounted Police* in ripe red color or *The Plainsman*; nothing was any good as far as she was concerned and as she made a point of seeing bad movies, she especially enjoyed dragging Maddy and Jack to what she called "the triple native show" at the Majestic up the cross street the other side of that wide bruising avenue the Fox was on, below the east brink of the Heights, brown Tahiti stomachs and flowered Hawaiian behinds.

That cross-borough artery had altered no more than the approach to the city he was taking now twenty-odd years later in the rental car he would probably have to pay somebody to drive back to Mount Mary Station. The West Side Highway squeaked, the heat had hardly flattened the tar-smooth eruptions, the other side of town Ivy and her club were listening for that squeak-squeal that you in a sharp instant sense has gone too long, the accident is occurring at last. Or Ivy says again that when she got pushed into the river in April she had no choice she was grabbed immediately by that wino, she didn't have the chance to call for help. Or saying again that they should not allow anybody new into the city unless someone already residing here should leave—that is, on a permanent basis, otherwise what had now started in Watts would start here.

Hind looked away from the almond extract billboard. He went down at the Nineteenth Street exit, went through a red light, and crossed to Park, where he turned uptown. Then east again, and south a block, and right: Carmen saw him approaching between the banks of linked cars, and as Hind heard the guitars of the problem kids on the brownstone steps of the church Carmen took away the garbage can and the two slanted slats so Hind could take the undertaker's illegally reserved but now legally occupiable space. Carmen disappeared as Hind backed in.

West to east, late sunglow filled the upper areas of the street's volume and, in the floor of this strict stone pass hazed the taxi roofs so you couldn't tell which cabs were free. No matter what language you resolved to think in, this metrovision was indeed of a sheer and dazzling canyon, the sun made it so. A sparrow dropped from the white fire escape at Hind's right and swung away into the light. The eye could for a moment make out in the second-floor windows of the ad art studio two pale cylinders—coffee—also the detached fingertips and knuckles stuck to the cardboard containers. Then, as you looked, the designers appeared, the man, the girl, and she (like Cassia) was delicately devouring what might well be a Mounds Bar.

Carmen stuck his head out: "Got a new car? Didn't see your wife and the little one." But Carmen had directed Miss Tree to Sylvia's flat! Hind said, "Up north for the summer."

"Yeah. The boss spends all his time uptown at the gym and restaurant."

"And The Assembly Club?"

"His political cronies, you know—his father was water commissioner so he shows his face at The Assembly for old-time sake; but he's at the gym-restaurant most of the time, he's thinking of turning these first two floors into apartments, air conditioning, a couple of bare brick walls, closing the business after ninety-five years." Carmen forgot Hind. "Well *look* at that crazy–!"

The livestock-rental truck was parked the other side of the street, a woman was carrying a gray goose in the main door of the ad art director's just as Hind saw the other, garage-like door roll up. A girl was backing a yellow Lynx convertible down the ramp, bulbs flared at her, somebody laughed way back in the dark room the car came from.

New improved Hydragena blew from a radio somewhere. It followed him upstairs into the closed air of the neglected apartment.

The dishes in the rack were dusty, like the leaves of the philodendron.

No more leaving phone calls for Smitty. If Hind was here when the phone rang, he would receive it as was.

He phoned Oliver, but no one in the department office answered; too late. And the night session would deliberately not know who Ol was. In one of the backyards a very small boy was singing "Winston tastes good" to one repeated tonic chord on a guitar that was too big for him, and the woman Hind had seen playing it days or weeks ago looked around from her smoking brazier and called something curtly, and the child changed to "The Oak and the Ash" keeping the same chord, and she turned again swinging in her halter a pair of breasts Hind was sure hadn't been so big last time, and reproved the kid again–"Greensleeves, Herbie." In the next yard a bigger bird box had replaced the other, and, the lid and wire frame off, fat twitching pigeons jostled inside but showed no sign of wanting to flutter out. Straight ahead, in the yard that abutted the undertaker's rear parlor (where a yard would otherwise have been), the husband and wife were hanging and lighting Chinese lanterns, their canvas-topped annex was finished and they were having a party.

Start to look for Oliver. Hind idly lifted the turntable's record up the spindle-rod to the changer notch and started the machine, but it was Ravel's "Left Hand," Laura's hand was on the jacket and you could not escape her voice reading—take her away, let Oliver Plane be saved as an end from being a means—but her accent comes, and the read words are clear until—"first theme heaves itself from the depths, first, and unusually, on the contrabassoon, rising by degrees"—engulfed by reed, string, orchestral fortissimo, by the gold lamé purse—Hind stepped toward the bedroom but the tragic sound brought him back to reject the record but instead his hand reached for the pink jacket to see Laura's words on the London ffrr, Blancard piano, Ansermet in charge, but the wrong kind of truth was trying to trap Hind, for the words Laura had read had been written by someone named: H. G. *Sears!*— "dance figure somewhat reminiscent of 'Pagodas' in the *Mother Goose Suite*"—he pinched the reject and went to the bedroom but at the door turned instead into the study and flipped the RECORD switch on one of his portables and erased a Laura tape. Oliver could be anywhere, however long your reach. You could canvas Canal and try for the Chapel of Laughter.

Most of the mail was advertisement; he'd take it back down and get it out of the house. But if he missed a call?

The designers were working through the evening. They seemed to laugh a lot. Coining it. Hind sat on the dirty radiator at the window by the ticking picture and listened for a call.

Oliver's True Confession, with behind it the awful facts that Cassia had gone down for him, still was like a Grimms tale, but if you thought of the giant's aged mother or the smell of flesh you fell into disarray. The guardian gave him the Brothers Grimm from the original German, rendering it steadily until Jackie, lying propped on an elbow, worried that he'd drop off into deep water just when Joringel, having lost Jorinda and become a shepherd in a strange village near the witch's wicked castle, had not yet dreamt of the means by which he would turn Jorinda and the myriad other birds back into their maiden selves: if you failed to stay awake Jorinda would stay forever a nightingale, and yet, facing the marvelous deep greenwood seabeds of sleep Jackie believed that if he lost faith in his own lucky blessing, and looked back, he would lose it all.

Tell that to the two designers in a midnight clinch and then—when Hind woke to a new, very late August cool in the air—in another, early morning clinch, in the window across the street; but now they broke it up and went back to their Anglepoise-lit tilted boards.

Hind's radio station would be running out of "Naked Voice" tapes. The guardian had only once expressed doubt: "but what does any one of those tapes *mean*?"

Hind was surprised to get through to Oliver shortly after eight-thirty.

"Hoo, what a relief. I was suddenly afraid you'd still be up-country."

"Maybe so, but you weren't afraid enough to stay on my job. You left when you pleased. And left quite a rumor behind you which got stuck to me, for Christ's sake. But then who am I? My students are wondering if I am Plane. Now tell me, what have *I* got to do with a plot to infiltrate CDNV and what's this old girl up to? Is she Extension? Well, she phoned to tell me to tell you about a kidnap and could she have an appointment with me, when were my office hours; and then when I told her she was confused and must have signed up for the wrong course, she said quote unquote, 'Plane, you're in this up to your teeth, don't try to back out, you don't know what could happen walking backwards.' And proceeded to tell me what to say when you came hanging around this week. How did she know you'd be seeing me if you didn't even know I was down from the country?"

"I don't want to hear what the Old Woman may have said to you."

"May!"

"No."

"But I'm about to tell you. Say listen Mighty Mouse, is there a lot you don't know about yourself? If you say you'll do something for a friend, you do it."

"I did. Your courses were a shambles. Half the kids didn't know who you were."

"Well, now you got me involved in—what? a criminal case? Before, I was my own man, now an aged crone is telling me I'm up to my eyeteeth in a kidnap."

"I'll hang up if you try to tell me. Forget the kidnap, be yourself, try to unquote the person you've been alluding to or invoking."

"Invoke! Why would I invoke her? Wait—so she came in to see me this morning, right on my heels in fact—"

"I won't listen to this, Ol. I want to see you tonight. Let's make it that steak place—"

"What steak place?"

"The Palm"—ominously what had been this now nameless city was shifting back into the old markings—"on Second Avenue mid-town west side of the street. On me. By the way, do you recall our True Confession game in 1944?"

"No, make it lunch out here at the Caf tomorrow, The Palm's too expensive. I got all these exams you didn't pick up for me. The old gal comes in in a cord suit a bit young for her, white hair, black eyes, a regular fury, I figured her for a C she wanted raised to—"

Hind hung up.

He put off calling Smith Answering Service.

In Oliver's old apartment now newly, variously painted and ruglessly echoing, a short swarthy man and his three unleashed Schnauzers looked Hind up and down.

Back in the neighborhood later, Hind learned that Knott's seventeen-year-old son had at last left home: to a one-room walkup round the corner, in a building his father had nothing to do with. Hind passed several times during the next two or three days, and there was young Knott three floors above the German deli with his back to the window banging and rattling his traps to recorded rock so it sounded like the room was full of players. The woman who made the German potato salad and the pea soup complained to Hind about young Knott with a lot of neighborly rhetorical questions; but then she refused blankly to cash Hind's check and asked if he knew young Knott.

Late in the day, the phone trilled, and true to his new dekidnaping policy Hind picked the receiver off the cradle.

A woman's strong manner: "This the answering service?"

"This is Hind."

"I want the answering service."

"But this is the real thing, me."

"I had hoped to leave a message with your answering service. That's how we've been working."

"Maybe you want Smith Answering?"

"That must be it. But since I've got you we may as well cross words."

"Why do I think I've heard you before?"

"You've been hearing *from* me."

"What *is* this? I'm a busy man."

She seemed to be making a laughing sound. "I won't ask you why you told your friend Oliver Plane not to speak of the Laurel case, though I'm glad you've guessed that Cubic Campus is no longer the relevant setting. But why do you go back to Plane, he's finished."

East Coast English, the "r" and "a" drawl—even, at a wild guess, a professor of math or classics at Radcliffe, a floor of a fine frame house on Washington Avenue.

"Isn't he still out of town?" said Hind. Ol would throw a girl over for a new one's pad.

"He has no more information for you. Was your wife eager to talk to you?"

"Don't you understand, I'm finished with the case. I won't even name it, familially or categorically."

"Mercy, Mr Hind! Well, you at least picked up a mission from your distinguished guardian; you genuinely want to rescue."

"Rescue what?"

"You of all people shouldn't ask *that*—didn't you pick up any of your guardian's keenness for language?—any more than a teacher of education" (ironic) "should hesitate to use the verb 'discuss' intransitively. One discusses. One rescues. Or, *you* do."

He had to pop the question to the Old Woman. But consequences were a threat to his new plan of not using people.

But instead ask about the guardian. That too was shifting ground, it too led to self. Or to the terrible tendril of conversation years behind, so far you would never catch up, words between the guardian and perhaps Thea.

"Why do you bring up my guardian? Did you know him?"

"How could you know him as I do?"

"Are you an old friend?"

"Certainly not that, or not for a long time. But stick to my subject: your wife talked; she talked of a visit perhaps, someone coming to see her. When I phoned her late yesterday to check on you—"

"So *Staghorn* was to be next! But wait, Sylvia has no violet mole on her back. I don't know who you are—" he must break his new rule and refer to the kidnap—"but if you know all about who knows what about the kidnap, go and rescue Hershey Laurel yourself."

"He's right here in the city."

"Good-bye!"

Yet to avoid speaking directly to her you'd have to wait for eleven rings so Smith Answering would pick up.

The ground-floor buzzer, Hind pressed the answer button and after half a minute went to the door.

Grimes, Red Grimes, was puffing there in dark olive summer straw and rumpled blue-gray acetate. "Finals over?" He grinned and stuck out his hand. He was subtly having it both ways—at once present colleague (very senior very junior) yet longtime friends no see (very senior very junior).

"I don't work there. I substituted."

"I haven't of course followed you these last few years. Your guardian..." Grimes had got past into the hall, and with a choice of living room, bedroom, or study, had drifted promptly into the last, and was humming at the books.

The murmur his words now came in was, given the situation, grotesque. "Oliver Plane, *he's* an, uh, associate of yours, mmm?, now where does he hang out, I seem to miss him whenever I go looking for him, you kids nowadays are so busy, mmm, batting out papers on, mmm, you never keep your orifice hours."

"I told you, I don't teach. I substituted."

"Mmm, yes. Mmm, well what do you know, Fossy's Ariosto, mmm, part of your dowry."

"Why shouldn't I have it?"

"This Harington's worth, mmm intacta, fifteen dollars, full contemporary calf albeit rebacked. I'll buy, if you'll sell. A memento of your mmm—"

"My...?"

"Mmm, *Perspectives in Linguistics*, Waterman, well well, mmm—"

"A lot were in storage till early this year."

"You don't have Oliver Plane's address? They were unable to give me any but the vacated. Seems to move around. That boy will lose his instructorship one day if he doesn't get a settled residence. I don't see *my* books here. Mmm, oh yes by the way, the Chapel of Laughter, you know it?"

But looking for Oliver three days ago Hind had looked for Grimes thinking he might know or be with Ol, for Sylvia had said Grimes was looking for Oliver. Hind got to the lecture room too late and found only evidences of Grimes on the greenboard; the small scrawl packed a lot into one panel:

$$\text{Time-Depth} = \frac{\log \text{ of \% of cognates}}{2 \log \text{ of \% of cogs after milliennium}}$$

from vocab samplings differentiate among true cogs, deceptive cogs, false cogs—Distinguish between "probably" > "prob'ly" (or "literary" > "lit'ry") and "habeo" > "aio"—For final be prepared to deduce by glottochronology the kinship through vocab similarities and divergences, of French/Latin or English/German.

More notes followed; and angled at the four corners of the panel the small scrawl left the janitor a ghostly warning, "Save."

You would have a hard time imagining that Hind and Grimes had not met in five years, considering Grimes' behavior now; it seemed to assume that they had never been parted.

Oliver didn't want this elderly persimmon crowding asses with him against the wall at a table in the Good Guys Saloon. And Hind moreover had so far to go, even assuming he passed safely through the Plane dekidnaping stage to Dewey—considering how much time Dewey (so Captain Kidd said) was putting in at the FHHC (for, so Ivy grudgingly had told Berry Brown, Dewey's weight had suddenly become another problem entirely and he was doing exercises to put it *on*), Hind might have to renew his membership, perhaps merely monthly at the Former Members' Rate. What Dewey would have to show you, be to you, become to you, once he had been freed of his role as a kidnap "carrier," might be staggering even for Hind.

"Nothing shocks me," he said to Grimes, who had the guardian's Ariosto in his hand.

"No, mmm." Grimes had not caught him thinking aloud. "Well, if Oliver Plane, say, were to go out tomcatting tonight, where d'you suppose he'd mmm gogo," the well-tempered glottis produced a joky rasp.

Send him goosing, goosenecking, let Grimes try one of Buck's live South African lobster tails and a mug of freezing English Red Barrel. "Go to the Good Guys Saloon—" Hind did not know after all these years what to call Professor Red Grimes, but you had that trouble a lot lately, like Buddy Bourne addressing Lief and Hind, Jack and Lund.

As Grimes left, refusing a drink, he turned at the landing and said, "We must talk some night, I have scads of memories you might be interested in. 'Course you know most of it, I suppose. The whole thing. Your mother and your guardian and all. Well, you know how lucky you were to inherit all those books, not to mention—what was the address of the Good Guys?" Hind listened to Grimes go to the third floor, the second (where he met Carmen waxing), and on down to the vestibule.

Hind could give Grimes without a tremor the address of the GGS and the distinguishing features so Grimes could find the GGS no matter which way he came from. But a few weeks ago—perhaps taken too readily by Maddy's dejection and his concern that the roller-skating guy might do something to him or to the old brick apartment house on Grace Court—Hind could have felt that only a dullard, or a tramping tourist from Hershey, Pa., (his family following him in a neat rank behind) or a tourist of the spirit, like Grimes in his antiquarian toponomasiology, could accept the old names of the city and of its parts. But now for the first time in ages Hind found himself forced to rehearse these names, or some of them. The guardian said he had designed a city-country counterpoise for young Hind, that Jack's experience should be not merely of both but of the true human whole they made, though anyone who looked could tell that the guardian would rather skip the regular cycle that, as if by a probate judge, was designated to be spent in the city.

Grimes was offering, had just now been offering, guardian memories, when all Grimes wanted was Oliver Plane's address; and what after all had he been to the guardian but a tenured mooch.

But the guardian had not minded being used or even nasty things children said behind his back about the annual treasure hunt and the nearly invulnerable clues.

"Well, Jackie," Grimes had said, "if you ever want to let me steal that Harington, you know where I am. I knew your guardian *such* a long time ago."

"*He* left you some books."

"He left me some books" (let the words of my mouth and the meditations of my heart). "A strange man. Fights he used to get into with Thea Dover. I just sat merrily on the sidelines with my crème de menthe, mouthing my Housman. You see, Thea never knew the secret. Apart from you and me and maybe one, maybe two others, no one knew. Though I suppose you've told Sylvia. A queer quirk in a remarkable, if mmm thwarted man 'musing among the ruins of the Capitol, while the barefooted friars were singing vespers in the Temple of Jupiter.' If, like monarch and consort, the ill-fated Hinds had not emplaned *together*, how different would your life have been."

Having said good-bye, Grimes seemed to go very slowly, speaking idly yet slyly, seeming to suspect Hind knew more about Oliver Plane's whereabouts than he was telling.

And what was that *guardian* secret? Academics gossip brilliantly or, as if half-leaking a scholarly scoop to a student, gossip vaguely, tapping their omens to hear them click cluck clock. Was the secret that the guardian loved Hind's mother? Or that the guardian—but this was *Grimes'* view—was a failure, or worse? Hind had always known just how extraordinary the guardian was, in his own way a giant.

But Grimes here mattered only mmm vis-à-vis OP. And here, he knew less than Hind.

By the hour, Hind received phone calls, and having sounded the caller for info or echo of Oliver Plane, Hind erased the call.

Was he afraid to go to sleep? After three hours'
sleep he was having a hard time erasing...Dewey Wood
inquiring why Hind had dropped the FHHC, "they" said
DW might be getting a detached retina but thank God
and the City Council you got these things diagnosed early
nowadays...Mr. Morales, of all people, tight and truculent
at eleven P.M. repeating, "So what are you willing to do
for Siggofreddo?"

At eleven-thirty A.M., with sore eyes, Hind was turning
his key in his Segal safety lock when the phone started
inside and he thought of Marina phoning home from a
party so her Russian Blue and her Kerry Blue would find
solace in the companionable sound, the cat would open
one eye, the dog would slowly clear his throat.

At the twelfth ring Hind let himself back in. Thirteen,
four—

"Hello?"

"Smith Answering. We got a party calls *us direct* to leave
a message for you. This isn't right, Mr. Hind, it reduces
our efficiency. This once, we pass on the message, but we
can't take any more except through your number. The
lady said to tell you the following: 'Beulah Love stirred
up her sister-in-law the week of the Laurel kidnap.' This
is all the message, Mr. Hind."

You had to steer that right out of your mind just as you
had to put the Bean caul story into proper perspective,
Cassia's Oliver Plane, Oliver's Cassia, you must discipline
imagination, unquote guardian.

Oliver's university's college's staff Caf herewith:
mottled brown agronomite trays, you slid them along a
thirty-foot rack made of four parallel steel tubes at the
level of a girl's waist ahead of Ol, at the level of the top
of Ol's fly and the lower end of Hind's. Oliver lifted down

a plate of Green Noodles Chasseur and moved past the kosher and to-order sandwiches to the desserts, leaving Hind to push both trays. Beyond the cash register the serve-your-self corridor opened left into the Caf proper, a promise of Formica surfaces. All this pertained, though, not simply to Plane but also.

To Grunewald, natty in the far left corner of the Caf near the side door to the private dining room into which a distinguished group was even now moving, and Hind caught the plump angle of who but Grimes' rear who walked always at a slow, inclined slight jerk as if in constant readiness to occupy a passing chair. Oliver went toward Grunewald's corner. Oliver was all but ignoring Hind. Had Hind finished once and for all the relation between them by having used OP as a lead means in the now forbidden "case"? You almost expected to see, arrived out of retirement (to, say, give a "service" course in criminal detection) Inspector Praid. A voice under Hind's tray said, "Good afternoon, Members." A young pudge in a blue silicon suit and a marigold tie stopped Plane and said quietly, "Are you aware of what's been happening this session? Look there—" Grunewald had risen looking hopefully toward them—"and there" where the persistent fellow with the olive-green attaché case (he was opening it) sat at another dish-strewn table with two very young girls: "Students have been sneaking in here where they don't belong, under cover of status as staff assistants in linguistics lab, theater lab, anthro lab. Would you sign a petition?" Oliver kept moving, looking for a table. "Supposedly the student caf is too crowded, they tell them to move on as soon as they…" The pudge added mildly, "I haven't actually made out the petition…." Now he was addressing the blond briefcase, who had greeted him as "Member."

Grunewald stood quite near. Holly Roebuck was approaching.

Oliver, his fork up pronged full of noodles, was saying to Hind, "What do you mean I should '*just talk*'? What do you mean? I'm not receiving you."

"That boy over there with the olive-green attaché was thinking aloud with me one day and came up with an essential quality (though not, as he thought, a definition) of a real comeback: it can't be foreknown by its speaker or drawn from any repertoire, it must be spontaneous."

"You've lost me. Listen, what're you doing out here?"

"You know I didn't want to come, I wanted to meet in mid-town."

"No, no—" Ol wiggled his head impatiently, frowning— "I don't believe you. First, it was that old woman, then it was you refusing to speak of the kidnap she mentioned and with which I might add she threatened me. Then Poplar came asking for you and said he was sorry but he thinks he put an elderly woman agent, a government agent, onto you. And on top of it all, I find in some of these finals, my God, what is going on here? are you working for the university steering committee?"

"Please get off the subject of the old woman and what she was saying. Just talk to me."

"What subject? You brought it up."

"Forget it."

"It's your bag, baby; I had no connection with it—"

"I give in on one small detail: what did you mean in your letter from Mount Mary?"

"How do I know what I said? The girl wrote it. Her writing is illegible since she decided it was not charismatic to write a good linear hand."

"In that letter Oliver you said quote unquote, I could have '*rested*' on my '*laurels*.'"

"Forget it. I should never have let you fall into my pathetically banal life. But you always took things too hard, too soft....Remember Cassia?" A faint, tired, stubbly shadow of glee.

Keep lines clear, words measured: Oliver, thirty-five and a half, two upturned arc-creases under each eye, a hundred seventy (according to driver's license) (stripped down to the gray bathing suit he long ago rented from the Cuban attendant at FHHC and then bought because he liked it), unpredictable in his use of sauna (ten, eleven, fourteen, seven minutes), given both to nausea hangovers and highly spiced chicken molés, had (up to about a year ago) never (so he said) except twice in his life himself used a contraceptive; likes steamed clams; gave away Dewey Wood's incomplete set of Frazer, once smoked grass with the guardian's Jap on the guardian's beach with Hind; sometimes breakfasts in the park Sunday; played the cello, still occasionally joins his mother's Heights madrigal group The Muses; told Cassia Meaning in May of 'forty-six he was going to "ship out" for the summer, but did not; met the guardian once in the meat market on Montague in 'forty-three or 'forty-four and said, "You better do something about Jack." Here, you were trying to do right: receive Oliver excised from the kidnap conflations—don't even *think* the word, recall Christ's in-depth condemnation of the very thought of an adulterer, the very words in which the thought thinks—Ol was the bill of fare, but you found yourself slipping like a roving arbor seed into the dark confining earth of your own past fixing you, ending what good you could do for—cut even the seed analogy, for the dekidnap was to have been couched in plainest words.

"I remember *you*," Hind answered as Ol swallowed.

"Great cynic, Cassia. At thirteen she was promising.

My God she was smart. Remember her as the poet Bunthorne in *Patience*? Poor Jack, how you bring it back to me, in beige velvet trousers, and a brown-and-violet cravat puffing out at her neck, hadn't thought of it since the last letter years afterward she wrote me from London and said the truth was she'd been looking at me all through the 'what a very singularly deep young man' number—and she and I'd never spoken then. Had we?"

"How do I know? No, I don't think you had."

"And at the party in her school gym afterward I got close to her and she was telling you and Maddy and the music director in a red corduroy jacket that of course *Patience* is full of light, but it's too fetching, its intention declines into an innocent English drawing-room pastoral. That impressed me, until I heard your guardian say just those words a month later at my parents' party, but Cassia said it well and it impressed me almost as much as her elocution onstage hotted me up." (Two days later Hind had taken her to the Fox to see *Sahara* and *Crime Doctor's Strangest Case*, and five days after that she received *So Little Time* from Hind for Christmas.)

Grunewald stood ready two table-widths or -lengths away. Holly Roebuck had sat alone at an empty table nearby.

"—those four-syllable words. I wanted to get up onstage and stop her mouth in mid-rhyme. You thought she was singing. She *talked* her way through half the lyrics."

"When you leave here tonight, where do you go?" said Hind. "I mean, what's your address?"

"How's the song go? There's one line there that's the greatest they ever collaborated—you have to lead in with two preceding lines: 'And convince 'em, if you can, that the reign of good Queen Anne—'"

"'—was Culture's palmiest day.'"

"'Of course you will pooh-pooh'"—Oliver was singing

now—"'whatever's fresh and new, and declare it's crude and mean,'"

And Hind joined him: "'For Art stopped short in the cultivated court of the Empress Josephine.'"

Plane got a forkful of noodles into his mouth. "But when she stared at me really was a second later and she didn't even know I knew she was staring. 'If he's content with a vegetable love which would certainly not suit *me*, / Why, what a most particularly pure young man this pure young man must'—"

"We were talking of your plans, are you keeping this job?"

"No, 'Then a sentimental passion of a vegetable fashion must excite your languid spleen,/ An attachment *à la* Plato for a bashful young potato, or a not-too-French French bean!'"

"But I said—"

"Sorry, I was humoring you." Plane put down his fork.

"Humoring me! By ignoring me?"

"What am I being used for? A 'Naked Voice' tape? Where is it? Grunewald's pocket? And I just turned over a new leaf."

"You're being used for nothing."

"But 'sentimental,' you see, was exactly what I saw she was when I'd clocked her through a couple of times. I was disappointed in her. All of a sudden, there was this ordinary Cassia I hadn't seen but that I now saw had been there all the time staring at me. She started phoning. One night she drank a chocolate coke with Camel ashes in it and tried to be hysterical, said she thought she was pregnant, and I said, 'What, at fourteen?' But there was something to her. All that about refusing to go to Smith, and then college *period*. I tried to get rid of her but the lousier I got the more she was there. Where? At the end of the line. Or up in my room, my thoughtful father would never think of disturbing me. She was getting close to me in the wrong way. You know she was her best self with someone like you she wasn't really interested in."

Grunewald was on top of them, and spoke: "I thought I was taking Mr. *Hind's* exam, but now you seem to be back in the saddle, Dr. Plane."

Plane looked up at Grunewald: "It was a fair exam no matter who grades it."

(Confidentially) "Have you gotten to mine yet?"

"No."

"Maybe you're glad, considering Mr. Hind's stuff I gave you on the—"

"Say, yeah, what *about*—"

"I mean—Dr. Plane, what are *you* teaching in the Fall term? I suppose the sections are full up?"

A blond woman in a black silk suit edged in front of Holly as Holly stepped up beside Grunewald, and Plane turned from Grunewald.

"Oh, Mrs. Rosenblum."

"You were sick, Dr. Plane, how are you? I have something to explain to you. May I ask you a personal question? I wrote a long paper, it's too long and it's late, can I hand it in?"

"Sure."

"I've been looking for you, in terms of certain concepts, my paper was inspired—well" (smiling as at a private joke) "in a sense by the media—but mainly by a thing my daughter said recently—you remember you had my daughter—about the overture to *The Abduction*, how Mozart neutralizes and draws apparent depth into dense surface, she also quoted one of her professors about how all this was related in terms of the relation (do I have it right?) of the surface grating of one of the college air vents and the deep distance from which the sound comes, does that make sense?"

"Yes, Mrs. Rosenblum, I *will* take the paper." Ol slid his chair back as Holly reached around Grunewald to put her hand on Hind's. Ol said, "Oh, Mrs. Rosenblum, this is a friend of mine in the media, Mr. Hind."

Hind said, "I thought you were only teaching *two* courses this summer."

"I want another chocolate milk," said Ol and got away, but Hind saw on Ol's tray the dark shadow of the contents three-quarters up the waxy side of the half-pint carton.

"I have to too," said Hind to Holly, to Grunewald, and to Mrs. Rosenblum, and went after Ol.

Holly called, "You had iced coffee."

Then Ol was saying quietly to Hind at the counter, "I have to cope somehow with what they've cribbed from you into their finals. Haven't you done enough?"

He walked heavily away past the Watts Relief table and out the electric glass doors into an adjacent cloister, and then he stepped without missing a beat through the blue-and-brown ceramette transit hole molded in the high south wall.

In those other days Cassia didn't really limp. But you saw she'd rather lie propped on a deliberating elbow, or sit. "At the end—if there ever *was* one—Plane told me he loathed sickness, but you can see why I didn't believe that was it, I mean why he ditched me." She and Hind were thirteen, fourteen, fifteen, sixteen, and she would tell him more and more. Occasionally Oliver consented to see her.

Hind would go away to Charley, to her big mellow house with its platform ledges extending out from the

two tall first-floor windows—you could straddle the gap
between them in an inside-out hide-and-seek game—and
there was her mother's shelf of old cookbooks beside the
house phone in the kitchen; and there was her father's
barking seriousness about the market and his squash
seedings like a Christmas tree on end, and the programs
at Goya planned mostly by him and his pal Elder Plane;
also her father's respectful inquiries about the guardian
which gave Jack a sense of possession and increased
his confidence that the guardian was an extraordinary
man. What Charley's father didn't know, her big brother
didn't like. But big brother seemed to act with interested
discretion as chauffeur if not pander; he had the keys
to the summer house in Remsenburg, if not exactly a
risk-taker himself or a lookout—he had a second girl out
there himself, a townie whom the parents worried about
who waitressed at the beach club during the season.
("*Waitressed*, did you say?" was the guardian's pained
reaction. "That's carrying formation by analogy a bit
far.")

But now through the cerami-rounded lip of the wall-
hole (the cross-disciplinate artist's name on an ethyl-gold
plaquette on the wall proper), you could see the south-
southwest corner of the big Plazette being fast traversed
by Oliver Plane.

Behind came Mrs. Rosenblum's voice, "He had iced
coffee."

But in the familiar, changing Plazette no voices fled after him, and in the examination quiet nothing beckoned
his pursuit, no ends, no vents. If you could not walk away
from Oliver you couldn't receive him as an accidental
whole self end, yes taken apart from Mrs. Rosenblum or
Holly or Cassia (and apart from the magazines she consented to look at with Hind, the *Desert Song* ad the week she
was in *Patience*, with Dennis Morgan looking like a rouged

fond-eyed corpse (Cassia said), and the very next day the three regulars and Plane the newcomer—no, exactly a *year* later—played True Confessions, and that night the guardian went to hear The Downtown Glee Club and the Trinity Choir Boys sing and he joined in on "Adeste Fideles" at the end.) The air in the Plazette seemed dry now, but a metal odor penetrated your energies so you seemed to be smelling something originating inside you, like your smell when you blew your nose after a dank walk through Cassia's London smog even masked. Ivy's hippie burglar was still at large. Oliver Plane could—yes, it was coming as you slouched gratefully down on one of the five new single-stem transparent benches added since the last time you looked, yes, coming: OP could not be received freely if pursued and caught, any more than you could do anything for Siggofreddo Morales if he couldn't receive what you did. What time did old man Morales call? Sleep, however deeply dark, was what you needed.

Maybe you wouldn't finish Ol in the old, guardian sense. Would that be bad? You a bum on a beach, you legs occupy more space than you paid for.

Gray in the air mildly blurred the mid-city outline. A single bomber banked west and began to seem smaller. Sunshine was reflected from its fuselage. You worded only what you saw, no matter how tired. But words had this tendency to turn into things. Witness BUMPER STICKER and BUTTON.

Dewey was sick, you couldn't take the chance of his ending up bandaged in an eye hospital or ending somewhere worse before you had a chance to erase your use of him in the revised case.

The yellow bulldozer was stationary on the lawn that lay between the open south side of the Plazette and the south-side class buildings. What would your face look like from under this bench? You shouldn't come up for air before you finished absolving yourself, then repossessed Sylvia.

But Oliver was Oliver's sake, and you mustn't think ahead even to why. Unthink Plane in order to be ready for him should he come. Lose your marbles if you don't.

Central Plazette is an exactly irregular pentagon, the one fully open side of which faces south. Its adjacent southwestern side is one-third open, the direct exit to the Meditation Shelter and Underway, where you might ask those interested in your collegiate advisory service to meet with you; the other two-thirds is of bone-blanched concrete, an end wall of the Life Support Sciences Building—itself an oval whose bending longitudinal façades (which from your transparent bench you see a small part of) are broken by chunky pilasters that in turn create an opti-concert of shadow structures through which personnel are to enjoy walking and in case of emergency may be easily seen and herded into or out. Hind's words were softening. The Plazette's longest (west-northwest) side is one wall of Social Sciences: dark colorfast mineral-surface panels are lit up and opened by bright cadences of window-inserts—you felt you knew that wall, for you taught behind it. The dark sandwich-panel facing occurs inside as out—chip-free, self-maintaining, incombustible; the material appears flat to the eye, it won't "oil can" or "pillow"; it has many uses—Hind once inspected the fascias between moldings. The building will not die of natural causes. Plane teaches there too. To your right, two unplanted trees (which will finish the line of trees in front of another building) stand like uncapsizable—stand firm in their burlap—. The building is going up. The top three floors are orange and black girders, the bottom four are bone-white concrete, unwindowed but for two narrow, vertical, deeply recessed ports at opposite ends of the façade and at different levels. To Hind's far left and

422

right ramps led into Central Plazette, and at his back he could feel the bright heat of the northwest wall of a high heavy administrophic cube. He hadn't energy to turn and see if the pediment's inscription had progressed beyond ADVERSITY.

Concrete and Santos-Dumont grass floored the Plazette. He felt he'd been sitting on this transpara-bench a long time but he thought he would stay, para-bench, stay. He was gratefully tired. You were welcome here, and alone.

Think of the eyes you gave your tall tilted houses in the church nursery school, which was at that age secular enough for your guardian to let you attend. At age four.

What windowing there was in this Plazette wasn't oculohumanoid. Just oblong windows.

When Hind pivoted (as if the para-bench helped him) on his buttocks, and lay out on the bench, his head at one end, his calf muscles resting pressed on the edge of the other...Where was anyone? Central Plazette, sunlit, was not exactly a (Natural Wood) pine grove, no wild unmetered free-gro: and you did have some final dust filling your lungs and cutting your warm forces. But why not like the Plazette? If the edifices seemed poly-purpose prerenovated architecture that you would and could airlift anyplace and put down around too many different kinds of groups of folk, it was nonetheless intelligible. If the bench was softer than the grassy ground, you must not in any case frequent that grass, it said so. And anyway, Corbusier was all for rediscovering the city soil. Ah yes, but by raising buildings off the ground.

You were interviewing relevant personnel at your ease afloat on a transpara-surface. Far down the line the guardian could not wait, and left. The olive-green attaché case snapped open and a mini-city unfolded like a Jack-in-the-box with a bang, "for your children, a creative playthink," said the case. Lame legs, both right and left, faced Hind's supine eye, and tongues flicked from the poor mossy kneecaps: "Leave Plane alone, you cannot *help* using him. Look at yourself instead—but in terms of how you *are known!* By grass and stone." Then a startled, golden velvet mike, stunted to eye level, was gargling at him a "singularly deep young man" and he tried to ask if it was related to the greenvents. And as the interviewees filed by, Hind was trying to say, But you are rooted and can't move, you know you can't move, and you must be watched over, because you are rooted and can't move and need services, what's the meaning of this?

But the sky's crust was tilting up at this the ADVER-SITY end, and the sun slid to the mid-city profile, passed through it, and poured its now broken glow back east-ward, and a voice was saying, "—ol' sock ol' bean, what you up to?"

And in his sleep he protested that he had not received his regular sinal rinse yet and his interviewing had been tampered with and indeed truncated ere one of the prime in-depth prospects could reach the head of the line, one Professor Red Grimes, who had extraordinary information to be interviewed of; but what came out of Hind's waking mouth was a reply to a newly demustached Pop Poplar, spiral notebooks at the hip.

"Pop!"

(Palms up, pacific protest smile) "I've changed. I'm not 'Pop' now."

"What are you?" A sparrow? Pallid, hatless attaché case. Brilliant army boots, sharp chinos, white-on-white short-sleeved button-down.

"You always were a character, with your blind handshake and your height, and now you're lying on a park bench."

424

"Well, that's what *you* were, a character, what little I saw of Pop Poplar."

"I'm not Pop now, I'm Laurey, if you don't mind."

Hind's hand went up a few inches, but just as smartly as in the old rescuing days. "You look different. What's with CDNV?"

"You got to learn the code and you don't get to stay a kid. You meet felt needs. This all came to me the other night. My parents cut off my source of supply, so what do I do for basics like car insurance and public relations and a hundred other expenses indigenous to the way I was living? And the university leaked word they were cutting off subsidies to my organization; the relevant assistant dean evaded the issue by saying merely that it was felt that CDNV was not ultimately creative enough—get that! *creative*—to rate a cut of the Infra-Colleges Activities Bank. Circumstances, you see. But life is circumstantial, fight it you wind up convicted every time, look at Shepard, look at Oswald. So I'm hitting the books."

Perhaps some fresh ripe Plane was here yet. The sky's dilute gray was turning silvery gold, and the crashing end of the dream was wrong, for the sun had perhaps two August hours left: "Anything new? What books are you hitting?"

"Since I still have a little leverage here and there, although it's not my bag any more, I was able to get into Plane's An-thro-Lang. 11C, I heard he's worth catching, he made a name for himself during second and third summer trisessions, they're saying he's got a new thing defining the locus of all disciplines, and that's what I need at this point, my cousin's mother says the new theory is something called Infra-Structural Non-Depth Perspective and can be applied to any field. Gibbon, Dürer, Watts Towers. *You* know Plane. He's quite uninvolved, wouldn't you say?"

"I can't say. But where is everyone?" Plazette lawns, bright bulldozer, settled preparation for masses that might or might not occur.

"Gone home or in a three-thirty-to-six exam."

"What time is it?"

"Chocolate time."

"That's old and bad." But peculiar.

"I've *gone* kind of old-fashioned. When I get a free evening I go see one of the lyric films of the Thirties. What about you?"

"Receiving." If that wasn't clear, tough. Poplar could take care of himself.

"Mmm," said Laurey. "Look, I regret putting that old dame onto you. Did you lose your cover? I don't want to know who she is, but I very much regret my part in putting her onto you, for I learned last week that you may not have been exactly committed to us, but you weren't against us either. I hope you, well, have something to do. Listen, one of my CDNV researchers told me your name can be found in Webster's Dictionary. I said to check further, but then CDNV folded."

"The time?"

"I stopped wearing a watch because of radiation sterility, but I happen to know it's about four-thirty. The grass is good this time of the afternoon. The leaves and grass are treated so the sulphur dioxide won't turn them tan or ivory; in fact, they're green year round. The quiet here is, well, almost sacred. Look at the city off there."

"But does *Plane* speak of himself as uninvolved, or do others. Is he regarded as a rebel?"

"*There's* an old word. I never heard Plane in person. I believe he says you have to stand apart if you're going to be together. That's what I *believe* he says, someone I know copied notes from a friend of hers in Plane's class. And he also believes that the great menace today is health, particularly *qua* idea. If you could see my kid sister, seventeen and already happily married, apartment in Long Beach, she's a freshman and Jim's an upper sophomore, they both worked in Sears during vacation and they're going to during Christmas."

Yes: in that wishful "*stand apart*" was the key: "Plane ever talk about his roots?"

"Plane? I believe he believes that you stand apart in order to stand together, cut your roots in order to grow. I bet he isn't a native New Yorker." The name reached you from far far away, last year, even a *few* years ago.

He never shipped out, those school summers, and later he never for God's sake even went to Europe; he never did things he told Cassia he'd do. This was the truth about Ol.

"Two-family house in Long Beach only a city block from the ocean, though they don't see much of it. You get into their three-room either through a closet in the adjoining apartment or a side door up some rickety porch steps. Walls were very close together and dirty. Rust on the shower floor. Couple of old peeling cabinets in the kitch, and when you moved them, they left rust marks on the linoleum. Kitchen sink very wide, very shallow, old-fashioned. Well, those kids, you should see how they transformed that pad. It's been an inspiration to me."

"I haven't time now, Pop, I have to run over and see a guy just for a minute."

"But *I* was the one who was in a hurry, man. *I'm* not keeping you. I only wanted to explain that you have to live with what there is, and these kids, you wouldn't recognize the apartment—"

"I can imagine—"

"—they put stuff in that maximized the rooms: dark blue rug in the living room and foyer—I went out to

inspect when they finished cleaning and painting–orange
Danish modern rocker facing a striped blue-and-lettuce
couch, end tables with lamps, and in the bedroom they
centered the bed on one wall–hey Hind! wait, don't go–in
the kitchen they put a walnut Formica set and covered
the cabinets with contact paper. Add yellow curtains and
accessories, she calls it her–"

"But I don't care about them, I have a rush errand, see
you around, Hershey."

"–her dollhouse is what she calls it, and she commutes
to school four days a week on the subway from Long
Beach–hey! 'Hershey' did you say? My name is–wait, I
really regret–oh I forgot, what are you doing *back*?"

Over the shoulder, headed for Plane's Temporary,
Hind called, "I sort of reversed direction."

It was going to be possible to get Dewey Wood in
sooner than foreseen.

But Oliver Plane had gone. He had left behind three
neat packs of finals.

So Pop's staff had traced Hind to Webster's Dictionary.
Once Hind had thought he would grow out of that name
into the guardian's. What if you were a word? Did you
live up to it or away from it?

Think of Pop presuming he was the one who had
started the Old Woman after Hind. And yet could you say
the now unmentionable Hershey kidnap had begun with
*Hind*? With only a matter or two of unfinished business to
do with Oliver, there was even less point wondering why
the Old Woman cared so.

"Did Joringel use the wonderful flower of the gall-
spitting witch when he went in to turn the nightingale
back into Jorinda?" the guardian asked.

"No," said Child Hind sleepily. "He paid no attention
to her."

Maybe so, but he did dekidnap the other six thousand nine hundred and ninety-nine nightingales caged in and along and up and down one wall in the witch's poisonous air.

Someday, instead of one of the auto culprits exhausting hydrocarbons and nitrogen oxides into part of all the air we have to breathe, you would board a nonair-burning private-person pod, hook in, and go. (The very air turned Hind's words into remote control tricks, and as the guardian said, language is the trap.) On top of one pile of bluebooks was one that began, "Spending hopefully an average of two hundred dollars a year more on the slum child than the middle-class child, our Board of Education still can't teach ghetto kids to read. Our ancestors progressed from drawing pictures, to picture symbols, to writing vis-à-vis an alphabet; but today we regress, the educationalists make the child use the look-say method, develop a sight vocabulary, and thus ape no less than the CHINESE tongue. But when I listen to Ravel's 'Left Hand' there is in a flash no Red China, no Vietnam, no Watts, no Bomb, no palm, everyone is free and evil has been erased from the surface of the earth. Altruism is the purest self-motivated force within the individual: likewise—"

Likewise when, later that week, after Oliver had first been reluctant to talk and then, waving a handful of bluebooks, had cursed Hind for intruding unfamiliar ideas of antiperspective into the normal syllabus—and then a book salesman from Boston chased Hind to shelter in the blond briefcase's office, who welcomed Jack with "Hi, Member, you and I are on the adoptions subcommittee, small *a* small *s* small *c*," and in the Waiting Vestibule a girl who did not look like Sylvia rushed at him in a quiet fit saying, "Let me identify myself, I wrote that paper on the use of 'of' in the titles *Songs of Innocence* and *Songs of Experience*? I signed up for your course in the

Fall but the department says you don't exist, there's no Hind on the faculty, but I signed up, I signed up," Hind put a moratorium on visits to Plane's university's college, for before you knew it you would be getting deterred by endless people there, like a thermal inversion causing air to stand stagnant like a modern hung ceiling, even if language *is* the trap, as the guardian said to curious undergraduates at fine old smaller well-elmed private colleges who came voluntarily to hear him inquire what they thought of themselves, what words they tended to think of themselves in, though after Cassia's words to him that Plane-haunted Christmas of 'forty-four, he was not inquisitive about her.

Here, Oliver's new girlfriend was phoning behind his back to complain to Hind of the Old Woman's calls to college: Ol, she said, wasn't involved in any Old Woman's kidnap, he was just trying to get out from under a raft of finals, and who did Jack Hind think he was? To which Hind, who had merely undertaken to keep Ol from getting plowed under and becoming a sophisticated hobo and was now tramping around (sore feet and all) merely trying to dekidnap Ol by receiving Ol as an organically accidental whole end, replied by requesting the irate girl's phone, he would call the Old Woman and see. As it happened, the radio station, still pleading for new NV tapes, was able to get her address through her phone number.

The bell on the fruit-and-vegetable man's horse-drawn wagon out in the street made Hind think of the bell that he had never heard ring for the fishermen when they came home where May and Sylvia were.

He had forgotten May's birthday.

Young Wade Knott was drawing small crowds of mini-folkers who hung around the kraut deli and got mixed up with the bus-stop people, looking up to his window where hour after hour he rattled and slashed and cracked his traps, stopping only to change a record, it sounded like a triple combo.

Smith Answering relayed messages to please call, from Maddy, Peg, and Dewey, the first two (so the new Smitty confided) so upset you could hear.

You had to give Ol one last open chance to unwrap and let go as accidental organic personal end, as nonmeans.

It was a second-floor loft and Hind had to pay off two ageless colored winos in order to get through to the buzzers and the vestibule door, which in any case was latchless, so you could just walk in, away from the young trenchcoat that was shouting to Hind from the sidewalk, "You opt for private sentimental charity rather than systematic government aid-policy, I know *you*."

Oliver's girl's door had a big square pane backed inside apparently by corrugated paper. The note said, "Museum of the City, The Dive, Chapel." This initial stage of the dekidnap was going on too long.

Subway was better than cab, the museum way uptown.

Oliver was not in the ship room on the first floor of the museum nor, upstairs, in the dark room with the full-size period tableaux embalmed behind their huge picture windows as if by electric light. But then there was Ol in the corner dollhouse room conversing openly behind the case containing the five-floor nineteenth-century brownstone. No.

No, he was talking to Mrs. Rosalind Rosenblum; and a girl, whose airy-limbed fragility in a horizontal-striped orange-and-lime shift was belied by a tough, legs-apart stance and a frown which meant she wanted to go, stared away into the front of the delicate house, its hinged façade swung out. She saw Hind first and, apparently because of his height, murmured (he thought) "Jesus!" Her round dark glasses had reached the end of her long, dainty nose.

Plane came around the glass case and said, "Hi" quietly (as if not to disturb other visitors), then turned to Mrs. Rosenblum and reintroduced her, adding that Hind knew Laura, and said, "Wait a minute, there's something I want to show Barbie in the tableaux," and sauntered out.

Mrs. Rosenblum was coming toward Hind, "You know Laura. I wish I did. God, when she was a tiny baby I could just eat her up in one gulp, *you* know what I mean. So I was visiting the hospital today and thought I'd expose myself to the Museum of the City–I've lived here so long, even if Laura doesn't think where *we* live is the city–and also I had to discuss with Professor Plane; so he said meet with him here. He's so sensible, he says let her keep on in this apartment of hers–I'd hate to tell you where it is, maybe you're familiar with it–she's well known around for wearing gold, she won't take more than twenty dollars a week from my husband, and she just doesn't fit in, I wish I could make her over, but–she's been talking Mexico now–not Europe, Mexico–I can't tell you how upset I am, she'll broaden her perspective she says."

"But I don't *know* her," said Hind–a glance at the doorway, shoes on marble–"know her I mean as a person, no that's not exactly my meaning–but why do you go to Plane? he was making it with her this spring." Light steps down the marble stairs, no waiting for the elevator. What's the play?

"A *plan* with her? making a plan to go to Mexico?" Mrs. R's handsome cheeks had sunk a notch into general but almost imperceptible disorder, she didn't know how to catch up, how to get even, how to move from where she was.

"You hold it, I'll get him." Oliver and the girl were absconding.

"I studied her face all her life and now suddenly what I thought I saw, I don't see any more, the whole face it's different, it isn't even there, that was a sweet kid, and she says, 'What's Hitler to *me*?'–"

A gray-garbed guard pivoted on one scratchy sole to see Hind cross the stairwell. The guardian was saying, "'Abscond' is a verb *in*transitive," and behind him there hung the early-nineteenth-century city's delicate crowd of buildings staked out by shipmasts and steeples.

Outside, Hind saw them neither south nor north nor straight out west among trees or on a slope of granite beyond the wall bounding the park. Maybe they dashed round the block or caught that bus now two blocks down.

He simply could not get back downtown to The Dive, the trees of the Park on his right would not end and would not; he was slowly skating in an oblong of maple or bicycling over an aromatic perspective-expanding glue that might be easier to ride on when it finished drying but *in* that setting process might fix him. You could almost feel the bus's tires print their endless tread on the avenue's summer tar. South, south.

The former owner of The Dive had given up trying to sell the bad antiques that packed the place and had sold out to a gentle, soft-tongued Texan, a retired grad student from Austin. He used the Thirties stuff for his customers, and gave away some chipped and loose late Victorian chairs. No one knew how he made ends meet, he didn't buy a Gaggia pump.

Oliver and Barbie were not in evidence when Hind went out of the noisy midafternoon heat down the steps and through the open door of The Dive, but then, like some inevitable triangulation begun long ago, the three of them (Ol from the His door, Barbie from Hers) were walking toward the same round table on which were pale green mugs and a Danish sliced in half. The low ceiling was sticky with thick mold and cobwebbing, and Ol and Barbie were looking at him with a certain indirection as if there were someone behind him about to do something. Ol was not talking *to* him.

Hind had caught them, Ol said; now what? Barbie was asking if Hind didn't recall their exchange over the phone.

Moving of mugs, another coffee and a Danish, stops and starts and quick silences broken.

A sad girl sitting in a bentwood straight chair on a low platform read loudly enough to be barely inaudible.

"All right. You trailed us ninety-odd blocks down here. I am afraid, Jack. Do you understand that? Afraid. Your old woman phoned the other day to find out what had passed between you and me, and to threaten me that if I didn't stay out of the kidnap I'd be up to my teeth in it, and not to listen to you. Now what do you want?"

"Just to listen to *you*."

"I don't know a thing. I have no evidence of anything."

"Can I sit here a while, till you're finished?"

"Don't"–Oliver got mad and loud, and Barbie shushed him–"don't pull that humble unaggressive act. You want something from me that I don't have. I'm a terrifically ordinary person, granted I didn't know this a while ago. I'm just a normally ignorant, normally lazy teacher who is normally interested in his subject and his normally–"

"*You* don't believe you're ordinary, *that* isn't the Plane I know from the Heights, from school, from the newspaper–remember you did the 'Gasp' column? I could quote some of those rhymes today–"

"You give me the creeps."

"And Byron Bean's caul?"

"The creeps. Yes, I guess I remember and would rather not."

"I'm sorry I subbed for you at the college. It was from

the wrong motives. It was the kidnap, I hate to use the word, I'm trying to escape it, but that's why I'm coming to you now."

"Just go away and do whatever you have to do, but don't take me any further from what *I* want to do. Before I left and went to Mount Mary I was multiangulated between communications—crossfired ten times over from all the administrations at the college, and behind that—University Central. So I went away. I'd have gone whether or not you came along with your self-help self-determination project, you always act with this surpassingly mild intentionalism as if no one could know what you're doing, like a guy who slashes you to bits but always only by condemning your own faults in another guy—and thinks he's the subtlest but you see everything right on his envious surface plain as—"

"But Byron Bean's caul is part of this picture too."

"Yes? I thought you just wanted to listen to me. What, haven't you recovered from Byron's caul?"

"What you didn't know was that I loved Cassia, I was so crazy about her even my guardian sensed it and didn't say what he felt."

"I did know."

Barbie murmured, "Aha, he did know."

"Then you went the limit with her—"

"The old words come back, they're so funny and serious."

"And you advertised it in order to punish me."

"No. You give me too much credit. She said she wasn't a virgin, but she was, and then she got possessive and I thought I was a cruel bastard and I was coming down with a cold that day and I thought you needed a lesson like By-By, and I thought she could use one too, she was always telling other people's secrets, yours and Maddy's.

But next day she came back for more, you know."

A Negro had taken the little platform, though there were only a dozen customers. He was reading what appeared to be a poem: "The two hundred thousand dollars damage in Watts last week is like the loaves and fishes. But like the loaves and fishes before or the loaves and fishes after?"

"You talk as if I'm still thinking of how you played Cassia."

"Great goodfather Hind, at the appropriate time it will be leaked to us that you were undertaking such and such, deviously getting a job for that jig Berry Brown's girl so that he might indirectly gather new hope in order that they might marry in order that they might Fly Delta on a honeymission—well, I knew you were *way* up to something this time."

"You merely used me to get away from the city during the heat."

"If I really wanted to I would have walked out of the trap at college. But Barbie showed me I really didn't want out."

"You've been going with her for all of two weeks."

Oliver and Barbie rose as if in unison, stepped sideways around the table into the aisle, and Ol said, "We've gone from strength"—and she joined him with feigned facetiousness—"to strength."

In the street they tried to outwalk him, ten blocks, fifteen, going south, Negro loaders leaning up against man-sized crates in the middle of the sidewalk waiting, high old loose trucks shaking as they pulled away from their warehouses and tried and failed to beat the light.

"Leave us alone, Jack, we're going home."

But Barbie's was northeast. "You're going the wrong way." No answer. "You mean you're not staying at

Barbie's?"

"I never told my father off. I still visit them in the summer. My mother doesn't get up in the morning so right wing nowadays, and my father gives off a tincture of real human bitterness now, and says, 'Sex is the only body contact sport a man can get fat on, eh boy?' I haven't many close friends, and they're all pretty ordinary."

"Hey," said Barbie, "cut it out."

"I even like my family a bit now. Look, Jack: what will do it, what will get you off our back? We have a kind of date."

The Chapel of Laughter. Not yet. And *it* will come to *you* at the right time.

"Because I didn't know for a long time whether the students needed me except as a punchcard clerk; so I behaved like a kid; but because I know the ground now— even though I do get called 'Hind'—why, I'm getting married, and accepting a raise, and a fine new course in Amero-Europics."

"You slugged Cassia in the drug store."

"She touched me and laughed, reached out and put her cold fingers on my cheek, and I slapped her and the druggist told me to go, said I was worse than the boy scouts horsing around Friday night."

"You may need me yet. In an advisory role."

"*We'll* call *you*."

"That's what people say in this city. The main thing, you're an end in yourself, what I wanted you to be."

"God I'm not. But this is what Barb and I were saying last night, the idea that—" she grabbed hold of his hand and they looked into each other's eyes as if to say soberly, "I'm rooting for you, Sam dear, jointly we will be granted a child."

"—that we" (said Barbie) "are means in the old process,

and as old as...the fields of goldenrod, or you could say the fields of grazing coral deep in the sea—I was going to major in marine zo before I quit."

"It's a way out, Jack," said Ol, and a block south the Santos-Dumont Juxtaposition Division metro rumbled across. "A way out of death." (He addressed Hind as if Hind were an unstable, convalescing child to whom one might say, "Let us reason together.")

"Now," said Ol, "we have unfinished business downtown. Before we really settle. So we have to go."

"Go," said Hind.

Rooting indeed. Roto-rooting.

You were sorry for the rooted, but each was always there in his plot to be needy and helped.

A block down, moving quickly away from him, Barbie looked over her shoulder. She might last another month with Ol, who was stuck more than halfway between shiftlessness and the old curbs of the Heights where he'd sat very calmly trying to fix his right skate clamps so they wouldn't loosen. But more than halfway toward which?

You hoped the dekidnaping of Dewey Wood wouldn't take so much time, you finished what you started, stayed the course (as the Coast Guard officer at FHHC said), you didn't let down in mid-lap or when you had logged a comfortable lead, even if you suspected that you ended with something simple—for instance, Ol and Cassia contained between them the whole truth.

Hind did not listen to the rush voices he fed into his solid-state recorders three and four days running, but only to the playback quality; he saved tape by operating without the capstan sleeve, but the audio interference, especially when he was in the Fieldston lobby, increased. Art Courage had left word with Smith Answering and at

438

the Fieldston, where Hind stayed until Dewey got back from a rainy week at Greenwood Lake; but Art didn't show.

The afternoon before Dewey's return, Hind was back at the undertaker's. The latter was cordial, a body was coming in around suppertime, he had phoned his wife in Branchville, Connecticut, he wouldn't be up.

Hind checked with Maddy, who regretted having been in a state when he spoke to Smitty the other night, he was over it now, he had wanted merely to tell Jack that Corbu had died swimming off Cap-Martin.

At the buzzer, and thinking Dewey had come home early, Hind said good-bye, buzzed the visitor up, and went to his door, which he was now leaving unlocked.

On television a State Department spokesman had announced that we would—and he labeled it only an indirect quotation—we would stay the course in Vietnam.

At his threshold Hind was looked up at by the Old Woman. She moved by him putting down a large paper bag from Bloomingdale's as if she were getting set to neaten up the flat and tell him her day.

As if he was one of her familiars, whom she took brusquely for granted, she said, "What a lot of funny names your friends have! Plane, Ivy, Ash, Beecher, Wood—do you expect anyone to believe those names? Where did Plane's father grow up? Not on the Heights, did he?"

And names made you think. What about the Ken Rosewall racket Julio Loggia had asked for money for a down payment on last week? If you watched through Julio's eyes and words as two Negro boys simply, earnestly ping-clapped an S-D heavy-duty tennis ball against concrete on a soft, shining Sunday morning, the racket became a golden harp. But to hear Julio now had grated on Hind's ears: "I ast you before. What about that racket?" (Two little Puerto Rican girls in the former Sunday scene pass conversing, with not even a glance at the handball court, then suddenly at the corner as their light turns green they disappear into a newspaper-store-soda fountain and almost as quickly emerge biting the unwrapped end of a candy bar.) "Yeah, so I gotta watch two dinges their old lady gives the road sign test at the Motor Vehicle Bureau, they're playing tennis every Sunday like there was a net when all they got is a handball court, where's the net?, instead of a net it's a blank wall."

"Well?" the Old Woman said, and on the table her Bloomingdale bag fell over on its side.

# ii

But Hind couldn't say to the Old Woman "Get out," any more than the guardian could. And unlike that Greek she-monster the Chimera she had neither snake tail nor goat body nor lion head with or without optional flame-vomiter. She was snooping in the bedroom and now gazing into the street. "Where did the child sleep?" (In what was now the study, don't answer her.) "*You* could afford more than this." She was dark against the light window beside the ticking picture.

But now that OP was finished with, Dewey Wood must hold the temporary center (court, field, ice), though *Say it plainly*, says the guardian in the picture's ticklish cycle, to which the Old Woman seems deaf. Well, then, DW's the next and only next stop in the dekidnaping process, and all your guilty power like a giant growth you hope you can hibernate on must go to erasing D's relation with Hershey Laurel, and to receiving Dewey as one simply accidental organic whole end, now indeed watched by Ivy Bowles from her concerned, though sometimes shaded, window across the street from him. And as a means to that end, though according to Ivy's sad news about Dewey the means was supererogatory, Hind took the special one-month FHHC membership afforded former members only.

Hind had not examined the handsome Old Woman's face, but from his first glance at the front door he believed he knew it.

"Don't be backward, don't be shy," she said like a brusquely fond parent. "I know you have questions. Ask."

"But I haven't." Yet did he mean to himself, that he knew the face from the distant encounters since April, or from another deeper, closer time? Hind tried to say silently, "I made a vow to Sylvia–"

"Rubbish. Your wife's your wife. You've more interesting commitments which in my more wicked moments I think are my duty to inspire–"

"I vowed to Sylvia not to use persons as means; therefore, I now seek out"–hide the sequence–"*simply* seek out my friend Oliver: lest he be used as–"

"Look here," the Old Woman came up to him and he couldn't avoid her dark blue eyes and the smell of verbena, and around her long young hands the aftertouch of a half-vellum Lady Ottoline Morrell in, say, the open Gladstone back at Angel Mews, and lemon tea and cream of wheat for breakfast, and gray opaque stockings even in the heat, and down one diagonad in a long corner of time a knobbly little boy spirited away one Saturday afternoon to see a loudly elocuted, pastoral-ramped performance of the children's play *The Bluebird* at the Academy of Music, yet it was not she, it was someone else who had taken kiddy longlegs at the last moment.

"–lest Oliver Plane be used as, well, a mere means to get to the root–" mere gap over which the spark of my former revived kidnap inquiry shoots–

"So," she said, as they scuffed over the sooty hall floor into the living room, "you think the kidnap the *only* occasion to use people as means, and you think too that persons may not be *ends* in the kidnap itself. Your thought was never so crisp as your hapless guardian's. Now *there* was a man who was an end in himself; unlike him I never expected much out of you. By the way, would you like to tell me what you found out about Plane that's germane to the Laurel case?"

Hind could almost hear Hershey Laurel somewhere nearby growing. Where did she know the guardian from? A billow of regret swept Hind to her, as if into a relenting "O.K. I give up—I will serve you—tell me where to go—vouchsafe to me what Hershey Laurel is to you," but then (the intimate child sassing a comfy protectress) "Hershey Laurel isn't *any*thing to *you*." But he said nothing, and resolved to ask Sylvia what made her think they'd encountered the Old Woman long ago. But then he'd be using Sylvia, and he had vowed to return to her as uncumbered, in as straight, plain a way—as a Christy on Sunday skates or a Buddy Bourne singleheartedly meditating a kickoff reverse.

You would not let the Old Woman into your plan any more than you could nag yourself over what those other six thousand nine hundred and ninety-nine nightingales did after their emancipation, any more than you could go to the police garage across the river to redeem the Mount Mary rental Chevy towed away one hot night while the designers in their private chocolate-covered city were working and playing hard.

The Old Woman should be offered refreshment, but he did not like to ask her anything, and she wouldn't want what he had lying around the kitchen, and anyway he could smell her Luden's Eucalyptus coughdrop. Did she know he was moving on to Dewey Wood?

"When you were impersonating Plane, I sent you this right in your department box:" (she read) "'From the old stag whose vale is cut by a fisherman's brook, you learn why Sears was a sucker not to use violence to forestall further demonstrations.' But one of those dreadful students pinched the note before you got it. Otherwise you'd never have been shunted off to Sylvia. I know you knew Beulah Love's sister-in-law came to visit her around the time the Laurel child was stolen. But did you know that one of the Love youngsters who now works in Boston keeps as a keepsake a familiar beanbag even though she is in her mid-twenties? You had a beanbag; you know what a beanbag looks like. You gave up this kidnap once, are you going to do it all over again?"

Hind shook his head pursing his lips as if to say, I can't speak of these things, I'm not involved any more. Where did she get her knowledge from? She seemed to follow only the tracks he had not had time for.

They were getting nowhere. She would speak of the kidnap as if to entice; then edge onto the guardian—ah, his devotion to Gibbon and Burke, and, poor man, his charitable despair over the new political state east or west—then she retreated with a cryptic insult like, "How could *you* know? Isn't it a simple matter of blood?" said with mild resignation; "you're hardly the man he was." So that was it: vengeance upon the helplessly interloping adopted son, vengeance by a relative.

"Definitely," Hind said, "I'm not."

"Ah very well, but how can you not be interested in this information I freely give you? Can you imagine the time and money it costs me to find out about the Laurel search and still maintain my name in Rehabilitation as an inspirer of retarded children? Surely you, as an heir to a considerable competence, acknowledge the obligations of...whatever it is you have."

"I tell you I abandoned the affair you refer to. For I will not treat people as means. Which is the next thing to objects. Gobbling up their talk, using a hint here, a disaster there. And I have some voices to tape. I'm sorry."

"You want me to go." The voice familiar, yes, one he had heard, Sylvia was right. But at this distance the voice

444

turned like the color of a man's blood a hundred feet undersea. A *green* voice?

Hind rudely walked back into the bedroom and stood at the window half-hoping to see the Old Woman materialize on the sidewalk when he knew she was still in the apartment.

A white desert wagon backed slowly in ten feet west of the awning, and Carmen came out of the house to help the trade embalmer with a stretcher on which the new body lay wrapped in brown paper.

Six-thirty was way late for a rush hour jam, but at the window Hind heard still the mass of idling motors, the odd horn maybe from a cross street vainly warning cars in the main avenue north not to get caught in the intersection when the light turned green for the west-bound traffic.

Somewhere you heard a folk hymn harped, horned, and drummed, "Ride around, little dogie, ride around them slow,/ For the fiery and snuffy are rarin' to go." At FHHC you had the air-cooled music, no interfering words.

When Hind turned from the window and the little Dürer ticking finely away, he heard the Old Woman's steps going down. He hadn't heard the door.

He went out to the landing as if hospitably, heard Carmen whistling and looked into the well. The Old Woman's steps halted, and she called up, "You're afraid to question me, afraid I'll say what you don't want to hear. Is it something out of the past? way be*fore* the kidnap?"

"Yes," Hind said quietly, and even that echoed. If he tried to seem honestly frank, maybe she'd lay off.

"Something about your guardian? You afraid I'll remind you of his distinction?" She went on down, and he thought she said something like, "And his one little tragic slip."

Hind shouted, "His distinction I know, having lived with him."

She had seemed, and for months had perhaps tried, to catch his mind in one notion in order to keep it from seeing another notion perilously close to it. Which slip of judgment did she mean?

Time runs out: outward from a Center. Why had Ivy's news not shocked Hind?

Dewey's weight loss and anemia had been diagnosed.

Though he still took Honey Gulden's vitamin E "Bombs," Dewey was now a terminal case, and Ivy was grave as she said the phrase, first giving the abbreviation "t.c."

The Group did not provide cobalt on the standard major medical Dewey had.

But then, looking hard at Dewey, you didn't see anything new.

"You were born to aid others," he said "—which is a great thing, you see." And as Hind turned his face away smiling casually, the squeal of power steering on a sharp getaway from a curb park sent Ivy's shade right up. Dewey chuckled. "That's why you're a giant." He moved his hands from his knees to the chair-arm antimacassars. "Of course, I'm softening you up. It looks like I won't live to develop this brainchild of mine. However, I have every hope that *you* will come to my rescue and flesh out the roots I've hatched. That's why I asked you to come." But Hind had come on his own.

"So much happening today so fast. This morning my fellow Americans in Missouri have been experiencing a generally east-bound weak low-pressure area and you and I will most likely get it tomorrow unless we stay in Greenspan, Junior's, controlled air.

"Now years ago, when my beloved wife, who had a year at Georgia Southwestern College, said one afternoon she wished we could turn back the clock, the seed of this idea came to me, and only now I see that elsewhere in the world scientists are also interested in this question—I may as well let the cat out of the bag to you—this question of *time*." So Dewey Wood was doing original work on time. More to come.

"These fellows could not have taken over any of my own speculations, for as yet I haven't ever written up any of them; and after all you know very well people do approach ideas independently. For example, you and I arrived independently at a knowledge of the Connecticut kidnap, independently via the media, as I recall, and the case isn't broken *yet*."

"But no," said Hind, "no, that's something else. However, you were saying, about turning back the clock?"

"When the man in the subway change booth quoted his son's schoolbook, 'You can't *choose* how you save,' it was then I conceived that you do something only insofar as there's someone to do it for. The phil teacher at the library course puts a saying like that on the board like a theme to be aware of, he says. When the subway change booth man said that an effective acts only according to the powers of that which receives its action, I saw that he and I—on different tracks, or at different levels—what?—"

What must have been Hind's look stopped the old man: the guardian's untenanted legs were leaping from cell to cell of a deep memory bank and across a slippery stream as he approached slowly shooting at you such elderleery queries about infectious Babelingual airs to mask yourself from, that you hardly knew him and you tried to explain charitably to him that your electives were your own, whether History and Method of Science (for the large view deproblemized delabbed) or, say, a shirt-sleeved hunk of real live Research, to wit, a one-term inquest into the Physio-Thermonics of the Voodoo Lily's Sex Sequence.

"I said something? Jack? you have stomach distress, Jack? You're sort of green, I mean under your tan you're white. The way I looked before I joined Fieldston years ago. The sun and the semiclassical music, and the exercise, took me right back to my childhood I felt so good again."

"No. Go on."

"No, you're holding something back. Don't ever do that. Is it something I said?"

"The subway change booth man, go on." Where did the old boy's nerve come from? Against the backdrop of his immediate future, his grotesque courage winked and blinked like a neon ad flood-fed with polluted voltage. At least he did not air his terminal symptoms. So long as DW did the talking, all these verbal imprecisions were merely part of life observed.

"Would you like an apple or a chocolate-covered coconut bar?"

"I wouldn't." Your smile swelled your own upper cheeks into your view.

"I saw that he and I had inevitably found the same *terminus ad quem*, as our phil teacher puts it, and neither of us with any formal higher education until recently, he's in the change booth under Park Avenue there for years, and I put in my time laboring in my own chosen line of work. *Why* we should have arrived at almost the same conclusion I leave to an observer of the human heart like yourself. But the idea was seminal, it gave me the clue to what indeed I had all my life secretly weighed—one day my wife said she wanted to turn the clock back, those were her words—and the secret was kept even from myself—somewhere inside, the idea in captivity was growing unbeknownst. Even while I answered Mr. Herder's phone and inspected old Kelvinators and the scratched paint in the elevators in apartment buildings he owned, and tried to explain to tenants that Mr. Herder wanted only their comfort, that there was, let's say, no need at the particular time to replace the defective housephone or install an outside buzzer program, there was so little danger in that neighborhood—even through all this useful but not very philosophical day labor, my mind that had reached out and nailed the idea that lay unfelt in my beloved wife's conversation let that idea grow in the creative captivity of—"

"Your wife came from...?"—accidental whole end—

"A gentle town in Georgia named, I believe, Americus. But when her father lost his job at the basket company they moved to Atlanta, where her father often wrote letters to the press urging the completion of the three famous figures on the north face of nearby Stone Mountain. Just could not help writing to the editors. Drawn to the media, you might say. Sucked right in. Her parents, Jack, urged her not to adopt a child, and I concurred in her wish not to disturb them. Have kids, you have something to talk to the wife about, says Phil at Neighborhood Drug, but my wife and I never had that trouble. Jack, the idea I am coming to makes me sometimes think that perhaps I still *have* a wife, perhaps our wedlock is preserved inviolate."

How did Dewey go about this bequest so cheerily when, standing behind him, between the bad Dürer reproduction and the back of his neck, Nature's master plot beamed neutrally in ever-lessening yet slowing sweeps toward that old last day when his heart's FM would jam beyond fixing, the harvest of goals would end and the old team field disappear like the TV picture which, untouched in scale or brightness, races to collapse its length and breadth when your potent thumb and forefinger snap the set off in mid-ad.

"In what?"

"Inviolate."

Dewey was adopting an alarming little "eh," a cocky punctuation he punched out for emphasis.

"My idea's this. You do a front flip off the Fieldston springboard (eh?), you go one way (eh?), you enter the water, slow down (*you flatten* on the bottom, I seen you), and you come up. Yes, provided you don't get chopped by Min the Model backstroking the width of the pool, you surface (eh?) *older* than when you *dove* (eh?), and by the same token you can't very well reverse the dive and suck yourself back reverse-wise onto your board like you were going forth and back between alternate spots on a green beret trampoline (eh?), it's one-way." Dewey shook a finger. "And you never get it back. When I first conceived the seed of this idea, my dear wife used to sit watching me lick my mouth thinking, and she wouldn't crackle the pages of her *Daily Mirror* or reach under there for a *Geographic*, or a Sears catalogue (eh?), she had to keep quiet."

But the guardian always came back. Thea and, by significant juxtaposition, Bee Bee Barker are due on the eleven-five for a long weekend, and the guardian has tramped down there into blueberry and higher thickets beyond the stream, which from the drive you can see only at the stream's one wide point at either end of which it narrows sharply to lose itself in thicket and scrub. You are standing by Pliny, whose faded convertible top, threadbare at the ribs, will need patching near the plastic back-window. But its flowing fenders are waxed to a deep green shine and the prow-stem Lincoln Zephyr grille is rust-free, though from year to year the guardian prefers not to see if the undercoat does what it's supposed to. (*You* know that small rough patches have dropped off.) Then suddenly it's eleven, and there is a blob of platinum glare bemusing you where the left fender's arc passes down forward. You yell down toward the high bed of thicket and glance further to the far hazy break that signals the sea—"e*leven o'clock* and *let's go*" and again and again: and for a long moment you believe that he, he, has grown into that sea of—"No, Jack, not 'sea'—great Scott, what has all that thicket to do with sea, call it what it is"—that sea of vegetation, which is therefore even more articulate now that it has come into possession of its human owner, but articulate or not it looks back at you under the silent sun and says to the child in you, You will never die, just as you were never or never exactly born. The sight of this expanse of growth expands across your mind, then exhales itself smaller, than expands again, larger here in Dewey Wood's humid parlor than it even was that hot summer day toward which Bee Bee and Thea's train rolled certainly. And as the shallow narrow valley looks back at you as if to divulge something even better, there's the khaki shirt bobbing and there the blue jeans and like a madman the guardian trying to run free of the thickets and then suddenly free with, Buddy Bourne would say, a big hole in front of him, and as if sprung forward by the branches that had held him he was now quick-stepping over the stream careful to touch every last flat rock. But the strange thing was his apparently instant appearance at your side out of breath. "Don't waste time, Jack. Don't follow my example." Falling sideways into the driver's seat he said this again, and added, "And for blueberry honey at that." And then as they drove up the first rise of the pale, stony road and they heard the familiar hammering under them, the guardian was complaining again that the Shell man couldn't even screw the brackets up tight enough on the (now two-month-old) muffler-tailpipe assembly, there was no end of worries, little ones, you couldn't depend on workmanship and were constantly distracted from your real work.

Dewey said, "And I said to her, 'Maybe somewhere a clock is turning backward, you talking about turning the clock back,' and she, she was like a child she blinked those gray eyes at me and says wonderingly, '*No!*' It is lonely, Jack, having these things inside you, nobody at home to tell them to (eh?). All right, then, your dive's like a three-year-old battery on a fifteen-degree morning, oh yes you'll get juice from the wrecker if and when he comes, but tomorrow you find your old coils didn't hold that juice. *New* battery maybe dead as a handful of wet cement first thing on a subzero morning; but get juice from the wrecker those coils *will* hold it (eh?). What am I talking about? I'll tell you: a oneway process, like an H-bomb, like our earth aging, like our universe growing."

Dewey was apparently himself out of juice or for a second daunted by his thoughts.

Hind took leave of him, arguing Dewey's condition but also admitting he had other things he wanted to do, to which Dewey replied maybe Hind was getting selfish in his old age.

Waiting a moment on Dewey's landing, Hind heard the TV come on with the hourly forecast. DW had a vision of All-America farmed gently and epicentrically by a complete set of coordinated weathers.

At home Hind was at loose ends. This stage of the dekidnap seemed indiscriminate and not inevitable. You could be doing push-ups on the cobalt carpets of FHHC just as well as

Waiting for the Old Woman to arrive unannounced, you soon heard her feet making the marble steps echo, doubtless welcoming the cool stone.

Were her eyes preoccupied—or really dull? Her shoulders were not straight. He wondered if he had a tea bag and if the milk in the small pitcher in the icebox was sour.

She seemed to ignore the tone of their last talk. "May I?" She sat.

"Ow Wow Ow Wow" down the southbound avenue, then fire engines grating like bulldozers.

"My Bloomingdale bag from the other day?"

"It's in the bedroom closet." Hind turned to go.

"Why do you go back to Plane? He can't help." But then the Old Woman shook her head as if to clear it. "But wait—you're off the kidnap entirely? Ah—" she made one abrupt laugh-sound, stretched her legs out straight—"I followed you and followed you in the old days, you were easier to inspire then, and indeed then I had nothing directly to do with you; and then your guardian died without telling you he knew of the kidnap, but he did. And I could have told him you would waste your quite ordinary powers on something like the kidnap or, as it has also turned out in your 'Naked Voice,' something crass in the media. I could have told him. But I spoke once years ago and that was enough. What could you know of the suffering he went through in his private and public life?"

"What public life did he have? there was the college advisory service."

"In his private life pursued by guilt, in his public life seeing all avenues of activity soiled by the very social principles he tried masochistically to espouse."

"I didn't find him quite like that."

"You are difficult to inspire."

"I loved him, he was a father."

"*You loved*—a man you couldn't begin to equal, much less understand? who could have done anything on God's green earth he wished to do, and who made indeed in his subtle way a rather remarkable life for himself. And who would have been the last to warn you you ought to finish what you start."

"But he did often say that to me. And as for this unspeakable case, I decided that I *didn't* start it, and so needn't finish it."

"Hershey Laurel is—there you are again, the *names* you populate your life with, your heartfelt beneficiaries—Hershey Laurel is *in this city*. And you haven't the imagination to wrap up the case."

"I told you I won't go on using people."

"Your humanitarian charity, if you will pardon me, stinks."

"Charity! But," Hind found himself saying, "I always expect a return."

"Don't go back to Plane, he cannot help."

Hind wanted to ask her why she did not inform the authorities where young Laurel was, what her sources were, and how they could be made final use of—assuming the police thought of Hershey any more.

But instead—for she showed signs of leaving—he hoped she would leave, disappear into one of the green-and-silver avenue buses with their advertising spaces rising lighted from roof edges like decoration, and he said as she went to the bedroom, "I will, I really will, finish with Plane. Give me time." This had been in his tone, though not exactly what he had said, to Sylvia's father when the old man had caught him on the phone at last, "Give me time," and the angry old man guessed wrongly that Hind had no intention of returning to Syl.

The Old Woman, yes, she was out of the house, and again he had not heard the door open and close.

Hind missed the camphor and eucalyptus of the gym, the yellow-green false promise of indeterminacy which the pool offered you before you sauntered out of the massage rooms onto the cold tile. He missed even the cigar-chewing lifeguard's invisible transistor.

454

Oliver Plane phoned to ask what Hind had done with the Self-Contained Meditation of a pupil named Max May. Sylvia was able to leave word with Smith Answering that she had the list of calls SA had sent to the island and she had now brought down to the city.

While Carmen watched a TV glass on which a small boy in a bow tie skated and skied over a kitchen floor new-waxed to a well-known glo, Rain's granddad told Hind that what hurt more than any other thing done by the new management of the redesigned (national chain) bar on the corner which he had run for thirty years until the rent went up last year to six-fifty a month—hurt even more than the trashy clientele—was that on Saturday night now coat and tie were compulsory.

Outside the Fieldston a cat had got up under a taxi fender on the tire and was sparring at hands that were trying to get it off.

Hind had seen the amorous designers out on the street looking strangely smaller than when Hind from his fourth-floor lookout watched them in the second-floor studio room; and now, approaching the Fieldston, he had seen Honey Gulden in Salad City looking so mild in his gray slim-brim staring at a mirror waiting for his lunch that you would never have placed him in any of the health club's key administrative posts.

Hind wanted to black out the kidnap but felt that nearly everyone he met had eager information. The old Cassia game was reversed: he was "it," but everyone was after *him*. You tried now not even to look for Dewey. Greenspan, Junior, explained that the black spot on his forehead had been a tiny growth now removed; he was afraid it might have been skin cancer. Why on earth was Dewey doing such strenuous waist turns? When Art Courage walked past the Juicearama on his hands, Hind had to leave; Art was saying, "Make love, don't talk war."

Back home he phoned Sylvia and at the other end of the line heard, "Smith Answering." When he asked, "Sylvia?" the unfamiliar "tock" sound of a hang-up was followed by nothing: but then that nothing seemed to have been a mistake (rather than evidence that Sylvia was on) for the disconnection drone flowed in. No one but no one hung up on *Hind*, needy or not. Mrs. Loggia phoned to ask if Hind had seen Julio and to say that luckily the area redevelopment had been stalled, so their block wasn't coming down yet.

When the Old Woman turned up around teatime as if she had never gone off on a bus but merely slipped back into an FHHC-type mirror-surface system or had merely had a rest on the first floor, she asked what Hind had been doing for the past four days. He could not believe it had been so long. She was tossing Laurel data into the air. "One" could see the boy from a distance, if "one" preferred to plot one's plan slowly and safely. He would probably be playing Stolen Base at the beach Saturday, weather permitting. The OW was tired, too tired to answer questions she knew he had—like how did she know so much.

She seemed even too weary to ask for a drink; in her elegant weariness she seemed to drop the Laurel case, and think only of the beloved guardian. "An affinity between us, you know; the way he would arm one in to dinner in the old days..."

Precisely because in certain dreams the guardian was telling Hind point by point that (and how and where) he was his adopted son, Jack would think—in the middle of diving practice, or on the early morning local express under the river taking the paste-work dummies to the printer's on Twenty-third Street the night after putting the school paper to bed, and then even at the instant of confronting rather proudly the brusque stocky printer in his long fifth-floor shop seemingly filled only with the unresonant cross-cut slug slug of the linotype—Hind would think that the guardian had never actually spoken of the adoption in so many words. This strange possibility—like a dive so well sprung you thought you lay out indefinitely in the higher volumes near the wire-basketed roof-lights—turned you down into reaches and reaches of special kinship accumulated under the knowledge of the guardian's foster-paternity. That inviolable understanding grew up as a tiny shell imperceptibly forms, or a great impossible suspicion, or, one day on your beach (after you and he laughed at the waving Portagee Chief offshore there in his Coast Guard picketboat he called "waterborne logistic craft") a sympathy made of need and habit you are surprised to see alive in the vectors of your limbs as the almost naked guardian straightens up to show you a palmful of ("very common, *Nucula Proxima*") Near Nut Shells and lowering his voice as if to the proper scale touches with his little finger the one of these which has still on it what you seldom get in sea-wrack specimens, and your strong, long, tan legs seem to say, "*He* is as he is, partly because of *you*," and you look past him down the beach.

"What," continued the Old Woman, "have *you* ever done for his memory?"

"I thought of writing his life."

She had broken in with an almost vulgarly disparaging sound, a sinal groan. Then, "and his gentle wish to change others, to use his position, but my goodness, the change in *him* after he met your mother. She took possession of his senses perhaps; and when she was dead her memory reduced his powers, though he always had charm, heaven knows. He could playfully call a girl a snob and it gave you gooseflesh. But later it wasn't women any more, though of course there was that Thea Dover who monopolized him."

"That's nonsense about Thea."

"But it was mainly men friends and instead of the old tall-tale-telling magic some solemn male force of mind I confess I got pretty sick and tired of—even comparing ailments, oh *his* enlarged heart from all that track at Eaglebrook and Deerfield and Harvard, versus *Grimes'* unspeakable skin problems that suddenly one year cleared up. Oh, you should have heard years before that, the stories your guardian *told me*—elegant, divine imaginations that took you far far away from anything, till you found yourself years later alive and relaxed in that leather chair he'd sat you down in a moment before in the Harvard Club and hazel eyes flickering uncertainly at you—you'd have seen if he'd ever told the story about— it was as gossamer as one of those silly things Mummy made us memorize, 'Montana the Shepherd His Love to Aminta'—yet different, dark. You should have heard...oh, of the adulterous lovers turned into hawthorne bushes far from each other and so hybrid the girl's husband could not even find them to cut them down and avenge himself, till one day—" the Old Woman, perspiring along her upper lip where there was faintly dark down, had lost Hind, had gone away into a grove where she need not avenge herself on him by inspiring him, and where it was possible to re- enact the guardian, all undisturbed even by the strangely near and low-flying racket of the helicopter that drowned her words and then for a few seconds did not pass but stuck overhead as if taking exception to some motion along Hind's street, then passed away toward the west river—"he was a polytheist, you know, and found holy virtues in tree bark and beach flowers and in stones, once I caught him with an ordinary, garden-variety rock in his hand on the old patio half naked saying to it, 'Tell me what do you think of me,' though I could not know if he had caught me watching him, and he turned as if seeming not to be startled and said, 'This chunk of feldspathic stone'"—how did the Old Woman remember *that*?—"'is in possession of my hand'—Well, this wasn't exactly charm, it was eccentricity of a dangerous sort, which he was guilty of in his tantalizing use of women, too. The only other time I caught him talking to himself was in the later period when he was changed, he was alone in the Heights flat and I made no sound on the hall carpet, he was alone reading very loud, this was in the later stage when he had gone very theoretical, atheistic (not that he was ever much of an Episcopalian), and much on the phone to some iconographer in Chicago and to Grimes in Cambridge on scholarly topics, I couldn't deal with him, he was a different chap, full of sententious conclusions about the honor and finality of marriage vows. Which I suppose was how he put Thea Dover off, and it was shortly after you came onto the scene, where was I?, he was throwing his hand about so wildly he must have thought he *was* Burke and reading how Louis *pitied* his subjects for turning into brutes and just before he saw me out of the corner of his eye, he was reading about Marie Antoinette when she was dauphiness, how does it go?, I suppose you wouldn't know, with your head full of babbling naked voices—no, *there* it is—'I saw her just above the horizon, decorating and cheering the elevated sphere...glittering like the morning star...I thought ten thousand swords must have leaped from their scabbards to avenge even a look that threatened her with insult.' Then he saw me and clapped his calf-bound volume shut and said so hurriedly I thought he was pressed for time, 'But-the-age-of-chivalry-is-gone.-That-of-sophisters,-economists,-and-calculators-has-succeeded....'"

Gymnastics, Gibbon, theories of death, the treasure hunt—most of this Hind knew already. Yet for the first time since the April clue, and exactly because, there so magically still in Sylvia's chair, the OW had been ruminatively flaunting facts which Hind already in effect knew, he was sorry for her, and he could almost bring himself to ask those Laurel questions. Almost.

"It was very well to preserve his fondness for another," she said, "but adopting a child—I told him one night—was going a bit far—unless he took a wife to assume some of the crucial responsibilities, like keeping you off chocolates."

"What relation are you?"

"I am a cousin. Not a first cousin."

Hind wanted to end the puzzle between them by letting her have it: "Why don't you want to allow me to be even a man who knew him well? Do I have to prove my possession? by telling you his habits, talents, and hopes? by acting out—by assuming his face, his voice? Go away!" (Getouta here, said Buddy Bourne when he wanted to get out of having to debate a point—getouta here, when Hind tried to explain about the reverse and about Byron; but not getouta here when, embarrassingly to both Bourne and Jack, the guardian buttonholed him at the Garden to find out why he had it in for Jack.) Instead, now, as the guardian would have done, Hind protracted the established form of the meeting with the Old Woman, was polite if not gracious, offered her his full face if not a cup of tea or an aspirin, concealed his relief that for the moment she wasn't offering him some new variety of Laurel information.

"You haven't acted upon the inhibited sentiments expressed in the letter that got sent to all the freshmen in your college class."

"It was first of all a letter sent to *me*."

"Yet originally written when you were a baby palpably unfit to receive a letter." The Old Woman smiled meanly, and Hind again had the dragging sensation that she tried to fill his eyes and ears with one idea in order to keep him from seeing a second perilously close to it. Her long arms extended, she had placed her young-looking hands so the fingertips touched the top of her knees. There was a strain of angry play in her way of moving the talk, so that as he felt he was finishing one line of disagreement she'd begin a kindred line. Did Hind let her adjust the conversation because he pitied her (as you pity a dangerous person whose menace is less oppressive than its causes alluring)? or because he wouldn't mind if foreign powers (*mutatis mutandis*) helped him finish or even only restore himself (honorably) to the warm and normal air Sylvia breathed?

But what if the Old Woman does not come back again?

"But Jack," Dewey simply continued from last time, "I have reason to think this one-way process is at most a mere half of your over-all story. Here's why. You look at your tongue in the bathroom mirror, watch your waist at the Fieldston, take a gander at your left hand with your thumb branching to the right: and then by God you bring your right hand up beside the left and what do you see in all these? Better still, Heather Fordham (while Winky's knocking them back around the block) knocks a cue ball up and back for break, and if she taps it right what do you see? You look at a twig in cross-section; even if you can see a difference in the Fall cells versus the Spring cells, that annual boundary which their difference forms is an annular mark, a ring, like the other cambium rings, and it and what's inside it make a—what word comes next, Jack? I'll tell you: *symmetry!* Yes, it's in your tongue, your pair of hands, your cue ball like atomic particles bouncing one way or the reverse, your concentric vegetational growth. And symmetry, my lad, is not a one-way process."

Hind was up again, he would visit Dewey again tomorrow, he didn't want Dewey tired; furthermore it looked as if Dewey would last.

"But Dewey, when did you see this? You didn't just *think* this up, did you?"

"Aha, Jack, you are the captive of your preconception just like my pal Skinny Hirsch that I visit each and every summer at the lake who says I'm out of my bird. Of course he's a nature lover and thinks a city person don't know any more than a public library course, 'course I came originally from upstate."

But when, intending to end the interviews with Dewey, Hind looked for him early next morning and three mornings after that—for they were the simplest times, when DW was fresh, perhaps least downcast by what Ivy had referred to as D's terminal illness—Hind couldn't find him.

The little girl Rain was outside Buck's shop watching three boys dash and dance across the avenue in mid-block challenging cars whose acceleration would rise against Wade Knott's combo blasts, then fall away north.

Captain Kidd, who never looked *at* Jack but merely straight ahead into his collarbone, said Dewey was working out.

Though Hind couldn't believe this, he phoned the Fieldston and was told by Greenspan, Junior, (against a sedative backdrop of endless strings and oiled horns) that Honey Gulden put Dewey on a new alternate drill. Was this Dewey's way of ignoring the death sentence? Hind did not ask.

And did not betray his new knowledge when he did catch Dewey at home one bright dry breezy morning when both Grimes *and* the Old Woman had threatened to come by.

And Dewey, as if ignorant of the gap in the sequence of his expository bequest to Hind went right on, first while dusting window sills, later in his chair.

"But a public library course gives you perspective. You see how much others don't know, who don't take the course but live just day by day like Josef—he's experimenting with TV color adjustment and living for the day—which came last month—when I break down and purchase one of his reconditioned black-and-white models. Or Gold who really doesn't like the remote-control finder-track that all the finished work's hung on now so you only touch a button and hold it till your coat and pants come rolling up. Installed it for his son who he's proud of but now Gold isn't so happy in the shop and all the time he's across the street in Josef's drinking coffee."

But Dewey had his work; oh yes, he said, had his work ever since his dear wife one Saturday as she was just going over to Neighborhood Drug said that about turning back the clock—and though she'd say she was only going round for some Anacin she stayed two to three hours, which was lucky that Saturday for he had wanted to dwell upon what she said—he all these years had been staring at the "implicit possibilities, Jack, the way you stare into your bookcase that is so familiar you can't spot the one book you want. *The Yearling* or James Truslow Adams, name it. But as my wife would say very quietly now and again when the topic of church came up, 'I know that *my* Redeemer liveth,' (eh?). This was what I too felt about my idea's implicit possibilities."

The Old Woman was proceeding as if her last series of remarks had not been broken by her departure and return: "What were you able to know or feel about a letter like that? Your father, years dead and writing when you were barely able to make a consonant sound, speaks of the long dream of changing, of preparing one's life, of finding a ground on which to act so there shall be no waste."

"I know the letter by heart," said Hind.

"The Dover woman—" the sentence stopped, and the kidnap evidence abruptly recommenced. How, asked the OW, was it possible for a child to be taken, hidden, raised, moved—didn't Hind care that in an open society like ours such muted atrocities…? (*Like* ours? had Hershey then been picked up from another, perhaps parallel, society?)

Hind recalled the famous letter, his mysterious sense of it, and Thea's surprisingly unreasonable view of where it came from. But to get going on it with the OW would violate the guardian's axiom voiced repeatedly during the lazy summers, yes the summer Jack turned twelve and was being taught real writing, taught toughly to name, show, examine: "Do not end in such a way that you seem to open up a whole new beginning."

Jack had known of the letter, had put it out of his mind long before he went to college and the guardian raised the issue first with him and then with the dean. The dean believed indeed that the letter from Hind's late father would "inspire the average freshman to better work habits whether he be an aspiring scholar or–" and it was printed nicely and disseminated to Hind's class the third month of first semester:

> Dear ————,
>
> Your mother and I have talked of how you might turn out. And unbeknownst to myself a great sadness came over me that indeed I had made wrong turnings all the way–school, college, university, work, family, etc. And though your mother firmly dissented from my view, I state it here with a certain melancholy confidence: not merely that I did not work hard enough at college and later, not merely that I did not even approach what I was determined to approach, but that I did not become myself. I share with you what follows, in hopes that in the end you may be better pleased with your achievements than I with mine.
>
> What you study matters not, nor whether in the end after college you choose the life active or

the life contemplative. One envisions the grim, pivotal mysteries of the managerial giant in the public world, better still the reined energies of the statesman-orator. I, for one, can imagine—and wish I had taken for myself—a life of persistent inquiry. After thirty years of studying, say, visible nature or its derivatives—rocks, insects, the deflection of the winds, the impact of the Murex snail on declining Rome and the early Church, or even the bachelor tree ceremonies practiced in India; or of studying, if you will, the logics of language—yes, after thirty such years it would be enough simply to contain in my self knowledges worth saving. No need to prove or claim—merely to possess in oneself and to be possessed by, the few knowledges one's small originality desires. To settle for such a possession is not to be a coward, but a shepherd.

In your self, if you can see deep enough, you may find the choices that are properly yours. And you will find that in order to be an individual you will need old models. Yet do not follow Authority simply for one of its regimental styles that look so easy to adopt. Your own distinction will be partly in the freedom you appropriate for yourself: and the best kind is freedom of the mind, which if you seek it with the tenacity of a bulldog and the grace of a gentleman will make you yourself. Indeed, in this freedom where you will find your own style of action and of words, you will find the force with which to contemplate this very Authority of which I speak, the great scientist-philosophers, the ethical teachers, the epic narrators, the historians—to see past the easy evidences into the difficult and spreading forms of truth, as a lexicographer never assumes his etymology to be the answer till he explore other implicitly possible derivations.

Make your choice: let it be a choice to work hard, yet not slavishly: to work toward the end of knowing your self as it can best become. And having chosen, do not look behind you, but be in yourself the past present.

Turn words into deeds.

As Jack stood in the town P.O. quickly seeing where guardian or dean had deleted the "lower orders" breaking loose from the "sheep fold of natural authority and legitimate subordination" as well as references to the lost City of Is, its meaning not only to Celtic studies but metaphorically to the recapture of the past—a fellow frosh for whom this letter was the morning's whole post murmured amiably at Hind's elbow, "same old dog shit."

The Old Woman said, "Whenever I see Plane I don't see you with him, so you may be finished with him and haven't told me."

Did she need Hind because she was by a technicality disqualified or divorced from action in the affair and could act only in him?

You wanted to honor her knowledge of the guardian—the cold beans, the chocolate prohibition (Jack was allowed only a small ration Sunday), the rather too-narrowly-based college advisory service, the little essay on Dürer—she knew so much: yet she didn't want you to honor her knowledge, she wanted only that you convey her caprices to the places she wished them conveyed. And if Hershey Laurel would as she promised be attending the Sunday night hockey games at the Garden this coming season, still Ashley Sill was in trouble, Dewey Wood unfinished.

On the way downstairs into the mid-town heat, she was calling Grimes an upstart pansy who if he hadn't worked like a black would in any case have given his right arm to go through Harvard, hanging around in the very old days, saying, "*Happiness* is the best organizer of one's time, Fossy."

"Exactly what relation are you?" Hind again asked the OW looking into the stairwell.

She stopped and looked up so wearily she might have been going *up*stairs. "Cousin by marriage."

"Ah."

"Arranged marriage, at that, and not such a bad idea, when you look around."

When did Dewey begin speaking again?

"And then it came to me," said he, "like Gold's innovation he's forever harping on."

Life trembling in the vicinity of a familiar thought which is roused blearily by a familiar-seeming occasion: Grimes sipping something green and reading a book and humming (as if its deathless power could be rendered out of the page's silence into the minor interstices of human air only in protomusical code); and Thea and the guardian arguing over a passage in *Measure for Measure* they were reading aloud from the same volume: and the tremor calmed by the invasion of another vicinity, a second familiar thought so risky it conveniently occluded the first, namely that the beloved guardian...well, he tended to be a bit dogmatic at times.

"So says I, says I," Dewey went on, "what if these one-way processes are just untrue facts, get me? You could say a round-trip to Greenwood Lake last month is two one-ways, now couldn't you? (Don't answer.) You could. And my idea is this, and my dear Iris would be proud, and it would even tie in with her own faith, y'know (eh?): *this*, that the whole shebang *is* symmetrical, and best of all, so is—look out, Jacko—*time*. This is my key contribution, in terms of my own work in terms of time, and it is this that I'm hoping you'll work out the details. For I have so much else to accomplish"—he winked—"ere my days are numbered. *This*: that time can be symmetrical only by being reversible. (Steady, Jack, it's a new concept, as wild as a Greek hillside and just as simple.) In this other, reversed time, what's happening? Maybe you can guess, but I'll tell you.

"Time goes the *other* way as *well!*

"But where? Where does it? Steady now: time goes the other way: in a universe, but another universe, a second one (eh?), and a second one that is right here around us and even–look out, Jackie–passing through us: but Jack, in our city of material miracles, and in our nation where our weather in the Great Plains is a matter of concern to *me* thanks to the thoughtful TV programing I have and thanks in turn to my neighborhood dealer–in this world we're insulated (eh?) from this other realm, aren't we?, like we'd been abducted and held *incommunicado*. And *yet*: it's congruent with our own universe yet without ever shaking us up or smothering us or cutting off the light like an eclipse, get me (eh?)? A few of us, to be sure, have intimations of this other sequence, but only a few."

Dewey was so unnaturally alive, his thesis so hopeless at its root and so stolen in its prospects, that Hind found sitting with the poor old boy a pain.

This was harder than a double split-session at the FHHC; and avoiding the Old Woman or what she called up; and now dreading Grimes and the uncharitable animus he roused–and pressing guiltily through the dekidnap toward a luminal surface afloat somewhere ahead, a last light emanating from a free life with Sylvia and May. But next thing you'll find yourself airily asking–as if He were secure in his fame, "Whatever became of Hershey Laurel?"

Honey's random body count at FHHC when Hind arrived was thirty-three. A voiceless "September Song" accompanied two naked businessmen, one English: "Don't miss the Astrodome, even if you got only half a day–take the client there." "I hear it's rather splendid. Leave it to you lot to do away with the seasons." "Yeah, well baseball on that grass isn't the same old summer madness, but what Judge Hofheinz created has got to be a miracle in terms of–"

Crossing the north-south avenue at four Hind stopped to aid Rain's granddad and his "walker." But he glared ahead and told Hind not to get run down himself, what the hell did he think he could do, fly him across? Somewhere from a window the Beatles were calling, "Help!"

On afternoon TV young wives told a sympathetically clapping studio what bugged them about their spouses (spice?); and one towering brunette told what positions her "old woman" of a "hubby-poop" slept in.

In the night the wall picture ticked Hind awake, and at the window he saw–it must have been past two, his clock had stopped–lowering his eye to the window sill he could just see through the top panes of a tall second-floor window across the way into the rear studio, where an actual shot was being taken. There was the silver-rimmed tube-end the photographer looked through; and the staging his camera box sat on; and below, under light, the end of a king-size bed with two separated feet under the blanket; the feet came together under the blanket, then together moved to one side; a flash then seemed to widen the scene though the frame of the top panes permitted Hind no true widening. A diagonal strut, part of a stepladder. A photographer out of sight.

Returning to sleep, Hind heard a cozy transistor quote a famous prospect as saying that in terms of multilevel aims the Vietnam tail was wagging the global dog; then dimly the weather forecast moving off toward the north-south avenue. Hind reached for someone else in the bed, and he saw the still surface of the dark pool at FHHC.

In the morning he appeared at Dewey's door promptly at eight-thirty; Dewey wasn't expecting him.

"There it is: congruent yet insulated—where time runs the reverse of what it is here. Ah then. The individuals *there* run timewise in the exact same polarization (eh?), but they run from death to birth instead of our way of doing things. For them, life ends at birth (eh?). Independent of my own findings, some fellow in Europe, I think, found an atomic particle, a whole set of them I guess, called an Oad (eh?), that some of them live lots longer than they're meant to, so he thinks these might have done a flip (eh?); but—watch out, now, Jack—I arrived at *my* view by unaided reason, Jack, unaided reason, that's an extreme point you got to make in your implementation. Now what's the implicit possibilities here? Twofold, communication, transportation: *a*, these people in the other universe moving opposite to us go from what is our future toward what is our past, so they may be able to see what's going to happen to us, and if it's anything we wouldn't like, maybe we can sidestep it, think of the amelioration there. And second, transportation: it figures that if you can get flipped into the other stream, if you can slip, say, off your train and cross over to catch the car going the other way—bringing it just down to your daily experience—why then you get a new lease on life (eh?)—and not only the Oads: what if a man disappears, leaves his wife and kids, the police do all they *can* do but have to declare him missing, maybe he flipped over into the other (eh?)—could happen to anybody—maybe he'd take his family *with* him. Why, years later, after you've been back toward birth (eh?), you get off and go over to the old universe that you're in now. The big thing in implementing this idea is how to flip out and over. Better than calisthenics and soy oil any day, and at *their* health clubs the symphony begins at the end and goes straight to the beginning. The setup is like tumescent-detumescent, tumescent-detumescent. I told Iris and she promised not to tell any of her chums at Phil and Phyllis's. She looked it up in the dictionary, 'tumescent,' 'detumescent.'"

Poor guy? Well, this was better than physical fitness, better than dear Charlotte's theochronic doctrines of Return taught at the Secret Temples on Willoughby Street, folding chairs and black velvet surplices and privately printed testaments (with appendix outline guide) written by the woman architect who had been literally running what looked like, but was not, the same Alsatian round the Heights for thirty years.

"*You* can do it. I sometimes think that though I've had a perfect life full of nice nice, good good people helping one another, if I had known what I know now when my dear wife was around looking up words in the dictionary—"

"—*tumescent...*"

Dewey tried to resume but stuttered. "Poor Iris, she used to call kids 'little strangers' and 'heavenly bounty'— I mean, kids you have. But..." Dewey was pointlessly wagging his head back and forth. In denial? "Health, TV, my new weather studies, good neighbors like you, and then the implicit possibilities in this project of ours. I got *so* much to look forward to...."

"*Health*?"

"Perfect. I'm in a relatively stable high—"

"Ivy said, two or three weeks ago—"

"Countdown has stopped," said Dewey with quiet triumph.

"What do you mean? You're not going to die?"

"My body healed itself. Negative biopsy. And between you and me, I had a dream the other night that I got Oads in my arteries, so I may be going through *negative decay!* Anyway, a return to normal weight problems." Dewey guffawed and reached to slap Hind's knee but it was too far.

"Problems?"

"Same old problems. Diet, ekcetra."

"But I thought I was listening to a *terminal* case. For God's sake, I thought you had cancer of the—didn't you have cancer of the—...?"

"Dear old Jack, you've been eating yourself up with worry. But that young doctor at the medical group checked and checked. He admitted maybe the other biopsy was wrong, after all they gave a routine X ray to a Puerto Rican girl and got it mixed up with a person who was really sick—'course then they discovered (in fact *she* just discovered) she was three months pregnant. But then he said my other biopsy couldn't have been wrong, and I was just suddenly all better, but of course I hadn't been able to believe in the first place. I've been saved in order to finish—well, who knows what I may not finish? A famous man named Heard said that by the time they unearth the cancer cure, it would have cured itself."

"Two, three weeks ago, though..."

"I knew by then. Thought you'd been informed. Thought you'd hear through the Fordhams or Carmen or little Rain or Phyllis or Knott or one of the Old Chestnuts. Even told the men who spray that new tree they planted on your block in April. The negative biopsy was three days prior to when I met with you." (The guardian abolished that usage "met *with*.")

"But you asked me to develop your brainchild?"

"That goes as per program, Jack. You go *ahead* with these Oads. There's so much else I have to initiate. Before I die. *If* I die." (Twinkle, twinkle.)

You were standing looking down at Dewey and his hairless hand lying on the crocheted antimacassar, and at the gold-threaded speaker of his Japanese AM-FM on the narrow table with the book trough underneath.

"You do mean, then, to die?"

"Meaning?"

"To follow your dearly beloved wife?"

"What's your meaning? Say'd you hear the old gent fell asleep at a fifty-degree angle on the sit-up pad had a cerebral at the Fieldston last month?"

"You had a nerve taking my time."

"Where you going? Now Jack—" Dewey's face, though the same, had drawn together, tightened into something else: "I was a *good* husband to Iris, don't think I was anything but good to her, there isn't anything but good *in* me, and it was so long ago—by God it was before Phil began giving out samples of chlorophyll gum. Hey remember my 'peaceful olive...oriental plane'?—don't think—I was good to her I promise you, I know what you're thinking, *real* good to her I can tell you. Hey, *you* should talk, never sharing your money with that lady cousin of yours who lost her job in rehabilitation!"

If you admit neither waste nor inability to finish, how do you deal with the tableau you've just left—the portly putterer among his possessions, the pot Oliver had "pawned" on Dewey as a Roman lachrymatory one of Ol's old girls had allegedly thrown for two night credits on the Craft Center wheel. And how do you absorb the fact that it isn't possible to dekidnap effectively receiving each earlier lead now as an accidental organic whole end? These people quite simply refused to be dekidnaped. Oliver had to remind you all the time, keep an eye on you. These people made you rehearse the Laurel case; made you use them as means by which to inhale the past; they disappointed your hopes for them. So you had to use summary measures.

And the time they took! (The Good Shepherd bells were playing "September Song" as the noon concert opener.)

And you could insulate DW from OP or OP from PP or LR. Such a mess of unpasteurized guidelines run from one to several that though these doomed unhappy people be rooted to one spot, plot, trench, or wench—the guardian's hand is raised in anger—they could cause Hind constant motion.

One day Berry Brown wanted Hind to accompany him to the pier. But it was too soon. Would the next step be so plainly Ash Sill if Hind had not that other morning with May been thinking of the kidnap revival as a *dive* from which he must work back systematically to the surface? But like the past, these kidnap offenses were all *on* the surface, in your old and ill-used and overused mind. Berry was saying, "The old man Wood got no time for me. He's taking notes on the weather report, said he was busy." Dewey's system of coordinated weathers was pastoral, musical, and mechanically endless: and Berry Brown believed that it was partly because of weather coverage in the nation at large that Dewey Wood had faith that right would prevail in the Asian deltas, where he had heard their weathers were simpler and easier to monitor and/or control.

Oliver Plane was irritably calling to say that Ashley Sill wanted to see Hind at such and such an address, and Hind might be able to straighten him out, he was in a dangerous state, and Peg was in town staying with Maddy and Flo. But as OP went on, still worried that he'd been drawn into a kidnap, parrying where there had been no feint, sounding Hind for kidnap data he didn't have, Hind could not listen: for the guardian was holding up to Hind's eleven-year-old eye that tiny, exceptional *Nucula Proxima*, and its olive-brown skin, quite a rarity among sea-wrack specimens.

Hind phoned Angel Mews, but when the American desk clerk answered with his mouth full and Petula Clark behind him reiterating the joyous dissolution of the dominant into "*Down*town," ha ha ha haaaa ha haa "*Down*town," Hind didn't have the Old Woman's name and could only describe her. And although, since this phone voice must be no more Laurel-primed than Staghorn would have been, it might as well be led toward kidnap particulars (perhaps it was swallowing a Hershey bar), or even asked point-blank, "What would Staghorn have said if I (and not Pop) had nabbed that clue in Plane's department box and driven up to sound him out?", Hind said, "Is her name by chance 'Foster'?" and the clerk, after a ringing gulp, said, "There is a Miss Foster, lives here for years."

"Please ask her to phone Jack Hind." It's bracing to say your name like that now and then.

Dark against bright fading panes, now she was the window itself standing near the Dürer still periodically ticking on the wall.

When Ash's Peg called from the Beechers', someone took the phone away from her to say he thought Ash had unwittingly gotten in with the roller group who had threatened Maddy, and Maddy should institute a thorough prophylactic check of the old incinerator system in his building, should in short start turning some very square corners for a change.

Later, Smith Answering reported that a "Mystery" Beecher phoned. (Joke? dialect?)

And Ash, on whom Peg had not yet sicked the police, was leaving with Smitty messages so humanly detailed that the service again threatened Hind with discontinuation.

## • • •
## *iii*

Hind was eleven. And behind the guardian through trembling midday heat which made them at once individual and imaginary, the familiar platoon were fruitfully deployed down the beach. Engleman Deal, dug in up where the sand was dry as dust, blasted a hollow perforated ball out of imaginary traps; further down, Red Grimes on hands and knees in a limp white infantine sunhat, turned a page of the Sunday *Times*; still further, Thea, turning to walk back, had scared up a mass of sandpipers, who flew around her over the water and back behind her.

Jack had found then, but not till the words came, that all through the childhood he now suddenly saw ending, one certain tremulous tact had guarded him like an enchanted bequest, and he was not violating it: "You never got married. Didn't you want to?" The guardian seemed to be examining the olive-brown *periostracum* and the hinge's regular teeth and on the shell's inside its pearl stomach—features so unquestionable no words need identify them—but he said promptly, "Gibbon speaks of *odium novercali*, stepmother hatred." Then he threw the shells away and put a strong arm on Hind's shoulders and as they set off at a long pace, the guardian said, "It comes just before his piece on the perils of city life." Thea thought she had caught their eye, or the guardian's, and she called; but they couldn't make it out.

If now, with Ashley Sill's anxiety coming like time into your thirty-five-or-six-year-old head from the dusty telephone receiver, you could reach down to that old beach from the city undertaker's top floor and find your guardian, left like a huge curved bone whole and independent, then you could possess it and turn wholly to the Sills of this world.

"No, don't give me your address, I can't come today. I know you've got trouble with Peg because she called, but I can't come."

But unless you abandoned this new series of accidental organic ends, Ash was indeed next on the dekidnaping line. Can you make sacrifices forever?

The guardian once said, "Ashley won't thank you for getting him into this, you know," when Hind had sidestepped the guardian's real wish and had left the Independent Advisory Service assistant's job for Ash to fall into. Hind was at loose ends then right after college, and the draft didn't want him for Korea or anything else, and the guardian was sorry Jack didn't want to take on what the guardian felt could blossom into something quite remarkable. So along *with* Ash, who grew grimly puzzled about the job, Hind went on two of the first (and only) few IAS junkets.

"Now this is not an insight I can *impart* to a young man soon to graduate. But I can help him to draw it from himself," the guardian observed.

Well, what?

"A glad and proud acceptance of what he is *able* to do, and hence what he *should* do. Your boy Beecher fell in love with slabs, cloverleafs, slate facings, freeze-free fountains, and the Amsterdam South development plan. He followed me around the house discussing research into quartz iodine theater lighting, and the tragedy of the Maillart bridge in Switzerland that was never done because the jury couldn't decide, and the tragic consequences to Coney Island and New York City of the 1911 Dreamland fire. Maddy has that mysterious collaboration of appetites that turns a man toward architecture; I'd love to have had it.

"On the other hand, the last thing Jimmy Commons wants is law, he's too bumptious, too uncertain; who will tell him? His mother has fallen in love with Virginia Law School, what can I say? And three to one he marries someone unsuitable, too. I watch your lot make mistakes I've seen over and over in my own generation. Red Grimes even when he was a Harvard junior already knew that shivering satisfaction, that condensed finality of a sound scholarly sentence, the tip of the iceberg, weeks of consideration dehydrated into one fact. Red knew what he wanted because he knew what he was."

Fondly, Hind took the sensible and dropped the dubious. After all you could be a soldier, film-cutter, gymnast, tree surgeon, or hotel clerk–but *should* you?

"It was here at Tanglewood last August the idea came to me," said the guardian, mainly for Hind's newly graduated ear, and Daisy Deal looked at the guardian with affectionate resignation, though not because he had butted in on Engleman Deal contrasting MacArthur's background and Truman's. "Yes, right here; and as I looked at those people spread-eagled sunbathing on the lawn outside the Shed waiting for their music as if it were background music–"

"Those *people*–" murmured Daisy Deal, and suddenly tipped her broad straw hat in the waiter's descending face and ordered jellied madrilène and sweetbreads in the southern cadence she saved for public places or for parties where she knew hardly anyone.

"–many of them Jack's age," the guardian continued, "and mind you, I don't question their right to camp there day and night to get fragments of a Munch tone poem–"

"They *can't* stay all night," said Hind, and spotting Ash and a girl (not Peg) through the restaurant's glistening porch screen and the branches beyond, he got up to go into the street and stop them, and Charley put her napkin on the table as if to follow, but didn't.

"—it's the dumb condescension as they look at you. If I had an hour alone one at a time with those young people I swear I could help them discover—"

The girl was driving to New York—she was in a hurry to get going—and Ash was skipping the evening concert. He gave Hind the ticket to give away. Charley and her parents always spent the night at Fox Hollow School. Hind in any case had not been asked to join Ash.

Back at the table Daisy Deal picked up her blueberry muffin, put it down and picked up her soft roll. Charley, who always tried to be nice, asked Engleman Deal if he would like to be a judge, and he smiled back and said. "I'll do anything that's fun."

"But," intrudes from a dark foreground an imaginary Sylvia you won't meet for seven years yet, "what if Mrs. Deal does say 'Booorbon' sour? She loves the Boston and can give real musical reasons why the late quartets are original in their freedom, and she can accompany a Schubert song, and she gave me her older son's Goya which I still only play a few diagram chords on."

But the guardian was proceeding to outline his plan to Marie Verity's father, who was there mainly because Marie was studying cello at Tanglewood that summer, and he was bobbing his silver brush-cut above his fruit cup at each point the guardian made. But the guardian seemed distracted. Engleman Deal was promising Charley that the AP correspondent who on July fourth in Prague had got ten years for alleged spying would be released.

Now fourteen years later Hind still kept the sparse file of Independent Advisory Service correspondence and breakdowns.

Daisy Deal had on her mantel a Gerber's jar full of sand from the guardian's beach.

The Old Woman would love to see the letters the guardian received from deans. Hind phoned her every day but she was out. Ashley hadn't phoned for seventy-two hours but Hind knew from Maddy that Peg was still with him and Flo.

The strain of angry play in the Old Woman's manner might mean she intended him to pay for something. But would he know what? Wasn't it insane of her to acquire and then ration out these alarming Laurel facts? Yet she used them only as a means for something else, yet that too turned out to be a kind of means: the Laurel case faded to the sides of the conversation like cars hearing the Emergency Wagon Ow Wow behind them; and she cared only in the end for the topic of the guardian; yet here again she wanted Hind to know only what she unwisely felt would diminish him—and both helplessly and by design she flirted—that was it, she flirted—with knowledge she wanted him to come so close to he would palpably reckon his failure to possess it. The last time, on the stairs, she was alarmed but tired. Maybe she wished to inspire him to a certain pitch of social service, self-examination, or rehabilitatory rescue, then leave him on his own. But she was alarmed: for, when he reported that Grimes was hanging around hoping to get hold of the guardian's Ariosto and a few other books with the familiar *toison d'or* plate, the Old Woman hooted up the stairwell, "Don't ask *him* anything—what's *he* know," and called him an upstart pansy.

Two things were plain: she had been crazy about the guardian, and he wouldn't have her. (Certain WASP ladies began to get handsome in their forties and were stunning by sixty.) ("Not scallions, eggs, basil, or pine nuts can make you want a lady if she isn't right," the guardian had said to Ash and Hind on the road the first IAS trip they had taken; "and if she isn't, it won't take the Sun-god to put her wise.")

Now a week ago Ashley had said he was speaking from the Chapel of Laughter, and Plane was with him. Your ideal solution was to discover the Old Woman, Grimes, and the Laurel child (if he wasn't dead) there too. Why not invite Maddy as well and double up the last two dekidnaping phases? AS & MB.

It didn't work out that way.

But then suddenly when he phoned, the Old Woman *was* in at Angel Mews. After admitting it was she, she remarked, "The answer to your unasked question is that if you *had* picked up my lead in Plane's department box and gone to Staghorn you'd have *contrived* to find evidence in something or other he said—he says a lot."

"But my guardian! Why didn't you say more? It was wonderful, about his theories of death, and the Burke passage on the dauphiness above the horizon—can't you go on?"—even if he *had* heard most of what she would say.

"What *about* the dauphiness? Is that all you called about?"

"Thea called him a prince among kings—no, *of* kings."

"What a way to put it!"

"I'm sorry. I would love to hear more. You knew him when he went off to paint in the High Tatras before Hitler. And you knew him at the time he adopted me."

"You don't really know about that," the Old Woman said with a quiver in her voice.

"I don't know much, I admit that. But what *is* there to know?"

"Ah, you couldn't understand. It would take insight you weren't born with." Her pause intruded. "Any more than those two devious Chinese understood my instructions—well, who knows *what* they were, Chinese, Korean, Laotian, Cambodian, Tibetan—I mailed each a micro-dossier on the Laurel case knowing they sometimes met at lunchtime on the pier—"

"*This* has nothing to do with the guardian. You're hiding something."

"—and knowing that the big one"—big pier or big Chinese? her will seemed to be rising again, but now droning with a kind of efficiency—"was still a drug consultant for your friend Beecher's firm. But I did not expect them to go right to Santos-Dumont that day—"

"If you won't discuss the guardian," said Hind, "I think I know where to ask." But what precisely did she fear?

"But the kidnap is your real chance to be someone," she said.

"You watch, I'll ask Grimes, and Thea, and Van White—"

"—but that day I took no chances: I telephoned Santos-Dumont, and judging from the peremptory response, I must have got one of the Sisters." She laughed at her end, but now said harshly, "You will *not* call Grimes and that crowd. You know all you need to about your guardian." The quiver again.

"If you tell me all you know."

"That would take more time than we have."

"What about his Independent Advisory Service?"

"You know all about that, and that wasn't the real Foster in any case. Don't you want to know about the new Laurel tenants? Don't you want to know how, ah, in the field of Love one night two people concealed a precious theft and as a consequence of their failure to take precautions were trapped into conceiving a wild brainchild of a plan which all but dictated their future for them?"

Into her pause of tense satisfaction, Hind dropped four words: "So long, Miss Foster."

If she knew he was serious, she might compromise and return over old ground familiar to them both. Whereas once–before he met Hind's mother?–the guardian believed that in sudden death the last idea you had was destined to live on, he came to think that sudden death means you have that much more power to give to the Nature that receives you. Yet he hoped to have plenty of time to collect himself when the time came, and–"Let me not die in hospital, but on an island, purely drying, burning, blanching, cleanly starving," yet there was always company for lunch at the Heights apartment or a weekend at Greengage, and always invited, though like Grimes often self-invited.

Postpone dekidnaping Ash. The Independent Advisory Service rings a bell.

Three in a Lincoln Zephyr. Green. Pliny.

Find, to tell this story, words the guardian would approve: plain and exact rather than rich; solid and silent as objects; and clothed in a middle tone.

They were away early on a gray, late-October day. Ashley was hung-over; he had gargled with Listerine before going to bed at the guardian's but forgot to swallow two tablets of buffered aspirin. You were glad the car had no radio, but you hoped the guardian would talk: college was behind you (a Negro statesman addressed the commencement exercises) yet even closer behind you in the back seat sat this sour anxious classmate: other classmates off to study navigation at Newport, canine limb transplants in Baltimore, ballistics in Texas, Chaucer in Los Angeles, sociology in the Field, geology in New York, Hitler in Germany; three classmates dead, one in a car, one in his firm's plane, one of brain tumor discovered while on active duty with Ridgway in Korea;

one classmate just last week off to a severe houseparty near the nation's capital for initially screened diplomatic trainees; and Maddy married, and Peg standing by—and a lack of depth in the future like the wall a blind man senses and stops shy of.

Ashley said from deep in the back seat that he wasn't sure what was going to happen when they got there, and the guardian explained that the dean would probably have lined up several appointments for late afternoon and early evening. Ash's unasked question was, "What am *I* supposed to do while you are trying to counsel and draw out these guys?"

Six miles south of the western Massachusetts line the guardian stopped for lunch at The Green Man Inn. Ash was half through a frosty, twelve-ounce bottle of Budweiser before the guardian could conclude an exchange at the desk with the dapper little assistant manager who had been laying out the full Hotel Ad curricula at the university from which he had lately been graduated, and of whom the guardian said, striding through into the dining room of which his party were the sole occupants, "There's a young man who knew what he wanted and is running a first-class country inn. He may be posted to a city hotel next year."

"I will vouch for the beer," said Ash, who soon had a second and third to go with his toasted club from which he meticulously picked out every flake of the thin layer of tuna between the tomato slices and the pale boiled ham.

The assistant manager came and put a book of matches under one table-leg, and while he stayed to talk, the guardian kept his head tilted back for two minutes holding above his plate a loose-packed chunk of rare Chopped Round Steak.

"To pass the practical I had to integrate and cook a duck dinner for seventy Lions. I'm thinking of pursuing an advanced degree."

"When did you know this was what you wanted?"

"My father ran a restaurant about twenty miles from here. Do you know McLean Game Refuge? He was not as successful as he could have been, but I inherited the desire to serve others. Are these your two sons? May I ask what line you are in?"

Hind answered, hoping to rescue the guardian's hamburger. "He's versatile. He has extensive gardens—"

"—oh, nurseries," said the assistant manager.

"—and he is a linguist—"

"—*that* helps in *this* business—"

"—and he is a counselor—"

"—well, *there's* a profession all right."

The guardian said, "He didn't mean 'at law'—I am merely an unofficial adviser to college seniors who may need help in finding out how to make the best use—I wonder if it doesn't sound conceited of me."

"Just devious," said Ash, and the guardian proceeded to discuss something.

At three o'clock the Lincoln Zephyr rolled down Fraternity Rise, and Hind was alarmed that he had come. White plantation pillars and dark Norse wood and Georgian brick and farmhouse colonial led, as if through the world and time, to an arrested-Gothic administration building. Here the guardian, with Ash and Hind, was directed by a secretary to an office located above the science museum.

"Dr. Planter passed you on to me," said a broad man who received them there. "It's a pleasure. Have we met? I didn't think so, I don't have the chance to meet with as many as I always hope for. But you've been back often."

The conversation puzzled the guardian and, giving the man the benefit of the doubt, he replied, "I've been back every year, though I'm not what you'd call an old grad. No, I'm not that."

"Class of...?" asked the man and grinned with unmistakable excitement.

"Harvard, 1920."

"Business? Law?"

"No, just Harvard College."

"Transfer?"

"No."

"You didn't graduate here?"

"I didn't *go* here. Great Scott no. Nor did my son," the guardian nodded at Hind.

"You neither?" the man asked Ash. "Well this just isn't my day. I was led to believe. Well, we are always deeply interested in our various endowment funds, this being a *private* school."

"Who are you?"

"Assistant Director, Alumni Affairs. Dean Planter passed you on to me. He firmly believed you might have a significant contribution to make in terms..."

"Talk English."

The man's tone now turned normally indifferent. He did not smile now.

And he did not accompany the IAS to their first afternoon interviews.

In a recently unfinished library annex behind the nondenominational chapel, they found the room and, waiting at a desk, a boy of about seventeen. When Hind agreeably said, "You're here...," the boy thought he'd been asked why, and said with genuine modesty, "For a laugh or two," speaking of himself not the IAS program. After the introductions Ashley went off for another chair and the guardian observed how young the boy was. "Yes, I'm only seventeen and three-quarters."

"But you're only a freshman then."

"No, a junior."

"You're too young for a junior."

"I know."

"The program is only for seniors."

"But I'm a junior."

"Why, then, did you come?"

"I wanted to talk to someone. I'm rather shy."

Since the guardian wished each interviewee to be his natural self, the guardian could not at first voice his impatience.

"Take public speaking," Ash needled. "No, come to think of it, you better not."

The pause, here at the outset, was tempting; the guardian could have filled it with his own questions and answers, nice contrasts between his early notion that death distributed one's self among various appropriate powers of the pantheon and his recent discovery that death spread one's disintegrate self into the forms of the Nature one pretended to stand above–brainchildren evoked with plain words and floated on the very same fluency that a bit too buoyantly replied the night before to Ash's incoherent challenge *why* the guardian wanted this IAS–"Simply because my life as I once conceived it is forfeit, and here is something I can give and that can be received freely." The ring of the words had been, Hind thought, rich enough to forestall elaboration–of which, of course, the guardian was quite happily capable. "Say again?" murmurs an imaginary Sylvia to you from that dark foreground in a military idiom she probably doesn't know.

Say again? But it is always different, like each new phone call from Ash here fourteen years later, who is angrier and angrier that you won't meet him, but with whom you wish only to discuss those old trips he doesn't want to take now and would be further angered to hear you recall. He is somewhere in the city trying to get hold of you, but you know that some change in his link with Peg is what will turn the trick.

"And so," the guardian is saying, his red and blue silk tie still tight at his neck, blue blazer still buttoned at the middle, "you are unhappy, but you know the one thing you need to know at this point: namely, what your ability is, your natural bent. Maybe when you are forty you will decide it would have been wiser to risk failure as a bassoon virtuoso than be a mere voice in the ensemble. I think you're mainly right in knowing what is possible for you to do, and pleasurable, and reasonably difficult, and to plan to do that."

"Well, I have to go now," the boy said.

Ash had gone out into the hall again, though not this time for a chair.

When he came back, the guardian was busy with the second candidate, who was possessed of a thick head of short blond hair and a set of red cheeks. He had just been asked the sixty-four-dollar question as Ash entered blowing the last of his last drag into the air of the room.

The blond fellow bowed his head in honor of what he was about to say. "I want service."

Ash made an ironic catch with tongue against roof of mouth that sounded like a dentist's mouthdrainer interrupting. "I.e.," the blond continued, "I want to serve. I'm serious, I want to serve my country at *all* levels."

"This," said the guardian, "is not freedom, but its reverse."

"*Oh* no," said the blond quickly and with the firm smile of an executioner who acknowledges his turn in an unflinching process. "*Oh* no you don't sir; I wish to achieve a position at the top of the business community from which I can reach out both to government and to ordinary people. A year ago I worked out a philosophy of life, partly through the influence of a slightly Bohemian friend of my older sister who divided problems into *ex*tensive and *in*tensive and then proceeded to dismiss them one by one."

"But which business?" asked the guardian.

"Nowadays it hardly matters, sir, it's method that counts. Find the key to other people's behavior and— well you've got them hooked and your job licked. I might go into automated braille, but I'd have little or nothing to do with particulars like research or the psychology of the demand-to-production-volume ratio. It would be policy dynamics, person to person. It doesn't take much of a brain to see through the theory you get in the classroom. The secret is to find the simple principle of policy dynamics. You wouldn't find it in a book. But you might in a man's face or voice. Now why do you take an interest in me? Why are you up here on a weekday with two young friends? What are you *really* investigating?"

"*I'm* asking the questions," said the guardian.

"Ask," said the blond.

"You're like a disembodied spirit, aren't you?" said the guardian, and Ash snapped his eye up to the guardian.

"I don't see it that way, sir."

"You will probably make out in business."

"*We* think so."

"We'll get *you too*," said Ash, as the blond fellow bowed his way out of the room.

Almost immediately there was a third interviewee, and the guardian looked at his watch and became urgent, even combative, in his questions.

The youth answered, "But *why* must I be one thing?"

"It's probably all you can."

"I'll be a lot of things. I'm going to ship out for a while. And then I want to be a cook in a good San Francisco hotel, kill two birds with one stone; then I want to write a mystery; then I want to work six months in a body shop to learn how to fix my own car—"

"You never will; everyone says that," the guardian interrupted.

"—and ultimately I shall marry a rich young widow and go to med school…and be a specialist, yes."

"You have to begin medicine right after college," said Hind, at which Ashley groaned. "It's all that interning later on."

"Why?" said the guardian to Hind; "there's no reason you can't start a career late. But," turning back to the interviewee, "what makes you think you're a doctor?"

"Because I want to make a lot of money and I have top grades."

"Healing, then, is a mere means to the end of money?"

"Oh," and a laugh, "money isn't the end—there *is* no end in itself. For example, why are you sitting here grilling *me*?"

Granted, said the guardian over dinner, a boy will behave rudely under pressure; but having walked in of his own volition, number three should not then have charged them with grilling him. The last thing the guardian would wish to do, he said, was "grill" a boy. He had himself in his time been guilty of words that caused despair, and since the person in question died during this period he couldn't help blaming himself. So the guardian was cautious, and with his words too, for one never knew when a word would become a deed, though of course he didn't think kindness was an end in itself.

"What did you do to this man?" Ash asked. "How did he die? Did he kill himself?"

"I don't enjoy discussing it," said the guardian. "Elder Plane knew the man, and didn't like him, but that's neither here nor there."

"Well," said Ash, "it *is there*. But," getting up from table, "if you'll excuse me, I don't think I was much help today." Ash had a pint of Old Mr. Boston in his room, and at that stage of the first IAS trip, he did not particularly want to confuse his anxieties about himself with his gathering animus against the group leader. The guardian canceled the one evening appointment saying he had contracted to talk only to seniors.

Hind walked under cool, dark trees with the guardian, bumping shoulders and by tacit agreement taking a path here, a road there. Once, a door sprang open and out of the light a guffawing student lunged onto the walk, kicked a paper cup as if in self-defense, and ran past them as someone slammed the door.

Hind was glad to lose the half-formed resentment he'd had since June graduation. The endless hole he'd fallen forward through wasn't the guardian's fault. And Hind's graduation was in a way the guardian's loss. Thea said, "Long ago when I first knew him, he used to speak of Harvard as an ancestral home of the Fosters—and naturally he was sorry when you didn't go—and of Kittredge's white suit (or was that Mark Twain?) as if it were a costume agreed on after consultation with the Foster family. And accompanied by Daisy he would sing, 'I Dream of Jeanie' and, the second go-through, hold the 'I' deliciously long with a very pear-shaped 'ah' and the 'ee' only at the gentle finish falling into 'dream'—and after a few more

he'd explain really a bit tiresomely, Jack, the familial tie
between his Boston and New York Fosters and the Fosters of Stephen fame. But then he stopped all that. Was
it when *you* came along? Perhaps. Spoke no more of the
clan Foster, and little of himself really. Which of course
isn't a bad thing, is it?" she asked with a hint of plaintive-
ness intimately woman-to-man but ritual and vague.

"Of course," the guardian went on as they turned from
a road into a path, and Hind wondered if Ash would assert himself by throwing an empty Old Mr. Boston out
the window onto the rear porch roof in the middle of the
night, "of course, I was painting in the High Tatras before
the Crash—yes, receiving the strange fantasy compensa-
tions you get only in a landlocked country, and painting
more and more out of my head till one day I examined a
thing I'd done from recent memory of the fields sloping
down from below Stary Smokovec to the town of Poprad
and saw with pain and relief that alas unintentionally it
lacked all depth, all plasticity, and then I saw it was accidentally abstract and the broad wedge of pasture adrift
upon a dark panel of forest and above pressing the cluster of Poprad on its flat land up against a sky that I had
got all wrong, was really a view of part of Greengage, and
I felt the sea pushing at my back and the house just off the
canvas—but it was also a delicate smudgy water-color
frock my dead sister wore in such a way that one thought
(and one was right!) that she'd nothing underneath."

And *now*, with Peg phoning from the Beechers to ask
if Hind knew someone named Grimes, Hind heard their
steps—his and the guardian's—gently skiffing along under
the guardian's mood, sustaining the gentle changes of
subject and seeming to steer him not too close to some
things he was afraid to show Jack Hind, the adopted son;
and as Hind now fourteen years later told Peg he was
going to meet Ash on Thursday at an address downtown
and would see what he could do, and heard not relief

but intimate anxiety in her "You'll let me know how it comes out" as if she feared she might have to change in order to fight her subtle husband on new ground that reflected a new time, Hind was instantly (until he cradled the receiver) fourteen years back in the drugging lucidity of the October night finding he and the guardian had looped round to the college inn and were praising Ash's last poems and doubting his talk of diving into a Wall Street odd-lot house to get in touch with *something* real where for God's sake (unquote) you really had to know your beans: while at the same time the guardian and Hind knew Hind was the true point. Then they were in the inn bar, a loud spoiled ten-year-old in a bow tie was kicking and slapping the pinball even though "Tilt" was showing, and on stools three undergrads in blue blazers and white button-downs open at the neck nodded sagely as a big young bartender told them, "See, I never apologize to nobody for nothing!"

"Sounds like something he's said before," was Ash's reaction when the guardian repeated it in the car driving north next day. "It's a comfort to repeat yourself. That's why I'm miserable, I can't stand to."

The guardian tried to conduct a discussion. "But if one knew one's past so well and had grown so strong that one refused to re-enact blind or craven errors one—"

"*Santayana*," Hind and Ash said, and then chuckled as if at their own absurdity, though Hind then beneath his public embarrassment at the guardian's not citing Santayana, found actually something very like what, an instant before, he had pretended to himself he felt. Absurdity. But later it occurred to him that others besides Santayana must have said the same thing.

"—refused to make mistakes over again one would still be finding oneself in highly similar situations; otherwise one wouldn't have the option to *make* those same errors."

"I only meant talk," said Ash, "words. Not reiterating. Which means you never can say much. It has to be new. Conversation and poetry, eh?"

"On the other hand," said the guardian—and the smooth gray trunk of a beech tree and the blooming bronzes and cherry reds of the hardwood leaves overhead made Hind want to fight his way back to the city and look for a job—"on the other hand," and the guardian seemed happily surprised at himself, "one doesn't *get* a chance to re-enact one's errors. But one does get strange second chances. Take this advisory service. I thought I'd lost my chance to be a teacher, which was once one of several things I wanted to do. Yet now look at me, teaching in another key you might say."

"Yeah," said Ash; and Hind and the guardian heard a settling in the back seat, fabric against fabric.

The first of two seniors that afternoon looked remarkably like Ash except for a big white tennis sweater. After some fumbling, and Ash getting up to close the window against the rainstorm, the conversation developed.

"Well what are your questions?"

"I have none," said the guardian, and looked at Ash and Hind inquiringly.

"You mean you're going to *tell* me?"

"What would I tell you?" asked the guardian.

"Why you're here? I heard this was outside guidance. That's what you need, you see, help from *outside* the system, so what you receive isn't always your own blood type, so to speak, your own air you've just breathed out—like my father's disappointed I plan to go out for hockey, why don't I play squash, he plays squash, and squash will be something I can play all my life—which is exactly what I give the old man back in his face, squash *is* something I can play all my life, and you can lose an eye in squash just like you can in hockey, and when my roommate says why worry about a petty thing like sports when the Rosenbergs and the bomb are staring us in the face, and he slips off into fine points of the German peace treaty—but it's the principle involved, my father actually thinks he's losing face if I don't go out for squash, can you believe that?"

"No," said the guardian, "I can't. What do *you* think are your talents?"

"Furthermore my roommate, nice guy and all that, is Jewish. We laugh and I say you're just a Bronx Jew—so he's saddled with a special viewpoint, he doesn't see the Procrustean country club; and if my roommate was tied to a gravestone all night in the Bronx in nineteen whatever it was, I still have *my* life to fight out, and the hockey-squash issue is a microcosm of my father and I. And as I pointed out to my roommate, this Greenglass was just as guilty as Julius and Ethel. My roommate is going to transfer to Chicago, he doesn't know why he came here, but *he* plays a good tricky game of squash, isn't that ironic?"

"Are you in doubt about your future?" the guardian asked. "That's why I'm here."

"Do you mind if I take off my sweater?" The interviewee raised his arms, but then said, "No, I just—I gotta get to the library. Mr. Foster, what business are you in?"

"I try to do many things," said the guardian, and Ash leaned way forward in his chair and stared at the floor.

"He's a humanist," said Hind.

"Oh. You got money," said the boy in the white sweater. "So's my father but the crazy fool takes the train in from Connecticut five days a week."

"And you will too?"

"One thing to be said for being in the market. You're not shucking the responsibility you bear to your own money and to the industrial enterprises behind which it stands."

"Have you never—"

"No, I mean I want an interesting position with a challenging future. I wish I were a born doctor or a born lawyer or diplomat—but most of us don't have a real vocation—do you read me?—"

"But," the guardian rose, "you're precisely the kind of man I want to help, and you—my friends on the Heights—in the city, where I live—all have children like you earnestly discussing futures that are not real alternatives—"

"Do you want to be a dull man?" said Hind, and Ash groaned.

The interviewee stood up and pulled down the back of his sweater and smiled without speaking. Then he left.

He was succeeded by a girl named Gloucester—"my married name, but I'm separated, and I shouldn't be here because I'm not"—she lowered her voice to a husky, lubricious range—"a matriculating student." She laughed. "And not a male either, but anyway you're not doing a land-office business today. I'm just living at home and sitting in on my father's experimental Italian course he just started. No kids, twenty-two years of age, and don't think you're going to send me back to my husband, I'm hoping if I stay away long enough he might get to know himself."

Ashley was laughing and the girl was addressing her remarks mainly to Hind, who now said, "We contracted to help graduating seniors only," and thereupon felt disastrously slow and young. Was he saving the guardian? But the guardian objected wearily, "No no, if she can't talk to us, whom can she talk to?"

"Quite a lot of guys," said the girl. "But Daddy's upset I'll corrupt them, and I don't drink or smoke, it causes bad breath."

"What did you do before marriage?" the guardian asked, but the girl was looking sullenly at Hind, then at his legs, and didn't seem to hear.

"What does any girl do? Think about it. It's terrible once you've been married, and guys know the spot you're in, like the bastard Jimmy who was just in here."

"And why take Italian?"

"Why not?"

"It spends time, and you ought probably to be in the city living on your own."

"Researcher in a PR firm? Third reader in a trade book department? I don't have the credits to be a teacher or a social worker. Listen, a polite traveling salesman in a fur-lined driving coat and the premature gray hair and strong face from the beer ad with the rec room ping-pong table in the background asked me in a bar if I was a prostitute—like he was merely asking for truth, like was my father still alive, politely."

"Maybe he was too polite," said the guardian. "Maybe I am. Maybe all we can tell you is that in your present state of mind you shouldn't stay in a small college town. There's nothing wrong with struggling a bit in the city—taking a night course in design—"

"I'm a woman, so I shall be artistic, huh?"

"You don't want someone to talk to. You want someone to punish."

"*Why* should I leave here? I love my father, can't you get that into your head? You *could* help me by giving *me* five thousand instead of this goddam snob institution of higher learning."

That was what her father had, well, told the boy in the white sweater when he said he might try this visiting adviser. Her father had heard about it from a dean, the money angle.

to prosecute that past, that shyly beckoning guardian, till (diving–whether down or up–toward that mysterious surface of things) you find a tall tale you don't honestly know you're looking for. And it will not do to recant under pressure these varieties of familiar pattern lingering in your upper gums and the middle mass of your mind– in favor of random data today fourteen years later, the random close smell of roto-chickens fresh-spitted after lunch turning all afternoon behind the butcher's window in whose moving surface you see not only a pair of thick female eyebrows but across this random upper West Side street an old movie marquee billing prices of cabbage, carrots, tomatoes, beets; any more than it will do to lose yourself in, so to speak, the undertaker's man Carmen La Branche's sight, no, the sight of Carmen La Branche, as he stands, knees very slightly bent, in line at Kold Kut City; or, right around your corner, in a neighborhood you must admit is recognizable, to lose yourself in the sound of a can of calorie-free pop which in answer to your coin bangs down to the lower opening where your hand, like a mind (of its own) waits to grasp. No, the patterns of adoption, of possessed and possession, of male purpose, female laurel, filial paternity, of fore and aft, of illusory deep and delusory flat, wait for you as steadily as the greasy-haired woman (ostracized from Phyllis's genial fountain though never originally accepted there) whom you see here at your corner, whom you may chalk on your score slate as another pitiable breast in the pitiable mass of accidents but who cannot help telling you much more than that pastoral chaos of random data wound in naked tape: look at her trudging across Second: with her cigarette hand, which thus scores the act with a stroke of white against her linty black coat, she crosses herself again coming across the cobbles before the waiting, idling cars, one of which guns heavily as she passes for she is oblivious even of her very own, though transitory, red light.

If, back in April or May, someone had asked Hind point-blank what the avenue was called, he might have had trouble saying "Second" or "Third." Why was the city now again insisting on its names? After all, he and Maddy had agreed that much of the city, if not the Heights, was now part of a coastal density and was identifiable more by sinister peculiarities in its air than by its famous curtain-wall sky-points much less by Greek cornice moldings or Dutch gambrel roofs—or the secret antique compositions when you wheel around to look across a street, and find the great bridge lurking above the steep-pitched roofs of little eighteenth-century commercial buildings at Peck Slip which, poised for demolition, stand delicately warped as if by a painter's hand, their fine dormers gone but the old unifying spread lintels waiting personally to see you in or, barring that, receive your name—J. Hind, Fostermonger; Murphy's Fillets.

But now he found he had to admit, This is Third Avenue.

Right under his nose now a neatly trotting schnauzer turned off at an angle-iron post yanking its master halfway round on the taut leash. Diagonally across the avenue, though there the dog and master were, respectively, larger and taller, the same jolting connection occurred at a green storage mailbox, dog snapped by its lead after its master had been swung so as to seem to suddenly grab for something he'd inadvertently passed. Buck Field stood on the front step of his shop reading the paper; facing Hind was the headline GREEN BELT SOUGHT.

Trees on Hind's undertaker's street had no real crooks, for there wasn't enough tree: the crooks in the guardian's trees were full of the dark sweet smell of the wood, and you were careful not to plant your sneaker in a crook that was angled too acutely.

Hind did not have to look at the traffic light or the word spelled below it, for the racing flank of cars barely led by a new Bel-Air, having paused for an impatient breath at the changing light a block south, now mowed ahead, and Hind jumped out and ran for the other curb without looking.

He walked again. He was approaching the undertaker's. On the top step of the house four doors from his and next to the house where Rain and granddad lived, Leather Man, like a natural landmark, stood staring down at Hind. He was bare to the waist, just as if it were winter, and his skinny shanks in their breeches and high bright boots looked stiff and fragile. He nodded once to Hind and glared away toward the intersection Hind had crossed.

Halfway up the block the girl with the flowered cast sat on the steps of the Good Shepherd strumming an un-plugged electric guitar. The day child-Hind had listened to the guardian's tiff with Thea slip suddenly into an in-audible register as if it had been inhaled by the bedroom into which they passed slamming the door, he had put on his new reversible and gone over to Cassia's. She had not been expecting him, and that made the joke she had just finished secretly building into their joint block-chute system the harder to suspect. By a casual tick of her pin-kie she could now flip a horizontally-laid pillar-block at the top entry-point so as to govern whether your mar-ble eventually came out at the proper hole below, or, as now happened to Hind unbeknownst, your marble stopped, dropped, stopped, dropped, and then as if in a new soundproof dimension stopped dead somewhere in-side the maze—when Cassia calmly indicated a two-inch window halfway up one wall of the maze where Hind's marble had come absurdly to rest. He did not see Cas-sia tick the pillar-block back into place, and her cat's-eye marble, after an incredibly long and varied rattle, issued forth from the proper hole onto the rug; he tried three more times, but his anger sharpened his eye and it was then that he caught her altering the entry hole for her own next descent. But he was so angry that rearing up on his knees he clapped her in the cheek and she was so startled at Hind's hand raised against her she wept in self-defense but then, he suspected, she recalled he'd never seen her cry and stumbled out of the room and didn't return though Laurel scuffed back and forth attempting to mediate their differences. After adjusting the hole again, he had sent a marble on down, and this time it had not come out either hole; and because Cassia was not right there with him, kneeling on the rug speaking to him only as an explosive interruption of her constant low humming, "Mairzy Doats," "Blue Champagne," "Elmer's Tune," "Intermezzo," "South of the Border," Hind could not bring himself to take a surplus block and bomb the chute-system.

Climbing the undertaker's marble stairs Hind recaptured last night's dream that had escaped him as he reached to turn off the alarm this morning that was not ringing and had not been set. A patrolman sat reading in the station house. Deposited on a silver radiator you couldn't turn off except from Centre Street HQ, a note on a white sheet came alive as he looked: words came out, Burkean references to the lower orders breaking into the sheepcote of legitimate subornation (no), and Hind tried to recall the features of the man who put the white sheet down on the silver paint. But no: now new words appeared: ALL I WANTED WAS TO TAKE THE CHILD AWAY, NOT FAR, THEN BRING IT BACK AGAIN. As the letters came out, the kidnaper's voice receded like a hearing test; the patrolman turned a page, and the captain appeared and walked to a gumdrop-lit panel to activate the daily Pan-City deodorant program. A young man in mufti counted down, "Five four three two one—Chocolate Cedar and Mentholated Camphor!" and the captain activated.

All the way up the marble stairs Hind felt someone waiting for him. At the south window of the living room he was immediately seen by the man who, with his wife, had put up the canopy. The man called to him, so he had to raise the window, they didn't know each other—"Listen what happened to *us*. You see our little patio here and the flagstones?" Hind grinned, and the man frowned and hesitated. "So I took a cab downtown and got a seventy-pound bag of crushed rock, all white, for between the flags, all sparkling." The man thrust a palm out and down. "So where did they go?"

"*I* don't know," called Hind.

"Wait, I'm *telling* you—birds ate them, starlings, sparrows, you name it, even these broken-down pigeons next door, *ate* them. Seventy pounds in a week."

"That's too bad," Hind called back. "A guy I know who runs a gift shop planted a hundred tulips in his garden on Fortieth and because of the office building that overlooked the garden he lost every single one."

"Yeah? Well what do I do, get seventy pounds more?"

"Guess how the tulips were destroyed."

"I can't guess, my wife always asks me guess how much she paid for a dress, but what do I do about my stones?" He turned and moved away toward the canopy. As he stopped to tinker with a Chinese lantern, Hind called out, "Paper clips! That's what destroyed those tulips, would you believe it?" The man looked back over his shoulder, shook his head, shrugged, and passed on under the canopy.

The telephone was ringing. It would be Ash, and Smitty would pick up.

Maybe Hind would have to have Sylvia back even without pursuing the dekidnaping program through to its proper end. He lay down, he had forgotten to close the windows, he felt the bad air stuffing his nose, he opened his mouth to sleep.

He didn't know during the dream whether it *was* one. So the circumstance seemed endless and unhallowed, though not till then had he seen that he felt dreams ought to be hallowed. A surgical patient in a green sheet with trap door in front stood near him, but Hind couldn't know if this person was to help out at the table or merely observe. They were going in, the numerous hands around him; they were not incising, for the incisions had occurred "before the dream began" unquote, and that occasional costive chill in his bowels when he was a child was the only remembered sensation like what the slippery hands made him feel. But now his neck got longer until, since it was in danger of extending its head too far so the head might lapse off the edge of the table, he swung it sinuously upward, neck and head, and was looking down to the terribly clean hole in him which the glassy hands manipulated. ("*Hands mani*pulated?" said the guardian; "look up the root.") He saw his heart—with its truncated spouts, it was a seahorse, and the wet made it seem in a kind of mucus house; and a transparent roof of green asbestos shingles was unconvincing. And one of the curling constipating fingers said, "This heart was always cold—as cold as a tall peg in a short hole, as cold as anything else in the world. But no, this isn't a heart: this giant's heart is hidden many beats away in case of surprise attack. But when Hind, with once again that sinal clearing (as if you had wept) woke and re-enacted the dream, he feared it was a dream he had set out to have. But then he found he was still dreaming, for Miss Cassia Meaning in starched gold leaf waltzed up out of the ward to report that Dewey Wood died of a nightmare, she had been there and had started waking him when he began to call for Hind and to strain as if his hands had been lashed to the mattress; but close up, Miss Meaning then gleefully told him, "It was really 'Iris' he called."

The phone was ringing, it seemed never to finish, and the room's dusk was almost untouched by the afterlight on the other side of one hundred folded feet of Dow Handi-Wrap. The man was short and broad, as short as the Düsseldorf weight-lifter behind whom Hind had stood hunched at a mirror combing his hair and who had hated Hind for occupying that upper reflective space and for being over a foot taller, and suddenly whipped back a combful of hair-drops onto Hind's necktie. *This* man in Hind and Sylvia's bedroom—who could not have entered through the impenetrable Handi-Wrap—said, "I have not been sent by your wife, yet I confess I am a doctor, like so many others today. I call your case the Laurel File." Behind the man across the street the fire-escape sparrow sniffed Red Cedar, wobbled on the high rail, and would not fall into its metamorphosis from bird to thing.

"Let's see," the man went on. "*Hershey* would be not merely the small city in p.a. deeply American in its all-electric school and its cocoa soap, but also L. B. Hershey, director of Selective Service (Mr. Draft himself!). But ultimately Hershey is the chocolate firm. Ever stuck a dime in one of those subway vendors?"

"No," Hind was a long time saying, "the name is simply his."

"I don't say it isn't. I don't say that at all. Let's move on to the child's last name, or what *was* his name, since he is probably dead. *Laurel* is indicative, don't you think, since in Maryland near the Peoples Drug Store where a certain tall man possibly named Dove bought five hundred Super Complex Vitamin Vessels, is the well-known track called Laurel Park."

"So what," said Hind, "you could as well say it's an adjective lured from the first name of Laura Rosenblum, who was–"

"*We* know who she was. But"–and the short man held up his rough chunk of a gold ring–"I wasn't the one to say it, was I?" And the roughness then became a raised design, a harp, a gold harp. "The great Parkinson, in his *Paradisus*, has the laurel growing in 1629 in London–in Highgate, to be exact–where you once walked with Miss Meaning–and if you bruise the lance like leaves they smell like bitter almonds."

Dreams are facile. Bring everything together. The guardian's abortive language lore and the Children's Theater of the Hershey, Pennsylvania, TV station. Side by side.

But you're not going to get what you want. Even if you stop the dekidnaping and concentrate wholly, through negotiables like the Fossy Ariosto, or the twelve-inch Heightscape oil Van told you Thea coveted, on Grimes, on Thea, even on the Old Woman, if she is still available and has not left behind in her room merely a whiff of lemony cleanliness. You still have your commitment to meet Ash tomorrow, Thursday, at the Chapel of Laughter and your suspicion that what you must now ask him about the IAS fiasco fourteen years ago will neither dissociate neatly from, nor associate naturally with, the dekidnap of Ash inescapable in any point-blank negotiations.

To reach Sylvia in April you had to face the kidnap. From which you found your way to Sylvia only to discover that dekidnaping was your sole means of satisfying, and thus having, her. Only in turn to find that you could not pursue the dekidnaping without turning up the guardian in newly revealing disguises. Instead of Jack climbing the Beanstalk three times, strength to strength, hiding place to hiding place, treasure to treasure–you were thrust back through a Chinese box of integrity-challenges-in-terms-of-vested-commitments, so that seeking the golden bird you got mortally contracted to seek the golden horse first, but then even before that you must level a mountain. "A lesson in that tale somewhere," the guardian murmured, closing the Grimm beside Hind's bed.

Plane was at the Chapel of Laughter too; Hind caught his voice off phone when Ash was giving directions; the approach to the Chapel of Laughter seemed zigzag–get off at Houston, then walk east, south, east, south (you couldn't go a decent diagonal in this grid city, and a damned tourist was telling you how to bus downtown). ("To *bus*?" a voice incredulously asks; "surely we have not sold out the noun so cravenly!")

The bus you hopped just around the corner might be the same one the OW took at the start of the revived kidnap; perish the word. Berry Brown waved in front of The Green Dragon Restaurant in the shopping complex at the west foot of Rivervale Villas; but near Hind and approaching the bus stop at a rapid limp a jaundiced, heavily clothed beggar had his hand already out and Hind did not know what to do as his bus then ran a red light and floated violently to a stop at Hind's very shin and he and his twenty-cent fare were on and in and the beggar was grinning at the window Hind sat down by. "Fiorello never would have let it happen," a woman's voice said, and a man's, "But the problems aren't the same." "So what's it matter," the woman's voice again, "you're voting Lindsay just like me."

Why did Peg and Ash want Hind's intervention? The best kind would be mild, perhaps not even advisory. See if Ash would tell the truth about himself in front of an old and devoted friend like Jack Hind. Accidental organic whole end. But Ash thought Hind had exploited their interstate and longtime friendship to tap the golf course (hole by hole if need be) to extract a track leading to the solution of a seminal contemporary dilemma. And Ash was right–though wrong if he thought Hind disloyal.

But what was Ash doing here? Too late for the Pope's U.N. visit or for the World Series, though the Series, God knew, wasn't here this year. Did "Ash" the problem call for a solution by force or by ecological adjustment?

By a wall clock in a counter-and-booth eatery a sign said, "Welcome N.Y. Police Academy–Police Laboratory, Youth Investigation Division, Bomb Squad, Ballistics Squad, Homicide Squad, Burglary Squad"–there were musics everywhere, near your seat and out on the passing street. You reviewed anything Ash might have said, but, like the eyebrows and cauliflower prices reflected in the window while through it you saw turning chickens tucked along stainless spits, Ash's "Before Peg hooked me I was the same man as after" got involved with the Old Woman's "a lot of funny names your friends have–Plane, Ivy, Ash, Beecher, Wood, Cassia–do you expect anyone to believe?" But this wasn't an issue, for if your friends (and associates) were trees or possessed of tree connections, you received them regardless of sex, verisimilitude, or depth, as a life which you year by year had enacted for yourself.

In May–June?–Ash had been as unwilling to talk of himself as he had been unwilling to come on the second IAS trip ten days after the first. The guardian persuaded him; and Hind had been similarly effective this past spring though God knew the information received had had as little to do with the kidnap mission as the kidnap with IAS.

"On top of this," Ash said when Peg had discreetly left the dining room after that numb lunch above the golf course–"I made one of my rare visits to the locker room and listened to a foursome analyze the *Big* Fellah, yeah, the *Big* Fellah playing a big series at a big club in South Africa, yeah, playing with another one of the Big Three, meeting at the summit of their game; and then the youngest of the foursome—fairly and smoothly like your guardian in the old days—said the club in question was segregated, and last year a black player who worked his way up into the South African National Open had had to be escorted round the course four days running by two of their official green blazers. But one of the others said, 'Segregated! What are you talking about? *All* the courses are segregated. You make it sound as if just that course was.' And added (which genteelly shut up the young guy who was probably putting for a junior partnership), 'Furthermore, J. M., the Big Two I believe issued a statement to the effect that we play golf not politics.' I came back to the house, aware again of the lucidity with which my class has been educated; and I wanted to pack my soft Italian luggage and leave. I thought, 'I am a divot someone neglected to replace, a divoted husband, the Big Fellahs go round the world under par, putty putt putty putt, concentrating manfully and grinning with simply modesty, raising a hand when they run one in."

How negotiate Ashley's dekidnap without using him as a means?—a means to get back not simply to Sylvia but to the lined vanishing face of the guardian at which now all-points aimed. Like your plight between genes and judgment, between inbred and bred up, you stood (at the behest, it seemed, of your mad Old Woman and maybe even his worship your loved guardian) between the bracing and punitive hint and the terrible troth. And the ugly trouble was that you never caught up with these lost and found revelations on your own but must receive them from persons who only half-possessed them and in whose throbbingly ignorant fingers they could never, like the guardian's municipal bonds, appreciate, or like your deeply legal kinship with that wonderful man, grow.

May and Sylvia in white vinyl boots waited in the sun for the bus to pass, and as it did they seemed to look through it. Were they going to the Medical Group? Why else down here? Friends Hind did not know?

Two blocks farther on—the bus pausing for a light to change, then slowing for a couple waiting at the stop who then turned and strolled on—Julio Loggia in a white cardigan was walking along with a pressed and green-covered tennis racket under his arm, his hand on the end of the head like Berry Brown holding a folded newspaper. Hardly to be pitied.

The military solution might be best for Ash. But Peg would have to do the certifying. Ash would never even chide Hind about Sylvia, he would just be sternly sorry. And he would not talk about Peg the way Art Courage talked of his long-standing high-geared engagement with little Miss Manikin and her Yoga-programed parts. At least by omission Ash was honorable. How much more could he have said to the guardian the night the IAS officially achieved fiasco status? He said enough about the guardian and next day capped it with, again, the letter to freshmen. They drove back and soon afterward Hind conceived of "Naked Voice."

"Now, Marie Verity's a smashing girl," the guardian said at dinner the final night of IAS in 1951. The guardian had just been suggesting in a hushed and therefore even more demanding voice that Ash not marry Peg right away but go to France and write, see how a foreign language clears and centers and enforces from the mass of rich English in your mind your own voice. Ah, he has found his own voice, the pundictum goes, as if growing up were a case of laryngitis. ("Yeah, well...") The guardian liked Marie the sweet girl in dirndl skirts, and made no secret of wanting her for Jack. But Marie Verity at the Young People's Concerts at Carnegie Saturday mornings let herself go, God did she. And on the subway, though she was always, almost companionably, there in the lead car, Hind could not possibly sit with her; for he was engaged in combat at the window and she, with both patent leather pumps tight to the gritty floor, would be checking the concert notebook she kept just as Ernest Schelling said, with all the programs and little information projects; and when she garnered a second place tie at the end of the season, she reacted just as when they played the concluding *allegro non troppo* of the Brahms C Minor—tears (actually, awfully) coming, and then, turning to Jack Hind next to her in the box, such a smile, which made him look back again at the orchestra his heart racing with embarrassment, feeling then at eleven or twelve that for this girl the music (which in her later classroom mood would be "Beethoven's Tenth, according to von Bülow") meant that everyone (especially on the Heights) loved everyone else, from President Roosevelt (who made her father's eyebrows go red with hate) down to the Meanings' maid Laurel. In those days Marie had been to her gentle, curt mother somewhat as Charley's bird-haunting mother had been to Charley; but no, Charley was an amiably unsatisfactory daughter who never did find out who she was though she knew damn well that at twenty-eight she wasn't going off with her mother to look for the vociferous Killdeer's orange rump on some city golf course in late October. How could Cassia like Marie? And why didn't the guardian encourage Jack to see more of Charley, even though Jack's interest in her was the mildly incestuous intimacy of long, long acquaintance—taffy pulls, sandy wet bathing suits, mock street-wedding at age seven or six, years and years of tennis, shut-outs and conquests, tears on both sides, mutual awakenings.

But how could you, pushing open the bus doors now, prolong, like love or a dream, this guardian recollection through the confused interview approaching? But look at the city renewing its sprawling needs each day like the air that at five A.M. tasted different but by six was caking your (sorry to be a bore but, your) upper gums. You couldn't go much further away from that night with the last IAS interviewee than this rubble-laid lot poised for recreation into a vest-pocket park. Two kids sparred under the city's signal dove and its caption "Smile, for your lover comes." And how far between these two framed memorials did, say, Thea come with her current passion to intervene on behalf of whatever was vanishing— for example, that skeptical koala she color-snapped in Australia looking like a big pussy willow bloom up in a fork of its diet-eucalyptus (save koala, guard Australia, fly Qantas).

Why not chuck the dekidnap, hire a car, drive up to find that Lynnfield girl and recheck her evidence?

The address Ash had slowly directed him to, and to which now a tree-hopping sparrow seemed to be leading him, was a three-story warehouse of darkened brick. But nothing said "Chapel of Laughter." Probably speed. Gold skirtlet, Sylvia had said, or Grimes had said. Laura Rosenblum wasn't the only goldie.

At the door you couldn't help hearing the tone of that letter to freshmen: unbeknownst, derivatives, tree ceremonies, free dorn. Sounded like the guardian, perhaps he had decently edited it. Or maybe Ash was right, the guardian had written it.

At the doorway of the Chapel of Laughter—"of" it how?—Hind thought of his dead parents far far off in each other's tangled arms; and as he thought to himself, "Why didn't I wish to go to see their graves?, Elder Plane never said much about Mr. Hind"—there stood Ashley and Oliver through the pane of the inner door, and also, whether reflected from behind you or simply there through the shadowy glass, Sears (like the Connecticut man who closed his store in Ridgefield and set off to find his son himself) observed that the police investigation of his boy's precious disappearance was inadequate.

"Mr. Story's demolition crane will soon be playing ball with *this* place," Hind quickly greeted Ash and Ol—but the guarded perspective of clear language has been hopelessly betrayed by now.

"Barbie was right," said Ol, "old time sake wouldn't have been enough to get you here, we had to bribe you with the chance of a good turn."

"What did Peg have to do with you coming?" said Ash, who, in his Brooks Brothers brown herringbone and with his long jaw clean, looked too neat to be a considerable denizen of this place, out of whose dirty dusk a pale face now said, "Remember, no fair bothering the ones on the third floor."

"Is this"—Hind with quick words was trying to fend off all this foolishly collaborative talk in order to protect his new review of the guardian past—"the Chapel of Laughter?"

"We have serious business to finish," said Ol, and a deep southern voice from the first landing said, "Who you got there, he's O.K.?" and higher there was a fine vein of laughter, like music from the vibrating saw Father Amondson bowed and rippled one summer's eve for Christy and Sylvia, who in bed once said to Jack, "Poor man, it sounded like electronic whatchamacallit."

The second floor, much better lighted, was the kind of fifteen-hundred-footer Sylvia wanted to lease, if you put up a couple of thousand for plumbing and walls. The sweet hint of grass, sharp but distant, was around, but it didn't seem to come from one crowded quiet corner by a window where green cigarette packs and quarts of Budweiser were on the floor among the cross-legged people whose discussion seemed just now to have petered forth and ceased.

"If you want the truth," said Ol, "we *both* have to settle with you."

"I finished you a month ago," said Hind, but how in this setting did you receive Ash as accidental organic whole end?

Ash said, "Don't mind these people coming out of the woodwork. A couple of parents were looking for their kids and now they come all the time but I don't know if they found the kids. Probably."

"But," said Ol, pointing Hind to three director chairs in a far corner, "of course this isn't the Chapel of Laughter as it properly was, you understand."

Hind answered Ash: "What is there to mind? These people aren't saying anything."

Someone in the crowded, quiet room, as if retorting after a long time, said, "But as I said to my son, you don't want to throw out any of this, you need the old perspective where you know where you are and your eye is arrested at one point. *And* you need the cubist multi-view, you can't be so narrow." The deep southern voice came back after a considerable pause: "Listen, brother, you left out Versailles. Don't tell me about Versailles, I saw that house and garden last summer, and that's another kind of space, man." "Bored the end off me," said an English voice. There was a remarkable amount of unoccupied space on this floor considering how many people were packed into that quiet discussion corner. Someone said, "You can make this place anything you want it to be—it all depends on the individual."

Laughter and stomping upstairs, shuffling and door-banging downstairs: and all you wanted was to atone, for having illused Ash, conceived him as several stereotypes and employed him in the now no longer prosecuted town-and-country kidnap. But how atone if your receptivity to him as an accidental organic whole end were to be fogged, bugged, and jammed by–"What did Peg say?" "I said I was worried about you–as I *am*" (Hind added, and heard his benevolence conspiring in a void) "and that when I got time I'd come and talk over whatever you wanted to. I told her you were just having a vacation." "For over three and a half weeks?" said Ash, but Plane said, "The real point is as follows: now I warn you, listen: Your guardian's friend Grimes phoned me at Barbie's, he got the number from you–" "He didn't." "–of course he did–where had I *been*, what was I *do*ing, as if I even know him–how come he prolonged his curriculum consulting at the department, which is pretty peculiar for a big name scholar, you'd think he'd–" "What's this to do with me?" said Ash, "Then he said–and first I thought the old bitch Grimes was after me myself–your guardian's cousin phoned to say if he didn't get on the shuttle to Boston in twenty-four hours, he was going to be *entailed* (her word) in a kidnap inquiry that he was in fact already linked with. And he asked what I knew. Now I don't know what this is, but I gather you involved Ash in it too." "I wish you'd tell me what Peg said."

When the second and final IAS trip ended as it began, inconclusively and in New York, Ash went to see Peg, and they were married so quickly the guardian wondered if she was pregnant, but she wasn't.

Grimes wanted the guardian's Ariosto. "Did Grimes say anything else?" "And on top of this, Sill says you believe his golf course is part of the kidnap." "*I* didn't say that," said Ash, "I only said I thought that was how Peg felt." "Don't back down," said Ol. "She's given up on me, hasn't she?" Ash asked, and upstairs that laughter shivered again. Was this setting the way you had to take Ash? But what the hell, you were giving him a fair chance to be an accidental whole organic end chaos of human being, weren't you?

"Business," said Ol, "and quick to the point. An Englishman who hangs around Sylvia and has tough pals is going to expose my connection with you and your kidnap if I don't fork up three months' rent for this place. I don't have the rent. The landlord is poised to evict, convert, and relet. Three lofts at three-fifty per. And I can tell you Ash is going to be in trouble too. But they know who you are, vis-à-vis Sylvia, and I'd be surprised if they didn't put the screws to her." "But if they want the money from you, why bother Sylvia?" "They know I'm trying to get the money from you." "But what did Grimes say? Why did he swallow what he heard over the phone?" "It rang a bell, long ago, something to do with your guardian and a kidnap he mentioned to Grimes." "How long ago?" "But," said Ash, "you didn't answer me about Peg. How is she *really*? *She* has nothing to do with your old man."

"But," in the same plane years ago, "why does he care if I marry Peg or not? Why does any man? No, I can see why sometimes your friend thinks you need to settle down, like you're getting too much sex and he pretends he's worried; but what's your old man care about Peg and me? I thought he was such a square, you know." "He is," said Hind, as the guardian strode out of the washroom and they went to meet the dean. The dean knew his "counterpart" at Ash and Hind's college, and was sorry he had not lined up more than one interviewee for the afternoon. The IAS appeared doomed. The day was pale and raw; the dean invited them to join his country-dancing group that night, but the guardian declined on the chance another interviewee might materialize.

The first and only one didn't turn up until four-thirty. He was tall and had dark wrinkles under his eyes; he looked older, a veteran; he certainly had on a broad-shouldered sharkskin double-breasted.

"Suit and tie," said the guardian, who must have noted white-on-white and the spread collar, the heavy silver tie and its tight small Windsor.

"I thought we would be going on from here," said the interviewee. He looked at his gold wristwatch. "I'm Morgan H. Story. You know my mother's maiden name–" and the guardian winced up at him too quickly, for he hadn't wanted to look at Morgan on the occasion of his remark; the guardian looked away and his mouth drooped a bit open as if casually. He had not known that Morgan's mother had married a construction contractor or that they had a place on the Island or that she had told Morgan so much about the guardian he almost thought he knew him. "She said you were class."

The guardian smiled slightly and asked what were Morgan's *other* reasons for consulting IAS.

"No," said Ash, here in the Chapel of Laughter once more, "I didn't recall the names till you said them. I know I got mad at your old man out in the hills that night. And Peg came into it." ("Yes or no?" said Ol.) "Then driving down the next day," said Ash, "wow! I balled him out, I guess. And back in the city that night I had a date with Peg and danced on the Astor Roof–that I remember." "You proposed to her that night." ("Look, yes or no?" said Ol.) "Why does that stick in your mind?" "Because almost as soon, I started 'Naked Voice.'" ("Look, yes or no, Hind?" Ol got up, motioning back two men and a girl who stood half out of the dusk behind the main doorway to this second-floor loft.) "And when I thought of it a month later, I was sorry I hadn't taped Morgan Story. Where did he take us for dinner? Forester's. And especially at the Green Bat Cave later, but that might have been a bit wet, but *he'd* have been happy." ("The big guy?" one of the ones in the door asked.) "Morgan H. Story said his kid brother might need IAS but Morgan didn't, for he was going into his father's racket even though his mother disliked his father, but that was for being a night school clod who subscribed to the Art Book Club because he liked the pictures and never *read* a book except the World Almanac sports statistics, on the john."

"Peg was really furious?" "Well, to be quite frank..." "Really angry?" "Well she's not exactly—it'll take more than flowers, Ashley." "I had a few drinks the night before I drove down here. She goes on to bed, leaves me drinking; or if I'm on the emergency wagon and just sitting around with my hand on a cigarette, she'll come through the living room, stop in the middle as if she remembered something, but ignore the fact that what I'm going through isn't exactly a picnic and I'm not taking cranapple nectar and Hershey bars for it either: and even stopping like that she manages to ignore my whole presence. Then politely leaves by another door. And see this pencil? The eraser's rubbed right off. This is me. I can't erase any more. So you're a godsend to be telling me Peg is in a rage. Because otherwise how would I give her credit for it? Whatever your reason. Let's face it, you loved taking over my car years ago when we had that slight mishap with the frozen tree." "*You*," Hind intervened, "you couldn't even fix a kid's swing after your own wife told you how." "Well, this little chapter has gone on too long," said Ash, "I'm pulling out of here, pick up Peg, get back home to our land."

But in the middle of things that night fourteen years back Ash hadn't been able to pull out in the middle of his assault on the guardian: "Why didn't you phone the dean at his country dance and tell him to stuff his bag? He's using you. He let you grease his elbow and invite yourself up here among the heavily endowed trees because he thought you'd pay for the well-spoken privilege by footing another elm." Then Ash had shut up, the guardian pocketed the dean's note, and Morgan H. Story told them his life and paid for the double whiskies and the double lamb chops and the triple sec he had insisted they all have, and drove them to the Green Bat Cave, which was at first—through sawdust-buoyed shuffleboard challenges and Mario Lanza's screaming white "Be My Love" spun over and over again by the middle-aged blonde in a green basketball jacket who sat there in New England in a booth with a blond man much younger—merely a woody, no-dancing roadhouse that advertised meatball sandwiches to keep its licensing status.

When Story was in the john, the guardian said to Ash, "Fraternities are an evil as they're maintained here. He doesn't belong to one. Why should he come up here among these Ivy sons of alumni fathers—"

"He's a snob," said Ash, "and so is his mother, and in self-defense so is his father."

"Ah, then, what *is* a snob?" said the guardian, and Morgan Story, his thinning dark hair newly slicked, stopped to challenge the blond man to a game.

Hind said to the guardian, "He's a waste of your time," and Ash added, "There's something kind of sick about this whole IAS trip."

The guardian, who was drinking tea at the bar, said, "You wait and see. I'm selfish perhaps. The coincidence that this rather pathetic city slicker should have known of me in another world, so to speak, that he should know all that old silliness, the Polytheist Club at Harvard, the sixteenth-century lyrics I would quote helping a charming maid over a stile, the idea of one's death distributing one's unique force among those godly potencies signally receptive to one's own nature—how I must have talked about myself to that girl his mother. God, the nonsense I talked. And felt! In those days I made much, to myself, of my family, my name. Though, as I recall, I professed exogamy."

"*Every* marriage is outside the tribe," said Ash gloomily fourteen years later. (Oliver and the three others had gone from the doorway, there were steps going up to the third floor, someone turned Albert Ayler on—the new Fantasy recording spread its flat accidental energies through the building.)

"Yes," said the guardian, "I know you know the meaning of exogamy the *word*. But can you at your age guess what meaning the idea bears concealed beneath its dictionary sound? What is freedom?—"

"I'll tell you in a second," Morgan Story called, "as soon as I crush my opposition."

"—Is it, to be able to choose anything at all that loiters beyond oneself?"

"The lie active or the lie contemplative?" said Ash.

"Ah good," said the guardian, "but the point is, you may not have it in you to be both, I mean the *life* active, the *life* contem—"

"But you need the past," said Ash naggingly. "The old models."

"Where did you hear that phrase?"

"Nothing special about it. Any more than there is about bachelor tree ceremonies in India, and by the way what *about* bachelor trees?"

"I see, you're ragging me about that letter to freshmen—Jack's letter."

But it didn't stop Ash, who told the guardian he'd heard him telling Hind the first night of IAS in the inn that the guardian had gone on with IAS not only because it might blossom into something rather remarkable, but even more, to help Ash, give him a hand at a bad time.

And what did he mean by setting out to do a thing like this, and why did he go around telling people? It made you feel, Ash said, about two feet tall.

Morgan's last disc was a hanger and he won a dollar from the blond man, who objected to Morgan's quitting and said truculently as Morgan came and stood behind the guardian, "I don't see you here Saturday I betcha. That's when it's tough around here, you don't just..."

The guardian thought he was pacifying young Hamlet by, instead of acknowledging the bachelor tree allusion, badgering Ash genially about freedom "–any more than my mother knew the Latin names or even the family traits of the trees and shrubs she and Father loved–" and Ash, "don't treat me like an invalid, deal with me," politely, querulously, quietly–"for she had no wish to possess them. Whether buds of something had leaf scars or chambers of pith mattered not. She didn't read gardening books, nor visit nurseries."

"I seem to have gotten out of phase," said Morgan, he thought archly. "Weren't we talking about me?"

But the guardian finished: "Yes, yes, the thing is, early on to see the hard but proper price of freedom. Time was that I wanted to surrender myself, to work for Roosevelt in the beginning, or before that to commit myself to painting–I've told you about working in the High Tatras before the Crash. But then it came to me. I saw that one must–or *I* must–become my own innate independence."

"So very becoming," said Ash.

"To possess nothing finally, if you see. And then not *be* possessed. Take my scholar friend Professor Grimes: he has, in effect, *chosen* his antecedents: by, do you see, first assuming his own independence of family and birthplace, even birthright. Sounds cruel but it isn't. But, possess and you are possessed." The guardian swung round on his stool and grinned handsomely at Morgan, whose beard had begun to show and who looked sallower even than the green shades and yellow bulbs made him.

"Well," Morgan said, "no magic about it, you have to know who you are—no mysteries allowed, there isn't time. Then, if like me you are bound to be a big success, what you do is you husband your ambitions with a fiendish patience."

"Oh Morg," said the bartender's wife from a booth.

"Ever think? patience *is* the key. You don't have locks?—drop and wait. Girl coming along sluggish? slow?—wait for her. Your peers don't recognize your superiority? your existence even?—don't press till it's time. Talk only to those who are listening. Money. Women. Power. Anticipate the correct moment. My old man did O.K., and I'm going to show him I understand, because I'm going to triple that business, and he knows it. But *he* couldn't always wait, y'see. My kid brother who couldn't care less about construction, my father's actually glad Artie wants to be something else—when Artie was a tiny child my father used to follow him around the house, y'see."

The guardian got an elbow on the bar, and stared at the floor. "It seems rather abstract," he said. "And 'anticipate' means 'forestall.'"

"And one day my old man told Artie, who was only eight, that my mother and he had *had* to get married, and Artie said oh sure was it because they loved each other and my old man smiled and then said, 'And I was going to night school then.'

"Well, there it is. No magic about it. I, Morgan H. Story, am the product of impatience.

"Learn from everybody. Eclecticism. I take what I need. Take Toynbee: the destined man prepares by retreating (which is me here in the hills), thinking, planning, waiting; grows strong—then returns. To civilization. And wins.

The whole rest of Toynbee is just to prove his moral, and I wouldn't buy it."

"Nor would I," murmured the guardian.

"But my mother bought it for my birthday. Or take old George Holly, with his blued hair: when he picks up my fellow students hitching over the hills to their sister college, if he gets the wrong answer to his ritual gag 'Do you mind getting up there with a flat tire?', he respectfully drops the guy wherever they are on the road, drives back, and starts again. But if you're a prude and you discard George, you lose a remarkable man who knows the history of roulette, pinochle, hearts, dice better than any professor at either college, y'see.

"Eclecticism and patience. But patience."

"Where are the caves?" the guardian asked the bartender, who, as if in self-defense, reached for the wet towel bunched on the counter.

"I guess there's one back in the hills a mile or so. If there *is* one, it's on this land."

"Why are the bats green?"

"It's just the name. You be surprised—summer people drive through, stop the night at one of my wife's cabins behind here, and they'll never ask about the green bat caves."

At the end of the evening, which, because of all the driving, seemed part of the next day's melancholy trip to the city, Morgan H. Story was saying, "She definitely remembers you, you have the dubious distinction of being her last boyfriend before me—"

"—she was at normal school in Boston, as I—"

"—I mean, before my father."

In the Lincoln Zephyr in the bright morning, the purple hills lay above unwatching, and clean concrete and tar never failed to be there ahead.

The southern voice you'd heard from the landing: "What's the big guy on?" and Ash: "No, he was just dreaming, that's what he was staring away at," and the southern voice: "Hey, that's O.K., turning on by thinking back, why not?, that's O.K., I'm not knocking heads that turn on like that, better than speed, better than grass, better—" then Ash came back in and stood by Hind's director chair. "Before I met Peg I was the same man as after. But being married gave me a place to fix my inaction in. But for her to really blow her sock as you said, it's got to be a new situation. I don't want to disappear any more. That night on the beach with that Jap junkie reciting translations, I wanted to dig through to China. Or was he Chinese? Sometimes I think they're all the same in at least one thing, Orientals: they're all waiting to do us back our favors. I got to go. It's getting dark out. I want to catch her." "Do you recall what my guardian said on the way home?" "No, except I told him he ought to get away from his own class." "You said more." Laughing upstairs broke through to the landing above and was coming down. A man tried to speak through his own hilarity, "—depth I never never guessed, depth, there is *only* depth, no breadth no end, just deep, man."

"Of course, Ash," said the guardian, "what you say is true of this Independent Advisory Service and of its leader. One doesn't get the chance to break through onto clear ground, and make wonderfully necessary changes. There I was painting in the High Tatras at the time of the Crash. But oh to have been in Czechoslovakia just a few years later, you see. Now *that* could have had the significance this little junket of ours may seem to you to have lacked. On that cold day in Prague, 1939, the Jewish husbands naked in the park, their ladies naked— no, nude—in the trees chirping like birds. Oh Ash, to have been standing at the window of my old red-carpeted second-floor restaurant down the hill from the university and as Hitler came along that tree-lined avenue, to have shot him. And then to be shot oneself on the spot. But by 1939 I'd written a mystery, I'd started to study the market and write a little essay on Dürer; Jack had been left an orphan by that dreadful autogyro accident, and I had seen Jack's adoption through with the great help of Elder Plane's cousin, a fine fine lawyer—hectic days—"

"But we're not going to turn away from what's been going on here," said Ashley Sill in the back seat.

The guardian tried to interrupt, Ash could be his Boswell, or no he'd be Ash's, think of the city they were returning to now as the London of young Samuel Johnson, surely there was for Ash in the heights and depths of New York someone like Mr. Cave, the editor of *The Gentleman's Magazine* who went under the singular name of Sylvanus Urban and evoked the reverence of—

"Seeing you kid yourself, Mr. Foster, up in these middle-class upper-middle-class pastoral spas has cleared my head. Don't you see, you concern yourself to advise not guys who might really need you but these future leaders on whom our country is banking, most of them backgrounded just like me and Jack; and seeing you—well it's more pathetic than dangerous—it's cleared my head. I know what I don't want. You've drawn *me* out anyway, even if your IAS—" a few more words, and Ash slept the rest of the trip. And the pity Hind felt for the guardian: who seemed even less consolable to your left in the driver's seat (left elbow out the open window, left fingers and right hand gently but firmly on the tortoise-shell wheel), than if you had been in the back seat. You wanted him, you wanted to listen to him talk and talk—he didn't quote poems then the way he had used to—you wanted his fluent voice to cover you like a skin, fill your eyes, take total control of the air.

You wanted to stop Ash, who was in the doorway obviously leaving the C. of L.: "Hop and Daisy all alone?" asked Hind. "Don't you worry about Hop and Daisy. Save yourself."

I may not like myself. But I know who I am.

If there was time to dekidnap Mad—who now believed that should the Plante people make an attempt on his apartment house (just parallel to the guardian's, which fronted on the next street north and whose west windows overlooked the harbor) they would probably leave a heat-sensitized but shock-resistant micro-soybomb in the kitchen trash which would go up when Flo put the trash down the incinerator chute—Mad's accidental organic whole performance would have to be superrelevant. At least Ash was done.

Eleven blocks north and west Hind squeezed into a street-corner phone booth past a boy who stood his guitar case big end up and didn't move.

Into the receiver you said, "It's me, Jack, Hind."

"Changed your mind about Fossy's Ariosto?"

"*What* kidnap did my guardian mention to you, and *when*?"

"What's it worth, dearie? mmm, ah, what was it Fossikins used to intone to his ladybirds?—'Whoso list to hunt, I know where is an hind,' etcetra etcetra. He played Bunthorne to my Grosvenor, you might say: he the fleshly poet, I the idyllic. Mmm, in reply to your truculent inquiry: *your* kidnap. I'd like to see you, you know. Of course, I'm just an old fart with a little heat left, plus a thwarted but undirected wish for a bit of mild vengeance, plus a few jokes. At the moment I'm going about your city collecting instances of this odd verbal identitism, I think there's a book in it—bumper sticker reading BUMPER STICKER, button reading BELLY. Mmm in reply to your truculent inquiry, I know nothing else about your kidnap except that Fossy knew you were conducting a private investigation and was concerned you not waste your vital, however public, spirits. What about it, may I drop up tomorrow?"

"No, just your voice. I can handle that."

"Don't go 'way mad. The old gal Fossy's cousin can't bear to be in the vicinity of those who knew and were fond of your strange misguided father, perhaps that is why she—"

"He *knew*."

"About the kidnap, yes. But you know how he was on certain topics—couldn't bring himself to speak out honestly."

"Don't you talk about honesty, Red."

Thea might speak out. A dozen blocks farther north, a transistor standing on a pile of *World-Telegrams* on a newsstand discussed the value of Michigan State's giant defensive end, six-seven. A cat played soccer with a dented ping-pong ball. A transistor still farther north was pacifying the countryside. Thea's phone didn't answer. Mannikins in Fall and Winter coats had huge paper flowers instead of heads.

Why rush? Time on that last IAS ride passed slowly, the guardian choking with silence but then rambling painfully, and time though thus slow accumulated length as Pliny the Lincoln Zephyr passed not simply south to New York and Brooklyn Heights but deep into the flatlands of November, and winter: Burke's view that "the rights of men are in a sort of *middle*"—Johnson's lexical excesses—the fallacy *falsum in uno, falsum in omnibus*, which the guardian had found to be entertained most often by members of the working or lower-middle classes—until Ashley (after another silence raced past a dog track, a shopping center under construction, a Sears, a tall old dun brick public school with a circular swing in front, and later a golf course), said, "You didn't only *edit* that letter to freshmen, you *wrote* it." Which the guardian never answered—as if, Hind then had guessed, Ashley's charge was self-evidently in error.

Thea was still out, when Hind passed through his unlocked vestibule door and his unlocked apartment door upstairs and phoned her. The guardian's flower books, with the sheep bookplate, the pictures, the smell of lemon on his hands turning pages and telling how bumblebee flowers often have pressure release mechanisms that flowers catering to the smaller honeybee don't have—and then on a walk inland from house and beach, toward the town road and among the treasure-hunt trees, and then stopping for a brief analysis of that simplest and loveliest of pollinations—the wind and *its* humble flowers—look at these grasses. But of course you must wait. It's only November.

# iv

Hind stopped. But not for an emergency.

On a Sunday looking up- and downtown crossing Lexington and then Third, he recognized the sunny Manhattan hills. Let goldenrod—or some of Thea's reddish-brocaded coleus, or hawthorn, dogwood, or even laurel!—grow up out of the so-called John Plante's fertile head; but these coasting hills were real.

Hind caught and boarded an uptown bus. He'd wound Sylvia's alarm clock and it actually went off before he woke. In Buck's shopwindow, before a backdrop collage of Blackout headlines and photos featuring in the asymmetrical center John Lindsay's serious smile, stood FUN BIRD a fiery rainbow cock made of dyed and spotted Kleenex.

Two Afro-Americans in red football shirts with white shoulders slowly dribbled a basketball past Captain Kidd's headed downtown. Farther up, the avenue was an aisle of less undifferentiated executive blocks; Hind had not only made Sylvia's clock work but had both no memory of a dream last night and, then, the conviction as he woke of being—perhaps by virtue of waking up—on the brink of a dream telling Maddy sorry he couldn't help—no, simply couldn't advise him to invest or not in the paintbrush firm. But if Maddy joined the FHHC as Hind's catch, Hind got five free massages. Finally one morning promptly at ten when it opened, Berry Brown did use Hind's free passes which in fact any member could just pick up off the front desk. Berry brought his airplane luggage, and according to him the cauliflower ear with the blue nose who was supposed to look at those passing down the hotel lobby stairs to the club looked at Berry's topcoat and his black-and-red basketball sneakers, and raised his nose to speak, but at the last second as Berry slowed for the first marble step beyond the lobby carpet this serge and overweight senior citizen looked away with stunned serenity. Still, Berry didn't have the guts to go into the gym and walk the blue carpet among the mirrors; so he sat in the sauna reading the four newspapers he had packed. Weekdays he met the nine-forty commuter train at Track 27, and after the crowd had come through and the butt filters and coffee containers were being swept out Berry could go down the platform with new passengers to the train that had become the ten A.M. for Boston, and in the end compartments by the doors he would pick through the slanted stacks of *Times, Wall Street Journal, National Observer, News*, and perhaps a fugitive *Monitor*, preferring papers not left at financial, food, or sport pages but decently restored. Today he'd be at the pier if it wasn't too breezy.

But Hind was off the bus at the broad towering corner of Forty-second almost without thinking "Grand Central." The Sunday subway steps were as continuous in their free silence as the apparently distant hum of the subsequent escalator whose steps plated with knife-sharpened grooves moved endlessly down to the Queens level.

For you must look again at the Orientals' map. Even if it's nothing now but cardboard undercoat with a few poignant initial histories hinting east, west, south—flash portraits jammed down in pencil or ballpoint as the train came in, or doodled lies to fill time while trains did or would not come: the white, featherweight windbreakers; the wool jackets labeled in script across the shoulder blades STORKS; the rich brown leather motorcycle jackets studded in silver; all crowding in to write, throwing an elbow, palming a waist, brushing an eager breast—and, yes, recorded live across the curve of your watery cornea though now clear since you have learned to allow for refraction at this depth you once thought full of pathos—Honey La Grange at the subway map rubbing out her number, seeing it still appear, then incising over it fictional—but could any be fictional?—digits. The beloved guardian's old ideal of Plain Language was dead, wasn't it? or if alive, alive in the great carbometabolic map of Cupidine reaction, elation, synthesis, hooked and arrowed in para-musical notation, scoring not Glutamate to Glutamine, but vis-à-vis inner goals, disinterested to infrastructured weedhead in terms hopefully of face, screed, or "Other"—embracing icecapade and aquascape, escapade and even vanilla, its bean and its pod—and, guarding the frontiers of "nice," "of," and "you" as well as (if it needs guarding) the honorable derivation of "achievement" in the French for "finish," becoming like old Skoldy in retirement trying without success to grow in a cold frame out in Bay Ridge Hairy Bird's Foot from that Hampshire golf course smuggled live past Kennedy customs.

Well then, did the guardian emerge from the wilderness of phenomena poignantly sized as an ineffectual dilettante? or did he fade like a fireless cremation back into his enduring background which in life it became him both to cling to and to step apart from? (See in Dürer's unfinished treatises a parallel to one's own life: the need to balance theoretical and [k-k-k-] creative: to Morgan Story that night, with love and a wild grin, "Those two big books of Dürer's weren't a waste of time, you see. Dürer wasn't content to be merely a maker. It's imperative the maker not reach final answers but be muscularly, instinctually tying into life palpable materials." "Yeah," said Morgan, "it's O.K. if you got locks. Well, *I* know perspective. I had a course in it. Well, not *only* in—")

The penny you put in the chocolate machine years ago has turned to a nickel though the Hershey recipe hasn't changed; and on this quiet platform, reached by dying pulsations from the street, your nickel keeps coming back. The Flushing local in the mirror behind you isn't "waiting" in the station, it's just there; nor could you ever "catch" it. Was there bread to be smelled at the Rawson Street elevated stop on Sunday too? Turn from the Hershey mirror and saunter toward the empty car, not meaning to get on: and the door drives shut as you reach it.

And likewise it came to pass that two or three weeks ago, not from that very Beecher apartment you soon must visit, but from a hotel, the resonant and breathing phone voice of a weirdly talkative Peg Sill said, "Thank you, Jack, even if your motives escape me. But you did something to him, you surely did, for he was in a corner, a long corner, and he came and took me away from Maddy and Flo's right in the middle of a super ragoût Vietnamese she invented for some leftovers; and he balled me out and I—hit the ceiling literally. Whatever you said got home. Ash said to tell you not to worry, Oliver doesn't want it known he arranged some parties at the Chapel of Laughter. He's bucking for promotion at school."

But Hind had already paid the C. of L. rent requested, though he didn't tell Peg.

Might as well give Grimes the Ariosto, whether or not Grimes had something to give in return.

Thea wasn't answering her phone, unless she was away.

Another day Hind ordered by mail a set of toy animals advertised as the product of research: lead them to water, they grow for weeks—secret of growth educational. Eddy might appreciate them; he wasn't at all well, according to reports.

Early on another morning a model emerged from under the great roll-up delivery door of the ad studio and a clear vinyl chair was brought for her to be photographed in. Afterward when she unplugged the inflated chair she bent so far over that what there was of a hind skirt pulled right up above her undercoating, whereupon the chair began to sink and she pushed and turned until at last she had it in an oblong section, which she carried down the street while the photographers went back under the slowly down-rolling door.

But why would Thea be not answering the phone? You could combine a visit to her with a visit to the Beechers around the block.

He didn't know what day it was. He walked, to make the trip longer, all the way south to the Brooklyn Bridge, then across under high arches like the abandoned beginning of a Perpendicular nave, but as if he were crossing not merely East River but the entire harbor itself in wise steps from the Hoboken clam house to Staten Island's Willowbrook School for defective kids (cheek by jowl with the Latourette Golf Course)—then to Liberty Island (careful not to bust off the torch she's been carrying so long) to South Street Viaduct (hold your lane) to the Poplar Street station house, a five-minute skate from (or to) Thea's, though she was surely not home.

"Ah for God's sake, Jack! Have you been trying to get me? First, it was the agent, then I was in the country—during the bivouac (that's what Van calls the Blackout, he was having a drink at a convention in a mid-town hotel, said it was just like the war)—then when I got back the agent phoned again and I'd seen Maddy Beecher's commie friend who made me so guilty about this big apartment that I told the agent I'd think over the rent and the smaller flat upstairs, but then I thought for God's sake this is just like Chamberlain at Salzburg or wherever it was, and when the agent called back this morning exactly when he said he would, I didn't answer."

"You have too much, Thea. We all have."

"I know it, darling, but what could I do with my tables and chairs? They're as bad as children or books. By the way, you can have my old butter pats."

Her incandescent-fed red-brocaded coleus thrived. To simulate a lightning stroke she had stripped a vertical line of bark off a cypress bonsai.

"And the war," she said. "*Paris-Match* says we can't lose. But think of the investment. General Hershey says the draft board's keeping an eye on the progress of deferred students."

"General L. B. Hershey's specifics."

"Democracy's all very well for overdeveloped nations, but sometimes I wonder if we're not sort of *using* the Vietnamese rather than they us. Or am I being idealistic?"

"No. If we only *were* truly using them. But I didn't come just to see you."

Thea was pouring a cup of tea and said mildly, "Oh for God's sake, Jack, don't rub it in." Her visible possessions here weren't, after all, so many. She didn't crowd her piano, and she didn't clutter the walls with grouped etchings, water colors, whittled reliefs, abstract shots of beach and bog and suspiciously near-genital surfaces all interfitted as if when you took one down you'd have to take down a whole hinged system.

Her great-grandfather had made the plain, inlaid Hepplewhite tables, and in the drawer of the one directly under the guardian's tiny oil of Greengage's east porch, there were packs of cards Thea never used.

"You used to make cinnamon toast in the afternoon." On rather hard Thomas Protein. Harsh transitions are bad manners.

"And one day you were here for tea you stayed the whole night and I gave you a bath, you were nine and weren't at all sure you wanted me to, you were just in that phase. And when Fossy poked his head in and said, 'Made in the image of God,' and went away again, you forgot your little embarrassment and said, 'Does God have to wash?'"

And when you were eight (no more), sitting on the floor of his room with a knee on the bathroom threshold Thea had to undress in front of you because she was taking a bath; and she didn't mind—you recall, perhaps wrongly, that she seemed to like it, taking her time, going to the chair and the bed and bureau laying things down; and when she hadn't a stitch on (looking less thin than with clothes, though she didn't wear a girdle), the front door opened far away as you said (as if "at last"), "*He*llo, Thea," and you heard Fossy's approach and she hustled into the bathroom and bumped your knee shutting the door, and then the guardian appeared.

"Did you used to say 'Ho hum'?" That night conversation, the woman unidentified.

"It was only a facetious tic, I never said it when I was bored. Funny thing to remember. Do you still see the Beechers? The little boy's terribly bright. I think they're worried about him."

"It was a conversation you had with Fossy."

"What? There were so many. Right to the end. You're quizzing me, Jack."

"I don't know about what."

"He had a secretive way too, just like you. Though God knows there wasn't much he kept from me. The day he died—"

But the fireplace at Greengage, and the knowledge that the rainswept beach was a short walk away—did Thea possess this?—on the peeled top of the log, flame floated on sap, and rootlets of fire in twos or singly slipped back and forth like eyes, not even eyes in the wood, eyes afloat on burning surface—did Thea possess *this*?—and your guardian expounding the city-country imperative, the balance that was, mmm, richly related to all the other balances in a cultivated man's mind.

"—he was disturbed that day about you. Also he didn't feel well. He said it was the cold baked beans, and so-called country sausage. And he, well he smiled, as if he loved me. I put my arm around his waist. He was afraid you weren't finding yourself. I said I thought you lived quite an original, intelligently domestic life. He said, 'I'm so damn conventional.' He said he knew I was right, but the great professions—law, science, scholarship, service, art—he said he kept thinking of them as points at which to permanently stop, 'get off the endless belt,' he said, 'you think it's taking you into the future but you're walking in the wrong direction.' I gave him a consolation kiss and said—why yes!—'Ho hum, dear, ho hum,' and he smiled at me then, with the breakers behind his great gray head because he knew what my infrequent 'Ho hum' meant and it didn't mean exactly I was impatient. Oh, he said there was a thing he must talk out with you. Your trip abroad with Sylvia had brought together, he said '*in his eye*,' all the past and present elements of this 'thing' he must talk out with you. He sounded almost afraid. Now suddenly I feel guilty. We made a fire. He put a gray gull feather in my hair. Anglo-Saxon squaw trying to look indifferently gay, feeling desperately sentimental. And he spoke again of Gibbon, the religious toleration Rome showed. And he was flirting with that old polytheism of his—or is it pantheism, I always forget—"

"But *why* did my European jaunt bring things together? Was it the kidnap?"

"Oh *that*—I'd completely forgotten. Yes, perhaps he *was* worried about it. What sticks in my head is how he told about the personality of the sea and our fire and the wind, and he was very affectionate that afternoon, Jack, as long as it lasted."

"Guilty, you said?"

"I *felt* guilty. Yes. I'll show you. It couldn't have helped you or Sylvia. It was my oddly reassuring keepsake of him, this more than anything else, I wonder why. It was in a shoebox. A letter to your father which I gather Fossy retrieved. Not even fairy light-foot Grimes snooped into this."

Thea went down the hall at the end of which were the two bedrooms. And then Hind couldn't hear her.

But the pitiable or sordid would tell no more than, say, the floral note card the forest wife sent:

> I got your name from Farmer Love, who did some work for me and when I described you, laughed a lot and recalled someone like you investigated the Laurel case once. But I'm contacting you because of what I'm supposed to get. A fabulous old lady visited my home and said there would be a very tall man coming through the country doing market research into Welcome Wagon follow-up, and I should say to him all that about city noise that a real city person doesn't hear, and to throw in the dew idea, remember? And if I said those things I would be the recipient of a year's supply of the disinfectant of my choice. Well, where is it? (But I really liked you, and it was true that I take creative non-fiction at the Base.)

Hind did not read the letter Thea now handed him, and thinking he meant not to take it, she said, "No, I don't want it now you know I have it. You can't imagine what your mother's death meant to Fossy."

"You knew his cousin Miss Foster?"

"An intellectual snob."

"She fell out with my guardian?"

"More than once. Their fight was indirectly due to you, though you were only five or six. She made peace by ordering tickets for a children's performance at the Academy and came down from somewhere—Boston, I think—to take you. Red was there. He was on leave studying Indian that winter."

"I can't recall."

"That termagant said something, I wasn't there, and before Fossy could rescue the conversation it went its logical way."

"But he knew about the kidnap later on."

"Foster did say Grimes goaded her."

"How?"

"You know how he used to sit about and half-read while people talked, so he would dip in when he jolly well felt like it? Once later, Fossy and I were fighting over a passage in Proust, Fossy was maintaining that Swann's later rationalizations were not credible as those of a real man, and Red said, 'Stop fighting, kids, I'll read you the real thing—great scholar, great poet—hold on...' he began to read *A Shropshire Lad*, didn't he, but Fossy forgot himself and said, 'Shut up, Red; Housman didn't even get his topography straight in those poems.' But this earlier time with the cousin Foster, so he told me, he forgot you were watching from a doorway. Yes, that's it."

"Grimes goaded Miss Foster?"

"Oh goodness...well, your dear guardian told me Red read part of a poem softly, as background to a few bad words that were passed—nothing serious—with your mother's name in it—I mean the poem—all very witty. Who is it? Lady Winchelsea? I'm hopeless. No, it was a man, and I think it's Wyatt. And your mother's name figured in it."

"In what?"

"Then Fossy changed the subject of course—I mean, with me, later—and said he and Grimes once debated it. Wyatt."

"What?"

"Ooo, please," Thea moaned, "give me a rest, darling. All right, Grimes said...of course it's a love poem; so is... some other they'd been haggling over, which Fossy insisted was about the Goddess Fortune—well this other one with 'Hind' in it he said was about cupidity not love."

Thea took a deep breath and blew it out. "*Your mother.* When she died, he went to the country. I was just beginning to know him. Through Elder and Engleman and Daisy and Van. Fossy said things like, 'She knew how to make herself your prey without your knowing it. You were free in her hands'—oh Jack I have to dress and run—or if you want to come along we can talk, no you don't want to come along—"

"I have to go to Maddy's."

"You see I couldn't say, 'Fossy, *any* woman's a bloody human being. I don't care how complete a companion—that was what he called her too, it made her sound like a bedside subtreasury. But you can't trust a thing I say. Except that—Poseidon and Aeolus and the Muse of Love, whoever she is, were all there that last afternoon. It was Ike's sixty-ninth birthday, wasn't it?"

He was kissing her good-bye at the door and she said, "Let me know how the little Beecher boy is." At the elevator she pressed the button for him, talking about the poor little nocturnal lemurs at the Bronx Zoo who might have caught cold in the Blackout if the keepers hadn't stuffed blankets between the bars.

Now you should be ready to dekidnap Maddy. They were right round the block. But the giant Recollection was sneezing in your mind as cataclysmically as the guardian when he rushed the season in mid-March and had a fit of them: As Hind passed down the familiar street which he believed now he could not help inheriting, passed as slowly as Rain's granddad with his walker, and all around came that sequence of guardian sneezes, shriek-puff after shriek-puff: the dependence of vowels on tongue-advancement (: Grimes); the use of a grill only when your vanishing point is beyond the edge of the paper (: Byron Bean), but what if you couldn't draw, no matter how many guardian lessons; beginning Safari amaryllis bulbs *now*, in mid-November, if you want that red (so easily forced) bloom by Christmastime (: guardian); grudging surrender to the now-pedigreed neologism "defoliate" but deep (if posthumous) resistance to the use of "leaflet" as a verb, as "to leaflet villages suspected of Vietcong sympathies." But this wasn't the guardian. And yet something of this: and if that Poseidon of Ike's sixty-ninth birthday was tender romance for Thea, it was stern (if delusive) *consolatio* for him, dimly a benign threat of religion in the salt spray and the incredible clear contour of the October swells; Poseidon was even more urgently that Gibbonian account of subtle Roman order rooted in toleration as tenuous as the law was plain; and yet again more urgently, here was the tentative figure of Gibbon more amply complete in his eighteenth-century scholarship than brawny Johnson marbly toga'd, sir: Gibbon at those "Fashion suppers" in Paris, or listening to Burke whose reflections on France were as humanely formed, if somewhat uninformed, as the guardian's on Detroit and Harlem in June of 'forty-three, his heart somewhat enlarged not merely from middle-distance running in school and college, but more from anxiously knowing that the sunlight of Ariosto and the deep sense of Johnson's lexicon lived in a space of inheritable air guarded by brownstone stoops and the Poplar Street patrolman (whom Heights people always called "Clancy") who right here along Maddy's street yelled for fifteen long minutes when he caught Jack Hind and Lief Lund scaling the elegant face of the Lunds' house—inheritable heir guarded even now by the televised commissioner first licking his lips waiting to be told he's on, then proudly declaring, "This city is the greatest city for crime in the U.S."

"Rhodes scholars grow like trees around here," Elder Plane said in Oliver's hearing; "the Heights record is remarkable." But not so remarkable as a twelve-, thirteen-, fourteen-year-old who was busting all records for height, so when you mounted the high board ladder at the St. George Hotel pool under the gleaming gaze of balcony spectators (so close you could almost have benevolently dragged over the rail that wise public school kid) you felt like an omega-headed octopus, and when you proceeded down this very street toward the harbor you felt your height like the old soldier's nose that grew so long that his comrades had to walk and walk to find him at its root prostrate, and when you confessed this to the beloved guardian who after all had read you "The Nose" in *Grimm's Fairy Tales* in the beginning, that sage had first answered by alluding to the same tale—"But Jack, on the contrary your amazing growth is like the horn that could not but make beautiful music." But seeing that this merely met riddle with riddle, he added that whatever one was, was a fine thing to be, and to think of one's born attributes as separate from one's self verged on suicide, didn't it? Of course, when you put the guardian's body next to Van White's, Engleman Deal's, the portly Jap tenant's, much less Grimes', there was no comparison, so the guardian could afford to be reassuring. "Your head," Buddy Bourne choked, "was up in the cotton-picking clouds!" The guardian seldom raised his voice, not even when

Buddy angered him that night at the Garden hockey game; to Jack, only once, when he found out about Jack and Charley after her brother spilled the beans, and even then vague words weakened the anger—"in the depth of your fourteen-year-old wisdom you cannot imagine the consequences that might—...." Far away inside, farther even than May had seemed to be when Sylvia was six weeks gone, you felt that because you were a freak the (nonetheless beloved) guardian hadn't the right and even couldn't reach you. But there were, as surely Gibbon and Johnson (even Boswell and Savage) agreed, many things one would never say—Shirley Laurel telling a Dane in Norway that long ago she liked her husband—but "never say" wasn't precisely what the guardian meant when he called "unspeakable" the fifty-two Danish children aged one to twelve being packed off to Germany by rail from the Copenhagen freight station just before Christmas 'forty-three.

Maddy's elevator tried to sing the words it sang so many months ago, "Lowell, Lawler, Laura," but instead Jack was coming in from his movie date with Cassia the Christmas of 'forty-three or 'forty-four and the guardian's party were departing for dinner in Manhattan, the guardian sternly disagreeing over Gilbert and Sullivan with the organist Willoughby and with Thea and two other couples whom the guardian introduced to his "boy." The guardian asked if he'd wrapped his present for Cassia Meaning, he thought he knew a passage in So *Little Time* to show just how thin Marquand was, though in his way thorough. "I wrapped it"—the lie came naturally, and didn't matter, and the septet trooped out, one of the men archly asking if the maître-d. would seat Willoughby in that old red corduroy jacket. The sleeve of which Fossy in reply grabbed, saying Willoughby was not Bunthorne the fleshly but Grosvenor the idyllic—for the guardian didn't know these two couples very well, and neither did the good-natured Willoughby.

But now Maddy Beecher did not take Hind's arm when the door opened; nor did Hind feel adminicular. Flo called out rather softly from somewhere, "Jack, what a surprise, Bee Bee's coming for supper, I've got tons of risotto." As if he hadn't heard, Maddy said, "It's Eddy. We've been sort of worried."

Hunger moved like radio storm static across Hind's stomach from left to right.

Thea's old bedtime *Kinderscenen* were coming from Maddy's living room stereo, Maddy disappeared through the pantry door and was heard talking, and Hind saw, on entering the huge green fitted rug and hearing the piano broaden before him, that on the silent TV screen a golfer was just putting. Maddy came in from the kitchen and turned up the sound as the putt rolled, a black hand took away the flag, and a woman's rising wail was with the white ball all the way to the cup until at the lip the wail became a brief shriek and the ball hung poised there on the lip and did not drop. "Player says golf is the most humiliating game," said Maddy.

Hind receiving: accidental organic whole end is the play.

"Eddy's been going to bed earlier. For a long time we let him push himself, and we pushed him. A kid that bright, you don't want to lose these good years, and with his appetite for new skills you want to feed him as fast as his system can take the work. But he went too fast perhaps. Or I did. Or maybe something else."

Get back to Maddy.

Flo watched for a second from the kitchen doorway, then went back. Her hair had turned auburn since May. Thea's *Kinderscenen* never sounded like this. Hind lay in bed hearing—and maybe in the foreground the newspaper rustling—endlessly independent piano music, earnest as the child who was almost playing to it, gratuitous as the child's hunt into a flickering wood where the firm run of hopeful octave-crests and returning melodies was like a companion substance yet, like the wood, puzzling you forth to the rim of a hidden clearing where, unlike the guardian's fairy tales in which from that clearing came the noise of a giant brandishing a branch, only a sweet unknown wind waited to join the substance of those simple piano promises you thought had kept you company through the trees but which, now that you don't go to sleep so easily any more, you know was never with you when you idly hunted but was itself that sweet wind beyond the wood hunting you as you it—until, puzzled to the rim of that clearing, you stopped, for your eye was lured up sharp to the guardian's tree house: but when you moved back to get a real look your foot felt the stiff green shoots cupping white lilies of the valley among the twigs and needles: the music took you back and forth, circled you in your bed till as you were carrying the music to sleep feeling the guardian's and Thea's hands playing over you you almost forgot to slide one big foot out from under the covers to breathe. Thea's Schumann wasn't this definitive stereo guarded by upholstered boxes either side of the changer and amplifier and programed so extensively as to contain, if you knew how to tune in for it, the total dossier, the river he tried to kill himself in, the daily hand of Clara, even the flutist Baron von Fricken's adopted theme and Robert's passing fiancée the Baron's adopted daughter Ernestine. But in those bedtime days the *Kinderscenen* weren't even Schumann; they were Thea, and the music was familiar possibility—it was like sleep, the sea-rhythm and danger, emergency and deep rest; and on the bedtable your deerskin sack of marbles lay on a book of ancient Chinese knights in black armor.

And what collateral did you get for agreeing to an unconditioned withdrawal from that bed of childhood scenes, man?

"I apologize for not getting in touch," said Maddy. "I'm sure you've needed friends these last many weeks, but right now I see everything in terms of–" he raised a hand cocking his index and hammered twice toward Eddy's room.

"On the contrary, I meant to call you after you phoned about Corbusier–and honestly, *is* it Eddy? Isn't it really the old thing we discussed in your office in May? Give you brown boards and shingles, the attic where it's meant to be? remember? trapped by administrative and architectural cowardice?"

"Yet," said Maddy, "maybe there's justice in you of all people coming today."

From the open kitchen doorway Flo's voice gave off an odd, flat caution: "Maddy"–as if to stop him. When he turned off TV and stereo Eddy was calling, "Mom, is that someone?" and Flo went down the other hall to see him.

Justice? in Hind *of all people*? How much did Peg tell?

Why the hell was Maddy describing their Experiences of the Summer? Futile perfunctory adjective susurrus, and Eddy on the brain–for which Hind did not have time now, since the point was, Maddy's accidental whole organic end.

But he was at a table showing Hind the bridge and landscape he had made for Eddy at the island but Eddy hadn't been receptive.

Ah, but here, collapsing his derivative vision to a summer toy for a not-quite-scale-model little man, Maddy was perhaps betraying himself truly–yes, a toy clamped into a nature exact if not sublime, a Swiss gorge over which that silent, leaping sickle slab, Maillart's veering Schwandbach-Brücke, subsumed the chasm within sublime statutes of stress and strain and torsional backlash that ruled not only naked, shallow bearing-slab but chasm too–

"—all for Eddy, only for Eddy. He was in such a peculiar bind, I thought I could help pull him out of this nose dive he'd—"

No. Steady now: Maddy not Eddy. Maddy was the accidental organic whole end-of-the-moment to be dekidnaped.

"The school warned us in June he could not be retained if he continued uncooperative—he was waiting for things to be *assigned* to him! My God! Eddy? uncooperative? He was promoted, of course, though they don't actually promote at that school from one grade to another, because they don't have grades, they don't have years."

"But you were commuting all summer. Weren't you concerned about Plante and his anarchist rollerskaters?"

"How do you know Plante? Oh, Sylvia told you—"

"*You* did."

"I wanted her to get May into Eddy's school, and one night—but after what happened to Eddy, though I'm not blaming it all on them as I imagine you can guess—"

"But Ash said Plante's people were still a threat to you."

"Now that I've had to face the truth about Eddy, Plante's friend's soy bombs are a fantasy I haven't time for, like Santos-Dumont backing two new Harlem nightclubs as an integration project. No, it's like this: Eddy's become ironic. Not sarcastic; ironic. At nine going on ten. A tweaking facetious echo. But he didn't get it here. Say I'm explaining active surface to him, or torsion in concrete, or why we have to go beyond old-fashioned *diagonal* concrete reinforcement; and Eddy breaks in with 'Dad, you're one of the Good Guys'—he's got a T-shirt that says 'Good Guys.' Or Flo puts out his cereals and almost seriously he says, 'Builds blood, you better believe it.' But the way he says it, you don't know whether *he's* using the media clichés or they're using—"

"Media's not just advertising, any more than Santos-Dumont's only building."

"But I don't bring it out in the open because it will make him super-self-conscious—"

Maddy stopped to listen.

Hind diverted him into the main track: "You pushed Eddy a little too hard to make up for what you too modestly think are your own failings. I remember—do you?—what you said when you came back from London when S-D sent you as advisory troubleshooter to the County Council on gutting or replacing those Regency rows and you used to walk up from your friend's flat deep in the City early in the morning and through the Temple, and you saw fellows running through Lincoln's Inn Fields in sweat suits and you walked to Covent Garden vegetable market for breakfast and when you came home to New York you didn't care about Santos-Dumont electronic solid-state homes any more."

"And got plugged into monorail ecology that was little more than statistics, but—Eddy can simplify, can generalize, God!—but he won't work out just how to implement his concepts: for instance, to replace greenboards with"—Maddy raised his eyebrows and rolled his eyes—"Instant Communicare Telscreens which the speaker inscribes instantly with a palm-size remote typer-Tel-graph (as Eddy christened it), but Eddy won't work out operating details for the typer, it's the *idea* that's relevant. But there's where genius lies. In his head are ideas that outdate every gadget in Flo's kitchen."

It was Eddy calling, "Is that Jack out there? Jaa-aack!"

Hind handed the little pause to his worried host, who now resented Hind's imputation: "Pushing Eddy? Believe it or not, it's these busted marriages. Not to get personal, but Peg and Ash—and then last summer *three* of our married friends visiting us separately just during a period when I'd gone on the wagon, and their divorces depressed Eddy, he said so, and I believe him."

"Jaa-aack!" Eddy's voice was followed by Flo, who smiled sweetly and passed through to the kitchen.

Maddy whispered, "It's this nine-year-old irony—to Peg he said, 'As Daddy doesn't drink too much if at all any more it is no longer possible for me to tell him a bedtime story for him to doze off.' Though he did finish his serial about the man in the Sing Sing death home, I think I told you about it, but you missed the end—"

"And the beginning."

Maddy's voice was up again. "But you know the ads where the sponsor kids his own product but in fact is—wink by knowing wink—bombing out those bald clichés meaning them to stick in his well-manured consumer's brain precisely because the ingratiating wit of the ad implies we're all in this together." (The guardian in the driver's seat of his antique ideal says, "Can you give me an example? Can you document this?" and Ash answers, "It's self-evident and we don't have *time*.") "The sponsor seems to facetiously know the clichés are a joke but implies to comrade consumer that, well, under all this *we* know the product is not merely a ball—the pudding creams your heart, the green cigar filters your lung—but not too good to be true too, and reliable by virtue of the sponsor being cliché-cool—drop the bombs yet not be possessed by them. Eddy didn't pick this up from me, not from his home atmosphere, but from the media. And he thinks he's using this tone, but it's using him. Well we were discussing whether a city can be planned. And I got onto Washington and poor old neglected L'Enfant who designed it, and how in 1909 they dug him up out of the roots of a Maryland cedar and buried him overlooking the city—and Eddy murmured, 'I'd be lost without my Roto-Rooter.' But this spoof of nonmeaning coincides alarmingly with his new view of science; he's abandoned science, Jack. It was all I could do to keep him from throwing down the incinerator his bedscape seaside stabile."

"Hey Jaa-aack!"

"–sea*scape* stabile, I mean. And this summer he deep-sixed his decomputer. And he doesn't invent any more. It's a general depression. When he understood from something Peg said that you and Sylvia were divorced too, he cried–and *I* never knew he was so fond of May. I was hoping he could go back to school, even though he'd been low all summer–asking me for permission to drown himself! Flo called off the colored kid we were going to have up to the island for two weeks. But Eddy not only abandons science, he reads only fairy tales. God knows I don't veto these tales–I *favor* imagination–and God knows I don't even know where *I* am. But–"

"But I haven't divorced Sylvia."

"It wasn't *only* your divorce that got him down. It was something else."

"Maddy," said Flo, who was in the room again.

"Jaa-aack," called Eddy less urgently.

"I'm out of place here."

"No," said Maddy. "You know how he admires you, ever since you brought that baby tape recorder. And your height, you know. Do see him."

"Better not," said Flo.

"I'm going," said Hind.

"No," said Flo, "stay for supper. Bee Bee's coming."

"But he *wants* to see you," said Maddy. "See him and *then* go."

"It'll upset him," said Flo.

"Maybe it's my divorce he says he's troubled by, but that isn't the true cause. Maybe he isn't a scientist. Maybe you've encouraged him too much."

"I'm sorry, Jack, I'm very very sorry, Flo and I may have our differences, but there's nothing but good in us and we've given incredibly to that kid."

"Maddy," said Flo, again in that new flat tone undecided between bland logic, defensive nerves, and quiet indictment. "He doesn't understand what we've been through."

Who was "He"? Eddy? Hind? What *did* Eddy know?

Maddy said, "Better not then," but Hind was across the green carpet in three strides and into the hall leading to Eddy's room. Maddy called out, "Plante's sculptor friend came on a twenty-one-day and stayed—we have a mutual friend, guess who."

Eddy lay on his neat bed dressed in tight gray flannels, white athletic socks, blue button-down, and a dark knitted tie. Hind closed the door and leaned back on it, and Maddy and Flo's apartment went away like the lead BMT car whose front window, so keenly disputed on concert Saturdays, could seem to leave it behind.

Eddy held out a hand, palm up, both grandly receiving in the manner of Good Queen Rain of Murray Hill and wanting to touch the large body of his visitor.

"I could have come out but they think I'm taking orders from them. Even though they don't give any."

Judging from what stuck out of the huge Jolly Green Giant carton by the vast white Formica desk, Eddy had lost interest in various laboratoid devices. They would not include anything so slight and lyrical as Hind's old Gilbert Chemistry Set—that valuably rattling triptych of tiny wooden kegs—sulphur, cobalt crystals—and glass tubes and tin accessories and a fresh wick'd burner. The gray-on-green SANTOS-DUMONT SISTERS pennant sharp on Eddy's wall over the bed pointed, if you took it seriously, toward a closet door illustrated with a spangled op puzzle which, depending where you moved, was either a target-shaped Old Glory or a bearded head of the President.

"What's up?" said Hind.

"Anything."

"I missed the death-home serial."

"Didn't *they* give you a rerun? It was clever but pretty depressing. I didn't believe it. I don't *really* like death. I don't want to die."

"Care to tell me one of your stories?"

"Noop."

"Or the daily fairy tale?"

"Where'd you get your inside information?"

"Maddy."

"A boy's best friend."

"His dog? his mom? his dad?"

"All of them. Or his banker. Or his bank account. Or his airline."

"Got something against Maddy?"

"Dad's got problems."

"Have you?"

"I've stopped running, Jack." Instant words, add your poor humid breath, and blow: yet for a second despite the cliché you *saw* him stop running. And the Impala SS full of reporters and photographers that overtook him did not run him down, it just passed apparently through him. "Yeah, I've stopped running."

"Maddy's got problems?"

"I been running and running, but I found out you *can't* break the tape."

"You're only nine."

"Ten next month. But you don't get the idea." Eddy shut his eyes. "You still looking for that kid?"

So Eddy knew. Did the search then end here? Under a Santos-Dumont flag and with the guardian shadowing all other issues?

But Eddy was telling (about) his fairy tales to Jack and their conversation evened into magic narrative communion.

Take Hansel and Gretel. Yes? Yes, that's what I said, Take Hansel and Gretel. And the rest, too, they all come down to two things—luck and being good. Hold it, what about dropping the white pebbles to blaze a trail home after they were left in the wood by the father and wicked stepmother? Yeah, but what about Hansel breaking out all his bread for the same purpose the second time? Ingenuity. No, ingenuity's no good unless you're a good guy. The tales all come down—But Eddy!, *way* down—I don't get you, but it's like this, Hansel and Gretel comes down to this: don't trust anyone who has candy windows. What about stepmothers? Well, that's prejudice. Why's the stepmother got to get it all the time?—the wicked step-mother, big deal. But it's on what's behind the prejudice that the tale turns, the fears, the things people do to each other. Yeah, the neuroses our teacher discussed with us, don't give me that stuff, I got that from Marina one night she read me "The Water of Life" and told me what it meant and I let her have it. She's not so tough.

"Are *you*? You cried, I heard."

"Once! Oh yes I guess I did." Since he'd been staying in, Flo gave him two minutes of sun lamp a day, and he had a tan pallor. "I been quite depressed, Jack. People going away, people getting divorced. And Adam moved to Garden City."

"*I'm* not divorced."

"I'm glad"–gently avuncular, but as if it mattered not much after all. "I wish some others weren't."

"Not your mom and dad at least."

"What I couldn't make anyone understand. So I don't tell anyone."

"Tell me."

"*I* don't understand it."

"Tell me."

"They were getting a divorce but now they're not."

The need for it having died, as an appetite dies...but some appetites cannot be re-enacted: Shirley Laurel told Beulah Love that when she was carrying Hershey she ate ten chocolate bars a day, and Beulah said she was surprised the child came out white. Bella Church, having taken her bite out of the department store's branch doughnut-concept, sold her house and her foul-breathed Boy's garden to an unidentified contractor for an unannounced sum. Santos-Dumont? The Sisters were doing a good turn of land speculation out there, and to keep taxes down left some barren areas unimproved–for instance, where the great pentagonal batting cage stood. Maddy and Flo unseparated, the long-limbed crone a princess–money back.

"And they don't know I know," said Eddy. "I was rowing around Needle Point, it doesn't come out far, so I was close inshore, and I heard their voices, the elevation and the position of the pines and the ravine and air current I guess happened just right. I don't want to tell what they said."

"Of course not."

"But I know they don't want to live together any more. And then I saw them by the beach shed, Daddy burning trash, I saw the smoke but they didn't see me, so I started rowing like mad and caught a crab–I tried to–so they saw me before they could think I'd overheard. But a couple of nights later I got up to hear them and they were saying they wouldn't break up after all. But only because of me. She said to Dad, 'Jolly white of you,' and Dad said, 'Jolly white of *you*.' Which started it again, which isn't anyone's business, and anyway I don't think I understood it."

"But I'm *glad* they're sticking it out, I mean together," said Hind, and sat on the bed.

"Yeah," said Eddy; "maybe I am too, but–"

"*But what*?"

"But now they're staying together, and it's my fault."

"You're too intelligent."

"Yeah"–serious or kidding. Hind understood. He could stay here incommunicado with this child. How long could he stay?

Back to school soon? A regular school "hopefully" ("An imprecise vulgarism": unquote guardian; would he ever be definitively unquoted?)–well maybe try the "gifted" school next year, but. And meanwhile duffing off? I'm learning all the time, never knew the fairy tales were so good, take you way away, better than Sylvania color TV, but bring you back down to earth, like "The Water of Life"–the youngest son gets the water of life for his father the king who gets it but only after it's been stolen by the wicked elder brothers, etcetra–Marina told me all about the tight gorges the bad brothers got stuck in, and the magic iron rod and the two loaves that never could get eaten up and the fountain where the water is, but she's full of shit, the story means you got to be pleasant to poor people, dwarfs, etcetra, they can do a lot for you; and don't be haughty. "Everyone's in these stories, Jack, even you."

"Is there anything you'd like?" A transfusion? "Shall we go to a hockey game some night?"

"Like Jack and the Beanstalk, but I don't see how it fits you. *I'll* call *you* when I find out. I like giants. You don't look so big as when I was a child. Some giants are good, some are bad."

"I know," so quietly, so tired.

"Some win out and eat their victims, some get beat. Will you take me with you when you do a 'Naked Voice'?"

"Sure."

"Because I phoned you after Aunt Peggy said you and your family split up. And there was a colored woman said she'd tell you I called, and called me 'Honey.' But you didn't call back." Mystery Beecher, Smitty had said.

"Yes, I'll take you." No thing Grimes could say could matter more than Eddy.

"I want to get out of here, Eddy, O.K.?"

"Sure. You got to go."

"But I'll come back."

"Sure."

"With May?"

"Sure. Wait. The *point* of my execution serial was not what Dad or Bee Bee said. The man in the death home wanted to be alone, but no one let him. Puncture-proof tune-tubes squeezed music on him all day, and people kept coming. He tried to remember walks alone when he was young. He was happy just to be around then. Now he just wanted to be alone to think. But his family kept coming. He was innocent but he didn't worry about that. Bee Bee said I was brainwashed. He just had to think about what was going on. And they kept bringing him chocolate roses to eat, as if each meal was his last." (Flo had Marinetti's *La Cucina Futurista*.) "You know about the kid that grew out of a begonia? It was watered by its mother every night." (Last spring Eddy began wetting his bed.)

Flo and Maddy stood in the living room, aware that Eddy's door had now been left open by Hind, who was coming down the hall—but no readier for him than he for them.

"You see," said Flo, and took a breath, "how he is."

"Plante's sculptor friend, as I was trying to say," said Maddy, "knows Cassia Meaning. She's taken to wearing a therapeutic copper ring around her ankle."

"I think Eddy's O.K.," said Hind. "I have to go. Give my best to Bee Bee and Marina. You said they're coming to supper?"

"It's only Bee Bee," said Flo. "Maybe I should have asked Marina."

"What'd you think of EB honestly? What can *we* do?" Maddy asked, but not for a reply.

"I'm afraid to tell you."

"What'd you talk about?"

"Your summer projects. He's tired. But he thinks you're great, both of you. Did you know that?"

"Well," said Flo, "it hasn't been a real emergency."

As the elevator door opened, Maddy was in his doorway suddenly and said, "This English sculptor claims Cassia taught *him* all that *Plante* knows about this flattening perspective thing, just a few accidental droppings at a party in Kennington. She doesn't see him any more."

Watched now, again, by the Heights trees, whose silence holds under its sway all the emigrant probability the harbor voices—from the white Coast Guard weather ship thirty miles out coming in from near Greenland after a month on station, to the class of Negro ("Please, 'Afro-American'") children on the ferry, some rattling the chains on the deck aft, some below staring at a pile of tarnished sauerkraut in the hot dog man's basin—you tried to remember about monkeys' stereoscopic vision, was it the result or the cause of their becoming arboreal?, the guardian would have known, on a Sunday at the Museum of Science and Industry, where at a button's touch (–ambiguous! ambiguous!–) a duct blew at you as from an imprisoned trachea, Dentyne breath like Siggofreddo Morales'.

The excellent four- and five-story houses along Remsen Street, their dark or almost pinkish tan sandstone perhaps hiding little that you couldn't unearth in Georgetown or Beacon Hill, turn before your very eyes into a nature not unlike what the guardian said we must wipe away the human smudges on to clearly see, like the deep skies looking at us and the blue shade dropped by boulders upon snow crust, which (in a lower, later mood) he said you might not see until you could give your life a semipermanent historectomy of all these human relationships, what Eddy seemed to partly want just now, but–halfway between Hicks and Henry the Deals' house was, is, and shall be where at a monthly meeting of Goya the guardian read his belated and unfinished paper on Dürer's two major treatises.

At Montague and Clinton where you caught the BMT for Carnegie, the guardian once looked up at his bank, The Franklin Trust, a Romanesque mini-tower scraping the immediate Heights heavens shared with the Commercial Gothic Holy Trinity tower across the street, and he quoted the Archbishop in *Henry V*, "The singing masons building roofs of gold," and smiled privately.

But now here for heaven's sake is little Mrs. Byron J. Bean, Senior, and "*Well,*" she does not say, "imagine running into–" does not recognize you, but this is because she does not see you, because in her extreme nearsightedness she does not let her eyes wander north, south, down, or up, lest she see somebody she thinks she ought to recognize (in that positive cautionary manner of hers in which discussing By's unexpected rejection for military service two weeks before Eisenhower defeated Stevenson, she said to Hind, "But you see By-By hasn't found himself yet; you have; you *know* who you are).

As simply as from one slab of the past to another, you cross the shallow surface of the city, and, emerged like a drunk at noon, stride the Bowery's Old Indian Trail, and feeling comfortably at your elbow the windows of the restaurant equipment stores with their big plain implements, you become Big Nose, the Bowery's Paul Bunyan, marching with butcher's cleaver at the belt; or then you are Joe Gould, affronting Lady Astor or sitting in Washington Square imitating a seagull's cry.

Has the President proclaimed Thanksgiving? Of course he has, by now. Will Sylvia go home to her mother and father's next Wednesday? You can hear the red, white and blue chips on beloved Daddy's table; but she won't go home for Thanksgiving without *you*.

And, too, half an hour ago just when Mrs. Bean came opaquely by, you could hear (though in another street of the Heights past) the abrading roar of Christy Amondson's skates approaching that crucial test-sewer, for at last, rather than accept and appear to ignore his father's public affront, he has acknowledged and publicly rejected the prohibition. And, as your Liberal Conservative guardian breathes in and out of the present, Christy's skates come together like skis and he crouches for that famous jump and is deafeningly upon you; and as you are destroyed, there is silence except for the traffic mildly moving behind Mrs. Bean here in the present, there is silence because he has in one great piece left the ground—silence among the watchers, silence even as airborne he breaks through into the present, clearing two four-foot black-iron sewer-grates (-grilles, -grids) and three feet of tar between!

But time, whether flat or deep, is short, whether for Maddy, whose Sears Belt Massager will not boggle his evening watch, his afternoon watch, or his watch that tells all the foreign times, or for you, who know Sylvia won't wait forever.

But Grimes, logging his daily true, false, and deceptive cognates, is on his way over, invited for Fossy's Ariosto.

And Hind had not noted the day until, hearing the Thanksgiving parade and looking way out his window to see green silk soldierettes playing a slow, brassy "My Funny Valentine," he felt the more palpable sense of Grimes' "Well, that's very nice, you're a darling" over the phone. Grimes was coming, Hind now saw, not only for Fossy's Ariosto but for Thanksgiving dinner.

They went to Fisherman's Net, Third Avenue near Thirty-third. Going and coming, they heard Knott's son at work above them drumming against his background of recorded reeds, brass, and strings.

A small postprandial cherry liqueur was on the house, and Red had Hind's as well, to go with the Manhattans he had drunk right through dinner. He found himself telling Jack about a night at the Princeton Inn during an academic meeting one weekend—and Oliver Plane, whom Red had met just that afternoon, told Red there was a new "perfectly unnatural" practice Red would do well to acquaint himself with (winky wink)—it had started in a West Side Turkish bath and had spread, said Ol, drunk but deliberate—and it was called "consolatio." Red had tried to get Ol to describe it. Now he looked sadly at the empty liqueur glasses. Doubtless acknowledging the gift he was soon to get his hands on, Red seemed to feel he must remember the guardian on this day, and Hind did not ask after all about the kidnap or the Old Woman.

"Fossy used to say there should be a President's commission on language; yet, as I patiently told him, he wanted a Johnsonian retrenchment. After all, Johnson's *Dictionary* isn't a lexicon at all—'windward' and 'leeward' come out meaning the same, mmm?—but rather, a work of moral fiction. Oh I knew Fossy. If one knew him, one found his lovely inconsistencies all on the surface, but one had to know him. Lovely in his transparence for those who knew."

A very fat young couple adjusted their illustrated red-and-white lobster bibs. Grimes sighed, staring at the portrait of Jackson on the bill Hind laid upon the placemat.

"Though even his errors were charming, mmm? Telling young Plane's mother 'madrigal' came not from Latin and Greek 'fold' and Italian 'herd' (correct enough) but *madre* (which is involved only very remotely, either in association with *materna lingua*, 'mother tongue,' which may have caused *matricale* to come to mean 'mother song' in its application to primitive Italian pastoral songs; *or*, in association with the early Italian variant *marigale*, since in North Italian *madre* became *mare*).

"Mind you"—they were in the street, Hind bending to hear Grimes, and Hind saw ahead Rain's granddad and the two Old Chestnuts standing at the corner by the new bar—"Fossy sang a pleasant light baritone—*and* your 1530 Wynkyn de Worde music book—which he owned without being an authority on—reminds us Fossy knew precisely what he was" zzzmmming Gibbons Byrd—as the endless syllables, transparently devious, trail into the undertaker's steadily improving street and to his green awning and up the marble stairs.

"Why do I find *your* Fossy so unsatisfying?" asked Hind.

"That must be *your* Fossy, not mine," said Red. "A handsome chap, and a loyal—why, like Dr. Johnson, he would have written a quick treatise against the elliptical arch in Blackfriars Bridge just to support a friend. Yet he had a communication problem, as we all know."

Hind did not know what music he put on, he was so eager for Grimes to go, it made him feel taller and taller, the ceilings of the top-floor flat more and more cramping. In one backyard the little boy was doing a steady thumb-and-two-finger accompaniment to the slow charcoaling of a foil-swathed turkey.

"Yes, like many men who talk a lot, he couldn't, I gather, find out how to discuss certain things that I for one should have liked to see aired. I gather he seldom spoke to *you*, for example, about you know what."

What? Charley and her virginal grace the first time? her bewildering anticipations expert—never forgot her legs, forgot nothing except that her brother was coming back at a certain hour from his date with the town girl. And the guardian knew before the next week was out, and was obviously frightened.

"I know what?"

"I thought you knew about her. The woman Foster who bothered me. You were present at her expulsion, long ago, though you were very young."

"How old was I?"

"Age five, six? Fossy wanted to make it up with her."

"Make it up—?"

"And said it was a nice gesture for her to travel down on the train to take you to the Academy of Music."

"But we didn't go. Or did we?"

"You went, but not with her. Friends had tickets and at the last minute you went with them and gave away Miss Foster's ticket at the box office."

"She didn't take me?"

"She went right back to Boston or whatever eminence she had entrained from. She was furious. And quite a dish, if I recall. She could easily have been, I mean happily become, your mother."

"Who did I go with?" Hind asked insincerely, Grimes was losing interest.

"And she made some rather unkind allegations."

"O.K."

"About your mother. Whose married name, of course, was Hind. And suddenly Fossy became another man, told his cousin to get out, and she walked past him to give you the tickets, and he was rather stunned to find you there."

"What did she say about my mother?"

"Called her jealous names. Tart."

Grimes wandered into the hall and stood looking toward the study wheezing cigarette smoke in.

"You knew my parents."

"Funny how you put it. Yes, I knew your mother."

"Were they happy together?"

"It wasn't easy. And the whole thing was so short."

"Was my guardian very friendly with Mr. Hind?"

"God no. What gave you that idea?"

"Oh."

"Frank Hind wasn't, shall we say, receptive to Fossy's interests. But though Fossy was too well-bred—and something else too much or too little too, I think—he did not go into the subject deeply. But children knew, and boys find out. I suppose he rarely talked of who you were—in the long broad family-tree sense; but an adopted child, any child, any child, comes on these facts like sex, and they just come to possess the knowledge, don't they."

"He asked if I wasn't curious about the Hinds."

Grimes walked idly over the undertaker's creaking floor into the study, and Hind against the background (behind *him*, not Grimes) of "This Land Is My Land" sung in a harsh boy soprano to that backyard guitar, barely heard Grimes say, "Confusing enough to be adopted by your own father. That would have given me enough to think about for my whole life." Music off. "You were a sweet little boy. It was a mistake John Foster never could quite face having made."

"You underestimate him." How do I go on talking? How does one save face?

"I tend always to over- not under-."

"You despised him."

How do you go on talking. Hasn't he destroyed you?

"I loved old Fossy, pursuing the mmm point of his life, but it was always a bit ahead of him. Charming man."

Which mistake? Hind? or not having married? Not having married *her*?"

Grimes was again in the hall between study and living room, peering at him. "You're irked. If I said anything wrong. No one ever tells me anything. So your father had it off with your mother. Don't you find that reassuring? Your phone's ringing."

The answering service would pick up. But they were slow, and maybe Grimes would slip away, given the chance.

"Hello," said Hind. To be adopted by your own father.

"I got you at last. This Hind? This is…Dove."

"Yes? Dove?"

"*I* know you know me. The woman told me you did. She said you might make a deal, even though she knows I can't make no deal."

"I'm not thinking." Separate photographs, never the pair together except in the separate photographs on the childhood bureau, the guardian and Jack's mother.

"You better *do* some thinking." Floor creaks, door latches, measured toe touches marble. Grimes is gone. "Because if you try anything it'll cost you more than you going to want to pay. I know who you are, I seen you." Beulah and Ken had always been on the outs with Beulah's sister-in-law, and Dove's voice came now like an extension of the Old Woman's threatening clues. "Don't know what you think you are, a cop or welfare, but the kid stays with us, we're his parents now and he's happy with us, I'm warning you." What about birth certificates? Maybe he looks like them. And meanwhile why did Frank Hind get it into his head to take an autogyro ride? "–his parents and he's happy with us, and if you try anything I hate to think what's going to happen to your family. Remember that. She told me all about you." (The Laurel muse alone in her mid-town hotel fidgets, flails, tries expiringly to bring together the abandoned quarry and the vanishing hunter.)

"*She's* after you. Not me."

"That's a lie and I'll tell her when she phones."

"And tell her my name is Foster."

Maybe you rang off too soon, maybe he wanted some unilaurel collateral, but it isn't every day you trap a dad.

You breathe a shallow "Well!" Grimes receding from his Thanksgiving toast: guardian to the fore, mud in your eye: foreground and background like interpenetrating sieves: but Grimes' clicking steps down the undertaker's stairwell echo your own nearer words: "Nothing new here," as the guardian one participating Saturday afternoon said of sssssss*Son of Tarzan;* "nothing new." And nothing has really happened.

You go to the record shelf by the phonograph and find that letter Thea gave you where you stuck it unread between two jackets. "Mine or yours," the letter starts onto the page after the salutation "Dear F:"

The simple thing is to say she's yours. Yours by a right we all three might not fail to acknowledge. But why *should* I give her up? And is she really willing to give up the child? Maybe I could not hope to have her *and* the child. God knows I don't easily forget–

Yet if the menacing Dove did not want some unilaurel collateral, maybe you for one have persevered in being a unilateral colaurel.

*v*

God knows I don't easily forget the damn moral superiority you never stopped insinuating you possessed, some advantage above the ordinary simple things I for one was brought up on, the corporate integrity of the family group.

Will you think of this when you try to kiss her? Will you think of your betrayal of *me* (even if we were seldom more than acquaintances) when you try to kiss her? You laugh in your holy strength when I say your kisses of her are truly and deeply (though I know of them) behind my back.

Is the order torn? The bottom edge is ragged, the bottom margin minimal.

The guardian could no more write "kisses of her" than the actual correspondent here, obviously Frank Hind, would write the letter to freshmen with its bachelor tree ceremonies in India or the lost City of Is. Any more than the slimmer slimmer vinyl virgin motomorph, lately bedeviled by the shaggy-haired assistants who would not let her leave her bike on the street, could have turned into the veteran heifer photographed in all seasons. Any more than the guardian could or often would have claimed to be a botanist like his father, much less an authority on hawthorn.

Or Hind a chip off the old block.

Yet since you have faithfully gathered into the fold of accidental organic whole ends Oliver Plane, Dewey

Wood, Ashley Sill, and Madison Beecher, even at the expense of missing May's birthday—you must guard the ancient Foster-rule of achievement: You finish what you embark. Therefore, the pier. But who would you find there in December?

Across the street through the fire escape bars the ad art director's CPA could be seen checking back and forth; sometimes his head moved, sometimes just his eyes. Illusion or not, you always felt when you finished a perspective lesson (with or without grill) that you'd commanded nothing, even indeed that you were being watched skeptically along with a number of other objects by that omnivorous vanishing point which was like the guardian's eye on you.

Too tall for your age long ago, you knew you stuck out; and you wished not to; and so—so?—you were a generous giver but not a generous receiver, which is the test of generosity you now see. You couldn't help it, but you wanted to give back the school cup for most improved athlete. Ditto, the guardian's oval cardboard photo of your mother in a slip when she was three; and Christy's second-best skates he solemnly gave you after his mother unexpectedly bought him new ones with rubber-coated wheels; ditto the unfinished manuscript of Plane's Siggofreddo poem "The Diving Accident"; and the two-dimensional tiger Eddy bequeathed you when he changed schools, that he'd cut out with a coping saw and painted thickly gold and black; ditto the gift of Brooklyn Heights itself, whose circumference was everywhere and whose center elsewhere—bounded on the west by docks below and huge flat view of Wall Street above; on the south by an Atlantic Avenue beyond which across Pacific, Amity, Congress, Warren, Baltic (less real than Cassia's in her "Monopoly"), President, and Summit lay dreary commercial wharves and respectable brick tenements which (though Jim Commons once made a thing of taking friends to the pool at the Red Hook low-income development) were an indefinite sector between Buttermilk Channel and Gowanus Basin to get *through* if you were driving south-and-east to the Park Slope or to get *over* if, once the Belt Parkway western loop got started, you were driving to Fort Hamilton to visit Skoldy or to Lindy's for lobster or on toward that ominously flowering Parachute Jump the guardian wouldn't let you go on; bounded on the north by the partly hidden, vaguely inspiring stone and network of the Brooklyn Bridge and, from a certain angle, the Manhattan behind it, together a tangential intimation of impersonal purposes but still, if you wished, an antique and honorable barricade; as wisely definite as the prospect to the east was ambiguous and risky particularly if, when you left the stamp man's musty wood floor on Fulton and walked up past the Tivoli where there had been first burlesque then the thing in which Hedy Lamarr floated nude—and Cassia lied she had seen, one afternoon all alone—you turned down Myrtle under its darkly echoing El: for then, if you had the imagination of Daisy Deal, you could foresee far down Myrtle an undifferentiated Negro unison moving every day, week, and month block by block toward and then into the Hill section and ultimately to the Washington Street post office at one of the very corners of the Heights. Yet the center was elsewhere, if anywhere, though how it had slipped past the circumference Hind did not know in those days when he loved the sound of the harbor sky overflowing into the eminent privacy of the Heights, almost as much as he loved the guardian, and more than he loved him resented this nonreturnable gift of place with its landscaped encumbrances: the center as far as you could go in yourself or out along one of your arms, a center only imaginary, a perspective from which planes of present as fixed as the cocoa mat of the springboard you once stood on, conveniently part into scheduled pasts re-enactable in such a way as to demonstrate to the incredulous guardian where the time of his life went after all, or become radially tethered ticks on a shockproof economic geography under glass.

(Take a breath, the Heights waits to be free of your spell.)

Gifts, in short, fed to you until you thought you would die of bounty (just as, in the school pool, of growth); you wished to grind the gift into the ground to repay the giver and humble yourself.

Or, sitting near him at the Deals' the night Fossy gave the belated paper on Dürer's treatises, you feel thrust to your adopted credit some familial or physical part in the distinction cautiously on view in those scattered, suggestive, tenuously individual insights—Dürer's sacrifices in pursuit of completeness; his catholicity of reception (for instance, the Italian strain, the Venetian laurel); his interest in America; and the desperate tenacity in his late perceptions of how necessary his theoretical...treatises would be to...the image of his own...completeness. And the guardian's middle style, supple, even if his belated paper was not wholly finished. This you wanted to explain to the swarthy guest in the green wool shirt and black-and-yellow plaid tie who, at the end of the reading and before Engleman Deal slid open the doors to the dining room, smiled as if he had dug up one of the guardian's bones unbeknownst, and had a number of vague remarks to make—was Dürer, after all, that good even as an artist, you know in terms of (k-k-k) of creation....There wouldn't have been time to explain even if you, Hind, had had the background—and that night you felt like an object that stuck out.

Smith Answering terminated the arrangement with Hind the first week in December. Calls were getting so personally detailed that neither patience nor politeness from the switchboard girls could simplify the messages coming in. The Black Agency advertised that they could and would answer any phone in Manhattan, and Hind contracted with them. But during the two uncovered days between Smith and Black the Old Woman caught him.

Dove would have told her "The name is Foster," but she made no direct mention. But she did find out what he had received from Thea.

"She should not have given you anything like that."

"You haven't seen it."

"No disposition of it in the will."

"Nonsense. And why anyway resent a letter he wrote... to my father saying how he loved my mother?" If the Old Woman wanted to believe he didn't know, let her.

"Ah. Then I do not resent it." She couldn't understand. "Even if it *was* unearthed and appropriated improperly— which was and is my point. As well as that I am disappointed you've abandoned a case that might have made you famous."

She would bother him again, but she was tentatively placated with the vision that he had not after all found out who he was.

She would be charmed—if such an ungenerous muse could be—by his feeling that he was *innately* adopted.

Grimes deserved the Ariosto he had walked off with without asking Thanksgiving Day. Hind phoned the storage people to find out if they had the Wynkyn de Worde, but they wouldn't root through all the cartons; Grimes could easily have walked off with that one too.

Since Hind did not wish to break the kidnap he was afraid that Dove might phone and say too much to Black Answering. Someday he ought to have a word with him.

The pier remained a problem, a loose end as ticklish as the Buddy Bourne "nonreverse" for the guardian until accidentally he had a chance to try to fix things with Buddy.

When Sylvia had first come into the scene she was in the process of walking a new part of the city each weekend. When had she come here to the pier, and would she have taken the overpass or merely looked from the hospital side of the Drive?

The guardian's ruminations upon the possessive case or the tantalizing city-country perspective a civilized man ought to achieve, seldom if ever brought him down into the "*other* ghettos," his disingenuous dig at the Heights. Sylvia didn't describe for him, though Fossy seemed to want her virtually to reenact, her Sunday trips; her shyness was in part her earnestness, which in turn she would earnestly hate to be accused of, for though she daydreamed her way through every grade of potato knish from Market to Delancey, she had studiously begun with (and could not, nor would want to, erase from her letters home) the significant surfaces of that truncated segment angled by the Williamsburg and Manhattan bridges, from the Sea and Land front with its three-over-three severity and clarity and its Georgian Gothic brownstone arches—to St. Augustine's Chapel on Henry Street where Boss Tweed, on the lam, probably *didn't* hide in the slaves' gallery in order to attend his mother's funeral—to the round arches and the star in the center window of Bialystoker Synagogue, which Van White would hasten to remark was once (cluck cluck) Methodist Episcopal.

Answer: you didn't *know* whether Syl would have taken the pier overpass or left the pier alone. In April one thing; perhaps in December another.

Wind from the bridge upriver struck Hind as he went up the steps on the hospital side.

You could still walk both piers, but the city would soon fill up the slip with sand and gravel. No one was on either the larger plaza pier where baby carriages had parked and the green, nicked benches still stood, or the narrow pier where the regulars had come.

How, then, treat as an end in itself the *place*, divorced from the kidnap and from people?

But there was music as you got closer, or, first, a broadly shuttling beat like a giant bouncing on an expensively and subtly strung box spring (not unreminiscent, say, of the 510- (foundation) coil Posture-Mate Sleep Set Sears was offering). And then, as you came nearer, it became an ozone ensemble, sprinkling supersoft extract of young lungs, sweet hearts, late-postwar roller-fugue, and wash-white whiffs of effluent socianity but out of nowhere: until you were near enough to spot the small gray oblong standing where Charley the Pole used to sit. But now the drums' thunderette, and the cymbals' mild splash included a strangely human synco-tick-tick-tick under the pier. Was Berry Brown below looking for his gear, or working for the Coast Guard?

Across the water the crane and wrecking ball were not in evidence, nor the wall. Leashed above the stern of a white dragger struggling gulls seemed trying to slow it down.

"We're not even supposed to be here," a familiar voice said behind him. "This is the beginning of the end, they're commandeering it for eminent domain."

"No," said Hind turning to greet Ivy Bowles, "it wasn't *private* property."

"Well, anyway, I'd have noticed you anywhere."

"We're a long way from April sun," and from women on the other pier in densely dark glasses apparently dozing but often actually watching you.

How many are part of your life's process before you know them? like anxieties you can't yet find the plug to hook in to actual paraphernalia.

"I've not seen you here for months." Ivy's long blue raincoat seemed to have extra buttons low down, so the wind from the Queensboro Bridge couldn't if it had wished to, flip even a corner hem. "How come you're here?"

"Hoping to witness an accident, Ivy." Hold it, her eyebrow twitches up wary. "No. Reminiscing."

"Of a time that was better than this. When there was *space* for decent people. Look at that open burning"—she flung out a prophetic finger at a barge bearing a smoking pile of something. "I for one believe there's room for one new person in the city when and only when one resident leaves. What right have they to the air space?"

"No one has a *right*."

"Just what I meant exactly."

"We just take *up* the space. No getting rid of us."

"Just what I meant. I'm not just talking. I'm saying I won't give up my air rights to a newcomer of *any* race."

"Then don't."

"It's all very well they tell us, Love one another, 'love' is a word like any other word, and it's one thing to say it and another to do it. You love if you've got it in you. Now the young vicar at the Good Shepherd with his chime machine and his school for kooks, he has a lot to learn."

"But he's right, Miss Bowles, he's right: *Love*—" and after a second's hesitation Hind added with wicked quickness, "and intermarriage beyond that."

"What's this 'Miss Bowles'? You called me 'Ivy' last spring."

"I mix up names. I can't recall if the undertaker's man is La Grange or La Branche." Sometimes you had to collapse a name for expedition's sake: OW, IB, MB, AS, DW, OP, SH, JF.

"So I'm willing to love my neighbor. So long as I can choose who he is. I don't love some of my own flesh and blood, as I told the vicar. Words are one thing, flesh and blood's another. I didn't have any objection to those Chinamen used to come here at lunchtime—*let* them run a lottery probably or worse the way they huddled together. One day last spring, they just stopped coming."

"You recovered from your dunking."

"Imagine pneumonia in the summertime! But wasn't that weird about Mr. Wood?" Hind moved away from the hammering and they walked slowly toward the Drive end of the pier. "You didn't hear?"

"Which story? I know he was diagnosed wrongly."

"Twice, no less. *Well*: he was losing weight faster than his gym exercises should have been, and he went back to the Group and they got out his records and tested him again and by accident that first diagnosis of someone else happened to be Mr. Wood's as well. And he *is* terminal, just as I heard and told Phyllis three whole months ago."

Maybe the undertaker would get the job. Carmen was afraid the house would be sold.

"I'd sue," said Ivy. "Say, why'd you stop coming to the pier in May? Find something better?"

"Work."

"You weren't a plainclothesman, now were you? I bought a Lafayette 'Guardian' Police Radio, it's better than TV any day—it was after the steer broke out of the abattoir in Brooklyn, you hear the emergency all-points and you feel like you're first on the scene. Charley thought you were following the young fellow who had the tape recorder for the Baptist Blind."

"Maybe he was following me."

"It's certainly possible in this world of modernity we live in." Ivy, a regular reader of printed material, continued: "In this decade since 1955 our population is up 17½ percent; the death rate is dropping alarmingly in my opinion; you're getting an average forty-three births per thousand, and by the time I'm ninety-five there'll be seven billion people on the face of the earth. It's Mao and the Pope. As for you, you stick out in a crowd," said Ivy, taking Hind's arm in a pretense of friendly joking; "but these people are coming and they're going to engulf the ordinary thinking person. Like me."

"The paranoid," said Hind, "endows his supposed persecutor with a vitality the latter might well be glad to possess."

"Speak English."

"English is heavily inflected—see, saw, seen; Chinese is at the other end, an isolating language, invariable elements strung together; and smack in the middle you find agglutinating languages."

"You've got me," said Ivy, relinquishing Hind's arm and slowing her pace. He turned on her and she quickly said, "Yes; well, and what's an example of *them*?"

"Finnish, Ivy, Finnish."

And was this what the guardian had set out to do, having trapped himself in languages of love and having lost his heart to that woman and having accidentally—but *was* it accidentally?—caused Hind to happen? Had he set out to finish what he started?

Too late to ask the late guardian. Who could not in any case answer. Perhaps you grew so, because you were a child of ecstasy, because the guardian, in perhaps the only true possession of his unfinished life, possessed that woman and was possessed of her as an end in themselves. (Mmm, yum yum, a Cubic Campus phil bluebook blends like instant pudding with lore panned from the Golden Age Family Advice Service Welcome Leaflet.) An end not in terms and tokens of other mean ends. For though you hale into the inverted tree of your body mediairs from random tran-Sisters and median doseinfectants from a consumer-guided video tube, so that from one perspective you are an endlessly beginningless dream of tokens—in your case, little John, a green giant watching through the night over rich panhandles and vegetable deltas and high crops of woods which because you're green puzzle you as to whether you're farmer or farmed; yet from a second perspective, you were (from that woman and man) a procedural Grace as sublimely unnecessary as the thought of a child if it had come to mind on that lucky if foreshortened afternoon with darling Charley you were possessed by knowing amazement as you joined the puzzle of her clutches without dissolving it, while for a long hour her name escaped, and with it the clay court out the window and the village circling beyond—you and Charley in green Remsenburg, Long Island, as if your profound Brooklyn Heights street, Remsen, had dreamed its way out into Long Island earth, a dream like Sears Laurel's when he transplanted Shirley's heart beyond familiar city limits, if you were not guardian against the kidnap's recollection.

But by learning who you were you finished what the guardian started.

You were coming to a standstill. At night from bed a bad accident at the Third Avenue intersection sounded like the mere *BOCK* of a car hood being securely shut.

What you really wanted...was basketball, but the guardian urged gymnastics and/or wrestling so hopefully that you went out for and in for diving, and he was sympathetic.

Dewey didn't answer at home. The Group divulged the identity of his doctor but the doctor's nurse "simply could not" give out any information.

Greenspan, Junior, took Hind's $35.00 for a one-month (former-member) membership at 9:55 A.M. and at 10 Hind was at poolside just as the Cuban tossed in the chlorine tablets.

He ignored Hind and went back to his folding chair, his *Strength and Health*, and his radio. He probably didn't know that a year ago he had resentfully put his case to this very Hind passing by: during his daily fifteen hours at FHHC he vacuumed the cobalt-blue carpet; mopped tiled corridors outside sauna, steam, and showers; sieved and inspected the water in the pool (which he drained and squeejeed fortnightly); dried his skivvies behind the rock-full bright steel sauna stove; ate quick meals upstairs in the FH drug store where his girl worked part-time, and always had for dessert downstairs a handful of protein candies from the machine; had a weekly trim in the FHHC barber shop, where his girl manicured part-time; did his radio-listening, his periodical-reading, and his weights—yet when he asked to rent a hotel-staff bedroom upstairs in order to live the other nine hours on the premises, he was flatly turned down.

At this hour his pool was so smooth it might have been dry. In the old days at school the single best thing in diving (if you could get down before the squad chopped it up slogging back and forth on the kicking boards) was to feel this transparency vacant below your body as you hopped off the right foot, pointed your toes, let the board bend and hold you, then release your spring almost straight up toward the basketed roof light—for then at the static turning point (if the dive was any good) your flat water had vanished and you headed down not into pale lime water armed with a breastful of air (and figuring to miss the treble-wrapped abrasive end of the board by twelve to eighteen inches) but into another air whose celled floor was so softly far that your own gross length and then some would disappear long before you could even hope to reach and jab your fingers and bark your knuckles.

On the way out Hind stopped at Greenspan's desk to ask about Dewey, but Greenspan didn't know anything.

Long after May's bedtime Hind arrived at Sylvia's and told her about the guardian right away, that the guardian was his real father. She shrugged, then preceded him down the long hall to the living room. When he looked in on May the whirr of the humidifier covered the *crake-crake* of the door hinge. Two large watermelon pits were stuck on the grille of the humidifier. Sylvia had asked him long ago—"I don't know if I want the dehumidifier or the *hu*midifier"—and he got it at a discount.

"What's this?" said Sylvia holding out a brochure as he came into her living room. "Are you a foster parent of a child from Hong Kong, South Korea, Philippines, or Vietnam?" She stared at the brochure as if making conversation.

"I arranged for them not to tell me who the kid was."

"Why?"

"Because of what you've said against me."

"What in particular?"

"I thought if Foster Parents, Incorporated, withheld all personal data about the child—"

"The Unknown Child."

"—then the gift wouldn't seem self-congratulatory."

"Hell, I'd love to see a picture of the little..."

"Actually, I think it's a girl. 82.4 percent goes to child and family."

"You do know who she is. You're kidding me."

"No and yes."

They sat, and May cut loose a quick, sighing sentence down the hall, or was it a momentary up-cycle in the humidifier?

Hind went on, "We'll be receiving a full history and photograph in the next few days."

"Your name is still legally Hind, of course."

"Yes. But you haven't anything to say?"

"Too late to do anything about your guardian."

Then Hind was asking what May wanted for Christmas. He wanted to get the presents himself, he said, and Sylvia murmured "Big deal," but she was apparently glad.

"So," Hind tried again. "He was my real father."

"You always felt like that in a way. Not literally, but."

"Now I've a different feeling."

"He never once told you. I suppose he implied it to me. But he loved you so much he just *was* your father."

"Why didn't he tell me? The Old Woman and Grimes knew. Grimes didn't catch on, Thanksgiving Day, that he had just revealed it to me, he thought I'd known, maybe he was even showing *off his* knowledge to me, he cared much more about one of Fossy's false derivations. The Old Woman tried so hard to come close without telling me, like birds bombing a cat—it was vital to her not to lose what she thought was her edge in my not knowing."

"Once in the kitchen at Greengage and once on the beach, I thought it possible. I discounted it."

Next morning, Hind had trouble finding not the toys but their significance; for he was going to the very stores May had mentioned and buying the very things she had asked for and now expected to get. What did *he* contribute?

The FHHC secretary readily revealed that since Dewey was in the hospital an FHHC get-well card with Honey Gulden the Golden Superguy soaring through a high-rise gorge with cape out behind him, had been mailed to Dewey automatically as a member in good standing.

The Old Woman was correct: if from Plane he had gone originally not to Sylvia but to Staghorn he would have found a lead of some kind in Staghorn's severe conversation, even perhaps in his work.

Having seen people as leads, Hind had been trying to turn the leads back into people.

One of Staghorn's Sylviascapes looked more like a wooded ravine under a blanched sky. In the summer of 1941 Hind hid the Jesus-puzzle portrait in the drawer where he kept, embalmed in the original powder, the fishskin prophylactics Ford Free's eldest son had traded him for his treasure hunt prize.

Why didn't you feel bad about Dewey? Certainly not because Dewey wasn't a lead any more. The double goof in the Group diagnosis was like a tired gag, and now Dewey's Group did not cover the quantity of blood he would need to waste in order to keep his head above water three or four final days.

A woman at a desk looked at Hind's card and said, "This is old stuff for you."

You sat in the bright empty room in a nylon lecture seat molded in one of several fresh impregnated colors. An Irish nurse came out and led you in. As you waited for a doctor to finish questioning the woman about to give her six-monthly insurance pint guaranteeing her family up to forty emergency pints, you recollected that Dewey was another type. But no, your blood simply went into the pool–"Pool?" queries the guardian, his copy of Johnson's immortal lexicon open at "laurel." The starched uniform swished by with a clear plastic sack of dark blood. The doctor beckoned, and Hind went to the desk and sat and answered the familiar questions. The guardian would never go along with Thea to give blood during the war; he didn't like the idea—had it anything to do with his fear of blowing his nose?—and when in the summer of 'forty-five Elder Plane said he had cautioned Thea, who was giving it every eight weeks, and then said how many gallons it had come to since 'forty, the guardian said he was disgusted at the thought of it.

Off the jabbed end of Hind's middle finger the doctor took a spot of blood which he put into a small beaker of blue copper sulphide testing for anemia. Hind would like to tell him about Dewey. The blood formed a Cheerioat, the doctor rapped the beaker with his fingernail disintegrating the doughnut, but then the blood formed a new one clean and substantial as clay, finely holed and subtly flattened. It sank monumentally and reached the bottom safely. Hind was about to point out the successful integrity of the blood doughnut and the success of the test, when the doctor said, "Good deal, it floats"—the doughnut was irrelevant, a splotch lay on the surface.

When the nurse slipped in her needle and taped it, you wouldn't mind letting out two or three pints. What did the holy sisters do with Robin Hood's rich blood when they let him die? The Irish nurse seemed to have gone away. A filament conveys your blood stream direct to Dewey—brings back syrupy singing and harsh talk, Negroes move slowly through shop windows which shiver into exquisitely dimensioned slow panes that swish like the Meanings' maid's slippers, and other Afro-Americans rise and fall on the evening breeze lyrically looting, chorally embracing, wafted on the evening as if it were water: while against their attenuated tender "I Got a Shoe," Engleman Deal with a violent case of hiccups sums up late at night. "They have had their chance and will continue to have in this society. My grandfather shoed horses for a living, but look at me. No one, of course, dares say, 'Send them back to Africa where they came from (never mind *how* they came),' or 'Races imply differences, performance indicates capacity.'" To which the guardian, violently checking his anger, stares at the Arabian horsemen deep in the red carpet and murmurs tensely, "You compare the incomparable. Education is the key, education." In another room now turned on like an adjustable space in one of Maddy's S-D Sisters' electric-field houses, "Sex education," declares Flo, and Jim Commons with his violently bluff, down-to-earth surprises, "I tell 'em the first thing they gotta do is learn to keep it in their pocket."

"Wakie, wakie," the guardian has his head through the blood doughnut, but his shoulders are too broad and the life-ring sinks gracefully with him in it, puzzled, trapped, calm. "Wakie, wakie," it's the Irish nurse sealing your bag, and your instant dream cleared your sinuses and though it's going away now—in the dark sack—you say, as if to put an appropriate end to it, "—in my blood, trapped in—" "All right, dear, keep your arm closed for a minute, then you can have your orange juice and cookies."

Another night, close to Eddy's birthday.

Hind was drinking.

"*Why* did he not tell me?"

"Because he decided to be ashamed." Sylvia was trying to take Hind's presence in her flat as a normal thing.

"But why? Because he was an adulterer? Wouldn't that have seemed to him independent, strong?"

"No."

"Or because he thought he should have taken her right away from Frank Hind and married her."

"Well, she might not have died then."

"No, he was conventional. It was legitimacy, the same that appalled the Old Woman."

"No. It was that he loved her. More than you."

"So by not marrying her in time he finished what *I* started."

Saturday, a week before Christmas, Hind found his

disused Ken Rosewall missing from its corner in the study closet; and as if resuming the long-ended Thanksgiving chat he turned directly to the space where the Ariosto had been. Presume it taken by Grimes—not an ungraceful gesture after all—who had inadvertently turned him on with the revelation he brought as his poor harvest offering. Had Grimes mistaken those casual references to the Wynkyn de Worde? Hind looked for it all over both bookcase walls like the guardian abruptly hunting a citation.

Later he found May and Sylvia in line in Kidd's. "Roman Pizza is like everything else," a hooded child quoted, browsing, but did not finish the ad with its endlessly climactic series contradicting the first proposition.

"The big question," Sylvia was saying after dinner, "is how could he hide it from you all this time? You must be stupid."

"No, the big question is, why do I feel less his son now?" "I can understand that," but she wasn't telling why.

To see Fossy anew—now, in his perpetual absence—would be to erase him as he was alive and (as if reflected) yourself as Foster, not adopted son or Hind-Foster, or Foster-Hind.

"Your English friend Plante," said Hind, "told the university about Oliver Plane's drug assemblies at the Chapel of Laughter, even though I agreed to their demands and paid the rent."

"It's nothing to do with poor me," said Sylvia.

"But Oliver's researching a monograph on the C. of L.'s background, so the university has cited him for involvement in urban interuction"—(insurrection, interaction, instruction)—"which they call a phase of para-publication."

"You use the material you've got," said Syl, with an unattractive lack of irony.

Hind wanted a walk, and said he might not be more than half an hour. In Rivervale Complex playground.

Surrounded by proven grass and among stilt-borne, free-holed stomach forms, the seesaw at rest was from a distance tonight an abstract attenuation of a howitzer, if they used howitzers any more; but on arrival Hind found it only a rather literal sculpture, a slick stone remembrance of real things—or a *petrified* seesaw. Hind touched the splinter-free ramp and found it not stone but composition, or a compofaction. But you could, after all, in terms of superveiled recreation, play upon this seesaw even if it did not respond.

The Knotts were moving into Rivervale Complex, "hopefully" as soon as she pried the old man loose; he wouldn't have to give up all his superintendencies, and there were no objections to animals. She felt the great thing about River-vale was that at night you'd always hear someone walking behind you since walking on the grass was prohibited.

But here, slowing down near Hind, was Sylvia, smooth and brown from the great white bulbs on their high black tubes and the emerald glow of the lawns. "He didn't tell you everything, though God knows he paraded his body in front of us often enough. But why *should* he tell everything? But he was more than a father to you. He was a man, and he's more alive the more you know him."

Hind had to look at his hockey ticket but pulling out his wallet now would be impolite. "And why did *you* leave *May*? That front door, the police-brace slot is broken, it doesn't lock. God knows what's going on back there right now. Did you leave her because you're more than a mother to her?"

"I didn't think about it. Can't you see me without seeing May lying in bed behind me? with a dehumidifier in her room so loud she wouldn't hear a thing?"

Since there were several disparate ends you wished to prosecute, two or three continuations to finish, other initiations in terms of ancient preoccupations, others just curiosity—you must learn to use Syl more vividly than heretofore.

Hind and Sylvia didn't finish the Sunday papers Saturday night. They went back to them Sunday morning.

Sunday afternoon you were tired of reading about Rome Ploughs knocking down Hobo Woods and the attraction Coke cans possessed for those concerned with booby bombs, not to mention Mighty Mouse Rockets or the CBU dispenser and its three-pound bomblets; tired, too, of reading about the Gemini rendezvous.

Hind's mother indeed was what Fossy saw through Hind, and as truly a "slip of wilderness" (from his favorite play for reading aloud, *Measure for Measure*) as in that poet's exact sense the natural son Hind himself was. Yet in his surface self Hind had been real enough for the guardian to be actively sick on the beach in 1950 finding Jack with the Jap tenant and Plane in the shack and being asked by the Jap if he, as one of the great ones, had ever smoked grass; real enough years before when the guardian (rather dashing in pea jacket and molasses corduroys) mortified you at half time by buttonholing Buddy Bourne on the way with the squad to the field house to ask why Buddy yanked you after the kickoff—then starting the argument all over again at the hockey game in December. Real enough to ask point-blank what you did with Charley that spring day in 1944 and privately ask Charley's father's garage if they knew how her brother wrangled the gas to joyride a hundred-odd miles out to the Island and back. Real enough another time to make Thea almost cry and make her move out.

There was in the end more to your abortive re- and dekidnap than an April to X-mas tour of salient wood, stone, steel, or synthetic points, wasn't there?

Sylvia intently knits the heel of a large sock and listens to the old movie you are watching. There *you* are: the guy on your gently convex screen saying to his strong, vulnerable girl early in the drama, "I can't now, I got something I gotta finish first." Plain talk, steadfast brow, justice in the nostril, clement lashes. "Yeah, kid; unfinished business," and plants a considerable stiff kiss o'er her opening mouth, then moves tall-ly off: off to the mob's funeral-parlor-front cave on the east side: or toward the rock foothills of Mount Mary where in a cabin Boyd Birch's boys play five-card stud all day all night awaiting (for) you while venison ripens from a juniper and—in town—no sir, a dead sheriff he can't raise a live posse. On the other hand, when you possess information as hard as the Old Woman's last gasp—the Garden seat locations following up her earlier report that Dove took poor Hershey Laurel to the Ranger Sunday night home games—you didn't go and waste it.

Why did so many lines empty into that unremembered Garden game years ago? Sunday afternoons Buddy took his summer camp prospects to see the Rovers at the Garden, but Charley's father was a trustee of Hind's school and a contact with extra Ranger tickets had unloaded two blocks one of which Charley's father gave Buddy as a fellow Knight of Columbus (though socially of course, like Fossy and the soccer coach Blum, they rarely met), and Charley got two tickets for Jack but didn't want to go herself, she had taken him to the Hit Parade the end of November, was it 'forty-one?—

So many lines. Yet they did not seem to empty into that bluey-white rink—what you paid for—the sauntering glide of one bald bulging giant idling along the boards before face-off; the stuffed goalie snowing the crease and then just before face-off touching blades with his team as they circled by the cage; then, as the guardian standing up muttered, "Irrelevant," Our National Anthem transfixed the players and the neat referees, and you thought rather it wasn't at all irrelevant, whether, like the gray-haired lady in the next row down in a wool athletic jacket marked HARTSDALE H.S., you sang loud and looked around you, or merely stood at attention like Buddy Bourne at the very brink of the upper deck who picked up his brown pork pie from under the seat and clapped it to his chest, not irrelevant at all but a precious delay conceived by grownups to guarantee the clash official, to make you appreciate the clash all the more when at last the organ ended, a clash whose result would appear in the *Tribune* standings.

The rink, yes: yet Hind couldn't reclaim that game—either who the Blues were at home to—Red Wings, Hawks, Leafs—or whether Brian Hextall had done anything or there had been a fight: for what mattered was here back in the upper deck away from the enormous glowing ice, the center, back in the dark crowd surrounding the rink and its motions: had it been Montreal, like tonight? but what mattered that night years ago was in the upper deck at the end of the second period.

No need to tell Sylvia that he'd had tonight's ticket a month, or that the game wasn't exactly a gratuitous escape: for she knew he'd had the game in the back of his mind (if there was such a place). No need to reveal the Old Woman's magically particular information—upper deck, section and row: for Sylvia wouldn't understand any better than Hind himself this hazardously guarded coincidence.

Granted, years ago at that other game (won, lost, nor now recapturable even by micro *Times*) Jack and the guardian, and Buddy and his old campers and new prospects, were all diametrically across the Garden from Hind-Foster's surveilling seat tonight, a diameter infinitely unlikely to escape its circumference yet very long through aromatic twilight as live and broad as that glamorous gap where, in this same old Garden, the B & B high-wire toes pedaled and danced and in whose upper reach the tiny roof trapeze in its spot of light swung choppily and was a form of pantomime whose climactic properties equal that whole space from bar to tanbark which, also, teems with gravity.

Climbing the Garden stairs that night, Jack was, Hind-Foster was, you were, so crowned by your wild tottering height you thought that in the happy patient crush you and your height fairly glimmered, were ogled, judged, and found too much: and your pursued heart kept saying, That is my height but this is me: whereas tonight, much much taller, you hardly bother to slouch rising from the side entrance in the escalator's smooth order, and if your six feet seven smugly whispered that children were especially drawn to you and your height, you hardly heard, and hardly now, as before, saw yourself as the English social worker Sir Basil Henriques, six foot seven (according to Cassia), just before the war pleading for the poor London-County-Council-adopted kid deprived of visitors by the LCC-adopted technicality governing County Hall visitors' passes—hardly saw, hardly heard—for past and present were organizing a crash parley and it was touch and/or go whether the participants would find the Garden a congenial locus.

The Garden was big enough, its sounding air bigger than the city around it as separate as if you turned a long corner into Dewey Wood's alternate or alternative world, or found for Ivy's sake new room within the jammed air of New York, though everyone here in the Garden had left a space outside. The organ rolls beneath the smoke. You pass a short man stepping steadily ahead with a packed cardboard tray of hot dogs and high beer-cups.

From the open corridor where Hind walked above the upper deck he saw his section, and turning down the steep steps did not look for Dove and Hershey's section for there was time and Dove might be watching. Hind read the program and looked across the Garden to where he and the guardian sat that night.

You could say to yourself, At least there's the extra motive of the actual NHL game tonight. The Rangers are out to snap an eleven-game losing skein (streak, string). When, a week before that other Garden game, Fossy took you to the New Jersey airfield where the Hinds' auto-gyro came down, Thea refused to go along. You felt at that other Garden game that if you fell off deep into that rink from this bright smoky upper deck, you were the guardian's only son, a real responsibility—like when you pictured killing yourself on the end of the springboard, having, like Siggofreddo in the end, gone up too straight; or like, in the shuddering sighs of the sea in front of the Jap's shack, swallowing away the Postum-sweet laryngeal bruise left by the marijuana—the guardian's valued adoptee.

But tonight Buddy and the guardian were gone, and if Dove and the kidnaped kid were here tonight, Dove would find your plunge to the rink below an inconvenience because it might lead to new questions. Sylvia, and May too, would care, though Sylvia would think, What an incredible ending, it must have been suicide. (Not a full house, but over fourteen thousand.)

: To drop off into that great eye where a cluster of white Canadiens and blue Rangers now swept their pointless puck up and back between the cages and behind.

For fear of being caught looking, Hind hadn't checked the Dove seats; but he had a place for them in the corner of his eye and felt them empty till well after face-off.

The fat boy bawling obscene greetings over the edge of the upper deck changed his tune at 8:19, the Rangers had made it 1-0.

Early in the second period they added another.

When the fight broke out and spread down the boards, and the bench leaned out to join in, Hind at last looked; but he saw no one like what he thought Dove and the boy Laurel would look like; yet the spaces were full, and he got up to stretch while others rose to cheer the unsteady blue and white shirts bloodying each other.

Yet years before, he was watching the steampad-truck on the ice; for the second period, unlike tonight, had ended—and the guardian rose saying there was your coach Bourne. And while the truck breathed away the mass of skate-blade lacerations, there a few rows down in the upper deck was Bourne (, Buddy, K. of C., B.S., V.F.W., collector of matchbooks and possibly the widest variety (in private hands in Brooklyn) of college-monogrammed mugs, glass and china) lifting his broad back unhappily as the guardian's profile against the ice below offered Buddy a lively, beneficent welcome.

Slowly as a rheumatic, you rose to go down to the brink to join them.

Where Dove and the boy Hershey should be, were two thick heads, red and black cropped close to the glistening skin. At least he'd ask them who they were.

The beneficent welcome continues (though God knows the guardian doesn't own the Garden) and Buddy's regular headshakes make his unheard words seem repetitious.

At the brink of the upper deck you looked into the second row at Blackie and Red, who turned and stared with contented hostility.

· · ·

"*You* ask *him* why I yanked him. *He'll* tell you. Get *his* side. Ask him what about the kickoff reverse, Hind to Lief, or Lund to Jackie, case may be. Get *his* side, that'll make you feel better prob'ly." Oh, the betrayal of Buddy Bourne—your own coach honorably allied in victory and defeat irregardless: saying such things to your meddling beloved guardian. The betrayal of Buddy Bourne; his act but possessed fully by John Hind alone.

"Those your seats? I don't think so."

Red and Blackie grinning at each other, then continuing to stare.

"*Hindie* din't feel...what you said. He knew the reverse could have meant a TD right there on the first play."

"But Bourne, don't you see, his improvisation was ingenious. *They* saw Lief Lund cutting across toward Jack and *they* doubtless inferred the very reverse you'd planned, whereupon Jack kept the ball. Why make a boy feel guilty for a play like that? You removed him summarily, Bourne."

"Athletics builds character," said Buddy, bobbing his head as if undecided whether to nod or bow. "Ask any company commander, he'll say, 'Athletes some of the finest characters I've known.' Not your *Mexican* athletes you know what I mean by a Mexican athlete, I could name a few do the absolute minimum in PT and get doctor's excuses, got white in the corner of their eye when they come onto the field, they didn't even wash their face before they came to school—working on the yearbook, newspaper, you name it—they don't make *my* teams, that's one thing Hindie never was, a Mexican athlete, Mr. Hind."

"Not decent to treat a boy like that, Bourne."

"Well," said Bourne, reflecting upon the program in his hand, "you wanted to help him. *That's* O.K." The steampad-truck was breathing away the last crisscrosses.

"Your job is to help, too."

"And to win. But I have faith in our system. Initiative, individualism, calisthenics, the world of sport, private enterprise. Kid don't achieve his full potentiality, 'f he doesn't get out and fight, get out of his background, ekcetra."

"Ah, detach himself from it. Is that it?"

"So to speak. Yeah. *You* said it, not me."

"From his family. You mean 'family' by 'background'?"

"My meaning was—" Buddy turned up his seat so he could stand more freely. He knew nearly enough what he meant so that he resented not so much not being able to say it, as being asked to. "My meaning, Mr. Hind, was... their *fathers* is what I mean. O.K., go on tell the trustees Bud Bourne said that."

"I am not, I regret to say, a trustee," said the guardian, and Buddy Bourne's eyes changed, he wanted to make up, he had mistaken the irony in the words.

And Hind saw now what years ago he sensed in his own smarting eyes: that Buddy, though he didn't know it himself, was sorry the guardian (he thought) felt badly *not* being a trustee. The steampad was off the ice, several fans turned their attention to Buddy and the guardian, whose difference they had heard but discounted.

"Who wants to know?" said Red.

"Whadda, *you* got tickets for here?" said Blackie.

"Where did you get your tickets?" asked Hind. "Who gave them to you? I know who bought them originally."

As he turned back up the steps, either Blackie or Red, invoking the justice of custom, called out, "We moved down from in back, you can do dat, everybody does it."

· · ·

You hear the guardian behind you partly from the crowd partly from that eyelike rink beyond and below: "You see what a beanstalk that lad is," an apparent pity circulating through all the years since, and yet accepted as the bountifully becoming style of Adopter in his nice relation vis-à-vis and/or in terms of Adoptee. (Now Jack my dear, says the adopter, that rink has nothing a-tall in common with—an *eye*.) (Nor you, you remind your lengthy self, the adoptee, anything in common with Rhodope's giant babe Athos sired by—none other than Neptune.)

Cassia could very well catch herself (after saying, "You're only adopted; adopted children don't have exactly the same insides as real children") by adding unconvincingly, "Wish *I* was adopted." You two were leafing through the medical book the guardian had shown you when you were six and hadn't even met Cassia, in which not only the words but even the pictures had to be read to you, it was part of the brain, which Hind now with skeptical Cassia—eleven? twelve? he had an erection but mightn't have to stand up for a few minutes—explained to her was a longitudinal (prime) cut of cerebellum labeled *arbor vitae*, which (turned into English for her) explained the tree look: then the guardian that earlier time—and child Hind had up to that point been bored—said, "That's your brain, isn't it astonishing?" by which he meant the arborescent cast of the pictured slice, while *you* thought it was astonishing *you* had one, you—a queer accident—though those weren't your words at six, and the guardian had explained "astonishing." And you thought of the soft mass of Cassia's insides, unknown to her, and bubbling away, different from the outside skeleton of membranes, hair, crust, and polish, each with untamed intersections of message while behind and below were dark bubbling insides loved but almost never seen.

·  ·  ·

Neighbors returning to their seats: 2-1, Rangers, who now, like the Canadiens, ready for the last period, came stepping onto the ice as if into a subtly varied current. And the fat boy in the front row of this upper deck right under Hind's nose was bawling at the Number Two goalie Simmons that the Rangers didn't win since the night before Thanksgiving and they blow this one too. Two periods were enough, Hind got up to go.

In the rear window of the car ahead of your cab going south on Ninth, a couchant dog hooked into the ignition winked brightly.

Coach Blum, who had an apartment on the church side of Monroe Place (where Charley and sometimes Cassia watched Hind, Lief, and sometimes Plane, squeezed between two hard, gleaming banks of parked cars, play rather tense stickball with public school kids) mentioned the guardian a bit too often; shortly after the little left-winger broke his leg, Blum, to his delight, was asked over for a drink one Sunday noon. "Your insides aren't strong finishers, really, are they," observed the guardian with serious sympathy; "your halfs lay it in, your outsides center well. But where are the goals?" Hind—but was the guardian speaking now or was Hind recapturing his own thoughts?—Hind, the "useful" fullback; de Forrest the Unwilling (plus of course Jacob Fay in goal), racked up the lowest one-season goals-against in school history even facing five public high elevens. And Hind had not minded the forward line's meager output (, attack; harvest of goals). Earlier he had grown to feel too big for football, but in any case preferred soccer's open flow, and the naked rigor of hand-less, armless heads and chests and stomachs, and independent legs.

Finish now: just go home. Sylvia. May. An honorable peace.

But you could have done that in April. It was what you meant to do, rushing down the undertaker's cloudy white stairs. So why now?

You could find Dove if you tried. And he knew it.

Hind got out at the undertaker's (this driver echoing others, "Kinda late for a wake"–"I'll look you up if I ever need a–"); sat in the study till past twelve; heard the throbbing west wind; heard the regular Ow Wow Wow of Emergency, the natural sounds.

The ad folk had left evidences of last night's annual wassail: parked at the curb, the only signs of life across the way, stood the two green Port-O-San johns wired to the building by colored bulbs strung above the sidewalk and advertising a certain self-sufficiency in the piece of pipe that stuck out of each roof.

After the news and weather, Hind switched off the transistor he had forgotten he owned.

On the other hand, finish with Sylvia–("*with*?" sounds the big toe of the long foot of Berry Brown's liberally white power dominoad turning restlessly from "of" toward new fields of verbiculture crux, but Bee Bee Barker stretches smiling to take it in her teeth and, missing, calls, "Fascist! what's a univocal sentence to a black peasant?" but the big toe turns hopefully back to her mouth as she holds up her end of a discussion in a Manhattan living room: "Dead? I'd miss sex most.")–: yet how *finish* with Sylvia when the beginning was hers as well as yours in the first place?

Your planted feet go deep in the past, you barely keep your soft heart, neck, tongue, eyes above ground. On the other hand, you then shoot up terribly–you *are* the beanstalk, Jack.

Or, in a moment's lull looking down at the Jesus-puzzle portrait on your desk in front of your wooden Cruiser

Indianapolis, and touching her hand and discovering that she does not move it, you and Cassia are suddenly visited by your guardian, whose dislike of her takes here the form—and in his ridicule—of the Jesus-puzzle. Religion needs entertaining tricks like this, he says, and the face, look at it, it's wretchedly drawn, who couldn't do better?—and for a second the hatched, tangled puzzle-face oscillates to and fro, fading into the penman's mass-produced undergrowth then emergent, alone and individual the white Christ rather Christy-like with hair longer—the Heights son neuronically unfit for all but risky and unusual work, likely alas to remain his parents' Problem—apparently unlike *old* Amondson, that desperado father whom, when he came to demand Christy's skates back and stood at the door showing under the entrance to his nostrils like a murderer's or condemned man's ominous mark, the tiny arc of single dark bristles his razor had not reached, the guardian summarily dismissed—though next day Hind took back the skates.

That Jesus is not Fossy's large, fine, disturbingly bland face, any more than *you* (a specialist possessed of so many varieties of kidnap that the felon who just last month left the parents dead in the baby's playpen is to you no more original than the one who left the child and took the parents)—*you*, are certainly no *unilateral* colaurel, hijacked to the American plantation.

You can unlearn (or unquote) your beloved guardian's face no more easily than the hardware man's son can overlook his guilt over letting his bat slip off into the air to strike Hershey over the eye. But it can now be told that this guilt is also pique over having been fooled by the grand change-of-pace floated at him, instead of her notorious fastball, by Ken Love's tomboy daughter who now works in Boston's own Jordan Marsh.

"Social sentimentality," grumbles Bee Bee Barker, who happens also to be fed up with Marina's constant cooking—"What good would it do if Hershey Laurel *was* found? But if you say the only ransom is what the Lindberghs bought—a dead child and a ladder identified by that cop the wood expert—then there's no sense trying to change anything. Well, history will do the changing despite John Foster, Jack Hind, the Heights, or a laureate thesis founded on ruling-class sentimentality. I'm not kidding"—words she never spoke but could have felt. Yet the lemony hand with the bone bump on its back an inch forward of the wrist, replies, "The city is not *only* man's high-risen pretence, for instance the Babel Development Complex Center; it is also David's Jerusalem with the temple at its core." Bee Bee didn't reply "You and a hundred other Eames barber-chair architects live most of your life in the country."

Papers. Destruct. "Destroy these files," that was what a letter in the first file had said when you went through it the night after Fossy's death, having sneaked away to *North by Northwest* at Loew's Met in the afternoon when visitors, received by Thea and Sylvia and denied the sight of your guardian's body, were wondering where you were. "Destroy these files," the first file still said.

You looked at random, but though nothing was complete, much was begun.

Here was a poem Fossy had included in that taped reading successfully intended for the memorial.

And then here was the bachelor tree ceremony. In India when a bachelor marries a widow, he must marry a tree first; when the tree is then cut down he achieves equality with his projected widow-bride.

Or quote: "In *King John* Shakespeare's Bastard after speaking of the strumpet Fortune (II, i, 391-4) follows with 'How like you this...?'—a clear echo of 'They Flee from Me' and proof that Shakespeare read Wyatt's most famous poem as a complaint against Fortune." Unquote.

Unfinished diary shots. Or here: what? a fugitive sciental love letter? sent and retrieved? meant for Hind? The soft mass of the deciphered words themselves like a *place* you sank inevitably into—or like the trees in that newly neutral yet comforting vale Sylvia never had a chance to finish telling about during their wait in London airport—to whom was the guardian writing?—

> It was as if in that moment of real love (which life tried to unfit me for and from which I emerged as from a background of whole cloth into something partial) the fluid (bad word!) came not from my loins and the hot foot of my spine but from all motions current in my gathered body going on and on.

To Hind's mother? No telling.

But it needn't be in some attic scryne that you find the secret semblance between *hero* and *eros*, for you knew already somewhere in your own scrinial skull that be it god upon girl or man upon goddess, Socrates was right, heroes spring from love; yet you can't then decide if Fossy ever in real words said, "*Hero* in the old Attic is only *Eros* altered."

Or here: you knew it so well you never wondered if it was about her, if the setting was foreign—Czechoslovakia? impossible; the later trip to Scotland?—and now if it had lain in your little, hedged wilderness fading out of focus or rushing into focus and as irrelevant as Fossy quoting Johnson's undervaluation of laurel in that stately lexicon—lain waiting for some inadequate re-enactment:

> I looked back through the brief steep vale between the two eminences—remember?—and there was a slope cutting across my sight of the east reach of

the city's seaward fringe. The slope was greatly and intimately green (bad phrase!), and hence very (though not really) near: yet a minor dash of movement caught my eye; it was a dog and a woman so small they were embedded in the hill which itself rose back as if to become properly distant: but the air, or the adjustment of angle, dimension, and color, or maybe my eye—forestalled the change, and the slope remained unnatural in scale.

The guardian often had to wake Jack three or four times in the morning during his eleventh and twelfth years. "O.K." "No. Now." "O.K." "Don't say 'O.K.'" "O.K. I just got to finish up this dream—" "No you don't." "—tidy it up...."

Like the forgotten transistor, now the phone: made itself heard; called from the dark living room as if buried; tinkled; revealed itself glimmering in a remote nest of this abandoned flat; twanged; rang; instantly replayed; continued.

Out in the dark wind (that came from behind Central Park hustling through the Ramble and through linden, dogwood, ash, maple, pine, and gingko, mingling them with True tobacco and Scope mouthwash), you could nearly see the Black Answering Service list of unfinished business:

BLACK ANSWERING CENTRAL: Your Calls

1. Someone phoned about Mr. Wood. Call tomorrow.
2. A lady phoned about Dewey Wood. Contact tomorrow.
3. Heather and Phyllis phoned about Dewey.
4. Did Julio Loggia phone asking why Jack phoned him?

5. Ah, perhaps Herbie phoned from deep in a downtown dividend. Perhaps he would like you to call back. Re: your wife and/or his sister or foster sister.

6. The New York Rangers made it 3-2 at 9:12 of the final period.

7. "How long," according to Pan Am, "has it been since you had an affair with an island?"

8. How many children did Ken Love get?

9. At the memorial gathering Father White played Fossy's tape first without replacing the capstan head so in the beginning Fossy sounded like the Fugue-a-rooney roller-contraltos prevocalizing. Did Mrs. Hind forge Frank's John Hancock to the guardianship instrument? How soon before the autogyro disaster?

10. How could you, on October 15, the day after Fossy's death, snatch three hours to stroll down past the stamp man's brown building, the court house you and Maddy got caught once at night using as a shortcut from Fulton through to Livingston, the King's County Trust, Schrafft's, all the way to Loew's Met to see *North by Northwest*?

11. What ulterior motive was the man at Goya in the green shirt possessed of who challenged the guardian's view that Dürer's approach to perspective was not conventional Renaissance?

12. Herewith Sylvia's father's list of talk topics for when Staghorn came:

    Lyons' string bean: at odds with landscape? or become part of it?

    Sports: as much the opium of masses as religion?

    Do we act from choice or are we mere effects?

Sylvia's vocation: how use time and talent for greatest fulfillment? how is her art progressing?

13. The guardian did not deduct for tax purposes the fifty dollars he sent to the school for orphan boys (1909–) in Dauphin County, Hershey, Pennsylvania.

14. Did Mrs. Byron Bean call Fossy a great man because he invited her, a widow—for whom, as everyone knows, there is no place—to sit at his table at the Yuletide Ball?

15. Herewith Hind's provisional stanza to end Oliver's unfinished ode on the diving accident of Siggofreddo Morales, who is now expanding his father's Superette:

> The dive goes on, like space, like death,
> Stopped only on the cocoa mat,
> Which interrupts the diver's depth
> Only to let him off to find
> Another slower, endless lens
> Deep as the nothing behind is flat
> Toward which his twisting heart descends
> Hunted by abandoned breath.

16. When you came back from *North by Northwest* people were waiting to pay their respects. Late that night you and Thea listened to the "Appassionata" on WQXR.

17. Sylvia phoned.

18. When Charley came out at the Yuletide she had a yellow rose in her hair and like the other girls she danced the first dance ("The Anniversary Waltz") with her dad. Meanwhile you and Maddy and Lief postponed your appearances in the ballroom by drinking underaged and postprandial martinis

at the St. George bar, and you for one thought of Cassia and Charley at the same time, but then they drifted apart.

The iron ground-floor door clanged, and feet slipped and tapped over the stone and on up onto the steps, dropping very steadily.

19. You couldn't call up Master E. Beecher (saying first, "In case I forget your birthday on the 25th") and share with him your sublime out-, in-, up-, and down-sight that you have become what you were—the very beanstalk you shinned up. You should belong to Illegitimates Anonymous. Or send a contribution to the Children's Theater Company of WITF-TV, Hershey, Pa.

The steps (you could say to the guardian without risk of ambiguity) altered only in that, being nearer, they were louder.

She's *humming*! She?

20. Cassia Meaning hugged you the night of her last sailing. She said, "Sweetie, it's all awfully original as you tell it, but how can you be *sure* his thing was to end like this? *Such* a peculiar view of perspective, I mean all out of proportion—I mean, I don't know Dürer—well, I mean—hell, maybe I wish *I'd* thought of it, maybe I'd have found myself, sweetie. Mind you, your guardian's own painting was chocolate box stuff, wasn't it.

Now Sylvia's not humming.

21. Did Dove's wife, Beulah Love's unwelcome sister-in-law, send the anonymous notes from Europe that lured the Laurels there? By not setting the authorities on the Dove trail, did the Loves ensure that they'd never have to entertain the Doves again?

Sure. It's Sylvia. But what if the steps *aren't* Sylvia? coming up out of the human-made, though not yet airtight, Nature of this city.

Surprise the Old Woman, the muse who preyed on you: Begin the guardian's *Life* even against those rising now no longer humming steps upon the undertaker's plain stone stairs. The guardian's devotion to others, yes, and to the possession of freedom: yet then, his *true* power (don't lean on italics) in the very routines he dreamed he was not possessed by:

> This is a man who, possessed by a dream of freedom which he never, hence, possessed, thought himself a shepherd but found himself a tree.

Felicitous, but not Fossy—someone else—you—the inadequate re-enactor.

At the old landing the key entered the Segal lock unnecessarily.

Canvas all chances—still you knew in the shallows of your clammy skin that it was Sylvia, alone. She hadn't lit the green-shaded landing light; so, now inside, creaking over the floor, she was very dark. But then she was alone at his study threshold, her eyes in the mild overflow of his Anglepoise violet.

No pained grin. Not drunk. Not terribly tired. Presumably not with child. "Don't end it," she said.